Praise for S. M. Stirling's
Island in the Sea of Time

"A book you won't want to—and won't be able to—put down. An outstanding piece of work." —Harry Turtledove

"A perfectly splendid story . . . endlessly fascinating . . . solidly convincing."   —Poul Anderson

"A compelling cast of characters . . . a fine job of conveying both a sense of loss and of hope."
—*Science Fiction Chronicle*

"Meticulous, imaginative. . . . Logical, inventive and full of richly imagined characters, this is Stirling's most deeply realized book yet."
—Susan Shwartz, author of *The Grail of Hearts*

"Utterly engaging. This is unquestionably Steve Stirling's best work to date, a page-turner that is certain to win the author legions of new readers and fans."
—George R. R. Martin

"Stirling's imaginative foray into time travel should please fans of alternative history."
—*Library Journal*

"An enormously entertaining read."
—Virtual North Woods Website

AGAINST THE
TIDE OF YEARS

A Novel of the Change

S. M. Stirling

A ROC BOOK

ROC

Published by New American Library, a division of
Penguin Group (USA) Inc., 375 Hudson Street,
New York, New York 10014, USA
Penguin Group (Canada), 90 Eglinton Avenue East, Suite 700, Toronto,
Ontario M4P 2Y3, Canada (a division of Pearson Penguin Canada Inc.)
Penguin Books Ltd., 80 Strand, London WC2R 0RL, England
Penguin Ireland, 25 St. Stephen's Green, Dublin 2,
Ireland (a division of Penguin Books Ltd.)
Penguin Group (Australia), 250 Camberwell Road, Camberwell, Victoria 3124,
Australia (a division of Pearson Australia Group Pty. Ltd.)
Penguin Books India Pvt. Ltd., 11 Community Centre, Panchsheel Park,
New Delhi - 110 017, India
Penguin Group (NZ), 67 Apollo Drive, Rosedale, North Shore 0632,
New Zealand (a division of Pearson New Zealand Ltd.)
Penguin Books (South Africa) (Pty.) Ltd., 24 Sturdee Avenue,
Rosebank, Johannesburg 2196, South Africa

Penguin Books Ltd., Registered Offices:
80 Strand, London WC2R 0RL, England

First published by Roc, an imprint of New American Library,
a division of Penguin Group (USA) Inc.

First Printing, May 1999
20 19 18 17 16 15 14

ROC REGISTERED TRADEMARK—MARCA REGISTRADA

Printed in the United States of America

PUBLISHER'S NOTE
This is a work of fiction. Names, characters, places, and incidents either are the product of the author's imagination or are used fictitiously, and any resemblance to actual persons, living or dead, business establishments, events, or locales is entirely coincidental.

The publisher does not have any control over and does not assume any responsibility for author or third-party Web sites or their content.

To Marjorie Totterdale Stirling,
1920–1997. Ave Atque Vale.

ACKNOWLEDGMENTS

Lyrics from "Fogarty's Cove" used by permission of Ariel Rogers/Fogarty's Cove Music, copyright 1976, written by Stan Rogers.

My thanks again to the people of Nantucket (individuals too numerous to name), to the U.S. Coast Guard, and to the historians, linguists, and archaeologists.

Thanks also to Suzanne Feldman and Anne-Marie Talbott for their help, and to Lawrence H. Feldman, Ph.D. (anthropology) and M.L.S., for help—and help with the beer.

PROLOGUE

Since the Event, everything has changed. We've had to just accept it—those who didn't go into shock and never come out—like time itself, a mystery we'd never solve. Many *couldn't* accept it, and I think that accounts for a lot of the craziness that bubbled up in the first year or two. On top of it all, William Walker headed off to England with his band of thugs, to set himself up as a king, and we had to fight a war to stop him. If he'd stayed up in the twentieth, maybe Walker would never have been more than a mildly amoral officer in the Coast Guard instead of a warlord and emperor, and his bitch-queen Hong would certainly never have had the opportunity to rival Elizabeth Bathory and Giles de Rais in the atrocity league.

God knows, I like to think the rest of us have improved on the original history a bit, where we could—spreading potatoes and sanitation, putting down human sacrifice and slavery. Mind you, there are still times when I wake up and expect to hear radios and cars! Now we've had a few years of *comparative* peace, and things are looking up. For now. What really worries me is that we couldn't finish Walker off.

From the personal journals of Founding Councilor Ian Arnstein, as quoted in David Arnstein, An Introductory History of the Republic of Nantucket,

Ch. 4, the Crisis of the Second Decade

(Nantucket Town: Oceanic University/Bookworks Press, 57 A.E.)

(May, Year 2 A.E.—After the Event)

Agamemnon, son of Atreus, King of Men, High Wannax of Mycenae, and overlord of the Achaeans by land and sea, decided that he loved cannon.

"You did not lie," he said, smiling like a wolf at the shattered section of fortress wall. He inhaled the stink of burnt sulfur as if it were perfumed oil. "You can make more of these?"

The outlander bowed. "If I have the metal and workmen I need, Lord King," he said in fluent Greek with a whistling, nasal accent.

"By *Zeus Pater,* Zeus Father of Gods and men," Agamemnon swore. "You shall have what you require—and besides that, you shall have land of me, houses, gold, comely women, fine raiment, weapons—yes, and honor in my house among my *ekwetai,* my sworn companions!"

The outlander bowed again. *Wil-iam Walkeearh, that's his name.* Hard to remember the foreign sounds . . . there were murmurs at the king's back, from nobles displeased at seeing an outlander raised so high among them mere weeks after he arrived at Tiryns, Mycenae's port. *Fools.*

"Never have I seen or heard of anything like this," he said, as the gathering began to disperse. "Not even among the Hittites or the clever Sudnu, the Sidonians."

Agamemnon's personal guard fell in behind them, sunlight breaking red off the bronze blades of their ready spears, eyes wary under their boar's-tusk helmets.

"And to find such among the savages of the northlands . . ." The king shook his head. "Where comes this knowledge of throwing thunderbolts?"

"Ah, my lord king," the tall stranger said. "*That* is a very long story."

CHAPTER ONE

March, Year 8 A.E.
(June, Year 2 A.E.)

"Get that God-damned moa under control!" a voice shouted from the street. It was a quarterdeck soprano, trained to carry mast high through a gale; the accent was pure Carolina sea-island gumbo.

Marian, Jared Cofflin thought as he joined the councilors crowding to the windows, using his six feet two of lanky height to peer over their heads. One of the big birds was sprinting down Broad Street, heading for the harbor—or just away from the handlers with poles trying to catch it. People tumbled out of its way, bicycles toppled, ponies reared, a cart overset and bags of stone-ground flour burst in a beige mist.

"Damned funny-looking things, aren't they?" someone said.

Jared Cofflin agreed. *And they were a lot cuter as chicks,* he thought. Sort of fuzzy and about the size of a turkey; the *Eagle* had picked them up in a New Zealand that the Polynesians had yet to reach, during her survey voyage in the Year 2. *But, oh, how fast they grow.* The head still looked fairly chickenlike, although it was bigger than a German shepherd's, now; the eye bore a look of fixed stupidity leavened with terror. The bird itself stood twelve feet tall and weighed more than a cow, with a long neck, a bulbous body, and absurd, enormous three-toed feet—pile driver feet, and a man threw himself out of the way of a kick that could have snapped his neck. The ponies drawing another cart bolted, spilling barrels of whale oil, and the slipping, sliding chaos that followed would have been funny if it hadn't been so dangerous.

A steam-hauler puffed out onto Broad from Easy Street, pulling three wagons under tight-laced tarpaulins; it looked a little like an old-time locomotive, with the wheels of a heavy-hauler truck. The driver and fireman took one look and bailed out the other flank of their open-sided vehicle to get out of reach of the moa's six-foot neck, but they tripped the brake and exhaust valves first and it coasted to a halt in a huge *whuff* of white vapor that made the giant bird flinch and slow.

Then someone vaulted onto the tarpaulins, a tall slender black woman with a long curved blade in her hands.

Marian, all right, Cofflin thought. Which explained why she wasn't here already; it took a genuine emergency to make Commodore Marian Alston-Kurlelo late for anything. For a Southerner, she had a positively Yankee attitude toward punctuality. Maybe it was the twenty years she'd spent in the Coast Guard before the Event.

The *katana* flashed in a blurring arc as the huge bird tried to stop, turn, and peck at the annoying human all at the same time. Another flash of sunlight on steel, and there was a *crack* sound; Alston went to one knee on the tarpaulin, and shavings of beak spun free. The moa braked frantically on the slippery asphalt, then fell on its rear with an audible thud and an ear-stunning cry of *SKWAAAK*!

"Get that God-damned thing under control befo' it hurts somebody, Ah said!" she shouted again.

Before the moa could scramble upright the keepers were on it, and one of them clapped a bag on the end of a long pole over its head. A yank on a cord drew the bag tight, and the fight went out of the cow-size mass of gray feathers.

"CHHHHirrrr-aaak," it sounded in muffled protest, following meekly as the keeper hauled on the cord. Two more came behind and to either side, carefully avoiding the reflexive kicks.

"Come on, Tastes Like Chicken," the keeper said. "You've got an appointment with an ax."

"Whose bright idea was it to let one of those things loose in town?" Cofflin asked. *Actually they taste more like veal,* he added to himself.

Angelica Brand coughed discreetly. "Well, Chief, we're roasting a couple of them for the Event Day festivities, and . . . well, it's a lot easier to get tons of bird into town if they walk, and they're usually quite docile, this was just a little trouble . . ."

"Someone could have gotten hurt," he said sternly to the Councilor for Agriculture. He could hear Marian's quick step in the hallway outside. "Let's get back to business."

"Executive Council of the Republic of Nantucket will now come to order," the recording clerk droned. "All are present. Fourth meeting of the Year 8 After the Event, March twenty-first. Chief Executive Jared Cofflin presiding."

Damn, but we've gotten formal, Jared Cofflin thought. And single-digit years still sounded funny; granted, using "B.C." and "A.D." was just plain silly, since nobody knew if or when—when, if you listened to Prelate Gomez of the new Ecumenical Christian Church—Jesus

Christ was going to be born in this mutant history. The younger generation found the new system natural enough.

He brushed a hand over sandy blond hair even thinner on top than it had been at the Event; he was fifty-six now, honest, straightforward years even if he had looped around like this. Fisherman, Navy swabby, chief of police . . . and since the Event, head of state.

Christ.

"Okay," he said at last, when the reading of the minutes was over. "Let's get down to the serious stuff. Martha," he went on to his wife, smiling slightly, more a movement of the eyes than the lips.

Martha Cofflin, née Stoddard; ex-librarian, now Secretary of the Council, with a long, bony Yankee face like his and graying brown hair.

"First item is immigration policy," she said. "Before the Council are petitions to allow increases in the yearly quota of immigrants and temporary workers to the Island from Alba." The White Isle, what this era called Britain.

Odd, Cofflin thought again. There were plenty of islands, but everyone knew what you meant when you said *the* Island these days. *I suppose it was inevitable we'd develop our own slang.*

And our own feuds, he thought as hostile glances went up and down the Council table. On the one hand, Nantucket needed the hands. Everything took so *much* work, with the limited technology they had available; on the other hand . . .

Angelica Brand of Brand Farms nodded; so did half a dozen others. "I'm trying to get sugar-beet production started, and—"

"We need that next dry dock *badly*—"

"If we could only get some coal, there are surface deposits up in Nova Scotia—"

Our budding plutocrats, Cofflin thought. People on the Council tended to have useful knowledge and to be more energetic than most—that was why he'd picked them. Good people, mostly, but you had to watch them.

"Wait a minute!" said Lisa Gerrard of the School Committee, static crackling from her silver-white hair. "We're already overburdened. All these immigrants are illiterate—what with the adult education classes my people are working around the clock, the teacher-training program is behind schedule, *and* the crime rate's up!" Thoughtful nods.

Cofflin looked at his younger cousin George, who'd taken over his old job as head of the Island's police. "Ayup. Mostly Sun People. Can't hold their liquor, and then they start hitting. Or if a girl tells them to get lost, or they think someone's dissed them . . ."

"And besides that," Martha said, "if we're the majority, we can assimilate *them.* Too many, and it'll start working the other way 'round, or we'll end up as a ruling class with resentful aliens under us. And as George says, many of them just don't understand the concept of laws."

"Or why it's a bad idea to piss up against walls," someone laughed.

"Actually," a voice with the soft, drawling accent of the Carolina tidewater cut in, "we may have something of an outlet for their aggressions."

A couple of the Councilors looked over sharply; Marian was usually extremely quiet at Council meetings, except when her defense and shipbuilding specialties came up.

"From the reports," she went on, "Walker is leavin' us no choice but another war to put him down."

Thank you, Marian, he thought, letting one eyelid droop slightly. Her imperceptible nod replied, *You're welcome.*

"Well, perhaps we should move on to item two," he said neutrally.

"Item two," Martha said dryly, giving him a glance.

All right, all right, so I've learned to be a politician. Someone has to do it.

"William Walker," she continued.

This time the expressions down the table were unanimous. *Nobody* liked the renegade Coast Guard officer, or any of the twenty-odd other traitors with him. Nantucket had had to fight an expensive little war to stop him over in Alba—and had ended up with a sort of quasi protectorate-hegemony-cum-alliance over most of southern England.

Cofflin cleared his throat and looked at the Councilor for Foreign Affairs and his Deputy—Ian Arnstein and his wife, Doreen. They handed around their summary, and Ian began, sounding much like the history professor he'd once been.

"Our latest intelligence reports indicate he managed to get all the way from the English Channel to Greece, arriving about three months after the end of the Alban War, and—"

There were long faces at the table when he finished; many had hoped they'd seen the last of Walker when he fled Alba years ago. Someone sighed and said it out loud.

"Wishful thinkin'," Alston snapped. "We should have made sure of him, no matter what it took. I said so then."

"And the Town Meeting decided otherwise," Cofflin said. The Republic was very emphatically a democracy. Back then they'd decided that the margin of survival was too thin to keep hundreds under arms combing the endless wilderness of Bronze Age Europe.

And they were right, Cofflin thought. Not much prospect of catching Walker, and if they'd chased him hard back then he'd have settled somewhere deep in the continental interior, where the Islanders couldn't touch him. Leave him alone, and his arrogance and lust for revenge would make him stop within reach of salt water—planning to build a navy someday and come back for a rematch.

Marian had once said she was unsuited to Cofflin's job because she was a hammer . . . and saw all problems as nails. *But she's a very good hammer, and some problems are nails,* he mused, and went on aloud: "I think we can prod the Sovereign People into some action now, though." His statement was only half ironic. The people *were* sovereign here, very directly. "The screaming about how we're spending too much on defense ought to die down a little, at least. Marian?"

Marian Alston pulled out a sheaf of papers. "Here's what I propose," she began.

Little of it was a surprise to him. Contingency planning cost nothing, and he had a limited discretionary fund to work with for more concrete preparations. *At least we could lay the groundwork, since the Alban War.* The new Marine regiment was coming along fairly well, from the reports—young Hollard was a doer, and the Republic had grown enormously over the last eight years, in numbers and capacities.

Cofflin wondered grimly what Walker and his renegades had been doing in those same years. Walker wasn't the kind to let grass grow under his feet, damn him. If they *didn't* do something about him, eventually he would do something about *them.*

"Oh, sweet fucking Jesus Christ on a Harley," William Walker muttered in English, before dropping back into archaic Greek. *"Seventy alternative meanings?"*

Thick adobe walls kept the heat at bay, but light lanced in like spears of white through small, high windows. The room was a rectangle, whitewashed plaster on the walls and hard-packed earth covered in gypsum on the floor; it smelled of the damp clay in a tub, and of clay tablets drying in wicker baskets.

The Achaean scribe sat patiently on his stool. "Yes, lord," he said, humoring the newly-come stranger the High King had set him to serve. "There are seven tens of meanings for this sign."

His pen was a reed with a sharp thorn set in the tip, and his writing surface moist clay pressed on a board. The thorn scratched a circle divided by two straight lines, like a four-spoked wheel.

"This is the sign *ka,*" he said. "Also the sign for *ga, kha, kai, kas, kan. . . .*"

And you have to figure out which from context, Walker thought. *What an abortion of a writing system.*

The *real* joker was that the script wasn't even well suited to Greek. The main ancestors of these clowns had arrived in Greece as illiterate barbarian war bands from the north; they'd picked up writing from the

Minoan Cretans, along with most of what other feeble claims to civilization they had. The original script had been designed for a completely different language; all the signs for sounds ended in a vowel, and there were a whole bunch of Greek sounds that didn't have a sign at all.

Pathetic. Which was all to the good, of course. Not a day went by that he didn't bless Whoever or Whatever had caused the Event.

"Thank you, Enkhelyawon," he said to the scribe. *No fucking wonder nearly everyone's illiterate here.* "Now, how have you progressed with my people's script?"

In the original history, if "original" meant anything here, Mycenaean civilization was going to go under in another fifty years or so in a chaos of civil war and barbarian invasion; this writing system would be completely lost, and when the Greeks became literate again after their Dark Age it would be by borrowing the ancestral alphabet from the Phoenicians. The Romans would get it from the Greeks and then pass their version down to Western civilization . . . and here he was, teaching it to the ancestors of the Greeks. *More weird shit.*

"Lord, a child could master that script you showed me," Enkhelyawon said tolerantly. "Twenty-six signs? That is nothing."

He picked up another slab of prepared clay and quickly wrote out the Roman alphabet. "It is interesting, lord—I have yet to find a word that cannot be written in it."

"You won't," Walker said dryly. "And it *can* be learned by a child—that's the whole point."

The scribe was a middle-aged man, which meant mid-thirties here, with a few streaks of gray in his pointed black beard. Walker could watch the thought percolating through, and some of the implications popping up like lightbulbs. It was a look he'd become deeply familiar with since the Event. The locals weren't necessarily stupid; show them a concept and they'd often grasp it PDQ—the smarter and less hidebound ones. Not all of them thought that *So it was in the days of our fathers* was the answer to every problem, when you showed them an alternative. The trick was finding the right ones.

Enkhelyawon looked down at the clay tablet. "And . . . ah, I see. The sounds of the letters seldom change."

"Small need for us scribes, then," the Achaean went on after a moment, his voice subdued.

"No, *more* need for scribes," Walker reassured him. "The more that can be written, the more will be written. And here you write on skins as well as clay, true?"

"Of course, lord," Enkhelyawon said. "Clay is for rough notes, for monthly tallies. We transfer to parchment for lasting use; parchment is costly, of course."

Because it was a by-product of the sheep-and-goat industry, the hide scraped and pumiced until it was thin and smooth. Meat was an upper-class luxury here, and leather had a hundred other uses.

"Here is something we call *paper*."

"Ahh," the scribe said again, handling the sheet. "Like the Egyptian papyrus?"

"No. Notice it's more flexible. And it's made out of linen rags; this sample piece was made here in Mycenae. Nearly as cheap as clay, and it's much easier to write on."

More lightbulbs went on. Walker nodded and rose; one thing he'd learned in Alba, before those interfering bastards from Nantucket upset his applecart, was that power was like an iceberg—nine-tenths of it was invisible, the unspectacular, organizational side of things. At least here he didn't have to start from absolute ground zero with a bunch of savages who didn't even have the *concept* of organization beyond family and clan.

"Think about these things, Enkhelyawon," Walker said. "I will need a man who understands both the new and the old ways of writing and record keeping. Such a man could rise high, in my service. You must speak with my vassal Edward son of John." Who had been a CPA, before the Event. Double-entry bookkeeping . . .

He nodded to the Achaean's bow and walked out into the main hall-way of the house Agamemnon had granted him—his town house; there were also estates in the countryside down by Tiryns, and the land in the vale not yet called Sparta.

This was a typical nobleman's mansion for this day and age. The basement storerooms and the lower course of the wall were made from big blocks of stone, neatly fitted; above that were two stories of massive adobe walls and a flat roof. The outside was whitewashed, the walls inside covered in smooth plaster and then painted with vividly colored frescoes of fabulous beasts, war, and the hunt; the beams and stucco of the ceilings were painted too. In the center of the hall was a big circular hearth, sunken into the floor and stone-lined, surrounded with a coaming made of hard blue limestone blocks. Even in a summer a notional fire was kept going, the smoke wafting up to a hole in the ceiling; four big wooden pillars surrounded it, running through the second story and up to a little extra roof with a clay quasi chimney in it. A gallery surrounded the pillars with balconies from which you could look down into the great hall.

It all sort of reminded him of Southwestern style, Pueblo-Spanish, like the old Governor's palace in Santa Fe but gaudier. He'd been raised on a ranch in the Bitterroot country of Montana, but he'd been down that way competing in junior rodeos. It was a little gloomy, since most of the light came through the roof or from the antechamber at one end, but his followers were already putting up oil lamps. The local olive-squeezings weren't as bright as whale oil, but the still should be operational in a couple of days. Alcohol gave a nice bright light, when you knew enough to use a woven wick and a glass chimney.

Guards stood by the entranceway of bronze-bound wood, his own men from Alba. They wore equipment he'd made up there before the war, iron chain-mail hauberks and conical iron helmets with nasals; they carried steel-headed spears and round shields blazoned with his device, a wolfshead.

Another came and bowed his head, his helmet tucked under one arm. His blond hair was cropped at his ears like Walker's, and he sported a close-trimmed yellow beard.

"Wehaxpothis," he said—"Lord" in the tongue spoken by the Iraiina tribe in remote northwestern Europe, or "chief of he clan." "The men are settled and we are unpacking the goods. The *rahax* here has sent slaves, with many loads of fine things—cloth, and furniture. The Lady Hong and the Lady Ekhnonpa your wives are directing them."

"Good, Ohotolarix," Walker said. "That's *Wannax* Agamemnon, by the way. You and the others will have to learn Achaean, and quickly. It is needful."

It shouldn't be too difficult, either. The proto-whatever that Ohotolarix's people spoke was only about as different from this archaic Greek as French was from Italian.

"And your handfast man Bill Cuddy wishes to speak with you on the setting up of his *lathes* and of Martins's *forge*," the young guard-captain went on.

He managed the English words well; the twenty Americans among Walker's followers still used the language a fair bit, though he doubted their grandchildren would. *Probably there'll be a lot of loan words.* Even the civilized languages here lacked a lot of concepts.

"Let's go," Walker said, settling the *katana* and pistol at this belt. "We'll put in a forge, but the rest of the machinery's going down to Sparta. Oh, and get Alice."

Alice Hong was a doctor; he'd need to see to sanitation and water supply with her, here and at their other locations. Bad water was *dangerous.* He'd nearly crapped himself to death more than once since the Event. And she could get a start on modernizing the royal textile plant, too. The palace had hundreds of slave women spinning and weaving, but he had models and drawings for spinning jennies and kickpedal looms with flying shuttles; back in Alba they'd gotten them working well. After a lot of experiment, but it was all basic Early Industrial stuff, well within the capacities of a local carpenter. The machines would free up a lot of labor for other work and make the king properly grateful for all the extra wealth.

Hmmm, he wondered, *how long before we give the King of Men the heave-ho?*

Not for quite a while, he decided reluctantly. He'd have to thoroughly understand the politics here and make some allies first.

Walker laughed aloud and slapped his henchman on the shoulder. "Let's get to work," he said. "I want to be *ready* before we meet my old skipper again."

Ohotolarix was a hardy man, born to a warrior people. Nevertheless, he shivered slightly at the sound of his lord's laughter.

"*Got* it," Lieutenant Vicki Cofflin said, giving the bolt a final turn.

The new carburetor stood out against the pre-Event machining of the aircraft engine. It looked . . . clunkier, somehow. *Just make it easy to replace, make a couple of dozen, and switch as they wear out.*

She wiped her hands on a rag and then turned to Ronald Leaton. "You want to do the honors, Ron?"

The tall, lanky engineer shook his head, stepping back. "It's a Coast Guard project," he said. "Seahaven's just the prime contractor. All yours, Lieutenant."

Vicki nodded. "All right, then,"

She took a deep breath. The converted hangar near Nantucket's little airport was always cluttered, with parts and workbenches and machine tools. Right now it was even more so, with a big bag of goldbeater's skin—scraped whale intestine—hanging from the ceiling. A tube ran down from that to the Cessna engine mounted on a timber framework in the middle of the concrete floor. The rest of the team gathered around, in stained blue Coast Guard coveralls or the equally greasy unbleached gray cotton that Seahaven Engineering favored. The hangar smelled of hot whale-oil lubricant, and other things less familiar these days—gasoline fumes and a faint, nose-rasping hint of ozone.

Another deep breath, and she pushed the ignition button. The engine coughed, sputtered, blatted . . . and then settled down to a steady roar. Some of the watchers covered their ears, unused to something Nantucket had heard little of since the Event—an internal combustion engine at full throttle.

"Great!" Vicki shouted. "Let's take her up and down, and vary the mix. Stand by!"

The engine snarled, coughed again as the mixture of hydrogen from the gasbag and methanol altered. *Four hundred fifty horsepower, or thereabouts.* About what it had put out in its first incarnation as half the engines on a Cessna puddle jumper.

"Get that adjusted!" Vicki said. The tests continued, sweating-hot work on a summer's day, until at last she tripped the switch and wiped her hands again, smiling fondly as the engine sputtered into silence.

"Damn, you know, I think this is going to work," she said.

"No reason why it shouldn't," Leaton said. "Methanol, hydrogen, gasoline—it's all an inflammable gas by the time it reaches the piston."

Vicki chuckled indulgently; she was twenty-seven, nearly two decades younger than Leaton, and she still felt motherly toward him sometimes. One reason was the otherworldly way he had of forgetting *everything* but the task at hand.

"I meant the whole *Emancipator* program, not just the engine," she said.

"Oh. Oh, yes, that too. All right, people, break for lunch!"

He and Vicki and a young man in Guard fatigues walked over to a sloping table by the concrete-block wall. Plans were pinned to it, showing a tapering teardrop shape five hundred feet long and a hundred and ten wide at its broadest point, with a cruciform set of fins at the rear that looked like, and were, wings from light aircraft. Along the bottom of the forward one-third was a gondola curving down from the hull, with three engines in pods mounted along either side of it. Those looked like cut-down sections of aircraft wing too, and were.

"Never thought I'd be piloting a *dirigible,* of all things," she muttered to herself, feeling a rush of excitement. It would be her first command in the Guard, period, unless you counted a harbor tug. *If I get it,* she thought. That hadn't been decided yet.

The younger man—his name was Alex Stoddard, a fourth cousin once removed of the Chief's wife—looked up from examining the blueprints.

"If you don't mind me asking, Lieutenant Cofflin, what *did* you think you'd be piloting?" he said.

"F-16s," she said. "I was going to go to Colorado Springs, the year the Event happened." At his blank look, she went on: "The Air Force Academy, in Colorado. Up in the twentieth."

"Oh," he nodded, polite but somehow . . . *not indifferent. Just as if I was talking about flying to the moon. Real, but not* really *real.*

It was amazing what an effect it had—exactly how old you'd been at the Event. Even a couple of years, and the outlook was entirely different.

I was on the cusp, she thought. *Eighteen. Not quite an adult but not a kid either.* Alex had been sixteen on that memorable day; not a *little* kid, she judged, but unambiguously a *kid.* He had grown up in a world where steam engines were high tech, and schooners and flintlocks everyday realities. He probably didn't get that occasional feeling of alienation, as if a glass wall had dropped between him and the world.

Vicki ran a hand over her close-cropped reddish-brown hair and turned her attention back to the drawings. The frame of the airship was made up of two long strips that curled from bow to stern, criss-crossing each other in an endless series of elongated diamonds like a stretched-out geodesic dome. Inside that framework was a series of strengthening rings, each braced with spokes reaching in to a central metal hub.

"That wire's the only metal," Leaton said, his finger tapping a horizontal view of one of the rings. "Everything else is laminated birch-wood and balsa and wicker." He cleared his throat. "Only steel, rather. The clamps will have to be aluminum."

Everyone winced slightly. The Republic's new industries, here on the Island and the mainland and Alba, could turn out steel of a sort, iron, copper, bronze, and brass, but aluminum had to come from pre-Event stockpiles. Leaton had a plan for a small hydropower plant on the mainland to convert Jamaican bauxite; the only unworkable thing about it was it would take the entire national labor force ten years to get it going, in which time they'd all starve to death. Like so much else, it would simply have to wait a generation, or two or three.

"Good thing we can get the engines burning that liquid fuel-hydrogen mix," Alex said.

"Ayup," Leaton replied.

Vicki nodded. That way, the reduction in lift would precisely match the lesser weight as the methanol or gasoline or whatever burned, meaning you wouldn't have to dump ballast or valve gas, which extended range. So did the middle cell of the five cylindrical gasbags inside the hull. The forward and the rear two would be inflated with hydrogen, cracked out of water with a portable generator wherever the airship was based, to give the ship pretty well neutral buoyancy. The middle one was a hot-air balloon. *That* would provide the variable lift, again reducing the need to dump water ballast or release precious hydrogen to rise or fall.

Leaton rested one hand on Vicki's shoulder and the other on the younger Guard officer's. "Damned fine piece of work, if I say so myself—couldn't have done it without you. It's going to work." He cleared his throat again; it was a gesture of his, like knocking on wood. "Once we've got the bugs out of it, of course."

"Of course," Vicki said dryly. Then she snorted. "Commodore Alston was . . . impressed . . . too, when she saw the plans on Monday."

"She was?" Leaton said, brightening; Alex looked eager as well. "What did she say?"

"She said . . ." Vicki stretched her Yankee vowels to try and match the sea-island Gullah of the Republic's military leader. *"Do Jesus, ah'm glaaayd ah ain' goin' up on that-theah!"*

They shared a laugh. "Got to go," Leaton said. "Washington Street Mills is having problems with their new powerloom, and if they don't get it fixed the Commodore will flay me—they've got a big sailcloth order in for the new frigates."

The two Guard officers took their boxed lunches and bottles of sassafras tea to a bench outside. It was a warm day, for springtime in Nantucket—seventy-two degrees, according to the thermometer— and the wind in from the south smelled of turned earth from the spring plowing, a rich, not unpleasant odor of fertilizer, and a tang of sea salt under that. The airport no longer looked abandoned, what with the new projects; one huge shed was going up, the frames like giant croquet hoops spanning a stretch of unused runway that furnished a ready-made floor. Besides that, the scout balloon hung high overhead, looking like a miniature inflated version of the *Emancipator*'s plans with a two-person gondola slung underneath, toy-tiny at the top of a thousand feet of cable.

An ultralight was going up too, wheeled out of a hangar with ground crew hanging on to the wingtips as they wrestled it around to face into the wind. The fuselage below was a one-person plywood teardrop, with a little lawn mower–style engine and a ducted-fan propeller behind; stubby pylons extended on either side, bearing a brace of black-powder rockets.

Jesus, I hate those things, Vicki thought. The electric ignition system for the rockets was . . . *not very sophisticated*—that was a nice, tactful way to put it.

"You know," Alex said meditatively after a while, "I'm a little surprised that the *Emancipator* got approved. I mean, it'll be *useful,* having something that can scout way around and carry light cargo— and I'm damned glad I'm getting an opportunity to fly—but is it cost-effective?"

"Not here," Vicki said gently. "Not on the Island."

"Not—oh."

The younger officer nodded. Vicki Cofflin was the daughter of one of the Chief's sisters, a much closer connection than his to the Secretary of the Council.

"Well, let's get back to work," she said. "Don't you love being on the cutting edge of technical progress?"

"Damned right," Alex said, nodding.

Jesus, Vicki thought, as she followed him back into the hanger. *I thought I was joking.*

CHAPTER TWO

Ranger Peter Girenas grunted as he lifted the gutted whitetail from the packhorse's back and brought it to a nearby cache-tree. Two other deer hung from the white-oak branch already, and he quickly ran the dangling leather cord through a slit between the bone and tendon of this carcass's hind legs.

With one hand braced against the flank, he jerked the crossbow bolt free. Easier than digging out a bullet, and cheaper—it was only in the last couple of years that ammunition had gotten cheap enough to use for hunting.

"Here it is, Pete," Sue Chau said, handing him half the deer liver, spitted on the green stick she'd used to grill it over the low coals of the fire.

"Thanks. Perks says thanks, too."

She laughed and nudged the dog with her toe. Perks didn't normally allow liberties, but right now he was too occupied with the deer head to resent it. Girenas squatted by the fire to wolf the meat down; the smell alone was enough to make a man drool after a day's hard work. It went well with the green smell of summer forest, the leafy-yeasty odor of the mold on the ground, and the spicy sassafras tea boiling in the pot. The rich organ-meat juices filled his mouth and ran down over his chin as he bit into the liver.

Have to shave soon, he thought, wiping his chin with a palm. The bristles rasped at his hand. *Or mebbe start a real beard.* He'd tried two years ago, but it had grown in patchy, as well as three shades closer to orange than the ash-blond thatch on his head. Still, he was twenty-one now, old enough to raise a decent crop, and it would be a relief to stop scraping his face. Shaving in the bush was no joke, even with a good Seahaven straightedge.

He was conscious of the girl's eyes on him as he stripped off his equipment belt and buckskin hunting shirt and went to the edge of the creek to wash off. *Look all you want,* he thought, grinning as the water's pleasant coolness cut through the sweat and dried blood on his skin. He stood an inch over six feet in his moccasins, with long legs and arms and shoulders heavy with the muscle that logging and hunting put on you. His face was broad in the cheeks, snub-nosed, weathered to a dark tan that made the pale gray of his eyes all the more vivid. He flung back his head in a shower of droplets and turned, still grinning. Sue was a couple of years younger than him, but well past the gawky stage; a looker, too, with exotic slanted blue eyes, amber skin, and long black hair, the heritage of a half-Vietnamese father and a French Canadian mother.

Not that any of that old-timer crap means anything here, he thought, catching her eye and winking, chuckling when she blushed and looked away. You were a Nantucketer or not, that was the important thing here in the Year 8. So far all they'd done on this hunting trip was hunt, but he had hopes . . .

She frowned as his expression went cold and his eyes slid past her. "Pete—"

The man cut her off with a chopping gesture. "What is it, Perks?" he said.

The beast stayed in his stiff crouch, head pointing northward and hair bristling along his spine, the beginnings of a battle rumble trickling out of his deep chest; he was a mastiff-wolf mix nearly a yard high at the shoulder, and right now he looked to favor his wild father's side of the cross. Peter's eyes flicked about. They had camped by a little overhang, where the creek ran down from a stretch of rocky hills. A couple of elms had fallen here in some storm, leaving a clearing edged with thick brush. Half a dozen steps in any direction the woods began, white pine north, white oak and chestnut and hickory lower down, all tall enough to shade out most undergrowth. Now that the sun was three hours past noon, the shadows under the great trees were deep and soft, hard on eyes half blinded by the light spearing down into the open space.

Sue had gone silent, her eyes scanning as well. She took three casual steps sideways and picked up the Seahaven-made rifle leaning against a shagbark hickory, her thumb going to the hammer to pull it back to full cock. Pete walked toward his own bedroll and weapons, equally slowly . . . no sense in making whoever or whatever was approaching commit themselves.

A twig snapped, and four men moved through the scrub at the forest edge. *Damn,* Peter thought as he halted and stood at his ease, his face an unreadable mask. *Rather have a bear, or a cougar.*

"Heel, Perks," he said. The dog trotted to stand beside him, hair bristling on its neck and shoulders, teeth showing long and wet.

The Nantucketer raised his right hand with the palm forward.

"Peace," he said—the gesture was common here, and they might have that much English.

Although I doubt it, he decided. They weren't any group he recognized. Stocky, muscular men with bronze-brown skins, dressed in breechclouts, leggings, and moccasins much like his. Hide bundles rode their backs; two of them gripped flint-headed darts set in atlatls, spear-throwing levers; one had a steel-headed trade hatchet in his hand; another, an elaborately carved hardwood club. Their bold-featured faces were as impassive as his; he watched their eyes, hands, feet, all the clues that told of intentions. Each had the sides of his head shaved and painted vermilion, with the hair up in a roach above and trailing in a queue behind; all the tribes on the coasts near Nantucket did. These had bars of blue pigment across their faces at eyebrow level as well, and a strip of yellow from brow to chin.

Whatever the hell that means. Maybe from far inland. Or they might not be from any tribe at all, just homeless wanderers from bands broken up in the epidemics. One had heavy facial scarring; he'd seen Indians marked up like that from the chickenpox in the Year 3. *Or maybe measles from the year after.*

"Peace," he said again.

Uh-oh. They weren't looking at him; they were looking at the camp. It wasn't much, just two bedrolls and traveling gear, but it would be a fortune in steel weapons and tools to locals. And attacking strangers wasn't considered wrong by any of the tribes they'd contacted—not unless oaths had been sworn.

"You're welcome to share our camp," he said. *"Hinyep Zhotopo,"* he repeated in Lekkansu, the tongue of the seacoast people that the Nantucketers had most dealings with. Hunters from one of the bands who traded with the Americans would have replied in kind; they took hospitality seriously.

Damn. No response at all, except to widen out a little as they came toward the fire. He was conscious of a cold, sour churning in the pit of his stomach and a furious annoyance that Sue was here . . . and all of it was incredibly distant, like the drumbeat of blood in his ears.

"Stop!" he said, waving them back, scowling. *Can't just . . .*

The spearcast came with blinding speed. Girenas was already dropping and rolling as the ashwood shaft whickered through the space he'd been occupying to thud three inches deep into a beech tree and stand quivering. The second spearman was aiming more carefully when Sue's rifle went off with a sharp crack and a long jet of off-white powder smoke. The Indian folded around himself with a surprised *ooof!* like a man who'd been punched in the gut. He wouldn't be getting up again, though, not with an exit wound the size of a baby's fist blasted out the other side of him by the hollowpoint.

Girenas flipped himself back to his feet, and the eighteen-inch bowie strapped along his right calf snapped into his fist, then into a gutting swing. The hatchet-man jinked in midleap as he dodged back, his war shriek turning to a yell of alarm. His friend with the club was using it to fend off Perks, the dog showing an endless ratcheting snarl and making little rushes whenever he saw an opening. *Ignore it.* The world sank down to one man and a razor-edged piece of steel on a two-foot wooden shaft. They circled, crouched, their soft moccasins rutching in the fallen leaves and punk of rotten branches. Five seconds passed, and then the Indian feinted twice and swung in earnest, a blow that would have chopped halfway through Girenas's face. He met the descending arm with a bladed palm, and the hatchet spun away. The bowie slammed forward, cutting edge up.

The Indian's hand slapped down on his wrist. For an instant they grappled chest to chest, the heavy smell of sweat and the bear grease that the man wore on his hair rank in his nostrils; the warrior's body felt like a bundle of rubber and steel. Then Girenas hooked a heel behind an ankle and pushed. They went down; the Nantucketer landed on top of his opponent, one knee in his stomach. The air wheezed out of him in a choking grunt. Girenas pinned him with his left hand and ripped the other free of the weakening grasp, stabbed once, again, again. The body thrashed under him and blood splashed into his face, but he ignored it as he rolled erect.

That was just in time to see the third Indian grab Sue's rifle in both hands, trying to wrestle it away from her. In a less serious situation, the look on his face as she hopped up, kicked both feet into her attacker's belly, and fell backward to flip him up and over would have been comical. She spun around on her backside like a top, raising both legs and slamming her heels into the Indian's face as he started to rise—a move from the unmercifully practical school of unarmed combat that Marian Alston had made part of Islander schooling. She scrambled to grab the rifle, came up to both knees and pounded the steel-shod butt into the Indian's bloodied face again and again, panting with fright and rage.

The last Indian was writhing under a hundred and twenty pounds of wolf-dog, trying to hold the fangs away from his face. Girenas scooped up his crossbow from where it hung on a branch nub and put the short, thick quarrel through the Indian's chest a second before the wide-stretched jaws would have closed on him.

That was a mercy, in its way.

"Reload!" he snapped at Sue. She was pale and her hands shook. *"Reload! Now!"* She took a deep breath, let it out, and obeyed. He nodded satisfaction. "Heel, Perks."

Girenas pumped the iron lever set into the forestock of his crossbow six times, and the thick steel bow cut down from a car's leaf-spring ratcheted back and clicked into place, ready for the quarrel he slipped into it. The girl pushed up the breech lever of the rifle, her eyes enormous in a face gone pale, thumbing home a paper cartridge, closing the action and priming the pan. They both went to ground behind logs, eyes scanning.

"Perks! Circle!" he snapped.

The dog slipped through the underbrush and made its way around their campsite. The ranger followed, infinitely cautious. He found Perks nosing back along a trail and followed it for a few hundred yards, until he saw a place where all the Indians had paused in a muddy patch.

"Only the four of them," he said as he stepped back into the camp-site. Relief mingled with sadness as he cleaned the knife and looked at the dead men. "Damn—"

Sue Chau had been staring at them too. Abruptly she turned and blundered three yards away before going to her knees and vomiting up a rush of half-digested deer meat. Girenas nodded, sighed, and took her a pannikin of water.

"Rinse and spit," he said. "Then have a drink of this."

The silver flask had been his father's; it had Cyrillic lettering on it. The contents were pure Nantucket barley-malt whiskey, aged a year in charred oak. The girl obeyed, choking a little, then went to splash her face.

"Sorry," she began.

"Nope," Girenas said. "You did pretty good." He kept his tone cool. "Still want to be a Ranger?"

She looked at the dead men. The bowel stink was already fairly bad, and the flies were arriving in droves. "This sort of thing, does it happen often?"

"Nope," Girenas said again. "Sometimes, though. Mebbe once a year."

Sue took a deep breath. "Well, I'm not quitting," she said.

"Good," he said with approval. "Now let's cover them up and get going." He looked at the sun again. "Might make the base if we push it."

They broke out the shovels and dug, setting rocks from the stream on top of the earth; Girenas planted the men's weapons as markers at their heads. Silence reigned as they broke camp and headed south toward Providence Base; Sue went in the lead with her rifle in the crook of her arm, then the three packhorses with the kills and gear. Girenas brought up the rear, and Perks went further still, like a hairy gray shadow among the trunks of the huge trees.

It was hours before they saw sign of their own people. That was scanty at first, a buried campfire, hoofmarks, a nest of feral honey-bees, clover and bluegrass growing wild from seed dropped in horse-dung. Then breaks in the forest canopy where loggers had gone through, clearings scattered with stumps and chips or already rank with tall grass, brambles, flowers, and saplings. They stepped onto a rutted drag-trail heading downhill, and then the hills parted to show Narragansett Bay gleaming out before them, white-ruffled blue water, banks and islands green to the water's edge, sky thick with wildfowl. Half a dozen craft were in sight—a schooner, fishing boars, tugs hauling rafts. Below ran a road, gravel over dirt, and they could hear the faint shriek of a steam whistle.

"Home," Sue said.

She opened the breech of her rifle and used the cleaning rod to tap the paper cartridge out, stowing it in the pouch at her belt before blowing the priming out of the pan and easing the hammer forward. Girenas slipped the quarrel from his crossbow back into its quiver before pulling the trigger with a flat *whung* sound.

"Home," he agreed, with a sigh.

"Get sent to the past, spend all your time annotating reports," Councilor for Foreign Affairs Ian Arnstein muttered, in the privacy of his sunroom-office. "What a dashing life we exiled adventurers lead. Christ, I might as well be back in San Diego grading history papers."

Well, not exactly, perhaps, he thought, resharpening his goose-quill pen on the razor built into the inkstand and looking down at the report. *God, but I hate these pens.* The last ballpoints had run out years ago, and nobody had gotten around to fountain pens yet; it was the usual story—too much else with higher priorities.

God, but I miss my PC. Oh, God, for a laser printer.

He pushed his glasses back up his beaked nose—and losing *them* was something he didn't even want to contemplate, given what the Island lens grinders were turning out as an alternative—and read the paper before him again, winding his fingers absently in his beard. It was a long-standing gesture; unlike many on the Island, he'd had this back before the Event, when shaving was easy. It was bushy and curly and a dark russet brown where it wasn't gray, like what was left of the hair on his head, almost matching the color of his eyes.

He tugged harder as he read on. The Keyaltwar tribe over in Alba were building boats . . . probably war-boats for raiding abroad. Some bright boy in a leather kilt had figured out that while under the Treaty of Alliance they couldn't hitch up their chariots, take down their tomahawks, and hit the neighbors up for cattle and women in the old style—several punitive expeditions had driven *that* lesson home—third parties weren't covered.

Those people are like the fucking Energizer Bunny. There was a map of Alba in one corner of the room. A line ran from roughly what would have become Portsmouth to what would have become southern Yorkshire. Everything east and south of it was the various *teuatha* of the Sun People, the Indo-European-speaking newcomers William Walker had enrolled in his attempt at conquest; these days they were Nantucket allies in theory, a resentful protectorate in fact. West and north of that were the Fiernan Bohulugi, allies in fact.

Dotted lines marked individual tribes. "Keyaltwar . . . right, north bank of the Thames." The Sun People tribes weren't much for commerce. What they *did* understand was raiding, rustling, rape, and slaughter; and now they were playing Viking.

"Blond Proto-Celtic Comanches of the Bronze Age," Ian muttered, turning pages to look at the sketch of the ship. Up front was a figurehead that looked for all the world like a dragon's head. Some passing Islander trader or priest of the Ecumenical Church might well have *told* them about the Vikings, like dropping a catalyst into a saturated solution. *As if they didn't get enough ideas of their own. Have to be careful not to push 'em too hard, though.*

First, radio Commandant Hendriksson to send out more agents. The treaty forbade hindering traders and missionaries, which was convenient for espionage. Find out who exactly was doing this. *Note: we might use bribes and economic threats to lean on the Keyaltwar high chief, if he's not involved.* Then see which of the Keyaltwar's neighbors had the most blood feuds with them—inevitable that some would. *They* could complain to the Alliance Council at Stonehenge, saying that they felt threatened, and that would put it under the treaty's purview . . . if you stretched that deliberately ambiguous document a point or two.

"Note," he wrote at the bottom. "Consult with Doreen"—his wife treated Gordian knots the way Alexander had, and that corrected his tendency to on-the-one-hand-but-on-the-other himself into paralysis—"then talk it over with Marian, Jared, and Martha." He brushed the feather tip of the quill over his nose.

"Note," he went on. "Talk to Prelate Gomez. Missionaries?"

For a moment he chuckled at the thought. A thoroughly secular Jew, helping to spread religion among the pagans of Bronze Age Britain. Ecumenical Christianity at that—the federation of denominations here, something rather like very High Church Episcopalian with Unitarian overtones. Another dry chuckle; the snake was biting its own tail with a vengeance, with Americans bringing the Anglican faith to Alba.

Then he began writing up an appreciation for the Chief; they'd have to explain things to the Town Meeting. How the ancient Athenians had gotten *anything* done with all decisions made by a committee of thousands baffled him, all the more so now that he'd seen direct democracy in action.

He sanded and blotted the paper, rose, stretched, and looked at his watch. Four-thirty, and he'd been working since eight. "Christa," he said to his second assistant, ambling out into the sitting room and then down the corridor to *her* office. "Get fair copies of these typed up, would you? And run one over to the Chief's, and one to Commodore Alston-Kurlelo at Guard House."

Almost unfair, he thought, looking around at the filing cabinets and map boards. Preliterate cultures just didn't appreciate the advantage that being able to store and collate information like this gave you. *But then again, as Marian Alston-Kurlelo is wont to say, fair fights are for suckers.*

Ian trotted up the first flight of stairs, to one of the converted bedroom suites that served as Doreen's office. The former student astronomer looked up; she was sitting across a table from a short, dark man in a long woolen robe, flowerpot hat, and curled beard, repeating a sentence in something guttural and polysyllabic. Papers were scattered on the surface, some covered with ordinary writing, others with what looked like Art Deco chicken tracks.

Akkadian, Ian knew, with a shudder—the Semitic language spoken in Hammurabi's Babylon; he had to learn it too. Akkadian was the diplomatic language in today's Middle East, the way French had been in Louix XIV's Europe. At least they'd been careful with their language teacher this time, after the nasty experience with Isketerol of Tartessos in the Year 1. Shamash-nasir-kudduru—the God Shamash is Guardian of the Boundary Stone, or Sham for short—was a weedy little Babylonian date merchant whom one of the Islander ships had picked up in a brief initial survey of the Persian Gulf; he'd been living on Bahrain (Dilmun to the locals) and not doing very well. In fact, he looked a lot like Saddam Hussein after a long, strict diet.

"My lady," he said in a thickly guttural accent, with a sidelong glance at Ian, "here we have the . . . it is to say . . . symbol, meaning 'day.' " He drew one wedge with the broad end upright, and two more springing off to the left and slanting upward. "It to be is able also to be the symbol for a *sound*."

"Which sound?" Doreen asked with a sigh.

"It is sound *ud*," the Babylonian said. "That is first sound. Also symbol is for *tu* or *tam* or *par* or *likh* or *khish* . . ." He drew another, with an upright wedge, three horizontal to the side, and an arrowhead to the left. "It is sound *shu, qad, qat*. Can mean *quatu*, it is meaning in your speech, 'hand.' Also *emuqu*, 'strength,' or *gamalu*, 'protection,' or . . ."

Ian cleared his throat. "What say we commit some dereliction of duty?" he said.

"God, yes," she groaned. "Sham, you can knock off too. Same time tomorrow."

The Babylonian made a bobbing gesture over folded hands and collected his writing materials. Doreen tidied her own desk; she was neater than Ian, perhaps because as Doreen Rosenthal before the Event she'd been a budding astronomer in her late twenties rather than a bachelor—well, widower—professor of classical history just past fifty. She also looked *extremely* good bending over like that in a light summer dress, with her long black hair falling down and half hiding a wonderful view of décolletage. She'd been positively chunky when he'd first seen her, back the day after the Event. That was when she was working as an intern at the Maria Mitchell Observatory, where she'd used the little reflector telescope to pinpoint the real date from the stars. *Of course, we all lost weight those first six months, and God knows we're not likely to sit around watching TV anymore.* Nowadays she could have modeled for a statue of Ishtar, one of the sexier kind.

"Let's pick up David and grab something to cook down at the docks—couple of lobster, we'll boil 'em up and throw together a salad."

Their housekeeper-nanny had the boy in the kitchen with her while she sat with a cookbook, reading slowly, her lips moving. Back at the end of the Alban War the Islanders had insisted that the defeated Sun People tribes let all their slaves go free. Denditwara had been one of many who came to Nantucket, since she had no surviving family. The gap in living standards was so enormous that even the most lowly job here was luxury by Bronze Age standards.

Sort of like Mexico and California, only more so, Ian thought. "If you haven't started dinner yet, Denditwara, don't bother," he said. "We'll handle it—Quigley's Baths first, and then the evening's yours."

"Thank you, boss," she said, dipping her head; she was half his age and short, a round-faced blonde who looked extremely English, physical types evidently being much more constant than culture or language. The Alban gave them a shy smile of gratitude for the free time; she was seeing a young man who worked in the whalebone mill.

Ian and Doreen winced slightly. Getting her to use something else besides the Sun People term for "master" had been difficult. So had getting across the concept of being an employee and working for wages.

"Can I see the boats, Daddy?" David asked. He showed signs of sharing his father's height, but the face had Doreen's oval shape and olive tone and black ringlets hung around his ears.

"Yes, you can see the boats if you promise to keep close to me and your mother," Ian said. He could see the six-year-old considering the bargain.

"Will," he said. "I *want* to see the boats."

That's a relief, Ian thought, chuckling. Nantucket was a better place for children than L.A., but there were still street hazards.

"What a zoo," Ian muttered an hour later, as they watched Denditwara scamper off to meet her bone grinder and David started to tell them about a game of catch he'd played with one of the other children in the baths. The roar of traffic nearly drowned the child's treble piping.

"All right, all right, hold your horses, we'll get out of the way," Ian said, as a carter cried for space. He and Doreen were standing on the broad, flat expanse of the Steamship Dock, where the ferry from the mainland had tied up to drop off cars and trucks and tourists, back before the Event.

Arnstein looked up reflexively as he remembered that never-to-be-forgotten night . . . *God, eight years ago.* A little more, since the Event had been in March and it was into July now. The crawling dome of fire over the island, and then the terror next day as the impossible truth sank in. Then the even worse terror: seventy-five hundred Americans on an island that produced little besides daffodils and a few gourmet vegetables. Fear of starvation, food riots, cannibalism . . . Hell of a thing for a middle-aged professor of classical history to get himself caught in. Hell, he'd almost canceled his spring vacation on Nantucket that year.

"But we made it. Tight at times, but we made it," he muttered.

He looked over at Doreen as she bent to jerk their son back from a determined attempt to pet a pony. The shaggy, stiff-maned animal was sulking in the traces of a cart heaped high with barrels of maple syrup from Providence Base on the mainland. It had a look of settled discontent on its face, an I-am-about-to-bite-you expression. The Bronze Age chariot ponies they'd brought back from Alba usually did. The first generation crossbred from the Alban mares and the Island's quarter horse and Morgan and Thoroughbred stallions were a lot better, but still expensive.

"What was that, Ian?"

"I said we'd made it." The two of them nodded in silent agreement.

Fishing boats were unloading amid a raucous swarm of gulls a little to the southeast, at Straight Wharf and its basin and the row of long piers constructed over the last few years. That part of town hadn't been as densely built up before the Event, and the new waterfront there was full of fish-drying sheds, workshops, warehouses, and timberyards built since.

Here on Steamship Dock only the respect due Councilors kept a small bubble of space open. Half a dozen brigs and schooners were tied up—the classes that Nantucket's new merchant houses used for long-distance work. The ratcheting of the spindly cranes and winches that swung heavy loads ashore was loud even against the clatter of hooves and iron wheels on the pavement.

Factors and dealers and storekeepers dickered and yelled, customs agents prowled, sailors chanted their rhythmic *Heave . . . ho! stamp and go, stamp and go, heave . . . ho!* as they hauled to unload cargo. Indians in blankets jostled kilted Proto-Celtic warriors and priestesses of the Fiernan Bohulugi cult of Moon Woman from Alba in poncho and thong skirt, watched by an Olmec noble wearing a cloak of woven hummingbird feathers that shimmered in impossible shades of turquoise, scarlet, purple. A herd of moas—the smaller breed, only four feet at the shoulder—were being pushed clucking and protesting onto a barge, headed for Long Island and the farming life. The spattered by-product of their fright added its aroma to the thick odors of drying fish and boiling whale blubber, raw leather, horses and horse dung, sweat and woodsmoke, tarred rope and wooden hulls.

The fresh sea breeze kept it tolerable even in summer. Mostly tolerable. One reason the Meeting had authorized steam dredgers was to dig deep channels southeast up the lagoon, so some of the more odorous trades could be moved downwind of town.

They dodged around a cargo from the Caribbean going inland on steam-haulers—bulk salt from the Islander penal settlement in the Bahamas, a few precious sacks of coffee from plants set out on Trinidad the spring after the Event, chunks of raw asphalt, sulfur for gunpowder.

Plus quetzal feathers, jaguar pelts, chocolate beans, raw cotton, mahogany and dyewoods from trading along the Main, he thought. The list sounded more romantic than the hot, sweaty, dangerous reality; the Indians down there were corn farmers and therefore more numerous and better organized than the hunting peoples along the New England coast. There had been one short, sharp war with the Olmecs already.

Of course, that was that noble savage True Believer idiot Lisketter's fault. Rousseau, what sins have been committed in Thy name! Lisketter and her followers had ended up very dead, along with a few of the Islander military and a whole raftload of Olmecs. Lisketter's people had been sacrificed to the Jaguar God and eaten, most of them.

He didn't even like to *think* about what had happened to Lisketter before she died.

"And speaking of lobster pots," he said.

They pushed their way to the base of the Steamship Dock, along a waterside section of Easy Street, then over to the shallower basin beyond Old North Wharf, which now catered to the inshore fishery.

"Got 'em right here for you, Mr. Arnstein," the lobsterman said, hauling up a net dangling overside from his boat.

"Thanks, Jack," he replied, handing over a silver nickel, the Republic's own coinage, and accepting the change in coppers.

The former software salesman nodded thanks. David prodded the gently squirming canvas sack with his fingers and giggled at the sensation. Ian checked his turn at the fisherman's soft exclamation and looked to his left.

Another ship was being towed south between the breakwaters and into Nantucket's harbor. The design was American; to be exact, a scaled-up copy of the *Yare,* a two-masted topsail schooner that had carried tourists around the island before the Event. It wasn't Island-built, though. Countless small details showed that, starting with the stylized mountain on the flag at the mainmast top. Six small bronze cannon rested with their muzzles bowsed up against the bulwarks on each side of the craft.

One of Isketerol's ships. Ian shook his head; you had to hand it to the man . . .

"When you tell it, my sire, it's as if I can see it with my own eyes," Sarsental said, his eyes glowing.

Isketerol hid a grin. The new king of Tartessos was still in his thirties, with no silver strands in his bowl-cut black hair and all his teeth. He could remember what it was like to be a boy of twelve winters, just coming to a man's estate and wild for great deeds.

He leaned back in the courtyard lounger, smiling at the children sitting around his feet. Deck chairs were another Amurrukan thing. *The Eagle People certainly know how to make themselves comfortable,* he thought idly.

"Weren't you frightened?" one of his daughters asked.

Isketerol laughed. "Some of us were like to soil our loincloths," he said. "There we were, just two shiploads of us—the old ships, remember, small and frail—alone among the northern savages on a trading voyage. That was dangerous enough, they're wild and uncouth. Then there *it* was, the *Eagle* ship itself. Three hundred feet long and made of *iron*—"

They gasped.

"—and with masts a hundred and fifty feet tall. Three of them. Hull shining white as snow, with a red slash of blood-color across it and the great golden image of their Eagle god beneath the bows. Many of us wanted to flee right there, I can tell you."

"But you didn't, my sire," his eldest son said.

"No. Let that be a lesson to you." He reached out a hand and made a snatching motion. "Be cautious, but when the Jester drops a chance for advantage, take it! The Jester is bald behind, you can't grab His hair once He's past. I stayed by the side of the barbarian chief we'd been dealing with, and Arucuttag of the Sea rewarded me. For when the Amurrukan, the People of the Eagle, landed . . . one of them spoke Achaean, and I could act as their go-between with the natives as they dickered for grain and beasts."

He fixed an eye on his eldest son. "See what learning foreign languages can do? I'd have been dumb as a fish but for that. So study your Achaean and Sudunu and English."

Sarsental nodded, slow and thoughtful. *Good!* Isketerol thought. He didn't intend that his heir should fritter away the mightiness he was building here.

"That's when you met the Medjay chieftainess?" a daughter chimed in eagerly. "The Nubian warrior?"

Isketerol winced slightly. *Have I told it so often that children correct me?* Still, it was important that they all learn; there would be work enough for all the children of his wives. Little Mettri didn't look as if she'd settle down to spinning and overseeing the housemaids, and she loved this part.

"Yes," he said. "A tall woman, black as charcoal, was their captain. Alston was her name, a fierce warrior, good sailor, skilled with the sword and very cunning. She's still the Amurrukan war-leader, under their king, Cofflin."

"A woman," Sarsental said dismissively.

Isketerol reached out a hand and rapped him on the head with his knuckles. "Their customs are different. Don't underestimate an enemy! I've made that mistake, to my cost."

"Yes," he went on, "she was the one who invited me to their homeland across the River Ocean, to teach them the languages of these lands around the Middle Sea. On the *Eagle* I met *William Walker*"—he pronounced the Amurrukan name carefully—"and became his blood brother, for he was discontented with the rule of Cofflin and Alston and wished to find a land where he himself could be lord. And there I learned much; and from him I learned much. Together we pirated the *Yare* and her cargo from Nantucket, together we conquered and ruled among the Sun People and the Earth Folk of Alba. When the Amurrukan made alliance with the Earth Folk and defeated him, it was I who took him and his band to the Achaean lands, and I received in reward the great ship *Yare* and much of her burden of treasures."

"After you stopped here in Tartessos and made yourself king with his aid!" they chorused.

"Not just made myself king," Isketerol said. "Began to make Tartessos great—and after the Crone comes for me, you who are my children must make our city greater still. And to do that you must learn many things, so—"

They groaned but obeyed as he signaled to the servant to take them back to their lessons.

Isketerol stretched and sighed. Time to get back to work. He was a slight, wiry man of medium height such as was common in southern Iberia, dark of hair and eye and olive of skin, with thin white scars seaming the brown skin of his forearms and a mariner's calloused hands.

"Send in the king's chief of makers," he said. The mustketeer guards by the entrance to the courtyard stood motionless, but a messenger from the rank standing by the wall hurried out.

Soon the official came, with a slave bearing a long bundle behind him. Both went down on their faces in prostration, and Isketerol signed them up.

"Let me see it," he said. Then: "Yes," he went on, pulling back the hammer of the musket. "You have done well. I will not forget it."

The musket was solid and deadly feeling in his hands, stocked in beechwood, the iron blued to an even finish. Its smell of oiled metal was heavy and masculine amid the scents of flowers and sun-dried earth. He swung it to his shoulder and took aim at the figure of a warrior in the mural painted on the whitewashed wall of adobe brick across the courtyard.

Squeeze the trigger, he remembered. *Click-whap!* and the hammer snapped down. Sparks flew as it cracked the frizzen-cover back. A pouch of cartridges accompanied the weapon, each with one charge in a cylinder of paper, and a bullet shaped like a conical helmet with a hollow in the flat base. A *minié ball*, the books said—why, he didn't know, for it was not in the least round.

"Yesss," the king of Tartessos said happily.

His hands caressed the weapon. Much better than the first crude batches. In a few years they would have breechloaders, but this was well enough.

"How many?" he asked his Chief of Makers.

"Lord of the city and the Land, Bridegroom of the Corn Goddess, Favored Son of Arucuttag of the Sea and the Lady of Tartessos . . . fifty now, and ten more each seven days, to begin with. Each with *bayonet* and *ramrod.*" The man's tongue stumbled slightly over the English words.

That was not such pleasant hearing. The man hurried on: "Lord King, if you did not insist on the, the *measuring with screws* of each part—"

"Then the guns could not be repaired at need with ready-made parts," Isketerol snapped.

And if many had to be taught to repair the parts, they would start making them for themselves. William had left him a set of duplicate micrometer gauges along with the spare lathe, and he intended to keep the manufacture of guns his own monopoly just as long as he could.

"I do not understand this making of each thing so like another thing," the artisan said.

"It is not necessary that you understand, only that you obey!" Isketerol shouted in exasperation.

"You are the king, lord," the man said, bowing, turning pale beneath his natural olive.

Not only the king, but a king more powerful than the one who had fallen to iron-armored warriors and fire-powder bombs and William's deadly *Gurund rifle.* The old king had done nothing without consulting the heads of the great families.

Today many of those heads hung on iron hooks from the walls of the palace. Now when the king of Tartessos commanded, men fell on their faces and obeyed—men in the whole southern half of Iberia, and in the lands south across the Pillars, as well. He and Will had spoken much, those months in the White Isle, and his share of the *Yare*'s cargo included books to supplement what he'd learned in Nantucket itself. The history of the years that might-have-been was full of hints on the manner of ruling and how a king might gather all the reins of power to himself, on the keeping of records and maps and registers, on police and *bu-reau-cra-cy* and armies, on the coining of money and the building of roads. The problem was that he had so few others who understood. Most of them were young men he'd raised up from nothing, but that was good too—such men knew that all they had depended on his favor, not on their birth.

He reined in his temper as the chief of makers trembled before him; it had taken Isketerol long enough to understand the Amurrukan words *interchangeable parts* and *mass production* himself.

In that false history the Eagle People recorded, nothing remained of Tartessos three thousand years from now. No trace of the city or her people, of her gods or tongue or customs. If he was to build a house that would last forever, the foundations must be laid deep. His voice was stern but not angry when he went on.

"Work harder on the machines for the cutting of metal! Then you will make many, many more muskets, and everything else that the kingdom needs."

"Lord King, we hear and we obey," the man said, backing away.

Isketerol relaxed back onto the lounger and considered the list written on the paper before him, written in his language but using the Eagle People's *alphabet*. He frowned slightly; paper the Islanders would sell, glassware, tools, luxuries. But not lathes or milling machines. Well, Tartessians might not have the arts from out of time, but they were no fools . . . and he had the drawings, the books, the men Will had helped train in Alba.

Already they had done much; oddly, the most useful of all had been the machine with lead seals for the making of books—*moveable type*, in the Amurrukan tongue. He intended to see every free child in Tartessos schooled in it, even the girls.

All the common people of Tartessos called down blessings on his name; he'd given them wealth, made captains of fishermen and lords of farmers, brought in foreign slaves to do the rough work. Even the new customs, the burying-of-excrement and washing-with-soap rituals, no longer brought complaints. Not when so few died of fever or flux.

Hmmm. And now that I have an embassy there, we can—very slowly, very secretly—see if any of the Amurrukan with useful knowledge can be brought here and join me.

The Eagle People had godlike powers, but they were men with the needs and weaknesses of men. He could offer land, slaves, silver, wealth, power as nobles under him. It was a great pity Will hadn't accepted his offer, but William Walker was not a man to take second place, no matter how rich the rewards.

Rosita Menendez walked in, her robe of gold-shot crimson silk brushing the tiled floor. Isketerol winced slightly; silk was another thing the Islanders would sell in Tartessos, but the price was enough to draw your testicles up into your gut. And, of course, what one of his wives had, all the others demanded, leaving him no peace until he bought it for them.

"Hi," she said in the Amurrukan tongue, sitting on a stool by his feet. He replied in the same, to keep fluency.

"Hello, Rosita. How does your school go?"

"Fine, Iskie," she said.

Has she been drinking again? he wondered, but then he relaxed. No, it was just Eagle People gaucherie; they had no sense of ceremony or manners. *Well, she's far from her people, lonely sometimes.* Most of the time being a queen in Tartessos was enough compensation for her . . . although to be sure, he hadn't mentioned his other two wives when he'd courted her back on Nantucket.

"Actually, Iskie, some of the students could take over more of the basics, the way they do the ABC stuff now," she said. "Plus Miskelefol and a couple of others are good enough to do most of the routine translations of the books, if I help them a little with the dictionary," she went on.

"Good. You will have more time for teaching the mathematics and bookkeeping and medicine."

She rolled her eyes but kept her sigh silent. Even a queen wasn't immune from the knotted cords of her husband's belt. Especially a foreigner queen with no kindred in the city.

Well, she's pretty enough—and she'd given him one child, a son—*but her knowledge is more important than her loins.* She'd been a healer's helper back on Nantucket, a *registered nurse* in *Eng-il-ish*. Invaluable here.

Walker's woman, Alice Hong, would have been even more useful. A full doctor, a mistress of some of the Islanders' most powerful arts.

"Then again, no," Isketerol said to himself, shuddering slightly. "I am very glad the Lady of Pain is far, far away."

Far enough away that the thought of her was stirring. He drew aside the loincloth that was his only covering on this warm day and motioned Rosita closer. She knelt on a pillow beside the lounger.

"Use some of that Amurrukan knowledge," he said, grinning and guiding her head with a hand on the back of her neck. This was another thing he'd learned on the Island, and it was catching on fast here.

CHAPTER THREE

The scream was high and shrill, a wail of agony and helpless rage. Marian Alston-Kurlelo sat bolt upright in bed, then turned to shake the figure beside her gently on the shoulder.

"Wake up," she said firmly. "Wake up, 'dapa."

The Fiernan woman tossed, opened her eyes. They were blank for a moment, before awareness returned; then she seized Alston in a grip of bruising strength.

"I was—the Burning Snake had me, the Dream Eater," she gasped. "I was the Sun People's prisoner again, but *you didn't come . . .*"

Alston returned the embrace, crooning comfort and stroking the long blond hair. *Had my own nightmares about that,* she thought. Presumably in the original history—if "original" meant anything— Swindapa *had* died among the Iraiina. Her whole people had vanished, overrun and swallowed up. *And I went on alone, back up in the twentieth.* The room was very dark; an internal clock developed by a lifetime at sea told her it was the end of the midnight watch, around three in the morning.

She felt tears dropping on her shoulder and tenderly wiped them away. "There, there, sugar," she whispered. "I *did* come."

Rescuing Swindapa had been sort of a side effect; they were there to trade for stock and seed-grain, that first month after the Event. She certainly hadn't expected them to end up together. *In fact, 'dapa had to pretty well drag me into bed, after months of my dithering—all those years in the closet made me timid. Christ, was I stupid.*

The rest of the Guard House was quiet; evidently the children hadn't woken. Alston waited until her companion's shuddering died down into quiet sobbing, then turned up the lamp on the bedside table. The period-piece splendors of the house were a bit faded now, eight years after the Event, but with a squared-away neatness that was solely hers.

Swindapa wiped her eyes and blew her nose on a handkerchief from the dresser. Marian smiled a little, remembering teaching her to do that with something besides her fingers. The blue eyes were clear now, with the mercurial mood shifts she'd come to know since the Event. *The only thing reliable about 'dapa is 'dapa,* she thought with a rush of tenderness. Odd that they got on so well.

"What were you thinking?" the Fiernan said. "I could feel your eyes touch me."

"That you're my other half," Marian said. "And about that night down in the Olmec country."

She remembered *that;* one hand went to her left thigh, touching the dusty-white scar. Remembering the darkness and the wet heat, mud under her boots, the light of the flares and the burning temples of San Lorenzo breaking in shatters of brightness off the obsidian edges of the Olmec warriors' spears and club-swords. The quetzal feathers of their harnesses, the paint and precious stones and snarling faces. The cold sting of the spearhead in her leg; at the time all she felt was an enormous frustration that her body wouldn't obey her; that they might not get out with Martha Cofflin after all. And then Swindapa, sword flashing as she stood screaming over her fallen lover.

The Fiernan nodded. "Moon Woman has woven the light of our souls together," she said.

"And I was thinking that you're cute as hell," Marian added, grinning.

That's God's truth as well, the black woman thought. Swindapa was her own five-foot-nine almost to an inch, slender and long-limbed. There had still been a bit of adolescent gangliness when they first met, but it had gone with the years between. The oval straight-nosed face looked firmer now too, tanned to a honey color and framed by the long fall of wheat-colored hair.

"Woof!" Alson said, as the Fiernan's leap and embrace took the air out of her lungs.

"And you are as beautiful as the night sky with stars," Swindapa murmured down at her; that was as strong as compliments came, in the Fiernan Bohulugi tongue. It sounded pretty good in English, too. "Let's share pleasure. I want—"

Marian stopped her with another kiss; loving someone didn't make them more like you, and she was *still* embarrassed by Fiernan bluntness at times.

"Thanks," Vicki Cofflin said, taking the thick mug of sassafras tea. The warmth was welcome in her hands; the early morning was chill enough to make her wool-and-leather flight uniform only a little too heavy.

"Well, this is it," Alex Stoddard said, looking up at the huge structure that creaked above them, secured by a dozen mooring ropes along either side. Its blunt head was pointed into the southwest wind, and it surged occasionally against the restraining lines, as if eager to be gone.

She nodded, feeling the excitement hit her gut with a chill that counterbalanced the warm, astringent taste of the tea. *Scary, too,* she thought. She'd had her share of risky business over the past eight years, with the expeditionary force in Alba—she'd carried a crossbow to the Battle of the Downs—and bad weather at sea. This was a little different. The design studies said the *Emancipator* would work; she'd helped crank up one of the mothballed computer workstations to run the stress calculations for the frame and worked on the design phase as well as the construction. She knew it *should* work, but trusting yourself to this flying whale made out of birch plywood and cloth was still a bit nerve-racking.

"Especially when I was going to fly shuttles," she muttered wryly, then shook her head when Alex looked up from his checklist. "Let's get on with it," she said aloud.

The *Emancipator* did look a little like a whale, like an orca; some wag had wanted her named *Free Willy,* but the Commodore had stomped on that good and hard. Vicki did one more careful walk-around; checking everything one last time was something that was drilled into you at Fort Brandt OCS very thoroughly, and even more as a middie on a Guard ship. The strong smell of the doping compound on the fabric skin filled the air about her, and the scents of glue and birchwood.

The immense presence of the airship was a bit intimidating too. She knew objectively that it was light and fragile, but it felt formidably solid looming above her like this. And it was *big,* bigger than the *Eagle,* which was the largest mobile object in the world, this Year 8 After the Event.

"I hope you get the command," Alex said behind her. She concealed a slight start. He was a tall young man—six gangling feet—but he moved quietly. "You deserve it."

"The Commodore will appoint whoever she thinks can do the job best," Vicki said, then grinned. "Thanks for the thought, though, Ensign Stoddard. I'm supposed to have dinner with the Chief and the Commodore on Harvest Night, so we'll see."

The *Emancipator*'s gondola was a hundred feet long, a narrow swelling built into the airship's frame. When it was grounded, the craft rested on outriggers, wooden skis much like a helicopter's skids. The rear ramp flexed and creased a little beneath their rubber-soled boots as they walked up; everything on board was built as light as possible. Beneath their feet were the tanks for water ballast and liquid fuel and the compartments for cargo—or, under other circumstances,

Leaton's hundred-pounder cast-iron bombs. Three tall wheels stood along each side, with a member of the crew at each. Another came climbing down a ladder that stretched up into the hull above, access to the gasbags.

"Captain on deck!"

"As you were," she said, feeling a spurt of pride.

Captain for at least a day. The crew relaxed and went back to the preflight checkpoint. The Commodore's idea of discipline was strictly functional; ceremony had its place, but that wasn't getting in the way. Another good thing about working for her was that if she thought you were competent enough to do a job, she didn't stand over you or joggle your elbow.

Just deal with it competently, quickly and without unnecessary fuss, Vicki thought. *So let's get on with it.*

She walked forward, past the engine stations, the folded-up bunks, the tiny galley with its electric hot plate—no exposed flames on *this* craft, by God!—the map boards and the big, clunky spark-gap radio and smaller, smoother-looking pre-Event shortwave set. There was a swivel chair at the point where the decking came to an end, with the sloping windows that filled the curved nose of the gondola surrounding it on three sides. Low consoles surrounded it as well, mostly pre-Event instruments adapted to their new tasks; air speed, pressure, fuel, temperature gauges. The windows looked down on a shadowed section of the Nantucket Airport runway, mostly deserted in the predawn light. The whole project wasn't exactly clandestine, but it had been kept on the QT.

And I'm supposed to leave by dawn and come back by sunset, barring emergencies, she reminded herself, running an eye over the instruments. Everything still nominal.

"All hands to stations," she said. "Raise the ramp."

"All hands," Alex echoed. "Ramp up!"

Vicki Cofflin turned and looked down the long space. Engine crew, buoyancy control, ballast control, radio, navigation—that was Alex's department, as well as being XO; and vertical and lateral helms just behind her. *Good crew,* she thought. Fourteen in all, enough for watch-and-watch. Only the radioman was older than she, a ham operator back before the Event. Only five Albans, and they'd all come to the island as teenagers, Alex's age or younger, enough to get the basic education required.

"All right, people," she said. "We've all worked long and hard getting the boat ready. Now we're going to take her up and see what she can do."

Nobody on Nantucket had any lighter-than-air experience, if you discounted people who'd been up on rides in Goodyear blimps, which included Ian Arnstein, oddly enough. They'd all read everything they could find, but there was no substitute for hands-on experience.

She slapped the back of the chair. "*Emancipator*'s going to give us some surprises, unless she's completely unlike any vehicle human beings have ever made. So stay alert."

"Aye, aye, ma'am!"

Vicki nodded, took off her peaked cap, and sat. "Let's go."

"Sleepin' like babies," Marian whispered in the predawn darkness, moving carefully so that the armor wouldn't rattle.

"They *are* babies," Swindapa answered softly, giving her hand a squeeze.

The nursery down the corridor from their room held two beds, each with a girl and a stuffed animal—Lucy had a blue snake, and Heather a koala bear. The redhead was lying on her back, snoring almost daintily; the dark girl curled on her side, as if protecting her goggle-eyed serpent. More stuffed toys stood on shelves, along with dolls, blocks, puzzles, picture books, a dollhouse Jared Cofflin had made and Martha painted for a birthday last year, wooden horses carved in Alba, a fanciful model ship on wheels from Alston's own hands. The girls were seven almost to a day; they'd both been newborns, orphaned by the Alban War.

Well, Lucy's father is probably still alive, Alston thought meticulously. He'd been the only black with Walker, and they hadn't found his body. Her mother had died in childbirth and been left behind when Walker and his gang ran for it. *Alive until I catch him.* The big black ex-cadet from Tennessee hadn't gone over to Walker for wealth or power; it had been his damned fetish about the imaginary Black Egyptians, and Walker's promise to send him there with the secret of gunpowder and whatnot to protect them against the Ice People White Devils. That didn't make him any less of a traitor in her eyes. It was actions that mattered, not intentions.

"Let's go," she said quietly.

They padded down the stairs, the wood creaking sometimes, and into the big kitchen at the back of the house, flanked by the sunroom that overlooked the rear garden. For a moment they busied themselves with preparations for tonight's dinner, seeing that the wood stove was fed and bringing out the suckling pig from the pantry. Alston chuckled at that; two women in Samurai-style steel armor with long swords across their backs, feeding the nineteenth-century wood stove in a house last remodeled by a California investment banker in the dying years of the twentieth century.

And those girls upstairs were born three thousand years before me, but they're the future.

The breakfast oatmeal was bubbling quietly in an iron pot atop the stove, but it wouldn't be ready for another hour and a half. They cut themselves chunks of bread and washed it down with whole milk from the jug in the icebox, then fastened their boots and took the wooden practice swords in their hands as they let themselves out. Nantucket was cool in the predawn blackness even in late summer, the air damp and smelling of salt, fish, whale oil from the street-lamps, woodsmoke from early risers. The two women crossed over to the north side of Main Street, turned onto Easy Street and then South Beach and began their run, bodies moving with smooth economy to the rattle and clank of the armor, hands pumping in rhythm.

"Better you than me!" a wagoneer called to them, yawning at the reins.

Marian recognized him and gave a wave; he'd been with the Expeditionary Force in Alba. *Odd. So many got killed, and instead of throwing stuff at me, the survivors like me.*

"Easy day," she said to her companion. "Only an hour"— running out to Jetties Beach, down the sand cliffs, some *kata* on the wet sand, then back "and we'll have to head in to start dinner."

"It is a holiday," Swindapa answered, then sprinted ahead, laughing in sheer exuberance at the day and at being alive.

Very much alive, Marian thought. *And that makes me feel like livin' too.*

"I never thought I'd be *nostalgic* about living in fear of starving to death," Jared Cofflin said.

"You aren't," his wife replied succinctly. "You're just feeling hard-done-by."

The Chief Executive Officer of the Republic of Nantucket stared down at the papers on his living-room table; the tall sash windows of the Chief's House were open to the warm evening air and the sounds and smells of summer, and roses bloomed outside in the narrow scrap of garden. It'd been an inn just up from Broad, originally built as a shipowner's mansion back in the 1840s. Sort of a running joke between them and Marian and Swindapa, the Cofflins on Gay Street and the Alston-Kurlelos on Main.

"Balance of payments? *Balance of payments?* The whole damned island is sent back to 1250 B.C.—"

"That's 1242 B.C. now, dear.

"1242 B.C., and I'm supposed to worry about the *balance of payments.* Christ, I remember when we were all wondering about how we'd get through the winter."

"Marian! Get away from that!" Martha called.

A seven-year-old girl with straw-blond pigtails snatched her hand away from a cut-glass decanter and went back to pulling a wheeled model ship across the floor. Cofflin's expression relaxed into a smile. If the island had stayed in the twentieth, he'd never have met Martha—not beyond nodding as they passed in the street, at least. *No little Marian, then. No Jared Junior or Jennifer or Sam, either.* Two of their own, and two adopted from the orphans of the war in Alba. He and his first wife had never been able to have children and never got around to adopting, and then Betty had died back half a decade before the Event. *Strenuous, youngsters are, but worth it,* he thought. Of course, ending up with four at his age was more than strenuous.

"And then this bunch want to start a new settlement down in Argentina," he went on. "As if we weren't spread out enough already."

"Dear, there's no law against emigrating. We can scarcely send Marian out after them for leaving without permission."

"Speaking of which," he said, tossing down the papers. "There's young Pete Girenas and *his* group of let's-get-ourselves-killed enthusiasts. Christ. Should I have sat on them? They might have given up—"

"What's their average age, Jared?"

"He's the oldest, and he's all of twenty-one."

"Well, then."

Cofflin sighed. "Let's get going. I'll think about that later. Marian's expecting us for the anniversary party." His daughter looked up at the sound of her name. "No, sweetling, Aunt Marian."

Young Marian's middle name was Deer Dancer; that was what "Swindapa" meant, in English. *Damn, but I'm glad the* Eagle *was close enough to get caught up in the Event. God knows how I'd have pulled us through without Marian.* Or without Martha, or Ian, or Doreen, Angelica Brand, Ron Leaton, or Sam Macy, or . . . *well,* particularly *without Marian.*

He looked at his watch. "Speaking of which, where's—"

"Hi, Unc, Martha." Vicki Cofflin came through the door with a bound and scooped up the child. "How's it going, midget?"

Cofflin smiled as his niece tussled with his daughter and Martha rounded up the rest of the offspring. Vicki didn't have the Cofflin looks, but then, her mother had married someone *from away,* as Nantucketers said—from Texas, at that. He'd been off-island when the Event happened, a particularly final form of divorce.

Vicki was stocky rather than lanky, with a snub-nosed freckled face and green-gray eyes. She wasn't in uniform, this being a family-and-friends evening—he tried to keep *some* distinctions between that and government work. The jeans were pre-Event, her shirt was Murray's Mills product, Olmec cotton spun and dyed with wild indigo here on Island, the shoes hand-cobbled from Alban leather.

Our successors, he thought. Vicki's generation, who'd come of age after the Event. To them the twentieth was fading memory; to their younger siblings, hardly that. To Cofflin's own children it would be history learned from books and stories.

"Evening, Vicki. How's your mother?"

"Ummmm, fine, Unc. You know how it is."

He nodded; Vicki didn't get along all that well with her stepfather, and her mother had started a new family—one of her own, plus three Alban adoptees. *Well, you pick your friends, but you're stuck with family,* he thought. Though it was natural enough, seeing as how Mary had lost her elder two boys to the Event as well as her husband. Although presumably they were still—the word made no sense, but English grammar wasn't well adapted to time travel—all right, up in the twentieth.

He pushed down a crawling horror that they all felt now and then. *What if we destroyed the world, by being here? We could have. They could have all gone out like a match in the wind as soon as we changed something back here—all dead or not even that, all of them never existing, a might have-been.* The Arnsteins thought that the Event would produce a branching, two trunks on the tree of time, but nobody could know for sure. Come to that, nobody knew *anything* about the Event except what it had done.

He shook his head and kneaded the back of his neck against the sudden chill. Martha touched him briefly on the arm, a firm, warm pressure; the equivalent of a hug to them, and he felt the tension slacken as he smiled back at her.

It was a warm late-August evening as they stepped out, shepherding the children before them; the big American elms lining the brick sidewalks were still in full leaf, and the whale-oil lamps on their cast-iron stands were being lit by a Town worker with a long pole topped by a torch. The tower of the old Unitarian church stood black against the red sky ahead, still showing a little gold at its top in the long summer twilight.

"Ummm, Unc," Vicki dropped back a little to walk beside him, lowering her voice. "I'm a bit nervous. Having dinner with the Commodore."

He raised a brow. "Thought you did that as a middie," he said.

"Well, yeah, but that was . . . structured. Commodore Alston made a point of inviting groups of officer-candidates to dinner now and then."

"She doesn't bite," Cofflin said. "I read your report on the *Emancipator*'s trials, too. Looked good."

"We *did* have that problem with longitudinal stability."

"Ayup. That's why they call it a *test* flight, girl," he replied, hiding a smile. "And she's going to give you good news, next time you see her in her *official* capacity," Cofflin went on. "You can take the *second* off the *lieutenant*—but you didn't hear it from me."

"*Yes!*" Vicki whopped, pumping a fist, then self-consciously calming when Martha looked back over her shoulder with a raised brow. Cofflin had noted that the younger generation were a bit more spontaneous than his; probably influence from all the Albans around nowadays.

"I was a little afraid somebody else would be put in to command the *Emancipator* when it was finished," she said, burbling a bit.

"Doubt keeps you on your toes," Jared said, and then, "Evening, Ian, Doreen," when they met the Arnsteins outside the John Cofflin House.

"Evening all—hi, Vicki. Got the whole tribe with you, I see," Ian said. David was waving to the Cofflins' four from his father's shoulders, prompting a chorus of *"Give me a ride, Daddy!"*

"Ayup," Cofflin said. Then, "all right, Jenny, *up* you go."

He hoisted his adopted daughter to his shoulders; she wrapped her arms around his forehead and crowed gleefully. Cofflin gripped her feet, partly for stability and partly to keep her sharp little heels from drumming on his ribs. Marian went up on Vicki's shoulders, and Jared Junior on Doreen's; somehow, it didn't occur to anyone to ask Martha. She took a small hand in each of hers instead, smiling at the children's giggling and the mock horse noises coming from the other adults.

The bank and some of the shops were closing down, but the restaurants and bars on Main were full, spilling cheerful lantern light and noise and cooking smells onto the cobbles. He could see right through the Cappuccino Cafe to its little garden plaza beyond, hear the fiddle and guitar and flute from the trio performing there and the voices of the customers singing along, clapping and tapping their boots to the tune.

"That's a new one," he said.

> We just lost sight of the Brandt Point light
> Down lies the bay before us
> And the wind has blown some cold today
> With just a wee touch of snow.
> Along the shore from Eel Point Head, hard a-beam Muskeget
> Tonight we let the anchors go, down in Fogarty's Cove!

It had a nice swinging lilt to it. "Sounds different now, that sort of song," he said.

One of the many small compensations of the Event was that with electricity a strictly rationed rarity, most of the types of music he hated with a passion were impossible. He wasn't alone in that, either. Marian had told him once that to get rid of gangsta rap she'd have been willing to be stranded in the Jurassic with a pack of velociraptors in white sheets.

> *My Sal has hair like a raven's wing,*
> *But her tongue is like her mother's*
> *With hands that make quick work of a chore*
> *And eyes like the top of a stove*
> *Come suppertime she'll walk the beach,*
> *Wrapped in my old duffle*
> *With her eyes upon the masthead reach*
> *Down in Fogarty's Cove!*

A girl was up on a table, dancing to the tune, but he'd give odds *she* wasn't American-born. Fiernan, from the wild, patterned grace of the movements—dancing was a big thing in their religion and they got a lot of practice.

> *She will walk the sandy shores so plain,*
> *Watch the combers roll in*
> *'Till I come to Wild Rose Chance again*
> *Down in Fogarty's Cove!*

"Certainly does have a different ring," Martha replied. "For one thing, half the people singing it really *do* make their living at sea."

Jared nodded a little wistfully. His job kept him ashore and pinned to his desk much of the time—although he *did* insist on getting away at this time of year, usually to harpoon bluefin tuna. He could easily afford to pay the Town tax straight up in money, but there was a satisfaction to doing something useful with your hands. Not to mention doing a hard, dangerous job well enough to gain the respect of youngsters.

He worked his big fisherman's hands. It got harder every year, and sometime he'd have to let nature take its course. There was always the *Boojum,* his little twenty-footer. Someday he'd teach his kids how to single-hand a ketch.

"Folkie stuff was always popular here," Ian said. "Like you said, it has more of a, hmmm, *resonance* now. I understood a lot more about Homer once I'd seen a real battle with chariots and spears . . . although that's something I could have lived with not knowing."

"Let 'em sing," Cofflin sighed. "Got a difficult couple of years coming, unless I miss my guess. They've all worked hard, they deserve a party."

It was the last evening of what some bureaucrat at the Town Building had named, with stunning originality, the Civic Harvest Festival. They still celebrated Thanksgiving in November, of course, but this marked that first harvest of rye and wheat and barley, the year of the Event.

The Councilors nodded and waved to friends and acquaintances as they turned south up Main; Jared returned a mounted policewoman's salute as she rode by with her double-barreled flintlock shotgun on one hip; the horseshoes beat a slow iron clangor on the stones with an occasional bright spark.

Have to think about putting down asphalt here, some note-taking mechanism in the back of his mind prompted. The tourists had liked authentic Ye Olde cobblestones, but they were as inconvenient as hell now, unlike the other features—lots of fireplaces, for instance—of Nantucket's mainly early-nineteenth-century downtown. The noise when a lot of iron-shod wagon wheels hit them had to be heard to be believed, for starters.

"I'll be *damned,*" Ian said suddenly, craning his neck around so fast that his son whooped and buried his hands in the hair over Arnstein's ears.

"What?" Doreen said.

"I saw—"

"Saw *what*? Your jaw's dropping, Ian."

"I saw a tattooed Indian with a harpoon walking down toward the docks."

"Why not?" Cofflin asked. "There are a few of them working the tuna boats, they're good hands with a—"

Then he wheeled about himself. A barbed steel point glittered for a moment in the light from the streetlamp beside the Hub, but the bearer was quickly lost in the crowd.

"Gave me a bit of a chill," Ian said. Doreen nodded, and Martha gave a slight dry chuckle.

"Problem is," she said, "we've all had our sense of the impossible wrenched about, badly."

Cofflin nodded. He still woke up some days with that sense of dislocation, a feeling that the solid, tangible world he saw and smelled and tasted around him was just a veneer over chaos. Something that might spin away, dissolve like a mist at sea and leave . . . nothing? Or another exile beyond the world he knew. If once, why not again?

"What's wrong, Daddy?" Jenny said anxiously, feeling the moment of shivering tension in his shoulders.

"Nothing's wrong, Jenny," he said, reaching up with a reassuring pat and putting the same into his voice. *Jenny'll grow up with that,* he thought. The Event would seem quite reasonable, if you grew up with it. In a couple of generations they'd probably think of it as a myth, and 'way down the road some professorial pain in the ass would "prove" that it was a metaphor and hadn't happened at all.

They quieted the children and walked further up Main, past the Pacific Bank. Coast Guard House had been known as the East Brick back before the Event. A whaling skipper had built it and the two others beside it in the 1830s, red foursquare four-story mansions in the sober Federal style that rich Quakers had favored back then. All three and the Two Greeks, their neoclassical rivals across the street, had been owned by coofs, rich mainlanders who were not on the Island at the time of the Event.

Vicki swallowed and ran her hands over her hair—probably had memories of being called on the carpet here, since it was Guard HQ.

Jared Cofflin grinned; he'd turned the East Brick over to Marian Alston for residence and headquarters when the *Eagle* returned from its first trading voyage to Alba, that spring right after the Event, and he'd done it with glee.

Part of his pleasure in that was the thought of the California financier who'd paid three-point-seven million dollars for it just six months before and God knew how much in renovations and furnishings. One very irate moneyman, wandering through the primeval Indian-haunted oak woods of the Bronze Age island that the twentieth century had presumably gotten in exchange, looking for his missing investment. Maybe Jesus could love an investment broker, but Jared Cofflin didn't intend to even try.

He gave another spare chuckle as they walked up the brick sidewalk, careful of the roots of the elms that bulged the surface.

"What's the joke?" Ian asked.

"Thinking of the fuss back up in the twentieth, when they woke up and found us gone and nothing but trees and Indians on the Nantucket they got," he said. "Christ, can you imagine what the *National Enquirer* crowd must have done?"

It was an old joke, but they were all laughing when Cridzywelfa opened the door.

"The ladies are in the kitchen, Chief, working all day after the morning," she said with a quick, choppy Sun People tang to her English. "They said to park yourself, and I'll take the children on to the back yard through."

Cofflin nodded, chuckling again at the way New England vowels went with the Bronze Ager's accent. *Paak the caa in Haav'd yaad 'n go to the paaty.* With no TV or recorded sound to sustain General

American, it sounded like the native Nantucketers' clipped nasal twang was gradually coming out on top in the Island's linguistic stew.

Revenge of the Yankees.

"My ladies, they're here at the door," Cridzywelfa said.

"And we're *ready*, by God," Alston said, looking at the clock. Half-past seven p.m. exactly. Good. She'd always hated unpunctuality.

The cream for the bisque was just right, very hot but not boiling. She used a potholder to lift the heavy crock from the stovetop and pour it into the soup pot while Swindapa stirred it in with a long wooden spoon.

Thank you, Momma, she thought. Her mother had gotten her started as a cook, back on Prince Island off the South Carolina coast. And it had been on a cast-iron monster much like this; their little truck farm hadn't run to luxuries. *Though how she managed with six of us, I'll never understand.*

"Heather! Lucy!"

That last out the window to the gardens, whence came a clack of wood on wood and shrill imitations of a *kia.*

"Mom, we were just playing at *bokken,*" Heather wheedled. "You and Momma Swindapa play at swords all the time. Even with *real* swords, *sharp* ones."

"That's not playing, it's training, and you'll hurt each other with those sticks," Alston said, forcing sternness into her voice. "When you're old enough, you'll get real *bokken* to train with. Now come in and wash your hands and faces. You can play with David and the other kids until dinner."

"Oh, David's just a baby," Lucy said, with the lordly advantage of two years extra age.

The children dashed up the steps and through the sunroom.

"That all smells good, Mom," Heather said expectantly. "Really, really . . ."

Alston hugged the small form to her, meeting Swindapa's eyes over her shoulder. *All right, you were right,* she thought. *The kids were a good idea—better than good.* Alston had lost her own children in the divorce after John found out about Jolene . . . *God, was that fifteen years ago?* Or whatever; up in the twentieth, at least. No solitary chance of getting custody, not when he could have destroyed her career in the Guard with one short sentence *and* ruined her chances of being awarded the children in front of a South Carolina court. And Swindapa couldn't have any children of her own. Pelvic inflammation, from the way the Iraiina had treated her.

Alston cut two slices from a loaf and spread them with wild-blueberry jam; the bread was fresh enough to steam slightly. "That ought to hold you two for the long half hour until dinner's on the table."

"Run along," Swindapa said gently, bending to kiss the small faces. "Get those hands *clean*."

"Ahh," Jared Cofflin said, pushing the empty bowl away. "Now *that's* how to treat a lobster soup."

"Lobster *bisque*, dear," Martha corrected, helping herself to one of the broiled clams with herbed-crumb crust.

"Ayup."

The dining room had changed a little since this became Guard House. The burgundy wallpaper was the same, with the brilliant gold foliage around the top; so were the Waterford chandelier, the Philadelphia-Federal sideboard and the long mahogany table, but the rugs on the floor were from Dilmun at the entrance to the Persian Gulf. A pair of crossed tomahawks over the fireplace had bronze heads shaped like the bills of falcons, lovely and deadly. Those were from the Iraiina, a tribe settled in what would have become Hampshire—plunder of the Alban War.

Elsewhere were mementos of the *Eagle*'s swift survey around the globe in the Year 2 A.E. and voyages since: a Shang robe of crimson and gold silk made in Anyang; a square-section bronze sacrificial ax covered in ancestral Chinese ideographs; a blazing indigo-and-red-green tapestry of dyed cotton from coastal Peru, covered in smiling gods and geometric shapes.

Cofflin helped collect the soup plates and take them out to the kitchen to soak; off that, in the sunroom, the children were eating, with just as much noise and chaos as you would expect from ten healthy youngsters between three and seven, plus the housekeeper's two teenagers and the Colemans' youngest, who was still in a high chair. Cridzywelfa was presiding, with a smile that seemed genuine. He'd noticed that the locals just weren't as fastidious about mess and confusion as those born in the twentieth.

God knows I love 'em, but it's nice to eat without the kids now and then, he thought. At least *his* were all past the dump-your-porridge-over-your-head stage. Most of the time. The way Marian's redhead was squealing and waving her fork looked like danger to life and limb.

"Why did you name her Heather?" Cofflin asked idly, as everyone came back in with fresh dishes and exclaimed over the suckling pig borne aloft in glory with an apple in its mouth. Swindapa began handing around plates. He picked an olive from a bowl and ate it.

"Why do you *think*, Jared?" Marian replied, carving with quick, skilled strokes.

The savory meat curled away from her blade, and she looked down the table, visibly estimating portions; the Cofflins, the Arnsteins, Starbuck, Captain Sandy Rapczewicz and Doc Coleman—Sandy had been Executive Officer on the *Eagle* when all this started, and she'd kept her maiden name when she married the Island's senior medico. Victor Ortiz, who'd been a lieutenant back then; his wife was a relative of Swindapa's named Jairwen, hugely pregnant now, and the two were chattering away in the soft *glug-glug* sound of Fiernan, the tang and lilt of a language that had died a thousand years before Christ.

"Wouldn't have asked if I knew," Cofflin said, smothering a mild annoyance when most of the rest of the table got the allusion and he didn't. Martha was chuckling into her wineglass. Only Vicki looked as baffled as he was.

"Heather Has Two Mommies, dear," his wife said. "Don't you remember?"

"Well, of course she has two—oh." He thumped the heel of his hand on his forehead.

"It's a perfectly good name," Alston said. " 'dapa, this load is for the other table. One of my grandmothers was named Heather." A slight quirk of the lips. "Doubt she expected to have any red-haired great-grandchildren, though."

Steaming layers of sliced pork lay on the edge of the platter, cut with a surgeon's neatness. *Of course, doing that Japanese sword stuff was her hobby,* Cofflin thought, passing the applesauce. *Other hobby, besides cooking, that is.*

"Say," he went on—it was all old friends here—"do Heather and Lucy ever have much in the way of, ah, problems about that? Now that they've started school?"

"About their parents?" Marian gave a slight cold smile, and Swindapa looked briefly furious. "Yes, sometimes. A few times."

"Sorry about that," Cofflin said, flushing with embarrassment.

"Oh, no problem. They're very athletic little girls, for their ages." The smile went slightly wider at his look of incomprehension. "I gave them some pointers and told them to ambush whoever gave them serious trouble about their mothers, two on one, and beat the living shit out of them. And if the parents complained—well, they could come complain to *me*."

He looked into the dark eyes of the person who he knew was, after Martha, his best friend in this post-Event world. And the embarrassment turned, just for a second, to a jolt of pure, cold fear.

Shit, but I'm glad Marian never had any political ambitions.

"Barbarians," Swindapa muttered under her breath.

"What was that?" Martha said.

"Nothin' much," Marian said, smiling slightly. "Swindapa has a low opinion of some Eagle People attitudes, is all."

"Fully justified, in some cases," Martha said dryly.

People started passing things; gravy, bowls of scalloped potatoes, roast garlic, cauliflower au gratin, sliced onions and tomatoes in oil and vinegar, steamed peas, butternut squash, wilted spinach with shallot dressing, lentils with thyme, potato-and-lobster-claw salad, green salad, bread.

"Oh, Mother of God, but I got so sick of edible seaweed," Ortiz said, biting into a piece of tomato with an expression of nearly religious ecstasy.

"Saved us from scurvy the winter of '01," Martha observed, slightly defensive. "My Girl Scouts did a good job there, finding wild greens."

"Oh, they did," Ortiz agreed. "No dispute there. I'm just so glad to see vegetables again."

Murmurs of agreement interrupted the chomping of jaws.

"The economy's doing reasonably well," Starbuck conceded, grudgingly. *Christ, and they think I'm stingy,* Cofflin thought. The ex-banker went on, "Despite the lavish use of public funds on projects such as yours, young lady."

Vicki looked down at her plate for a second. "Defense takes precedence over affluence, sir," she replied.

Starbuck's shaggy white brows went up. "Nice to hear one of the younger generation quoting Adam Smith at me," he said grudgingly. "Well, I suppose it won't bankrupt us. Not quite yet."

Things *had* improved. Cofflin spread butter on a piece of the chewy, crusty whole-wheat bread. Butter, for instance. There hadn't been more than two dozen cows on the whole island, at first. The breeding program was going well, though.

"You Eagle People complain about the oddest things," Jairwen said, tossing back her long brown hair. "You've ways to have got vegetables in the middle of winter, and then complain you that they aren't fresh picked as were."

"You've got a point," Doc Coleman said. "This diet is actually healthier than what we had before the Event; a little heavier on salt than I'd like, especially in the winter with all the dried fish, but plenty of fiber and roughage, not much sugar and less fat—look how lean this pork is, even. Plus, I doubt there are fifty people on the Island who don't do more physical exercise than they used to, just getting around." Luxury transport these days was a bicycle. "And no tobacco or recreational drugs; thank God. Pass the gravy."

"It's back to dried dulse for some of us," Alston sighed.

"You're ready so soon?" Cofflin blurted. *Hell, I thought I was following things closely!*

"Oh, not for the real push," Alston said. "We need more ships, more—sorry, 'dapa, just a little business—but it occurs to me that we just can't wait until we've got enough ships and people to do it directly, so we'd better start laying the groundwork through the back door. Lieutenant Cofflin—sorry, Vicki—has her pet coming along right nice. We can run the tests on her, and then start taking it apart again."

The younger Cofflin glanced between her uncle and the black woman, suddenly alert. Alston smiled slightly and nodded. "Time you were brought into the loop. Everybody here's cleared."

She sketched out a plan, and a little way down the table, Ian Arnstein sighed and rolled his eyes.

"Oh, God," he said. "*Another* two languages to learn."

He couldn't quite conceal the grin that broke through. His wife hit him with her napkin and groaned.

"The first part, that'll be more in the nature of a long trip than a military expedition," Marian said. "Then . . ."

"Enough business," Swindapa said firmly. "I will work tomorrow. Today is for play. Dessert, and then we dance."

"All right," Jared Cofflin said, chuckling and leaning back with a cup in his hand. "You know, one of the few good things about this job is that it lets you meet every nutcase in the Republic, and just yesterday I met one even crazier than the gang around this table. Let me tell you about a young man named Girenas over at Providence Base and *his* weird idea."

Peter Girenas looked at himself anxiously in the small mirror by the washstand, checking his chin and his mottled-leather Ranger uniform. Then, swallowing, he glanced around the room. It wasn't home, just the place he lived when he was in town; the owner of the Laughing Loon was glad to let him have it in return for a deer every week or two. Bed and floor were mostly covered in skins of his own hunting, bear and wolf and wolverine; there was a Lekkansu spirit-mask on one squared-log wall, a coverlet of ermine pelts, a shelf of books, his rifle and crossbow, some keepsakes and a photograph of his mother. And on a table beside the bed was a sheaf of papers.

"Stay, Perks. Guard."

The dog curled up on his favorite bearskin and settled his head on his paws, watchful and alert. Girenas picked up the papers and took a deep breath, then carefully closed the door behind him and trotted down to the taproom of the inn.

It was quiet now, on a weekday afternoon, spears of sunlight through the windows catching drifting flecks of dust, sand rutching under his boots against the flagstone floor. Sally Randon was idly polishing the single-plank bar at one end with its ranks of bottles and big barrels with taps, and the chairs were empty around the long tables. Except for one. Girenas scowled at the sight of the three seated there.

He recognized them all. Emma Carson and her husband, Dick; they were big in the Indian trade. And Hardcase. He was a big man among the Lekkansu, one of the first traders with the Americans—and he'd been pulling together the shattered clans after the epidemics, trying to get them back on their feet after the chaos and despair of losing more than half their numbers for two years running. The Ranger didn't particularly like him, not like some of the Lekkansu warriors he'd hunted with or the girls he'd known, but Hardcase was an important man.

Or would be, if he could stay off the booze. The Carsons had no business encouraging him like this.

"I greet you, elder brother," he said in the Lekkansu tongue, walking over to them. "Have you come to trade?"

"Trade pretty good," the Indian said, in fair if accented English. "Lots of deer hides, maple sugar, hickory nuts, ginseng."

The two Nantucketer traders were glaring at the ranger, and the man made a motion as if to hide the bottle of white lightning the three were sharing. Dick Carson didn't bother Girenas, a beefy blowhard. But Emma . . . *heard a snake bit her once. The snake died.*

"Emma, Dick," he said, nodding. Then in the other tongue: "Will you get many knives, hatchets, fishhooks, fire-makers, blankets?"

"Hardcase trades smart," the Indian said, his grin a bit slack. "Other families will pay well for break-the-head water. Easier to carry than lots of heavy things."

"But when the water is gone, you will have nothing—not tools, or weapons, or blankets."

Hardcase's eyes narrowed. "Rifles even better than break-the-head water," he said. "You're such a friend to us, why don't you get us some rifles? Friends do that."

Dick Carson's eyes were flickering back and forth between the Indian and the Ranger in frustrated anger. Emma's were cold; he suspected that she talked more of the local tongue than she let on.

Girenas' eyes were equally chill, and his lips showed teeth in what was only technically a smile.

"You know, Ms. Carson," he said softly, "there are fines for exceeding quota on distilled liquor sales to the locals. And, of course, selling firearms is treason." Or the ratchet-cocked steel crossbows that Seahaven had turned out for the Nantucketers' armed forces before gunpowder production got under way.

"Hardcase must go. His brothers are always welcome in his camp," the Indian said abruptly, staggering a little as he collected his bundles and headed for the door.

"Goddammit, you punk bastard!" Dick Carson hissed. "What'd you have to go and queer our deal for?"

"After you've given him the third drink it isn't dealing, Carson. It's stealing, and that isn't the sort of reputation we need with the locals. I'm a Ranger, I'm supposed to keep the peace . . . and it works both ways."

"You'd better remember who you're working for, boy," Emma Carson said. There was no theatrical menace in her voice, not even a conspicuous flatness. She pulled a worn, greasy-looking pack out of a pocket in her khaki bush jacket and began to flip cards onto the board for a solitaire game. "Or the Town Meeting might remind you."

"Let's leave that to the Meeting, shall we?" he said pleasantly. "Have a nice day."

He forced his fists to unknot as he walked out onto the stone sidewalk of Providence Base, blinking in the bright gold sunlight. You couldn't cure everything in life, and that was a fact. All you could do was your best.

He was on First Street. The name was not a number. It was literally the first the Nantucketers had built when they made this their initial outpost on the mainland, not long after the Event. A street broad enough for two wagons sloped down the hill, bound in asphalt at enormous expense and trouble, lined on either side with buildings of huge squared logs. Down by the water and the wharves were warehouses, plank over timber frames; off to the northeast a little was the water-furrow and a row of the sawmills it powered.

The tall wheels turned, water splashed bright; steam chuffed and a whistle blew from others, for the need had outgrown the first creek that the Nantucketers dammed. Men and women skipped over the bloating tree trunks with hooked poles, steering a steady train of them to the ramps where chains hauled them upward. Vertical saws went through wood with a rhythmic *ruhhh . . . ruhhh,* while newer circular ones whirred with earsplitting howls—*errrrraaaaah,* over and over. The air was full of woodsmoke, the scent of fresh-cut wood, horses, and whale-oil grease, and the overwhelming smell of the sea.

Little of the surrounding woods had been logged off. The Meeting had decreed that, saying that only mature timber might be harvested and only a portion of that in any square mile. Even in town enough had been left to give welcome shade; the leaves were beginning to turn, but the afternoon was hot enough to bring a prickle of sweat. He walked uphill, past wagons and folk and a shouting crowd of children just out of school.

The public buildings of the little town stood around a green with a bandstand in the center; school, church, meetinghouse, and a three-story blockhouse of oak logs with the Republic's Stars and Stripes flying from its peak.

Peter Girenas took a deep breath, nodded to the guard—the town's main arsenal was inside—and walked in. The first floor was racked rifles, crates of gear, barrels of powder in a special room with a thick, all-wood door. It was also dim and shady, smelling faintly of brimstone. He trotted up the ladder-staircase, through to the third story. Broad windows there let in enough light to make him squint. It wasn't until he stood to attention that he saw who waited.

Not just Ranger Captain Bickford behind the table. Chief Cofflin, and Martha Cofflin, the Secretary of the Council. His eyes flicked back to his own commander. Bickford was smiling, so things couldn't be *too* bad.

"No, son," Cofflin said. "You're not in trouble over that fight. As a matter of fact . . ."

Martha Cofflin slid a paper out of a folder. "Had Judge Gardner expedite the papers a bit. On the deposition of Sue Chau and your own statement, there's no grounds for any proceedings. Self-defense."

"And why don't you sit down, Ranger?" Cofflin said.

Girenas juggled the sheaf of papers awkwardly for a second, then brought up a chair and sat with them in his lap.

Older than I thought, he decided, meeting Cofflin's level gaze; he'd never happened to see the Chief at close range before. The long, lumpy Yankee face had deep wrinkles around the eyes, and there was a lot of gray in the thinning sandy hair.

"How did you feel about it?" Cofflin asked.

Surprised, Girenas paused for a minute to marshal his thoughts. "Well, at the time, there wasn't time to feel much of anything, sir," he said. "They started it, so I'm not tearing myself up over it. But I'm sorry it happened. Usually I like the locals, get on well with 'em."

Bickford nodded. "Speaks Lekkansu like a tribesman," he said. "Lived in one of their camps for six months a couple of years back, done useful go-between work. Trade supervision, that sort of thing. About my best scout, and I'm grooming him for a lieutenant."

"Sir?" Cofflin looked up. "Speaking of trade, I saw something today you'd better know about."

Cofflin's face took on a frown as Girenas described what he'd seen in the taproom of the Loon, and Bickford's fist clenched on the table before he spoke.

"Chief, we *need* some sort of an executive order about this sort of thing. Better still, we need a law rammed through the Town Meeting."

Cofflin leaned back. "That's one opinion. What's yours, son?"

Girenas said, "The Captain's right, Chief. The Carsons are the worst, but not the only ones. The locals, they just can't handle hard liquor, even worse than Albans that way. But they know right from wrong well enough, when they sober up and realize they've been diddled. Just wrong one, and see what happens! We could stumble into a war if we're not careful. Already would have, I think, if it weren't for the plagues. A lot of them, they don't like us Nantucketers much, sir."

"Ayup. Can't say as I blame 'em."

Martha Cofflin spoke. "Problem, though. First—are we entitled to tell the Indians they can't buy liquor? They're adults, and not citizens of the Republic, either. Second, could we enforce a law like that if we did pass it?"

Cofflin smiled; Girenas had rarely seen a more bleak expression. "There was a little thing called Prohibition. Before your time, Ranger; even before mine. Disaster. Showed the costs of passing a law just to make yourself feel righteous.

Girenas frowned. "Is that a fancy way of saying we can't do anything, sir?"

The Cofflins smiled dryly, an eerily similar expression. The man spoke. "Not at all, son. We might have trouble enforcing a law; the Carsons or someone like 'em would find a way to wiggle around it. I *can* lean on them, though, until they cry uncle. Nobody can get much done businesswise if the Town's hostile—and that sort of thing operates by more . . . flexible rules."

His wife nodded. "We do need to establish a tradition of dealing decently with the locals. It's going to be more and more of a problem, anyway. Looks like our numbers are going to double every fifteen or twenty years, probably for the next century or two at least, between immigration and this enthusiasm for reproduction that everyone's showing."

Girenas nodded slowly. "Thank you, sir, ma'am," he said.

Bickford cleared his throat. Cofflin lifted one knobby paw slightly. "Ayup," he said. "Time to get to the main business we came for."

Martha Cofflin produced a sheaf of papers from a knit carryall lying on the table. Girenas swallowed; it was a copy of the document resting on his knee.

"I, ah, hadn't expected it to go so high so fast, Captain."

Bickford shrugged. "Advantage of having a small government, Ranger."

Chief Cofflin tapped the papers. "Had a tirade all set up," he said, his mouth quirking slightly. "About reckless young fools, and how we can't afford to divert effort, and how anyone hankering after adventure—which Marian rightly says is somebody else in deep shit far away—can ship out on a trader or join the Expeditionary Force. Then I realized I was starting to sound like the old farts I hated when *I* was twenty-one, and I took another look. Ayup, it *is* about time we got at least a survey knowledge of what's going on in the interiors of the continents, something like what the *Eagle* did for the coastlands in '02. And it is logical to start with this continent here."

Girenas felt a wave run through him, like a wash of warm water from his chest down to knees grown weak. *Glad I'm sitting down*, he thought.

"Two problems," Martha Cofflin's dry, precise voice went on. "First, are you the man to lead it? No offense, Ranger Girenas, but you're extremely young. Second, costs."

"He may be young, but he's not reckless," Bickford said. "Got as much experience as any of us post-Event, too; been in the Rangers since we branched off from the Eagle Scouts. If I were putting together an expedition like this, I'd pick him."

Cofflin was glancing through another file, as if to remind himself. "Hmmm. Your family's working in the mills here . . . immigrants before the Event, eh?"

Girenas nodded. "Three years before, Chief, from Riga."

"Let's see, a brother and sister, and your parents adopted two. Too young to go with the expeditionary force to Alba, but plenty of time in the woods here. Looks like you prefer camping out, mebbe?"

Girenas answered slowly, cautiously. "Yes sir. I . . . I'm good at it. Like to stick with what I'm good at, seems more . . . efficient that way."

"No argument. You've done a good proposal here, too, well organized, everything justified and costed out. I've talked with people who know, and they think you've got some chance of pulling it off. Let's see . . . six of you in all."

Suddenly he grinned. "Christ, I'd like to go with you myself, if I were twenty and single."

"Costs, Jared," the Secretary of the Council said.

"Ayup."

"I included an itemized list of necessities, sir," Girenas said.

Cofflin chuckled. "Son, they say I'm cheap. And I am, with the Republic's money. I *could* pay for this out of the discretionary funds, but I won't." He held up a hand. "Yes, it'll be useful, if you pull it off. Not essential, though, and certainly not an emergency. Remember, every penny I give you comes out of someone's pocket, will they–nill they."

"Sir, this expedition will pay for itself and more, and not just with information. The gold—"

"Would be mighty useful. *If* you survive. Meantime you're asking for horses, weapons, trade goods, the services of six strong young people, even a radio. And yes, we do have ships in the Pacific now and then"—trading for cotton textiles with the Chavin peoples of Peru—

"but running up to the California coast to pick you up is still a big risk. So, son," he went on, "it's up to you."

The ranger gaped at him. "Sir?"

"You're a free citizen of the Republic of Nantucket. Circulate a petition, then get up on your hind legs at the Town Meeting and persuade the other citizens. I'll even say I'm in favor . . . personally, not officially."

"Sir?" Girenas felt his voice rise almost to a humiliating squeak. "I'm no . . . no speechmaker!"

Martha Cofflin's expression mingled sympathy and unyielding resolution. "Then learn. You've got until spring." Then, kindly: "Your age ought to help. Lot of younger people will be glad to see one of theirs proposing something."

"Lord," Girenas muttered.

He scarcely noticed his dismissal until he was out in the street again. *Hell, I haven't been in Nantucket more'n once a year,* he thought. Then: *They didn't tell me to forget it, either.* Resolution firmed. "I *can* do it, by God!"

He turned west. Hills rose on the edge of sight, blue and dreaming. Hills and mountains, the rivers like inland seas and the plains full of buffalo, Alder Gulch and its gold . . . *grizzlies and Indians and wolves, oh, my!*

CHAPTER FOUR

September, Year 8 A.E.
(March, Year 3 A.E.)
(June, Year 4 A.E.)
(July, Year 4 A.E.)
September, Year 8 A.E.

Reveille, Marian Alston-Kurlelo thought as her eyes opened, waiting for the pitch and roll of a bunk at sea, the creak of cordage and lap of the waves and the way a ship's timbers spoke as they moved.

But it wasn't a noncom bellowing, "lash and stow"; it was roosters, and someone beating on a triangle. "Rise and shine, sugar," she whispered.

"I will rise, but I refuse to shine," Swindapa said, mock-grumpy, yawning and stretching; the corn shucks in the mattress beneath them rustled as she moved to give Alston an embrace and then swing out of the bed.

The ferry had brought them in late last night; it was a chilly fall morning, and the water in the jug and basin beside the window raised goose bumps on the black woman's skin as she washed and pulled on her clothes. The coarse blue wool of the uniform was clean by the standards of Year 8—it didn't have visible dirt and it didn't smell. Considering something unwearable after one use had gone the way of electric washer-dryer combos.

Fogarty's Cove was already bustling. Only an archaeologist would be able to find any trace of the Indians, less than a decade after the Event had crashed into their world; the stones of a heath, a scatter of chipped flint, a tumbled drying rack, gourds gone wild. The Islanders had done considerably more. Steel screeched on wood in the sawmills, while hammers and adzes rang in the boatyard down by the wharves, where a big fishing smack was taking shape. Faint and far in the distance came a soft heavy *thudump . . . thudump* as stumps were blasted out of newly cleared fields with gunpowder. The streets were full of wagons bringing in grain and meat, raw wool, eggs, pumpkins and apples, peaches and potatoes, wine and butter and cheese—all from the new farms stretching westward from this outpost. Storekeepers and craftsfolk were opening their shutters and doors; livery stable, blacksmith and farrier, doctor, haberdasher.

The air was full of the strong smells of horses and cattle, woodsmoke, drying fish. Over the rooftops she could see the bright yellows and crimson of autumn trees in woodlots and field verge, the old gold of tasseled corn, copper leaves in a vineyard, a wide-horned bull drowsing beneath an oak as mist drifted over the dew-wet pasture's faded green.

Lively, Alston smiled to herself. Crude enough by the standards of the twentieth, but those weren't the standards anyone with sense used anymore. *A lively little kid, growing fast.*

Swindapa came up behind her and wrapped arms around her, resting chin on shoulder. Alston sighed, a sound that mixed a vast content and an anticipation of the day. Words ran through her mind:

> *I rose from dreamless hours and sought the morn*
> *That beat upon my window: from the sill*
> *I watched sweet lands, where Autumn light newborn*
> *Swayed through the trees and lingered on the hill.*
> *If things so lovely are, why labor still*
> *to dream of something more than this I see?*
> *Do I remember tales of Galilee,*
> *I who have slain my faith and freed my will?*
> *Let me forget dead faith, dead mystery*
> *Dead thoughts of things I cannot comprehend.*
> *Enough the light mysterious in the tree,*
> *Enough the friendship of my chosen friend.*

They buckled on their webbing; knife, pouches, binoculars, and double-barreled flintlock pistols at their belts, *katanas* over their backs with the hilt jutting up behind the left ear. Saddlebags held their traveling kit; they carried those downstairs in their arms, slinging them over the benches beside them as they sat at the long trestle tables in the tavern's taproom.

Wild Rose Chance was an example of what "log cabin" could mean when the logs were a hundred feet long and a yard thick. The big room was already fairly warm with the fire in the long iron-backed fieldstone hearth and busy—a score or more sitting down to a hearty breakfast. Alston nodded to friends and acquaintances as she loaded her own plate and sank her teeth into a slab of hot, coarse wholewheat bread with butter melting on its steaming surface.

At least I don't have to worry about my weight, she thought. Not when things like traveling fifteen miles to Camp Grant meant half a day in the saddle, not fifteen minutes in a car.

"Hey, there anyone here who speaks Fiernan?" a voice called from the open street door.

Alston and her partner looked up sharply. A woman stood there, in ordinary bib overalls, but with a shotgun over her back and a star pinned to one strap. Behind her were a young couple, dressed Islander-style except for their near-naked toddler, but obvious immigrants. Behind *them* was a clamoring pack—she thought she recognized several farmers, a straw boss from one of the timber mills, and the owner of the boatyard among them.

Swindapa began to rise, then sank back as the proprietor of the inn went over, drying his hands on a corner of his apron.

"Thought you did, Sarah," he said.

"Thought I did too, Ted."

Swindapa did rise then, smiling, when mutual bewilderment became too obvious. She returned chuckling.

"They speak Goldenhill dialect," she said. "Thicker than honey—I'm not surprised the sheriff couldn't make hoof or horn of it and the poor couple were frightened out of the seven words of English they had between them. The sheriff will put them up in the Town Hall tonight and find someone to explain about contracts."

Alston nodded approval and threw down her napkin. Everyone was short of labor, but that was no excuse for taking advantage of ignorance. Her inner smile grew to a slight curve of full lips. *Jared's seen to that.* By the time the immigrant couple had put in five years they'd speak the language and be eligible for citizenship; a few years more, and they'd probably have a farm or boat or shop of their own, and be down at the docks clamoring for a chance at a hired hand themselves. *And* their kids would be in school.

There had been times in the Coast Guard when she'd wondered what the hell she was doing—on the Haitian refugee patrol, for instance.

Or "cooperating" with those cowboy assholes in the DEA and BATF, she thought. If you had to be hired muscle, it was nice to work for an outfit run by actual human beings.

They took their saddlebags out; the inn's groom had horses waiting, four-year-old Alba/Morgan crosses. Alston swung into the saddle, heeling her mount out into the road.

"Worth fighting for," Swindapa said, indicating the town with an odd circling motion of her head.

"Let's go tell it to the Marines, love," Alston replied.

* * *

"Yeah, it's coming along okay, man," the blacksmith said, his long, sheeplike face neutral.

William Walker was always a little careful around John Martins. For one thing, the Californian ironworker hadn't come along to Alba willingly, like the rest of his American supporters. That had taken a knife to the throat of his woman, Barbara. For another, Walker suspected that under his vaguely Buddhisty hippy-dippy exterior, Martins was capable of a really serious dislike.

"Well, should we go for a converter, or should we do the finery-chafery method?"

He looked around the raw little settlement. Walker had been to Greece a couple of times up in the Twentieth, once on Coast Guard business and once on holiday. This looked very different from what he remembered. The plain of the Eurotas River stretched away on either hand, about forty miles of it from where it left the northern mountains to where it reached the sea. More mountains lined it on either side, and they weren't the bare limestone crags of the twentieth century, either. There hadn't been nearly as much time for the goats and axes of men to do their work; these uplands were densely forested, pine on the higher elevations, mixed with evergreen oak and chestnut and ilex further down. The glade in which they stood was waist-high grass; the wind down from the heights smelled of fir sap. Not quite like Montana—for a bitter moment he remembered the snow peaks of the Rockies and the wild, clean smell—it was warmer, somehow, in a way that had nothing to do with the air temperature. Spicier, with scents like thyme and lavender.

"Hey, I'm just a blacksmith, man," Martins said, hefting the sledge in his hand. "You get me iron, and I can work it."

Walker pushed his face closer to Martins's. The Californian was a tall man, as tall as himself, and ropily muscular. Older, of course—in his late forties now—with a ponytail more gray than brown at the rear of a head mostly bald, and absurd small lens glasses always falling toward the end of his nose.

"Don't try to bullshit me, Martins," Walker said. "I know *exactly* what you can and can't do, family man. Now, I think I asked you a question?"

The sad russet eyes turned away slightly. Besides Barbara, there was an infant now, and Martins knew exactly what Walker was capable of, too.

"Converter will take six months, maybe a year, if we can do it at all, man—have to, like, talk to Cuddy too. Finery I can do right away, no shit, and blister steel."

"Then get started on it. We'll work on the converter later."

Walker turned away and surveyed the work site. Trimmed timbers were piling up fast, with teams of near-naked peasants and yoked oxen hauling them out of the woods. The Achaean architect Augewas and Enkhelyawon the scribe were standing near the stream, drawing with sticks in the dirt. Walker paced over, still feeling a little odd in the Mycenaean tunic and kilt. It was comfortable clothing for this climate, however, at least in the warmer seasons.

"Gwasileus," the two Greeks said, bowing. "Lord."

In classical Greek that would come to be *basileus* and mean king, but here and now it was simply the word for chieftain, overlord, boss man.

"How do things go?" Walker said.

"Lord," the architect said, "there is good building stone near here—limestone, hard and dense, a blue stone. And I can build a wall across this stream."

He nodded. The creek was about chest deep in the middle and twenty feet across. By southern Greek standards it was a major river; according to the locals, it shrank by about half in summertime. Flow was seasonal here, but not nearly as much as it would be up in the twentieth. The greater forest cover held water longer, and so runoff was slower. There were more springs, too; he wasn't sure if the actual rainfall was greater, but it certainly *felt* as if it was.

"But, Lord, why do you wish it to be built this way?" Augewas said, indicating the ground. He'd sketched the slight narrowing a hundred yards east, where they were putting in the dam, and a curved line across it with the convex end upstream.

Ah, that's right, they don't have the arch or true dome, Walker thought. He drew his sword and used the tip as a pointer.

"The weight of the water pushes on the dam," he said. "If the wall is straight, only the strength of the wall holds it back. If it is curved, the water pushes the earth and rock into the sides."

"Lord?" the architect said, baffled.

Walker sheathed his sword and looked around. *Don't underestimate them,* he reminded himself. They built good roads for this era, and aqueducts, bridges, towers of great cyclopean blocks; they knew how to handle stone, in a solid rule-of-thumb, brute-force-and-massive-ignorance fashion.

The problem is that they've got a set of rote answers to known problems but no concept of calculating stresses and forces.

Ah, he thought after a moment, and cut a branch. "Here," he said, holding it straight between his palms. "Push downward."

Augewas did, and the green stick curved under his finger. "Now," Walker went on, "I will bend it upward like a bow." He did so. "Push again. See how it resists the push? Now put it between your own palms and *I* will push. Held straight, only the strength of the stick opposes my finger. Now bend it into an upward arch. Feel how the push goes against your hands when it is bent?"

"So . . . so the force of the water will push against the *sides* of the embankment, where it butts into those ledges of rock!" Augewas said, pointing. Another thought struck him. "And we will not need to build it so thick, to be just as strong!"

"Exactly. That will flood all this land here."

Augewas, a dark grizzled man, nodded brusquely. Enkhelyawon looked slightly shocked at the lack of formality, but Walker let it slide. He recognized the attitude; it was a professional focusing on his work, not somebody dissing the boss.

"That, yes," he said. "That will give you a head of water. But where do you wish to take it, lord?"

He waved toward the valley of the Eurotas. Clustered, flat-topped peasant huts of mud brick showed here and there amid grainfields and olive groves, occasionally the larger house of a *telestai,* a baron. On the edge of vision was the megaron-palace near the site of classical Sparta. Like that later city, it was unwalled, but for a different reason—the High King of Mycenae forbade stone defenses, as he did at Pylos and a few other places directly under his gaze.

"We might use some of it for irrigation, eventually," Walker said. "But come, I will show you what the first use will be."

He led them over to a trestle table of logs. On it stood a model three feet high. "These are my handfast men Cuddy and Bierman," he went on. "And this is a . . . replica in small . . . of what we will build below the dam."

It showed a wheel of timbers forty feet across, with a chute to bring the water to its top and spill onto the curved blades within. At Walker's nod, Bill Cuddy poured a small bucket of water into the pan at the top of the model, letting it run down a wooden chute. The wheel turned on its axle, and the cams on the shaft moved hammers, pumped a piston bellows, turned a small round grindstone.

Augewas looked on in fascination as Cuddy explained the operation of the machine with patient repetition, turning frequently to look at the dam site, visibly struggling to turn the model into an image in his mind.

"The first thing the *water mill* does," Walker went on, backtracking occasionally to explain when he had to use an English word with no Achaean equivalent, "will be to drive the bellows for the *blast furnace.*"

"For the iron, lord?" Augewas said eagerly. He'd seen samples from the tons the *Yare* had carried, and these people knew about iron in the abstract—they bought small quantities through the Hittites for ornament or special uses. They just didn't know how to smelt it or work it properly yet. "There is ore, near here?"

Bierman put a sack of cracked rocks down on the table and spoke in slow, careful Achaean: "About sixty-five percent . . . that's six parts in ten, I mean . . . iron. Hematite ore—real nice, except I think there may be traces of nickel, maybe a little chrome."

"Besides the ore of iron," Walker said, "we need charcoal in large amounts and very pure, soft limestone for flux. We will need many hundreds of laborers, to bring those and all the other necessary things together. Metalworkers must be trained; I have a master ironsmith and a dozen men who have been learning from him. Then when we have the iron from the *blast furnace,* it must be further worked with heat and hammers—very heavy hammers . . ."

Enkhelyawon tossed his head in a purely Greek gesture. "The *wannax* has decreed that this must be so. Spend and spare not what is needed; I heard him say so, the royal word from the King's own lips."

Angewas nodded himself, more slowly, a beatific smile spreading over his lined face at the prospect of an unlimited cost-plus contract, or the Bronze Age equivalent. "That is a command worthy of a king indeed. One seldom heard in these sad times, when great lords clutch their bronze and silver hard and trade is so troubled. Then besides the dam, we must build channels for the water," he went on. "This furnace itself . . ."

"It will be of stone, shaped like a tower that tapers from the base to the top, but it must be lined with a special type of brick," Walker said. "My men are looking for it—fireclay, we call it. There must be ramps to the lip of the stack." He went on, pointing out details.

Augewas stood silent for a moment after he finished. "I see, lord," he said at last. "Then there are these buildings. And we must have roads, roads in the hill country here, to fetch the materials. Barracks and storehouses of food and other goods, for the workers. Houses for the masters and overseers. A great project, lord, one worthy of my skill. Here I will learn much, as well as do much."

Walker smiled. *Great,* he thought. *An enthusiast.* Now he could get back to Mycenae for a while and do some intensive politicking.

"Everything's a trade-off," Jared Cofflin said.

Martha made a noncommittal noise from behind him. "This one is an *expensive* trade-off," she noted.

Cofflin grunted in his turn and pushed harder on the pedals. The two-person tricycles were the transportation of choice for those who could get them, and he didn't feel easy commandeering a horse carriage now that Martha wasn't lugging around a nursing infant anymore.

Maybe they'd buy one in a year or two, when horses were cheaper. *Of course, then I'd have to rent space in a stable, and it'd take forever to get the damned thing ready.* Animals couldn't just be parked until you needed them.

They were moving out Hummock Pond Road, south and west of town. It was a bit eerie, having so many different landscapes in your mind's eye. The thick, tangled scrub that had covered the Island since long before he was born, then the frantic chopping and burning, and there were fields of grain and potatoes fertilized with ash and fish offal . . . and now changing again, to pasture and orchard.

Now and then they passed people at work, a farmer on a sulky-plow turning furrows as he rode behind two horses, wagons scattering fertilizer or pulverized oyster shells, long rows of harvest workers gathering late vegetables, a herd of close-sheared sheep flowing around the bicycle like lumpy white water as it was driven by two teenagers and an extremely happy collie. A wagon driven by a policeman went by with a dozen resentful-looking, hungover men in it; drunk-and-disorderly convictions, he thought, going out to work off a couple of days helping to mine Madaket Mall—the old landfill dump, which was full of irreplaceable stuff. He nodded and smiled to the peace officer. That was lousy work, worse than shoveling garbage in its way.

"Getting old for this," Cofflin puffed, glad of the excuse to stop when a hauler did, dropping off bales of coarse salt-marsh hay from the mainland.

"Not as old as you were the first year," Martha said, and he chuckled. *True enough. God, the way my thighs ached!* He felt stronger now than he had the day of the Event, and he'd certainly lost the small pot that had been marring his lean frame.

Farm wagons loaded with milk tins, vegetables, and crates of gobbling turkeys passed them on their way into town. He felt a little glow of satisfaction every time one went by, nodding and waving to the drivers. That was life itself, for his people and his family. Hard-won life; none of them except Angelica and a few others had known a damned thing about farming.

They came to a new turnoff, marked BESSEMER CASTING PLANT #1. "Well, here's Starbuck's Nightmare," Martha said, as they wheezed up a slight rise.

Cofflin chuckled breathlessly as they coasted down the new-laid asphalt and braked to a halt. This thing had swallowed a lot of money—since the Event he'd gained a new appreciation of the way money represented crystallized sweat. And using it for one thing meant *not* using it for another.

Ronald Leaton was waiting for them in front of the office shack, wiping his hands on the inevitable greasy rag.

" 'lo, Chief, Martha," he said.

"Morning, Ron. Well, I'm glad we persuaded you to put *this* out of town, at least," Jared Cofflin said, dismounting and peering around with his hands on his hips.

The complex itself was built on cleared scrubland, the buildings constructed of oak-timber beams and brick beside new asphalt roadways, with a tall wooden windmill creaking beside an earthen water reservoir. Smoke smut and charcoal dust coated everything, making even the fresh-cut wood look a little shabby.

"It ain't pretty, but it works," Leaton said. The engineer was grinning, the way he usually did when showing off a new toy. "This is the smelting stack of the furnace," he said, pointing to a squat chimney-like affair of red brick fifteen feet high with a movable top like a giant metal witch's hat.

"So that's a blast furnace? Cofflin asked. It looked formidably solid.

"Cupola furnace, if you want to get technical, since it's for remelting metal, not for refining ore. That's where we melt down the ingots. Now, we *could* just melt down scrap and cast it straight—I've been doing that for a couple of years, on a much smaller scale—but we don't have an infinite supply of scrap. And we are getting cast iron in some quantity from Alba. Pretty damned good iron, too; those little charcoal blast furnaces can give you excellent quality and Irondale is doing very well."

Jared found himself giving the riveted boilers an occasional uneasy glance. There had been some nasty accidents with those in the beginning.

"That's for blowing the blast into the stack," Leaton said, pointing to the larger engine.

A long *chuff* came from the little donkey engine, and the tender threw a lever. The wooden links of the endless belt rattled, and the ingots began to lift toward the top of the furnace stack. When they reached it, they fell against the side of the conical plug with a loud, dull clanging and down into the furnace. Another wagon brought up big wicker tubs of charcoal, and they went up the conveyor likewise.

"So once we've tapped the molten iron from the furnace . . . over here, Chief—"

They walked around the massive construction.

"We take it in the holding car here and bring it over to the converter."

That was the second structure, twenty yards away. The core of it was a tubby egg-shaped construction of riveted steel plates twelve feet long; it was rather like a fat cannon pointing at the sky. Beneath it was more rail, and men and women in stained coveralls were unbolting the bottom with wrenches a yard long and lowering it onto a waiting cart with jacks and levers.

"You can see where they've got it open, the inside is firebrick and calcinated limestone. . . . We really should have two, one up and one being relined. Anyway, we pour the molten iron in the top and blow air in through that removable bottom—it's called a tuyere, the long pipe thingie over there swings in and we get the blast from a blowing engine, two double-acting steam pistons."

"That what created that almighty racket last night? Had a couple of people riding into town hell-bent-for-leather, screeching that the Event had happened again."

"Ayup. Better than fireworks—exothermic reaction, great *big* plume of colored lights, flame . . . that's why we've got tile on all these roofs. Oxygen in the air hits the carbon in the iron and it *burns*. Took a while to get from theory to practice, but we're getting usable batches now. And heck, even the *slag* from a basic-process converter is useful, ground up fine for fertilizer. It's all phosphate and calcium."

Leaton's slim, middle-aged features took on a look of ecstasy; he'd run a computer store back before the Event for most of his living, but the little engineering shop in his basement had been his real love. He'd done nonstandard parts for antique automobiles, prototypes for inventors, some miniature steam engines for collectors. *And* he'd had a big collection of technical books; one of the most useful had been a World War II government handbook on how to do unorthodox things in small machine shops.

Seahaven was the island's biggest single employer now, if you didn't count fishing, and it had spawned dozens of smaller enterprises.

"And here's where the steel goes," Leaton went on. "We're using graded scrap in the smelter to alloy it. Hard to be precise with this Bessemer process, but it works in a sort of more-or-less fashion. Eventually we'll have to get manganese and alloying materials of our own, but for now . . . anyway, the converter pours the steel into this crucible, the insulation keeps the steel molten while we put a couple of batches in, we close it up and rotate it to mix 'em up and get a homogeneous product, and then we pour *that* into the mold."

The shape being swung up out of the timber-lined casting pit on an A-frame crane was nearly as long as the converter itself but much thinner, still radiating heat as it lay on its cradle with bits and pieces of sand and clay sticking to its rough-cast exterior.

"That's no steam engine cylinder," Cofflin said grimly.

"Nope," Leaton said regretfully. "Eight-inch Dahlgren gun. Still have to turn the exterior and bore it out, of course. The boring mill's going in over there." He pointed to a set of stone foundations and a pile of timber. His expression clouded slightly. "Marian *did* say her project had priority?"

"Ayup," Cofflin nodded grimly. "The Meeting agreed. Right now, that's the form *progress* takes. First priority, now that the *Emancipator* is off on its trials."

"You can see this is a lot of work, hard-sweat work, though," Leaton went on. "About that immigration quota—"

"Goddammit, Ron, save it for the Council meetings!"

The furnace belched smoke and sparks into a sky thick with geese heading southward. Their honking sounded forlorn through the rumble of burning iron.

Odikweos of the Western Isles heard the flat cracking sound of metal on hard leather and then the unmusical crash of blade on blade. He flung up a hand to halt his followers—right now, only a boy with a torch and a single spearman—and listened.

"Nothing so dark as a city at night," he murmured.

Not even a forest before the rising of the moon. Nothing that stank quite so bad, either. Sometimes he was glad his own rocky fiefdom was too poor to support such a warren.

The narrow alleyway where they walked twisted so that the light of the burning pine knot didn't travel far. High mud-brick walls rose on either side; this late at night few of the small windows set under flat roofs showed lamplight behind them. Only a scattering of stars glittered overhead, hidden by the high roofs—many of the buildings were enormous, three, even four stories tall, looming like black cliffs.

Voices now, men shouting in rage, and one shrilling scream of agony. He rubbed his beard. *It's the High King's business, to keep order in his stronghold,* he thought, looking up to the citadel of Mycenae on its hill above. Plenty of lamps glowing *there,* even at this hour.

"But perhaps we should take a look," he said. "Follow me, and be careful."

He drew the sword hung on a baldric across his body and shifted forward the round shield slung over his back, taking a firm grip on its central handhold. The sword glinted cold blue-gray in the torchlight; it was the new type, *steel* as it was called, straight and double-edged and nearly three feet long. The hilt was bound with silver wire and the ring-and-bar guard inlaid with gold, as befitted a royal man's weapon—it had come as a gift from Agamemnon, part of the new wealth he'd found. Harder to put an edge on than a bronze sword, but sharper once you did, and much more durable.

The spearman closed up on his left, and the torchbearer fell a little behind, holding up the burning wood until their shadows passed huge and grotesque before them.

The alleyway gave onto an irregular open space perhaps two or three spear lengths in any direction, covered with worn cobbles; thuds and groans and clatterings echoed off the mud brick. The light here was a little better, and the torch had room to spread its flickering glow. Against the wall opposite two men fought four; the two had an injured friend down at their feet, and the four had a fifth man sitting on the ground behind them moaning and clutching his belly. The attackers all had shields; three fought with spears, the fourth with a nobleman's bronze sword. The defenders . . . Odikweos's brows rose under his headband. One of them was helmeted, dressed in a tunic of some strange rippling dark-gray stuff that reached to his knees, and carried a round shield marked with a wolfshead. A short, leaf-shaped sword flickered around the edge of it. His companion was in cloth, but he bore a sword that *curved,* long as a man's leg, and he wielded it two-handed.

Rumors clicked together in the Achaean's mind. Here was a chance to see all that his curiosity had desired.

"Gods condemn you, bastards!" he roared, running forward. "See how you like an even fight!"

The retainer beside him also called on the gods, although in a rather different tone. Odikweos met the attack of one dim figure head-on, ducking under a spearthrust, levering the other man's shield aside with the edge of his own. That took a grunting twist of effort, but it left the man staggering and open. He ran the long steel sword through his opponent's body, careful to strike below the ribs. There was a soft, clinging resistance, a bubbling scream as he wrenched the blade back and brought the shield up with desperate quickness.

His alertness was unnecessary for once. His retainer had taken the wounded attacker, a short underarm thrust through the gut. Now he braced one sandal on the sprattling form and stabbed downward with a force that crunched his spearpoint through the dying man's neck and into the cobbles beneath. The strangers had moved forward promptly, blades flickering. The attacker with the bronze sword took to his heels while they were dealing with the last of his followers. The curved sword bit low and hamstrung that lone and luckless one, and the odd short sword rammed forward into his gut in an economical underarm stroke.

Odikweos lowered his own sword and waited, panting slightly. The dead added their bit to the sewer stink of the town. *Pity,* he thought, as the stomach-wounded attacker jerked and went still. *We might have made him talk.*

"Odikweos son of Laertes, *wannax* of Ithaka among the Western Isles," he said.

"Walker son of Edward, *hekwetos* to Agamemnon King of Men," the other man said. He looked as if he recognized the underking's name, somehow, even panting with effort and the pain of his wound. Odikweos swelled slightly with pride at that.

"My thanks," he went on; not an Achaean phrasing, but the western lord caught the meaning.

Walkeearh, he thought, shaping the word silently with his lips. This close, Odikweos could see more of the man, the one of whom he'd heard so much. His missing left eye was covered by a black leather patch and his brown hair held back with a strap of gold-chased doe-skin; a very tall man, six feet or more, well built and strong-looking, and quick as well, from the way he stood . . . except that he kept a hand to his side, where a spreading stain darkened the fabric of his tunic.

"Since we've fought shield-locked, shall I bind your wound?" Odikweos asked.

Walkeearh shook his head. "We're not far from my home, and it isn't serious. Come and take hospitality of me, if you may." He looked around. "We'll have to get my man here back as well, he's got a spearthrust through the leg." Walkeearh's hale retainer was binding it with a strip torn from a cloak.

"Indeed," Odikweos nodded in approval. A lord must look to the needs of his men. "That's not a matter of difficulty."

He turned to the nearest door and slammed the pommel of his sword against the beechwood panels. "Open!" he roared. "Open, commoner—a kingly man commands you!" It was a large house; there would be a door or bedstead within, and men enough to carry it. "Open!"

There were. The Achaean walked beside Walkeearh up the hillside road and through the massive gate with its twin lions rearing above the lintel stone. Their bronze fangs shone above him, for there were many torches and numerous guards there. They exclaimed at Wal-keearh's wound, but passed him through at his bitten-off command. The house he led them to was a fine one, a hall and outbuildings; Odikweos's own palace in the west was no better. He accepted that with only a slight pang of envy. Mycenae was rich in gold and power, Ithaka wealthy only in honor and the strength of her men.

He looked about keenly as they walked into the antechamber. It was brighter than he'd thought an inside room could be. Lamps were fixed to the walls, with mirrors of unbelievable brightness behind them— far brighter than burnished bronze, or even silver. The lamps were strange as well, with tops of some clear crystallike substance above them and wicks that burned with an odd bluish color and a fruity smell. The light made it easy to see the gear of the men who crowded around; their armor was tunics of small metal rings joined together. Odikweos smiled at the cleverness of it.

Although—hmmm—those rings look good to ward a stab or cut, but they wouldn't be much protection from a crushing blow.

They were hustled into the main megaron-hall, which made his eyes widen. A great hood of sheet copper stood over the central hearth, with a pipe of copper running up the full two stories to the terra-cotta smoke-pipe in the ceiling . . . and he'd thought smoke-pipes were the last word in elegance. There was a cheery blaze on the big round hearth, but despite that, little or no smoke drifted up to haze under the painted rafters. More of the wonderful lamps were being turned on by the servants, giving fine light throughout the great room, shining on weapons racked around the pillars and doorways. There were chairs in plenty, more than you'd expect even in a great noble's home, and fine hangings over them. Skilled slaves took his weapons and cloak and brought him heated wine with honey and a footstool. Another undid his sandal straps and wiped his feet clean.

Walkeearh swore as they lifted the tunic over his head, leaving him dressed only in his kilt. Odikweos looked at the wound with an experienced eye. *Not too bad.* A clean-edged gouge where the spearhead had plowed his side, perhaps touching a rib a little. It bled more freely without the wool of the tunic packing it, but it should heal if it didn't mortify, which was always a risk even if you washed the cut with wine as he did—an old Shore Folk woman had taught him that trick. His earlier impression was confirmed as he watched muscles moving beneath Walkeearh's skin; this was a fighting-man you'd be cautious of offending. From the scars, he'd lived through many a battle.

Two women with a flutter of attendants came down the staircase from the upper story of the house, straightening their indoor gowns. One was tall and blond with braids down her sides to her waist, well shaped but only passable of face. The other was . . .

Odikweos fought not to gasp in astonishment at the exotic loveliness. The other was short, with skin the color of fine amber and hair raven-dark. Above a tiny nose and impossibly high cheekbones her eyes *slanted,* with a fold at their outer tips. Who had ever seen the like?

And a wisewoman as well. She washed her hands in water and some sharp-smelling liquid that her attendants brought, examined the wound, then spoke in a sharp, nasal-sounding foreign language.

"Speak Achaean, Alice," Walkeearh said. "We have a guest."

"That needs some stitches," she said, then bent to examine the warrior with the wounded leg. "I'll have to debride this—that'll take a while. Kylefra, Missora"—that to two young woman who looked alike enough to be sisters—"get him to the *infirmary,* and *prep* him, *stat.*"

Walkeearh stifled a gasp when she swabbed out his wound, then set his teeth and ignored it as she brought out a curved needle and thread and began *sewing* the wound together, as if it were cloth.

"Sit, be at ease," he said tightly. "This is my captain of guards, Ohotolarix son of Telenthaur." A big yellow-haired man, young but tough-looking. "And my wives Ekhnonpa"—the fair woman—"and Alice Hong. Ladies, here's Odikweos son of Laertes, who probably saved my life tonight."

Odikweos bowed his head politely. Ekhnonpa spoke to Ohotolarix in a strange, almost-familiar language, then thanked him in slow, accented Achaean.

Hong kept at her work. *Strange name*, he thought. *Is she human?* Perhaps she was a dryad, something of that sort—certainly this Wal keearh was otherwordly enough to wed an Otherworlder. When the wound was closed, she painted more of the clear liquid on it and then bandaged it, securing the pad with a roll of linen around her man's chest and over a shoulder.

"Don't strain it," she said. "I'll go look at Velararax now, after I touch up that ear of your friend's."

Odikweos made himself sit still as she came up beside him. "This is going to hurt a little," she said. *No, human enough*, he thought; she smelled like a well-washed woman roused from her bed. The fingers touched his ear, and then something stung like liquid fire.

"Here, Lord Odikweos," she said. "That will heal cleanly."

When the women had left, a grave housekeeper brought basins of water to wash their hands and trays of food, bread and sliced meats, olives and dried figs. While she mixed the wine half-and-half with water and poured it into fine gold cups, Walkeearh shrugged into another tunic, moving cautiously.

"My thanks again," he said. "The gods witness"—

He poured a libation, but—curiously—not on the floor. Instead he used a pottery bowl with a rush mat inside it. Courteous, Odikweos did the same; it was always best to honor a man's household customs.

—"that I and mine are in your debt."

"May we fight again side by side someday," Odikweos said. That wasn't unlikely, given the coming war. "Who were your foes? Men sent by some rival?"

Walker smiled. "I have enough of those," he said.

"True, you've risen far among us in only one winter," he replied. "Far and fast, for an outland man." He looked around the curiously altered hall.

"And where one man rises, other men envy and hate," Walkeearh said. Odikweos nodded; that went without saying. "You're in Mycenae for the muster against Sicily?"

He tossed his head in affirmation. "My men and horses are camped outside the city," he said. "We came by sea to Tiryns. I've a guest-friend here and sought his dwelling, but he has blood-kin sleeping like the ribs of a sheep on the floor of his hall, and I was leaving again to seek my tent."

"Stay here," Walkeearh said. "There's room in plenty, despite the war."

Odikweos nodded, smiling. That was just what he'd hoped. "I will take the hospitality you offer gratefully," he said. Curious to see how this Walkeearh would react, he went on, "Although I'd be even glad-der to be sleeping beside my own wife, at home. If this was a war against other Achaeans, I would have found some way to refuse the summons."

Walkeearh smiled, an odd lopsided expression. "Pretending to be mad, perhaps?"

Odikweos laughed. "You have a godlike wit. Perhaps so, perhaps so. Well, there may be plunder in this war, at least."

You had to be more careful when the hegemon called his vassals for aid against a foe or rebel, of course; dodging that call looked too much like rebellion itself. He had no desire to see the black hulls of a hun-dred hollow ships drawn up on the beach before his home.

The foreigner didn't bluster about glory. Instead he nodded thought-fully. "Spoken like a man of cunning mind," he said. "When men who should be vassals of the same high king war with each other, the realm is weakened."

Odikweos blinked; that hadn't been exactly what he meant . . . al-though when you thought about it, the idea made some sense in an odd, twisty way. "Certainly the king of men won't get much tribute from the dead," he agreed. "And besieging a strong city—well, the ar-row of far-shooting Paiwon Apollo rain down on such a camp." There was always sickness when too men stayed in one spot for long.

"Leaving the realm weaker if outsiders attack, as I said."

Ah. A real thought. "I know of none such who threaten the Achaean lands," Odikweos said. "Although the Narrow Sea north of my hold-ings swarms with pirates these days. Many more than in my grand-sire's time; of course, we do more trade there, too."

"And the savages hear of the wealth of the Achaeans," Walker pointed out. He yawned, then winced. "It's time for sleep."

"It is good to yield to drowsy night," Odikweos agreed.

The housekeeper showed Odikweos to a room, offering to have a bath drawn first if he wished.

"Tomorrow," he said, looking instead at the lamp she carried.

It lit the dark corridor off the megaron well; a tall wax candle in a bronze holder with a handle, with another bulb of the beautiful crystallike substance around it. *The bulb keeps a draught from making the flame flicker or blowing it out,* he thought. Clever, very clever.

"What is that called, that crystal?" he asked.

"It is called *glass,* lord," she said, looking surprised at his curiosity. "I know little of these things, but I heard the master say it was made from sand, in fire."

This man must be beloved of Hephaistos, the Achaean thought. He'd seen beads of glass, from the eastern lands, but nothing like this. *Nor is he shunned by Ares Enuwarios, either.* An odd combination, the gods of craftsmen and of war.

They came to a bedchamber; unusually, it had a door of wood rather than an embroidered curtain. Another candle on a table beside the bed gave light. The girl waiting within turned down the blankets . . . *another new thing,* Odikweos thought. Over the mattress was a sheath of linen fine enough for a lady's undergown, and another atop it, beneath the blankets and sheepskins.

The mixer and wine cup beside the bed were usual enough. He filled the cup as he stripped and sat on the bedside. The girl unbuttoned the shoulders of her gown, stepped out of it, and waited with her hands clasped and eyes cast down; young and comely, with good breasts and hips. He patted the bedside, and instead of mounting her at once gave her unwatered wine.

"Tell me your name, little dove," he said.

She gave him a grateful smile and sipped. He smiled back at her. Odikweos son of Laertes was a man of medium height, his hair black with reddish glints and his eyes hazel, his face still unlined despite a weathered bronze tan.

"I am called Alexandra, master," she said shyly. With an accent, so that was probably not the name she'd been born with.

"I don't think you are a repeller of men, though," he said, punning on her name, for that was its strict meaning. The male form, Alexandros, made more sense.

She laughed, and he spent some time soothing her before he put his hands to her waist and urged her back, which made her ready to welcome him. Afterward they talked more, and it was easy to lead her mind.

Many men forgot that women and servants had ears, and tongues to talk with. Such men were fools. You could learn invaluable things from underlings, and he intended to learn all he could of this strange house. The gods had given him rocky islands on the edge of the world for his demesne. That wasn't to say that they meant him to spend all his life as a poor underking.

He didn't think this foreigner chief was a fool of the more obvious kind, either. Something could come of that.

* * *

"It seems Moon Woman has sent stars to guide my feet on the path of war," Swindapa said, with a sigh.

After most of a decade, Marian's mind translated automatically; the words were English, but the thought was Fiernan. An American would have said: *No getting around it.* Swindapa's birth-folk were a fatalistic lot.

"We've spent more time exploring and building ships than fighting," she pointed out gently.

"Truth," the blonde said with another sigh and reached over to squeeze the other woman's hand. "Moon Woman turned the years themselves in their tracks to give us that."

Alston laughed. "You know, that's about as good an explanation as I've ever heard," she said.

Swindapa stroked a hand down the neck of her mount. "The ships are wonderful," she said. "And horses are almost as much fun as babies."

They rode side by side, in the shade of the trees left uncut on either side of what was becoming known as the Great West Road down Long Island's north fork. Leaves fluttered down to meet those already in swales by the ditches and thick on the gravel, drifts of old gold and dark crimson. To their right were patches of wood, of salt marsh noisy with wildfowl, and glimpses of the sound. She reined in for a second to watch a schooner beating eastward, its sails white curves of a purity that made her throat ache for a second.

The other side of the road was a mixture of forest and plowland set out in big square fields—the Meeting had handed out square-mile farms to homesteaders, leaving half the land in forest preserve. Cornstalks rustled sere and dry in stooked pyramids amid thick-scattered orange pumpkins, next to the almost shocking green of alfalfa; where it had been mown for hay the scent was as sweet as candy. Wheat and barley stubble was dun-yellow and thick with the clover that grazed herds of crossbred sheep. Where teams of oxen or horses pulled disc plows the turned earth was a rich, moist reddish brown, swarming with raucous gulls squabbling over the grubs exposed by the turning steel.

The riders waved to the workers digging potatoes, to shepherds and their barking dogs, to passersby—farm wagons drawn by calm-eyed oxen, the odd rider, and now and then a lone pedestrian.

Alston smiled at the miles of post-and-board edging the fields, remembering the experiment with splitting black walnut for Virginia-style rail fences. Theoretically that should have been cheaper, but it turned out that the use of wedge and maul was something Abe Lincoln must have learned at his father's knee.

Sure as shit nobody on Nantucket could do it! she chuckled to herself. Anybody could nail boards, though, and one of Leaton's people had come up with a simple pile driver to set the posts.

The road dipped into a belt of trees along a creek; planks boomed beneath the hooves of their mounts. Alston felt her horse take a sudden sideways skitter as something squealed angrily. A sounder of pigs erupted from the mud beneath the pilings, scattering into the trees in a twinkle of hooves and brass nose rings. The air was full of a cool, damp, musty smell, leaf mold and turned earth.,

"Gone wild," Swindapa said. Her eyes raked the woods by the side of the road; they were closing in, as the riders reached beyond the settled zone. "Like that . . . and that.'

Deer Dancer had the Spear Mark tattooed between her breasts, the sign of a hunter among the Fiernan Bohulugi, and Alston was still surprised sometimes at how sharp her eyes were. She pointed around; at a patch of plantain, dandelions, dock, nettles, a honeybee buzzing between the flowers of white clover, a starling flitting between branches.

All things from Nantucket that sailed upstream against the tide of years, Alston thought. "Like me, sugar," she went on aloud. "Worse things than being a weed. Means you're hardy and difficult to get rid of."

Their laughter echoed in the cathedral stillness of the forest, and they kneed their horses into a canter. Traffic would be thin until they reached the training ground where the republic prepared an answer to Walker's ambitions.

"Rejoice, Oh King," Walker said, bowing low.

"Rejoice, *ekwetos* Walkeearh," Agamemnon said, nodding regal benevolence as he stepped down from his chariot.

The wind was blowing across the Lakonian Gulf, cutting the summer heat where the Eurotas River met the sea. All was bustle in the cove sheltered by the rocky headland; workmen, women with jars on their heads, slaves moving loads of all types, wagons full of grain or timber. Rows of mud-brick huts had been built a little inland, and a tall structure with long, armlike sails going around and around. Curious, he walked toward it and through the broad doorway at its base.

"Ah, another of your *mills,* Walkeearh," he said.

They were no longer so strange that they shed his eyes in bafflement, although this was different from the ones moved by falling water and the interior was dim and dusty, full of loud creaks and grinding stone. Up above, a long pole turned with the sails outside . . . *driven by the wind,* Agamemnon thought. *Clever.* As if the circle of sails was the wheel of a chariot and that pole the axle. That turned a toothed wheel, which turned another wheel on a vertical shaft, and that ran down to ground level. More wheels drove a giant round quern taller than a man, shaped in profile like an old figure-eight shield. Peasants walked up a ramp and tipped jugs of grain into the top. Below, flour poured out of a spout into still larger *pithoi*, storage jugs as tall as a man's chest. Slaves dragged them across the stone platform and into waiting oxcarts, some of them the big four-wheeled type that Walkeearh had made.

"Swift," Agamemnon said. "But surely you don't let your slave women sit in idleness? They can't earn *all* their keep lying on their backs."

The outlander laughed politely at his overlord's jest, along with a couple of the courtiers who'd driven down from Mycenae with the high king. Walkeearh bowed his head again.

"True, lord; this *wind-mill* does the work of five hundred women grinding grain. The women do other chores—work in the fields, or make cloth."

Agamemnon grunted and scratched his beard. *That sounds . . . sensible,* he thought dubiously. Just as the women in the palace at Mycenae could make more cloth and better, with the new looms and spinners that Walkeearh's wife the wisewoman (his mind carefully avoided the word "sorceress") had shown them. Many of the slaves the outlander was using in his *mills* and mines had been bought with that cloth—still more with the silver from new deep shafts in Attica that he'd shown the High King's men how to make.

And didn't Wannax Lakedwos of Athens bawl like a newborn calf when I took those for my own, the Achaean ruler thought with an inward chuckle.

Much of the metal was being stamped into little disks with Agamemnon's face and titles on them; convenient, since you didn't have to weigh the silver, and it spread his fame widely. A year ago he wouldn't have dared to seize the mines, but with cannon and mortars vassal kings suddenly felt far less secure. He chuckled, imagining Nestor in Pylos or Lakedwos in Athens sitting at meat and looking up now and then, expecting a bursting shell to crash through their roof-trees.

Still, there was something about all this that made him uneasy, something of the feeling of a chariot whose team had run wild, or even of an earthquake. He quickly made a sign of the horns with his left hand and spat to avert the omen.

"Show me the ships you are building," he said, as they came back into the sunlight and slapped flour dust off their tunics.

"This way, my king."

There was one floating at a pier with men swarming over it, and another half built in a timber cradle at the shore. Agamemnon bit his lip in puzzlement at that one. The way the carpenters worked on it was very strange; instead of mortising the planks together with tongue-and-groove joints and then putting in ribs to strengthen the shell, they were putting up thick ribs and crossbeams and then nailing a shell of planks to them. Several forges stood around it, red-glowing iron hissing as it was quenched in vats of oil or water.

"Doesn't that take much metal?" he asked, pointing to the crews nailing the long oak planks to the frame.

"My lord sees as clearly as Horus, the Falcon of Egypt," Walkeearh said. "But now we *have* much metal. And building a ship in this way is so much quicker than the old manner. Less skill is needed, and it's stronger as well."

Agamemnon almost rubbed his hands. All tin and most copper for the making of bronze had to be imported, and it was so expensive, especially the tin. Iron came from within his kingdom, and it grew cheaper by the day. Cheap for *him*, at least. The mines and smelters were a royal monopoly, by Walkeearh's suggestion and his decree—under Walkeearh's exclusive management, and Walkeearh could not be a menace, an outlander who owed everything to the King of Men's favor.

That gave him a hand on every vassal's throat. Gunpowder and cannon gave him a spearpoint held to their eyes.

"Show me the finished one," he said.

"This way. It's called a *gullet,* Lord King."

Footsteps boomed out along the wharf. He looked keenly at the ship; unlike any he'd ever seen before, it was fully decked, a smooth sweep of planking from pointed prow to rounded stern. Two masts stood tall, whole pine trees smoothed down and glossy as a table, with furled sails. On either side six small cannon waited, on stubby oak carriages with four little wheels. Crewmen scattered from the king's path as he came up the gangplank—and from the ready spearpoints of his guards, glittering steel-bright in the noonday sun.

"How is it steered?" he asked, going to the stern and looking over. There was a single steering oar, pivoting like a door on its post, but no apparent way to turn it.

"This wheel," Walkeearh said. "It turns ropes that draw pulleys under the deck, moving the tiller—the bar attached to the *rudder,* the rear steering oar—either way. Here in front of it is the *compass,* the north-pointing needle."

Agamemnon shuddered a little to see a sacred oracle displayed so casually. *Perhaps one should be put in the shrine of Zeus the Father and of far-shooting Apollo,* he thought. *Yes, with sacrifices and celebratory games.*

"Shall I show you how she sails?" Walkeearh inquired.

"At once," he said. Then: "Hold, a minute—who are those? Are they doing a sacred dance?"

Men in tunics were walking about in lines and blocks not far away, holding sticks. Overseers shouted orders, and the lines turned, advanced, marched away again.

"Oh, those?" Walkeearh smiled charmingly. "Just an idle thought of mine, Lord King. Men to handle a new type of cannon. Very *small* cannon, such as might be useful in rough country. Men of little account—younger sons, mercenaries, farmers."

"Oh," Agamemnon said dismissively. "*Poh.* Well, perhaps you can get some useful work out of them. Let us sail; I hear that your ship can sail against the wind."

He laughed again, and Walkeearh with him. "Not against, Lord King, unless it is rowed. But closer to it than the old ships, yes."

"Superior violence and intensity," Major Kenneth Hollard read on the last recruit evaluation form. That translated as "beats the hell out of opponents in training." The DI's notes went on: *"Problems with discipline largely overcome."* That usually meant "no longer has to be dragged away with ropes."

"We've got visitors," a voice said, breaking his concentration.

He looked up; it was his second-in-command (and younger sister), Captain Kathryn Hollard. Sweat stained her khaki fatigues and darkened her sandy-blond hair; on her the long family face looked reasonably good even under a short-on-sides Corps haircut. She'd had Second Recruit Battalion out on a field problem, open order in forest country—they'd gotten field drill down well, but you had to be flexible; massed formations were great for fighting spear-chuckers, but that approach would be too dangerous with Walker's men. Arnstein's spies said the renegade was doing far better than expected with firearms, and so were the Tartessians.

The sounds of a working day at Camp Grant filtered in through the outer room where his orderly had her desk—the rippling thump of marching boots with someone calling cadence, hooves clopping, a distant *shoonk . . . wonk . . . shoonk . . . wonk* from a mortar team practicing on the firing range, the crackle of rifle shots, the rhythmic sound of a smith's hammer.

His eyes flicked across the rough plank of the office to the board that had his schedule for the day chalked on it. As usual, it contained enough work for about twenty hours, which was fine if you left out little luxuries like sleep. *Hell, farming would have been easier work,* he thought. He could have gotten a six-hundred-forty-acre grant on Long Island and a loan from the Town for start-up; all the veterans of the Alban War had been offered that, and his older brother *had* taken one. He'd decided to stay in the Corps instead; memories of his father, perhaps, and things with Cynthia hadn't worked out the way he expected.

Dad would have laughed himself silly, seeing me a major, he thought. Gunnery Sergeant Hollard had refused promotion to commissioned rank four times. *Always said he preferred to work for a living,* Ken remembered with a wry smile. *Not to mention the way he'd get a rise out of a Marine Corps that was part of the Coast Guard.*

Commodore Alston had firmly squelched suggestions that her command be renamed the Republic of Nantucket Navy. Ken Hollard understood that, too. His father had had a dog, and if you asked Semper Fido "Would you rather be in the Army, or dead?" he'd roll on his back, put his paws in the air, and do a fairly good dead-dog imitation.

"Who the hell is it this time, Kat?" he asked. Visiting firemen had been far too common over the last month or so. "Maybe I can unload it on Paddy . . ."

"I don't think so," she said. "It's the commodore."

Oh, Christ, the boss, Hollard thought, shooting reflexively to his feet and looking around like a private caught in his skivvies by a snap inspection.

"Thanks for the warning," he said, suppressing an impulse to smooth down his hair and beard and tug at his khaki uniform jacket. Instead he contented himself with a quick look in the mirror. He saw someone a few years closer to thirty than twenty, with sand-colored hair and beard and the tanned, roughened skin of a person who spent much time outdoors in all weathers.

The face beneath was long and lantern-jawed, with a jutting nose and high cheekbones. It was a common enough face among old-stock Nantucketers—those lines had intermarried until there was a general family likeness. *At least Kat and I didn't get the receding chin.* Six feet and an inch tall; he'd been a skinny teenager, but the passing years had put solid muscle on his shoulders and arms. The Sam Browne belt held a double-barreled flintlock pistol and a *katana*-style officer's sword; his helmet lay on the table he used as a desk, out in his office-cum-ready-room. He took a deep breath and scooped up the flared metal shape as he went through, tucking it under his left arm and waving to the orderly to keep working.

If she wanted everything prettied up, she'd have just given us some warning, he thought. Commodore Alston made him nervous—she had that effect on just about everybody—but she had a reassuring tendency to concentrate on function rather than form. *There are a lot worse people to work for.*

She was waiting not far from the HQ block with her hands clasped behind her back the way he remembered her on the quarterdeck of the *Eagle,* with her aide Lieutenant Commander Swindapa by her side— Guard seafaring rank, easy enough to remember, given their blue uniforms. *And domestic partner as well as aide, remember that.* Wouldn't want to commit a social gaffe.

"Welcome to Camp Grant," he said, saluting. "Commodore, Lieutenant Commander."

Commodore Alston-Kurlelo returned the gesture, with the same precision he remembered from the gymnasium of the high school over on the Island, that day he'd volunteered for the first expedition to Alba.

"Needed to talk over a few things, Major," she said. "Readiness, and potential assignments."

He nodded stiffly, feeling a rush of excitement like a hand squeezing at his diaphragm. *Assignments. Hot damn! Real work?* He didn't like combat, not being a lunatic or an Alban charioteer, but peacetime soldiering could get monumentally dull.

"Ma'am!" he said. "Would you care to inspect the troops, ma'am?"

"I'll observe briefly, Captain. I don't want to interrupt training schedules, and we have some matters to discuss."

"Ma'am."

The blocks of troops on the parade ground flowed together into a column. Another series of commands, and the formation split and moved forward, opening out like a fan until there was a two-deep line stretching across the parade ground. Another, and they halted in place, the first rank going to one knee and the second rank standing. Another, and each left hand flashed down to that hip, drawing a long sword-bayonet. A rattling click and the knife-edged blades shone in precise alignment, pointing toward an earth-and-log berm along the far side of the parade ground.

Each right hand went to the knob on the back of the rifle's stock, and a lever came up like a monkey's tail to expose the breech. Another movement of the right hand, to the cartridge box at their belts. The nitrated-paper cartridges dropped into the open breeches of the rifles, to be pushed home with a thumb.

Slap. The levers went down again. *Click,* and the hammers were pulled back to half cock. Hands dropped to the belts again, this time to bring up the spring-loaded priming flasks. Those rattled against the frizzens, knocking them forward to expose the pan and drop in a measured amount of fine-grain powder. *Snick,* and the frizzens snapped closed, the sparking surface in position to meet the flint in the hammer's jaws.

"Ready . . ."

Three hundred and sixty thumbs pulled back the hammers to full cock, a ratcheting metallic sound.

"Aim . . ."

The rifles came up; there was a slight ripple as each muzzle pointed at one of the man-shaped timber outlines staked to the berm. That had been one of Alston's ideas; better to make the targets as close as possible to what the troops would actually be shooting at.

"In volley . . . front rank . . . *fire*."

BAAAMMMM.

A small fogbank of dirty beige smoke drifted sideways, smelling of fireworks and rotten eggs . . . *smelling of death,* he thought. The thought of what these breech-loading rifles would do was satisfying in a technical sense, but the pictures in his mind's eye were best put aside.

Both ranks came to their feet, grounded the butts of their rifles with a rattle, and stood braced. Alston walked down the files, her face an unreadable mask, her eyes appraising; he followed at her right hand, the courtesy position.

The uniforms were gray-khaki-brown linsey-woolsey four-pocket tunic and trousers with deerskin patches on elbows and knees, flared samurai-style helmet, rifle, utility knife and twenty-inch bayonet, webbing harness and pack. The faces were less uniform. Few of the rankers were Island-born; many more of the noncoms and nearly all the officers, of course. A scattering of Indians, they made wonderful scouts, but most were from Alba, about evenly divided between Fiernan Bohulugi and Sun People.

"Interesting," Alston said to him sotto voce. "I can't always tell which are which."

He nodded, pleased. You weren't supposed to have a past, in the Corps.

She stopped in front of one. "What's your name, Recruit?"

"Ma'am, this recruit is Winnifred Smith, ma'am!" The voice carried a harsh, choppy accent that had never been bred on the Island.

Must be an Immigration Office name, he thought. Replacing something a Sun People tribeswoman on the run from her kinfolk didn't want remembered. Probably on the run from something that got a woman pinned facedown in a bog with her head shaved and her throat cut.

"What's your tribe and clan?" Marian Alston asked.

"Ma'am, this recruit's tribe is the Republic of Nantucket and her clan is the Corps!"

Alston gave a small crisp nod and walked on; Hollard hid his gratified smile. The Republic of Nantucket had found them one way or another, from its bases in Alba or the docksides on this side of the Atlantic; adventurous youths, runaway slaves, absconding wives, taboo-breakers, the ambitious attracted to the promise of Islander citizenship and a land grant for six years' service. Many were simply uprooted from home and folk and custom. The Alban War and the flood of Islander trade and tools and ideas after it had left growing upheaval in their wake.

They smelled of dust, sweat, leather, gun oil, burnt powder, and healthy well-washed young bodies. Kenneth Hollard kept his face impassive, but he felt a glow of pride; this was *his* work, built from small beginnings—the Marines had started out as landing parties for Guard ships.

Following along behind the Commodore, he could see eyes flicking toward Alston reflexively as she passed. To the Fiernan Bohulugi she was the warrior who'd come from beyond the world to take the Spear Mark, rescue and court a priestess of the Kurlelo line, lead Moon Woman's people to victory and crush their ancient enemies. There was a star named for her now, folded into the endless chants that they sang at the Great Wisdom, what would have been called Stonehenge. To the Sun People she was more of an ogre, word spread by the few who'd gotten back alive to their homes from the Battle of the Downs. Her race heightened things in both cases; the Sun People had a tradition of dark-skinned demons they called Night Ones, and almost none of these Bronze Agers had seen a non-Caucasian before.

Not that there are many in Nantucket, either, he thought. Memories of the enormous variety of peoples on the mainland pre-Event seemed distant and dreamlike now.

"Very good, Major. Dismiss to duties, if you please."

The battalion scattered, trotting to their barracks and then to classrooms and workshops around the parade square. They were first and foremost fighters, but doctrine held that every rifleman should learn a craft or trade as well, so that the Regiment could be as nearly self-sufficient as possible abroad. And the teaching included the three R's and the rights and duties of a citizen.

He took a deep breath. "The next thing you should see concerns more recent recruits, ma'am. Punishment drill."

"What's the offense and sentence?" Alston asked.

"Article seven: sexual harassment; punishment gauntlet, defendant's choice."

With the alternative choice being dishonorable discharge and five years' penal servitude on Inagua in the Bahamas, digging salt from the lagoons. Not many chose that; he'd rather have a few weeks of pain himself.

"Ah," she nodded. "What were the circumstances?"

"Section seven, basically," he said.

Hollard had read the old Uniform Code of Military Justice, as well as the stripped-down version Commodore Alston-Kurlelo had drafted for the Republic of Nantucket's armed forces. The UCMJ looked incredibly complex and far too focused on procedure at the expense of results. The new code was quite simple on sexual matters, as on much else—no fornication on duty; none up and down the chain of command in the same unit, except between married couples and registered domestic partners; no unauthorized pregnancies; and a catchall clause allowing administrative penalties for *actions or speech prejudicial to discipline and good order.* Apart from that, what consenting adults did on their own time was their own business.

"This was the usual thing," Hollard went on. "Sun People man and Earth Folk woman. She decided she didn't like him anymore, and he couldn't get it through his head she could tell him to get lost. Thought it was just a fight, until it came out at the Mast."

He thought he heard Alston's aide mutter *"Scumbags"* under her breath, but it wasn't loud enough to hear. His inner smile was wry; having Fiernan and clansmen from the charioteer tribes in the same unit was murder sometimes; they just didn't *like* each other and their customs were about as distinct as you could get . . . and neither always meshed with Americans, either, to put it mildly. A complete set of national stock-figures had grown up already, with the same underlying element of truth that most stereotypes had—to the Americans, the Fiernan seemed like good-natured, happy-go-lucky slobs, and to the Fiernan the American Eagle People were detail-obsessed control freaks with a serious pickle up their butts. And both thought the Sun People were homicidal maniacs with hair-trigger tempers—and lazy, to boot.

It would have been easier to have an all-Islander unit, like back during the Alban War; he wouldn't have had to waste so much time running elementary literacy classes. The problem there was that there just weren't enough Islanders; everyone was in the militia, of course, but that was for home defense and major wars declared by the Meeting. For that matter, things would have been a little simpler if the Marine expeditionary regiment was all-male, but that ran up against the same objection—not enough recruits—and of course there was the long term to think about. Alston certainly wouldn't have stood for that sort of precedent, or Martha Cofflin, or his sister, Kat, for that matter.

"That is a problem," Alston said, in her soft, drawling voice. "Those tribes, they've got a confirmed case of the virgin/whore complex."

"This gets it out of them," Hollard said grimly, as they came to an area behind C Barracks. "Or at least convinces them to keep it to themselves. Second offense and it's off to Inagua, or the hangman, depending on circumstances."

A young man stood shivering and naked before a table. His eyes flicked to the newcomers and grew wide as they saw Commodore Alston.

"Carry on, Lieutenant," Hollard said.

The Islander at the table was young, around twenty. His voice was stern but not unkindly as it went on, "You understand the nature of the offense and sentence of the court-marital, Private Llandaurth Witharaxsson?"

"Yes, sir," the recruit said.

The junior officer paused for a translation; Llandaurth nodded again and spoke in his own language. A corporal said, "He understands, sir. He says he took the Eagle People's salt and agreed to obey their laws. The woman wasn't his, and he did wrong. He's ready to face his punishment."

"You chose the gauntlet?"

The man straightened, his pale skin flushing against the tow color of his hair and an archipelago of freckles. "Llandaurth Witharaxson is no coward, to run from hurt," he said in slow, careful English.

The lieutenant nodded. "Good. And remember, Private Llandaurth, that your offense is not only against the law but against your comrade-to-arms . . . your oath-sworn shield-br . . . sister. In battle, you must each ward the other's life. What you did is as if you turned away in battle and left a comrade to the enemy." A pause. "Translate that, please."

The fixed look of endurance flickered into puzzlement for a second, then a slow nod.

"Sergeant, execute the sentence."

A drum began to beat, and the drummer fell in beside the prisoner. Llandaurth turned and began to walk in step with it, a pause between every step, toward an alleyway made of thirty-seven standing figures. All of them were women, all the women in his company; they had their rifle slings in their hands, buckle-end outermost. The first was a private with a black eye and a puffy swelling along the side of her face. She gripped the leather strap with both hands, whirled it around her head and struck. Brass and cowhide snapped into flesh; a bloody welt and gouged wound appeared across the man's back and buttocks. Another strike smacked into his shoulders. He grunted in involuntary reflex, cupped one hand over his genitals and the other to protect his eyes, and kept walking to the slow beat of the drum as the musician paced down beside him outside the gauntlet.

Hollard pursed his lips. *Some of them are hitting almighty damned hard and fast,* he thought. *On the other hand, this is* supposed *to hurt bad.* If the offense had been a little more serious—real injury to the victim, for instance, or an actual rape—the punishment would have been a noose.

Halfway down, the condemned man's grunts changed to hoarse cries, torn out past clenched teeth. Llandaurth went to one knee for a second, and the drummer marched in place. That meant extra blows as he staggered back to his feet. Three-quarters of the way, and his body and scalp were a mass of blood and welts, sheening crimson in the sunlight. The rifle slings were spraying drops of red now, and the man fell forward, crawling the last dozen paces like a crippled dog. The drum gave a final flourish and fell silent. Two troopers with a stretcher came forward, and a medic hurried to his side.

"Carry on, Lieutenant," Hollard said again, as they walked on past the dispersing crowd. One of the women who'd administered the punishment looked pale, and two others were helping her sit and put her head between her knees.

"Unpleasant but necessary," Alston murmured.

Swindapa nodded vigorously. "The Sun People don't know how to behave with a woman unless you kick them," she said. Grudgingly, she went on, "Some can learn from that."

"I've met Americans who could use the same treatment," Alston said, her full lips pressed together.

"We've *given* a few Americans the same treatment," Hollard said. "Now, this is our armory; every recruit is trained to use the repair tools."

When the inspection was finished, he led them into his own office, and an orderly brought glasses of fizzy sarsaparilla on a tray. The room was plain boards for the most part, with a window opening onto a porch and the main parade ground. Soon it would be sundown, time for everyone to fall in as the flag was lowered and then be trooped off to dinner.

"Very satisfactory, all in all," Alston said after a long moment's silence. "What's your appraisal of the training program as a whole, Major?"

Oh, Christ, now isn't that *a question.*

"Ma'am, it's going smoothly now. Geometric progression, of course—train one, he or she trains two, two become four, four become sixteen, and so forth. Right now we can turn out as many per year as the original plan called for and expand that on short notice."

"Good," Alston nodded. "And you're satisfied with your training cadre?"

"Fully satisfied now, ma'am. In fact . . . well, a lot of them have much more experience than I do—pre-Event experience, that is. I'm surprised I got this appointment."

"We're not cursed with a seniority system here, Captain, and you did very well in Alba." She paused, looking at him; he met eyes so black that you couldn't see the pupil. It was more than a little disconcerting.

"In a way," she went on, "pre-Event experience is worse than irrelevant here. Commandin' this sort of unit isn't much like drivin' tanks into Kuwait City." At Swindapa's raised brows she went on, "That was a war we had, a little before we came to this time." To Hollard: "In any case, I couldn't spare any of my Guard officers; they're needed for the ships. I thought you'd do well here, and you have. In fact, you've pretty well worked your way out of a job."

"And into another?" Hollard asked eagerly.

"Anxious for a fight?" Alston asked, her voice unaltered.

I must be nuts. Kathryn certainly thinks so. He remembered the battles of the Alban War well enough. The way his balls had tried to crawl back up into his gut as the enemy host came out of their dust-cloud. The light sparkling on their blades, the sound of their chant as they advanced and the rhythmic boom of weapons hammered on shields. The way a man screamed with an arrow through him. The wounded later, lying across the field like a lumpy carpet that twitched and writhed, calling for water, or their mothers. Kathryn limp on the medic's table, her leg a mass of blood around the wooden shaft. And the stink . . .

He also remembered what Alston had asked him in the high school gymnasium, back right after the Event, when he and his younger sister had volunteered for the battalion.

"There's a job needs doing, ma'am."

She gave a small cool nod of approval, and he felt oddly heartened . . . *and now I have to provide that to* my *people. Christ.*

" 'dapa," she said, "let's see it."

Her aide opened a satchel at her side and spread a map on the desk. All three of them leaned forward. "This is our latest appraisal," she said. Only the slightest trace of the singsong lilt of Fiernan was left in her voice. "Including what we've gotten from our Babylonian, Shamash-nasir-kudduru."

She managed to roll the guttural Akkadian syllables off her tongue readily enough—Hollard was supposed to learn it himself, in his plentiful spare time. He'd made a fair start, but—

Well, she did *have an advantage on me,* he thought. He'd learned a good deal about Fiernans himself in the course of the past couple of years. The priestesses of Moon Woman had to memorize enough information to rupture a mainframe, starting when they were toddlers. Doing astronomy and fairly complex mathematics without written symbols absolutely required a science of memory.

Hollard examined the map carefully; it showed the Mediterranean basin and the lands beyond as far as the Persian Gulf. The outlines of coast and mountain were much the same as the maps he'd seen in high school—but the names of the countries were utterly different.

Swindapa's finger touched southern Iberia, just west of Gibraltar. "Tartessos holds the Straits, the Tartessos is no friend of ours—King Isketerol has an alliance with Walker."

"He also has fairly up-to-date sailing craft with cannon," Alston said. "Not as good as our ships, or our cannon, but there are a lot of them. We can't get steamers that far in any numbers, either." Her finger made a circle on the map. "He controls the whole of southern Iberia and northern Morrocco now. But the real problem is further east."

Her finger slid over the blue Mediterranean, past Italy.

"From what we've been able to gather—some of the Tartessians visiting here talk, and the Arnsteins have agents in place at our embassy in Tartessos—Walker arrived in Greece about six months after the end of the Alban War. Since then, he's been hard at work, taken over here and here and here. We *have* to stop him. If he gets control of much of this area"—her pink-palmed hand spread long, slender fingers to cover Greece, the Aegean Sea, and much of western Anatolia—"we're in deep trouble. Half the population of the world in this era lives between Greece and western Persia, countin' Egypt—and he's got an embassy in Egypt, too."

"So we can't leave him be, and we can't get at him," Hollard said.

"Not directly," Swindapa cut in. "But there's a back entrance to that compound."

She set out another map, ranging it below the first. It was a world map; again, the physical characteristics were much the same, but whole continents were blank, or had only a coastal entry or two where an Islander ship had visited.

"Not through here," she said, tapping the Red Sea. "Egypt is too close to Walker these days, and it's bad sailing, anyway. Here." The finger veered eastward, up the Persian Gulf to the point where the Euphrates and Tigris Rivers joined and flowed into the sea.

Hollard whistled soundlessly. "Iraq . . ." he said.

His own finger moved on the first map, up the rivers and over the mountains to Anatolia; a vague area marked "Hittite Empire," centered on the city of Hattusas, not far east of where Ankara would have stood, in a future that included a nation called Turkey. As far as anyone knew, the remote ancestors of the Turks were living somewhere in southeastern Siberia at this moment.

"Even with firearms and cannon, that would be a long way to march and fight," he said neutrally.

"Granted," she said dryly. "However, what we've got in mind is a diplomatic mission with heavy military escort. Land here"—she tapped the head of the Gulf again—"make arrangements with the authorities, move north to the Hittite area, and organize resistance to Walker. Hopefully, keep him busy, keep him off-balance, and limit the amount of territory he controls, until the Republic's in a position to open the Mediterranean and deal with him directly."

Hollard kept his face expressionless. *Well, the Council isn't thinking small,* he decided after a long moment's silence.

"Ma'am, that's not within my area of expertise," he said carefully.

Alston nodded. Swindapa suddenly broke into an urchin grin; he felt his own lips tug upward involuntarily.

"Glad you see that," the commodore said. "Actually, our diplomatic experts will handle that—the Arnsteins. You'll be along to provide an escort, to exert force to accomplish the political objectives that the Arnsteins—and the Council, we'll be in radio touch, of course—set, and to help organize local forces."

"Oh." A wave of relief made his knees feel weak. "Thank you, ma'am. I think . . . well, I can at least give *that* a good try."

"Excellent." At the black woman's nod, Swindapa set a heavy stack of files in front of him, all marked "Confidential." "Start studying these and set up Camp Grant to operate under your successor—make your recommendation as to that. We want to get goin' as soon as possible, in order that you don't get there too much behind the news of your coming."

CHAPTER FIVE

(June, Year 4 A.E.)
October, Year 8 A.E.

"**S**teady."

The mass of Siceliot warriors was three hundred yards away, coming at a dead run. Sunlight blinked off their metal, although for most of them that was only a spearhead or a knife. The sound of their feet and screaming war cries drummed in his ears. Four chariots came ahead of the pack, with chieftains dressed in armor much like the Mycenaeans.

"Speaking of which," Walker murmured to himself. Most of the Achaean host was still down by the ships; he glanced back over his shoulder and made a small *tsk* sound.

Getting their precious gee-gees and dogcarts out, he thought.

Odikweos was beside him, leaning on an old-fashioned figure-eight cowhide shield nearly as tall as he was, with his Ithakans behind him. The tall horsehair plume of his helmet bobbed over his head; the protection was rows of bone sawn from boar's tusks, sewn onto a thick boiled-leather backing. He was wearing a chain-mail shirt under that, though, not the cumbersome affair of bronze plates that was the native equivalent. The Greek hawked dust from his throat, squinted, and spat.

"I hope your savior God inspires you," he said calmly. His arms-men were shifting in place, wiping their palms on their tunics for a better grip on their spearshafts. "There are about four thousand of them . . . and only six hundred here ready to fight."

"Let me show you," Walker said. *Bright boy, this one. Steady nerves, too.*

He turned to his own men, four hundred of them, spaced in blocks two ranks deep between the six field guns.

"Ready," he said, his voice clear but carrying.

The front rank knelt. The second leveled their muskets and thumbed back the hammers, a ripple of motion like the spines of a hedgehog bristling.

"Aim. Gunners, ready. Fire on the word of command."

The gunners skipped aside, holding the lanyards of their weapons. He judged the distance to the charging locals. Two hundred yards, over ground as near flat as no matter—the heights of Epipolai, that later would be the core of Syracuse, were ragged behind them. He drew his sword and raised it.

"Fire."

The steel flashed downward. The noise that followed was stunning, a blow felt through the gut and chest as much as through the ears. The cannon leaped backward, their trails plowing furrows in the dusty earth. The crash of four hundred rifle-muskets was almost as loud. A huge cloud of dirty-white smoke billowed out, smelling of burnt sulfur. It drifted away rapidly, and there was a murmur and shifting among his men as they saw the results. His own eyebrows went up a little. The guns had cut wedges through the native war-host, as neat as if God had stamped them out with cookie cutters. Within the cleared spaces lay body parts and ground that looked as if it had been *splashed* with red goo. Further away, shapes twitched and moaned. A horse screamed high and shrill, dragging itself along by its forelimbs, then collapsed.

The half-inch minié balls of the muskets had done a fair bit of damage as well, leaving bodies scattered back a hundred yards or more.

Walker smiled like a wolf as he lowered his binoculars. "Steady, there," he called out. "Keep it going."

The gun teams were jumping in with swabber and rammer. Hot bronze hissed as the wet sponges were run down, twirled, and pulled free. Loaders came forward with cartridges of case shot, and the rammers pushed them down. Gunners stepped close and ran long steel pins down the touchholes to pierce the thin linen that held the gunpowder, then filled the pans with priming powder from their horns. Six men ran each gun back to its original position, and the cycle was ready to begin again. The musketeers were going through their own drill—bite open a cartridge, prime the pan of their flintlocks, put the butt between their feet, pour the rest of the powder down the barrel, follow it with the hollow-based minié bullet, ram the paper on top as wad, a thump-thump-thump sound. One man fired as soon as his weapon was ready, and an underofficer stepped up behind him and knocked him down with a blow of a baton to the back of his neck.

The rest came to the "ready" with no more than a tense grin or wiping of hands on tunics. The enemy were dribbling to a halt, stunned and bewildered. *They'll need a minute or so to get the idea,* he told himself. And it probably wouldn't be this easy again.

"Ready," he said. "Take aim. *Fire.*"

Point-blank range, less than a hundred yards. Thousands of lead projectiles slammed into the Sicilians, all of them traveling at more than a thousand feet per second. Dust spurted up, and smoke drifted away. When it did, the enemy were running for the hills, or hobbling or crawling; hundreds of them lay in the dirt, and the noise of their terror was like a huge sounder of pigs squealing.

Walker laughed. "Reload, fix bayonets, prepare to advance. one round of canister in the guns and limber up to follow."

About a mile thataway was the headquarters of the paramount chief of this district, the closest thing Bronze Age Sicily had to a king—he traded with the Greeks regularly, or had, before Walker talked Agamemnon into this expedition. Why make withdrawals when you could steal the bank? Besides, if his enterprises were to expand the way they should he would need a source of raw materials, labor, and food outside the Achaean system—there was a limit to what he could commandeer before the nobles revolted.

Goddam low-surplus economy, he thought. *I need to build up on the QT, until I'm too strong even if they do realize I'm undermining the system.* Luckily, the Bronze Age Greeks were—no, not stupider than their classical descendants, just not given to rational, systematic thought.

"We'll be first with the plunder," Odikweos said.

Walker nodded. *I like these guys,* he thought, not for the first time. *Straightforward.*

"And maybe a few girls worth fucking," he said; that was often fun in an athletic sort of way if they fought. "But the island itself is the real plunder."

Odikweos nodded. "If we can hold it," he said.

Yeah, this one is way above average brains-wise. Got to get him on my side.

The Achaean licked the sweat off his lips, looking sideways at the grinning, laughing riflemen and gunners. A drumbeat and the whole mass moved forward in step, bayonet points in a bristling line. "With these, we may be able to."

"If the right man is in charge," Walker said. *And I certainly don't have the time for it.*

Swindapa daughter of Dhinwarn, of the Star Blood line of Kurlelo, spun on the ball of her foot and paused, then sank slowly back down with both hands raised to the crescent moon in the last gesture of the dance. Her long hair floated down around her shoulders as she did, sliding over bare skin like a kiss.

"*ahTOwak hdimm'uHOtna nawakawa!*" she cried.

The others in the circle echoed her: *Silver starlight make a path for the children of Moon Woman.*

That was the end of the most sacred part of the ceremony. The circle stood silent for a moment, then gave a soft sigh together and became individuals once more. She stood watching the glimmering trail that stretched out over Nantucket Harbor as a singing peace replaced exultation.

Coming to herself, she looked up at the sleek curve of the hull that stood on the slipway above them, smelling of cut wood and fresh paint. The English word for such a ship was "clipper." It was not a bad name—there was something of urgent speed in the sound of it—but not a great one, either; it lacked the swan-grace, the eager dancer's leap, needed. The mind-mother of this ship had been called *Cutty Sark*, and that had a better ring . . .

Marian came forward from the shadows of the slipway. She wasn't a Star-Moon Dancer, of course—you had to be born as well as trained for that—but she'd been initiated into the Spear Mark, and that made her one of Moon Woman's children, so she could be part of the end of the ceremony.

"We must sing her a soul down from the stars," Swindapa said.

Marian closed her eyes for a second—she always felt awkward about speaking in public, even more about singing; it was odd, but an endearing shyness. Then she began:

> *See her bow break free of our Mother's sea*
> *In a sunlit burst of spray.*
> *That stings the cheek while the rigging will speak,*
> *Of sea-miles gone away!*
> *She will range far south, from the harbor's mouth*
> *And rejoice in every wave . . .*

"What is it, Doc?" Cofflin asked, looking up from his desk.

Dr. Henry Coleman looked grave; but then, the head of the Island's medical efforts usually did, even on a fine fall day like this. The round-faced man beside him was grave too, although he looked like the type who usually wore a smile.

"Justin Clemens, isn't it?" Cofflin said. *Twenty-five*, the filing system in his mind said. *In the medical apprentice program since the Event. Passed for doctor two years ago. Odd, I haven't seen him around much.*

"Yes, Chief."

"Been over on the mainland—medical extension officer," Coleman said.

Clemens made a slight face; Cofflin sympathized. There had been bad problems with uptime diseases in Alba, but nothing compared to what happened among the Archaic-phase Indians. Even *Alban* diseases were a major problem to the Amerindians. The Islanders had been trying to help, but it was debatable whether it did anything more than soothe the Town Meeting's conscience.

"We've got a problem," Coleman said. "Nothing on the mainland. A problem for *us*."

"Problems, worry, and grief are my specialty here," Cofflin said, rising and pouring three cups of cocoa from the pot over the spirit-lamp by the window, then handing them around.

"Now, what's the problem?"

He sat back, stirring his cup. The kids were all in school, Martha had spent the morning teaching and was back getting some Council resolutions drawn up as legislation for the Meeting to vote on, and he'd finally gotten down to the only *mildly* urgent stuff. The dock-workers union meetings specifically—he was giving them some sub-rosa encouragement, and the shipowners and merchants were complaining.

"Well, let them," he muttered.

"We have cowpox," Coleman said.

Jared sat up straighter, putting aside his cup. "What's cowpox?" he said, cudgeling his memory. *Doesn't sound good, whatever it is.*

"Justin here spotted it, had some Alban immigrants working on a dairy farm in for their chicken-pox shots." They'd worked out a live-virus inoculation that was usually effective.

Clemens kneaded his fingers together. "Ah . . . it's a viral disease in cows, sometimes jumping to humans in close contact. Fever, rash of red spots sometimes leaving very faint pockmarks."

"Sound like anything familiar?" Coleman added grimly.

Cofflin frowned. "Sounds like . . . Christ, no!"

Coleman nodded. "Smallpox is a very close relative. Best guess, back in the twentieth, was that it was a mutation of cowpox, probably started among pastoralists somewhere. Nobody knows where, exactly. When it hit the Mediterranean basin—thousands of years before the twentieth-well, call it the Red Death. Every bit as bad as bubonic plague."

Cofflin ran a hand over his forehead. Chicken pox had been ghastly among the local Indians, and it had killed more than a few Albans here on Nantucket before they'd gotten it under control. The fact that it took weeks to cross the Atlantic was a help too, since the voyage time exceeded the latency period and not many on the Island had turned out to have shingles, the chronic form. Those who did weren't allowed off, either. The thought of a *smallpox* epidemic . . .

"What can we do?" he asked.

"Luckily, there's no evidence at all that smallpox exists here,"

Coleman said. "What we've got is the *possibility* of it lurking in some backwater. That's the good news."

"The bad news is that we're poking into a lot of backwaters," Cofflin said. "Ayup. can't stop, either."

Clemens leaned forward eagerly, balancing his cup and saucer on his knee and gesturing with his free hand.

"We can do something," the young man said. "Vaccination originally meant simply infecting everyone with cowpox as children, and repeating the process periodically. I recommend we put it to the Meeting and have a universal program—everyone on the Island, everyone who *touches* on the Island, and everyone we can get to do it over on Alba, too."

Cofflin glanced over to Coleman for confirmation, then nodded decisively, and pulled a pad of paper toward himself. "Right. Let's get going on this . . . just a second."

He ducked into the next room, where Martha was dictating a letter to her secretary. "Sorry to interrupt, Martha, but could you handle Gerrard next? Doc Coleman and I've got a bit of a crisis."

"Certainly, dear, but you should see Hillwater after that."

He nodded. Paul Hillwater wanted this new Conservancy Office set up, to regulate things like whaling and forestry. Good long-term idea, and in the shorter term he needed Hillwater's friends Dane Sweet and the other old-line environmentalists.

I'll put Sweet in charge, he thought. Two good reasons for that; one, he'd do a good job of it, being a conservationist but not crazy, and two, then *Sweet* would be the lightning rod for complaints. Let *him* take the heat from both directions.

Martha smiled at him, the familiar dry, quiet curve of the lips. *Knows exactly what's going through my mind,* he thought. It was a profoundly comforting thing. Doreen and Ian were like that, too. Marian and Swindapa weren't, and he wondered how they stood it.

People are different, he decided. Just because it was banal didn't make it any less true.

"Well, you brought that off fairly well," Coleman said, as the two doctors pulled their bicycles out of the rack in front of the Chief's House.

"Thanks, Henry," Clemens said. "I felt a mite nervous, bearding the Chief in his den."

"Jared doesn't bite," Coleman said dryly.

"Yes, but he's the *Chief.*"

"You youngsters needn't put the reverential tone into the word," Coleman said. "He's our Chief Executive, not a king. Ayup. You've got a good eye, youngster. Doubt I would have spotted those pocks for what they were."

A shy grin. "I'm starting to feel like a real doctor."

Coleman stopped with one foot on the pedal. "Dammit, don't let me hear you say that again! You *are* a real doctor. Real as I am."

"Sir . . . Henry, you know I don't have everything a medical school up in the twentieth taught."

"You know *more* than a lot of those overspecialized machine tenders," Coleman snapped. "You're a damned fine GP and general surgeon, and you know how to improvise. You can do anything I can do, you know what works and why, and you're qualified to teach it. I'd call that being a real doctor, all right. I'm not immortal, Justin; none of us geezers are. If anyone's going to keep the torch lit, it's going to be *you,* and the others your age."

They pushed out into the traffic, pedaling easily. Doctors rated the cherished Pre-Event bicycles, not the heavier solid-tire model that Seahaven's spin-offs made. Gay Street had little afternoon traffic, only a delivery wagon pulled by a sleepy pony. Justin Clemens puffed a little as they wove among the heavier traffic on upper Main, dodging past a steam-hauler, a few of the well-to-do in one-horse buggies, and a stream of more prosaic wagons and cycles like their own.

The Cottage Hospital had picked up the name before it moved into its present gray-shingle quarters on South Prospect Street forty years before the Event. It had grown since the Event; new covered passages snaked out to neighboring buildings, tying them into the older block. Nineteen beds had grown to a hundred or so, not counting the out-stations at the mainland bases and in Alba, and this was now the only teaching hospital in the world, and the only center of medial research. The gardens were still lovely with trellised roses, though.

Those were Coleman's hobby, the sweet-scented, old-fashioned type. A trellised vine was blooming under the white-painted windows as well, shaggy and bee-murmurous. The head of the hospital thought the sights and scents were good for convalescents and worthwhile just on general principles.

Clemens broke into a beaming grin as he saw Andrew and Kate Nelson helping their eight-year-old son into a street-tricycle—room for two passengers in the back—waving to him.

"Feeling a lot better, sprout?" he asked the boy. *Smoothest appendectomy I ever did,* he thought.

"Sure am, Doctor," the boy said.

The smile slid away from Justin's face as the parents completed their thanks and another bicycle drew up. The rider was a woman of his owns age, a trim figure in green shirt and slacks and bobbed yellow hair, with a satchel over her back.

"'lo, Ellen," he said.

"Justin," she replied. Her eyes went to Coleman, and she patted the knapsack. "Brand had the poppy extract," she said. "I'm off to get it into the safe."

Coleman nodded. They *needed* that white ooze; it was the base for morphine. "Production's up?"

"Another quarter acre, and two more next spring, she says."

All three of the doctors shared a silent moment of thanks that opium-poppy seed had been available on the Island after the Event, even if it *had* taken years to breed up enough for full-scale growing.

The elder medical man sighed when Ellen Clemens disappeared through the double doors. "I don't suppose there's any chance of keeping you here," he said.

Justin shook his head. "That . . . wouldn't work," he said bleakly.

Coleman nodded with another sigh. A messy divorce was always bad news; in post-Event Nantucket, with nowhere to go, it could get very bad indeed.

"I suppose I could try Alba," Clemens said. "Not as frustrating as the mainland, and they need extension officers."

"Hmmmm," Coleman said. "I think there may be another alternative, if you've the itch for travel."

"Gorgeous damned thing, isn't it?" Marian said quietly.

"She will dance with the waves like Moon Woman's light on a waterfall," Swindapa agreed.

Ian nodded. *Well, in the abstract, I agree.*

The shipyard had started out as a boat-holding shed, where pleasure craft were stacked three layers high for the winter. The size had made it a natural for *building* ships, when the Islanders got around to it; the overhead cranes alone were an enormous convenience. Now the huge open-ended metal building was filled almost to its limit by the craft that lay in its cradle within.

"Two hundred and twelve feet long, beam thirty-six feet, depth deck-to-keel twenty-one feet," Alston said, caressing the words. "Forty-six feet of raised quarterdeck. White oak, black oak, beechwood, white pine. Nine hundred twenty-seven net tons."

He could barely hear the murmured terms of endearment under the racket. *Well, everyone has their own Grail.* His had always been to *know.* Before he met Doreen or held his son, it had been the strongest thing in his life, and it wasn't the weakest even now, not by many a mile.

Scaffolding covered the sides of the great ship, swarming with workers. Outside, the boathouse was flanked by new timber sheds almost as large. From them came the sound of blacksmiths working, *tink-whang-tink,* the screeching moan of a drill press, the dentist-chair sound of metal-cutting lathes. Over it all was the whining roar of the band saws; Leaton had rigged up enormous equivalents of the little machines used to cut keys, ones that would take a small model and rip an equivalent shape out of balks of seasoned oak. Steam puffed from boilers and from the big pressure-cooker retorts where timber softened so it could be bent into shape.

The fall day was brisk, but the heat of forges and hearths and the steam engines that drove the pneumatic tools kept it comfortable in the shed. The air was full of the smell of hot metal, the vanilla odor of oak, sharp pine, and tar bubbling in vats. Sunlight fogged through floating sawdust.

"Take a look," Swindapa said. "It's like being inside some great beast, a whale."

The Arnsteins scrambled up a long board stair built into the side of the scaffolding, splintery wood rough under their hands. It led into the ship through a section not yet planked, and they stood precariously on a piece of temporary decking.

"It *is* like being inside a whale," Doreen said into Ian's ear. "And it looks a lot bigger than you'd expect."

Ian nodded. This was a cockleshell compared to an aircraft carrier or an oil tanker back up in the twentieth, but close up it felt *big*. His eyes followed the long, graceful cure of the keelson and the sharp bow, and the way the ribs flowed up from them. She was right about it being like the inside of a whale, too—there was an *organic* feel to the ship, as if it were something that had grown naturally.

"What surprises me," he said to Alston, as she stood with legs braced and a roll of plans tapping on her palm, "is that this one is taking so much less time. *Lincoln* took more than a year—eighteen months."

Swindapa said something in her own language, then translated, "We have danced the play of numbers into wood."

Ian blinked. *Well, every once in a while you remember she's not an American,* he thought. Then she went on:

"I think you would say . . . learning curve?"

Alston nodded. "Everyone knows what to do. Besides that, we've got the jigs and such—we're buildin' these like cars with identical parts."

"That does give us an advantage," Ian said a little smugly. "Twentieth-century concept."

"Not really," Alston said, half turning, her eyes sardonic. "The Venetian Republic's navy did it with their war-galleys in Renaissance times."

"That's taken you down a peg, mate," Doreen whispered in his ear. "Clapped a stopper over your capers—brought you by the lee."

"You've been reading those damned historical novels she likes again, haven't you?" Ian said, grinning. *Actually they're not bad.* And they'd helped him understand Alston better.

One of the overhead trolleys that had once shifted sailboats lowered a great oak beam through the open space over their head and into the interior. An ironic cheer went up when it was found to fit exactly into the slot prepared, and a man with an adze stepped ostentatiously back. Figures in overalls and hard hats moved forward and there was a rhythmic slamming as the big deck beam was fastened home, spanning the whole width of the ship where her main deck would be.

"Heavy scantlings so she can bear a gun deck, but she's not really a specialist warship," Alston noted. "Good deep hold under there . . . had to modify the design a little, of course, because the *Sark* was a composite ship. We *could* do that, but maintenance far abroad would be too difficult, and besides, we've got more good timber than metal. Altered the sail plan, too; all those stuns'ls and studding sails took a lot of crew to work them, and we don't have the sort of competition they had, no need to squeeze out every half knot. And clippers have too little reserve buoyancy for my taste, so we—"

"Commodore," Ian interrupted—this *was* a semiformal occasion, in public— "as long as it gets us where we're going, I should care?"

"Councilor, you're a philistine," she said, with a tilt of eyebrow and a quirk of full lips.

"Hebrew, actually."

"Is either of them around yet?"

"Not the Philistines; they were probably mostly Greeks, with odds and sods from everywhere, part of the Sea Peoples—due to invade Egypt and get thrown back in the next couple of generations. Hebrews . . ." He shrugged and flung up his hands. "If Exodus records any real events, the Pharaoh that Moses dealt with could be either Ramses II, who's ruling Egypt now, or somebody a century either way. I doubt that real Judaism—Yahwehistic monotheism—exists right now."

"Yahweh probably still has that embarrassing female consort they discovered in those early inscriptions," Doreen said. "Good for her."

"Another month," Alston said, looking around the ship again. "Finish up, launch her, step her masts and rigging, get her guns aboard— and the *Lincoln*'s, too—then we load up *Lincoln* and *Chamberlain*, plus *Eagle*, of course, and at least one of the schooners, and we're on our way."

"You're going to be commanding personally?" Ian said, relieved.

"As far as the Gulf. I talked Jared into it. I need cadre who're used to these ships, we'll have four at least by the time we run the Straits, and a good long voyage is the way to train them."

Marian looked up at the ship and began to speak softly, under her breath. Ian recognized the words; he wasn't surprised anymore, either—there was more to Marian than she let on. In Alba he'd heard her recite from the same poet on a field where dead men lay in windrows. This time it was happier words as her eyes caressed the hull. He caught the surge and hiss of the sea in it, and the longing for places new and strange that he'd always suspected lurked under Alston's iron pragmatism:

> *A ship, an isle, a sickle moon—*
> *With few but with how splendid stars*
> *The mirrors of the sea are strewn*
> *Between their silver bars!*
> *An isle beside an isle she lay,*
> *The pale ship anchored in the bay,*
> *While in the young moon's port of gold*
> *A star-ship—as the mirrors told—*
> *Put forth its great and lonely light*
> *To the unreflecting Ocean, Night*
> *And still, a ship upon her seas,*
> *The isle and island cypresses*
> *Went sailing on without the gale:*
> *And still there moved the moon so pale,*
> *A crescent ship without a sail!*

CHAPTER SIX

November, Year 8 A.E.
(November, Year 6 A.E.)
(June, Year 7 A.E.)
December, Year 8 A.E.
(June, Year 7 A.E.)

"Lordy, but I hate giving speeches," Alston muttered under her breath as she stepped down from the podium on the steps of the Pacific National Bank at the head of Main Street.

"Tell me about it," Jared said.

"Maybe that's why you always give the same one, Marian," Ian said out of the side of his mouth, grinning as he applauded with the crowd. *"Thank you for your support. We'll get the job done. Good-bye."*

"Oh, I don't know," Doreen said. "back in Alba, she threatened defaulters with having their ice cream ration reduced."

"To hell with the lot of you," Marian said, seating herself and looking suitably grave. She cocked an eye at the sky; it was a bright, chilly morning, but there was a hint of mare's tail cloud in the northwest, and the wind was about seven knots, brisk up from the harbor.

Prelate Gomez rose to conduct the blessing service. Hats went off among the dense crowd that packed Main Street Square and the streets leading off it; expeditionary regiment Marines and townsfolk mingled. Alston kept her hat on her knees and listened respectfully. Gomez bore the red robes with dignity, despite looking to be exactly what he was, the stocky middle-aged son of a Portuguese fisherman from New Bedford. The Sun People among the regiment and ships' crews had had their ritual yesterday, sacrificing a couple of sheep to Sky Father and the Horned Man and the Lady of the Horses . . . *and at least you get to eat the sheep,* she thought.

Swindapa had led the Fiernan Bohulugi service last night, she being the senior of the Star Blood on the island at present. *Which makes her, technically, a Grandmother.* And wasn't *that* an odd thought. Alston had attended that, it being in the family and she being an adoptive

Fiernan of sorts—nobody cared if she actually believed in it, they didn't think that way.

"War is an evil," Gomez was saying. "But in this fallen world, we are often forced to a choice between a lesser evil and a greater. Our citizens and their Meeting have determined that the interests of our Republic demand that Walker be brought down before his power grows too great, and that is a just decision. He has shown himself to be utterly without scruple.

"To protect our people, our children, our nation, from such a threat justifies this war. But there is another and greater reason for it. Walker is one of ours. When he spreads death, suffering, slavery, among the peoples here in our exile home, *we* bear part of the responsibility."

Alston winced inwardly. She'd *suspected* Walker had something up his sleeve, but there hadn't been any proof . . . and he'd struck without warning, taking the *Yare* and heading out. Cunningly, too, using Pamela Lisketter as a decoy to give himself time.

"And since Walker is at least partially our sin, so we must pay the price of his suppression. Let us pray to Almighty God, God the Father, God the Son, God the Holy Ghost, that He does not require a payment more than we can bear. For whatever the price may be, bear it we must."

And on that cheerful note, she thought, bowing her head. Alston hadn't prayed since she was about fourteen, but whatever your opinion of his beliefs, Gomez was a man to respect. They weren't exactly friends—several reasons for that—but they worked together well enough.

The silent moment ended with a trumpet and bugle call. The crowds cleared the street, and the men and women of the Marines and the crews formed up to march down to the docks.

Alston picked up her cap and drew a deep breath. "Let's go," she said.

"Yeah, boss, this is more like it," Bill Cuddy said, holding out his wine cup for a refill.

A slave girl in a filmy kilt of Egyptian linen knelt gracefully and poured from a long-stemmed glass jar.

William Walker leaned back in the great terra-cotta hot tub set in the floor of the bathing suite and smiled at his machinist, enjoying the sensation of steaming water soaking the knots out of his muscles.

"What did I promise you back in Nantucket, Cuddy-my-main-man?" he chuckled. *Master of Engineers, technically.* "Gold, girls, all the comforts of home, within reason."

The new house—*palace, in fact*— was almost finished. He'd built it not far from the site of classical Sparta, on a rise overlooking the Eurotas valley. The basic materials were the ones the locals were used to working in, but he'd made some modifications. Pitched roofs of baked-clay tile, for instance; the local flattops leaked like a bastard in the winter. Floors of glazed tile, the way he had this area set up, or polished marble; he looked around with satisfaction at the mural frescoes, mostly battle scenes from the conquest of Sicily last year. Running water wasn't a completely unknown concept here, but the sort of full-suite setup he'd put in was, and that went double for the flush toilets with S-curve pipes. Central heating, too, with underfloor ducts, and furnaces and tanks for hot water on tap in the master's quarters.

"Yeah, you came through, all right, boss," Cuddy said. "Funny how much easier this was than Alba."

"Lot more organization to start with," Walker pointed out.

Although that has its drawbacks, he thought. His glance went to the tall French doors. He couldn't see much out of them, the best they could do for window glass still being sort of wavy and opaque, and it was raining outside on the terrace anyway. If it had been clear and he'd gone outside, he could have seen down the valley to the palace of the underking of Sparta, whose sons had all conveniently died in the Sicilian campaign.

He really shouldn't have tried to have me offed back in Mycenae, he thought. Of course, the guy was sick these days himself . . . courtesy of dear, dear Alice Hong. *God, but it pays to have a doctor on your staff.* And once Wannax Menelaos was gone, Walker knew *exactly* who the high king was going to appoint in his place. *Odd. I expected them to be brothers. More like third cousins once removed.*

But on the whole, operating in civilization of a sort was a hell of a lot easier than cobbling together a kingdom out of the tribes up in Alba. There was a lot the Achaeans didn't know, but at least he didn't have to teach them *everything.* He smiled at the vista beyond the windows; he'd left plenty of room for expansion later.

Something imposing, but not ostentatious, he thought. *Something along the lines of San Simeon.*

"Easy to get used to this sort of thing," Cuddy said, raising his cup in toast. He looked aside at the girl, who was kneeling, sitting back on her heels with eyes cast down. "Like, getting laid whenever you want, for example."

Walker nodded, although he wasn't the sort of three-ball man that some of his American followers were. Rodriguez, for instance, and even he'd slowed down a bit now that it was not longer a big deal.

"You deserve it," Walker said sincerely. "You've got the machine shops working fine now."

Cuddy shrugged and beckoned. The girl came over and knelt behind him, kneading his shoulders.

"The first part was the hardest," he said, tilting his head back against her breasts. "Like, one makes two, two makes four, you know? Lathes make lathes. Look though, boss—these guys I've trained, they don't really *understand* any of this stuff. Well, maybe one or two. It's all monkey-see, monkey-do for the rest."

"It's the results that matter."

"Surprised you sent Danny Rodriguez off to Sicily all on his lonesome," Cuddy went on.

"Oh, I put the fear of God into him well enough," Walker said. "Besides, Odikweos will keep him in line . . . and I can rely on Odikweos to see that our great good friend and liege-lord Agamemnon doesn't hear about exactly how *many* musketeers we're training over there. Christ, but these people don't have much idea of spook-work. Odikweos, he's the exception."

"Yeah, well, you got Odi the viceroy's job," Cuddy said. "He owes you—it's a fucking gold mine."

"Gratitude is strong; the bottom line's even stronger." Walker chuckled and finished his own wine. "He's raising a regiment of musketeers himself—most of these wog VIPs, you'd think getting out of their chariots was like cutting off their own balls. Odikweos doesn't think that way."

"He's keeping the sulfur and asphalt coming, too," Cuddy said with satisfaction. "And the other stuff."

Sulfur for gunpowder, of course. Sicily was rich in brimstone ores. The asphalt wells near Ragusa-that-wasn't were extremely handy too; you could distill something roughly like kerosene out of it without much trouble, and the residue had a dozen uses, like waterproofing these baths so the adobe brick didn't turn to mudpie. They were even paving some crucial stretches of road with it. Plus the slaves, timber, and grain that kept other projects going.

"Yeah, that's going pretty well," Walker said. "Pretty soon we'll be ready to start whipping on the neighbors again."

Cuddy looked at him. "Why bother, boss? Shit, we're practically running this place—will be, in a couple of years. Why bust our ass taking over more territory?"

"Two reasons, Cuddy. First, because I say so." He met the other man's eyes until they dropped. "Second," he went on more genially, "we've got to hit while the hitting's easy. We're not exactly building tanks and helicopter gunships here. Anything we're doing, the locals can learn, and we give them time, they *will* start picking up tricks—my buddy Isketerol already has, of course. So we've got to conquer as much as we can while we're ahead. That way, we'll have *numbers* on our side too. Quantity has a quality all its own."

Cuddy nodded thoughtfully. "Yeah, when you put it that way . . ."

"Besides, it's fun. Booze and cooze are all right, but you can only party so long."

"Ah, *try* me on that one, boss!" They laughed. "Yeah, I see what you mean, though. Sort of a challenge."

Walker went on: "Anyway, I'm off. Alice has something really *special* planned for those two that came in with the last shipment, and I've got a starring role."

Cuddy made a slight face. "Whatever, boss."

Walker laughed again as he heaved himself out of the tub. Water hissed over the indigo and white of the tiles, and the girls hastened over to rub him down with linen towels and dress him in a long embroidered robe imported from the Hittite country.

"Oh, she's a complete nutcase, I know," Walker said. "But it can be sort of diverting, for a change. *Hasta la vista.*"

And the screams and bodies keep the staff really *on their toes,* he thought, glancing back over his shoulder as he left. Two of the serving-maids were sliding into the tub, minus kilts, giggling and squealing.

Guards brought their muskets to present arms with a slap of hands on wood and crash of hobnailed heels on stone. Walker nodded back with lordly politeness.

"Philowergos, Eumenes," he said.

He'd seen a movie once, when he was young—*Battleship Potemkin,* that was it, about a mutiny in the Russian navy, sailors given rotten food and such. He still remembered his own reaction of contempt; what sort of doink shorted the hired muscle? *He* knew enough to spread around the vig generously, and that included knowing names. The thought warmed him as he walked past into the main body of the mansion.

Glass windows kept it reasonably bright even on an overcast winter's day, and fires boomed in proper fireplaces at either end; the floor was honeycomb yellow marble from a nearby quarry. He'd kept the traditional high seat on the southern wall, but added tables and chairs to make it more like a formal dining room. A curving staircase led to the second floor and Hong's quarters—Ekhnonpa and the children he'd had by her were over in the other wing, and glad to be there.

No mistaking Hong's door, dark oiled beechwood with silver bolts through it, and the mask of a skull in a golden setting above it with a candle burning behind the empty eyes. He walked through, past a sitting room with couches and a couple of beautiful locally woven rugs in front of the cheerful fireplace, and into the bedroom.

"You're late," Hong said. "But I haven't really started. Just sort of establishing the scenario."

Despotnia Algeos, the locals were calling her: the Lady of Pain, avatar of Hekate, with power over life and death. Some of the noble Achaean ladies were incorporating her suggestions in their rites. She was dressed in black gold-stamped sandals, a silver domino skull-mask, and an ivory-hilted riding crop thonged to one wrist, with a few straps and buckles elsewhere. He had to admit it all looked quite dramatic.

He didn't think the subjects today were concerned with niceties like that at the moment. One was a thirtysomething Sophia Loren type, spread eagled naked to the wall and bound with built-in ties at wrists, ankles, and waist. Her mouth was gagged with a leather ball tied with a strap around her head, and tears and spittle ran down her face and heavy breasts. There were thin silver needles through her earlobes, the webs between finger and thumb, and a few other parts of her body, and ivory alligator clips on her nipples. Thread-thin trickles of blood crept over her skin, disturbed by shuddering twitches.

The other, on the bed, was about fourteen, with small, pert breasts and a black fuzz of hair between her legs. He had a good view of that, because she was secured to the four-poster with a net of straps and buckles that held her arms stretched taut above her head and her legs spread wide and hauled back. There was a creaking and sobbing as she struggled.

Trays of polished instruments stood on wheeled trays above the gleaming tile of the floor; the rugs and tapestries were rolled up and safely elsewhere, leaving the half-done murals bare . . . and Hong had drawn those herself. She wasn't bad, sort of an Alphonse Mucha Art Nouveau style, but with subjects the Czech had never gone for. A bed of glowing coals burned in the fireplace, where other blades and spikes heated to cherry-red. Walker went to a sideboard and poured wine into an elegant shallow local cup, then sipped it. Too sweet, but not bad for all that.

Hong smiled at him sidelong, licked her lips and let the tip of the springy whip trail down from the bound girl's mouth, slowly drawing it across sweat-slick skin and down to her crotch, tickling with the tuft of feathers. Then her hand moved with blurring speed and thin red welts appeared on the inside of her victim's thighs.

Dr. Alice Hong gave a long shivering sigh at the squeal of helpless pain. "Just the right reception for visiting princesses, don't you think?" she said. The whip flicked again, a sharp, expert motion that brought a heaving convulsion. "Oh, does that smart, little princess? Shall I kiss it better?"

Actually they're the wife and daughter of an important rebel chief, Walker thought, watching her work and drinking again. An important *dead* chief; the rest of his relations were digging sulfur, hauling stone, and building roads in the new Achaean fiefs of Sicily—the ones who weren't hanging on crosses beside the roads. He pulled the robe over his head and tossed it aside. Alice would have been quite happy to include the chief himself in this little playlet, she was an equal-opportunity sadist, but he just didn't find that much of a turn-on.

Hong chuckled as she watched him. "Impatient as always, Will," she said, reaching out to tickle him strategically with the feathers. "But all right, let's start with the traditional defloration . . . or would you rather give momma there something to remember . . . ?"

"Decisions, decisions," Walker laughed thickly. "I think . . . yes, youth should be served first."

He walked toward the bed.

"Reveille, reveille, heave out, trice up, lash and stow, lash and stow! Here I come, with a sharp knife and a clear conscience!"

Alston opened her eyes as the brass bell rang. The big stern cabin of the *Joshua Chamberlain* was filled with light from the windows that formed a curving wall along the rear of the ship. The clipper-frigate creaked and groaned around her, the endless speaking of a big wood-built ship; water slapped at the hull, and the stiff breeze hummed through the rigging. The sound and the long, rolling pitch of the ship beneath filled her with a quiet happiness.

Swindapa stirred. The first voyage together they'd kept to the old no-fraternization-on-board rule, but the new NCMJ (Nantucket Code of Military Justice) allowed married couples and registered domestic partners to bunk together at sea. Above them they could hear the crisp *Sir! Crew turned out!* of the master-at-arms reporting to the officer of the deck. The ship resounded to a thunder of feet as the crew and the hundred-odd Marine troopers aboard raced up the gangways to stow their tight-rolled hammocks along the gunwales of the ship. Then another thunder, this time as water gushed from the pumps onto the immaculate deck planking, and hollystones and "bears"—heavy blocks of sandstone—began to growl as they were pushed over the wood.

"Time to be up and doing," Alston said.

"You Eagle People—always in a hurry," Swindapa laughed, rolling out of bed and tossing Alston's uniform to her.

Alston paused for a second to admire the sleek, graceful nakedness that smiled at her. *Eight years and I still get that catch in my throat,* she thought happily, then sighed and began her morning stretches. *Those* got just a little more difficult every year. The captain's cabin on the *Liberator* class had room enough, at least. With an eye to impressing foreign potentates, it also had paneling of curly maple, polished and stained to bring out the swirling grain of the wood, and strips of carving along the edges of the yard-wide planks. Even more likely to impress were the two long cast-steel twelve-pounder rifles that served as stern-chasers, bowsed tight in place with double lashings.

Gunnery practice again today, Alston decided, as she buttoned her jacket and adjusted the billed cap with fouled anchor that was Guard regulation. Drill was a damned nuisance on a ship crowded with passengers, but you had to find *some* time to get the hands used to their lethal tools.

They walked along the central corridor of the poop to the officers' wardroom, the hollystones loud on the quarterdeck above.

"Good morning, gentlemen, ladies," she said.

The wardroom table was crowded, since the two Hollards and some of their Marine officers ate with them as a matter of course. Barely two weeks out of home port and two days from the Islander outpost on Barbados they still had abundant fresh provisions. And coffee . . .

She added a filleted flying fish to her plate, anticipating the smooth buttery taste; several dozen had landed on the deck and made a short trip to the cooks. The coffee was harsh-tasting to anyone who could remember the twentieth; it was the offspring of ornamental coffee plants, the only option the Islanders had available after the Event. *Better than no coffee at all, by a long shot.* Which was what they'd had to put up with for long years afterward, as those first seedlings planted out on Caribbean islands struggled to maturity.

"Damn, but I missed this, the first few years after the Event," she said, sighing, after the first sip.

"It's like chewing nettles," Swindapa replied. "An acquired taste, but why bother to acquire it?"

"Could be worse," Alston said, looking through the night-watch reports presented to her—water consumption, miles traveled, positions, hourly records of speed, barometer readings—all routine. "Tobacco could have survived too." Doc Coleman had quietly squashed any attempt to bring *that* particular vice back to life.

"I drank decaf," Colonel Hollard said, lifting his cup of sassafras.

Alston's mouth quirked slightly, and she raised an eyebrow. She'd be handing over to Hollard's generation in time; it was nice to be reminded that they could remember America, the twentieth, as well. There were times she worried that they would disappear into this era like a drop of ink in a bucket of milk—not enough of them to season it.

A middie approached the table and saluted. "Good morning, Captain," she said. "The officer of the deck reports the approach of eight bells. Permission to strike eight bells on time."

"My compliments to Mr. Jenkins, and let him make it so," Alston said.

Swindapa stood with her, only a slight glance out of the corner of her eyes telling her partner what she thought of the Eagle People rituals of military courtesy. *It's still a bit of a game to her,* Alston mused. She performed it faultlessly, even acknowledged the reasons for it but . . . *deep down, I don't think she takes it all that seriously.* The Sun People recruits were a far more temperamental and willful bunch than the Fiernans, but when they finally grasped the concept of discipline they often embraced it with a convert's fanaticism.

There were times when she thought Swindapa's people were just too damned mentally healthy for their own good.

Up the companionway to the brightness of the deck, the sun now well clear of the horizon.

"Captain on deck!"

"As you were," she replied. She was acting as captain-aboard of the *Chamberlain,* as well as commodore of the flotilla; the Guard was still short of experienced ship commanders.

"Fair-weather sailin'," Alston went on.

She looked up; not a cloud in the sky. The deck of the *Joshua Chamberlain* tilted only a little, and she took the long blue swells with a smooth rocking-horse motion under all plain sail, three pyramids of white flax canvas reaching up her masts, a hundred and twenty feet on the main. The sails were braced to starboard, and the ship was moving at nearly right angles to the wind. *We should catch the trades in another few days,* she thought, reaching out to touch the rail. Then they could make better speed, with the wind abaft the beam.

The *Chamberlain* was lead ship in the Islander flotilla; behind her came the *Lincoln;* then the *Eagle,* the main transport, and the schooners *Harriet Tubman* and *Frederick Douglass.* They were in line astern, each separated by a thousand yards like beads on an arrow-straight line ruled across the blue of the ocean in cream-white wakes, their fresh canvas snow-white against the dark gray-blue of the hulls.

As a training ship, *Eagle* had been built for carrying people, not cargo; there had even been proposals to break up the big eighteen-hundred-tonner for her metal, on the theory that she was inefficient compared to wooden craft with proper holds.

Efficient as a troop-transport, though, she thought, watching the long hull with the red diagonal slash of the Coast Guard.

"Signal," she said aloud.

Swindapa took out her pad; the ships all had radios salvaged from pleasure craft. *Chamberlain's* was in a low deckhouse forward of the wheels.

"To *Eagle*;—prepare to drop targets." Those would be rafts of empty barrels that had held salt provisions, lashed together with poles and flags standing up. "Ships will pass at four hundred yards and then come about," she said. To the first lieutenant: "Mr. Jenkins, sound to quarters. Fighting sail only."

"Yes, ma'am," he said crisply and turned.

Orders flowed out and a drum began to beat, a long, hoarse roll of sound. Marines crowded out of the way as parties dashed to rig boarding nets along the sides and splinter-netting overhead. Crewfolk ran up the ratlines, and the ship came more nearly upright as the topsails were clewed up and sea-furled. From below came the sound of partitions being knocked down and struck into the hold. Alston stood quietly, glancing at her watch.

Better, she thought, as the bosun reported to the quarterdeck, still panting a little. *Ten minutes forty-seven seconds.*

Eagle had been making more sail, pulling ahead of the other ships. Alston felt her lips quirking in a smile as she passed in a sunlit burst of spray, sharp bows slicing the swells. Objectively the new clipper-frigates were even prettier ships, without the clutter of deckhouses on the quarter and around the mainmast, but . . .

I commanded her so long, she thought. More than ten years now, if you counted the time before the Event. *I've seen and done a lot on that deck.* And it was where she'd used a pair of bolt cutters to take the collar off Swindapa.

"Mr. Jenkins, bring us two points to starboard, if you please. And trim, by all means."

"Yes, ma'am." A turn: "Helm, two points, thus, thus." The two hands standing on the benchlike platforms beside the double wheels heaved at the spokes with a precise, economical motion, their eyes on the compass binnacle before them.

Jenkins's speaking-trumpet went up. "Haul starboard, handsomely starboard, there!"

The rafts splashed free ahead of them, and *Eagle* ran forward a half a mile to be out of harm's way, heaving to broadside-on to the other ships. Alston and Swindapa walked forward on the quarterdeck, down the steep wooden steps to the main deck, and then down a level further. The main gun deck of the *Chamberlain* was a single great room now, an oval space six times longer than it was wide, tapering to the narrow shape of the bows, lit only by the crosshatched light of the grating-hatchcovers above. It smelled of fresh wood still, and underlying that, brimstone, salt water, sweat, and the cooking scents of breakfast. Twelve eight-inch Dahlgrens crouched on either side, shaped like soda bottles and enmeshed in their cradle of carriage, lines, pulleys, and tackle.

Pity we can't do many rifled guns yet, Alston thought. Leaton's Bessemer steel just didn't have the consistent quality needed for those pressures, though; and the thought of a burst gun on these crowded decks was enough to make her shudder. There were the chasers, and a few rifled siege cannon struck down in the holds for the expeditionary force to use on land, but most of the Republic's guns were smoothbores. Good ones, at least, modelled on those of the Civil War era.

The gun teams waited, crouching, hands ready; many were stripped to the waist and had kerchiefs tied around their heads as they prepared for the shattering physical effort of serving the guns.

Or stripped to the waist except for bras, Alston thought; it wasn't *quite* the same as down there as on the gun deck of the *Constitution* or *Chesapeake* in the War of 1812. One young woman grinned at her for a second, then turned back and spat on her hands as she braced ready.

"Target's coming on to bear, ma'am," a middie said from his position near one division of the guns.

"Very well. Out tompions!"

The red-painted wooden plugs at the muzzles of the guns were whipped out.

"Run out your guns!"

A long drumming, squealing thunder of carriages across decks as the crews threw themselves on the ropes and twelve sets of two-ton weight ground across the oaken planking; sunlight pierced the gloom of the gun deck in rectangular shafts as the gunports rose.

"Fire as you bear!"

Alston took two steps up the companionway ladder; that gave her a good view of the target four hundred-odd yards to starboard as well as the gun deck, with the heel of the ship pitching the rail down.

"Time this, 'dapa," she said, and Lieutenant Commander Swindapa Alston-Kurlelo put on a grave official face and took out her stopwatch.

The gun captain of Number One, Starboard, spun the elevating screw and heaved at the handspike that moved the rear of the gun as the crew hauled likewise on the tackle that moved the muzzle. He glared over the barrel of his charge a final instant, then:

"Clear!" he bellowed, giving the lanyard of the friction primer a swift, hard jerk.

BAAAAMMMM!

A long jet of flame-shot smoke lanced out from the *Chamberlain's* side. Her eye caught the fall of shot exactly, a grooved splash in the surface of the water ten yards short of the target, and then another beyond it as the ball ricocheted like a flung stone.

Not bad, she thought, smiling a little behind the expressionless mask of her face. *That would have gone aboard a ship, right enough.*

The gun captain pivoted like a matador, arching his body over the massive steel bulk of the gun as it leaped backward up the inclined plane of its carriage with an angry squeal of wooden brake shoes. As it stopped, the rest of the crew went into a precisely choreographed dance around it, readying for the next round.

Meanwhile, the other cannon roared as the rippling broadside went down the gun deck, and the choking sulfur-tinted smoke coiled across the deck and turned it into a thing of fog and menacing shapes. More than eight hundred pounds of high-velocity iron lashed the sea around the target with stunning violence, as water gouted all around the target, and fragments of plank whipped skyward amid spray and froth as direct hits stove barrels.

The first gun fired again. "Two minutes ten seconds!" Swindapa shouted into her ear. A good many of the crew had wads of cloth stuffed into both of theirs; enough of this could damage your hearing.

Alston nodded. Seventy seconds to reload; not bad at all. Her eye sought the next target.

"Sail trimmers!" she called, standing back from the stairs.

The crews shrank as one from each gun ran up the ladders to the deck, taking their place in the sailing crew. Another period of shattering sound, the crews' bodies running with sweat at the physical exertion and the heat the guns were throwing off. The guns were jumping back harder as the steel soaked up heat, and she could hear grunts and harsh panting at the brutal labor of wearing them around. This time, only half the second broadside could bear on the target, and there was a concentrated move for the scuttlebutts—open-topped casks of water secured to the deck—in the short interval between the second and third targets.

Alston waited until the last second before she called: "Boarders! Boarders to their stations!"

The gun crews shrank again as another thirty left them, grabbing weapons out of the racks as they ran for the companionways. The result looked remarkably piratical, half-naked bodies bristling with flintlocks and edged steel.

And for a wonder, nobody's spearing anyone in the ass, she thought with satisfaction. That *had* happened once or twice, earlier. Middies oversaw four guns each, and they were running full tilt from one to the next, correcting aim and heaving on lines themselves. *For a wonder, nobody got their foot run over, either.* That could cause really nasty injuries, but the only way to learn to do this fast was to do it *fast,* exhaustion or no. You had to accept a certain percentage of training accidents if the training was realistic.

"One minute fifty-six seconds," Swindapa said.

Not so good, Alston thought; and the crews were collapsed around their weapons, panting like hound dogs on a hot day; she could hear someone retching dryly.

"Master gunner, house your guns and secure the deck," she said into a silence that seemed to echo in the aftermath of the cannon roar. She lifted her voice a little, waiting until the sail trimmers and boarders had returned to their stations. "Not bad, boys and girls. But it could be better."

The cheer that followed had an element of groan in it, but there were plenty of smiles as well. First Lieutenant Jenkins was grinning as he saluted her return to the quarterdeck, looking at his own watch.

"We beat *Lincoln* by a good ten seconds, ma'am," he said.

Alston nodded, smiling a little herself. Victor Ortiz had the other frigate, and he'd be fit to be tied; she knew he'd had the crew doing weight training at intervals, trying to beat her time.

"There's such a thing as overstraining," she said. The shriller bark of the eight-pounders and carronades the schooners carried ended the exercise, leaving only a fogbank of powder smoke drifting eastward as it dispersed.

Marian Alston took a deep breath of the clean air and looked at her watch again. "We'll heave to," she said. "Signal 'Captains repair to *Eagle* for a working lunch at thirteen hundred hours', Ms. Swindapa. Mr. Jenkins, we'll rig pumps, and have the masthead and a rowing lookout check for sharks."

Lines formed for the salt-water showers after the sails were struck; the gun crews' hands and faces were smut-dark with black powder residues. Luckily Fiernans didn't have a nudity taboo, and the Americans and even the rather prudish Sun People had gotten used to it. Body modesty simply didn't go with the sort of cramped quarters a mixed force in the field or at sea had to put up with; they'd learned that shortly after the Event. After a while it simply wasn't much of a deal.

In fact, she thought, *by now I feel much more self-conscious about being the only darkie among the* bukra.

By an odd quirk of fate she'd been stranded in the Bronze Age along with a piece of American real estate where blacks were rare—no more than a few hundred in all. Rare, and even more so proportionately with the influx of Alban immigrants; language and culture changed, but Sun People and Earth Folk alike *looked* very much like their Anglo-Saxon descendants.

The water felt cold on her bare skin as she turned under the pump; she took the bar of gritty ration-issue lye soap from Colonel Hollard with a polite nod, lathered herself thoroughly, and stepped up to the rail, handing the bar over to the next in line.

"All clear!" the lookout said; the ones in the longboat rowing around the ship carried barbed harpoons and rifle-muskets.

Alston poised, then leaped, taking the fifteen-foot drop in a knifing dive. That carried her deep into water that closed around her like a blue jewel; she turned and looked up, watching as Swindapa slid down toward her with her long yellow hair streaming out behind like a banner. They touched for a moment fifteen feet down, kissed in the discreet silence of the ocean, then kicked for the surface that hung over them like a rippling mirror. She tossed her head as she surfaced, watching as whooping crewfolk followed her off into the water.

Hollard scooped up his sister and threw her in, then followed in a clean dive. For moments it rained soapy Guard crews and Marines; many of them were cannonballing and landing with appalling splashes. She made a mental note to have more swimming classes.

Swindapa trailed her as she made for the stern at an easy crawl, matching her stroke for stroke. The warm Caribbean water caressed her, a feeling of tingling life buoying her. And if there were shark and barracuda in these waters, that was part of life too.

"On deck, there! Sail ho!"

Alston looked up sharply, catching the hail from the masthead at the second shout.

"Damn," she said mildly, spitting out salt water and stroking swiftly to the ship's side. Ropes hung over the railing; she swarmed up one hand over hand, then directly up the ratlines to the mainmast top.

"Where away?" she said to the lookout, dripping on the hot planks of the triangular platform.

"East by south, ma'am," the lookout said, in a faint but definite Sun People accent, harsh and choppy under the nasal twang of Islander English. "Ship-rigged or a bark, I'd guess."

Alston took her heavy binoculars and focused them. White shapes of sail, a three-master, bark-rigged like the *Eagle* but much smaller.

"On deck, there! Hands to stations, Mr. Jenkins, and notify the flotilla!" she called down. "And have my uniform sent up, if you please."

It came up, and Swindapa with it. They shared a towel and dressed, disregarding the slight stickiness of salt on their skins; that went with voyaging, since fresh water was never abundant enough to waste on washing. She put the sails in her binoculars again; the strange ship was flying the Stars and Stripes, but that meant little. Details of construction meant more, and she ran through a mental file of everything the Islanders had built in the past eight years, and what they knew of the Tartessian and Alban yards.

"One of ours, I think," she said after a moment. "Let's get down and ready to hail her."

You had to be wary, in a world with the likes of King Isketerol and William Walker loose in it.

"You haven't been letting the grass grow under your arse, by the gods," Odikweos said.

He held out his hand and looked around at stone-built wharves, streets, buildings, the ribs of ships on the slipways. Nothing here but a fishing village a few years ago, and now it was a city—*Neayoruk,* Walker had called it. *"New" I know,* Odikweos thought. *I wonder what or where Yoruk was or is?*

"A lazy man has no luck," Walker replied, taking the offered palm in the American gesture, which had become quite the fashion.

Hammers, hooves, wheels, and voices made a surflike roar of noise throughout the little town, full of pungent smells of sweat and dust and manure baking under the hot June sun. Foreign ships were tied up here too, looking tiny beside the craft Walker had built. Slaves carried elephant tusks ashore from an Egyptian merchantman, tapestries from one out of Byblos, purple-dyed cloth and clay jugs of wine from Ugarit, oxhide-shaped copper ingots from a Cypriot trader. So much wealth so close to the sea would have been an irresistible lure for raiders in the old days, but a fortress of earthwork and stone stood at the edge of the harbor, cannon snouting from embrasures along its thick, sloping walls. And armed schooners out on patrol had met the Ithakan's ship half a day's sailing away.

A groom brought a mount forward, one of the half-breed sons of the sixteen-hand quarter horse that Walker rode himself. The Achaean put a foot in a stirrup and swarmed aboard, competently, if not with the ease a lifetime's practice had given Walker. He wore trousers of fine kidskin as well as his tunic; those had become fashionable too, among younger nobles flexible enough to consider a saddle as dignified as a chariot.

The two vassal kings rode north up the valley of the Eurotas, with their escorts clattering behind and outriders ahead with a harsh, repeated cry of "Way, make way!" Odikweos stretched his eyes, taking everything in, including the way Walker kept an eye on his reactions.

The road itself was a novelty. Instead of graveled dirt it was a smoothly beveled curve of Sicilian asphalt mixed with crushed rock, twenty feet across, lavishly ditched, with young trees planted in rows on either side.

"How far north does this run?" Odikweos asked.

"All the way up the valley, and three-quarters of the way to Mycenae. We'll have it through to there by the fall rains."

"Through the *mountains*? In only three years?"

Walker nodded. "Gunpowder is a tool as well as a weapon," he said. "Blasting makes road building easier."

Not to mention unlimited slave labor. Chain gangs were moving up from the port, while down by the river more were at work on an irrigation canal, its stark geometric shape cutting across the softly patterned fields. Harvest was under way. Part of it was as always, men and some women cutting the yellow barley and wheat with sickles, others following behind to bind the sheaves. In other fields horses drew a machine that left a neat trail of reaped grain behind it. Odikweos nodded thoughtfully as he watched it, and he saw other fields that had been in grain in years before now planted with crops he didn't recognize.

"What are those?" he asked.

"The bushes are *cotton*," Walker said. "They make a fabric like flax but easier to work and finer. The tall stalks are a grain called *corn;* it needs watering in your dry summers, but it yields more heavily than wheat or barley. The low vines, those are *potatoes*, the last of them. They grow over the winter here. My guest friend King Isketerol of Tartessos brought the seeds and shoots from . . . a land far away and passed some on to me. Wait until you taste your first tomato, my friend."

"I see why you've been taking so much of the wheat from Sicily," Odikweos said. "Thousands more mouths to feed, and fewer fields in grain."

He nodded at a train of huge four-wheeled wagons rumbling along ahead of them, too large to make way for the kings; they guided their horses onto the graveled verge of the road to pass them by. Sixteen span of oxen drew each four-ton load.

"What are those called?" Odikweos said, pointing to one wheel. "I've seen the ones in Sicily, but nobody knew the name or the why of them."

"Double-bow springs," Walker replied. "See how they flex? That way, a jolt from the wheels doesn't harm the wagon's frame as much as it might, and the body is built like a boat—it yields and bends and so doesn't break. We call them *Conestogas*."

They rode north for most of the morning, speaking of many things, then turning left onto a branch of the road that ran toward the mountains that towered in the west, dividing the vale of Sparta from Messina. The traffic was still heavy; they were riding toward Walkeropolis, Walker's stronghold. The American pointed out features—the stone-lined channel that brought water down from the mountains, the four furnaces built into the side of a hill so that carts could bring fuel and ore to their tops. Smoke belched out of them, trailing away to the south; there was a deep rumbling sound from the furnaces, and endless clangor from the forges and workshops, and a clatter and bustle of uncounted folk in the broad gridwork of paved streets.

Not such smell, Odikweos thought, surprised.

This town must be nearly as big as Pylos by now, yet there was little of the shit-and-garbage stink you expected in a city. There were even slaves sweeping up dung with broom and pan and wheelbarrow. Even now, it still seemed odd to see so many male slaves together. In Walkeropolis they were marked out by the iron collars, and they were everywhere—hauling and pushing and carrying; there were great low-set barracks for them nearer the manufactures. Elsewhere there were no wells with lines of slave girls carrying jugs of water on their heads, but instead public fountains, fed by underground pipes. More pipes ran to the houses of the wealthy.

There were many other things even stranger—sometimes the little things were oddest of all, like wagons each keeping to the right side of the street. They rode through a great open-air market, past streets of shops and businesses, past chariots and wagons and *carriages* drawn by high-stepping Eastern horses.

Even shops for bread, the Achaean king thought with astonishment, watching a baker load loaves into the carrying-basket of a woman and take little copper disks in payment. Next door a leatherworker bowed low as a servant of one of Walker's Wolf People lords took delivery of a saddle; beyond that a treadle-powered lathe whirred, turning out the spokes of a wheel.

"One thing that does surprise me, my friend," Odikweos said as they turned uphill to the palace through elaborate gardens and the mansions of Walker's own *ekwetai.* "Is that you took no larger share of the credit for the war in the lands north of Olympus—and no larger share of the gold. You don't seem to me to be a man unconcerned with wealth."

Walker laughed.

The *Dolphin* was less graceful than her name; three hundred tons, three masts, but much tubbier than the *Chamberlain* or even the Guard schooners modeled on the *Bluenose.* She bobbed in the lee of the frigate, and her commander came up the rope ladder with a practical swarming motion.

"Permission to come aboard?" she called, with a wave of a salute.

"Permission granted," Alston said. "Captain McReady, isn't it?"

"Candice McReady at your service, Commodore," the merchant skipper said, holding out her hand.

Typical enough, Alston thought. No more than twenty-one, which would have made her all of thirteen at the Event, the twentieth century most likely a fading dream. A stocky, brown-haired young woman with a weather-red face and squint lines around her eyes that made her look older. She wore a floppy canvas hat and a sleeveless jacket of sealskin belted 'round with a cutlass, bowie, and flintlock pistol. The ironmongery looked as natural on her as the easy, straddled stance and the gold hoop in one earlobe. The hand she extended felt rough and dry and competent in Alston's.

The steward brought up coffee. "Thought I was sailing into a fight, ma'am," McReady said, sipping appreciatively. "Heard the cannon. Thought some damned Tartessian poacher needed his but kicked."

And just came boiling in with all four of your six-pounder brass popguns, Alston thought, nodding. *Fairly typical.* The youngsters coming up since the Event were *different;* not necessarily braver than their parents but harder-grained. *Entirely different attitude toward risk.*

Less likely to complain about bad luck, too. Of course, the attitude had its downside as well; the new breed seemed to be a good deal less shockable, more case-hardened than Alston would have expected or altogether liked.

I must be getting old, she thought. *I'm starting to complain about the upcoming generation.*

"They do show up here occasionally," Alston agreed aloud.

The Town Meeting had proclaimed the whole of the Western Hemisphere under the Republic's jurisdiction—sort of a second-millennium-B.C. Monroe Doctrine—but the Kingdom of Tartessos didn't acknowledge it. Iberian ships slipped in now and then, bartering with the Olmec chiefdoms, which had their own reasons to resent the Islanders; besides that little war back in the Year 1, the Republic frowned on human sacrifice. A couple of punitive expeditions had made that very clear, via cannon and Marine landing parties.

"Not this time, though. What crew, where from, and what loading?" she went on.

"My third trip this year," McReady said, jerking a thumb backward at her ship. "My first mate's my mate, my brother and his wife are quartermaster and sailing master"—Not an uncommon sort of arrangement; they waved from the lower deck of the trading ship—"and we've a crew of twelve besides. We shipped out of Nantucket Town to San Lorenzo first, picked up cocoa and dyewoods and raw cotton; dropped it in Pentagon Base in Alba, got a cargo of grain, hides, cheese, and wool, plus some steerage passengers, back to Nantucket. Out to southwest Africa in ballast and trading trinkets."

Alston nodded. "What loading now?"

McReady grinned. "Commodore, right now my cargo is absolute shit." She grinned more widely still at the raised brows. "Bird shit. Fertilizer from the islands in Saldhana Bay. One hundred ninety tons, all of it under contract to Brand Farms." She held up a hand, clenched with the thumb and little finger out as if measuring. "And the price is *just* right. Ought to pay off the Town share of our ship. A little other stuff, hides, horn, ivory—ten tusks—traded for it with the locals."

"Ah, the Namib," Alston said. The coast of southwest Africa, not far from where she intended to make landfall. "Any rumors of Tartessian activity there?"

"Yes, as a matter of fact; the locals drew pictures of what looked like a topsail schooner."

Alston scowled slightly; Tartessos favored that design, copied from the ship Walker had pirated in the Year 1.

"Couldn't be sure, though. They *are* putting in pretty regular further north, from what I hear."

This time the black woman forced her teeth not to grind. Slave trading, among other things.

"Thank you, Captain McReady," she went on, calm and polite. "Perhaps you could join the flotilla's captains aboard the *Eagle* for lunch. We could use any observations you have on how the trades are this year."

"Glad to—we're down to salt horse and biscuit," McReady said. "Trades're pretty steady, and further north than usual; haven't been becalmed yet on this trip. I'll get my logs."

Alston clasped her hands behind her back and rose slightly on her toes as the merchant skipper climbed back down into her skiff and pulled for her ship. The expeditionary force was supposed to keep William Walker off-balance, but it was a long-term project. Isketerol was making her nervous in the here-and-now.

God damn William Walker to hell, she thought. *If it weren't for him . . .*

"There's always a man like Walker," Swindapa said quietly. Alston started a little. Her partner had learned her moods *very* well.

"Fortunately, there's always someone like us, too," she replied, her head turning northeastward. Right now the renegade was having things all his own way, off in the lands of Mycenae. Some day . . .

Her lips showed teeth in what was only notionally a smile.

"There *is* a lot of gold up there," William Walker agreed, looking up at the portico of his house. A row of pillars marched across it— fluted marble, rather than the painted wood the locals used. *Greek columns, and the Greeks have never heard of them,* he thought with a slight smile. Servants were coming out to greet their lord.

The Mycenaeans had already had an outpost up north in what he thought of as Macedonia, a fortified border station. The locals were still at the mud-hut stage, but spoke something related to Greek. More important, he'd remembered where Philip of Macedon, Alexander's father, had gotten his financing—the gold mines of Pangaion, not all that far from the coast. Well worth an expedition.

"About a thousand talents a year worth," he went on. "I'm satisfied with my tenth." A talent was sixty pounds, more or less; call it twenty tons for the total output. Nobody here had ever seen precious metals on that scale before. They were learning about inflation, too, and the benefits and drawbacks of coined money.

"Why?" Odikweos said bluntly. "You planned the war, you found the gold, you built the works that tear it daily from the womb of *Gamater*."

"One of the things I like about you, my friend," Walker said, "is that you come right at things."

The Ithakan shrugged. "Paiawon Apollo speaks in words like a serpent in a reedbed, coil upon countercoil," he said. "But I've always been a better friend of the Gray-Eyed Lady of Wisdom, Athana Potnia."

"Let's put it this way—has all that gold brought peace to Mycenae?"

"As much peace as a piece of fat pork brings to a pack of hounds," Odikweos said. "Mycenae was always a knot of vipers, but now . . ."

"Exactly. Also, taking only a tenth, I'm not expected to spend men and goods guarding the mines—and the natives there don't love us for taking their mountain."

"Or for making their men dig in the ground," Odikweos said.

"Exactly, again. What's more, gold can't buy more than the land produces. Real wealth comes from increasing the yield of men's hands and then gaining command of that yield—gold is simply a tool. And third and last . . . well, there's a poem among my birth-folk. In your language . . ." Walker closed his eyes in thought for a moment. "It would go something like this:

> *Gold for the merchant, silver for the maid;*
> *Copper for the craftsman, cunning at his trade.*
> *"Good!" laughed the king, sitting in his hall.*
> *"But iron—cold iron—shall be master of them all."*

They drew rein before the portico with its green-white stone stairs. A small form burst through the ranks of guards and servants, followed by another, and then by a woman in a gown. He recognized Eurykleia, the household's chief nursemaid.

"Dad!" the hurtling bundle cried, and leaped with a trailing mane of white-blond hair. The second just leaped.

"Whoops," Walker said mildly and caught each under an arm. "Run along, the rest of you, no need for ceremony."

"I'm sorry, lord, they got away—"

"No problem," Walker said to the nursemaid. "They're eight. You'd have to put them in a cage like Egyptian baboons to keep them quiet."

The boy and girl wiggled delightedly; they were much of an age, the girl his by an Alban slave, the boy by his wife Ekhnonpa.

"Plain to see they've got spirit," Odikweos said, grinning.

"Althea has been misbehaving again, lord," Eurykleia broke in nervously. "And . . ."

Walker upended the girl. "What is it this time? Bothering your Aunt Alice again? Not safe, little one."

"Sneaking away to watch the warriors practice, lord," the nursemaid said.

"If Harold can do it, why can't I?" the girl pouted. She pronounced it "Haaar-alt," like the locals.

"Why not, indeed?" Walker said. He looked up at the servant. "If she wants to train with her brother, we'll see to it."

"But, lord, it isn't seemly!" she burst out, as Althea crowed in delight.

Walker's face went cold, and the nursemaid looked down, her own face gone pale. "Seemly is what I say to be seemly, Eurykleia. *I am the King.*"

"Yes, lord," she said quietly.

Walker hoisted his son over a shoulder and set the girl on her feet, delivering a swift spanking swat at the same time. "That's for not coming and asking me first," he said at her yelp, then gave her another. "And that's for disobeying Eurykleia. Now both of you run along and mind your manners."

He walked up the stairs. "My friend, we have a good deal to talk about," he said to Odikweos. "So that our children may inherit more than we hold today.

"Sicily grows dull," the Ithakan said. "Another man can chase bandits through the hills . . ." He paused. "Is that why you sent so many troublesome men to take up lands there?"

"Well," Walker grinned, "it *does* give them something to do, besides causing me problems."

"You are a man with a mind of many turns," Odikweos said admiringly, a little surprised when Walker laughed loud and long. "Troy next?"

"Troy, indeed," Walker said.

"That will bring in the Hittites."

"The worse for them, my friend. The worse for them."

CHAPTER SEVEN

January, Year 9 A.E.

"Uh-oh," Ian Arnstein said.

"Thunderclouds," Doreen agreed, looking at the Commodore as she lowered her binoculars.

"Mom?" David said. "Why's Aunt Marian looking so mad?"

"Shhhhh."

The Nantucket outpost on the uninhabited island of Mauritius was one of a chain the Republic was founding as time and resources permitted, staking out a claim to a global thassalocracy of trade and influence. Eventually it was supposed to be a jumping-off point for the settlement of the giant and equally human-empty island of Madagascar to the west and a base for trade throughout the Indian Ocean. The flotilla was two weeks out of a similar hamlet at the site of Cape Town, officially known as Mandela Base. *That* had met with Marian Alston's approval; neat little earth-and-turf fort, a well-built pier, a bored-log pipe to bring water down from a spring on Table Mountain, and half a dozen farms up the Liesbeck River to supply fresh produce.

Here . . .

The Islander ships stood in on an easting breeze, only a trace of white foam at their bows as they ghosted along at five knots. Eastward was a broad natural harbor where a river ran down to a silver-sand beach. Beyond rose mountains, densely green in the foreground, fading to blue-green as they rolled away inland. *Green* was the overwhelming first impression, huge broadleaf trees growing almost to the water's edge, and dark mangroves wherever a mudflat allowed; the white of sails, gray of hulls, and the broad red diagonal slash of the Guard along the ship's flanks were the only man-made color to break it. The settlement had run a pier out into the deep water, made of upright ebony logs and looking massively solid. Onshore . . .

Half-built, Ian decided; that was the best way to describe it. A couple of biggish buildings, but one of them had only the skeleton of a roof, and tiles were missing on the other. A windmill by the river looked broken, its vanes unmoving. Logs lay in untidy piles, and the patches of cleared land were weedy. Here and there were the signs of frantic last-minute effort that served only to make the rest seem more slovenly.

"By the mark, ten! By the mark, nine!" the leadsman standing braced in the bowsprit netting said, whirling the lead line around her head and throwing it far out to plop into the greening water. "By the mark . . . Christ, by the mark, *seven. Bye the mark, six!*"

"Captain Nguyen, I suggest you strike all sail," Marian Alston said tightly. "Signal to the flotilla. I'm not fully confident in the buoys marking the channel, here."

The officer nodded curtly, gave orders. Feet thundered on the *Eagle's* crowded deck, and teams bent to pull on ropes. Many of them included Marines, but the men and women clambering aloft in the ratlines all wore the blue sailor suits of the Guard; that was specialist work, hard and skilled and a little dangerous even in calm weather. They swarmed out along the yards and bent over them, gathering up armfuls of sail as the clewlines hoisted them up.

"Put your backs into it!" called a petty officer from the boats towing the *Eagle* up to the dock. The dark-blue water was fading to green as they neared the shore, and white foam curled as the ashwood oars stroked into it.

More thick ropes flew out, and the steel flank of the big windjammer kissed the coconut-fiber baffles. Further out, sails furled and anchors splashed, whistles sounded and the steaming ensigns came down, the national flag breaking out at the tops. He could see the party that stood ready to greet them on the dock bracing. Some had sickly smiles, others expressionless masks. The gangplank swung out and thumped down; Ian used councilor's rank shamelessly, crowding in behind the initial quartet of Commodore Alston, Swindapa, Colonel Hollard, Major Hollard, and Captain Nguyen of the *Eagle*. A bell rang from the quarterdeck.

"*Eagle* departing!"

"Welcome, Commodore," the commandant of Mauritius Base said.

Marian Alston returned his salute. He was a heavyset, balding man in his early forties, dressed in shorts and sandals and loose shirt and sweating until his scalp glistened through thinning black hair.

Might be the heat making him sweat, Ian thought. *Mebbe not.* He put Jared Cofflin's dry, skeptical Yankee voice to the thought.

"We've a luncheon laid on," the man—*Marvin Lockley,* he remembered—began.

"Later," Alston snapped. "I think we need to have a discussion, Mr. Lockley."

Not using his militia rank, Ian noted.

She turned. "Colonel Hollard, Captain Nguyen, please see to disembarking the troops and passengers," she went on in a flat, even tone that anyone who knew her recognized as the danger signal it was.

She turned on one heel and strode away, the luckless Lockley trailing in her wake. Ian followed, looking about. A cat lay in the shade of a thatched hut, nursing kittens. For a moment he accepted the sight, then grunted in shock.

That litter represents half a dozen feral cats in the making, he thought. *Dane Sweet will* have *kittens himself.* The Councilor for Conservation had been nervous about colonizing the home of the dodo anyway, and he and his faction had insisted on safeguards. Which, evidently, Mr. Lockley had let slip. A pregnant Fiernan girl waved to them; she was wearing nothing but a palm-frond hat and driving a sow ahead of her with a stick. *Feral pigs, too.* They were supposed to be strictly penned. A man in ragged shorts sat propped against a wall, a jug beside him . . .

"I notice that the water-furrow and the sawmill are incomplete," Alston said in a conversational tone.

"Ah . . . we've had some difficulties . . . hard to get parts . . ."

"I see. I think we should discuss this, Commandant."

They turned into what was evidently the commandant's quarters, a series of thatched rondavels. Swindapa halted outside and made a sign to Ian and Doreen; they did likewise and shushed their son. Voices came from within. He couldn't follow them for the most part, not until near the end, when Alston's voice rose to a quarterdeck bellow:

"This may be an island, *and it may be a* tropical *island, BUT IT ISN'T* GILLIGAN'S *GOD-DAMNED ISLAND—YOU HEAR ME, MISTER?"*

A moment later they came out. Lockley was gray-white under his tan, and shaking. Alston stood blinking in the sunlight for a second. The troops from the *Eagle* were filing ashore, then being dismissed; the civilian technicians and specialists and their families followed. Her eyes came to rest on Lucy and Heather, and a little of the stiffness went out of her shoulders.

"Mr. Nguyen," she said.

The Vietnamese-American officer came to attention as the commodore went on: "Mr. Lockley has decided to resign his position here and ship out on the *Eagle* as a foremast hand. Rate him 'seaman recruit' and see that he's assigned some fatigues."

"Yes, ma'am."

"Ms. Stearns."

The former commandant's second-in-command swallowed and braced herself. "Ma'am?"

"In the light of Mr. Lockley's resignation, I'm provisionally appointing you commandant of Mauritius Base. With the expeditionary force and the crews, we have more than a thousand pairs of hands here; we ought to be able to get things shipshape in fairly short order." A pause. "Shouldn't we?"

"Yes, *ma'am*."

"Good." She sighed. "Now, let's see about that lunch."

Doreen gave Ian a silent whistle behind the commodore's back and waggled a hand. He nodded agreement. As they walked away, Swindapa dropped back beside them for a moment.

"Ian," she said, frowning slightly, "who's Gilligan?"

"Let go, and haul!"

A squared ebony log jerked up off the pier, then swung out over the deck of the *Eagle* as the yard acting as crane pivoted on the mast.

"Heave . . . *ho!* Heave . . . *ho!*"

"Handsomely there, handsomely!"

Captain Nguyen lowered his speaking-trumpet and turned to Marian Alston.

"That's the last of them, Commodore," he said with quiet pride. He bent a critical eye on his ship. "I'm glad we finally got around to installing a proper hold. She trims well, even so."

"That she does, although I'd like to see her under way," Alston said. "She's a little by the stern."

"Better that than dead-level. I'd been meaning to come at the ballast and shift it a bit anyway. Less likely to press her forefoot down under full sail that way."

"She's your baby," Alston agreed, suppressing an inner pang. *Promoted away from ship command, goddammit,* she thought.

"That's the last of the cargo loaded, and we're wooded and watered," Nguyen said. He nodded toward the other ships of the flotilla. "Ready to sail with the evening tide, ma'am."

"Well, we're not in *that* much of a hurry." Theoretically, the stopover on Mauritius was supposed to rest the expeditionary force's people before the action at the end of it. Instead they'd spent an effortful week getting the base itself shipshape.

"Watch crews only," she went on. "We'll give everyone a day or two of leave, then get under way. Morning tide on Monday—oh-nine-hundred hours. Lieutenant Commander, pass the word."

"Yes, ma'am," Swindapa said, conscientiously marking it in the daybook to be issued as a general order.

Cheers and flung hats rose to the sky as Nguyen announced the leave and then exchanged salutes with the commodore. Alston removed her billed cap, sighed, and ran fingers over her damp forehead and close-cropped hair as they walked back up the single street of the little settlement.

"Looks better," Swindapa said.

Alston nodded. It did; the major buildings were all completed, the sawmill in action, livestock neatly penned, and the hollow-log aqueduct had filled the casks and tanks of each ship in turn as they were warped in to the dock. Good spring water too, not likely to go bad out in the middle of nowhere. Hollard's Marines were still putting the finishing touches on the fort, adding stone retaining walls below the earth ramparts. The colonel was lending a hand himself, stripped to the waist, sweat-shining skin rippling as he heaved an eighty-pound block into position. She caught Swindapa's frank look of appreciation and mock-scowled.

"*Just* looking," the Fiernan said. "I look at girls, too."

"As long as it's strictly a visual relationship," Alston chuckled. She added, "He's setting a good example for his troops."

Alston's expression softened into a smile as they came to the circle of children sitting under a tall, slender tree with a silvery-gray trunk— a tambalacoque. Doreen Arnstein was taking the class, pointing alternately to a live dodo in a wicker cage and a diagram on the portable blackboard. There were around three dozen youngsters, mostly children of the technicians attached to the expeditionary force. This was a long-term project, and you couldn't expect people to leave their children behind for an indefinite stay.

They waited for a moment while the assistant councilor for foreign affairs finished her rundown on evolutionary biology and younger children continued practicing the alphabet on their slates. *Nantucket's still small enough to be informal,* Alston thought. *I like that.* It was also small enough that Martha Cofflin had managed to thoroughly revamp the curriculum, and as a parent she liked that even better—they saw eye to eye on phonics and drill, and even Lisa Gerrard had come around on most of it.

Gerrard's not a bad *councilor,* Alston thought. *Just a bit stubborn.* She'd even shed most of her prejudices. *After nearly nine years of working with a real, live, breathing, capital-L Lesbian.*

The class broke up. Heather and Lucy came running, and Alston crouched, grabbed the redhead under her arms and swung her up.

"Do Jesus, either you're getting heavy or I'm getting older!" she said.

"Hey, Mom, did you know these gonzo birds could *fly* once but they got too lazy?" Heather said.

"No, it was their 'cestors who could fly," Lucy said from Swindapa's shoulders. "That's why you get sunburnt and I don't. 'cause of your 'cestors. It's evolutionary adoption."

"That's adaptation," Swindapa corrected.

"Like I said, Mom."

Heather stuck out her tongue at her sister, and Alston felt her heart turn over inside her. *Nice to know what you're fighting for.*

CHAPTER EIGHT

February, Year 9 A.E.

"The King comes! Eat dirt before *shar kibrat 'arbaim,* the King of the Four Quarters of the Earth! King of Sumer and Akkad, King of Kar-Duniash, King of Babylon, Ensi of Marduk. . . ."

The great audience hall of Ur was tense, dense-packed with robed clerks, priests in old-style wraps that left one shoulder bare, and soldiers with their beards freshly oiled and curled. The hot still air smelled of that perfumed oil, sweat, and fear. Light from the small, high windows stabbed into the gloom hot and bright, breaking off the colors of tapestries and murals that showed the king's ancestors at war, at the hunt, making sacrifice to the gods. Save for the ever-watchful royal guard, all went down on their bellies as the king entered.

"Shagarakti-Shuriash, son of Kudur-Enlil, son of Kadashman-Enlil, descendant of the kings who were before the kings, unto whom the Gods have given rule! *La sanan, sa mahira la isu!* The king who has no rival! O King, live forever!"

Shagarakti-Shuriash seated himself and made a sign. The crowd rose, standing with folded hands and downcast eyes, as was seemly.

"Let the king's servant Kidin-Ninurta approach! Let the king's servant Arad-Samas approach!"

Kidin-Ninurta cast a single burning glance at his rival as they prostrated themselves before the throne. When they rose, he found himself under the king's gaze.

Shagarakti-Shuriash was a man in his early middle years, with gray in his curled beard; he was perhaps a little lighter of skin and more hawkish of feature than his average subject, legacy of the Kassite hillmen and Mitannian princesses among his ancestors. His body was stocky and thick with muscle, beginning to grow at the waist but at ease in the gorgeous embroidered linen of his robe. Gray-streaked black hair was clubbed at the base of his head with gold wire and confined around his brows with a circlet of gold shaped like a city wall.

"I have come a long way from Babylon," he said. *This had better be worth my time,* came unspoken afterward.

The brown eyes were hard and weary; he had been on the throne for only three years in his own right, but much of the toil of kingship had been his during the long reigns of his father and grandfather, campaigning in the north and east.

"Let the king's overseer of trade with Dilmun and Meluhha speak."

"O King, my lord, your servant Kidin-Ninurta prays that the gods grant you long life and health! Your servant has met with the strangers from the south. Your servant has spoken with the strangers from the south. They approach from the south, in great ships; from the lands of Dilmun and Meluhha they approach. From the days of the kings your fathers all such affairs have been the province of my office; so decreed the kings who were before the king."

Arad-Samas was swelling like a frog with the need to speak. When the king granted permission, he burst out:

"O King, my lord, may the gods, the great gods, the mighty gods make your days many in the land! From the time of the kings your fathers, diplomatic correspondence has gone through *my* office. Letters with the kings your brothers of Assyria, of Hatti-land, of Egypt, of Elam, have passed through my office. It is my task for the king to—"

"The strangers appear from the south, in the direction of Dilmun and Meluhha! Precedent—"

"They are not of Dilmun! The are not of Meluhha! My office—"

"Silence!"

The bureaucrats bent their heads and folded hands; the king made a quick quirk of the hand toward his personal secretary. There was a swift juggling of tablets, and the man read:

"From the king's servant Arad-Samas to the king's servant Kidin-Ninurta; health, prosperity, life. You write once more of rumors of foreigners in great ships at Dilmun. What is this to me? The Assyrians have broken the Mitanni and prowl the northern borders like wolves about a sheep pen; Egypt and Hatti-land have made a peace and speak not of Asshur's deeds. The Elamites are hungrier than the jackal and more cunning than the serpent. I have greater concerns than the ships of merchants in the Southern Sea."

Kidin-Ninurta smiled within himself and bowed his head. *There are some things that should not be written down on the clay.* His father had taught him that. It made it so difficult to switch positions later. He thought fondly of the ingot of pure silver that rested in the strong room of his house, the gift of the strangers. The strangers who had come to the Land and shown that they *were* of consequence, as he had said and Arad-Samas had denied in writing . . .

"Let Kidin-Ninurta speak," the king went on. "Let others withdraw."

Amid considerable rustling and clanking, most of the crowd filed out the exits; except for the guard, of course, and some of the king's advisers and wisemen, and the king's heir from the House of Succession, his son Kashtiliash.

"O King, your servant speaks. For five years merchants returning from Dilmun have spoken of strange ships."

"How, strange?"

"Huge, O King. Larger than any ship seen before, and laden with goods so fine that they might have been made by magic and the arts of demons. I thought these tales to be wild—does not every sailor returning from Dilmun speak of wonders? Yet the tales are true; the truth is wilder than the tales!"

Shuriash nodded thoughtfully. He had seen some of those goods. Glass clearer than water, or in colors impossibly vivid; small mirrors better than burnished bronze or silver; most of all, knives and tools of the northern metal, *iron*. Better iron than any he had ever been able to get from his "brother" Tudhaliya in Hattusas; a knife of it was at his waist now, with the plain bone hilt replaced with gold wire. Small things, but beyond price.

"These foreigners—do they speak our tongue?" Working through interpreters was always an annoyance.

"A few speak it. Also, they have one of the king's subjects with them, whom they have trained as an interpreter; a merchant, Shamash-nasir-kudduru by name, of Ur. They desire an audience with the king's person."

The king stroked his beard. "They speak of trade?" Trade was a good field for a king to till.

"They speak of trade, and of alliance; they bring the word of their king Yhared-Koff'in." The bureaucrat sounded out the uncouth foreign syllables with care. "And they send gifts, that the heart of the king my lord may be made glad."

Shuriash's eyebrows rose. He clapped his hands together. "Let the gifts be brought forth. Let us see if these foreigners do my house honor; let us see if they are worthy of speech with the king's person."

Kidin-Ninurta bowed, smiling behind a grave face. "The gifts await the attention of the king my lord," he said. "At the *karum* of Ur they wait; by the waterside they are readied for his view."

Shuriash snorted. "Can they not be brought here?"

The bureaucrat bowed low. "O King, they are too many."

Shuriash's brows rose again. "This the king will see."

Like something out of Kipling, Ian Arnstein thought. *Well, some sort of mutant version of ol' Rudyard.*

The honor guard of Marines from the expeditionary force were in warm-season uniform—khaki shorts and shirts, floppy canvas hats, and cotton-drill webbing harness. The flared helmets were strapped to their packs, bayonets and bowies at their waists, flintlock rifles by their sides as they stood at parade rest. Their officers were in breastplate and helmet, *katanas* sloped back over their shoulders, sweating in the damp heat of Ur's riverside.

Karum, Ian reminded himself, which meant not only dockside but the association of merchants. *Sometimes I think my head is going to explode with all the things I have to remember.*

A huge, chattering crowd was held at bay by royal guardsmen, their spears jabbing a little occasionally to remind the common folk to keep their distance. The people looked much like twentieth-century Iraqis. Shorter, of course—nearly everyone was, in this century—dark of hair and eye, skin a natural olive that turned a deep bronze when exposed to this pitiless sun. The men wore kilts, or knee-length tunics, or longer robes; hats were shaped like flowerpots, sometimes spangled with bright metals. Here and there a near-naked laborer in a loincloth crouched, mouth open in awe; women were less numerous and dressed in long gowns and head-covering shawls, a few veiled. The crowd was dun-colored, mostly the soft natural browns and grays of undyed wool. Noblemen or rich merchants stood out in gorgeous relief, white and blue and purple and saffron-gold, often with attendants holding parasols over their heads.

Beyond them rose the walls of Ur—*but not Ur of the Chaldees,* Ian thought. It was half a millennium before the people the Bible called Chaldeans were to enter this land. *They call themselves Men of Ur, here, or Men of Kar-Duniash, or just Akkadians—*

Once this had been a Sumerian city, but that was a thousand years or more ago. The city walls were sixty feet high, surfaced in reddishgray fired brick, a brooding, looming presence. Bronze gleamed on the towers that studded the wall every fifty yards or so, or reared on either side of the city gates, but brighter still was the ziggurat that soared above those walls, nearly three hundred feet of step-pyramid into heaven. *That* was not dun-colored; it glittered, it blazed under the fierce Mesopotamian sun, it reared itself in a skin of paint and colored brick like some fantastic serpent.

"Impressive," Doreen said. "Even more impressive if it didn't smell so bad."

Ian Arnstein wrenched his mind away from a historian's dream made flesh and nodded. The sewer reek was already pretty strong; Ghu alone knew what it would be like in high summer. He looked back at the gates. Those massive bronze leaves were swinging open, with a squeal of hinges and a thunder of trumpets—ram's horn and brass—a pounding of kettledrums and a clash of cymbals. The royal party came in style, riding in chariots amid a blaze of spearheads, behind high-stepping horses that looked like miniature Arabians. The king's chariot was positively encrusted with precious metals and lapis lazuli, and the scales of his corselet were gilded; a crown of gold encircled his helmet. The crowd parted in a wave, kneeling and then going to their bellies in the dust.

I feel like a complete mountebank, Ian thought, stepping forward gravely.

In a way he welcomed the hideous embarrassment; it distracted him from the awareness that he was actually *here*, about to talk with a man whom the history he'd learned recorded as dead three thousand years and more. He'd gotten over that feeling in the other places the Islanders touched, but this was the ancient world he'd spent all his adult life studying. This city had been inhabited since men first learned to write on clay tablets.

Concentrate on not tripping on this goddam dress, you fool, he told himself.

He was wearing what their research and local informants had concluded would be impressive to Babylonian sensibilities—an ankle-length caftan of crimson silk embroidered in gold and silver thread and a hat plumed with bird-of-paradise feathers; in his left hand he carried a staff of ivory and ebony, topped by a golden eagle. Doreen was only a degree less gorgeous; even her clip-board was of rare honey-colored wood from the forests in the kloofs of Table Mountain.

As the King of Kar-Duniash dismounted from his chariot, Ian made a sign with his hand.

" 'Ten-*hut*!" Colonel Hollard's voice rang out. "Shoulder . . . *arms*! Present . . . *arms*!"

The Marine platoon snapped their heels together, and the rifles came up with a single snap and slap of hands on wood and metal. The officers' swords swept down, then up into a salute, with the hilt before the lips. Some of the king's guards bristled at the sudden movement, but Shuriash checked only a half a pace and came on with a regal nod. The handsome, hard-faced young man beside him clapped a wary hand to the hilt of his sword, then relaxed at a murmured word from his father.

"Greetings, O King," Ian said, halting and bowing from the waist.

Hard, cold brown eyes flicked from him to Doreen, to the great ships at anchor in the river with the sun blazing on their gilt eagle figureheads, to Shamash-nasir-kudduru flat on his belly and kissing the dirt at the king's feet.

"You do not make your obeisance to the king's person?" he asked. The voice was hard, and the guttural Akkadian tongue sounded menacing at the best of times.

But he's keeping it slow, Ian realized with relief.

"O King, live long and prosper," he said solemnly, holding up his right hand with the fingers spread in a V. *I always* wanted *to say that,* he thought, then there was a sharp pain in his ankle as Doreen kicked him; she hadn't believed he would actually go through with it.

"It is against our custom and the law of our god to bend the knee to any man," he went on with slow care. Shams had said his Akkadian was accented but understandable . . . but then, Shams had a disconcerting tendency to say what he thought would please.

Shuriash nodded, showing that he understood. Ian sighed relief and continued, "I greet you as I would my own ruler, Jared Cofflin." He *had* tried it out on the Chief, who'd almost ruptured himself laughing. "I bring the word of my ruler to the Great King, the King of Sumer and Akkad, the King of Kar-Duniash, of whose might and glory we have long heard."

Heard for several thousand years, but let's not go there yet

He fought down giddiness. The man looking at him was absolute ruler of several million souls—probably about as large a share of the world's population as the United States had had in the twentieth century—and unless first impressions lied he was no fool at all. You could get yourself into very serious trouble very quickly by underestimating the locals.

"Very well," Shuriash said. "I am glad to hear the word of my brother, Yhared-Koff'in. Does he send the son of his mother, the child of his wife, to greet me?"

Ian bowed again; by calling the Republic's ruler "brother" the Babylonian monarch was making a considerable diplomatic concession, granting him equality with the other great kings of the ancient East. Besides the Babylonians, only the Hittites, Assyrians, and Egyptians rated it.

"I have the honor to be Jared Cofflin's councilor for foreign affairs," Ian said. "It grieves me to report that our ruler's sons are not yet of a man's age." *And we'll leave the matter of elective government for a later date.* "I bear his instructions; I speak with his voice." *Oh, and I'm in contact with him by shortwave radio.*

Shuriash grunted; ambassadors were common here. "And I am glad to receive his gifts," he went on, glancing pointedly at the tarpaulin-covered heaps. "I do not doubt that they will make my heart glad."

Ian made an imperious gesture with his staff, and the Marines tasked to the job began to uncover the treasures; at another gesture the interpreter rose and followed them.

Shuriash did an excellent job of keeping his face impassive, taking only one step backward and registering a slight start at the man-high mirror that was revealed first. But a grin of unself-conscious pleasure showed strong yellowed teeth as he examined the weapons that lay on the table beyond; a suit of silvered chain mail, an elaborately worked helmet with a tall quetzal plume, a steel long sword in a sheath of inlaid leather, with a hilt of ivory and a gold pommel set with gems.

He slid the sword free and tested the heft and balance with practiced ease; the sun broke blinding-bright off the honed edge, and he gave a hiss of respect as he pressed it with a thumb.

"These stones shine brightly," he said, turning the weapon to catch the sunlight on its pommel. "How?"

"We call it *faceting*," Ian said; local jewelers merely polished their gems. Doreen nudged him slightly; the Crown Prince Kashtiliash was even more delighted with the silver-hilted long sword the Island's artisans had made for *him*.

"Behold," Ian said, moving on. "Spices from the far eastern lands for the king's table." Nutmeg and cinnamon were known here, but rare and unbelievably expensive. "Silver and gold for the king's treasury."

Shuriash picked up a gold coin the size of a dime and squinted at it, holding it at arm's length.

"Hard to make such a thing, much less hundreds," he said. "Why not ingots?"

"We call them *coins,* O King," Ian said. "Each is of a standard weight and fineness, guaranteed by the inscription stamped upon them. Trade is eased by these coins, commerce is made more swift by them."

A small exclamation escaped the lips of a plump official in the king's train.

"Bahdi-Lim, my *wakil* of the *karum*," Shuriash said. "He tracks a scent of profit more eagerly than a lion upon the trail of an antelope."

Minister of commerce, Ian thought, bowing slightly.

"Copper and tin, for the king's artisans."

The king's eyes lit up, imagining spearheads and arrowshead and swords. "My brother Yhared-Koff'in is generous!"

"Jewelery, for the king's wives and daughters," Ian said. "Ivory and rare woods, that the king may adorn his palace and the houses of the gods his patrons."

This time the murmur reached as far as the crowd surrounding the landing spot. The crisscross stack of ebony logs was taller than a man, and surrounded by threescore ivory tusks, all of them far larger than the Middle Eastern elephant could produce.

"Strange beasts, to make merry the heart of the king!" Ian concluded, with a sweep of his arm.

Shuriash burst into delighted laughter, and for a moment his face was a child's. One of the cages held a chimp; another a baby giraffe; and the third a moa, staring around with blinking wonderment.

"The king's heart is made glad by the gifts of his brother; his heart is full of happiness to see them." Shuriash's voice changed in the middle of the double-barreled formal sentence, suddenly didn't seem quite as delighted as his words.

"Remember, he has to return the favor, or lose face," Doreen whispered in Ian's ear. Kings here didn't do anything so déclassé as trading; instead they exchanged royal gifts that just happened to be of roughly equivalent value.

Meanwhile Shuriash was considering the honor guard. "Your kingdom is not poor," he said meditatively. "Nor are your craftsmen lacking in skill. I am surprised that you cannot afford armor for all your troops." His gaze sharpened. "Are those eunuchs?"

"No, O King. Know that some among us shave their chins, even as some of your priests shave their heads."

"Curious."

"In all lands custom is king," Ian said tactfully. "In every land the customs differ."

"And are those *women*?" Kashtiliash blurted in amazement. Even with cropped hair, the light summer uniforms made that fairly obvious, once a local started *looking*.

"Yes, O son of Shagarakti-Shuriash," Ian said, bowing again. "Such is our custom."

The prince snorted; he kept silent under his father's eye, but he fierce young hawk-features showed what he thought of *that* custom.

Shuriash went on: "And I see they bear fine blades, but no spear nor shield, neither bow nor javelin nor sling. Only those curious maces of wood and metal."

Ian smiled. "Would the king my lord wish a demonstration? I will call the officer who commands the troops my ruler Jared Cofflin has sent to guard this expedition; the officer will satisfy the king's mind. We call these weapons *rifles;* they are like a bow, like a sling, yet not like a bow or sling."

The king nodded eagerly; so did Prince Kashtiliash, and a number among the officers who followed behind. Colonel Hollard strode over and stopped before the Babylonian monarch, bowing his head and saluting.

"O King, may you live forever," he said. His Akkadian was nearly as good as Ian's, with perhaps a trifle less of an accent. "Does the king have an animal that may be killed?"

Shuriash nodded, intrigued. A moment's relaying of orders, and a donkey was led out and tethered to a stake a hundred yards downstream. Hollard pointed to a guardsman's shield, and took it when

Shuriash nodded agreement. He hung it carefully from the donkey's harness so that it covered most of the little beast's side.

"First section, front and center at the double!" he snapped when he returned.

Eight Marines trotted up and stopped in unison; Ian could see Shuriash's eyes following that, as well. Close-order drill and standing to attention hadn't been invented here yet; the king's guards were alert, but there was little formality to their postures.

"Oshinsky, kill that donkey," the Republic's commander said. "And *don't* miss."

"Sir, yessir," the Marine replied. She was a brown-haired young woman, a native Islander with corporal's chevrons and a Sniper star.

"There will be a loud noise," the Islander commander said in Akkadian.

She went to one knee and thumbed back the hammer of her Westley-Richards. Ian could see her squinting thoughtfully as she brought the rifle to her shoulder, exhaled, squeezed . . .

Crack.

Forewarned, the king and his son only blinked. A few of his courtiers made covert signs with their fingers, or clenched small idols that hung from their belts. The grizzle-bearded officers clenched their hands as well, on the hilts of their swords, and screams came from the watching crowd. The sulfur-stinking cloud hid the donkey from Ian for a moment; he felt a wordless prayer drifting up with it, to an atheist's God. The problem was that he knew that particular deity delighted in the perverse; otherwise he wouldn't be here in the thirteenth century B.C.

Th donkey gave an agonized bray, and seconds later it collapsed, going to its knees and then falling over sideways to kick a few times.

"By the brazen prick of Marduk," Shuriash said quietly, when a terrified guardsman ran back with the shield.

The men behind him were gabbling prayers under their breath, clutching at amulets; a shaven-headed priest extended his toward the strangers, chanting an incantation. The king held the shield up and then wiggled a finger through the hole the .40-caliber bullet had made through sheet bronze, tough bull hide and layered strips of poplar wood.

"You can throw thunderbolts?" he went on. His face was set, but sweat gleamed on it. "You must be a nation of mighty sorcerers."

Ian nodded to Hollard. "O great King, the earth lies at your feet," the young colonel said soothingly. "Not a thunderbolt. Lead shot, like a sling."

He took Oshinsky's rifle and raised the lever. "See, O King, here is the shot." He held up a bullet in his other hand. "Behind it is a powder that burns very fast. That creates a—" Hollard hesitated; there was no word for "gas" in Akkadian—"a hot swift wind that pushes the lead shot out of the iron tube, too swiftly for the eye to see."

"Like a sling bullet," Shuriash said. "Only too swift to see. It can pierce armor? How far?"

"A thousand long paces, O king. Shall I demonstrate?"

The king nodded, a tightly controlled gesture. *This is a brave man,* Ian thought. Several of the courtiers were still trembling; it spoke volumes of their fear of their monarch that none had run. Many of the crowd had, streaming back toward the city to spread Ghu-knew-what rumors.

Hollard pointed southward along the riverbank. The Islanders had planted stakes there, at fifty-yard intervals. Atop each was a local clay pot.

"Those are full of water," Hollard said. "But the *bullets* would strike through any armor a man could carry, and send his spirit to the realm of Nergal." He switched to English: "Squad, independent fire. Make it count."

Corporal Oshinsky snapped: "You heard the colonel. Llaundaur, you first, then to the right."

The Sun People trooper licked his thumb, wet the foresight of his weapon, and brought it up to his shoulder in a smooth movement that ended with another *crack;* the nearest clay jar shattered in a spectacular leaping jet of water. Colonel Hollard took out his binoculars and showed Shuriash how to adjust them; by the time the last pot broke, the king was looking more at them than at the firearms. Ian could see wheels spinning in the Babylonian's mind and gave himself a mental kick.

Hollard rescued the situation. "Let these tubes of far-seeing—these *binoculars*—be my humble gift to the king's majesty," he said.

"Out! Out!" King Shuriash bellowed.

The priests bent over the sheep's liver, the *baru*-diviners, the *mahhu*-priests who foretold in frenzies of madness, backed out of the council room where the king of Kar-Duniash had met with the ambassadors, taking with them the smell of blood and incense. Their lord resumed his pacing.

"Fools, dolts, wit-rotted tablet-chewers!" he roared, with a lion's guttural menace in his voice. "They can interpret comets and tell me to wear the same shirt for a month, but I ask them a question—I ask for an answer—it should be there in the liver of the sheep, and I receive nothing. Nothing of use!"

His son nodded. Sincerely, he thought. The generals and bureaucrats nodded agreement with their lord, too. With them, who knew what their real thoughts were? Over the years he had come to suspect that the priests, too, shaded their omens according to what he wished to hear, as well; or worse, according to how their temples wished to bend his policy.

" 'Great opportunity, but great danger,' " Shuriash quoted. "*I* could have told them that and saved the waste of a good sheep."

"The priests will eat the sheep," Kashtiliash pointed out.

"As I said, wasted," Shuriash replied.

There were smiles and a few shocked looks at the delicious blasphemy; only his son dared to laugh aloud.

"There are two questions here, O King," Kidin-Ninurta said. "First, what can the *Nan-tu'kht-ar* do for us? And second, what do they wish? What will be the price of their aid?"

The king nodded. "We know they are rich," he said.

Emphatic nods; the gifts they'd given the king amounted to about a year's taxes from Ur and its district.

"We know they are powerful, with their fire-weapons." Even more emphatic agreement; the *rifles* were bad enough, but the strangers had also demonstrated what their *cannon* could do.

"O King, they are more powerful than that," Kidin-Ninurta said thoughtfully. "Consider their ships. Consider *those*." He pointed to the binoculars on the table. "Consider the arts they must have to *make* all these things."

"O King my father," Kashtiliash said. "Consider also the most excellent order of their warriors. In their every movement they anticipate commands; like the fingers of a man's hand, they obey." He paused. "Consider also that each one was equipped and dressed exactly like the others—even to the shade of the cloth they wore."

Shuriash felt his heart glow with pride. *I have bred me a lion that can think as well as fight,* he thought. It was a good thought. The Nan-tu'kht-ar soldiers were like the marks of a cylinder-seal rolled many times on wet clay. The implications of that were . . . interesting.

"This Yhared-Koff'in must be a ruler of great power; his people must fear him more than the demons," Shuriash said. "They must obey as if he were a god among them."

"Women," Kashtiliash said thoughtfully. "All other things to one side, how can they be useful as warriors when half the time their bellies bulge with children? And if they can stop soldiers from fornicating, they are not sorcerers, but rather gods."

"Prince of the House of Succession," Kidin-Ninurta said. "Of that I asked the merchant Shamash-nasir-kudduru; for a brief time I was able to speak with him. The Nan-tu'kht-ar have a way of preventing conception. One that actually works without fail."

"Strange, even so," the prince said, tugging at his beard and disar-

ranging the careful curls that hot bronze rods and oil had put in it.
"How can a people grow strong if their women do not bear many
children?"

"That also I asked, O my lord; diligently I inquired. Their medicines ensure that few children die—less than one in ten, if what the
merchant said can be believed. They can bind Lamashtu, the de-
moness of cradle fever!"

That brought more exclamations, some skeptical, some wondering.
"This merchant," Shuriash said. "He knows their language; he knows
their ways. Such a man would be very valuable to us."

Kidin-Ninurta spread his hands. "O King, your servant thought of
this. But the Nan-tu'kht-ar guard him like a lioness with a single cub."

"Yet this Shamash-nasir-kudduru does not wish to dwell among
them all his days?" Kashtiliash murmured.

"No, Prince of the House of Succession. That is not his wish; it is
not the yearning of his liver. He wishes to dwell in the land of Kar-
Duniash as a great man, as a man of wealth and power."

"For which he needs the favor of the king, as well as the silver of the
Nan-tu'kut-ar," Shuriash said. "Something might be made of that."

He paused and leaned two palms on the table, looking at the strange
maps the Nan-tu'kut-ar had given him on their even stranger papyrus. His own scribes made maps, but this was fantastically detailed, and with the round glass on a metal holder—the *magnifying
glass*—he could read the small legends printed out in Akkadian writing. *What a tool of power!* he thought, looking at his land laid out as a
god might see it . . . and the neighboring lands as well. It wasn't perfect; the Euphrates was shown too far to the west. But that could be
corrected, they said.

His son went on: "With all their strengths, why do the Nantukhtar
come here to speak of treaties, of agreements? Why do they not
break down the walls of the cities, seize the wealth of the land for
themselves?"

"Ah, my lord prince," Kidin-Ninurta said. "I have thought on this;
I have pondered it. I think that the Nantukhtar are few in numbers,
very few. From what Shamash-nasir-kudduru let fall, their city of
Nantukhtar is smaller than Ur, far smaller than Kar-Duniash—rich
and strong but not large. Thither to that city and its lands they bring
many of their subject-allies every year to bolster their own strength, to
work and farm and fight."

"Perhaps that is why they use their women for many tasks,"
Kashtiliash said slowly. "Perhaps they have too few men."

"Perhaps we build a great ziggurat from a single brick," Shuriash
said dryly. "Also we circle the heart of the matter like vultures around
a dying donkey. These Nantukhtar have great powers, yes, but can

they foretell the future so much better than our students of the stars, of birds, of entrails?"

A long silence fell. "I pray to Marduk and Ishtar, to Shamash and Sin, the great gods of the land, that it is not so," Kashtiliash said. "What they said lies in our future . . ." He shuddered.

Shuriash nodded again, and his thick fingers traced over the surface of the map. He had read from the Assyrian chronicle the strangers had brought. It had made grisly hearing:

> *I forced Kashtiliash, King of Kar-Duniash, to give battle; I brought about the defeat of his armies, his warriors I over-threw. In the midst of that battle my hand captured Kashtiliash, the Kassite king. His royal neck I trod on with my feet, like a galtappu stool. Stripped and bound, before Ashur my lord I brought him. Sumer and Akkad to its farthest border I brought under my sway.*

"And the Elamites at the walls of Nippur," Shuriash said.

"Surely it is not possible!" Kashtiliash burst out.

"Long ago the Elamites burned Uruk, when Uruk was as Babylon is now," Shuriash said. "My son, you are a great warrior and a crafty leader, but I fear it is all too possible."

He could see the younger man contemplating it, as if an abyss had opened before his feet. When he spoke, his voice was slow and thoughtful. "In the time of your father Shalmaneser of Assyria broke King Shattuara and the last remnant of Mitanni, of Hangilibat, of Hurri-land. That frees his son Tukulti-Ninurta to turn all his power southward."

Shuriash sighed. "So, son of my loins, son of my heart, you see that Kar-Duniash is between the hammer and the anvil. Against Assyria, we are strong; against Elam, we are strong. Against both together . . . and *that* is why I believe the Nantukhtar. What they say of the years to come agrees all too well with my fears, with fears that have haunted my nights."

Kashtiliash had hunted lions and armed men with a smile on his lips; now he turned gray beneath his olive tan. Shuriash knew he was seeing the vision of himself brought bound and leashed like a dog before the altar of Ashur. Or of watching an Assyrian victory feast as a severed head hanging from a pomegranate tree in the gardens of Tukulti-Ninurta's palace—Assyrians were given to gestures like that. But fell fighters and grim, and their rulers crafty and war-wise.

"The Nantukhtar are too strange for my liver to feel easy at relying upon them. We might ally with the Hittites instead, or as well," the prince said. "They know Asshur's eye lies hungrily on their holdings west of the Euphrates."

"We might, if they did not have this new foe on their far western border, the Ekwesh," Shuriash said. "Now this rebel against the Nantukhtar king has risen to power there; he teaches the wild Ekwesh their arts; he gives them the secret of these fire weapons."

"So we will make alliance with the Nantukhtar, father and lord?"

"We will make alliance." His fingers traced the map again. "And then, once *our* enemies have been beaten, we will war against theirs—this rebel, the Ekwesh—if we can persuade the Hittites to it.

"It comes to me—perhaps a god whispers it in my ear—that the strangers bring a new age with them, one in which those who learn their arts will prosper and those who do not will be ground like grain between millstones and blown about by the wind."

His seamed face split in a broad smile.

"And Kar-Duniash," he went on, "is perfectly placed to benefit by this new age. Kashtiliash, my son, my heir, for all my life I have fought so that when my time comes to descend to the underworld I might leave to you a realm as strong and rich as that I inherited from my fathers. Now I see a chance to leave you a realm *greater* than I inherited; perhaps as great as Hammurabi's, greater than that of Gilgamesh. The Nantukhtar will need interpreters . . . as part of our alliance, I will suggest to them that a hundred young scribes be set to learning their language and their writing; and those young men will learn much of their arts. That for a beginning."

He raised his wine cup. "To the Nantukhtar! With them to pull our chariot, we shall spurn the four quarters of the earth beneath the wheels!"

". . . and it's the perfect location as far as controlling technology transfer goes," Ian said—a little smugly, Marian Alston thought.

The command group of the expeditionary force was gathered in the cabin of the *Chamberlain* for a last conference before the fleet left for home, and Ian was highly pleased with the way things had gone so far. So was she, but a contrarian impulse inclined her to look for the shadow side.

"How so, Ian?" Swindapa asked. "My birth-people in Alba started with less than these Akkadians, and they have learned a great deal of Eagle people lore already."

"Yes," Ian chuckled, rubbing his hands together, "but apart from the fact that we've encouraged that, *they* have iron ore, copper, tin, wood and coal for fuel. These Babylonians have nothing but water and mud."

"And petroleum," Alston pointed out. "Which we have to show them how to use, if we're going to get any benefit out of it."

"True," Ian said. "But they still can't do much in the way of metallurgy without ores or fuels."

"Probably can't," Doreen corrected. "We'll see."

"Expect the unexpected," Alston agreed.

Kenneth Hollard poured more beer from the jug into his tankard, then made a face as he tasted it. "Mebbe we can teach them to make something better than this gruel," he said.

"It's safer than the water," the chief medical officer of the expeditionary force said; Justin Clemens shook his head. "God, this place is a living farm of diseases."

"Whatever we do, we have to do it fairly quickly," Alston said. "I can't keep so many of the Republic's keels and cannon here on the other side of the world for long. Too much could go wrong back home."

"I'm a diplomat, not a—" Ian said, then hesitated. "Hey, it just hit me—I *am* a diplomat now, not a history professor playing at diplomacy."

"Well, duh," Doreen said affectionately, poking him in the ribs. "It's only been going on a decade now."

Ian cleared his throat. "I'm a diplomat, not a magician. We'll have to see."

"Don't underestimate King Shuriash," Kenneth Hollard said. "He's one smart cookie, if I'm any judge."

"I agree," his sister, Kathryn, said. "So's his son." She grinned. "And Prince Kashtiliash is cute as a bug's ear, too."

"I suppose so," Hollard said dryly. "He doesn't do a thing for me."

"That's because you're narrow-minded, Colonel, *sir*," she replied, to a general chuckle.

"Doesn't do much for me, either," Alston said.

"That's because *you're* narrow-minded, darling," Swindapa said. At Alston's mock glower she went on: "Well, I promised to be monogamous, not *blind*."

"I," Doreen Arnstein said, laying a hand at the base of her throat and looking upward, "will say *nothing at all*."

CHAPTER NINE

March, Year 9 A.E.

"Ayup," Jared Cofflin said into the microphone, looking down at the text of the treaty. *Christ, a treaty with Babylon.* "Those *are* good terms. Ian must have them buffaloed."

"Not exactly," Marian Alston's voice said, a little scratchy with distance. "I think they were gettin' worried about their strategic situation all on their ownsome—it's as bad as we thought from the histories, maybe worse. And this king of theirs, Shagarakti-Shuriash, he's one sharp man; Ian thinks so too. We'll have to watch him, of course."

"Of course."

Cofflin leafed through the terms again; trade, of course—a couple of the new merchant houses were already chomping at the bit—and alliance, first against Babylonia's enemies, then against Walker. That was excellent, *provided* they could get the Hittites in later. He read on. *Hmmmm.* An Islander base near Ur, under the Republic's sovereignty; joint courts for any civil or criminal case involving Islanders in the kingdom of Kar-Duniash.

"Good work, the lot of you," he muttered. Damned if he was going to leave any citizen, under any circumstances whatsoever, to what passed for ancient Babylonian justice.

"Let's see . . ." Right of passage up the Tigris and Euphrates for Islander transport, an embassy in Babylon itself, technical aid, mineral concessions . . .

"Crackerjack job, Marian," he said. "I'm not going to have any trouble getting *this* past the Town Meeting, I can tell you. It reads pretty much like our wish list. We'll post it right away."

"Ian's doing; I stayed in the background." A chuckle. "The locals are having to put up with enough culture shock as it is. Now, if we can just get past the Tartessians next year or the year after, it'll be Walker who's caught between two fires."

"Big if."

"Very big. We've finished disembarking and unloading and shipped our return cargoes, so we'll sail tomorrow—take a day or two to get

through those damned reed-swamps, and then it's 'all plain sail.'
Thank God the ships could get this far upstream. See you in two
months or so."

"Ayup. Give our love to 'dapa and the kids."

"Same to you and Martha and the tribe," Alston said. "Over."

"And out."

Cofflin sighed again and tossed the treaty into his Out tray; the
shortwave set stood on a side cabinet. It was a cold, wet, early-March
day outside. Branches were still bare; he could see a rider going past,
a blurred vision of a head bowed under a rain slicker and the pony's
drooping dejection. He half envied the expeditionary force, off in the
warm lands, and the hardwood fire crackling in the fireplace was
more than welcome. His hands hurt a little, the way they'd taken to
doing in weather like this.

"Linda!" he called aloud. His secretary came in, and he indicated
the treaty with a lift of his chin.

"Get this down to the Bookworks, would you, have them set it and
print up, oh, three hundred copies for the Athenaeum to distribute—
and tell 'em it's going in the next Warrant as well. Thanks."

"Sure, Chief," she said, leafing though it avidly; her younger sister
was with the expeditionary force, he remembered. "I'll run it right
over." She hurried out; he could hear a clatter as she grabbed an umbrella from the stand by the front door.

Printing that many would take a while with a handpress; it would
also put it on the agenda for the next Meeting. There were times when
direct democracy drove him crazy, but it had one great merit—when a
decision was finally made, *everyone* felt they'd had their say. In a way
he'd be sorry when the population got big enough for the House of
Delegates provision in the new constitution to kick in—that would be
soon, too, the way things were going.

"Next," he muttered, and looked at his In box.

A proposal to license and inspect day-care centers . . . *ask Martha.*
Leaton wanted to import a trial run of coal from Alba for the forge-
works . . . *ask him whether it's really necessary.* A proposal to establish a new Base down around the site of Buenos Aires.

Hmmm. That's a tough one. It was a *long* way away, and they were
already spread out thinner than he liked. On t'other hand, that was the
edge of one of the biggest areas of good farmland on the planet; also,
the preliminary survey said the locals were *very* thin on the pampas,
even by the standards of the 1242 B.C. Americas, which meant an Islander settlement wouldn't be too disruptive. In the very long run, it
would mean a big chunk of the world modeled on the Republic's ideals.

Put it in the discuss-with-the-Council file, he decided after a
moment.

And it looked like Peter Girenas was going to get enough votes before the Meeting to finance his expedition. He scanned down the list of names on the petition form, stopped, and began to laugh. After a moment Martha stuck her head in the office door.

"Something funny, dear?" she said, arching an expressive eyebrow.

"Mebbe, or mebbe I'm laughing so I won't curse. Take a look at who's backing young Girenas and Company's petition for a grant."

She came over to his desk. "The usual suspects . . . *Emma Carson?*"

"*And* all her friends." He shook his head. "I guess she thinks his chances of coming out of it alive are even worse than I do . . . and Emma never did forget an injury."

"Plus, she thinks with him out of the way, the Rangers might not be so hard on her," Martha said thoughtfully.

"Not if we have anything to do with it," he replied.

On impulse, he pulled his wife down into his lap. She gave a small snort and arched that eyebrow again, but put an arm around his shoulders and kissed him.

"Am I correct in assuming you want to quit work early?" she said, stirring strategically.

"Ayup," he grinned. "Why not? We do have a treaty to celebrate."

The door of the Wild Rose Chance opened, letting in a blast of cold air and a few drops of stinging March rain. Peter Girenas looked up and waved his friends over. They came, after they'd wiped their boots and hung their rain slickers on pegs driven into the wall to drip into the trough beneath. Several paused sheepishly when one of the waitresses pointed to a sign stating: NO WEAPONS ALLOWED and handed her their rifles or crossbows to be racked behind the bar.

Eddie Vergeraxsson was the first to reach him. He was a chief's son from Alba who'd been brought over as a hostage after the Alban War and decided he liked the Republic better and stayed; about twenty, brown-haired and hazel-eyed, lean and fast like a bundle of whipcord. He wore the fringed, camo-patterned Ranger buckskins as if he hadn't been brought up to kilts, and the bowie at his waist and tomahawk thrust into the back of his belt as if they'd grown there.

"Why so much ammunition?" he said, reading over the older ranger's shoulder. "Gonna be heavy."

Peter Girenas sighed a little, in the privacy of his head. Eddie was a good ranger—perhaps the best tracker and woodsman in the Corps, after Peter, good at languages, brave as a lion, deadly with any weapon. A nice guy to sit down and have a beer with, too. But he *was* Alban, and he had the *mañana* attitude of his tribe deep in his bones. His people took to guns like Lekkansu to firewater, though.

"Eddie, we're going a *long* ways from home. We can't drop over to the mill and trade some venison for another hundred rounds. That's why I'm taking two stallions along as well as a dozen pack mares. Just in case everything takes longer than we thought."

"Oh. Okay, Pete, that sounds sensible."

He leaned back and took a pull at his beer. The table they'd taken at the Wild Rose Chance was littered with notes and letters and files, plus plates and bowls and jugs. Peter propped the paper he was reading up against a milk jug and pulled his plate closer, forking up ham steak in red gravy with a hearty appetite.

"I think we're going to make it," he said. "What the Meeting voted, it'll just cover what we need."

Nods went up and down the table. "You did good, Pete—made those lost geezers back on the Island sit up and take notice," Sue Chau said.

He felt himself puffing up a little but suppressed it. "Not too hard," he said. "Hell, I even got the Carsons rooting for me."

Eddie laughed into his beer. "Diawas Pithair, won't they turn red and blue when we come back richer than kings? And even richer in glory."

Peter nodded. He wouldn't have put it quite that way—"glory" wasn't a word he was comfortable with—but there was no denying that was part of the reason. Even more than the gold or the cheers, though . . . *I want to see it. I want to be the first Islander to see it, while it's still . . . fresh.*

He looked around the table. There were probably as many reasons as there were people in his group; more, since each of the six probably had more than one.

Eddie wants to shine, and get enough gold to buy a big farm here and a horse-herd and throw parties and maybe take a vacation back in Alba and impress the hell out of his relatives, he thought.

Beside him was Henry Morris, the oldest in the group—over thirty. A big, slow, strong redhead, a pupil of Hillwater's; trained by Doc Coleman too. *He* had a thing about animals and plants and such; he was looking for a long-term career with the Conservancy Office. This would make up for a youthful indiscretion; he'd been involved with Pamela Lisketter, back when. Not much, but enough to make it difficult for him to get a government job. He'd be worth his weight in gold; no knowing when they'd need a sawbones.

Sue . . . *well, maybe I flatter myself, but Sue wants to come along because* I'm *going, I think.* Partly, and partly for the sheer fun of it.

Dekkomosu the Lekkansu was quiet, down at the other end. Beer hit him that way; he was short and stocky and muscular, hair still in a roach, but he was dressed in a white woods-runner's buckskins rather than his native not-much. He and Peter were blood brothers, and there wasn't much left of the tribesman's family; they'd been hit heavy in the plagues. *Figure he just wants to get far away and forget things.*

And Jaditwara . . . *she's just so goddam* strange. A tall, slim, blond Fiernan—she had the Spear Mark. Hard to tell *what* her motivations were; she'd just said that the stars told her Moon Woman wanted her to do it, and as far as she was concerned that was that. But Jesus, she could draw! No way they were going to let a Pre-Event camera and rationed film go along on this, and the Island-made equivalents were far too heavy and cumbersome.

"Good thing the Meeting wasn't held in Fogarty's Cove," Sue said.

Peter nodded, looking around the warm, crowded room. He had friends in Fogarty's Cove—that and looking at some horses was why he was here— but most of the Long Island settlers were against anything that distracted from pushing the frontier further west up-Island.

The taproom of the Wild Rose Chance was pretty full. They'd had a week of mild weather, but the March rain outside was near-as-damn sleet, and people near the door yelled whenever someone came in, bringing a little of it with them. Further in, that wasn't a problem; the big fireplace along the south wall was blazing. The air was thick with the good smells of roasting meat, baking bread, woodsmoke, and leather coats drying on pegs around the wall.

The staff were busy ladling and carving and running in and out of the kitchens with things that required more cooking than the hearth could provide; the bar was four-deep too.

"Hey, Judy!" Peter called. "Some of that mulled cider!"

"Here," she said. "And here." She unloaded plates for the others. "And I hope you all remember it when you're freezing and chewing on acorns in the middle of a snowstorm next winter, God-knows-where."

"That's a promise," Peter said.

"Bin'HOtse-khwon," Swindapa said, putting aside the sheet of daily returns from the flotilla that she'd finished reviewing.

Darling, Marian translated mentally.

"Mmm, sugar?"she said, looking up from the cabin table, where she had been pricking the map. They'd been making good time from Mauritius Base on their return; the crews were well shaken down and the wind steady . . . steady so far, at least. Two and three hundred miles a day from noon to noon, and hardly a need to touch the lines.

"What will we do, when Walker has been put down and the war is over?"

The Fiernan was sitting on the semicircular couch that lined the stern windows. Those were open, slid back to let in the mild, silky

warmth of the sea air above Capricorn, and strands of her yellow hair
floated free in the breeze. Alston gave an inner sigh of pleasure at the
sight, drawing a deep breath full of sea, salt, tar, and wood, of morning. *Woman, you are dead lucky.*

Behind the frigate ran her wake, a curling V of white against
aching-blue sea. The sun was in the east, adding the slightest tinge of
red to the foam of the wake, and to the sails of the ships following behind. It was very quiet, under the continuous creak-and-groan of a
wooden vessel speaking to itself; the rush of water along the hull, the
constant humming song of wind in the rigging, an occasional crisp
order-and-response from the deck above, the cry of a seabird. Above
that came the high piping of children's voices through the quarterdeck
skylight; with the expeditionary regiment's marines and civilians
landed at Ur, they'd brought Heather and Lucy on the *Chamberlain*.

Alston glanced upward and smiled. "Well, watch the children
grow. Look after the Guard, of course. Design some more ships." Her
grin grew wider. "Spend a lot of time making out."

"Oh, yes," Swindapa said happily.

"I was thinking, though," her partner went on. "Perhaps we could
get a place in the country, as well as Guard House? That's the Town's,
really. I'd like to raise horses, and it would be a place for our . . . what
do you call it . . . retirement."

Alston chuckled a little ruefully. She was eighteen years older than
her lover, almost to the day. *She means* my *retirement, of course.* Although she didn't expect Swindapa to stay in the Guard after she herself mustered out. She was a fine officer and loved the sea, but being
a fighting sailor was something she did only because it was needful.
And I don't intend to stay on after my usefulness ends, she told herself. One part of command was knowing when to let go.

"I thought you wanted to study more astronomy and mathematics?" she said. That was big a part of the Fiernan Bohulugi religion,
and in her quiet way Swindapa was pious.

"That, too. Doreen will be back then. She wants to start some
classes."

"Sounds good, then. We can pick up a place on Long Island, maybe."
Not a raw grant; clearing temperate-zone climax forest was full-time
work. Still, they'd invested their pay well, and developed land did
come on the market.

*That's actually a pretty good idea. I wouldn't mind having a garden
to putter in when I'm old and gray and baking cookies for the grandchildren.* "I warn you, though, I'm always going to need some salt
water now and then!"

"How not?" Swindapa grinned. "We'll get a place with a pier and a boat. And maybe we should adopt again. I'd like a little boy, too. Maybe more? A house lives with children in it."

"Mmmm, let's think about that," Alston said. Swindapa's enthusiasm for babies was a bit alarming—even more so than her newfound passion for horses. There wouldn't be any real problem. Even though the flood of Alban War orphans had died down, there was still a steady trickle; she could probably arrange it through her relatives in Alba.

The ship's bell struck. Alston and her partner stood and put on their billed caps before heading out and up the companionway to the fantail.

"Captain on deck!"

"As you were," Alston said, returning the salutes. "Lieutenant Jenkins has the deck."

"It's freshening, ma'am," the second-in-command of the ship said. "Coming a little more out of the north, too, and tending eastward, I think. I don't much like it, somehow."

Alston nodded, looking up and squinting a little. *Hmmm.* She felt the motion of the ship beneath her, looked at sea and near-cloudless sky, tasted the wind. Not quite as . . . soothing . . . as it had been. Swindapa nodded slightly as their eyes met; they went over to the low deckhouse forward of the wheels and down the three steps into it.

"Carry on," she said to the watch there; this was the radio shack, as well as holding map tables, digital clock, log readout, the new mechanical chronometer, and the barometer. "Give me the hourly readings."

Her eyebrows went up a little as she read them and then took a look at the current level. *Either the glass has broken or that's bad news.* She flicked the instrument with a finger. *Nope. Bad news.*

"Signal to flotilla; two points to the east and make all sail," she said. Out on the deck, she stepped over to the wheels.

"Thus, thus," she said, giving the helm the new course. To the lieutenant: "Mr. Jenkins, topgallants and royals, if you please."

"Yes, ma'am."

He went to the rail and relayed the order; she could hear it echo across the deck until the mast captains' voices called, "Lay aloft and loose topgallants and royals!"

The ship heeled as more canvas blossomed out high above their heads, thuttering and cracking, and the standing rigging funneled the force of the wind to the hull. At Jenkins's unspoken question, she went on:

"I want sea room, Mr. Jenkins; we're too damned close to the southern end of Madagascar, if it comes on to blow."

"Rig for rough weather, ma'am?" he said.

"By all means. Lieutenant Commander Swindapa, message to

the flotilla: *Prepare for heavy weather, be ready to strike sail.*" The orders went out, and she added, "Oh, and get those two imps of satan down from the maintop."

He grinned a little at that and called to the tops. A dark head and a red one peered over the railing of the triangular platform, with one of the crew hovering behind them, ready to grab.

"Mom!" came a faint call; then, in a treble imitation of the lookout: "On deck, there! Can we slide down a backstay?"

"No, you cannot!"

The wind blew away the muttered complaints. *They probably* could *slide down a backstay,* she thought; they were nimble as apes after three months at sea. *But not for a while; best to be cautious.* After a moment, her mouth quirked. The definition of "cautious" had undergone some radical mutations, back here in the Bronze Age.

CHAPTER TEN

April, Year 9 A.E.

"Lot of work," Kathryn Hollard said, looking up at the bulky three-step shape of the water-purifying works.

"Worth it," Clemens said fervently. "Come along—you should see this."

The base hospital's priority had been high enough that it was more or less finished. The walls were thick adobe brick, whitewashed inside, with a number of bays off a long L-shaped block and smooth tile floors. Light came from tall, narrow windows high in the walls, under the cross-timbers that supported the low-sloped tile roof. The wards were airy and cool; adobe made good insulation. Mostly they smelled of fresh mortar and new wood, and of disinfectant; but Major Hollard wrinkled her nose slightly as Clemens led her into one of the bays. An orderly pushed past with a basket of soiled cloth pads.

"Sorry, but there's only so much you can do when diarrhea hits."

They walked down the line of beds; a few near the door were Marines; the others, several dozen locals. Their faces were alike, though, drained and pale. Another orderly was pushing a wheeled cart down the row of bedsteads, stopping at each to make the occupant down a glass of what looked like water. Several of the locals were alive enough to try and reject the dose, squirming in mute terror. Their hair and beards had been shaved, a dreadful shaming thing to a Babylonian of this era.

"What is it?" Hollard asked.

"It's the reason we spent so much time on that slow-sand filter setup. Specifically? Damned if I know. It's a form of bacterial dysentery; I think I've isolated the causative agent. It's not cholera, but it works a lot like it. Rehydration with sugar-and-salt-laced water works fine, or by IV for the worst cases. A fair number died before we realized what was happening. The locals are afraid of our *magic;* I had to get a guard detail to bring some of these men in. That's what I thought you might help me with."

"You need a couple of squads?" Hollard asked.

Clemens shook his head, frustration turning his naturally sunny expression to a scowl. "No, what I need is *help*. More hands. I need some people who can be taught basics—changing bedpans, giving them the solution, getting them to the jakes if they're ambulatory. It would help if they could speak Akkadian. I thought of using some of the laborers, but they're too frightened—and the peasants . . . well, the term 'thick hick' might have been invented for them. They're even more ignorant and parochial than an Alban fresh off the boat."

Kathryn nodded. "I'm not surprised. Albans have to look after themselves, mostly. These peasants, they're pretty firmly under the thumbs of their bosses, and they *don't* encourage them to think, from what I've seen." Suddenly she grinned and snapped her fingers. "Tell you what—I think I can do something for you. Come on."

She turned and strode decisively away. Clemens followed, walking a little faster than he liked to keep up with the tall woman's stride, squinting under the brim of his floppy canvas campaign hat.

The tent they came to was theoretically the officers' mess; in practice, a lot of the work of the camp was done there, especially with most of the permanent buildings still under construction. Tables and benches stood under an awning, with the sides drawn up to let what breeze there was circulate. Clemens stopped and pointed to several plates of bread, cheese, and cold meat.

"There!" he said. "That's what I mean!"

Colonel Hollard and a pair of other officers were sitting talking to the councilor for foreign affairs and his assistant, with stacks of papers in front of them. The commander of the First Marine Regiment looked up at the doctor's outburst.

"What is, Lieutenant?" he asked mildly.

"That sort of thing is why we're having this problem with dysentery," he said. "Sir," he added after a moment, remembering hasty classes in military courtesy.

"I thought it was the water?"

"It's *usually* the water. But the locals *won't* dig the latrines deep enough, or remember to throw in dirt after they use them. Flies to feces to food—it's a wonder we don't have more than a couple of dozen down as it is."

"A wonder and your good work, Doctor," Hollard said. "What's this in aid of, Kat?"

Kathryn grinned, sat, and tossed her hat down, reaching for a pitcher of the weak, cloudy local beer and a straw. The Babylonians drank it that way, to avoid sucking in the sediment.

"Now I see why they avoid the water, after what Jus has been showing me," she said. "This rush of runny guts is overburdening his sick bay, and he needs some help. I thought it might kill two birds with one stone, so to speak."

"Ah, yes, the king's embarrassing generosity," Ian Arnstein said, stroking his beard.

Rumor made the councilor an absentminded polymath genius. Clemens hadn't seen much of him, apart from a few dinings-in with the commodore, but he suddenly wondered how much of that was a pose. The russet-brown eyes under the shaggy brows were disconcertingly shrewd.

"Generosity, Councilor?" he said.

Doreen Arnstein sighed, in chorus with Colonel Hollard; they looked at each other and chuckled. The Marine commander took it up: "King Shuriash decided to be *really* hospitable, so he just sent us two hundred palace servants," he said dryly. "Slaves, to be precise."

"Oh," Clemens said.

He knew the Republic's policy; they couldn't go crusading against slavery all over the planet—or a dozen other abominations—but the Islanders didn't tolerate it where they had the option. Ur Base was sovereign Nantucket territory, and there were severe penalties for any citizen who dabbled in slavery. *Doing a Walker,* it was called informally, the name for any sort of unethical dealings with the locals.

"At the same time," Ian said, obviously following his train of thought, "we can't just manumit them and turn them loose. For one thing the king would be mortally offended; for another, they'd starve or get re-enslaved or something of that nature right away."

"That *is* a problem," Clemens said. "Ah . . . sorry I hadn't heard about this, Colonel."

"We're all busy," Hollard said tolerantly. "As a matter of fact, we're all insanely busy. Kat?" He looked at the younger Hollard.

"Well, we've got them understanding that they're free," she said. "And they understand *who does not work, does not eat;* this place is run along those lines anyway. So when Jus explained his problem, it struck me that he could use fifty or sixty of them—start them off at fifty cents a day and keep, like the construction workers."

That was about a third of what an unskilled worker made back on Nantucket, but extremely generous by the standards of anywhere else.

"Not the singers or dancers or most of the . . . ah . . . entertainers," Kathryn went on. "But the cooks and housemaids, it wouldn't be a big change for them."

"That would be more than I need," Clemens said, alarmed.

"It'd be part-time," Kathryn said. "They could do the language and literacy classes say, two days a week, and work four."

Hollard nodded. "Good idea, Kat, and it'll free up our own people. All right with you, Lieutenant?"

"Ah . . . yes," Clemens said. "It'll pay off in the long run. I'll keep an eye out and have the brighter ones taught real nursing when we get some time."

"*Good* idea," Doreen Arnstein said. "If—forbid it, God—we've got a really big war on our hands, that could be crucial." She smiled, a hard expression. "And it'll give us an advantage over Walker. I doubt he wastes his precious time on clean water."

Ian Arnstein shook his head. "I only wish that were so, Doreen. More's the pity, I think he's too smart not to. And he has Alice Hong."

"She's a monster."

Clemens cut in: "Doctor Coleman says she was a monster, all right—but a pretty good physician for all that. She'll be able to give him good advice, if he takes it."

"With our luck, he probably will," Kathryn said mournfully. The pitcher made a gurgling sound as she sucked on the straw. "Pah! That last mouthful was solid ground barley. Well, Jus, let's go—you can look over the dancing girls and make a selection, like a sultan!"

Clemens cursed the blush that rose to his cheeks. *At least the sunburn hides it,* he thought. Small compensation for increased likelihood of melanoma, but you had to count your blessings in this post-Event world.

And at least I don't have to see Ellen every day.

"So, we have to ask ourselves, before we can *become* virtuous, what *is* virtue?" Doreen said, nibbling a pistachio.

The priest of Ninurta began to answer, then stopped, suspicious. He was an old man, his beard white and his olive face deeply seamed; the years had left him sunken and scrawny in his flounced, fringed robe, but his eyes were snapping with intelligent anger.

"Virtue is the knowledge of what the great gods our masters require of us!" The priest thumped the inlaid *sissu*-wood of the table for emphasis.

"Ah, thank you," Doreen said politely. "Then knowledge is something that can be taught?"

"Of course, woman!"

"Then from whom should we learn it?"

"From the priests of the gods, the great gods our masters—they who know the wisdom of old, that which is written on the clay, that which is difficult to learn."

"The high *en* priest of Marduk, here in Dur-Kurigalzu, he would be a very wise and virtuous man?"

The priest permitted himself a dry, wintry smile. "Of course. Although he is not of my temple, his piety and learning are well known; all this city knows of it." He was also a collateral relative of the king, which made the priest's words wise in themselves.

"Thank you again, O priest of Ninurta," Doreen said. She paused for a moment, then went on, "I suppose priests would strive to teach virtue to their sons, then?"

The priest settled back on his stool, arranging his robe. "Surely."

"Then, for example, Yasim-Sumu, the high priest's son, should be a man of exceptional virtue?"

The priest opened his mouth, closed it again, and flushed darkly. But he was an honest man, in his way. "No," he bit out.

Doreen smiled politely and inclined her head. *I'll say.* The relatives of several ex-maidens had come looking for Yasim-Sumu with pruning hooks; his relatives would probably be able to buy them off, but the sons of a nobleman he'd killed in a drunken brawl might be less forgiving.

"Then apparently virtue is *not* something that can be taught, O *en* priest of Ninurta?"

The Babylonian stabbed his bronze stylus into a fresh clay tablet. "Well, what in Nergal's name *is* virtue, then, woman?"

"Oh, I don't know either," Doreen said cheerfully. "It seems we're both equally ignorant!"

A few seconds later, Ian Arnstein stuck his head through the door and caught her still giggling.

"What had *him* storming out so fast?"

"Oh, I used the First Sophistic on him," Doreen said, taking another nut out of the bowl. "The negative elenchos. Have a pistachio."

Ian accepted, groaned, and sank down on a stool beside the table. The room was dim but quietly sumptuous; light came from an opening in the ceiling, that could be closed at need with a mushroomlike cap of baked clay.

"Doreen, you've got to *watch* that. Remember what it got Socrates?"

"Well, yes, but he didn't have diplomatic immunity, did he?"

"Jesus, Doreen, we're supposed to be making an alliance here! These people believe in omens the way Americans believe—believed—would have believed—in vitamins. If we get the priesthoods against us, how do you think every divination will turn out? And no, we *can't* bribe them all. For one thing, some of them are honest."

Doreen hung her head slightly. "Sorry . . . but old Samsu-Indash is *such* a doddering reactionary twit! I'm supposed to be teaching him our math, and he's utterly incapable of believing I can add up to twenty without looking at my feet, for God's sake."

"Yeah, but he's a Babylonian, you can't *expect* him not to be a sexist pig," Ian said. "Anyway, there's news."

She sat up at his expression, alarm chilling her despite the hard, dry warmth of the air.

"From the fleet. The broadcast was incomplete, but they've run into some really bad weather."

"I want everyone on a line," Marian Alston said grimly. "Storm canvas, and do it now. Signal to the flotilla."

The swell had been increasing for hours, and the light had taken on a weird, sulfur-tinged quality. To the north was only blackness, towering up to swallow the late-afternoon sky. *And heading our way very fast.* She set her teeth and looked around, trained her binoculars on the other ships of the flotilla—four of them, since they'd left the schooner *Frederick Douglass* at Mauritius. They all looked as ready as possible.

Her skin was prickling all over. *This is bad. This is very bad.*

She waited impatiently until the last work aloft was done and ran her eyes over every inch of it, sails on top of the yards and lashed with double gaskets; the forward staysails, the gaff and two close-reefed topsails still up, to keep way on her once the hurricane hit. A ship without sails couldn't be steered, and that meant death. There was an ominous, naked angularity to the masts with only those scraps of storm canvas up.

"Commodore," a petty officer panted, "the kids are strapped into their bunks, and Martinelli's with them."

"Thank you, Seaman Telnatarno," Alston said. That was all they could do. Now she had a ship to sail, and that would require all her attention.

Something was racing toward them across the sea from the north, a mile or more before the darkness. A line of white, as if the sea were being churned by an invisible laser.

"It's coming across the swell," she said mildly. "Damn."

Jenkins shouted a warning through his speaking-trumpet, and those on deck braced themselves, clutching at rigging and rail.

The air went . . . *limp,* she decided. Just for a moment the single close-reefed topsail sagged flat, all the roundness out of it. Then the wind struck, and tore the tough storm canvas out of its bolt-tops with a single shrieking burst, turning it to vanishing scraps and tatters that snapped like whipcracks. She could feel the whole thousand-ton weight of the *Chamberlain* heeling as the wall of air and water hit— over, further, further under the fury of the blow, and she watched the port rail go under with fascinated horror. Above her a line snapped with a crack like cannonshot, and something whirred by her. The scream from the wheels would have been deafening normally; she could barely hear it, or see through the froth of seawater that filled the space between. She leaped for the circles of wood, staggered as a body slammed into her, then fell to the deck clutching at its ribs.

Alston plunged on, vaguely conscious of Swindapa at her side. There had been six deckhands at the wheel; now one was just *gone*, two more down, their blood turning to pink froth in the Niagara that was pouring over the side. The two women leaped to the platform beside the wheels, waited until the spokes slowed, then grabbed them with a shock that thudded through arms, shoulders, and legs. Alston bared her teeth in a grunting rictus of effort. The frigate had heeled to forty-five degrees, and she had to brace her foot against the mount of the wheels to stop herself from hanging down like a loose rope end.

Slowly, slowly, the *Chamberlain* roared upright again, shrugging tons of water overside and through her scuppers as if she were a submarine broaching—familiar except for things that should have been there but weren't. Lieutenant Jenkins was back on his feet, yelling orders through his speaking-trumpet. Alston raised her eyes beyond him, squinting through the stinging spray, twisting to look astern.

At least it isn't freezing, she thought; she'd gone through storms in the North Atlantic where the spray turned to ice three inches thick on every exposed surface. Then she saw the size of the wave that was bearing down on her ship . . . bearing down on the *broadside* of the ship.

"Do Jesus!" she yelled. "Jenkins, get the staysails over!"

Thank God. He'd heard her and plunged down to the waist to get the dazed line crews hauling. The wind was trying to force the nose of her ship toward the monster wall of water that would crush it like a cup under a boot.

"Haul! Bring her around!" she shouted and felt Swindapa's long, slender body straining beside hers. The other two hale steersmen were with her, she could hear one of them screaming a prayer, but it wouldn't be enough. Then one of the men whose face had been lashed open by the broken line staggered up onto the platform across from her, his teeth showing in a grisly smile through a loosened flap of cheek.

"She's coming 'round!" Alston shouted exultantly and heard her lover's long hawk-shriek beside her. The staysails and gaff were keeping steerage-way on, and it might be enough.

Do Jesus, I wish I could put on more canvas. Impossible; nothing would hold in this. *What I've got up may be enough. May be.*

Or might not be. The light had vanished as if the sun had never risen, and the blackness was lit only by endless stabbing flashes of lightning. *Come on, sugar, point a little further south for me,* she thought to the ship. *Come on, come on . . .*

The stern began to climb, slowly at first and then faster, as if they were climbing backward up a cliff of blue-black tipped with darkling white foam. Alston saw the curl hanging above her and to the starboard, waiting, waiting . . . *now.* The cliff fell on them, and she could hear the ship's frame screaming in protest, the rigging humming like some great harp in agony. The water cataracted forward, and she took a deep breath to hold as it broke over the quarterdeck.,

Sea filled eye and nose and ear, battering at her body with huge, heavy hands that tried to tear her away from the spokes of the wheel. The ship heeled again, further this time, over on her beam-ends, and the sharp bow dug deep into the trough of the wave, as if the *Chamberlain* were going to run down the side of the wave and straight to the bottom.

She's broached deep, ran through Alston. *Hatchways caved—she'll never come up from this.* Fear of death was distant; an immense irritation was greater—there was still too much to *do*—and grief for Swindapa and Heather and Lucy harder still. At least her lover was by her side; the children were so *young,* and all alone in the dark—

Air broke around her; sin-dark, full of flying wrack, but the scream of the hurricane through the *Chamberlain*'s rigging was the sweetest sound in the universe. The wheel bucked under her hands, and she felt the ship's living movement flow up through her feet. Waves buffeted her, a formless savage chop that twisted the masts, bending them like whip-antennas, and the ghastly flicker of lightning saw identical stunned grins on the faces of the others at the wheel. Jenkins fought his way back up to the quarterdeck, with a party at his heels to carry off the injured—those who weren't just *gone*—and relieve them at the wheel.

"I thought we were sunk, skipper!" he yelled in her ear.

"So did I, Lieutenant!" Alston said, grinning in relief. "Keep her so—if we get any more big surges, it'll be from that direction."

"Aye, aye!"

Lightning flashed again and again, closer, closer. Then a *crack,* and a flash that blinded her through an upflung hand. The change in the *Chamberlain*'s movements beneath her feet and the crackling roar of white pine snapping told her their story in the second before sight returned.

Her eyes confirmed it. The frigate's hundred-and-twenty-foot foremast had been struck by lightning, had leaped in its socket like a living thing writhing in pain, and then snapped off three feet above the deck. It plunged to port, drowning its flaming tip in the wild water. Already it was swinging the ship's nose away from the south, into the wind. Caught in a cradle of rigging, the great mass of timber pounded on the ship like the stick of a mad drummer as wind and wave swept it about.

"Jenkins, take the helm!" Alston shouted. There was no time to think, only to *do*. "Everyone else, follow me. Axes! Axes!"

She led the rush down the quarterdeck and into the waist. They snatched the tools from the ready-racks as they passed—axes, hatchets, prybars, cutlasses. Then forward, past crew down moaning or crawling with the heave of the ship, injured or stunned by the fall of the mast and yards, the furled sails, and the huge tangle of cordage that was rigging when whole and a demon's spiderweb dragging them all to death now. Crossing the two hundred feet was as much swimming as walking, more like tumbling in heavy surf on a rocky shore than either. The wild water and tearing wind wrenched at them, flinging bodies into each other and the unyielding fabric of the ship with bruising force. Even over the banshee scream of the gale she heard the slamming drumbeat of the mast against deck and hull, booming up through her feet with the promise of wreck.

She and the others dragged and pushed crew to the crucial lines, the remnants that held the ruined mast to the hull, as well as slashing themselves. Blades flashed, thumping into hemp rope and wood and more than once into flesh as desperation and the mad heaving of the hull sent them staggering.

It's going, it's going! she thought, and brought her ax around in a two-handed swing. *Thunk*. The last of the six-inch-thick stayline parted. Out of the corner of her eye she could see the next monster wave running down with the cold inevitability of a glacier. The mast swept away, then back one last time like a battering ram in the hands of Poseidon. Oak shrieked under the impact, but that added its bit to the straining helm and shoved the bow away from the oncoming water. Alston threw down the ax.

"Hang on!" she shouted. Some of the crewfolk were still hacking mechanically at dangling bits of wreckage, heedless of everything else. She staggered to the nearest, looping ends of line around their bodies, vaguely conscious of Swindapa doing likewise.

There was a moment of almost-stillness. She rose from tying off a line under the armpits of a crewman and saw the wave strike her ship on the port quarter. Feet skidded out from beneath her as the *Chamberlain*'s stern flung upward and the ship pitched on her beam-ends. Water poured toward her, driven by winds building over a thousand miles of ocean. She felt her body leave the deck, hurl toward the bow and the railing, then slam into something unyielding. Pain lanced through her chest, and the hands that scrambled at rail and rope were strengthless. Everything moved with the slow-motion inevitability of dream.

Always expected to drown eventually, ran through a corner of her mind, even as her will doggedly forced her arms to lock in an effort she knew would be futile. The wave would take her overboard, and that would be the end.

Swindapa fell down the canted deck toward her, hair like a banner of yellow silk, shocking in the lightning-shot darkness. The younger woman's right arm clamped around her waist with desperate strength; the left was wound into a bight of line.

"Don't you leave me!" the Fiernan screamed in her ear. "Don't you *dare!*"

Wasn't planning on it, she thought, sucking in a last deep breath and holding it despite the salt spray that rasped at her lungs. And *Christ, 'dapa, you'll get yourself killed too!*

The wave struck, lifted them, slashed them backward and then smashed them down again against the decking with casual brutality. Alston let the last of her consciousness drain into her arms, locked around Swindapa and the rope.

Blackness.

CHAPTER ELEVEN

(May, Year 8 A.E.)
March, Year 9 A.E.
(May, Year 9 A.E.)

"You know what your problem is, Alice?" William Walker said, leaning back on one elbow.

Picnics had gone over big with the locals. It was funny that way. Sometimes they loved notions from the twentieth, sometimes they were horrified, and sometimes just bewildered. Snacking out in the open air they liked. *Maybe because they're so hot on hunting,* he thought lazily.

Alice looked at him sullenly. "My problem, O Enabler? Well, if you want to get technical, my problem is that I'm psychotic—a clinical sadist with paranoid tendencies, borderline sociopath, possible disassociative elements. So sue me."

"No, no, that's your *hobby.* I asked you if you knew what your *problem* is."

The royal party were alone on a hilltop in the foothills of the mountains. Summer was a little cooler here, under tall oaks; the grass crushed under the blankets gave off spicy scents . . . very much like a spice rack crossed with a sachet, in fact—marjoram, thyme, lavender. There were a few bees buzzing around as well, and a lot of birds.

Always birds around, since the Event, he thought idly.

From here he could see downslope to the Eurotas valley, but a fold of the ground hid the restless growth of Walkeropolis. There was only the soft palette of the farmlands, green and dun-gold and reddish-brown, the low silver streak of the river itself broken with yellow sandbars, and the hills rising blue and dreaming on the other side.

A little further back, Harold and Althea and a bunch of his retainer's kids were throwing a Frisbee—boiled-leather variety—with a big, shaggy dog loping between them trying for a catch. Ekhnonpa and Eurykleia were standing under an umbrella pine, slowly fanning themselves and watching. Other parties were scattered around the hillside, and a little lower down was the business side of things—a company of his Guards, and the servants, slaves, and whatever with the horses and carriages.

"Okay, Fearless World Conqueror, what *is* my problem?" Alice said, picking apart a piece of bread.

"It's simple," he said, grinning widely, nibbling at a pastry and taking a sip of lemonade. "You need to stop and smell the flowers."

Unwillingly, Alice's mouth turned up. There were slight lines beside it now. She'd aged well. Good bones to begin with; none of her vices were bad for you in the physical sense, and like many doctors she was a bit of a hypochondriac, so she watched her diet and exercise. *But if we had tobacco she'd be chain-smoking.*

"Look, Alice, *querida mia,* you've gotten out of balance," he said. "Your *chi* isn't flowing properly."

"Hey, roundeye, *you're* giving me the Buddhist shit?"

He chuckled. "C'mon, Alice, we've been together a long time. Open up."

"Yeah." She paused, sipped from a flask of wine, sighed. "You know, I never really did much like getting drunk. Buzzed a bit, yes; drunk, no—opens too many cupboards, like dope. So, okay. Yeah, I've had this feeling recently that I'm . . . drifting away, somehow. I mean, this is great here, it's my dream setup, but there are times I feel . . . odd. Cold. Out of control." She rubbed her hands over her upper arms, and her voice took on a slightly shrill overtone.

Walker put a hand over and kneaded the stiff muscles of her neck. "All right, Lady of Pain. You feel like you're drowning, right?"

"Right." She gave him a glance, half mocking and half relieved. "You know, Will, for a cast-iron bastard, you can be almost human at times."

"Hey, that's the *point,* my little Madama Butterfly. You gotta let it flow. *Indeed, he who has achieved satori may without sin steal the peasant's ox or take the last bowl of rice from a starving man; for he has become the eye that does not seek to see itself, the sword that does not seek to cut itself, the un-self-contemplating mind.* Or to put it in American—chill, babe."

"You going moralistic on me, now that you're a responsible *family man*?" she said, with a hint of danger in her voice. It dissolved into mere irritation as he shouted laughter.

"Christ, Alice ! There's something you haven't grasped yet."

"What's that, O guru?"

"Look, Alice, when it comes to the atrocity division, you're a *piker* compared to me. You're a little artisan, a back-to-the-land one-off maker of small, handcrafted gems. I'm mass-production assembly-line industry. Fuck, woman, I killed every third human being in Sicily.

We crucified two *thousand* slaves up in Macedonia after the revolt in the gold mines. And you know what? It didn't mean *shit* to me. Just part of the job, part of the game. And you're letting the edges of your personality fray because you flay one here or amputate a few organs there and it gets your rocks or female equivalent thereof off? Hell, and I thought you were tough, Alice."

"Why am I getting the feeling I'm missing something?"

Walker stretched out a hand, prisoning the woman's jaw. "You are, Alice. You see, we can do anything we fucking want to here."

"I know that!"

"No, you don't. We can torture and kill one day, and go roast marshmallows with the kiddies the next—just as we goddam well please. *Relax*, for Christ's sake, Alice! You don't have to look over your shoulder anymore, waiting for Big Daddy to come and take your toys away. *You're* making the rules now—after me, of course. You can take it or leave it. Whatever."

He held her eyes, until she heaved a sigh and relaxed. "Yeah, Will, I think I see what you're driving at. Yeah."

"Good. Wouldn't want the Avatar of Hekate to go dysfunctional on me."

Alice hesitated, then went on: "You know, Will, there's something . . . all these people, you know, the Agamemnon, that creepy daughter of his, Odikweos . . . you know, sometimes I feel a little weird being around them. You know, it's like there's this big mountain of *fate* hanging over them and I'm going to get caught in the avalanche."

Walker snorted. "Fate is what I arrange to happen to other people, babe," he said. Then his eyes narrowed. "Hey, that gives me an *idea*, though . . . yeah . . . oh, that *would* be fun. I *am* fate."

She shivered a little. "You know, Will, sometimes I think you *are* badder than I'll ever be."

His laughter lifted over the hillside, full-chested, and the children playing below looked up and waved, laughing themselves.

I hate this, Marian Alston thought.

Rousing from unconsciousness was *not* like getting up in the morning. You *hurt*. Pounding headache at least, litterbox taste in your mouth, nausea, and this time her entire body felt like one great bruise. *I'm getting too old for this.*

She forced her eyes open, made herself breathe deeply and move. It was the stern cabin of the *Chamberlain*; she knew a moment's relief that they hadn't sunk, at least. *Oh, start thinking, you useless cow. If we'd sunk, I wouldn't be waking up at all.*

Two small faces peered solemnly at her. She smiled—that hurt, too, but it warmed her inside. "You all right, punkins?"

"We're okay, Mom." An antiphonal chorus. Then Heather plunged on: "Momma Swindapa says to say she's okay too. *We* weren't even scared."

A knot of worry relaxed.

"Yes we *were so* scared," Lucy cut in, pedantic as always. "We were *really* scared."

"You were, I wasn't."

"Yes, you were, Heather, you were crying and yelling."

"Was not!"

"Were too!"

"Girls," Alston said, wincing at the rising volume. Her children stopped at once and brought her a glass of water. She sat up to take it, hiding her wince at the sight of their round, worried eyes, and hugged them to her. Lucy solemnly handed her a pair of pills in a twist of paper; two of their hoarded Tylenol tablets. Even after eight years in the bottle they should do *some* good.

A crewman with his arm in a sling and a bandage around his head was sitting in one corner. He shot to his feet and winced himself.

"At ease, sailor," Alston growled, hiding sympathy. "You can tell them I'm awake. And apparently we survived."

"Yes, ma'am. The foremast going, that was the worst."

Alston sighed again; she always hated it when they got that hero-worshiping look in their eyes, when all she'd done was her job. As he left she swung her feet out of the bunk; someone had put her in a long T-shirt. There was a bandage around her chest, but it didn't feel—quite—bad enough to be cracked ribs.

"Please get my clothes, would you, girls?"

The Tylenol was taking effect, and she was beginning to feel more nearly human, when Swindapa came in with an ensign behind her. She hugged the children and scooted them on their way with the injured crewman.

"Good morning, Commodore," she said, saluting; it was a formal occasion, after all. "Shall I report?"

"Good morning, Lieutenant Commander," Alston replied. "Let's have it. I'm functional. Mo' or less."

"Lieutenant Jenkins is in sick bay—broken arm, dislocated hip," Swindapa said. "We have nine missing and presumed dead, seventeen seriously injured, and contusions and sprains for nearly everyone." She moved her right shoulder. "Dislocated, but it works."

Alston nodded. *God damn*, she though sadly. It could have been worse, but she always hated losing any of her people. Words ran through her:

We have fed our sea for a thousand years—
Yet she calls to us, unfed.

Seafaring was dangerous, that was all there was to it; doubly so in
these small sailing ships. *I should visit sick bay as soon as I can.* She'd
have to visit the families of the dead when she got back—she hated
that too, but it was duty. They'd earned it.

"Ship status?" she said.

"We lost the foremast, of course. The main's cracked just below the
lower top—we woolded it with capstan bars, but it's not going to take
much strain. What's really worrying is the hole forward where the
mast kept hitting us before we cut it clear. We just finished fothering it
with a sail"— that meant sliding a sail over the hole as a canvas
patch—"but a lot of the seams are sprung, and we're still taking on
water. And with this cargo . . ."

Alston winced again, this time for her ship. Two hundred tons of
dried barley in the bottom of the hold, with dates, wool, and sesame
oil in big jugs on top of that. The rest didn't matter, but the dried grain
did; as it soaked up water it would swell, and if they were unlucky the
soggy, swelling mass could push planks right off the frames, the way
expanding ice did when a barrel froze.

"What time is it?"

"Fourteen hundred hours, Commodore."

"What news of the flotilla?"

"Radio's out—the deckhouse hatch caved in when the second wave
came over the quarterdeck. Everything smashed up, and the operator's one of the dead. The rest of the radio shack crew are in sick bay
too."

"Damn!" Alston took a deep breath. "Let's go take a look."

The feel of the ship under her feet was more alarming, down by the
head and sluggish, with a counter jerk after each roll; that was water
or loose cargo surging in the hold. Teams were working the pumps,
sending solid jets of water overside.

"What's the depth?" she said, when the junior lieutenant and the
chief warrant officers had gathered, together with a CPO or two.

"Four feet in the hold, and we're keeping just ahead of it, ma'am,"
a warrant officer said—he was ship's carpenter. "But God help us if
the grain blocks the pumps; it's chaos and Old Night down there, oil
two inches thick on the water and bales and jars floating around."

"Carry on, Chips," Alston said, looking aloft and narrowing
her eyes.

The ship looked naked, ugly and lopsided without the foremast, of
course. The mess on deck had been policed up, loose line secured and
a jury-rigged forestay had been erected from the mainmast to the

bowsprit. Her eyes traced the mainmast; a deep crack up at the fifty-foot mark, with a ring of twelve-foot capstan bars lashed around it. Even with the tight woolding of line around it she could see the crack flex. *Plus we lost most of the boats,* she realized.

"We put the cords on wet when we woolded the mainmast and it's getting a little tighter as they dry," Swindapa said. "But it still looks ugly to me."

"Damn right," Alston said, concealing a rush of pride. *Couldn't have done better myself,* she thought.

The mizzenmast looked all right, and the mizzen topsail was up as well, but with all the sail aft like that the ship would be a stone bitch to steer. "We have to get some sail for'ard," she said.

A couple of the faces grimaced. "Ma'am, if we put too much stress on that mast, it's going overboard."

"And if we don' make shore, we may founder," Alston said. "If we get another blow before we've had a chance to repair her, we *will* founder." She paused for a moment, thinking. "We'll try rigging a jury staysail up near the bowsprit."

Nods all around. "Are we going to try and make Mauritius Base?" the junior lieutenant—Sherman was her name—asked. "It's only six or seven hundred miles."

Alston shook her head. "Not with the wind out of the north, and at this time of year chances are it'll stay that way. We'll try for the mainland, and as far north as we can reach," she said. *Hopefully not too far south.* An iron-bound shore, given to sudden storms and waves even more monstrous than the ones that had hit the flotilla yesterday. Back—or ahead—in the 1940s, one had gone right over a British heavy cruiser, putting the turrets all six feet under before the ship resurfaced. Plenty of other vessels before and after had just vanished there.

"We're all going to be very busy, ladies, gentleman," she continued. "Ms. Alston-Kurlelo, please draw up a new watch schedule, spelling everyone on the pumps—and I do mean everyone without broken bones. Next, we're going to have to get some of that cargo overside." It was that or jettison the guns, and she wasn't going to get rid of the weapons if she could help it. "We'll rig a boom on the mainmast just below the crack; Chips, find out what suitable spars we have for that. Next . . ."

She finished with: "And I want a careful lookout kept."

That was all she could do for the rest of the flotilla. With an effort of will that got no easier with practice, she forced herself not to think about the other ships. Either the sea had eaten them, or not.

* * *

Melanterol son of Suaberon stopped to buy a skewer from a street vendor down New Whale Street; it was chunks of lobster meat with onions, savory and hot, filling his mouth with the water of hunger. The woman took his copper and laid the food in a split roll, deftly stripping out the thin wooden sliver and adding some of the biting hot peppers the Amurrukan imported from the Olmec country. Those were becoming popular in Tartessos as well; they were called *chilly*, which he thought a stroke of wit.

The spring wind from the north really was chilly—Nantucket was usually cool compared to his native Tartessos, and the winters were enough to rot the testicles off an ape. He was in Amurrukan dress—trousers, boots, jacket, and knitted wool cap—and that kept him warm. Besides that, it meant no one would take him for a foreigner at first glance; there were enough Amurrukan with his sharp olive-skinned looks that a casual glance would slide over him. It was obvious when he opened his mouth, though; his English was good, but not that good. Yet.

". . . Still no word from the commodore . . ." he heard, unobtrusively circling near a party of dignitaries who stood around, waiting for the ceremony to begin.

Ah, he thought. The Islanders' black she-devil war-leader was still lost, then, after that storm on the other side of the world. The king will be interested to hear that. If it came to war, the Republic would be weakened considerably without her and those ships.

He swallowed the last of the roll and clapped with the others as the Islander ruler walked up and cut the ribbon. This too was information; the king wished to know every little detail, for it might bear on the Island's strength. The great building behind him had formerly been the *A&P*, whatever that was, a merchant's dwelling, from the way they spoke of it. Since the Event the Islanders had used it as a whale rendery—he could still smell that—but a new channel had been dredged east up the harbor for the whale-catchers and their prey. The A&P and its wooden extension running down to Old South Wharf were now to be a huge covered market for farm produce and fish; many of those watching were excited at the prospect of renting stalls. All of them were relieved at getting the stink and greasy smoke of this trade out of the center of their city. He could understand that, since tanneries and smithies were banished outside the walls of Tartessos by law.

Melanterol strolled through the crowd, listening. Some were alarmed over the fate of the flotilla; others still believed that Alston would bring it through. Still others chattered of the fishing and the crops and exchanged gossip that wouldn't have been out of place in his native city. He looked northward; the harbor was crowded too, a leafless forest of mast and spar, and many of the ships were very large; he could see barge-loads of beam and plank being towed eastward to the shipyards, where new *clipper-frigates* were abuilding. The sound of hammering, of power-driven saws, the chuffing of steam engines came over the murmur of the crowd. He shivered a little. That was the noise of weapons being forged, a spear that might well be pointed at the heart of his folk. Perhaps they should strike first . . .

There were a dozen steam tugs or whalers in sight as well, their paddles churning the cold blue waters; a flight of gulls took wing at the melancholy howl of a steam whistle. *I hope the king's artificers are doing better with the engines of steam,* he thought. That was turning out to be endlessly frustrating, even now that they knew the principles.

A young woman in smoke-grimed overalls applauded next to him as the speech ended. "Lot of new stuff going up," she said. "Extension to the casting plant, too. Double shifts."

"Ah," Melanterol said. "You work there? A great thing. Even in Alba, we've heard of it."

"You Alban?" she said, turning to him. A snub nose with a smut of charcoal across it, blue eyes—and by her accent, not a native speaker of this tongue either. "I don't hear where you're from; I'm from the Glimmerfish country, myself."

He touched head, breast, and groin in a gesture of Alban formality he'd learned. "I'm from the Summer Isle—Ireland, the Eagle People call it. I trade—cloaks, horses, gold dust. My tribe wished to see if it would profit us to send here directly, and not go through Pentagon Base in Alba." He grinned at her. "And I wished to see its magic and marvels for myself."

She smiled back a little wryly. "Wonders, yes. I wondered and marveled at how much they would pay for work, until I saw how fast the coins flow away from you here!"

"Then let me buy you some of the wonderful bitter ale they serve at the Brotherhood," he said.

The woman gave him a considering look, up and down. *Fiernan Bohulugi,* he thought; they were even bolder than Amurrukan women, in some ways. *And she works for Leaton. Works at the Bessemer casting plant.*

The king was *very* interested in the place that made cast steel for cannon. There was a general description of the process in one of the books the palace had, but experiments had produced nothing but disaster and unusable spongy metal. Walker had been curiously unhelpful as well.

"Why not?" the woman said. "You get a thirst, pouring steel."

*   *   *

Marian Alston-Kurlelo stepped back from the pump handle, working her fingers and then wiping a forearm across her forehead. *Hell, at least I don't have to be afraid of sunburn.* Poor Heather had to watch that carefully in these latitudes, or she peeled like an onion.

"Reliefs on," she said aloud.

A new shift of twelve stepped up to the bars and began working them, up and down like the action on an old-fashioned rail handcar.

"Chips?" she said, walking forward and looking over the side where crewfolk were fothering another sail over the hull.

"It's gaining on us again, ma'am," the warrant officer said. *He* looked lobster-red; he'd been in the water a good deal. "It's not just the damaged planking. With that cross-chop during the storm, she spewed oakum from half the seams. We're taking water in trickles over big sections of the hull and I can't get at it with the state the hold's in. Every time the pumps clog we lose ground."

"Damn," Alston said, squinting up at the sky.

No more bad weather, thank Ghu, as Ian would say. The *Chamberlain* was making four knots across the wind, heading west by south; all the mizzen sails set, the main course, main lower topsail, and a big improvised triangular staysail on the line that led down from the mast to the bowsprit, through the area where the foremast should be. *Hmmm . . . we could use the upper half of the mainmast as a jury foremast, cut it off right where it's cracked.*

A figure emerged from the forward companionway, naked except for a pair of shorts and covered in oil, water, and swollen barley. Swindapa walked across the deck, plunged off the windward bow—there was a slick of sesame oil stretching downwind from the ship on the other side—and came up a line seconds later, glistening and reasonably clean.

"We've got most of the whole jars out," she said to Alston as she walked up, drying herself. "But there's just too much of the barley and it keeps *shifting*. The reed baskets it was in are all ruptured, and it's sludging around the ballast and *everywhere*."

Alston nodded soberly. They needed to get in to shore, maybe even beach the ship. That would be risky—this hull wasn't made for it—but it should be possible if they could get the right ground, soft sand or, better still, mud. Then they could recaulk, replank the smashed-in section of hull on the port bow, and *really* clean out the hold.

Hmmm. If worst came to worst, we could break up the hull, use the materials to build a couple of sloop-rigged pinnaces, and just sail down the coast to Mandela Base. She hated the thought of losing the ship, but they could salvage the cannon and come back for them later. Walking was out of the question; according to their best estimate, they'd make shore nearly two thousand miles from the Cape.

A belch of air came up the companionway, smelling of rancid sesame oil and spoiled barley. Her lips thinned.

"Quartermaster, have you finished checking the stores?" she said.

The warrant officer nodded. "Eight thousand gallons of fresh water in the intact tanks," she said. That sounded like a lot, until you considered how much two hundred thirsty humans could use in a day. "The others are repairable, if we can water somewhere. About half the dry provisions are salvageable, if you don't mind a little mold on the edges."

"On deck, there!"

Everyone not doing something that required close attention looked up. The lookout continued his hail: "Ship ho!"

Alston cupped her hands around her mouth. "Where away?"

"Three points on the starboard bow. Hull down. No masts!"

"I'd better take a look," Alston said. "Ms. Alston-Kurlelo, you have the deck."

"There," Prince Kashtiliash said softly into the hot stillness of the morning. "There, see? Where the reeds move against the wind."

The horses sensed it too, snorting a little in the chariot traces, the sound of their hooves on dirt sharp through the endless rustling murmur of the ten-foot sea of reeds. Kashtiliash shifted automatically and brought up his bow as their stamping hooves shifted the war-car. It wasn't rigged for war, now, of course, but hunting lions wasn't all that different. There was a quiver of arrows with broad-bladed, barbed heads strapped to the frame, and a bucket of javelins, plus a long spear and a hunting shield. His robe was plain wool, kirted up to let his hairy muscular legs have full play, with a new steel sword and dagger at his waist and leather bracers on his forearms.

The Kassite prince bared his teeth in sheer happiness. There was no better sport than marsh lion, unless it was elephant, and hunting lions was a royal man's duty as well as pleasure, so he needn't even feel guilty at neglecting affairs of state.

You will deal with the Nantukhtar all your life, his sire had said. *These warriors of theirs are young men, however eldritch they may be and whatever their powers. Drink wine with them, hunt with them—thus you will know them as men, and they you.*

It had been good advice. Except, of course, that some of them *weren't* men. They were women, something so strange that it slipped out of the grasp of the mind sometimes, like a fresh-caught fish out of a fisherman's hands. *Warriors in truth, not camp-followers.* It was like something out of a tale, of the ancient days of gods and heroes, of a piece with the eerie strangeness of the newcomers. He felt an excitement like a child's at the New Year festival when the images of the gods traveled to Babylon, swaying through the streets amid the throngs, and all things became possible.

"I see it, by God," one of the Nantukhtar said—O-Rourke, he was called, a man with the copper-colored hair you saw sometimes among the northern hill tribes in the Zagros. It seemed to be much more common among the strangers.

Which god does he swear by? Kashtiliash wondered.

The Nantukhtar pulled their *rifles*—how he longed to possess one, as he already possessed a pair of the marvelous far-seeing *binoculars*— from leather scabbards by the saddles of their horses.

He glared eagerly across the twenty yards of damp earth that separated the hunting party from the first of the reed thickets that stretched on southward out of sight, but out of the corners of his eye he watched the Nantukhtar general, Hawlahard. No, Holl-ard; Kenneth-Hollard. Instead of riding back toward the rump, the Nantukhtar rode on the middle of the horse's back, on a padded, built-up seat called a *saddle*. As well, they had metal loops—*stirrups*—on either side, where they could brace their feet. He marveled at the cleverness of that, and even more than at the iron horseshoes on their mounts' feet. Big horses, too. Shoulder-high on him, a good double handspan taller than the best chariot team he'd ever seen. Much heavier than Babylonian horses, yet long-limbed and swift. Kenneth-Hollard had promised him the stallion's services for his mares.

The reeds moved again, and the horses laid their ears flat. Kashtiliash's attention came back to the matter at hand with a snap. His nostrils flared, taking in the damp, beer-smelling scent of the marsh. Then it faded as the wind backed and came around into the north.

"They come!" he said.

Kenneth-Hollard and his officers swung down from their saddles and handed the reins to soldiers of theirs, readying their rifles. Then the roar came, shatteringly loud; the Nantukhtar beasts reared against the hands on their bridles, unaccustomed. The chariot teams of the prince's party were trained, but their glossy hides were damp with terror. More of the grunting-moaning sounds of big-cat anger, and then more roars . . .

There.

Two males first, full-grown but young, thickly maned—brothers, probably, joint lords of the pride. Seven lionesses; some with swollen dugs, so they would have cubs back further in—sure to make them fierce. There was a confusion of tawny hides and glaring amber eyes, great, graceful forms eeling among the edges of the reeds, milling among themselves.

Kashtiliash shouted his pleasure and heard it echoed by the nobles behind him. The animals roared again, paced, snarled, bristled at the intruders in their territory.

"Mine is the one on the right," he called to the Nantukhtar as it suddenly lowered its head and fixed unwinking eyes upon him, moved its haunches, stiffened the lashing tail to stillness—sure signs of a charge.

As he spoke he brought the bow up and drew smoothly to the ear, until the keen bronze of the arrowhead brushed the gloved fingers of his left hand on the grip of the bow. Muscle bunched in his arms and shoulders, horn and sinew and wood creaked, and he gloried in his strength. The release was sweet, his mind following the arrow as it met the lion's bounding rush. It took the animal behind the right foreleg; another was on its way before the first struck, and the nobles in the other chariots were shooting as well.

Hollard took one step forward and knelt, bringing up his rifle. *Crack.*

The chariot teams surged aside at the unfamiliar noise; Kashtiliash cursed and grabbed the edge of the war-car with a hand as the motion threw off his third shot. When he looked up, the other male lion was tumbling, its smooth, lunging charge broken by the impact of the bullet. His eyes went wide with surprise; an angry lion was *hard* to stop.

He grabbed the long spear and the hunting shield from the chariot and jumped down with a shout; his driver followed with another spear. *Crack.* O'Rourke whooped as he fired, an exultant sound that made Kashtiliash laugh in admiration. *A man of spirit, with fire in his liver.*

The horses started again, but this time it didn't matter. A lioness went down, then came up again and dragged herself aside, moaning, her hind limbs limp—broken spine. That was Hollard's second-in-command, the woman Kat'rin.

Kashtiliash took a fractional second to look at her; he'd wondered how a female would do in a lion hunt—that was as close as you could get to a battle without fighting one. She seemed calm; the face beneath the cropped hair was impassive under the sweat of a hot day in the marshes, and the startling blue eyes narrowed as she scanned for another target and brought the weapon to her shoulder. The smooth motion was unfamiliar in detail, but his warrior's eye recognized long training.

Then his lion arrived, and he swung the shield around. It had two large, staring eyes painted on it, sure to draw the attention of one of the big cats. This one was no exception. It leaped for him with a roar that seemed to shake the earth, but the beast was slowed by the loss of blood and the pain of the arrows. The long, keen bronze of the lance took it in the chest. The prince let the impact shove the butt-spike of his spear deep into the soft earth, then released it as the lion kicked, moaned, and died. His sword came out, the Nantukhtar metal balanced and deadly sharp in his hand.

Crack.

This time Hollard's bullet broke a charging lioness's hind leg, but she was up and coming in swiftly. Kashtiliash crouched and presented his shield to draw her, stumbling backward as a great paw smashed the wicker-and-leather surface back against him. The beast reared, and the gravemouth reek of its breath swept over him as it snarled. He struck underarm, and the steel sword slid into its belly with a soft, heavy resistance; he twisted it free and jumped back, landing with legs spread and feet at right angles, ready to move him in any direction.

Crack.

The woman warrior fired again, this time at less than five paces, and the lioness died at her feet, a last savage reflex driving it to bite the dirt.

Perhaps she has a man's soul, he thought. It would be intriguing to bed such a woman . . .

With the lions safely dead, the hunting party drew aside to a place where a few wild palms gave some shade. Servants watered the horses and fed them, set up an awning for shade and passed around the contents of baskets and flasks. Kashtiliash took a glass bottle from the strangers' stores and sipped, raising his brow. To begin with, it was *cold*—almost ice cold. That was a great luxury; the king had an icehouse in his palace, filled with blocks brought down from the mountains in winter, and perhaps a few great nobles and rich merchants had likewise.

Kat'rin-Hollard leaned on her elbow on a blanket nearby and wiped at her face and neck with a cloth, resting the cool bottle against her cheek for a second and sighing. Kashtiliash watched out of the corner of an eye, fascinated, as she sprawled at ease.

I have never seen a woman who moves *like that,* he thought. Not with a harlot's brazenness, although that was how it appeared at first. *As if she moves her limbs and body without* thinking *of them—as a man might.*

"Your land of Nantukhet is colder than Kar-Duniash? Like Hatti-land, or the mountains."

Kenneth-Hollard nodded. "Somewhat colder, in summer—a warm night here would be a hot day there. Much colder than your land in the winter—cold rain that turns to ice, and much snow."

Kashtiliash had campaigned along the edges of the Zagros in winter, and he shivered a little inwardly at the memory. "Great forests, too, I hear."

"Not Nantucket on," Kathryn said—her Akkadian wasn't as good as her commander's—"On mainland not far away, yes. Trees half as tall as ziggurat of Ur, cover land many thousand . . . how do you say . . . thousand day walks. We cut, cut fuel, cut timber, cut for farms, still always more."

"All the logs you want, for the cutting—it seems unnatural, like picking gold up off the ground," Kashtiliash said. Kar-Duniash grew nothing but poplar and palm and had to buy abroad for anything that required large, strong timbers, or hard and handsome ones. "But doubtless you need the fuel."

"We show, you have the black oil that burns?" Hollard said.

He puzzled at that for a second, then realized she meant the black water; he'd never thought to call it "oil," as if it were sesame pressings or pig lard.

"Yes, that will burn, but only with a stinking smoke," he replied.

"If you—" she hesitated, frustration on her face, and talked with the other two Nantukhtar. "Our word is *distill* . . . distill it, parts burn clean, it will. For lamps, for make . . . for making bricks. And for firing our steam boats."

He hid a slight shudder. Many had gone on their faces—or screamed and run—when the first of those came walking upstream without oars or sails. It still caused uneasiness, fear of ill luck. Yet already some of the merchants of the *karum* had hired those boats to haul cargo upstream. And—

"Those could be very useful to us when it comes to war against the Assyrians," he said.

Kathryn and the others nodded. "A road for supplies right into the heart of the enemy's country," she said.

"We have a saying, O Prince," Kenneth-Hollard said. "That . . . ah, novices talk of the clash of arms, and experienced warriors speak of supplies."

"That is true; it cannot be denied!" Kashtiliash agreed.

They not only have wonderful weapons, but they understand how weapons should be used, he thought with relief—he must tell his father of this. That was the difference between a civilized realm like Babylon and mountain tribesmen or Aramaean sand-thieves; the scribes and storehouses and skilled men to keep bread and beer and salt fish, fresh horses and arrowheads, flowing out to the armies in the field. *And the silver to keep soldiers longer than the smell of loot, and the engineers to build fortresses and bridges.*

He had a sudden, daunting thought; did the Nantukhtar view *him* as he might a chief of the Aramaeans? For that matter, his remote forebears *had* been hill-chiefs, hungry strangers who came down into these rich lowlands during the chaos that followed the fall of Hammurabi's dynasty.

Kashtiliash followed the conversation, appreciating how skillfully the Nantukhtar picked up slivers of information in answering *his* questions, and equally how they avoided telling him more than they wished him to know without giving offense. *Here I am, discussing affairs of war and state with a woman, and it seems quite natural*, he thought. Disturbing and intriguing at once.

At last their minds turned from larger matters to the hunt, through discussing what the rifles could do.

"My thanks to you," he said. "You killed five. Perhaps if we had many of these rifles, we could finally kill the vermin faster than they breed, and our stock and the peasants' children would be safe."

The Nantukhtar looked at each other again. "Well," Hollard said, "that's one way of looking at it."

"I proclaim these men free!" William Walker shouted. "Slaves no more!"

He stepped forward and twisted the metal collar around the first man's neck. The soft wrought iron had been filed nearly through, and it parted easily under the strong, wrenching pressure. The man fell to his knees, tears leaking down his face, and gripped the king's shins, babbling his thanks. He had a thick accent and pale eyes; he'd probably been bought in trade with the barbarians of the north. They were always willing to sell their tribal enemies for silver and wine. For steel swords, sometimes their relatives.

"If you wish to thank me, work well and faithfully," Walker said, restraining an urge to kick the new freedman loose, smiling and patting him on the shoulder instead; the guardsman dragged him back. *Mustn't spoil the tone of the occasion.*

He went on down the line of slaves who waited in the strong sun; there were thirty men and twenty women, about average for a week when he hadn't been away. As he took the collar off each, a clerk handed the new-made freeman or woman a certificate of manumission on parchment and a small leather bag of coined silver. When he was finished, he climbed the steps from the floor of the stadium and stood once more at the front of the royal box.

"Let all men know," he went on, "that these royal freedmen are now citizens of the kingdom, for they have labored hard to make those things we most need. Let them be paid a wage; let them be free to marry and establish their own households, to own land and to bear arms, to testify on oath in court. Let any children of theirs be enrolled in the royal schools, and let all men know that they have earned the king's favor, and the honored title of *Stakhanovites!*"

A long, rolling cheer went around the stadium, buffeting his ears. There were about ten thousand here, nearly all the free population of

Walkeropolis and their families, minus guards and the duty roster of the garrison, plus the most favored element of the slaves—most favored next to this crop of ones being manumitted, of course. It was walking distance from town, and they'd run out a spur from the city's wooden-rail, horse-drawn trolley system as well.

The public stadium was a compromise between what he remembered of Greek Odeums and an American football stadium. From here everyone could see him when he stood and stepped forward to the gilded railing of the marble-and-lapis king's box to speak, but a few steps back under the great striped awning one could enjoy shade and privacy without sacrificing a good view.

Walker walked backward three paces to seat himself on the throne, raising his hand high to acknowledge the roaring of the crowd. A fair number of them had been freed themselves in ceremonies of just this kind—less elaborate in earlier years, of course. Around the edge of the royal box stood a platoon from his guard regiment, in their gray chain-mail tunics, helmets, and cloaks, their bayoneted rifles across their chests. On every shoulder was his wolfshead badge, red on black; in the smooth marble front wall of the box the same symbol was set in orilachrium and onyx, and it flapped from the flagposts all around the amphitheater.

Pity we don't have good enough lighting for night games, he thought. *Or that pillars-of-ice effect that kraut Speer got with search-lights. Cool.*

The new freedmen were laughing now—some still weeping as well—and waving as they were led around the circuit of the sands by a brass band and drum majorettes tossing flaming batons; that had been Alice's idea and surprisingly popular. Alice was sitting on his right hand in a big silk lounger, occasionally giving the silver chain in her hand a bit of a jerk; it was attached to the choke-collar around the neck of one of her latest toys.

That one won't last long, Walker thought, looking at the circles beneath the staring eyes where she knelt on the marble tiles at Hong's feet. *Pity. Pretty little thing.* Soft, though. The harder ones sometimes came through the Hong Re-education Process alive.

Although they were always . . . changed.

She had half a dozen of her friends there, too. Wives and daughters of various Mycenaean bigwigs, mostly—members and prospective members of that cult thing she'd been working on for years, the Sisterhood of Hekate. It stroked her various twitches, and it was useful as well. Some of the Achaean noblewomen were wearing the new fashions that Alice and the women of Walker's retainers had spread—a knee-length tunic, sash belt, loose trousers, and gold-stamped sandals, in various combinations of color and cut, embroidery and jeweled additions.

"I don't know why you make such a big thing of these manumissions," the doctor said sulkily.

"Hey, do I object to your human sacrifices?" Walker said, chuckling. He considered a date stuffed with minced nuts and took a handful of popcorn instead, making a mental note not to forget his sparring practice later that day.

Aloud he went on, "Alice, Alice—you really don't understand personnel management all that well. Why do you think we go in for all this slavery to begin with?"

"Ah . . . because it's fun?" she said.

"That's *your* hang-up. Me, I just want to get the work done the way I want it done, as cheap and fast as possible. If I could, I'd hire 'em— less trouble if they find their own rations and flophouses. Thing is, there's no proletariat here. Damned few people here work day to day for wages, and those mostly only for the harvest or something like that."

"The *telestai* squeeze the peasants fairly hard," Alice objected.

"Yeah, but the barons don't *employ* them. The peasants manage their own land and hand over a share of what they grow. The artisans were all contractors, except for the slave women working the looms. There just isn't a hired labor force available. The only way to get big groups of people doing unfamiliar things under supervision in this setup is slavery—only way to get them working regularly to clock-time, too; they just purely hate that. Not that I've got anything *against* slavery, but mainly it's a management tool. But you've got to have a carrot as well as the stick. Manumission's a safety valve."

"I don't understand it; you're the one who enslaved them in the *first* place, Will. You knock someone down, then give them a hand up, and they're *grateful*?"

"Mostly they are. Hell, if you wait for human beings to be rational, babe, it'll be a long, dull month of Sundays. These guys are useful."

Walker looked over to where Althea and Harold were sitting with their minders. *God, they grow fast,* he thought. There were a few more coming up behind them, too—for that matter, Ekhnonpa was pregnant again; he still slept with her occasionally, for old time's sake.

"Remember this," he said to them. "It's part of the art of ruling, knowing when to use rewards and when to use punishments. It's not how much you give, but how much it is in relation to what the man had before. If he's a slave with nothing, a little can get you a lot."

The boy and girl both nodded solemnly; they knew his teaching tone. Then excitement broke through again and they bounced on the cushions, forgetting the bowls of ice cream in their hands and endangering the upholstery.

"What's next, Father?" Althea asked.

"Hmmmm—Alice, you handle the programming; what *is* next?"

"Well, it's *on* the printed schedule, Will—honestly, sometimes I don't think you appreciate my work at all."

Oh, but I do, babe. Particularly the medical school, and the library project—getting everything she knew down in print, with multiple copies. And training assistant healers, not up to full doctor status but able to do extension work in teaching things like sanitation—she'd gotten that idea from the Chinese Communists, of all people. *Without you, I'd have goddam epidemics gumming up the program all over the place.*

The cheering in the stands had settled down to a steady hum as the freedmen were led out through a gate of wrought iron; criers were going up and down the stairways chanting their offers of cold watered wine, sausages in buns, popcorn, and candied fruit and pastries. Walker inhaled with a nostalgic pang; it wasn't quite the scent of a high school game, but it wasn't entirely unlike it, either.

"Let's see, kids," he said, unfolding the sheet lying on the table beside his glass.

Nice crisp printing, and they're getting the engravings better, he noted.

That was Selznick's department. He glanced over; the man was in a lower box two places over in the nobles' section, with one of his concubines wiping grease off his double chin and another holding a tray of souvlaki next to this thick, ring-bedecked fingers. Walker felt the detached contempt he always did for a man who couldn't control his appetites. The information minister's vices didn't interfere with his job, much, so they were tolerable, and they did make him easier to control.

None of his original American retainers were stupid enough to think they could get along without him, and one thing he'd insisted on from the first was that they trained plenty of understudies. He was increasingly able to get along without *them*, and they knew it.

"Footraces first," he said to his son and daughter. "Then long jump and javelin. Then the ironworks boxing champion versus the road haulers' man, for a prize of three hundred dollars to the winner."

"That ought to be good, Father," Harold said eagerly. "That's even better than a soccer game."

Walker nodded; none of that nonsense with gloves or Queensbury rules here, it was bare knuckles and last-man-standing.

"Then it's three women with spears against a tiger," he concluded. His eyebrows went up, and Althea squealed with excitement.

"A *tiger*?" the blond girl said. "Oooooh!" She lifted a bored-looking Egyptian cat from its basket beside her and kissed its nose. "Wouldn't you like to be a tiger, Fluffy Fury?"

Walker looked over at Hong. "Maybe I *don't* appreciate you enough, *querida mia*—where did you get a tiger, of all things?"

Lions were available in Greece; you found them all over the Balkans in this era, though they weren't common. Bears, too. Tigers, though . . .

"Colchis," Alice said smugly. "I wanted it to be a surprise, so I got the captain of the *Shark* to pass the word there when you sent him around the Black Sea on the show-the-flag cruise, and then I kept it out at my country place. It's big, and it's *mean*. The women are all re-captured runaways, lots of spirit. They look very fetching too, all buff and fierce." She smiled and patted the head of her toy. "I trained them and designed the costumes myself."

"That *will* be interesting," he said.

"Three gets you two on the tiger," Cuddy said. "Hey, tell you what—I'll bet those litter-bearers you liked against . . . whatever-her-name-is there. That's four-to-one."

"Done," Alice replied, ignoring the sudden wild flare of hope in the toy's eyes. "She's sort of boring, anyway."

A clerk came through, with a murmur to the guard. He bowed and handed Walker a sealed message marked with the high-priority stamp and with Enkhelyawon's sigil in the red wax. Walker split the wax with a flick of his thumbnail and read quickly.

"Trouble?" Alice said.

"Intelligence report."

He snapped his fingers, and another servant glided forward with a silver tray and pen-and-ink set. She knelt to present the tray as a writing surface, holding it motionless as he scribbled, "Received. Well done." Definite news of the Nantucketers' arrival in Babylonia was worth interrupting him for. "We will meet in my sanctum to discuss this after dinner tonight." Then he would schedule a cabinet meeting for later in the week. The clerk bowed again and left, moving with the same unobtrusive swiftness.

Damn, the one drawback with being ruler of all I survey is that I spend so much of my time reading reports and holding meetings. Sort of like being a CEO. Of course, most corporate executives couldn't crucify the people who really annoyed them.

Walker stood again. "Let the games begin!" he called.

"You have not been idle," Kashtiliash said mildly. The sun of Shamash was declining toward the west as they approached the Nan-tukhtar base.

His face was impassive, and only the formal phrasing showed how startled he was. He'd heard reports that the Nantukhtar were building on the land his sire had bestowed; the *kudurru* exempting the grant from all tax and service stood in the courtyard of the great temple in Ur. He'd even heard that the foreigners had hired many peasants after the harvest, paying well and barging them downstream by the thousands.

But I expected an earthwork fort, not a small city! Walls defined a space the size of a minor nobleman's estate, several hundred acres; a broad road ran down through cultivated fields to the water's edge, where stood piers and slipways and a cluster of buildings.

The walls were like nothing he'd ever seen either. A low mound, a deep, broad moat, and then massive low-slung ramparts sunk behind the protection of the ditch. They formed a square, with triangular bastions at each corner and more before the gates. The surface . . .

"Is that all baked brick?" he asked, amazed.

Hollard nodded. "Look there, lord," he said, pointing. Down by the riverside was a series of low structures, shaped like long half-tubes.

"Kilns fired by . . . *dis-till-ed* black water? I did not know there was a spring of it here," Kashtiliash said. He would have known; the stuff had many uses, although it was costly.

"We drilled a well for it. That is what our *steamboats* burn here, too."

The prince nodded, hiding a shiver. He'd heard the Nantukhtar explanation, and it was true—a sealed vessel of water put on the fire *did* explode, so there *was* much force in the vapors of heated water. It was still eerie.

He glanced at the lavish, manyfold thousands of bricks. *We should look into using the black water thus ourselves.* Building was one of the primary duties of a king, and the better the buildings, the greater the *mana*.

"The residue is bitumen, also useful," Hollard went on.

"What is that other building, then, beside the kilns?"

"That is where we turn your reeds into . . . into a stuff like Egyptian papyrus. We call it *paper*, and it was our thought that your merchants could make it and then sell it to ours in return for our goods. We show them how, there."

"Excellent, Kenneth-Hollard," he said. The scribes sent to the Nantukhtar schools were sending good reports, but there was so much to learn here . . .

The roadway was thick with traffic; Nantukhtar wagons, one of them pulled by yet another *steam engine*, and men of Kar-Duniash as well. He looked keenly about at the land itself. New canals had been cut, and plants were growing whose like he did not know. Many peasants were at work, weeding and digging. None were occupied in lifting water with bucket and shadoof, though. Instead, skeletal structures of wood, with whirling vanes at their tops, stood at intervals, and from their bases water gushed as if by sorcery, running out into the furrows that laced the fields.

"Those are some new crops we thought would be useful here," Hollard said smoothly. "Sugarcane, cotton, citrus, rice, others. We can supply your farmers with seeds and slips from here."

Kashtiliash rolled the foreign names over in his mind. *Well enough.* In the end, all wealth came from the land.

They passed under the frowning gates, and under the muzzles of cannon. The Kassite prince looked at those with what he knew was an expression of pure lust. *With cannon, a king need fear no rebel.* They could pound down city walls like the bull-horn of Marduk—sieges would last only days instead of army-destroying months in camps where plague walked.

After a few hours' tour, his mind reeled.

Everything was alien, and much was so strange that he could stare at it and not see. Sometimes when he *could see*, the disorientation became worse—as when Hollard explained the *lathes* as being like a potter's wheel for the shaping of metal. When he heard those words there was a *click* somewhere behind his eyes, and suddenly he could see through the bristling foreignness of the machine to the principle behind it. Some things familiar were even more disturbing; to learn that pipes underlay the new streets and took away waste. . . . It was not that he didn't know of sewers and baths. Such things were common enough in the greathouses of kings and city governors.

It is that such things may be given to common soldiers, to servants, and laborers, he thought. *That* awed him, in a way that even outright sorcery like the fire-boats did not.

And the Nantukhtar have come not for a day, or a year, but for a lifetime, he thought a little uneasily. Nobody would go to this much trouble otherwise. *My father knew I would be dealing with the Eagle People all my days*, he remembered. *A wise man.*

At last he seized on something his mind could grasp. "This is a school?" he said.

The two-story building had a bronze disk over its entrance, with a bas-relief of an eagle clutching a sheaf of arrows and a wreath of olive branches; he'd noticed that symbol before among the Nantukhtar, as the gilded figureheads of their ships and the smaller figures that topped their battle standards. *The eagle must be their guardian god, then.* The corridors within rang with chants. He smiled, remembering his own long tutelage in the House of Succession, with the sons of nobles and priests for company. How the rod had fallen on their backs!

How they had hated the scribes and scholars who beat a little wisdom into their hard heads!

"Yes, lord," Hollard said. "Many among us brought their families with them, and it is our law that all children receive such teaching."

Kashtiliash nodded, walking down the corridor that divided the building. Then he stopped. "Those are the women my father sent!" he said.

They were dressed in Nantukhtar clothing, mostly, but they recognized him and sprang up from the benches facing the chalkboard to prostrate themselves.

He signaled them up and turned to glance at Hollard. "My father was not well pleased to learn that you had spurned his gift, sending away the servants he bestowed," he said. "Now I see them here. What is this?"

The Nantukhtar inclined his head. "Lord Prince," he said, "there has been a misunderstanding—such is inevitable when tongues and customs are so different. No offense was meant, and we did not spurn your father's gift. We did manumit the slaves, for such is our law, but they labor here for us nonetheless, as you see. And we thank the king your father greatly."

"You teach servant women to *read*?" said Kashtiliash.

Anger awoke—he was not accustomed to spend his time gaping at a new wonder around every corner, like some Aramaean sheep-diddler seeing his first city. He fought it down. *Look and learn*, he thought. The Nantukhtar were men, whatever the peasants might believe, and what some men could do, others could as well. *If we learn how.*

"Why not?" Hollard said. "Good for them, more . . . how you say . . . more useful for us."

Kashtiliash nodded grudgingly. The scribes his father had sent were being trained as interpreters . . . but the Nantukhtar would not want all such to be in the service of the king of Kar-Duniash.

"I understand," he said after a moment.

Only a fool whose alliance was worthless trusted an ally completely.

CHAPTER TWELVE

March–May, Year 9 A.E.

"**D**uck up!" Marian Alston said crisply, leveling her binoculars. The clewlines hauled up the mainsail. Through the space cleared she could see one of the ship's whaleboats beating up toward the *Chamberlain*, its small triangular sail bellied taut and the six sailors of the crew sitting on the windward rail as she heeled sharp over.

They'll be alongside in one more tack, she thought, and even as she did the boat came about. *Neatly done, by God.* The tiller over, the boom across, and the crew paid out, tied off, and switched gunwales in a single motion, neat as dancers.

As she watched, the factors were running through her head. Fine weather, a six-knot breeze out of the northeast, and a moderate swell under a blue sky scattered with small, fluffy clouds. The pumps were keeping pace . . . just. A steady hose-stream of water was pouring over the leeward rail.

I could clear the land and run down along the Wild Coast, she thought.

The problem was that this was the Southern Hemisphere's fall season—weather season, and as soon as anything *but* a moderate swell came up, the pumps started losing ground. Badly. And she was so damned *slow* under this jury-rig, not to mention steering like an ox. All along that ironbound coast, rocks, and reefs, with sudden squalls down off the mountains and freak waves rolling up out of the Roaring Forties—

The deck crew were going about their work in dogged silence, exhausted with the pumps and the endless sail trimming needed to keep the *Chamberlain* slanting across the wind. Meanwhile, the whaleboat skidded into the lee of the frigate, throwing a fine plume of spray off her bow. The sail and mast came down, the oars unshipped, and she came in under the anchor chains, fending off as the middie in command came up a line, as matter-of-factly as climbing the stairs in her own home.

"Permission to come aboard?"

"Granted," the OOD said; the middie saluted the quarterdeck and came up to salute again and remove her billed cap from short sun-streaked brown hair.

"Ma'am, it's a bay, all right. Narrow entrance, headland to the south and a sandspit to the north."

"A bar, Ms. Harnish?"

"Yes, ma'am, but deep—twelve feet at low tide, something like twenty-two, twenty-three at high. I think it's been scouring lately. Here's the drawing, ma'am."

She handed it over, and at Marian's gesture Swindapa, Jenkins, and a few others came to peer over her shoulder as she spread it against the compass binnacle. The bay within was liver-shaped, with two streams running into its southern portion. The middie had marked broad areas of marsh and tidal mud; beyond that, brush and dense forest of tropical hardwoods came down almost to the shore.

"Durban," Marian said. Not very much like what the twentieth-century charts showed, but they were used to that.

"No lack of timber, ma'am," the officer-candidate said. "A lot of them a hundred, hundred and twenty feet to the first branch. But we wouldn't be the first there."

"Locals?"

"No, ma'am. Found some marks of big fires on the beach, piled wood, and this."

The chunk of square-sawn wood was about a foot long, obviously broken off from a larger timber. Through it was a short piece of iron bolt. That brought whistles from the spectators. Alston brought it close and tilted it to catch the sun, brushing off a crust of rust with her thumb.

"Hammer-stipples on the bolthead," she said grimly. "Not Nantucket Shipyard work, or any of the contractors."

They machined their bolts; the only thing formed by lathe on this was the actual screw thread. King Isketerol's artificers were still short of machine tools, although from the reports of Ian's agents they were making up the lack with shocking speed. *Well, scratch that thought of a signal fire,* she decided. The cannon and gear on the *Chamberlain* would be a prize beyond price in Isketerol's kingdom; no sense in putting temptation in their way.

"Tartessian," Lieutenant Jenkins said, wincing slightly as someone jostled his slung and splintered left arm. "Well, they've got the ships and the maps—I suppose we should expect they'd be snooping around the Indian Ocean too."

Marian made a noncommittal sound and closed her eyes in pure concentration for a moment. "We'll do it."

"Ah . . . ma'am, twenty-two feet's chancy, with the ship this heavy."

"We'll have to lighten outside the bar, of course," she said and cocked an eye at the sky. *And pray for good weather while we do it,* went unspoken. *Not to mention that our Tartessian friends don't show up while we're hauled down.* The Republic and the Kingdom of Tartessos were formally at peace; that didn't mean that the Iberians wouldn't do their best to stick a thumb in the Islanders' eye if they thought it could be done quietly.

"Dispatch," the messenger wheezed, obviously having run all the way from the communications ready room. "Sir."

"Stand easy, Marine," Colonel Hollard said, looking up from his desk and putting down the cup of coffee.

The evening was cool and dark outside the slit window, an hour before the rise of the moon, the stars a thick frosting across the desert sky. From outside there was a low murmur of voices, the neigh of a horse in the distance, the burbling moan of a camel—they were finally getting some of them in from the southern deserts. He took the transcript of the radio message and read quickly, whistling silently under his breath.

"Thank you, corporal—and this had better not leak," he said. "Dismissed."

He swept aside the duty rosters and stores reports and opened a folder of maps that Intelligence had put together in the two months since their arrival. *Hmmm.*

I need to talk to Kat about this, he thought. His second-in-command would probably be in her quarters; she'd been out on a field problem for the last two days—forced marches, among other things, getting the troops used to moving in this heat.

He left his office, returning the salute of the sentries, and walked briskly across the lane behind the praetorium headquarters—Officer Country was a row of cottages behind the central square where the routes from the main gates met; the design was based on a Roman legionary marching camp.

"Kat!" he said, walking into the sitting room. "News from—ooops."

Major Hollard couldn't actually shoot to her feet; not with the Babylonian woman on her lap clinging so hard and facing away from the door. She did manage to disengage, rise, and brace to attention, flushing visibly even in the light of the single dim lamp and making an abortive effort to button her shirt. There was a flask of the local wine on the low table beside them, and two cups.

Hollard's eyebrows shot up; the local woman was one of the ex-slaves King Shuriash had sent as part of his gift to the Islanders. Then further. *You know, I could have sworn to God Kat was straight as a yardstick,* he thought, shaken. *Not that I mind, but it's a bit of a shock. And . . .*

"I presume this isn't a violation of Article Seven, Major," he said coldly.

A blow to his chest startled him. It was the Babylonian; she'd slugged him at eye level to her, she being about five nothing and wearing neither shoes nor anything else except sweat and a few hickies. This close, he was suddenly aware of her scent, a musky smell that made him momentarily but acutely conscious of how long he'd been celibate. She had probably hurt her fist a lot more than she had hurt him, but she was winding up to try again; a plumply pretty young woman, round-faced and olive-skinned, her blue-black hair falling to the small of her back.

"Whoa!" he said, holding up his hands. This time she punched him in the stomach; her small, hard knuckles rebounded off the muscle.

"*Stop* that," he went on, remembering to use Akkadian. Kat cleared her throat and seconded him, and the woman . . .

"What's your name?" he asked. That seemed to surprise her, at least enough to stop her hitting him.

"Sin-ina-mati, lord," she said automatically.

"Sin-ina-mati, do not strike me," he said. "Instead, explain why you are here with this officer. You do understand that you need not lie with anyone you would not?"

Sin-ina-mati looked as if she was going to hit him again. "I am here because the good Kat'ryn praised my beauty and my singing, and gave me sweet wine to drink, and *talked* to me! All my life lords have said, 'Woman, come here!' or 'Slave, bring me this!' You looked upon her with the eyes of wrath; you will not harm her. I say it, Sin-ina-mati!"

Well, I guess the self-esteem classes paid off, Hollard thought.

"Ah, assuredly, I shall not harm her," he went on aloud. "Yet we have business of war to attend to. Perhaps you should leave."

The Babylonian seemed to shrink a little as her eyes lost the brilliance of exaltation and she realized what she'd done. She gave a quick bow, scooped up her robe, and left—into the other room, he noted, not into the street.

"Sorry, Kat," Hollard said. "I just lost my temper—too many goddam Article Sevens. And . . . ah, I was a bit surprised."

"Well, so was I," she said frankly, buttoning her shirt and tucking it in. "I just got so damned *horny,* and there *isn't* anyone else here of my rank, and . . . Mati's a sweetie, though. This is business, I presume?"

"Yup." He handed over the note. "From Councilor Arnstein's office in Dur-Kurigalzu. The Assyrians have attacked, and according to

King Shuriash's spies the Elamites are mobilizing. There are rumors of strangers from the far north at both courts."

A grin. "Well, we *are* going to be busy bees tomorrow."

"No, sir," Vicki Cofflin said. "Ten days minimum. I won't swear to anything under fourteen. It's a big job, and we don't have the facilities we did back on the Island."

"Damn," Kenneth Hollard said, looking up at the cone-shaped forward section of the *Emancipator*'s frame. They'd shipped it in from the Island knocked down, since it was far too large for a ship's hull, and putting it back together was a long job. Particularly since building a landing shed here at Ur Base would take even longer.

Most of the rest of it lay scattered in carefully calculated pieces over the vast level field; the engines were up on frameworks, with the maintenance crews going over them. Bundles of oil-soaked reeds burned in metal cups on poles, giving light for round-the-clock labor. It was cool, almost cool enough to be chilly, and despite the lamplight of the Nantucketer camp, the stars were many and very bright. Two dozen laborers heaved on ropes under the ungentle direction of a pair of Marine noncoms, and the bow section swayed upright.

"Do the best you can, then," he said. "I think we're going to need it soonest."

"Belay! 'vast heaving!"

A hundred and fifty of the *Chamberlain*'s crew collapsed into the sand and scrub grass of the beach or around the capstan on deck. The spiderwork of cable that connected the ship to half a dozen of the bigger trees that grew nearly to the high-tide mark went slack. Stripped to shorts and singlet, Marian Alston waded through the thick mud around her ship; it squelched up to her knees, smelling of dead fish, mangrove, and seaweed.

She's steady. Thank you, Lord Jesus, she thought, reflex of a Baptist childhood.

The ship creaked, groaned a little, and settled into the improvised cradle; her gunports were all open and the deck covers off, letting the sun and air in and a waft that smelled strongly of spoiled barley out—rather like a brewery gone wrong, with heavy overtones of badly kept Chinese restaurant kitchen from the sesame oil.

That ought to hold her, Marian said to herself. *And we can use the raw wool for caulking, better than oakum.*

Hmmmm . . . if we find a tree of something like the right size, we could use it for a jury-foremast. Then they wouldn't have to stop long at Mandela Base, just head for Nantucket and the dry dock for full repairs.

"All hands," she said to the second lieutenant. The crew gathered, exhausted but cheerful, and the commodore stood on a barrelhead to look out over them.

"Well, gentlemen, ladies," she went on, "you've done it. Now we can get her ready and go home."

"Three cheers for the skipper!" someone shouted.

Marian ducked her head and endured it. She expected discipline and precise obedience; it always surprised her when she turned out to be popular.

"We'll spend the rest of today and tomorrow getting the camp shipshape," she went on doggedly. "Right now, I suggest we call it eight bells—and splice the mainbrace with lunch. Dismissed!"

There was another cheer. She looked at the sun; about noon. Swindapa came up as she jumped down from the barrel, herding their children.

"Marian," she said—in informal, family mode then. "Could we take a minute?"

"I think so," Marian said. Her quarters weren't far away, a tent made of sailcloth over spars and oars, and another smaller one for the children. They ducked into the hot beige canvas-smelling gloom.

Swindapa went on, "Heather and Lucy want to apologize."

I very much doubt it, Marian thought, forcing her face to sternness.

"What for?" she said.

"Uhhh . . ." Heather said. "Um, we went for a little walk."

"In the woods."

"Just a *little* walk—honest, Mom."

"But we didn't tell Seaman Martinelli. We're sorry. *Real* sorry."

Swindapa cut in. "They told him they were going to the latrine," she said.

This time it took less of an effort to scowl, despite the frightened, guilty faces. "This is serious, both of you. This isn't a prank. There are leopards and lions out there; you could have been *killed.*"

"Yeah," Lucy said in a small voice. Heather nodded. "We heard stuff, so we came back fast as we can. We remembered to mark our way. And we're *really* sorry."

Marian nodded. "And you *lied* to Seaman Martinelli. You could have gotten him into serious trouble."

Heather sniffled, and a tear ran down her cheek. "Sorry."

"Sorry isn't enough. Come here."

Swindapa's lips firmed into a thin, furious line. She glared at her partner and then turned her back. *I know, I know,* Marian thought angrily. The Fiernan Bohulugi thought spanking was stupid and barbaric, the sort of thing the Sun People did. Children were shamed or talked into behaving.

This isn't Alba. We don't have thirty grandmothers and aunts and cousins and siblings and whatnot around to watch every breath they take and talk them into the ground, she thought.

Neither of them needed to say it aloud; they'd been over the same ground too often. Marian's own parents in rural South Carolina had thought an occasional clip to the ear or swat across the bottom to be as essential as food and love to bringing up a child. They'd brought up six, and *none* of them had ended up in jail or on welfare.

She and Swindapa didn't quarrel about it in front of the children, though. Marian turned one small form over her knee and administered six carefully measured whacks, striking just hard enough to sting without bruising. Then she repeated the process.

"Now go and say you're sorry to Seaman Martinelli," she said to the tear-streaked faces. "You stay where he can see you, you don't get lunch, and if you *ever* do this again, this is the last time you'll ever get on a ship. If you can't be trusted to obey the rules, you'll have to stay home on Nantucket when your mothers are away. Understand?"

"Yes, Mom," they said, their voices trembling and wrenching at her heart. Heather was feeling her rear with two careful hands, but the threat affected her more than the spanking had.

Lucy went on, "Mom . . . do you still love us, Mom?"

She sighed and hugged them both close. "Of course I do, punkin. Your momma loves you more than anything. I just want to keep you safe, that's all. Now give Swindapa a kiss and scoot."

She sighed again after they had left. "I know, love," she said softly to her partner's back. "But I'd rather they had sore bottoms now than get dragged off by a leopard—or have to leave them behind every time we set foot off the Island. It's bad enough when it's a fighting voyage and we *have* to leave them."

An imperceptible nod. "Let's go have lunch," Swindapa said in a neutral tone.

"Well, how do we know for *sure* that Marduk and Ishtar and all the other ones they talk about aren't really running things?" David Arnstein said. "Making stuff like the weather happen, I mean. Or what Auntie 'dapa says about Moon Woman? You can't see them, but you can't see atoms and currents and co-ri-olis . . . that stuff . . . either."

"We don't know for sure," his father said.

The steamboat was making good time downstream, past the endless rows of date palms and the equally endless long, narrow fields and dun-colored villages of flat-roofed, mud-brick huts. After several months, fewer of the peasants ran screaming at the sight of the little side-wheeler, although they were still flinching. The Arnsteins were sitting under an awning, resting their feet on the track-mounted twelve-pounder gun and sipping herb-flavored barley water.

This has to be the butt-ugliest country the notional gods ever made, he thought. The palms could look romantic and beautiful . . . for about fifteen minutes at sunrise and sunset. And it was *hot,* even in May. At least he didn't have to wear a robe of state now; shorts and a T-shirt were bad enough. *Thank God everyone in this family tans.*

"We don't know for sure because you can't *prove* a negative," he went on to his son, laying down his pen. Doreen gave him a smile, as her quill went scrutching on over the paper before her. "That means you can't—"

"Yeah, I got that part, Dad," David said, kicking his sandals against the legs of his chair. "It's the rest I don't get."

"Okay. Well, first, when you've got an idea about why things are the way they are, a *hypothesis—*" The seven-year-old silently shaped the word. "—a *hypothesis,* you've got to *test* it. If things in the real world, things you *can* prove, work out the way your hypothesis says they should, then chances are your hypothesis is right."

"Yeah," the boy said, frowning in concentration. "Yeah, but what about stuff we *can't* test? Negatives, like you said."

"Well, we've got two rules for that," Ian went on patiently. *God, I've got a sharp one here.* "The first is that the simplest way to explain something is best, if it explains everything you can see. That's called Occam's razor. Don't make things more complicated than you have to."

"Hey, that makes a lot of sense!" David said, his face lighting up.

Sharp, indeed. There were a lot of adults who didn't get that; on the other hand, it would have been more flattering still if his son hadn't sounded very slightly surprised. David was moving from the parents-are-infallible stage toward the parents-know-nothing stage earlier than most kids, obviously.

"What's the other rule, Dad?"

"Well, this is a little more difficult," he hedged. "It's called finding out whether your hypothesis is *falsifiable* or *nonfalsifiable.*"

He was still deep in the toils of Sir Karl Popper's epistemology when the whistle beside the tall smokestack tooted. They were coming in to Ur Base, and it was time to get back to work.

"Hey, I can explain all this staff to the other kids!" David said enthusiastically.

Ian nodded, wincing inwardly; he could see the same expression in Doreen's eyes. They'd both liked doing that too, as children. David would have to learn for himself exactly how popular it made you.

* * *

Swindapa made a gesture with her right hand, palm down. Marian froze, eyes scanning the tangle of jungle ahead. Insects buzzed, some of them pausing to sip at her sweat or to sting; the thick vegetation was full of rustles, squeaks, clicks. A brief wind murmured through the dense green, bringing a little relief from the humid heat.

"There," the younger woman murmured, turning her head so the sound would not carry.

The antelope were in the clearing ahead, cropping at bush along its fringe. Fawn-colored with whitish bellies, twin spiral horns, big dewlaps below their throats, about the size of a large ox. They were eland, six of them, a bull and five females. Alston lifted her rifle, careful to make the movement slow and gradual. The sharp *click* as she pulled the hammer back to full cock with her right thumb made one of the big antelope raise its head, still chewing but scanning for the unfamiliar sound. Her mind closed in, limiting the world to a patch of pale brown hide behind the shoulder.

Stroke the trigger. *Crack!* Swindapa's shot followed, so close to hers that the two reports might as well have been one.

The eland gave a twisting leap and staggered a few steps before collapsing, with blood running bright crimson and frothy from its nostrils. Its companions had already left at a plunging trot through the scrub and vines, heads held high and eyes wide. Swindapa's went down even faster; when they had slung their rifles and advanced to the bodies, Alston saw that it had been a neck shot, clean through the spine.

"Show-off," she said.

Swindapa laughed, then sobered as she cut a branch and dipped it in the blood, shaking it to the four quarters of the compass and chanting. Alston remembered that from the first time they'd hunted together—on Nantucket, back when the Island had to shoot out its deer to protect the first crops. Now she could understand the words in the Old Tongue, apologizing and explaining to the spirit of the animal why this was needful, singing the ghost home to the Mother. She waited respectfully until the ceremony was done, then turned and put thumb and forefinger to her lips to whistle summons.

"These are not as the others," a small brown man whispered to his companion.

"They use the sticks that make a noise and kill," his companion replied. "Like the other Bad Ones."

The men—alike enough to be brothers and actually cousins—crouched easily in the upper branches of a tree. Neither was more than an inch over five feet; their cheekbones were high and their eyes slanted in yellow-brown faces. The hair of their heads was naturally twisted into tight peppercorns, that on their bodies was scant. An observer could have seen that easily, since neither wore more than a piece of soft leather drawn up between the legs and over a thong belt; they carried small bows, and quivers of arrows whose chipped-stone heads were carefully wrapped in leaves to preserve the sticky vegetable poison that tipped them. Their language was full of sharp tongue clicks and plosives spat from the back of the mouth.

"See, though, they are women," the first man said, pointing to the figures in the clearing downslope. "The others were all men."

"Well, they had to have women somewhere," his cousin replied. "Unless they crawled out from under rocks, like grubs."

"And one has yellow hair, while the other has skin black as the rock that burns," the first man argued. "None of the Bad Ones looked so. The hides they wrap their bodies in are different, too."

"Perhaps they are another clan of the Bad Ones."

"Perhaps. We will follow them."

"Carefully," the first man to speak said. "These are not quite so clumsy in the bush, either."

King Shuriash was far too proud a man to show emotion before a foreigner, particularly anguish over so slight a thing as a concubine's likely death in childbirth, and that during a war as well. But Lieutenant (Medical Corps, Republic of Nantucket Coast Guard) Justin Clements recognized it well enough.

"Can you save her?" the Babylonian asked abruptly.

"My lord king, that I cannot answer until I have seen the woman," the doctor said. "It may be that I can; it may be that it is beyond my powers or that it is too late."

Shuriash's heavy-featured face showed somber approval. "It is well," he said. "So many promise more than they can do, especially to kings." A wry, difficult smile showed strong yellow teeth. "But I have noticed that you Nantukhtar are more likely to throw the truth in my beard than to dip it in honey. Will you try?"

"It is an honor to help the household of our host, lord king," he said—or hoped he'd said; this archaic-Semitic language was awkward in his mouth, despite nearly a year's drill.

"Very well," the king said. To the eunuch guards: "Show him to the women's quarters, him and his assistants."

The journey wasn't long, although the tall, dim corridors of the palace were a labyrinth. *And the eunuchs make my skin crawl,* he thought. *Poor bastards.* It was mostly the thought of deliberate mutilation that disgusted him, but part of it was sheer elemental repulsion. *And maybe it's because one reason they don't look more mutinous than they do is that I'm clean-shaven*—which no man in the land of

Kar-Duniash was—*and because, face it, I'm a little plump too.* Objectively the eunuchs knew he was a whole man. Subconsciously, they probably perceived him as one of their own.

The passages of the palace wound inward, hung with bright knotted or woven rugs up to head height while the walls above bore scenes of palm trees, griffins and fabulous beasts, winged hawk-headed men bearing objects that probably meant something if you knew the symbolism. The floor was terra-cotta, covered in woven mats of rush or straw dyed in pleasing colors; the whole effect should have been gaudy but wasn't, and it lightened the massiveness of the adobe architecture. At last they crossed an open courtyard, and thence into a last suite of rooms.

We should supply them with bicycles or skateboards, Clemens thought. *This place is bloody enormous.* Although a palace here was far more than a king's house; it held warehouses, barracks, armories, libraries, and office space for most of the civil service as well.

"Here is the birthing chamber," one of the eunuchs said.

Clemens's nose and ears had warned him. Most of the palace smelled slightly of wool and people, with an underlying hint of wood-smoke and incense. Now he could detect sickroom odors—sweat, blood, urine. Two smooth-cheeked guards brought their spears up, then lowered them uncertainly as the escorting eunuchs waved them aside.

The room within was not very large but crowded. Mostly with women and eunuchs, although he recognized a few bearded figures in the fringed shawls of priests, and others who were probably priestesses. They flickered across his consciousness without much impact. It was the naked figure on the birthing stool that caught and held all his focus.

Too young, he thought at once; fifteen, possibly a little more. Thin, and slender in the hips, so that the swollen belly showed all the more plainly. A ripple went across it as he watched, but the girl was too far gone to scream. Blood dribbling down between her legs, but not the arterial gushing that would mean it was too late—

"*Out!*" he roared, turning on the small mob of spectators and flushing them out the door, nearly pushing when they jammed. "Smith, Kelantora"—to his assistants—"get her up on that!"

"That" was a table off to one side; he grabbed it and dragged it into the center of the room. A cloth from one of his bags went over it, and he glanced around. *No time to transfer her. We'll have to do it here. God help us, what a germ farm.*

It was then that he noticed a third figure helping transfer the panting, sweat-slick figure of the girl to the table. A woman, gaunt-faced under a plain headdress but young, in her twenties; a big hooked nose and receding chin, huge dark eyes. In a long robe with a shawl pinned over it, stained with blood and fluids that also splashed her strong, long-fingered hands.

"Who are you?" he snapped. "The midwife?"

Level black eyes looked at him. "No," she said. "The *sabsutu*"—midwife—"and the *ashipu*"—sorcerer, his mind prompted, or witch doctor—"have left. I am an *asu*."

That meant "physician," or as close as Akkadian came to having a word for it. Extremely unusual for a woman to claim such a title, but she couldn't be lying, not here in the royal palace. Of course, a witch doctor had higher prestige; to a Babylonian's way of thinking, physical treatments were superficial, a mere tending of symptoms. Only a supernatural approach got at the root causes of illness.

"I am an *asu* as well, of the Nantukhtar, the Eagle People," he said, as he laid out his instruments on another sterile cloth. "The king has asked me to save this woman's life."

"That cannot be done," the Babylonian woman said flatly. "The child is misaligned and cannot be turned—the midwife tried, and she is skilled in her craft. The woman will surely die within three hours."

Clemens looked up. He found not the cool indifference the tone suggested, but an utter and burning frustration.

"Perhaps, and perhaps not. Do you wish to help?" he said. She nodded, a single sharp gesture. "Then you must obey my orders without argument." Another nod. "First, go tell them that I need water. Water in bronze vessels, several of them, heated until it boils—have them put more on the fire and keep it boiling until I need it. And clean cloth—boil the cloth too, first. And wash—rub this on yourself, wash in the boiled water, and dress in this. Put this mask across your mouth. *Hurry!*"

The operation that followed was a nightmare that he never remembered very clearly, except for an occasional question—questions that somehow didn't distract him, that soothed his mind away from gibbering panic and allowed his training to move his fingers.

Tapping the hypodermic . . .

"What is that?"

"An extract of poppyseed. It banishes pain and makes the patient sleep . . . Smith, is the autoclave heating?"

"Yessir." The safety valve hissed, and the assistant swung it off the charcoal brazier with tongs and popped it open.

"You will use the *sipir bel imti*?"

His Akkadian seemed to improve under stress; "the way of cutting with sharp bronze" came through easily.

"Yes. The child must be removed from the womb."

"Then the girl must die, as I said?"

"No. Although it may happen."

The first incision, and the skin peeling back from the cut like saran wrap under tension. Smith and Kelantora setting up the saline drip . . .

"What is that?"

"Very pure water with salt and a few other things. It replaces some of the blood lost during an operation. Blood is better, but it must be matched or it will be poison." He switched to English. "Smith, type her. We might luck out. And type *her*, too. I don't like the way the hemorrhage is increasing."

Deeper, through the subcutaneous fat. Clamps, the cut held back with extensors, sutures for the spurting veins—clamp and tie off . . .

"What is that?"

"Catgut—thread made from sheep intestine. Kelantora, get the extensor in here—and move that lamp closer, I need to see what I'm doing."

The Babylonian woman picked up a cloth and imitated Smith, swabbing off his forehead to keep sweat from dripping into the working area.

"Will such a wound not rot, even if she does not die at once?"

"Infection is caused by very small animals, too small to see with the eye—you need instruments such as we have. If you kill the animals with *disinfectants*—cleansing medicines—the wound will heal cleanly."

"Invisible demons?"

"No! Animals—no more demons than you or I. Just smaller than a mote of dust." In English, *"Ahhh, got it!"*

Christ, he thought, as the flow of blood increased. The muscles were still contracting, and they must have torn one of the veins toward the cervix.

"Clamp, clamp!"

"Sir, she's type O-positive," Smith said, bending over his kit. *God, what'll we do when those run out?* They were working on substitutes, back on the Island. "So's the local."

"Good. You—what's your name?"

"Azzu-ena daughter of Mutu-Hadki, the *asu* of the palace."

"Azzu-ena, we need blood to transfer to this girl's veins. Yours is of the correct type. Will you give of your blood? It will not harm you and it may save her."

A very slight hesitation, and the Babylonian touched the unconscious girl's forehead. "Yes," she said.

"Good. Get up here. Bare your right arm. Kelantora, get her set up, stet! Azzu-ena, squeeze this with your right hand until we tell you to stop."

At last he reached in and lifted the small form out, hands clearing the mouth and nose. Then one further incision . . .

"What is that?"

"The uterus—the womb. Better to remove it. She can't bear children normally after this, anyway, and it's less likely to get infected that way."

And . . . *oh, hell, sometimes there's no substitute for tradition.*

A swift slap, and a thin, reedy wail.

"Out!" he roared again, as heads poked through the doorway. He handed the baby over to Smith and began the long, delicate process of closing the incisions. When the last running stitch was done his hands began to shake; they always did, and this time worse than usual. The assistants painted the area with a surface disinfectant.

"What is that?"

The Babylonian's voice was as calm and abstract as it had been that first time as he drew another hypo.

"A cleansing medicine. It kills the small animals I spoke of, in the blood."

A crude form of penicillin they'd finally stumbled on in the Year 4. It worked—far better than antibiotics did up in the twentieth—although God alone knew how long that would last.

Clemens gently covered the girl, then checked pulse and temperature. "She may make it," he said in slow wonder.

He went to the door. "Tell the king that his concubine lives and that he has a daughter," he said. "She cannot be disturbed . . . *quiet, I tell you!* She hangs between life and death and cannot be disturbed and will be weak for some time; nor will she bear more children. Take my word to the king, and leave this place in peace! You, you, you—sit quietly over there, on that bench, and wait in case something is needed."

The Islander doctor turned back in, pulled down his mask with a weary sigh. Azzu-ena was standing and drinking the water-and-supplements Smith had handed her, looking frail and out of place in the green surgical gown and cap. She put the glass down and faced him.

"What is your name, *asu* of the Eagle People?"

"Justin Clemens," he said, and added with a wry smile, "Clemens son of Edgar."

Suddenly the Babylonian woman's reserve broke. Clemens blinked in astonishment as she fell to her knees at his feet.

"Teach me, Jus'hikin son of Eg-gar!" she said.

"What?" he said, bemused.

"Teach me!"

Words poured out of her in a torrent, until he gestured and she slowed the stream down, pronouncing each word with desperate clarity so that the foreigner would understand.

"I am the daughter of an *asu*, and because he had no sons he taught me. Because I am a woman and raised in the palace, they give me some work here in the harem. My father was a wise man, a good man—and all he taught me is nothing, nothing. I have watched the sorcerors, and the spirits do not hear them, for those they treat live or die as they would if nothing was done. *Sometimes* I can help the sick, but so often I try and try and still they die, and I can do nothing but at least I *knew* I could do nothing and you *can* and I must know—"

She took a deep breath. "I own a small house in the *babtum,* the city-ward, of Mili-la-El, near the Eastern Gate. I will sell it and give you all I have." She clutched at his trousers, "I have no parents, no brothers to object—I will be your slave, scrub and clean and weave, if only you will let me learn—if you will only let me *watch* what you do!"

Clemens opened his mouth on a refusal as kind as he could make it, and then closed it again, remembering.

He remembered the pain of it, the lost tools, the knowledge useless without technologies that Nantucket did not have, facing parents who had to be told that their child was gone, husbands, wives, brothers. It had been even worse for his teachers, Doctor Coleman and the others. They'd never despaired, never stopped teaching, never stopped *looking* for ways to make up their lacks.

"*I will impart by precept, by lecture and by every mode of teaching . . . to disciples bound by covenant and oath, according to the Law of Medicine . . .*"

"What? What do you say, lord?"

"The words of an oath," he said in Akkadian. "Rise, Azzu-ena. If you would learn, I will teach you, as best I can."

CHAPTER THIRTEEN

June, Year 9 A.E.

A camel gave its burbling moan, and that set off the whole train of seven pair that were hauling the headquarters wagon. *God, but I hate those things,* Ian Arnstein thought. The Babylonians of this age knew little about camels and were convinced they were possessed by demons. He wasn't altogether sure they were wrong. They stank, they bit, they spat green mucus at anyone who came near, and they complained every waking hour in voices like guttural damned souls. Their only merit was that they could carry or haul three times what a horse did, further and faster and on less water and rougher forage.

The army of King Shuriash of Babylon sprawled out over the dun-colored flatness of the landscape in clots and driblets and clusters, half lost in its own plumes of beige dust. The king's paid men and the retinues of the nobles near the capital had been brave with banners and polished armor when they left Kar-Duniash, but now everything was the color of the grit kicked up by feet and hooves or the homespun of the tribal contingents and peasant levies hurrying to join them from every side.

Sometimes there was a hint of hills on the eastern horizon, the topmost peaks of the Zagros. Sometimes there was a hint of a breeze, like something out of the mouth of a smelting furnace but still welcome when it dried the sweat. Ian unhitched a canvas water bag from the big six-wheeled wagon's bed and expertly directed a squirt into his mouth. It tasted of silt and the chlorine powder used to sterilize it, and it was no more than tepid from the evaporation. It was still utterly glorious, especially if you kept all memory of ice-cold beer firmly out of your mind.

And now they were approaching a belt of intense green, where the Diyala River spilled its moisture onto the plain. That made the air very slightly muggy, hence even more intolerable, and there would be bugs. *Oh, will there ever be bugs,* Ian thought.

"Could be worse," Doreen said. Like him, she was wearing khaki shorts and shirt. Beads of sweat ran down the open neck and made the cotton fabric cling to her in ways that would have been more interesting if it wasn't so hot. "We could be marching and carrying packs."

Ian nodded. The Marines' khaki uniforms were wet with sweat and stained where multiple layers had soaked in and then dried to leave a rime of salt. The faces under the broad-brimmed hats were set, remote, fixed in a mask of endurance. Now and then one would hawk and spit, the saliva colored like the earth that lay thick and gritty on everyone's teeth; every hour they broke for a ten-minute rest, and the noncoms would check to see everyone was taking their salt tablets and enough water. Once every day or so someone would keel over, swaying or staggering or just falling limp as a sack of rice; the more extreme cases ended up on the wagons with a saline drip in their arm.

"Hup! Hup!"

Colonel Hollard came riding across the plain on his camel, the beasts's long, swarming pace spooking the horses drawing a Babylonian noble's chariot into a blue-eyed, flat-eared bolt even in the heat. *Or maybe it's their smell. Probably their smell.* Another camel paced beside him, carrying a short, swarthy man with a wide white grin and streaks of gray in his beard; Hassan el-Durabi, an ex-Kuwaiti whose wealthy family had raised racing camels and who'd been vacationing on the Island when the Event came.

The two men pulled up their mounts beside the headquarters wagon, saluting.

"Good beasts, Councilor," Hassan said, stroking his camel's neck and then giving it a flick on the nose with his quirt when it tried to turn its long, snaky neck and bit him on the kneecap. "Those Aramaean pigs we bought them from know nothing of handling them, nothing."

Ian nodded, smiling pleasantly; the Kuwaiti had been gleefully pleased to end up making war in Iraq, with the king of Assyria standing in well for Saddam Hussein—they *did* seem to have a good deal in common, methods-wise.

The nomads to the southwest had taken to using camels recently, but they were still trying to ride them sitting on the rump rather than on a proper saddle over the hump itself, and their pack-loading arrangements weren't much better. Most of the Aramaeans herded sheep on foot, with their gear on the backs of their donkeys and women. The Arabs' turn wouldn't come until long after the end of the Bronze Age.

Or would have come, if we hadn't showed up, he thought.

"What's the word?" Ian asked the Marine colonel.

"The Assyrians were supposed to be massing their forces on the middle Tigris," Hollard said, pointing north and westward with his quirt. "We're coming in this way to threaten Asshur from the rear. Prince Kashtiliash thought they'd be unlikely to guard it because it's considered too hard to cross these rivers. However, from the latest reports they *are* there in some force. The usual thing—enemy not cooperating with our battle plan."

"I presume we can cross the river?" Doreen said.

"Oh, yes," Hollard said simply. "A matter of firearms and combat engineering, really."

The game path was narrow, where it led down from the ridge above the bay of Port Luthuli. Marian smiled to herself as she looked around; in the twentieth century she'd been born in, this had been a very exclusive—and very *white*—suburb of Durban, South Africa. Her party was strung out along the slope on a dense-packed trackway of sandy earth, with trees towering a hundred feet and more on either side. The ground was thick with brush, including a particularly nasty type with hooked thorns that made it impossible to move off the trail; one of the Alban Marines had named it the wait-a-bit bush, for what you had to do whenever it snagged your clothing.

She shifted the rifle sling a little with her thumb and looked backward. Swindapa was next in line behind her, then a Marine who'd stripped to the waist in the humid heat; behind him were the ones toting the kills of the hunt, carrying the gutted carcasses on poles that were thrust under their bound feet. Marian smiled again, letting it grow into a rare public grin.

Damn, but it does *look a lot like a Tarzan-movie safari,* she thought.

Except, of course, that the one in the lead with the rifle and khakis and floppy hat was black as coal, and the native bearers were white. Nordics at that . . .

Great black hunter and faithful companions. Daddy would have laughed himself sick.

Swindapa caught her eye and looked a question. Marian replied with a gesture that meant "later" between them; the Fiernan found uptime racial divisions hilarious.

The answering smile died away to a frown, and Swindapa looked back over her shoulder. Marian threw up a hand, for a halt and silence. She couldn't hear anything, but Swindapa's ears were younger, and better trained.

"Pass," she said, waving a hand; the party filed by her. "What do you think it is, 'dapa?"

"I don't know," the blond woman said. She took off her hat and threw herself down on the ground, pressing an ear to it. "Whatever it is, it's heavy and coming this way." The frown grew deeper. "But those . . . those are footfalls, I think. People."

"Uh-oh," Marian said, unslinging her rifle and scanning the brush.

Nothing, except the insects and swarming colorful birds, and grunts and whistles and screeches crashing off in the bush.

The Fiernan came upright, checking the priming on her rifle. Marian raised her voice: "Corporal, you and the party with the game continue." It was only about a mile and half to base by the water's edge. "Miller, Llancraxsson, get your weapons ready, but do *not* fire without orders." The path was far too narrow for that; Swindapa's shoulder was nearly touching hers. "Be ready to pass your rifles forward, in fact."

Now she could hear the thudding too, or feel it through the soles of her feet. Salt sweat ran down onto her lips, and she licked it away. The sight of two small human figures a hundred yards away was almost painfully anticlimactic. A little closer and she recognized them, the race if not the individuals; San, the little yellow-brown hunters Europeans had—would have—met at the Cape twenty-five hundred years from now. Here and now they were the only inhabitants of southern and eastern Africa; Islander ships had met them all the way from what would have been Angola around up to Somalia-that-wasn't. They varied a lot from place to place, but they weren't usually hostile if you didn't give them reason to be; the ones near Mandela Base traded eagerly with the Nantucketers.

"That can't be all . . ." Swindapa began.

One of the San hunters was helping the other along; a sprained or broken ankle, from the look of it. They were looking back over their shoulders, too; so intently that they weren't aware of the Islanders until they were barely fifty yards away. Then the hale one looked up, saw the strangers, gave a cry of despair, and launched himself at a tree by the side of the trail. Agile as a sailor in the rigging, he disappeared up it in a single swarming burst of speed.

"Maybe they had a bad experience with the Tartessians," Marian murmured. She let the rifle fall back on her shoulder, turning the muzzle away from the San hunter, and held up her left hand.

"Peace," she said, and used the equivalent in the tongue of his Cape relatives, or as close as a tongue reared on English could.

He probably can't understand it, she thought. It *was* two thousand miles away, after all, and her accent was probably terrible. *But the sound will be more like what he's used to than English.*

The small man looked at her, then over his shoulder, then he hobbled toward the Islander party, using his bow as a crutch. As he came he was shouting something in his silibant clicking tongue, pointing behind him. When he fell nearly at Alston's feet he squeezed his eyes shut and put his hands over his head.

"Uh . . . ma'am?" one of the ratings behind her said. "Maybe if something's chasing him, we ought to move?"

"I'd rather see it coming, Miller," she said. "Quiet now."

A noise came echoing down the trail, a long shrill sound like . . . *like a trumpet. Trumpeting . . . what sort of an animal trumpets . . . oh*, shit.

Marian and her partner were experienced hunters. The problem was that neither of them had hunted elephant.

Clairton, she remembered, at Mandela Base. *Of course, Clairton said that the best way was to get behind them and brain-shoot them just behind the ear. That's a really* big *help right now. . .*

The ground-shaking thudding grew louder, and the shrill, enraged squealing sounded again, ear-hurting loud. *Can't run*, she thought. Elephants were a *lot* faster than people, and they could trample through thick brush that would stop a human cold. Swindapa was chanting under her breath, a song of the Spear Mark, asking the spirits of her kills to witness that she'd never hunted without need or failed to sing home the ghost of the dead beast.

"Jesus," Marian said, the words passing through her mouth without conscious command. "That's *big*."

The animal that turned the curve of the trail two hundred yards upslope *was* big. *Thirteen feet at the shoulder, maybe fourteen. Jesus*. An old male, with sunken cheeks and one tusk broken off a few feet from the tip. There were black stains dribbled down below its eyes, marking them like kohl—the sign of a beast in *musth*. It slowed as it saw and scented the newcomers, tossing its head from side to side for a better view, raising its trunk and letting loose a squealing blast of rage. Then the absurdly tiny tail came up, the head went down, and the elephant charged—swinging along with a steady, quick stride, each pace taking a good ten feet, faster than a galloping horse.

And me without a peanut on me, some distant part of her gibbered. Then her mind was empty, calm as a still pond, the way Sensi Hishiba had taught. She was on the mats again, the *katana* rising above her head. . .

Third crease down from the top on the trunk, the only spot you could get a brain shot frontally. There was a lot of thick hide and spongy bone in the way, but there wasn't any choice. Breathe out, *squeeze* the trigger.

Crack. Crack.

"Gun!" she shouted, shoving the empty Westley-Richards behind as Swindapa fired beside her.

The elephant tossed its head, trumpeting again, staggered. Then it came on, a moving cliff of gray-brown wrinkled hide, looming taller and taller, tall enough to reach into a second-story window. Eighty feet away, sixty, forty. Long spearcast away, and the six tons of living destruction would cover it in seconds. Three heartbeats away from the crushing and the pain.

Cool beechwood slapped into her palm, and she brought the rifle around with careful smoothness.

Munen muso—to strike without thought or intention. Sword or hand or gun, there was no difference. The sights drifted into alignment, and there was all the time in the world. The rifle, the trigger warm beneath her finger, the bullet, the path of the bullet, the target, all were her and not her. *Munen muso*, no-mind.

Crack. And she could *feel* the rightness of the bullet's trajectory, a completeness that had nothing to do with its goal, a thing right in itself.

She stood, drawing a deep breath and releasing it, the rifle hanging in her hand, ignoring the loaded weapon thrust at her. The elephant's charge continued, its head down, then lower, the tusks plowing into the packed sandy dirt, sliding forward, throwing a cloud of dust and leaves and a fine spray of blood before. Stillness, the elephant's body slumping sideways with its head held upright by the tusks, a huge release of steaming dung as the muscles relaxed in death. Marian stared into the beast's dark eye as it went blank, feeling an obscure communion that could never be described.

Another breath, and the world returned to its everyday self. "Woof," she said quietly.

"My uncles aren't going to *believe* me," Swindapa said, with a slight catch in her voice; her hand came over to grip her partner's shoulder.

Marian touched it with her own, then looked down. The San was slowly lifting his hands from his head and looking up, then even more slowly looking backward. The ridge of earth plowed up by the elephant's last slide touched his injured foot; he jerked it away sharply and hissed with pain. The he grinned, a wide, white, triumphant smile, looking up at her.

The American smiled back and went to one knee beside him, propping the rifle against the roadside brush. "Here," she said, uncorking her canteen, sipping from it and then offering it to the local.

He turned over, wincing, and sat up to accept it. Swindapa slung her rifle and went to examine his ankle, washing it with water from her own canteen and then manipulating it with strong, skilled fingers.

"Miller, Llancraxsson," she said. "We'll cut some poles for stretchers." For the first time she took in their white, shocked faces. "Miller?"

The noncom shook himself and lowered the loaded rifle he still held outstretched. "Ah. . ."

"Very well done, Miller, you and Llancraxsson," she said gently. "It was one of the rifles you two loaded that got him."

The man nodded, licking his lips and straightening. "Right, ma'am—thanks. A stretcher, we'll get right to it."

There were two red holes precisely .40 in diameter within a finger's breadth of the third corrugation of the elephant's trunk, each weeping a slow red trickle. Another was six inches higher and to the right, just in from one eye. God knew where the fourth shot had gone; still, not bad shooting at all. No telling whose shot had drilled the beast's brain, of course.

Swindapa was standing by the head; it was nearly as tall as she was, and she wasn't a short woman. Tentatively, awed, she reached out and touched it.

"I feel as if we've killed a mountain," she said softly.

"I know what you mean, sugar," Alston answered. "I surely do."

First big battle, Clemens thought, swallowing his nervousness. *It can't be too different from skirmishes, except for the scale. I hope.* He restrained an impulse to wipe his hands—they were already clean—and looked over at his Babylonian assistant.

Azzu-ena was big-nosed and scrawny, and there was the faintest suggestion of a mustache on her upper lip. When focused in total concentration, her face was still beautiful. She bent over the bilingual text, lips moving slightly as she read down the list. It was the same technique the Babylonians used themselves to teach Sumerian, the sacred language of learning and religion that was long dead as a spoken tongue.

"*Izi-iz:* stand!" she murmured. "*Luzi-iz:* let me stand. *Lizi-iz:* let him stand. *Iza-az:* he will stand. *Aza-az:* I shall stand."

She looked up to where Clemens and Smith were setting out surgical instruments from the portable autoclave on the trays, then covering them with sheets of sterile gauze. Reluctantly she set the folder of reed-pulp paper aside and rose, folding back the sleeves of her gown and beginning to scrub down in the sheet-copper basin of boiled water diluted with carbolic acid. They all had roughed, reddened hands from it; she seemed to regard it as a mark of honor. Word had come back that the allied forces were going to force the crossing of the Diyala River against opposition, and that meant business for the Corps.

Justin gave a quick glance around the forward medical tent. It had been set up on a slight rise, far enough back that the dust wasn't too bad, far enough forward that the wounded wouldn't have to be carried too far—timely treatment was the great secret of keeping mortality low. The tent had three poles down the center and one at each corner of the long rectangle; the canvas of the sides had been rolled up and tied, leaving only gauze along the walls. He checked over the contents: three operating tables, ether, oxygen cylinders, instruments, the medical cabinets, rows of cots, tubs of plaster of Paris and bandaging for splints. The personnel—himself and the three other doctor-surgeons from Ur Base, their assistants, a dozen of Shuriash's palace women who'd proved to have some appetite for nursing, corpsmen waiting with stretchers.

The light was good, bright but not blinding. The big tent smelled of hot canvas, steam from the autoclave, and kerosene from the burner underneath it; big vats of water were boiling not far away outside. *Must remember to have anyone brought in checked for live,* he thought. Lice were a wonderful thing, from the point of view of bacteria that wanted to spread.

"Heads up!"

Off to the northeast there was a distant thudding, and then a long brabbling, crackling sound.

At Azzu-ena's enquiring look, he spoke: "Guns. Rifles, cannon—our weapons."

She nodded, thoughtful and without the edge of fear that most locals showed when gunpowder came up. "What are the characteristic wounds?"

Clemens heard a chuckle from one of the other doctors. Nevins—she spoke pretty good Akkadian too. He felt a big grin spreading himself. *She knows the right questions, at least!*

"Tissue trauma, of course," he answered. "Long tracks of damaged tissue, with foreign matter carried deep into the body. Treatment is to remove all matter and debride the damaged tissue." You cut out everything that had been torn, and you eliminated the necrosis that was the greatest danger for gangrene. "Broken bone—shattered, splintered as well as broken."

A two-horse ambulance trotted up outside, swaying on its springs. Corpsmen sprang out and brought in the stretchers. Clemens ran over, swallowing. *I hate doing triage,* he thought, and then pushed the emotion away. He'd pay for that later, but later it wouldn't hurt his patients.

There were five figures on the stretchers, one thrashing and moaning. "Morphia here!" he snapped, continuing his quick examination.

All arrow wounds; two in the extremities, no immediate danger.

"Sedate and stabilize," he said. "I'll take the sucking chest wound. Nevins, you're on the gut. Thurtontan, you're on the one in the face— I think you can save that eye. Let's go, people!"

Some distant corner of his mind wondered how the fighting was going, but that wasn't his proper concern. Everyone who came to him had already lost *their* battle.

CHAPTER FOURTEEN

June–July, Year 9 A.E.

"Hey, *hup!*" Kenneth Hollard said, tapping his camel on the joint of its foreleg.

At the second tap the beast folded itself like an organic leggo set and knelt, front legs first. He stepped off, whacked it on the nose with his riding crop as it considered biting him—it was a skill you acquired quickly if you wanted to keep a whole hide—and looked right and left at the belt of reeds. They were ten feet high and about the thickness of a man's thumb, their tops feathery and swaying in a breeze that couldn't be felt here on the mosquito-buzzing edge of the damp ground. The air was heavy with their green, papery smell and the mealy odor of mud. A few paces forward, and the ground began to squish slightly under his boots. Bubbles of decay rose and popped in it, like porridge boiling very slowly.

"Reed marsh, then cultivated land, then the river, and the Assyrians on the other side, the scouts report," Prince Kashtiliash said from his chariot. His silvered chain mail rippled in the harsh sunlight, almost too bright to look at, but he'd sensibly left the helmet off for now. "It is likely that they have crossed the river themselves, to hinder our passage through the marsh."

"Kat?" Hollard said.

Kat wore the combat engineer hat in this outfit, as well as commanding Second Battalion; the Corps wasn't big enough for much specialization. She and half a dozen assistants had been working with theodolites and laser range finders. *Marvelous little gadgets, but eventually they'll go bust,* he thought.

"There's a natural levee along the river," she said. "The land drops off a bit to this belt of swamp, then there's another slight rise, and then it's all downhill out into the desert."

Ken lifted his hat and used it as a sunshade as he looked around, relishing the tiny moment of coolness as moving air struck his saturated scalp. *Thank God for brush cuts,* he thought abstractedly—everyone had one now, the medicos had made it regulation here.

"Drain, fascines, then a pontoon bridge?" he said.

She nodded. "We could use some hands for this, though." A glance upward. "We could use some air reconnaissance, too."

"If wishes were horses, we wouldn't have to use sewage for fertilizer," he replied.

The Kassite prince had been waiting patiently . . . although Hollard suspected he'd picked up more English than he let on. Certainly the hundred young scribes the king had assigned to learn it had made remarkable progress; but then, just learning to read in this country required a good memory, and the literate all learned Sumerian as well—though nobody had spoken it in a thousand years.

Kashtiliash was also sneaking an occasional fascinated look at Major Hollard, Kenneth Hollard noticed. *Well, I can't fault his taste,* he thought. The problem was, he had a horrible suspicion that Kat was returning the glances. *Christ, the complications! I like this guy; he's a fighter, and smart, and pretty decent for a local . . . but Christ, Sinina-mati would raise a lot less in the way of problems!*

"We'll cut through this section of ground in two parallel trenches," Kathryn said in English. "That will drain some of the swamp. We'll push the trenches through to the drier ground by the river. Then when we get to the river, we'll build a bridge of boats."

Kashtiliash tugged at his beard. "The Diyala is wider than bowshot here," he said. "That means . . . oh, I see."

His grin wouldn't have looked out of place on the lions he hunted, and the Nantucketers answered with an identical baring of teeth. They were all contemplating what would happen if the Assyrians tried to block passage of a river too wide for bows to shoot across . . . but well within range for rifles and cannon.

"Do cross river. How would you do, Prince?" Kathryn asked. Her Akkadian was much less fluent than Ken's, but it had improved considerably.

"Goatskins," the prince answered. "Men swimming with inflated goatskins, or rafts of them. A bridge of riverboats, if they can be brought up by water in time. A bridge of bricks, if we had much time and no opposition. Round boats of hides over saplings, such as can be carried in the baggage train."

The Nantucketers nodded.

"If some soldiers to work, we could have?" Kathryn asked. "And carts—tools, and three, four tens of carts. Dry soil is needful."

The prince nodded and turned to give orders. Many of the messengers who ran to deliver them were on horseback now, with saddles made at Ur Base. Before long a swarm of peasant levies came up, men in linen kilts and tunics—some stripped to their loincloths in the heat, as they would have been when working their fields at home. The better-equipped among them had bronze-headed spears and wicker shields; many carried bows or slings, and most had knives. Gear ranged on down to hoes and clubs, but the men looked strong and willing. The chariot-born noble who commanded them, and probably owned the land they worked, looked hot—anyone would, in a leather tunic sewn with brass scales and a metal helmet, in this heat—and decidedly less cooperative as he went to one knee and bowed his head.

"Command me, Prince of the House of Succession," he said.

Kashtiliash nodded regally. "Your men will work under the direction of this officer of our allies to force a passage to the river."

The nobleman did a quick double take. "Under a *woman*, Lord Prince?" he said.

Thunderclouds began to gather on the prince's hawk-nosed face. "You will obey a purple-arsed Egyptian ape if I command it!" he snapped.

Kathryn cleared her throat. "Prince?" she said. He looked over at her. "With granting leave, will handle this."

Kenneth Hollard nodded. Kashtiliash caught the gesture, shrugged, and signed assent.

"Settle this quickly," he said, and to the nobleman: "The war will not wait on your vanity."

Kathryn tapped the Babylonian nobleman on one shoulder. "You have problem, working under me?" she said mildly.

The Babylonian sneered. "Women work *under* me," he said, accompanying it with a gesture.

She smiled, shrugged, and kicked him in the crotch. Her brother recognized the technique—*sekka no atari*, to strike without warning.

Well, thank you, Master Musashi, as the commodore would say, he thought. Aloud, he continued to Kashtiliash, "Doesn't pay to underestimate an opponent."

The prince was grinning openly, and the injured noble's personal retainers—the bronze-armored spearmen who grouped around his chariot—saw it and checked their instinctive rush. The file of Marines behind Kathryn kept their rifles at port arms, ready for instant action.

"Harlot!" the Babylonian nobleman wheezed, straightening.

From the sharp sound of the blow, he'd been wearing some sort of cup protector, probably of boiled leather, but the impact of the Nantucketer's steel-capped boot must have been painful nonetheless.

Slow learner, Hollard thought, as the man reached out for the woman with a grasping hand.

She stepped forward and to one side with a gliding lunge, grabbed the wrist with her right hand, and twisted it to lock the arm. Then she turned with a whipping flex of the waist and torso, smashing the Babylonian's muscular forearm across her left. There was an audible crack of breaking bone. like a green stick snapping, and the man's face went gray. He gave a small choking grunt of pain and stood motionless—understandably so, for the point of Kathryn's bowie knife was resting on his upper lip, just under the base of his nose. Hollard jabbed with delicate precision, just enough to raise a bead of blood, then stepped back and bent to clean the blade by stabbing it in the earth before wiping it on the seat of her shorts and sheathing it.

Kat's feeling good-natured today, her brother thought. *Just broke his arm.* With a little luck, that would heal. She could have broken his elbow—that strike was usually aimed there. *That* would have crippled him for life.

Kashtiliash's grin had turned into a laugh; the generals, aides, and courtiers around him took it up. "You have displeased me, Warad-Kubi son of Utul-Istar. You may withdraw to your lands until your wound is healed and the anger of my heart abated. Do not show your face in the city until you receive word."

He looked down at Kathryn Hollard.

"That is an interesting art of fighting you have," he said. "I would like to learn it sometime. A wise man never passes up a chance at knowledge."

To the elder Hollard he went on: "I will array the host. If we can pass the chariots and infantry through on your bridge, we will deploy on the riverbank. I go; send word when all is ready."

And there goes our prestige if we screw up, Hollard thought, watching the prince's chariot trot away in a cloud of dust and a flash of plumes and bronze. That was the problem with being the magical strangers from Beyond the Land. You had to keep delivering.

"Smart cookie," Kathryn said pensively, hands on her Sam Browne and fingers tapping the buff leather. "Seems a lot more open-minded than most here."

"I think he's more concerned with results than process," Colonel Hollard said. "Of which I heartily approve. Okay, let's get moving. Scouts!"

That was Captain O'Rourke. "Sir?" he asked, in a voice with a slight trace of a brogue in it; he'd been an Irish student working on-Island when the Event came. About Hollard's age now, and his broad snub-nosed face was the color of a well-done lobster sprinkled with freckles. It clashed horribly with bright-blue eyes and carroty hair.

"I want the other side of this marsh under observation," Hollard said.

"Well, that's what we're for, Colonel," O'Rourke said cheerfully.

The recon company spread out and waded into the muck, testing the footing and holding their rifles, priming horns, and cartridge boxes high over their heads. Hollard lifted the handset to his ear.

"Testing. Hollard here. Over."

"O'Rourke here," came the reply. A few of the Babylonians made covert gestures or clasped the talismans at their waists at the voice that came from a box.

"Sir, the reed belt's about six hundred yards broad." A pause. "I'm on the edge, Colonel. It's about a quarter mile to the riverbank, stubble fields and fallow, and a big irrigation canal about halfway there." Another pause. "Definitely movement by the river, on the south bank as well as the north. I can see small parties of what looks like bowmen retreating toward the river—probably we flushed them out. Shall I investigate?"

"That's negative, Captain. Remain in place and prepare to bug out. What's the footing like?"

"Bad, sir, but it's not impassable if you're careful. Try running and you'll sink to your waist in no time. Definitely not suitable for vehicles, horses or troops in heavy gear, or in any numbers. You can sort of walk on the roots, but if you trample this muck it turns into glue."

"Do you think the enemy still has scouts in there?"

"Impossible to tell, if they're quiet, sir. You can't see more than three or four feet through these reeds."

"Good work, Paddy. Let me know if there's any movement. Over."

Wonderful things, handheld radios. Another pre-Event convenience they might as well use while they could; the batteries were already dying one by one. *Hmmmm. Now, I could just shell and mortar anyone who comes close—but that wouldn't hit their morale the way a stand-up fight would. Let's see . . .*

"You," he said, indicating one of the departed nobleman's retainers. "Get us reed mats—several score of them, at least. Now!"

The peasant levies might not have been much at a pitched battle, but they certainly knew how to work—and Babylonian organization was well up to seeing that there were plenty of sickles and mattocks.

Kathryn's battalion stacked arms, stripped to their skivvies, and set to, marking out the lines for the ditches. The Babylonian peasants waded into the swamp as well, bronze sickles flashing; they tied the reeds in neat foot-thick bundles and carried them back on their heads. More of them went at the ditches-to-be, cutting through the low rise that blocked off the riverside swamp. The loose columns of the Babylonian army were gathering further back in the desert plain, gradually coalescing into clumps and sorting themselves out into lines, with much blowing of bronze horns and waving of standards.

"They're not going to miss that," one of Ken's company commanders said. "They'll be able to see the reeds falling from the higher ground along the river. And they must have been watching our dust since sunrise."

"Right," he replied. "We'll deploy First Battalion in double line, ready to move up in support. C Company in reserve. Move the field guns and the launchers up—guns loaded with canister and short-fused shrapnel shell. Hmmm. Get me the local who's running this bunch now that Warad-Kubi's gone."

Okay, let's see. Practical range on the bows is three hundred yards max. The locals used a horn-and-sinew-reinforced model that had plenty of range. The best ones were expensive, though, hence rare. *On the other hand, that causeway's going to be fairly narrow.*

The Marines spread out along the edge of the dry land. Carts creaked past, carrying dry desert clay to mix with the layer of mud that went over the bundles of reeds, and more mud flew from shovels. Now that the endless desert march was over, he could hear laughing and joking from the working parties, despite their being smeared with the thick, glutinous soil of the swamp.

Kathryn came up, grinning through a mask of mud as dense as that on any of her troops; the salute was a little incongruous coming from someone dressed in a pair of regulation-issue gray cotton panties under an inch-thick overall coat of Diyala ooze. He returned it with a snap anyway; the causeway was a good job of work.

"Going faster than I thought," she said. "We'll be through by midafternoon at this rate."

"Glad to hear it, Kat. Think the causeway will bear the traffic?"

"Once, at least."

"Good. Make sure your people move their rifles along as it extends."

"*De nada*, boss," she said and plunged back into the ordered chaos of the construction. There were about a thousand men and women working on it now. He studied one of the two-wheeled oxcarts that was bringing up soil, looking carefully at the way the wheels sank.

"Captain Chong!"

The artillery officer came up at a trot. "Captain, I want you to get ready to move two of your field guns forward onto the causeway."

"Yessir." The face of the artillery officer was calmly intent as he pulled out his binoculars, studied the causeway, then trotted over to walk the ground. "I think it'll take it, sir," he said when he came back. "Better to manhandle the pieces and limbers forward separately. I'll need a couple of platoons to help." The guns weighed two tons apiece and were usually drawn by six-horse teams.

"By all means."

"The mortars?"

"Not yet. We can't observe the fall of shot well enough."

Hollard forced himself to take a swig of water, although his stomach was suddenly sour. *Christ, the last time I went through this I was a grunt.* The Marines had been out on punitive expeditions since, teaching Olmec priest-kings and restive Sun People chiefs to mind their manners, but that didn't really count beside pitched battles.

Arnstein's informants—and King Shuriash's—said that mysterious envoys from the north had been seen in Asshur. Rumor made them sorcerers . . . envoys from the Hittites? *If they're from Walker, they could have shown the Assyrians guns.*

The radio at his waist beeped, rescuing him from the gnawing anxiety of speculation without facts.

"Hollard here."

"Sir." That was O'Rourke. "Enemy advancing from the riverbank; two to three thousand. Light troops, archers and slingers. Over."

"Keep them under observation as long as you can, Captain. Out."

All at once the strain fell away; he reined himself in. Light-headed overconfidence was as bad as worrying yourself into paralysis.

Aloud: "Get the locals out! Everyone else, stand to your arms! Set sights for two hundred yards, rapid fire on the word of command."

Messengers went out, and the naked mud-spattered peasants poured through the Nantucketer ranks, heading back to where their arms-cum-farming-tools were piled. The Islanders who'd been working with them climbed up onto the causeway, scraping off mud and snatching up their rifles, weapons, and webbing harness—that went rather oddly with the nudity and wet dirt, but neatness bought no yams when you were in a hurry. A dense bristle of rifle barrels pointed into the swamp now, and the more usual line of the rest of the battalion two-deep along the edge of the reeds.

"Sir." O'Rourke again. "Sir, they're sending men into the swamp, daggers and spears."

"Pull out to the flanks and keep me informed," Hollard replied. "Over."

"Sir. Withdraw to flanks, keep enemy under observation. Over."

Fairly soon now . . . More locals came by, these carrying bundles of reed mats up to the causeway, behind the massed Islanders. There was a crackle of fire from inside the swamp itself, yells, the *crump* of a grenade. Hollard strained to see what was happening, but nothing *could* be seen, only swaying reeds and a few drifting puffs of powder smoke.

"Sir! The enemy are massing along the edge of the swamp! Numbers around twenty-five hundred. We've disengaged and have them under observation."

"Thank you, Captain." A hundred and fifty yards away, or a little less . . . Hollard drew the *katana* slung over his shoulder and raised the blade. Platoon commanders turned to face him, their own swords raised, eyes on the curved sliver of bright steel in his hand.

There was a massed snapping hum, like thousands of out-of-tune guitar strings being plucked, then a long whistling rush. Light sparkled on the bronze arrowheads rising in a flock over the tall reeds, winking as they reached the top of their arcs and began to descend.

"Fire!" The sword slashed down.

BAAAAAMMM. Eight hundred rifles fired in less than a second, the cannon adding their long plumes of off-white smoke and thudding detonations to the mix. They recoiled and were run back with enthusiastic hands while the infantry were busy with breech-lever, cartridge, and priming horn.

The humming swish of the arrows turned to a whistling as they fell. Mostly short; one of the gunners dropped kicking with a shaft through his throat, and here and there a Marine was dragged back wounded. There were shouts of "Corpsman!" and stretcher bearers ran forward, then back with their burdens, heading for the horse-drawn ambulances.

The return fire was a continuous crackling roar, like a mixture of Event Day firecrackers and heavy surf; the massive fist-blows of the cannon were punctuation. Smoke rose in a heavy bank, drifting back slowly with the light breeze; Hollard coughed and waved a hand before his face in futile effort to see better. What he could see was enough. The Marines of the First Expeditionary Regiment could all fire six rounds a minute—more here, since all they needed to aim at was a waist-high point in the general direction the arrow storm was coming from.

At this range, every bullet would be traveling at gut height and a thousand feet per second when it reached the enemy archers. At those velocities, projectiles cut through the giant grass with the neatness of a straight razor, but each semicircular cut glowed for an instant, precisely like a piece of tissue paper touched with a soldering iron. Even through the dense fogbank of powder smoke Hollard could see to the other side of the reed marsh now; it was patchy, as if some enormous animal had been grazing on it. What was left thinned as he watched. On the other side were the massed archers the enemy had put forward to harass the construction of the causeway.

Or what was left of them. Hundreds were down, still or kicking or writhing. Hundreds more were fleeing, despite the efforts of sword-armed officers to keep them to their duty—often by a quick thrust to the kidneys of a man who seemed inclined to turn. Less than half of them were still shooting, and the arrows were now more of a dangerous nuisance than a threat.

Poor bastards, Hollard thought. They'd done about as well as men could, facing weapons entirely outside their experience; that so many of them were still trying to fight was a miracle of courage and discipline, in its way. The sympathy was real but distant; right now he could be nothing but a will that thought *The commodore will give us a "well done" for this.*

Hollard clicked his handset to the company commander's frequency. "Aimed fire!" he called.

With most of the reeds out of the way, the Marine infantry had targets. So did the guns, and the rest of the battery that began firing over their heads with shrapnel shell, and the three-unit battery of rocket launchers. They weren't very accurate, despite all Seahaven could do with machined venturi units and carefully aligned fins. They did land in the general area they were pointed or, more often, exploded above it, scattering their loads of heavy buckshot like a chain flail in the hands of a giant. Their trails of smoke arched over the battlefield like monochromatic rainbows, twisting as they drifted away, sending men into fresh panic with the moaning scream of their passage.

Pack mules trotted up bearing panniers full of ammunition. Their drivers handed out ten-round cases or cylindrical packets of fine-ground priming powder. Here and there a rifleman swore and stopped for an instant to insert a spare flint in the hammer jaws of his weapon.

Four minutes later Hollard swung his sword down in another arc and called out, "Cease fire!"

Silence fell, broken by a single shot and the scathing curses of a noncom directed at the luckless private who'd been too lost in his loading routine to hear the order relayed down the ranks. The Republic's commander lowered his binoculars and winced slightly; the only Assyrian archers surviving were the ones who had run first or who had been very lucky. He was suddenly conscious of the thin whine of a mosquito near his ear—and that it was fainter than it had been earlier in the day. This much noise probably wasn't good for your hearing, long term. If the long term mattered much, in the circumstances.

"Major Hollard," he said, as he walked out onto the causeway.

The troopers grinned as he passed, a few of them pumping clenched fists into the air. *Well, they're Albans, mostly,* he thought, nodding back.

"Sir?"

"Push two companies out past the swamp—it's only a hundred yards, and if you lay those mats I had brought up over the fallen reeds they should hold. That should discourage any thoughts the Assyrians have about trying to interfere with us again, and then we can get this causeway finished."

She nodded. "Dumb sons of bitches," she said with a trace of sadness, looking at the piles of enemy dead.

"They probably won't be as stupid the second time," Hollard said grimly. "Certainly not the third."

Sitting at the edge of the marsh had been about the worst thing the

Assyrians could have done; that made it a contest of pure firepower, which was no contest at all when you stacked breech-loading rifles against bows. *Let's not get overconfident*, he reminded himself. There were no prizes for Gallant Last Stands in the Republic of Nantucket's military.

"They'll learn," his sister agreed. "They'll try a couple of massed rushes. I'd say—and pick up on tricks like using dead ground where our guns don't bear for shelter."

"And ambushes, night attacks, all that good guerrilla shit," Hollard agreed, his long face gloomy. "It never stays easy."

"Still," Kathryn said, looking at her virtually unscathed command and then at the ground where Assyrian dead lay two-deep, "It'd rather have *our* problems than *theirs*."

Marian Alston suppressed a satisfied belch. The bonfire was sending sparks trailing up into the night, warm against the cooler splendor of the Southern Hemisphere's stars. Shadows from this fire and others flickered along the beach, showing the lines of dancers who paced and stamped and turned to the insistent beat of the drums in their finery of ostrich-shell beads and civet-tail skirts. The sound of the bone rattles strapped to their ankles added an almost hissing undertone, along with the rhythmic chant. The air was cooler with the recent sunset, full of the smells of roasting elephant and eland and bowls of heaped greens gathered by the San women, with an oil-and-vinegar dressing from ship's stores. The food made a wonderful change from ship's provisions.

They were simply enchanted by chocolate, though, and by the wine and beer—she'd ordered the stronger liquor kept in the kegs; pre-agricultural peoples were just too vulnerable to it. They were like their Cape kinsmen in appearance, too; very similar, in fact, except that the women didn't have the enlarged buttocks that the desert clans further south did, storing fat like camels. Doreen had said that was a sign that the same population had lived in the same environment for a *very* long time, adapting generation by generation. The people here were a little taller besides; she supposed this lush green countryside was easier to make a living in. Certainly the hunting was good, even if the animals did get a little testy at times.

The San hunter with his ankle in a pressure bandage belched enormously—it was probably good manners here, although she couldn't bring herself to follow. Being less inhibited, Swindapa did and was rewarded with a broad white grin from the little brown man—and giggles from their daughters. Alston smiled herself and leaned an elbow on the log she was using as a backrest. It was surprising how well everything had gone, considering that neither the Islanders nor the local tribesfolk spoke a word of each other's language. Treating the injured hunter and returning him with gifts had helped; so had indicating that his clan was welcome to help themselves to the elephant carcass.

Remarkable how many of them showed up, she thought—and even more remarkable how fast they'd managed to demolish the great mountain of flesh. *We can probably trade with them for fresh meat and greenstuff. That'll save time.*

"Go'od," the little man said, and hiccuped.

"Good," Alston replied.

Out in the darkness the party was probably getting a little rowdier, to judge from the squeals and giggles. *There are times not to notice things,* she thought—that was one of the secrets of command. The crew deserved a rest, and the locals would reduce the three-to-two male-female ratio that sometimes made a shoreside luau a little tense.

Swindapa caught her eye and slowly touched her upper lip with the tip of her tongue. Alston's smile grew broader.

"Euuu, mushy stuff!" Heather said, as she and her sister returned from the dance, reading the signs with an eight year old's lack of tact.

"Aw, c'mon, moms, don't send us away to sleep yet!" Lucy protested. "This is *fun.*"

A faint *pop* from across the harbor interrupted their parents' chuckle. Alston's face went cold and intent as she followed the arch of the signal rocket.

"Blue burst," she said. That meant *foreign ship in sight.* Her voice rose to the command call: "All hands, turn to!"

The San looked around in bewildered alarm as the Guard crewfolk dashed for their weapons and fell in. Alston stood and waited, watching the blinking Morse of the signal station. It was on the two-hundred-foot bluff that closed the southern arm of the harbor mouth, which gave it a wide field of view, and they had telescopes and night-sight glasses.

"*Two . . . Tartessian . . . vessels,*" it said. "*A large . . . schooner . . . and . . . one . . . larger . . . ship . . . rigged . . . craft. Landing . . . party . . . heading . . . for . . . harbor . . . entrance . . . in . . . one . . . longboat.*"

"Company," she said grimly, as the cabin steward ran up with their weapons belts.

"An attack?" Swindapa said.

"No, not in one longboat," Alston said. "But I don't like it."

I don't like anyone else in these waters, she thought, slitting her eyes against the dark. *God damn Walker to hell, and Isketerol too.*

A lantern showed out on the water; the Tartessians had probably realized they'd been seen. *Two ships . . . that could be anywhere up to three hundred men, if they're carrying war crews.* And they well might be. This would be a voyage of exploration for them, not just a trading run.

She turned to the injured hunter and made signs. "Bad," she said—they'd gotten that far in the impromptu language lesson. Then she made gestures of firing a gun and of a wide-winged ship. He scowled dramatically to show he understood.

"Ba'ad!" he replied, putting an indescribable tongue click into the word.

The longboat came into sight, at first a ghostly white of water frothed by oars, then an outline. A good-sized ship's boat with six oars to a side and several men seated in the stern, and a light mast with no sail bent to it; they'd probably struck that to stay inconspicuous when they realized someone was using the harbor. *Not a bad piece of work,* she thought. Differences of detail from anything an Islander would build; the bird-head carving of the forepiece, for instance, and the tongue-and-groove fit of the planks. For all that, it was modern, as modern went in the Year 8; it had a rudder, for instance, and the mast was rigged for a fore-and-aft sail.

The oarsmen bent their backs and then tossed their ashwood shafts up as the keel grated on sand. The crew hopped out and shoved the boat further up the beach, and then a man who flashed with spots of gold in the firelight vaulted down to the sand, his cloak a dark billow behind him.

Alston walked forward; a file of a dozen armed crewfolk under a petty officer followed behind, and a pair of lanterns. So did her children . . .

Damn, should have sent them back. Still, let's keep it casual.

The Tartessians made a clump on the beach, the small waves breaking white behind them, and the dry scuttering sound of land crabs coming with a flicker of movement from the edge of the pool of light.

Make that "mostly Tartessians," she thought.

From Arnstein's reports, King Isketerol's fleet was growing fast enough that Tartessos proper and the kindred groups the king had incorporated by conquest and intimidation couldn't supply enough men. Most of the ones she saw were Iberian in appearance, olive-skinned whites with bowl-cut dark hair and linen tunics considerably the worse for wear. One or two looked like North Europeans, burly and fair—of course, Spain and Morocco *did* produce that type now and then. Another was unmistakably an Egyptian, shaved head and sphinx headdress and pleated kilt; astonishingly, there was also a black, tall and lean and ebony-dark, with looping tribal scars on his face, and an Oriental.

The leader wore jutting chinbeard bound with gold wire, a sea-stained purple cloak, and silver-and-gold buckles on belt and sandals.

He had a short broad-bladed steel sword and dagger and a flintlock pistol; most of his men had blades at their belts as well, and muskets in their hands—several of them, she noted with displeasure, copies of the Westley-Richards breechloader. The African had a spear with a broad, shovel-shaped head and a long bow and quiver, and the Oriental wore a two-edged bronze broadsword slung over his back.

Chinbeard held up a hand in sign of peace and smiled. Alston told herself that the patent insincerity was probably her imagination.

"Hello, Islander," the man said, then checked as he saw her properly. He turned a little gray then, and his men stirred and murmured until he glared at them for an instant over his shoulder.

Alston smiled thinly. *Helps to have a reputation.* "Hello, Tartessian," she said in reply. "Do you speak my language? We have interpreters who know yours."

Swindapa spoke it fluently, although Alston had never managed more than a few words; Tartessian was distantly related to the Earth Folk tongue, and the Island's experts thought both were kin to some Bronze Age ancestor of Basque.

"Alantethol son of Marental is a New Man of the king," the Tartessian captain said proudly. *Ah—one of Isketerol's protégés,* she translated mentally. "I speak well your Englits tongue. I have to Nantucket itself sailed. Welcome you to our anchorage be!"

"Yoda," Marian thought to herself. *"You seek Yoda!"*

He looked around, taking in the hull of the *Chamberlain* in its improvised cradle and the gaping hole where the smashed planking had been removed. She could see his eyes taking in much else, as well—particularly the Islander camp, with its sand-and-palm-tree ramparts, and the snouted muzzles of the frigate's cannon mounted on them. And the dim ranks of the Guard crewfolk standing behind her.

"Tartessos has no claim on these waters, and the locals are under our protection," Alston said.

The man made a dismissive gesture. "Let not civilized men—ah, civilized folk—quarrel over savages," he said ingratiatingly.

If you only knew, Alston thought, fighting not to grind her teeth.

"What are you doing here!" she said.

"Trading!" the Tartessian said, swelling a little with pride. "For jade, jewels, spices, silk, rare woods—widely trading. Also we take a word of the world to our king, and our king's word to the world."

Uh-oh, Marian thought. With that list of ladings, he might well have been as far east as Indonesia, or even up to the Shang ports.

"I see you have storm damage," Alantethol said. "Help sailors should render each other—and my crew has been long at sea, needs shore time, green foods."

He scanned the Islander ranks, checking a bit at the sight of Heather and Lucy between Alston and her partner; especially on Lucy, with her pale milk-chocolate mulatto complexion. *I can pretty well hear him think, "How the hell did they manage that?"* Marian thought with bleak humor.

"We could share a feast," he went on.

"I don't think so," Alston said dryly. "And as I said, the locals are under our protection."

Alantethol flushed. darkly enough to be visible in the flickering firelight. "The world is the world's world," he said, his accent thickening. "Not for only your Island to say, 'Go here,' 'Don't go there'!"

"And I suggest you sail on," Alston replied. The Tartessian's face looked ugly. "But before you go, observe this."

She took one of the lamps from a sailor and shone it toward the bluff across the harbor, turning it away and back to make the dots and dashes of Morse. Five seconds after the last signal a red spark rose through the darkness from the observation post, arching halfway across the distance between them before the deep *thud* of a cannon's report reached them. The shell exploded an instant later, throwing up a column of shattered water. Any ship trying to enter the harbor would have more like that dropped right on its deck.

The Tartessian nodded curtly and turned on his heel, sand rutching under the sandal. The longboat surged backward as the crew shoved off, then turned with a flash of oars.

"Mom?" Heather said in a small voice. "Is there going to be trouble?"

"I hope not, punkin," Alston said gently. "Let's go back to the fire."

I hope not, but I think there will be, she thought to herself.

CHAPTER FIFTEEN

July–September, Year 9 A.E.

Ian Arnstein watched King Shuriash's white-knuckled grip on the hilt of his sword as they walked toward the landing field in the cool dimness of predawn. The ruler's face might have been cast in bronze, but there were beads of sweat on his forehead. The councilor for foreign affairs wasn't all that certain about riding in this wooden balloon himself. In fact, he was probably more worried about it than the Babylonian was; Shuriash knew that the magic of the Eagle People *worked*. He wasn't burdened with memories of the *Hindenburg* newsreel, or the knowledge that hydrogen was highly flammable.

And I know *that Ron Leaton isn't infallible*, Ian thought. He'd spent several exquisitely uncomfortable weeks bending over a sickle, back in the Year 1, because Seahaven Engineering's first attempt at a reaping machine had failed. And he'd seen Marian Alston's fury when it turned out that the first percussion primers decayed in humid conditions.

RNAS *Emancipator* looked formidably large, sitting here on the flat clay of the landing field outside the walls of Ur Base. Arnstein swallowed and bowed the king and his attendants up the ramp at the rear of the gondola.

"In only a few hours, we will be outside Asshur," he said.

Even then there was a little jostling over precedence in the seating. When it was over, he clipped on his seat belt, a retread from one of the commuter airlines that had flown into Nantucket. The seats were wicker, broader and far more comfortable than those in the deregulated buses-with-wings he'd had to ride in up in the twentieth.

They were seated just behind the working quarter at the head of the gondola and forward of the first of the engine control stations. Lieutenant Vicki Cofflin—captain of the vessel by function—was in her seat at the forward edge of the floor, with an intercom set on her head, checking instruments.

"Three hundred pounds heavy at ground level," she said, snapping a switch. "Feather props."

"Feathered."

"On with engines!"

A coughing roar started up; Arnstein saw the Babylonians flinch. *Good ol' internal-combustion noise and stink,* he thought—the six motors were burning kerosene, distilled right here at Ur Base, but it was burnt hydrocarbon nonetheless. Outside he could see a crowd of spectators, many of them surged back at the unfamiliar blatting.

"All engines at forty-five positive."

The six crewfolk spaced on either side of the gondola heaved at the wheels that faced them. Through the big, slanting window Arnstein could see the sections of wing and the cowled pods of the engines tilt, pointing the propellers away from the long axis of the dirigible and toward the ground.

"On superheat!"

A clicking, hissing roar as hot air rushed into the central gasbag, inflating it. And a soft, mushy feeling under his backside, as if the dirigible were sliding on a surface of smooth, oiled metal.

"Positive buoyancy! Prepare to cast off."

"Ready to cast off, Captain."

"Stand by engines. Horizontal controls, forty-five degrees." The man at the attitude helm spun his ship-style wheel. "Prepare to release . . . Release mooring!"

There was a series of heavy *chunk* sounds as the line-grabs along the keel of the gondola let go, and the *Emancipator* bounced upward, pushed by the air that outweighed the volume she displaced.

"Engage props, all engines ahead full!"

The six converted Cessna engines roared, pushing the lighter-than-air craft northward and up, into the wind. Acceleration shoved Arnstein back into his seat as the nose rose above the horizon, a sensation he hadn't felt in nearly a decade. King Shuriash swore by the private parts of Ishtar, then exclaimed again in delight, pointing with one calloused swordsman's finger.

"Look! We *fly,* Ian Aren-s'hein! We fly like the birds of the air, like the gods themselves!"

Shuriash had four attendants with him—a great concession, considering how important the king's dignity was—and three of them shared the king's childlike enjoyment; they were young noblemen, followers of his son. The fourth was Samsu-Indash, and the elderly priest was sitting rigid in his chair with his eyes clamped shut, lips moving in silent prayer. Ian suspected that the command to attend the king was something of a royal joke. Shuriash was not a cruel man, for an ancient Oriental despot, but he was an absolute ruler, and men forgot that at their peril.

The figures below shrank to the size of dolls, then ants. *It's like rid-*

ing a bicycle, Ian thought. *You don't forget*. At the same time it wasn't like taking off in an airliner, either. There was a surging lightness to it, sort of like riding Pegasus —if you could imagine Pegasus as one of the Clydesdales that pulled the Budweiser wagon.

"Neutral buoyancy at twenty-two hundred feet," the second-in-command of the *Emancipator* reported. "Wind is from the north-northwest at three miles per hour."

"Engines at zero inclination," Lieutenant Cofflin commanded. The wheels spun, and Ian could feel the airship move forward more rapidly as the propellers came level with the keel.

"All ahead three-quarters." Vicki glanced down at the instruments. "Airspeed is sixty-seven miles per hour."

Wow! Ian thought, half ironically. *Fast!* Considerably faster than he'd traveled since the Event, at least. He translated for Shuriash and saw the king's well hidden amazement.

"Navigator, lay me a course for Asshur," Vicki went on.

King Shuriash was looking down in fascination as the city of Ur slid beneath them, the great ziggurat reduced to model size. The rising sun silvered it, and for a moment canals great and small flashed metallic.

"I see now the excellence of your Nantukhtar maps," the Babylonian ruler murmured. "Strange to see the lands so . . . there are no boundaries to mark the realm of one king from the next."

His glance sharpened on Arnstein, and his smile grew sharkish. "Not that there would be, now, between Kar-Duniash and the lands of Asshur."

Ian nodded. "Together, our armies have been victorious," he said piously.

To himself: *Meaning, we shot the Assyrians up until they ran, and then your boy Kashtiliash chased them until his troops got tired.*

Of course, from what Hollard and Hollard said, it worked both ways. The Islanders could shatter the Assyrian armies in pitched battle, but there weren't enough of them to hold ground—without Babylonian manpower, they wouldn't have controlled more than the land they stood on. Less at night.

"Yes," Shuriash said. "And I admit it, we could not have conquered without you Nantukhtar. Certainly not without paying more in blood and treasure. We are much in your debt, and the debt shall be repaid. For now I rule from the northern mountains to the Sea-Land, and the way is clear to the Hittite country."

"Indeed, all these lands are now yours to rule as you would," Arnstein said.

The Babylonian looked up from beneath shaggy brows. "When a

man says that, he is about to tell me how I should rule as *he* would have me do," he said sardonically.

Ian spread his hands. "I would offer advice. Whether the king hearkens to it shall be as the king thinks best." Shuriash nodded, and the Islander went on: "It is one thing to conquer a land, and another to hold it."

Shuriash nodded again. "True. Hammurabi ruled widely, but his sons soon found their thrones rocking beneath them—and if the stories are true, the same held for Gilgamesh! What is your thought, councilor of my brother Jaered-Cofflin?"

"First, O King, that your enemies are the king and nobles of Assyria, not the people of the land, or their gods."

That was enough to bring Samsu-Indash out of his stupor. "As the men of Asshur bow to our King, so must their gods to ours—to Marduk, King of the Universe!"

Ian made a soothing gesture. "Oh, none could doubt it. Yet the great gods of the land bow to Marduk in their own temples, where their own priests serve them, as men were created to serve the gods."

"Ah, I see," Shuriash said. "You think that the temples of Asshur should remain unplundered, and we should not carry off the images to Babylon."

"Unplundered, but subject to the control of the king," Ian confirmed.

That meant a 20 percent tax on temple revenues, and the temples were the largest landowners and bankers in any Mesopotamian kingdom.

Shuriash had been polite but wary at the start, then increasingly ready to consider his allies' suggestions . . . and since Dr. Clemens saved his favorite, downright friendly. *Mind you, he's still damned shrewd and nobody's fool. Leaving the conquered temples standing is in his own interests, even in the short term.* The Babylonians might not know the negative *elenchos,* but they were fully aware that you couldn't skin the cow and milk it too.

"So the hearts of the people will not be filled with hatred against the king of Kar-Duniash," Arnstein finished. "Likewise, if the land is not laid waste, it will pay much more in taxes than it would if it were plundered."

"True—although to tell soldiers not to plunder is to offend against the nature of men. You have other such advice?"

"Yes, Oh King. I think that it would be very useful to you if you were to summon the men of Asshur's lands and make known to them the laws by which you will govern them."

Shuriash frowned. "How might that be? Proclamations in each city?"

"Better than that. Let a royal decree be sent forth, that in every district all the heads of households—all the men of consequence—should gather together and select one to be their *delegate*. Let these delegates come before the throne, to hear the word of the king and take it back to their homes. You could do that at regular intervals, so that all the land would know the decrees of the king and hear of his deeds."

"Hmmmm." A tug at the grizzled beard. "Much as the *puhrum*—the assembly of a city—does. Hmmmm, that might well be useful . . . useful enough that I might summon these *delegates* also from my own ancestral lands. And if such men were gathered before me, I could consult with one here, another there—learn the mind of the land and what could be safely demanded of it."

He clapped a hand on Arnstein's shoulder. "You are a councilor indeed, and my brother Jaered-Cofflin is fortunate to have your wisdom!"

Well, the British history course had something to do with it, Arnstein thought as he inclined his head. *The English parliament had started that way, with magnates called together to hear what the king had in mind.* Arnstein smiled to himself.

Eventually, though, it started working the other way 'round.

The camel complained, a groan tapering off into a moaning sigh.

That's what they're best at, Kenneth Hollard thought, and pulled on the rein. *Complaining. I'm getting used to the way they smell, though, and* that *worries me.*

The rein was fastened to a bronze ring in the beast's nose, and it turned with a fair show of obedience. Hollard wiped a forearm across his face to get rid of some of the grit-laden sweat and stood in the stirrups to take a slow scan from east to west. *Hmmm. Something there.*

It was getting on toward noon, anyway, bleaching the landscape to shades of fierce white and umber. In this land you stopped for at least four hours in the heat of day and then traveled on into the night.

Not quite desert, he thought; it sort of reminded him of parts of northern New Mexico he'd seen on vacations with his family, back before the Event. Hotter, though—there was a sparse covering of grass, an occasional thicket of low, waxy-green tamarisk in an arroyo, the odd water hole. The vegetation had been getting thicker as they came closer to the jagged blue line of the Jebel Sinjar on the northern horizon, too. Beyond them was the heart of the old kingdom of Mitanni, the district the Semites called Naharim, "the Rivers," in the plain between the Taurus range and the Jebel. An Assyrian province now, although they'd received vague reports that it was rising in revolt. Or, from the sound of things, just dissolving into a chaotic war of all against all.

Three thousand years in a future that had bred him and wasn't going to happen—he tried to avoid thinking about that; it made his head hurt—these steppes would be part of the northern borderland between Iraq, Syria, and Turkey. Right now it was called, variously, Mitanni, Hanigalibat, the River Country, and God-knew-what, and it had been a marchland between Assyria and the Hittite Empire. Mostly it seemed to be empty except for wandering bands of sheep-herding nomads. Hollard smiled grimly to himself. Empty except for the remnants of the fleeing Assyrian army, the part that wasn't holed up in Asshur over to the east on the Tigris. The camel-mounted recon company had been traveling through the detritus for days; dead men and donkeys, their corpses seething with maggots, foundered horses, broken chariots, bits of gear—everything from bedrolls to weapons and armor.

He waited for the Babylonian liaison officer to come up. Ibi-Addad had learned to handle his camel fairly well, and like all his countrymen he'd gotten more and more cheerful as the campaign went on, which was understandable. He was even prepared to put up with traveling in the desert, among the wandering Aramaeans—truffle-eating savages, to a man from the settled lands between the rivers. And he could speak Hittite, which might be useful in a little while.

"What do you make of that?" the Islander asked, pointing to what looked like a set of low adobe buildings at the foot of a rocky ridge.

Ibi-Addad stroked his beard, which had gone from neat black curls to a tangled thicket over the past couple of weeks, and raised his own binoculars—that gift would have made him willing to come along even without King Shuriash's orders.

"I think it is the . . . " he began, and trailed off into terms Hollard couldn't follow.

The Nantucketer sighed. *Just when I thought my Akkadian was getting really fluent.*

"The manor of a Mitannian *mariannu*," Ibi-Addad clarified. "They were the ruling folk of Mitanni, before the Assyrians and the Hittites broke that kingdom a hundred years ago. A fragment of it lived on as a vassal state until my father's time, when they revolted and King Shulmanu-asharidu of Asshur destroyed them. I do not suppose many of that breed are left."

"Let's go see," Hollard said. "I think the Assyrians are paying a visit." He grimaced; they'd seen the results of that, in villages and nomad camps. "I thought this was part of their kingdom? They're acting like they were in enemy territory, though."

Ibi-Addad shrugged eloquently; he was in Marine khakis, but the gesture was purely Babylonian. "They are broken men fleeing defeat, and these are conquered provinces. The people here hate them. Except for the Assyrian colonists, and those are in the cities."

Hollard nodded and turned in the saddle. "Spread out and look alive!" he called.

The complex of buildings came into view as the camels paced northward in a long double line; a hundred mounted riflemen, and a mortar team with the pack animals. Another thing the Assyrians were having trouble adjusting to was how far a camel-borne outfit could swing into the desert and how fast it could move. The locals used donkeys for carrying cargo, and those had to be watered every day or so.

Oooops. Assyrians, all right—a couple of hundred of them, with half a dozen chariots. That meant some fairly high-ranking officers, given the shape of what remained of their field army. The men were milling around the adobes; those looked like they'd seen better days, with more than half of what had been a substantial village in tumbledown ruins. One or two of the large buildings seemed to have been occupied until recently; they were shedding mud plaster but still largely intact. There must be a spring of good water here, then, and the stubble fields indicated a hundred acres or so of grain, enough to sustain a big household if not a town, together with the grazing.

Hollard flung up a hand as the Assyrians broke into shouts and pointing, and the company came to a halt. *Careless bastards—should have seen us long before now.*

"Captain O'Rourke!"

The commander of the recon company whacked his camel on the rump and sped up to the commander's side.

"Business, sir?"

"Enemy up ahead. They've spotted us, and any minute now . . ."

Oooops again. A racket of harsh trumpet sounds and cries came from the cluster of beige-colored mud-brick buildings half a mile away.

"We'll be seeing them off, then, sir?"

"That we will, Paddy," Hollard said. "Six hundred yards, and set up the mortar. Open order. Let's not get sloppy."

The Assyrians were pouring out of the open ground, into the protection of the stout two-story building and its courtyard. The house was windowless on the ground floor, with narrow slits suitable for archers above, and from the looks of it the courtyard wall had a proper fighting platform on the inside. A short, thick tower rose from the rear of it, giving another story over the flat rooftop.

"Looks like a fortress," he said in Akkadian. Ibi-Addad had picked up a little functional English, but not enough for a real conversation.

"How not, Lord Hollard?" he said. "This is the edge of cultivation—the Aramaeans would be all over anyone not ready to fight like flies on a fresh donkey turd."

Hollard nodded; they'd seen *that,* too—small bands of Assyrian stragglers overrun by nomads out for loot and payback. They seemed to have a knack for skinning a man alive, from the feet up. He put the image out of his mind with an effort; the Assyrian had still been alive when they found him, one huge scab with eyes staring out of it, and *moving.*

"Looks like they've learned better than trying to rush us." O'Rourke chuckled. "Damned alarmin' it was, a few times."

Hollard nodded again. Whatever you could say about the Assyrians, they didn't lack for guts.

"Let's do it by the numbers, then," he said.

A thousand yards from the settlement the Islanders came across the first bodies. Hollard's brows rose; they looked like standard Mesopotamian peasants, men in loincloths or short tunics and women in long ones and shawlike headdresses. These had obviously been caught fleeing. One had a broken arrow stub in the back of his head, probably too tightly wedged to be worth recovering. Several others showed gaping wounds where shafts had been cut out for reuse, and the great pools of black blood were still a little tacky and swarming with flies.

"This morning," he said, not looking at a few very small bodies. *Those* had been tossed on spears.

"Sunrise, or a little after, I'd say," O'Rourke said, crossing himself.

Hollard looked eastward. The chariots had probably come in first and caught the workers out in the fields. A good place to halt, about a thousand years from the big flat-roofed house, and barley straw could be sharp enough to hurt a camel's footpads.

The camels halted and knelt, chewing and spitting, glad enough of a rest; some lifted their long necks and flared the flaps over their nostrils in interest at the scent of water and green growing things from the courtyard ahead. Marines dismounted, unslinging their rifles and exchanging floppy canvas hats for the helmets strapped to their packs. Others hammered iron stakes into the ground and tethered the beasts to them. The mortar team lifted the four-foot barrel of their weapon off a pack camel's back with a grunt, and there was a series of *clicks* and *clunks* as the weapon was clipped into its base and clamped onto the steel bipod that supported the business end. The sergeant in charge of the weapon was whistling tunelessly between her teeth as she unbuckled the leather strapping on the strong wicker boxes that held the finned bombs.

"Three up, one back?" O'Rourke asked.

Ken nodded; he wasn't going to second-guess the man on the spot unless he needed it. Patrick Joseph O'Rourke was possibly a little too ready to lean on higher authority—one reason he didn't have Hollard's job. Nothing wrong with his aggressiveness at the company level, though, and he had the saving grace of a wicked sense of humor.

The company commander turned and barked: "D Platoon in reserve, A through C in skirmish order. Prepare to advance on the word of command—and fix bayonets!"

The long blades came out and clattered home, their edges throwing painfully bright reflections in the hot Asian sun. Kenneth Hollard hid a slight grimace of distaste at the sight. He *knew* what it felt like to run edged metal into a man, the soft, heavy resistance. And the look in his eyes as he realized he was going to die, and the sounds he made, and the smell . . .

"Dirty job," O'Rourke said, catching his thought without the irrelevance of words.

"But somebody's got to do it."

Some of the Sun People rankers were grinning at the prospect of a fight. *But then, they're all maniacs, anyway.* Good soldiers but weird. Sometimes he worried a little about the impact they would have when they mustered out and got their citizenship. Up to now most of the immigrants had been Fiernan. Who were weird too, but less aggressive about it.

He raised his binoculars again. Plenty of the distinctive ruddy glitter of bronze along the edges of walls . . .

"Sir?"

That was Sergeant Winnifred Smith of the mortar team—Immigration Office name, she was obviously Alban by origin—Sun People, from the accent.

No questions asked, Hollard reminded himself. Your record started the day you took the oath, in the Guard or the Corps.

O'Rourke lowered his own glasses. "Let's start by knocking down the big gateway into the courtyards," he said. "With a little luck, they'll rush us."

"Yessir," the sergeant replied.

A broad grin showed as she worked the elevation and traverse screws; the muzzle of the mortar moved up a bit, and to the right.

"Nine hundred yards . . . one ring," she called over her shoulder.

"One ring, aye," the man with the mortar bomb in his hands said.

That was an elongated iron teardrop with fins at its base. A section above the fins was perforated, and around that his assistant clipped a linen donut of gunpowder. Then he slipped the friction primer into the base of the bomb, turned the wooden-ring safety and pulled it out.

Now when the round was dropped down the muzzle it would drive the primer in on itself, striking a light in exactly the same way as a matchbox and match. Seahaven swore that they'd have percussion caps available in quantity soon, but in the meantime this worked and they could make more in the field at need. Leaton swore he'd have a brass-cartridge rifle available next year too, but Hollard would believe that when it arrived.

"Fire in the hole!" the sergeant barked, and dropped the bomb into the waiting maw of the mortar. The team turned away, mouths open and ears plugged with their thumbs.

Thuddump!

A jet of dirty-gray smoke shot out of the muzzle. The bomb followed it, landing in the dirt about fifteen feet in front of the weathered wooden gates.

Whuddump! The bursting-charge exploded, throwing up a black shape of dirt that stood erect for a moment before drifting westward and falling in a patter of dust and clods. A small crater gaped in the packed earth of the trackway. Shouts and screams could be heard from the men within; the Assyrians had some experience of being under fire from the Islander artillery by now, and they didn't like it at all. A few stood up over the parapet, shaking fists or weapons.

Not enough experience, though, Hollard thought coldly, remembering the dead peasants and their children.

"Marksmen may fire on movement!" O'Rourke called out. "No need to let the insolence of them go unrequited."

Here and there along the line Marines with the sniper star began to fire, slow and deliberate. An Assyrian pitched forward off the parapet over the gates, landing with a limp *thunp* on the ground. Several others toppled backward, some screaming. The others ducked down, and ducked further when a bullet clipped the top of a bronze helmet barely showing over the crenelations of the defense. The helmet went spinning, ringing like a cracked bell. Fragments of the skull and brain beneath probably followed it.

"Lost his head completely, poor fellow," O'Rourke said.

Sergeant Smith gave the elevating screw a three-quarter turn. "Fire in the hole!" she called again and dropped in the second bomb.

Thuddump!

Another malignant whistle overhead, dropping away . . . and this time it crashed precisely into the arch over the gateway. When the smoke cleared the arch had a bite taken out of its apex—more dropped away as Hollard watched—and the wood of the gates was splintered, torn and burning.

"Lord Kenneth-Hollard," Ibi-Addad said, a frown of worry on his sun-browned face. "What if some of them drop off the wall on the northern side and run?"

"I hope they do," Hollard said. At the Babylonian's inquiring look: "All I can do is kill them."

"Ah," Ibi-Addad chuckled. "But if the Aramaeans catch them . . ."

"Exactly."

"And the tribes will be hanging about like vultures on a tamarisk above a sick sheep," King Shuriash's man said happily. Then he frowned. "More and more of the sand-thieves roam in these lands every year, though, and they press into the settled country whenever they get a chance."

Hollard nodded; according to the Arnsteins' briefings the Aramaeans were slated to overrun most of the Middle East in the dark age that the pre-Event histories said was coming, and their tongue and ways would stamp themselves on the region for millennia. Aramaic would be the state language of the Persian Empire, and the native tongue of Jesus. Or would have been . . .

Thuddump! Thuddump! Thuddump!

Hollard blinked and coughed as the harsh sulfur-smelling black powder smoke blew past. The mortar was firing for effect now, and the thick, soft adobe walls of the manor house and courtyard wall went up in gouts of dust. Smoke began to trickle skyward as the timbers supporting the roof caught fire. One round landed with spectacular— if accidental—accuracy square on top of the tower, sending a shower of wood, mud brick, and bodies in every direction.

"Roast, run into the wilderness, or come out and get shot," Ibi-Addad laughed.

Hollard nodded. True enough, although he still didn't like to hear laughter as men died. None of the choices available to the Assyrians were good.

"Heads up!" one of the snipers called. "Here they come!"

The rest of the line thumbed back the hammers of their rifles, a long multiple-clicking sound, as the enemy swarmed forward over the rubble of courtyard wall and gate.

So, they decided to die fighting, Hollard thought. Or trying to fight, anyway.

"Independent fire!" O'Rourke called.

The platoon commanders echoed it; Hollard heard "make it count" and "Aim low." Spray-and-pray was bad enough with automatic weapons; with a single-shot like the Westley-Richards, you really needed to take some trouble.

The rifles began to speak their sharp, spiteful cracks. Hollard estimated the Assyrians at a hundred and fifty or so, and they began dying as soon as they left cover, men falling limp or crawling, screams as faint with distance as the war cries. Other bullets kicked up puffs of dust around them; he saw one Assyrian stop and slam his spear at one, probably thinking it was some sort of invisible devil.

More fell as they drew closer, but none of the enemy turned back toward the shattered, burning buildings. The last one to fall carried a standard with a sun disk in gold on the end of a long pole; his face was set and calm, and by some fluke of ballistics he came within fifty yards of the Islander line before three of the heavy bullets struck him simultaneously. Hollard saw his face go from a set, almost hieratic peace to brief agony and then blankness as he toppled forward. The standard fell in the dirt and lay with the steppe wind flapping the bright cloth against the ground and raising tiny puffs of dust as it struck.

Silence fell, broken by a few moans and whimpers and men calling for their mothers—Holland had noted how that always happened on a battlefield, and he always hated it. Then there was a shout from the ruined buildings; another man emerged, this one waving a green branch torn from one of the trees within.

"Cease fire!" Hollard called.

He walked out in front of the Islander line and waited, one hand resting on the butt of his pistol. "That's far enough," he said, when the Assyrian was about six feet away. No sense taking chances with a possible berserker.

The man was obviously not a soldier; he was dressed in the long gown and fringed, embroidered wraparound upper garment that was a mark of high rank, and his curled beard was more gray than black. His face was a pasty gray with recent hardship and with fear, although you could see that before that he'd been well fed.

"Mercy!" he called. He went down on his knees and raised a clod of dirt to his lips; then down on his belly and crawled forward, kissing Hollard's boot and trying to put it on his neck.

"Mercy!" he bleated.

Kenneth Hollard restrained an impulse to kick the Assyrian nobleman in the face. "Surrender, and live," he said.

Ibi-Addad sighed and rolled his eyes as the crawling man began to babble thanks and call down benedictions from his gods, his teeth bared in an unconsciously doglike grin of submission.

"You Eagle People." he said. "Fierce as lions one minute, then like lambs. It makes no sense."

"Get up, get up," the Marine colonel said. "Go back there. Tell your countrymen that if they're not all outside in five minutes, we'll kill you all. We'll also kill you all if we find anyone hiding within, or if there's any resistance. Go! Now!"

O'Rourke was frowning at the enemy dead. "Notice something, sir?" he said.

Hollard did, and heard Ibi-Addad's surprised grunt follow. "They're all armed like a noble's retainers," he said.

Corselets of bronze scales, or bronze studs in thick bull hide; good metal-bossed shields, and nearly every man had a sword as well. His eye picked out other details: embroidered rosettes along the edge of a tunic, gold and silver inlay on a belt buckle or hilt, silver buckles on a sandal, a tooled-leather baldric. Some of the Marines were eyeing the same things with interest. Albans weren't squeamish about picking up valuables; he'd have to tell off a working party, when things were settled.

"Bind not the mouths of the oxen that tread out the grain," as the Bible said. Would say. Whatever.

The remaining Assyrians were scrambling out of the wrecked building, a score or so of them, including some badly wounded enough to require carrying or dragging. They went to their knees as the Nantucketers approached, touching clods of earth to their lips or holding out their hands to touch feet or thighs in token of submission, babbling in their rough northern dialect of Akkadian.

"Shut up!" Hollard barked. "Captain O'Rourke, give me a squad; we'll check the building."

"Ah . . . wouldn't it be better if I did that, sir?"

Hollard smiled for the first time in several hours. "No, it wouldn't, Paddy." Leading from the front went with the job in the Republic's forces. "Keep an eye on the prisoners and have the medic patch those that need it. And be careful: smoke draws more than vultures, here."

Hollard made sure that the *katana* slung over his back was loose in its sheath. Then he drew his pistol and used the weapon to wave the eight-bayonet section forward with him. The house wasn't exactly burning, but wood was smoldering and sending up black smoke here and there. *If there's enough left for shelter, we can put it out,* he thought. The shattered adobe was loose and treacherous beneath his feet as he climbed through.

The courtyard enclosed by the L shape of the main building and its own wall was substantial and had been handsome before it was shelled. A spring bubbled up in a stone-lined basin in the center; that would be priceless here. There were the remains of grapevines trained up trellises along the walls, and rows of fruit trees as well as banks of herbs, vegetables, and flowers. What attracted his attention was the six men and women impaled on tree trunks that had been cut down and sharpened in lieu of stakes. One of the privates behind him swore softly in Fiernan, another in English.

Well, he thought, swallowing hard himself and looking away from the contorted features of those who'd died in agony, *at least it makes you feel better about the job.* He was glad the heavy fog of dust and burnt powder was enough to cover most of the stink.

There weren't any living Assyrians in the courtyard, although the iron scythe of shell fragments from the mortar had left plenty of dead ones; he forced down a chilly satisfaction at that and walked through toward the building. There were two big doors standing open, leading into a sort of hallway. It had been a handsome space once, with painted frescoes on the plastered wall, and stone benches around the all-around, but the paint was faded and patched with plain mud, and the tile floor was cracked and worn.

The Assyrians had made modifications of their own. A table was draped in an expensive-looking knotted rug, and on it was a very dead man in armor of gilded scales, a purple-crimson cloak spread over him. His eyes were wide, and someone had slashed diagonally across his neck, a deep, ugly wound. A young man, with the heavy hooked nose, dense curled beard, and full lips common in these lands; deep chested as well, and judging from the muscular forearms and legs, very strong in life. The tanned skin was pale with blood loss, but seamed white scars were still visible.

And at the foot of the improvised bier, a woman was hanging from the ceiling, dangling by a rope looped around her wrists and secured to a notch in one of the exposed rafters. Her ankles were bound as well, and below her feet was a neatly prepared tepee of kindling and sticks ready to light. She wore the diaperlike undergarment universal here, and dried blood marked a scattering of whip marks on her back.

"Catch her!" Hollard barked, tossing the pistol into his left hand and reaching over that shoulder with his right. "And then get the corpsman."

The *katana* came out with a long *shinnng* of steel on leather and wood. Two of the Marines slung their rifles and obeyed; the rope was plaited leather, and it took two strokes before the tough hide parted. The woman gave a hoarse grunt as she fell back into their arms and opened her eyes as they lowered her to the ground. Her arms stirred only slightly as Hollard went to one knee and held his canteen to her lips; she drank eagerly, water spilling down her face.

Young, he decided. Not more than her late teens. Not quite like the physical type usual here, either. Her long black hair was feathery-fine and straight; it had russet highlights, while the eyes were a dark gray rimmed with amber-green. Her skin was a clear olive, features straight-nosed and regular, and her build more slender than the rather stocky local norm. On Nantucket he'd have said she had Italian in her background, or maybe Spanish. A memory teased at him . . .

Back before the Event. Who was it , . . yeah, she looks a little like . . . that woman who was prime minister of Pakistan . . . Benazir Bhutto, yeah.

The medic came running in, her red-cross-marked satchel in hand. "Diawas Pithair!" she blurted, in the Keyaltwar dialect, calling on the sky father who was overgod of the Sun People tribes.

The young woman's head came up, her eyes losing the glaze of pain. She looked at Hollard, then at the medic and a few others who were crowding around, and spoke.

"Dyaush Pitar?" she said, and then an eager string of sentences.

The medic looked baffled and replied in her own tongue as she began her work, which consisted mainly of ointment and bandages for wrists and ankles and whip marks. She shook her head and looked up at Hollard as she finished.

"Sir, it's real funny—I sort of feel I *should* be able to understand what she's saying, but I can't. Uh, she's okay—the shoulder joints are stressed, but they'll do fine if she rests 'em for a few days."

The woman spoke again in another language, throaty and agglutinative-sounding, and then in Akkadian; the Babylonian version of it, he noticed.

"Who are you?" she said.

Hollard sat back on his heel, resting his weight on an elbow across his thigh. "Colonel Kenneth Hollard, Republic of Nantucket Marine Corps," he said and then translated: "Kenneth Hollard, commander of a thousand in the host of the Eagle People."

"Ahhh! I heard the pigs of Asshur speak of you—an army of demons with weapons that spat fire and smashed walls like the fist of Teshub. I thought they lied, but I am glad that they spoke the truth."

Yet another non-admirer of the Assyrians, Hollard thought. *They have a positive gift for negative PR.*

"And who are you, young gentlewoman?" Hollard said.

Someone with a lot of guts, anyway, he thought. From the looks of things she'd been about to be tortured to death, and now she was surrounded by weirdly armed strangers, yet she looked cool as a cucumber, working her shoulders without even a wince at what must be considerable pain. *Probably near collapse underneath, though,* he thought—he could sense the quivering intensity of her control.

"I am Raupasha daughter of Shuttarna." The girl's chin lifted. "Who would have been rightful king of Mitanni, if the gods had not thrown the realm down in the dust."

Well, shit, Hollard thought. *That may complicate things.*

"Ah . . . if your father was here . . ."

A bleak expression; she turned her head aside for an instant and drew a deep breath. "No. He died while I was yet in the womb; the Assyrians killed him when they destroyed the last of the kingdom, and my mother died bearing me. I saw what they did out there; they made me watch. That was the lord Tushratta, the *mariannu*—the warrior-retainer—who bore me southward to this last estate of his and raised me as his own."

"Er . . . what happened here?"

A shrug, and she turned her face away, blinking rapidly.

"The Assyrians čame last night, fleeing defeat. My foster father greeted them as guests. What could he do, with twenty men only and they peasants, against more than a hundred in full armor? Then they demanded that I dance for their leader—meaning that he would rape me at his pleasure."

Her smile grew even bleaker. "And dance I did, and when he seized me—breaking the law of hospitality that all the gods hold sacred—I opened his neck with the knife in my sleeve. Then they slaughtered all here, save me—they gave over thought of ravishing me and after much argument decided that to flog me to death would be too merciful. Instead they hung me up as you saw. Not long after, I heard the thunder of your weapons. So my life was spared—Teshub, and Hepat, and Shaushga, and Indara, and Mitra, and Auruna, and the other gods and goddesses must favor me greatly."

Remind me not to get this chick mad at me, Hollard thought.

She struggled to her feet and made an imperious gesture; one of the Marines hastily picked up a long shawl, and she wrapped it around herself. Then she walked stiffly to the side of the bier and spat in the dead man's face.

"May dust be his food and salt his drink in the House of Arabu. My foster father and mother are avenged, at least."

"Who was he, anyway?" Hollard asked. *Time to get back to business.*

The girl smiled. It looked as if it hurt her face. "You do not know, Lord Kenn'et? That is—was—Tukulti-Ninurta. King of the Universe of Swine, King of the Four Corners of the Pigpen, King of Assyria, last of the seed of Shulmanu-asharidu, who slew my father and my people. Thus are *all* my kin avenged."

"Oh, *shit.*" It was time to call the Arnsteins and pass the buck. In the meantime . . .

"You will be safe with us, Lady Raupasha," he said. In English: "Sergeant, see to the young lady's needs." He dropped back into Akkadian: "Your pardon. I must see to my troops."

He turned and strode out, blinking in the bright sunlight. O'Rourke had taken down the impaled bodies, and working parties were hauling bucketfuls of water to splash and sizzle on charring timbers.

"So, Colonel, I hear it's a princess we rescued," he said. "A young, beautiful princess at that."

"Paddy, for once rumor does not lie—and there's all sorts of political implications involved."

"Better you than me, sir. You'd best take a look at this, too, though."

They went up a mud-brick staircase to a section of the house roof still strong enough to bear their weight. "Over there, southwest."

The figures he pointed to were ant-tiny in the distance. Hollard raised his binoculars and turned the focusing screw; the ants became men, leaping close in the dry, clear air.

Uh-oh.

A gray-bearded man on a donkey, in a long striped robe with a fringe, a flowing headdress, and a sword belted at his waist. Several men talking to him, arguing with broad, quick gestures. More donkeys with packsaddles, and men on foot—fifty or sixty, scattered over the bare steppeland. He studied them; a few in plainer robes than the chief, many in simple goatskin kilts. None of them had swords—most of them didn't even have sandals—but they all had long knives tucked through their belts. Bows, slings, and spears were in evidence too, and a few had hide and wicker shields.

They were lean men with vast black beards, their bodies looking as if they were made out of sun-dried rawhide. Leaning on their spears, or laying them across their shoulders and resting their arms on them, or squatting at their ease. He could see one spitting thoughtfully on a rock and honing a curved bronze dagger that would do quite well as a skinning knife.

Aramaeans, right enough, he thought. Aloud: "No sheep, no goats, and no women."

"War party," O'Rourke agreed.

"Well, that solves one problem," Hollard replied and drew his pistol again as he trotted downstairs.

When he stood in front of the prisoners he gestured with it; they'd learned enough to know that it was one of the fire-weapons that had broken their kingdom, and they eyed it fearfully.

"All right, you're free to go," he said.

The spokesman who'd kissed his foot looked up from giving a dipper of water to a bandaged countryman. "Free, lord? No ransom?"

"Free and clear." He pointed to the south. "Now get going."

"Go?"

"What part of *go* don't you understand, you son of a bitch?" he roared, the control that had kept his voice level suddenly cracking. The Assyrian flinched as if from a blow. "Go! Thataway! Or by God, I'll shoot you down like a dog here and now. All of you—go!"

"But, lord! We have no food or water or weapons or—"

"*Go!*"

"But we will die!"

Hollard smiled; it felt a little like a smile, though the Assyrian flinched again. When he spoke, his voice was calm.

"We have an old saying—as a man sows, so shall he reap."

He fired into the dirt next to the Assyrian's foot. "March!"

Ibi-Addad came out and watched the departing Assyrians with a moment's mild curiosity. Then he waved a leather sack.

"Look, Lord Hollard! Packed with salt, this will be perfect for keeping the head until you lay it before King Shuriash. That all men may know your victory!"

"Oh, *shit.*"

CHAPTER SIXTEEN

September–December, Year 9 A.E.

"**M**y lord king Agamemnon!" William Walker said, his voice loud and full of concern. "I will offer a hectacomb of white oxen to Zeus the Father in thanks that you live!"

The throne room of Mycenae was less bright than usual, despite the mirrors and lamps that Walker had installed for his hegemon years ago. Many had been shattered by the same grenade fragments that had flecked the walls. Blasts had scaled off a lot of the painted plaster, and blood was splashed across much of what was left of the magnificent murals of lions and griffons and Minoan-style sea creatures that sprawled in multicolored splendor around the great room.

The smell of burnt pork came not from a feast but from the body of the guardsman who'd fallen backward into the great circular marble-rimmed hearth, half-drowning the fire with his blood. Parties of Walker's guard regiment were at work carting out the bodies. He gestured to make sure one got the corpse in the hearth before the fire there went out—that would be extremely bad mojo, to the wogs' way of thinking. The hearthfire was the luck of the house and kin.

Not that I have to pay as much attention to that now, he thought. Still, no reason not to when it didn't cost anything.

"But the traitors around you have been found out and defeated," Walker went on, still in a loud public voice. "What a loss for all the lands of the Achaeans if you had been killed in the fighting!"

What a monumental pain in the ass for me, he added to himself. Right now he could enforce a claim to being the power behind the throne and make it stick at gunpoint, but he couldn't sit on the sacred seat himself. Not yet. Too many of the Achaean nobles would fight to the death if an outlander's low-bred fundament actually touched it. He needed them.

For now.

Agamemnon's face was still sagging with shock. *A lot grayer than when I arrived here,* Walker thought. *Lot fatter, too.* It made him pleasantly conscious of his own trim physique. The suit of articulated plate made for him back on Nantucket a few months after the Event still fit. So did the belt he'd won at eighteen in the Colorado state rodeo.

He looked up. Every Mycenaean palace—except his—had a four-pillar arrangement around the central hearth, with a gallery where the second story could look down into the great hall. Alice Hong was there, in Mycenaean robes but still looking as alien as the Beretta in her hand. She gave him the high sign and pulled a younger woman away, leading her by the hand.

"How . . ." Agamemnon began, then cleared his throat. His glance took in the ranks of musketeers along the walls, their bayonets bright—or in some cases, still sticky-red. "How did you know?"

"How did I know that evil councilors—surely men in the pay of the Hittites!—had attempted to turn your mind against me, King of Men? Had tried to persuade you to turn on me? Ah. Well, you see . . . you Achaeans are fine people, but you have your blind spots."

"Blind spots?" the lord of Mycenae asked, bewildered.

"Sorry. Literal translations don't always work." And he didn't always realize he was translating, since he thought in Achaean much of the time now. "*Blind spot* means things you don't see even though they're there. Like women. Just a second."

Ohotolarix saluted and bowed his head. "*Lord,*" he said, dropping back into Iraiina for security's sake, "we have the building in our fist. All the men you named are dead or in our hands."

"Good," Walker answered in the same tongue. "Now make sure none of their families get away either." These people were blood-feudists, and nits made lice.

"Women?" Agamemnon said again.

Dude's beginning to sound like a broken record, Walker thought.

Hong came into the hall, still leading the girl by the hand. There was a strong family resemblance between her and the middle-aged woman who trailed behind, strong straight noses and snapping black eyes. The rich fabric of their layered dresses rustled as they walked, with a hissing like snakes.

"Yeah, women. You see, the women in a palace hear everything—but you nobles, you act like they were doorposts or something."

Hong spoke: "And the Dark Sisterhood of Hekate is everywhere!"

Walker spared her a cold glance. "Yeah, well, secret societies, they're sort of more useful when they're *secret,* right, babe?"

"Well, sorry about that, Mr. Montana Maniac at King Agamemnon's Court."

His eyes flared like distant heat-lightning. "Not now, Alice!"

"Sorry, Will."

She didn't look sorry; she looked like she was lit up, a major glow on. *Hell, I feel like I've just snorted half an ounce myself,* Walker thought. *As if he could fight lions bare-handed and ball the whole cheerleading squad into squealing ecstasy and still run the Ironman triathlon. But I keep it under control, and dear Alice had better do likewise.*

"My wife?" the Greek croaked. "My *daughter*?"

"My lord king should remember that he was publicly considering sacrificing her for good luck in the coming war," Walker said.

"But that was for the good of the realm!" he protested. "The priests—"

And my lord king should have known, but didn't, that I was the one who bribed the augurs to say that we couldn't win unless you did. Of course, the idea wasn't completely mine; Alice sort of suggested it indirectly, when she got that hissy fit about fate. And she got it from Homer.

Now the augurs would explain that the king was "sacrificing" his daughter by marrying her to the new commander-in-chief. It was perfect, if he did say so himself.

There was an exchange of sign and countersign at the entrance to the hall. Odikweos of Ithaka came through with his hand on his sword hilt and a group of his officers behind him.

"Rejoice, shield-brother," he said to Walker, after a perfunctory bow to Agamemnon.

Even now the Achaean monarch started to swell with indignation at the discourtesy and opened his mouth to reprove it, but another glance at the armed men around his throne dissuaded him.

"The lower city is under control," Odiweos went on. "There was a little fighting at the barracks, but not much."

Walker nodded. "Sometimes you can shoot men more effectively with gold and silver bullets than with lead," he said. *Particularly if you see to it that they lose more than they can afford to well-trained dice,* he added to himself.

The Ithakan went on: "I have field guns commanding all the open spaces and patrols bringing in all the men on the list."

A figure in a long robe waited a pace to the vassal king's rear. "Enkhelyawon?" Walker prompted.

His chief of correspondence cleared his throat. "My lord, the scribes of the palace are in order and the telegraph office has been secured." He risked a glance at Agamemnon, but the high king was still staring in dazed horror at his wife and daughter. "The printed account of your crushing of the conspiracy and the list of proscribed families is already going out to Tiryns, Argos, Athens, Pylos, and the other citadels."

"Good. Carry on—see that normal message traffic continues until we have guard troops in place everywhere."

He turned back to the high king. "And we need some privacy, O King of Men, to decide how to safeguard you from future conspiracies."

Like, you marry me to your daughter and declare me lawagetas— general in chief—of all the Achaeans, for starters. And you don't so much as piss against a wall without my permission from now on. You'll probably die of natural causes before you stop being useful, though, so don't sweat it too much, dude.

"Treason," Agamemnon whispered, when the onlookers were gone.

"Not at all," Walker said with a charming, boyish grin.

"How not?" the Greek said with a certain haggard dignity. "Although at least you have not slain me who took you in when you were a fugitive and suppliant."

"Oh, I'd never have you killed. You're far too useful alive," Walker said. "As for the treason . . . well, among my birth-people we have an old saying: Why is it that treason never prospers?"

Agamemnon's head went back. "Because the curse of Zeus the Avenger of Right and the wrath of the Kindly Ones pursues the oath-breaking man who turns on his lord!" he said, his voice firm once more.

Behind Walker, Odikweos winced slightly. The American went on cheerfully: "Not exactly, Oh High King," he said. "We say that it never prospers, because if it prospers . . . why, none dare *call* it treason."

The Greeks stared in appalled silence as his laughter echoed through the great blood-spattered hall of the House of Atreus.

Prince Kashtiliash lowered his binoculars. "Their walls are open," he said eagerly. "As open as—" he coughed; speaking to Major Kathryn Hollard it might not be tactful to say *a woman's legs.* "—as the door of an unguarded house."

Asshur lay on the west bank of the Tigris. That meant something more definite here in northern Mesopotamia, away from the alluvial plains of Kar-Duniash. Here the land was higher, rolling steppe with copses of scrub oak in the ravines. Dust smoked off stubble fields, and sunset was throwing Prussian blue on the outliers of the Zagros mountains over the river. Ahead, the high stone wall of the Assyrian capital was black against the first stars on that horizon, with the triangular crenellations of the wall cutting the sky like jagged teeth.

More jagged than they were when we started, Kathryn Hollard thought.

She looked over from the little hillock where she and the Babylonian commander stood. The two rifled siege guns were further forward, on a hill their local allies had fortified with earthworks under Islander direction; a couple of the field guns were emplaced there too, and a brace of mortars to command any dead ground where the Assyrians might mass for an attack. The position was two thousand yards from the wall, nearly ten times the range of any weapon the defenders had. As she watched, a long jet of reddish fire shot out from the muzzle of one of the big guns. In the gathering darkness the shell was a red dot arching through a long curve of night. Another vicious red snap marked the spot where it drove into a section of wall still standing.

The deep *boooom* of the siege gun merged into the sharper sound the forged-steel projectile made when it struck stone. Half a second later fifteen pounds of gunpowder exploded within the mortared limestone of the wall, and a section of it collapsed outward with a roar like Niagara. A man came down too, falling outward in a trajectory that ended on hard, unforgiving ground. She was too far away to hear his scream, but the cheering from the battery came clearly, thin with distance.

Asshur was a lopsided triangle, with a long, curved wall cutting across the base and a sharp bend of the Tigris around the other two sides. Three hundred yards of the middle of the wall were down now, making a rough ramp that filled the moat and stretched out from the wall like a fan. Assault troops wouldn't need ladders to walk into Asshur now, only sandals and a good sense of balance. Fires were burning here and there within the walls, and a confused murmur of sound told of crowds in the streets.

The walls themselves were dark; if the sentries were still there, they'd learned better than to highlight themselves for bored riflemen. Lamps and bronze baskets of lightwood burned on the two higher hills over toward the riverside edge of the city. The bulky outlines of ziggurat and palace showed there; probably where King Tukulti-Ninurta took counsel with his noblemen and priests, although Intelligence hadn't been able to locate him since the Battle of the Diyala.

As if to seek him, a red spark rose into sight from the river; the flat, distant *thud* came a second later, and then the crash of impact. That would be one of the shallow-draft steamers patrolling under the river walls.

If Tukulti's there, probably nobody has a good word to say to him, she thought happily. *And I feel pretty good about that.*

In her opinion, Kenneth was a little soft on the enemy. Nobody who'd seen what Assyrians did to prisoners should waste much sympathy on them. From what she'd heard, they certainly didn't when *they* were top dog.

Kashtiliash's thoughts seemed to be echoing hers, with a more personal note.

"I don't think Tukulti-Ninurta will press my neck beneath his foot like a *galtappu*-stool," he said happily.

Kathryn chuckled. "No, I think he has better uses for his feet right now," she said.

Kashtiliash's smile grew into a laugh. "Yes—he runs with them, very quickly."

Glad he's got a sense of humor, she thought, enjoying the prince's wide white smile. They'd been working very closely since her brother took off after the western remnant of the Assyrian field army.

"That was a good idea of yours, sending flying columns out to seize the royal granaries," she went on. "A lot less strain on our supply lines."

He nodded. "A thing one can never remember too often: an army fights rarely but eats every day. Besides that, with more grain than we need we can give some out to those displaced by the fighting—thus they are less likely to turn bandit. Thus also, we have more troops for real fighting and need detach fewer to hold down the countryside."

Even more glad he's smart, she thought. This divided command could have gotten extremely dicey if Kashtiliash hadn't been both intelligent and flexible. *Snaps up military tidbits like dry sand does water, too.* He'd been agitating for a copy of Sun Tzu, after she read him a few passages.

Besides, she mused, *Kash here is just fun to campaign with.* The filth, fatigue, and general disgustingness of life in the field were a lot easier if the company was good.

She looked over her shoulder; the siege camp was lighting up there. Not as many campfires as there might have been, only about ten thousand of Kashtiliash's Babylonians and four hundred Islanders—most of the rest were strung out on garrison duty, or over west of the river with Ken making sure the Assyrians up the Euphrates toward Carchemish kept running long and hard.

He noticed the direction of her gaze. "Without your guns, I would not lay siege with so few troops," he said. "With them, the Assyrians dare not sortie—they must sit and be pounded."

She turned back, nodding.

As she did, something went *vvveeeewtp* through the air her neck had occupied the instant before. Reflex sent her diving to the rocky ground, and a hand around an ankle brought the Babylonian prince down right after her; he didn't have the instinct to hug the dirt as a soldier trained to firearms did.

Nothing wrong with his reflexes, though. He hit the ground on his forearms and crouched for an instant. Another flight of arrows went through the spot where he'd been, and then a dozen shadowy forms were rushing up from the ravine below the hill. The last fading sunlight glittered on the bronze of their weapons.

"*Assur!*" they cried.

"*Tukulti-Ninurta!*" using the name of their king for a war shout.

Kashtiliash bounced back to his feet with a springy grace despite forty pounds of armor, his sword flashing red in the firelight as he drew.

"To me!" he shouted. "Marduk conquers! *To me, men of Kar-Duniash!*"

The bodyguards on the rear slope of the hill had been squatting, or leaning on their spears. They wasted no time running up toward their charges, but the Assyrians were closer.

Far too close. Kathryn stayed on one knee as she drew her pistol and cocked the hammers by pushing it against her belt. Dim light, but you could make out the center of mass. Pistol out with left hand under right in the regulation firing position—

Crack. The recoil hammered at her wrists despite the leather bracers she wore. *Crack.* A man dropped abruptly; another spun and clutched at himself, screaming his agony to the night. Not bad shooting in this light, even at ten feet. The enemy weren't wearing armor, had probably shed it for silence and speed.

She came erect and drew the *katana*, turning to put her back to Kashtiliash's. *Must have been a souterrain exit,* she thought—a tunnel under the wall, intended for sieges. Someone saw the figure in fancy armor, realized they could get within reach, and took the chance. Just the sort of initiative you wanted officers on your *own* side to show.

A man came scrambling up the rocky hill, a narrow bronze sword in his hand, teeth gleaming in a face darkened by lampblack. He drew back to chop at her legs; she kicked him in the face, hard. The crunch ran back up her leg and clicked her own teeth together, and she felt the unpleasant sensation of crumbling bone. The Assyrian flipped backward and slid down into darkness. A spear probed at her. She beat it aside with the *katana*, let the shaft slide up along the sword's circular guard, then slashed at the wielder's hands. A scream, and something salt and wet hit her in the face, blinding her for a second.

Kathryn tossed her head frantically to clear her eyes. There was a *bang!* of metal on metal, and when she could see again Kashtiliash had reached around with his shield to give her an instant's cover, exposing himself in the process.

"Thanks!" she gasped, heaving the suddenly heavy sword up into *jodan,* the overhand position.

The prince's guard arrived, finally. There was a brief, ugly scrimmage in the darkness, and then nobody was left but the Babylonians.

"Are you well, Prince of the House of Succession?" the commander asked anxiously, falling to his knees and pressing his forehead to the ground. "Dismiss me, have me flogged or beheaded, son of Shagarakti-Shuriash! I have failed in my duty!"

"Nonsense. I commanded you to stay at the bottom of the hill. Get up, get up—take torches, search about."

He turned to his companion. "Are you well, Lady Kat'rin-Hollard?" he said.

"Blood's not mine," she said, wiping at her face; it was turning sticky. "Thanks, by the way."

The fear hit her then, as it always did—during the action you didn't have time for it. The thought of sharp metal sliding into your belly, the feeling of a hamstring being cut, a sword blinding you with a stroke across the eyes . . . She swallowed and ignored the cold ripple that turned her skin to goose bumps.

"Thank you," he said in English, startling her a little. Then he dropped back into Akkadian. "Now we have fought side by side."

The words were innocent enough, but something crackled between them. Kathryn's eyes narrowed slightly. *Jesus* . . . she thought, conscious of a tightening below her rib cage. *Jesus* . . . *not the first time I've thought about . . . oh, hell and damnation, why not?*

"Yes. I'm for a bath, though. Fighting's messy work . . . perhaps we could talk more later."

His smile was wide and white in the darkness. "That would be a good thing."

Am I being a fool? Kashtiliash asked himself.

He wore a hooded cloak, and it had taken all his authority to make his guard stay behind while he walked thus in the darkened camp.

Am I being a fool? Women I have in plenty. Even a couple along on this campaign, perfectly satisfactory ones. *But none who put Ishtar's fire in my belly and loins so that I cannot sleep even when sated. Or who tease at my* mind *even more than my groin.*

The Nantukhtar camp was a little apart from the much larger and more sprawling Babylonian one, set up with the obsessive neatness that the People of the Eagle brought to all they did. Approaching it in the darkness, he suddenly appreciated how exposed the cleared field of fire around its perimeter made him.

"Halt!" called the guards there, bringing up their rifles. From somewhere out in the darkness he heard the sound of another being cocked, and his blood cooled a little.

"Who goes?" came the challenge.

"A friend," he answered, conscious of the heavy accent that rode his few words of English.

"Advance and be recognized."

Recognition wasn't what he wanted, but he came close enough to speak quietly. "The countersign is *Gettysburg*," he said.

Even then, he looked around him as he walked through the camp; it was his first choice to see it without the pomp and attention that an official visit brought. Some things were the same as he had seen before, of course. The orderly layout of streets, always placed the same so that each camp was like a seal-cylinder stamping of the last, and the absence of stink and ordure—the Nantukhtar insisted that that caused disease, and certainly they suffered less from it than their allies, however much the priests and *ashipu* sputtered. There were smells of cooking fires, a whiff of livestock. Rows of small khaki-colored tents, some larger ones—officers' quarters, on the other side of a small central square, the infirmary—the picket lines for their transport animals off to one wall. A little donkey-powered mill grinding grain; oh, *that* would save on effort—one reason why the Nantukhtar didn't need camp-followers.

None were allowed in the Nantukhtar camp, although he'd heard that some of their troops sought out harlets among the Babylonians— there were more men than women in their ranks. He'd heard that Nantukhtar women were utterly without shame, and glimpses through the tent flaps showed that to be true enough. So did his passage past the bathing-place; that also made him glad he'd scrubbed with extra care and anointed himself.

Randy camp rumor also said that Nantukhtar women were as skilled as night-demons in the arts of the bedchamber, enough to drive a man to madness or death from sheer pleasure. He swallowed thickly. Rumor also said, with considerably more evidence, that a man who approached a Nantukhtar woman wrongly and gave offense was likely to be beaten within an inch of his life or beyond, by her and any of her countryfolk near to hand.

That made him pause for half a step. *Perhaps I mistook Kat'rin's intent?* he thought. That froze his blood entirely; he felt himself wilt. *But . . . I am the prince!* Surely nobody could beat—

I am not sure of that. The Nantukhtar were insanely oblivious to rank sometimes.

He nearly turned on his heel. *No,* he thought, gritting his teeth. *No. Kashtiliash son of Shagarakti-Shuriash does not scuttle in fear.* If he *had* been wrong, it would become obvious soon enough. She *had* asked him to come and speak to her. At worst, they would simply speak.

He passed more soldiers lying in front of their tents, some working on leather gear or sharpening blades, others throwing dice or drinking wine and talking. That was almost homelike; in some ways the Nantukhtar were indeed men like other men.

Around another fire some sat in a circle, playing on flutes and stringed instruments while a woman danced with a motion like reeds in the wind, her face rapt. The music set the small hairs along his spine to rippling again. It was the slower, quieter type of Islander melody; some of their music was of a hard, snarly sort like the pounding of their fire-steam machines, but this was even more alien. He strained his limited English and caught words:

> *Who'll dance with the Moon through the shady groves*
> *To summon the Shadows there?*
> *And tie a ribbon on their sheltering arms. . . .*

Beautiful in its way, with a plangent sadness. It brought to mind what little he knew of the Nantukhtar homeland—a green land of chill rain, fugitive sun, great forests without end, islands set in icy seas, mystery within mystery.

The commander's tent was larger than any others, set in some open ground of its own. Lamplight glowed through the canvas, and two sentries stood before the entrance, which was shaded by an extended flap that ran to two poles and made an awning.

"Gettysburg," he said to their challenge. And "Bayonet Chamberlain."

The rifles lowered, and the guards looked at each other. A voice came from within.

"That's all right, Corporal. Dismissed."

Another exchanged look, a salute, and the slap of hands on metal as the two sentries brought their rifles to *slope arms*—Kashtiliash had learned the Nantukhtar words of command well, at least—and marched smartly off.

Kashtiliash swallowed again; his mouth was dry, and the pulse beat in his neck until he could feel it against the edge of his tunic. He pushed through and let the flap of the tent fall closed behind him.

Kathryn was standing by a table that bore papers and documents in the strange flowing foreign script. From the rest of the lamplit gloom his eyes picked out a pallet on the groundsheet of the tent, hooks on the central pole of the tent for clothing and weapons, a chest with her name and rank stenciled on it in the blockier form of Nantukhtar writing. That was all in an instant, before his eyes fixed on her. She was standing grinning at him, dressed in what the Nantukhtar called a *bath-robe* of white fabric, her short, sun-faded hair still damp from washing. Her hands went to the cloth tie and unfastened it, letting the robe fall to the floor.

Ishtar, he thought. In Her aspect as the warrior who harried hell to fetch back Tammuz from the realm of the dead. Her skin was pale as new milk where the sun had not touched it, her breasts full and pink-nippled, and the hair of her body had been shaved—only a dusting of yellow fuzz across her mound. And in her eyes, something he'd never seen in a woman's before—a combination of friendship, a lust to match his own, and a total lack of fear.

She set hands on her hips and spoke:

"Well, what are you waiting for, Kash? Let's see what you've got."

Enkhelyawon looked around his office with satisfaction. He had a swivel chair behind a desk, almost like a king's throne, and glass windows behind him gave light; a trio of coal-oil lamps hung from the ceiling to cast their glow in the dark days of winter. Filing cabinets around the walls held summaries and reports. There were trays and slots for correspondence on the desk and an abacus set up for the new decimal arithmetic, although he seldom needed to touch it himself these days—he could hear the clicking of many more from the central hall where clerks sat in rows.

The Achaean ex-scribe nodded to himself. Here was recorded every estate, its fields and workers, how much it yielded, what its taxes were, who held it, and on what tenure of service. Here were marked and listed the roads and bridges and ports—those built and those building and those planned—the mines and mills and factories, the forests and the flocks and the herds. A *census* told of how many men and women and children dwelt in every province of the Great Realm, of what class they were and what property they held, from the Wolf People lords in their mansions to the rawest barbarian slave.

"Let any lord or commoner try to evade his duty to the *Lawagetas now,*" he said softly, with a deep satisfaction. All his earlier life he had scurried to the commands of *telestai* and *ekwetai;* now they moved to *his,* and his kin's.

A knock at the door, and his cousin's niece came in with a stack of files, each bound with a colored ribbon. She bent the knee and put them on the polished olive wood of his desk, standing to await his commands.

Enkhelyawon frowned slightly. He wasn't altogether sure that a woman working so was seemly . . . *but what the king says is seemly is so,* he reminded himself.

There was another saying abroad in the land, that Walker had a captive Titan in his dungeons, a being with a thousand eyes that could see all things and tell its master their secrets. Enkhelyawon's thin lips quirked, twitching the pointed salt-and-pepper beard beneath his chin.

I am the Titan, he thought. It was as well that the ignorant believed so, though. It made his work easier.

The top file was bound with a red ribbon. He opened that first—death sentences, sent to the palace for approval by Walker himself and returned. Those would be for men of some consequence. Twoscore names, and mostly stamped with a *C* for "crucify him." A few marked *R* for "hold for review." A lesser number still marked *P* for "pardon."

"These to the Ministry of Order, Section One," he said, and she curtsied again and hurried away.

The next was a report on the explosion at the new gunpowder mill in Pylos. He frowned and dipped his goosefeather pen in the inkwell, making a marginal note. The manager had a thousand excuses for failure, but the smell of incompetence wafted up from the page like stale onions from a slave's dinner pot.

The Achaean drew a fresh sheet of paper. *To the King's Eye Hippalos,* he began. *You are directed to investigate . . .*

There would be another *C* stamped by a name soon enough, he decided as he sealed the document with a blob of wax and a brisk *thump* from his personal sigil. Or if His Majesty was angry enough—and he might be, given the loss of skilled workers and machines—perhaps the manager would be turned over to the witch-girls in the black-leather masks, the Sisters in whose hands were the gifts of life and of death—of healing and of agony beyond all mortal knowledge. Then at least his blood and pain would serve some purpose, appeasing the Dark Goddess and Her servant, the Lady of Pain.

Enkhelyawon shuddered slightly, paused until his hand was steady again, and wrote.

"Why do you like the woods so much, Pete?" Sue Chau asked.

"Why?" Peter Girenas said. "Hmmm . . . sort of hard to say, Sue."

Choonk. Choonk. The gasping breath of the little steamer echoed back from the forest that walled the river, with a multiply receding slapping sound. It was a cool, bright day, with a fresh breeze out of the north that made his skin tingle, like fingers caressing his face through the short, dense new beard. Waterfowl lifted thunderously as the steamer's whistle tooted, and an eagle darted down to take one in a thunderclap cloud of feathers.

They were a fair ways up the Hudson, Long Island and its farms and Fogarty's Cove long behind them. Even the little fueling station on Manahattan was a fading memory. The floodplain of the river here was fairly narrow, swamp reeds were clamorous with ducks and geese. A passenger pigeon flock was flying by, just the tail end of it, like black clouds drifting past against the sun. The trees along the river were a blush of new green, the leaves looking sharp-cut against the twisted black and brown and gray of the bark. They were also huge, bigger than any he'd seen around Providence Base, or even on Long Island, some near two hundred feet. Beyond them hills rose, dark and silent—silent save for the bellow of an elk or the call of a wolf pack. A bear stood with its legs in the water; it raised its head as the sound of the boat grew louder, lips wrinkling around a huge flopping fish in its jaws.

Girenas looked forward. The side-wheeler was pushing its load of two barges, making a single articulated craft with the steamer at the rear. On the one ahead, Eddie was working with their horses, checking feet, joking with Henry Miller as he crafted a new bow. In the front barge the rest of their party were napping, or working on their equipment, or just sitting and watching the trees go by.

"Why do I like the forest?" he said at last. "Because . . . because it's clean."

CHAPTER SEVENTEEN

July, Year 9 A.E.–April Year 10 A.E.

"Well, thank you. You really know how to complicate my work—*both* of you," Ian Arnstein muttered as Hollard and Hollard finished their reports. "Has your family got a tropism for picking up royalty, or what?"

The Islander officers looked slightly guilty. *And I feel like I'm back in San Diego, raking some hapless student over the coals,* he thought. *Well, not really.*

Doreen wrinkled her nose and looked at the odorous leather bag lying out by the entrance of the big tent. It no longer held the head of the Assyrian king; *that* was on a spear in front of King Shuriash's tent. The Islander mission had settled in, with something large enough to be called a pavilion for the leaders and their office staff; it had started life as a feature of high school sports days, and the locals found the bright-yellow nylon impressive as all get-out.

"That's not really fair, Ian," she said. "Ken didn't *ask* to find this Lost Princess, or Tukulti-Ninurta's head either. They just sort of . . . turned up."

"Yeah." Kenneth Hollard ran his hand over his sandy hair, sun-streaked now after his pursuit up the Euphrates valley. "Look, I don't think she's just going to fade away, either, one way or another. Raupasha's that sort of girl, if you know what I mean."

Arnstein sighed his exasperation. "She's another complicating factor, is what she is—particularly now that the news has gotten out that there's a surviving member of the Mitannian royal family around. And believe me, we did *not* want another complicating factor at this point. It's put some fire in the belly of the Hurrians and what's left of their old aristocracy. More fire is not what that area needs. Everyone and his uncle has declared independence."

"Bad?"

"Bad. And the Aramaeans are burning, looting, running off stock, and generally having a grand old time. If something isn't done about it, the whole area will be trashed and the nomads will take it over by default, and . . . oh, sit down, for God's sake. And the Babylonians are stretched thin as it is."

"The Assyrian field armies aren't a problem anymore, and we've got all the cities," Kathryn Hollard pointed out.

Doreen gave her a baleful look. *"The flies have conquered the fly-paper,"* she quoted.

Ian amplified: "King Shuriash is enjoying himself, but he's also worried about getting overextended, and rightly so. He *can't* keep his levies under arms past fall; they're needed in the fields, and we can't do much about that for a couple of years. If his standing army and his nobles' retainers are tied up holding down Assyria, that leaves nothing for anything else. And the whole *point* of this exercise was to build up Babylon as a base for supporting the Hittites against Walker, you may remember. I said *sit down,* Colonel Hollard."

Hollard did; he still looked rumpled and stained from his long desert trek. "Yeah, well, talking of complicating factors, at least I'm not sleeping with Raupasha," he pointed out. "Christ, Kat. First it's whatshername—"

"Sin-ina-mati."

"Sin-ina-mati, and then *this.*"

Kathryn's tanned face flushed. "Look, Colonel Hollard, *sir,* it isn't an Article Seven, so what the hell business is it of anyone but me and Kash?"

Doreen's eyebrows went up further. "Kash, Kat? *Kash?*"

"Hell, Doreen, it'd be sort of weird if I was still calling him Lord Prince of the House of Succession, wouldn't it?"

"Getting involved with a local, and the fucking *crown prince,* for Chrissake—" Hollard began.

Kathryn's voice rose. "I suppose beautiful-local-princess syndrome is supposed to be limited to men, Colonel, sir?"

Hollard opened his mouth, visibly reconsidered what he had been about to say, and went on, "Look, Kat, I'm not looking for a fight, okay?" After a moment she nodded. "It's just . . . well, hell, his expectations are going to be *different.* This isn't the Island, you know. And yeah, there *is* a difference, in a . . . what's the word . . ."

"Patriarchal," Doreen supplied.

". . . patriarchal setup like this."

"I've noticed," Kathryn Hollard said dryly. "I've already turned down an offer to be the leading light of his harem."

Doreen stifled a chuckle. "How did he take it?"

"Offered to make me queen," she said. "Lady of the Land, if you want a literal translation."

Hollard shaped a silent whistle. Ian put an elbow on his desk and dropped his face into his hand. "Oh, and won't that put the cat among the pigeons—don't you realize that involves the succession to the throne, here?"

Kathryn snorted. "I turned that down, too, of course," she said briskly. Her face softened for a moment. "Though I must admit, I hated to do it, he was trying *really* hard . . . I did come back with a counteroffer."

"What?" Ian asked.

"Well, I said that if he'd make me queen, co-ruler, and general of his armies, and guarantee the succession to any children we had, and have them educated Islander-style, and a bunch of other stuff, I'd seriously consider it. *That* floored him."

Ian cleared his throat. "So you're breaking it off?"

Kathryn looked up, her blue eyes narrowing. "No, I am not, Councilor." She gestured helplessly. "I really *like* the guy, you see. It's not just that he's gorgeous and has enough animal magnetism to power a steamboat. He's also smart, and has a sense of humor, and . . . and it's mutual. We've agreed to see how things turn out."

Jesus, Ian whimpered to himself. Heavily: "Major Hollard, you're a free citizen of Nantucket."

She winced at that; she was also an officer of the Republic's armed forces, and a highly placed one at that. Rights came balanced with obligations.

Ian looked out the turned-back flaps of the tent, past the sentries and the ordered buff-colored tent town of the Marine camp. The *Emancipator* was circling over the city of Asshur, looking fairly large even at this distance. As he watched, a string of black dots tumbled away beneath it and the dirigible bounced upward as the weight left it. The bombs fell on their long, arching trajectories, and columns of black gouted upward. He could smell the smoke of burning from here; the gunboats on the Tigris were keeping the defenders limited to what water they could draw from wells and cisterns inside the battered walls, leaving little for fighting the blazes.

"King Shuriash has a whole bunch of delegations from the principal cities and tribes and whatnot of Assyria here under safe conduct," he said, changing the subject slightly. "We're running a bluff. If we can convince them that they *have* to give up, they will . . . and that'll get us out of a very deep hole. If anyone can pull it off here, Shuriash can."

"If," Doreen said. "The Assyrians are pigs, but they're stubborn, too."

"Speak of the devil," Hollard said, as trumpets sounded from the direction of the camp gate.

"Oh, he's not a bad sort . . . of cunning old devil," Doreen said. "I'm going to go interview our Flower of the Desert, okay?"

"Bless you, Doreen," Ian said. "Get me as complete a report as you can, soonest."

The huge-voiced herald began bellowing Shagarakti-Shuriash's titles as the chariots approached. The king sprang to the ground, waved a fly whisk in answer to the sentries' present-arms, and came grinning into the main chamber in a blaze of embroidery, civet-cat musk, and glittering gold appliqué. Prince Kashtiliash followed him, looking as subdued as his eagle features were capable of, and a trail of generals, priests, and officials followed. A brace of Assyrians came after them, richly dressed in long gowns and tasseled wraparound upper garments, but with rope halters around their necks in symbol of submission.

The Islander officers rose and saluted smartly; Ian came to his feet and bowed.

"Marduk and Ninurta and the great gods my masters have blessed our arms," Shuriash said, grinning like a wolf. "The great men of Asshur—the *turtanu*, the *rab shaqe*, the *nagir ekalli*, even the *sukallu dannu*—have come to see that the gods have given victory to the men of Kar-Duniash."

Commander in chief, chief cupbearer, palace herald, and great chancellor, Ian thought, impressed behind an impassive face.

"I have brought them here that you, our ally, may take their surrender as well—"

"Your pardon, O King," Ian said. "Your city of Asshur is getting damaged unnecessarily, then." He ducked through to the communications room. "Call off the bombing!"

"Strange," Raupasha said.

She put the cup of date wine before Doreen before she went to stand in the doorway of her tent and look down on the smoldering city of Asshur. The Mitannian's eyes were red, as if she had wept privately, but she kept an iron calm before the stranger.

"What is strange?" Doreen replied slowly; they were speaking Akkadian—not the native language of either—and having a little mutual trouble with each other's accents.

"That all my life I have dreamed of seeing Asshur laid waste . . . and now that I see it, it brings me less joy than I had awaited."

Growing up, Doreen thought.

From what she'd been able to gather, Raupasha had been raised in a little out-of-the-way hamlet, on tales of vanished glory from her foster parents. Well educated, by local standards; she could read and write in the cuneiform system, and spoke four languages—her native Hurrian, Akkadian, Hittite, Ugaritic—and a bit of what seemed to be a very archaic form of Sanskrit. Ian's scholarly ears had pricked up at that. He was working on a history of the Indo-European languages in his spare time. He would be working even harder on it if there were some way of publishing in the vanished world uptime. Not many people on the Island were interested.

"Of course, I never dreamed that wizard-folk from beyond the world would bring Asshur to its knees," Raupasha said. "I am forever grateful to you People of the Eagle, and to the hero-warrior Kenneth-Hollard—until I saw his face, I expected to die for killing the Assyrian pig. I was willing, yes; I had made my peace with it. But it is hard to die and know that your family's blood dies with you."

"I hope you've been treated well," Doreen said cautiously. *Golly, you've got to be careful with locals. Especially an unfamiliar breed. Got to remember they're as different from each other as they are from us.*

Raupasha crossed to a canvas folding chair, walking with a dancer's stride as the hem of the long embroidered robe someone had dug up for her flared around her ankles. She sat, cat-graceful, and curled her feet up beneath her.

"Very well, thank you," she replied. "Lord Kenn'et treated me as his own kinswoman—not what I expected, traveling alone among foreign soldiers. They brought as much as possible from my home, so I have some little store of goods here."

She gestured toward a bowl on a table, an elegant burnished shape of black ceramic, and her full red lips moved in a wry grimace.

Good thing Ken's a gentleman, Doreen thought. *That's quite a mantrap. Reminds me of Madonna, after she got the personal trainer.*

Raupasha went on: "So I have a dowry, of sorts. I may marry some tradesman of Kar-Duniash, I suppose, since I am still virgin . . . although I have no living kin."

Poor kid, Doreen thought. *Doing the stiff-upper-lip bit, but she's hurting.* The local value system meant she had to want to avenge her blood first and foremost, but the foster parents were the ones who'd raised her, and *they'd* been killed in front of her eyes. At some level she had to blame herself for that, fair or not.

"Well, you're under the Republic's protection," Doreen said. *Ian might not have wanted Ken to offer it, but it's irrevocable.* "We could find you something different."

"Perhaps carrying one of your . . . rifles, are they called?" A chuckle. "My people are warriors, but that is something I hadn't considered."

Her eyes went unfocused for a moment and she chanted softly. It was definitely poetry, not rhyming but alliterative. Doreen's ears pricked up; her mother had been Lithuanian, and she'd found that extremely conservative Baltic tongue helpful in learning the languages of the Iraiina and the other charioteer tribes in Alba in this millennium. This language had a haunting familiarity from both.

" 'Our . . . family of warriors'?" she said.

Raupasha's head came up. "In Akkadian it would be . . ." She paused for a second, her lips moving silently. "As nearly as I can put it—"

> Our race of heroes though they be Maruts
> Is ever victorious in reaping of men
> Swift their passage in brightness the brightest
> Equal in beauty, unequaled in might.

She shrugged. "That is in the old tongue, though, the *ariamannu*. Even in the great days of Mitanni few spoke it. My foster father . . ." Her voice choked off for an instant, and she drew a deep breath. "My foster father brought a few things written in it from Washshukanni, our capital."

Ian will be in historian's seventh heaven, until we get him back to practical matters, Doreen thought. Perhaps someday he'd have the opportunity to trace the migrations that brought Raupasha's ancestors from the steppes of Kazakhstan to be kings among the Hurrians at the headwaters of the Khabur. Speaking of which . . .

"We're actually rather concerned about the Rivers district," Doreen said.

"Now it is free of the yoke of Asshur," Raupasha said, nodding toward the flap of the tent with grim pleasure.

"Well, yes, but Chaos is king there right now. And we need the area secured. Has anyone told you about William Walker?"

"The rebel against your ruler? Yes, a little. He seems a dangerous man."

"That's far too mild. He makes the Assyrians look like . . . like little lambs. He's not all that far away, either."

The Mitannian nodded. "On the other side of the Hittite realm, yes," she said. "Lord Kenn'et told me. And his way will be made easier, now that the Hittites are at war among themselves."

She rang a small bell, and a maidservant—probably hired locally from among the Assyrian refugees—brought in a tray with bread, cheese, and dried fruits, and the local grape wine plus a carafe of water. Raupasha poured and mixed herself, before she noticed Doreen's wide eyes.

"You did not know?" she said. "Ah, well, in the northwest we had more traffic from Hatti-land. Yes, the lord Kurunta of Tarhuntassa has thrown off allegiance to Great King Tudhaliya in Hattusas."

Oh, Jesus, Doreen thought. She frantically skimmed through the reference material in her mind.

Tudhaliya's supposed to reign for another thirty years—that was well attested. Kurunta, Kurunta . . . wait, that was one of Tudhaliya's supporters—there was that treaty between them. Wait a minute. Tarhuntassa is southwest of Hattusas, about where Konya would be in Turkey in the twentieth, that's nearer to the coast and the Greeks, and by now Walker must have made some substantial waves in that area, upsetting trade patterns if nothing else, maybe mixing in the politics, so—

"Oh, *shit,*" she muttered.

They'd known that eventually events here would stop following the history books. Not only deliberate interventions, but butterfly-wing chaotic stuff; a glass jug would get traded hand to hand from Denmark to Poland and someone wouldn't be born because Dad was swilling mead out of his new possession instead of doing the reproductive thing at the precise scheduled moment. It looked like that had happened here even if Walker hadn't deliberately set out to split the Hittite realm. So now they'd lost another edge—the books were vague and full of gaps this far back, and sometimes just plain wrong, but they'd been a great help nonetheless.

With a wrenching effort she pulled her mind back to the matters at hand. *I'll tell Ian when he's through with King Shuriash for today, and we'll go over it. Meanwhile, the northwest is more important than ever.*

"Thank you," she went on. "That's very important news. And we'd like your opinions on what to do about your homeland."

"Mitanni?" Raupasha said. "Will the king of Kar-Duniash, your ally, not add it to his domains along with the rest of Asshur's realm?"

"Well, yes, but it's a matter of *how.* Garrisoning Assyria will be hard enough, even with our help. The Naharim, the Rivers, it's further away but right on the road to the Hittites. We need to get it pacified, and ideally we'd like it to contribute troops and supplies for the war against Walker . . ."

Raupasha brightened. "You ask me, a girl?" she said.

"Raupasha, in case you hadn't noticed, *I'm* a girl," Doreen said. "We . . . People of the Eagle don't think that a woman is necessarily less than a man. And you are of the old Mitannian royal family."

"A fallen house, and myself a fugitive in hiding all my life."

"But you must have had contacts—men who visited your foster father."

A long silence. Then: "I owe you a great debt. What I know, I will tell. Some did visit; not every *mariannu* family was slain or deported by the Assyrians—and of those who were led away captive to Asshur, some will wish to return."

"Good," Doreen said. "We have a saying: 'Knowledge is power.' "

"Ludlul bel nemeqi."
The voice of the priest rose in a chant, as the *ashipu* prepared his powders and bits of bone. Clemens found himself translating automatically:

> *Let me praise the Lord of Wisdom*
> *For a demon has put on my body for a garment;*
> *Like a net, sleep has swooped down upon me.*
> *My eyes are open but do not see;*
> *My ears are open but do not hear;*
> *Numbness has overcome my entire body . . .*

The Islander doctor grimaced at the thick smell of the Babylonian equivalent of hospital tents, the stink of the liquid feces that soaked the ground under most of the men lying in rows in the scanty shade. Flies buzzed, clustering thickly on the filth, and on eyes and mouths. *And carrying the bacteria, whatever it is, to the food and water of everyone else.* Stretcher bearers carried bodies away, ragged men willing to incur the pollution of touching a corpse for the sake of a bowl of barley gruel. The priest continued his chant:

> *My limbs are splayed and lie awry.*
> *I spent the nights on my litter like an ox,*
> *I wallowed in my excrement like a sheep*
> *The exorcist shied away from my symptoms,*
> *And the haruspex confused my omens.*

Then he broke off, seeing the American watching him; then his eyes went wide at the sight of Prince Kashtiliash, and he made a prostration. His duck of the head to Clemens after he rose was no more than barely polite.

"Honored guest," he said coldly when he had arisen. His eyes traveled to Azzu-ena beside him; she was still in Babylonian dress. "Although this is scarcely the place to bring a harlot."

"This is my assistant," Clemens said, his voice equally chill. It was a natural enough assumption for a local to make of a woman unescorted in a war camp. Natural enough . . . once. "Azzu-ena daughter of Mutu-Hadki, *asu* of the king's household. We have come to see the men I set aside yesterday. The prince comes with me."

"I see." The priest's eyes were dark pools of bitterness. "It is not well that men should be denied care. But come; the king's word cannot be denied."

A dozen men had been laid off in one corner of the enclosure; Clemens had had a couple of Marines stationed there, along with the local orderlies he'd trained, to see that his instructions weren't disregarded as soon as he was out of sight. There were ten sick men there now.

"The other two?"

"Dead," the priest replied. "As might be expected, with the demons of their fevers allowed to rage unchecked."

An orderly lifted one of the men with an arm under his shoulders, keeping a glass at his lips until he had swallowed all of its contents; then he made a check mark beside a name on a list and went on to the next.

Clemens nodded. "And the twelve treated according to your custom?" he asked.

The priest shrugged. "The demons are strong. Seven have died, and the others weaken."

"Yes," Clemens said. "Of the twelve treated according to our . . . rites . . . ten live. Of those treated by yours, five live. In another day, these ten will be alive. How many of yours?"

The priest made as if to spit on the ground. "That means nothing! The demons—"

"The fever demons seem to fear our rituals more than your gods," Clemens said.

"Blasphemer!" the priest began.

Kashtiliash cut in: "Silence!"

The priest bowed his head. "I am more taken with deeds than words," the heir said bluntly. "A man who shits himself to death is as much lost to my host as a man with a spear through his belly. If you will not listen, another will. Go, and think on this."

To Clemens: "You spoke the truth, and you have shown it by your deeds. The decree shall be prepared."

Clemens and Azzu-ena bowed as Kashtiliash and his guardsmen left. When they had gone, she spoke.

"What causes this disease?" she said. The corpsmen lifted another man off his fouled pallet and replaced it with a fresh stretch of woven straw, cleaning him gently. "More of the *bacteria*?"

"Yes," he said. "But the actual cause of death is lack of water; too much runs out with the diarrhea and takes with it salts from the body."

"As if a man were to sweat in the sun of summer and not drink," Azzu-ena said thoughtfully. "Yes, that will bring on the fever and delirium, as well. Such a man will die."

"Very good!" Clemens said.

"So," she said, "the cure is to drink much water?"

"It isn't a cure," Clemens replied. "But it keeps him alive until his body can kill the agent of the disease naturally and then heal itself. It must be *pure* water—boiled or distilled—with salt and honey or *sugar*"—Akkadian had no word for that—"in certain exact proportions. These replace what the body has lost. We don't have enough *antibiotics* to treat so many men, but this will work. Especially if the treatment begins before the disease takes strong hold."

Azzu-ena nodded, her big-nosed face somber, hands folded in the sleeves of her robe. "From bad water?" she said softly. "That explains much; why you Nantukhtar so hate the touch of excrement. . . . It was so my father died."

"Ah . . . I'm sorry."

She shook her head. "That does not matter. What matters is how we may treat these others." A toss of her head indicated the field of groaning victims. "The priest of Innana will not aid you, even if the prince commands—not willingly, and not quickly, and he will injure you by stealth if he may. I see it in his eyes."

"Right," Clemens said, frustration in his tone. He ran a hand through his short brown hair. "I don't know *what* the hell I'm going to do. There aren't enough medics or corpsmen with the regiment, or with the whole expedition. And I can't train them that fast . . ."

"You can train them for this one thing," Azzu-ena said, nodding her head toward the fire, where a huge pot of water boiled. "You cannot train them to care for the sick as well as you—we—would, but that is not essential here, no?"

"No," Clemens said. "What we need to do is stop this epidemic before it melts the army of Kar-Duniash like snow in Babylon."

"Then make up the medicine-water before, and have them boil it. Boiling water is not difficult. For the rest, nursing is what is required, no? Washing the men, keeping away flies . . ." She frowned. "For that, I think you should recruit among the women who follow the camp. They do much of the washing and repairing of clothing already."

Bright lady, Clemens thought. *Very bright.*

There were those, back on the Island, who said that it would have been better for the locals if Nantucket had stayed isolated, that every action would change the people whose lives they touched, and in ways beyond prediction or control.

"Yes, it will," Clemens murmured. "And I don't mind that at all."

Ranger Peter Girenas watched the sky, folding his arms behind his head and smiling at the clouds. The expedition was in what the maps said was central Missouri, but this place had never been mapped. He rested his head on a natural pillow of dropseed, the clump-grass that grows in the middle of the long swales of the tallgrass country. The grasses rustled and closed over his head, and he might have been alone save for Sue Chau sitting at his feet—looking, he thought, as pretty as the wildflowers as she sat in only her deerskin breechclout, combing her long black hair and chewing on a straw.

The dropseed beneath him was springy and firm, the intervals between the hassocks heavily matted with dried grass to make a perfect hammock. The soil beneath that was prairie loam that was like nothing he'd ever seen before—no clods or sticks or stones at all. He slitted his eyes and enjoyed the feel of the wind caressing his sweaty skin. A day like this, you could remember the crossing of the Ohio—the horse screaming as the raft overset, and the white water trying to topple it—without fear. Or the time they'd nearly lost Eddie to a cottonmouth bite, his body swelling, his mind raving, the two-week hiatus when they stopped to nurse him.

Long ago, now; it seemed long ago and far away. *Now* he could smell elk strips smoking over a slow green fire and the liver roasting for dinner. He saw dragonflies darting off below to the slough, a squadron of monarch butterflies flitting above the tall grass; he could hear a bobolink's bubbling song as it hung in the air twenty feet up, until that red-winged hawk silenced it by floating past far overhead. But the hawk was too high to be hunting, and too late to be migrating.

"Soaring just for the hell of it," Pete said. "He doesn't fool me. He looks busy, but he's loafing today, just like us."

High above the hawk were steady ranks of clouds, coasting on the westerly winds, dragging a shadow across the earth every now and then. He stood, only his head and shoulders above the grass, and watched the shadow cross the huge, rolling landscape, the grass rippling beneath it like waves on the sea.

Even more than the sea, he thought. It took some wind to move the sea, but the tall grasses bowed and moved to the slightest breath of it, out to the edge of sight. They were on a slight rise, well into the lowlands that stretched out to the line of cottonwoods and poplar along the levees of the Missouri River. From here he could see half a dozen other hawks, and a herd of buffalo along the edge of the woods, birds misting up from the water far away like black smoke . . .

I love the forest, he thought. He did—the endless silences of it, the multitudinous life from rotting log to forest crown. *But this, it feels like there's no end to the world.*

The others were not far away, lying around a tree—a fire-gnarled oak—that had rooted itself where the ground rose a little more steeply. That had provided the firewood they needed to smoke the elk meat and cook dinner—elk-hump steaks, liver, kidneys, marrow and wild greens. Henry Morris had had to bully some of the others to eat enough organ meat, saying it was the only way to get all their vitamins when there was little green food.

The fire was built on pieces of overturned knife-cut sod; the rest of their gear rested under groundsheets or was stacked against the tree. Hobbled, the horses drifted and grazed—this was certainly horse heaven, although now and then one of their three stallions would throw up its head and snort, at one of its own kind or at a scent of predator drifting down the wind. Mostly they hung around with their own group of packhorse mares, most of which were pregnant by now—Alban ponies were tough enough to take that sort of treatment. Perks lay growling softly in pleasure as he gnawed at a gristly lump of elk shoulder, while the expedition's other dogs kept a decent, deferential distance.

"Not going to be this nice come winter," Sue said behind him.

He chuckled. "Well, we're making reasonable time," he said. "It isn't a race. If we have to find a place to winter over, we will."

Dekkomosu came in out of the grasses, hand in hand with Jaditwara the Fiernan. He was grinned broadly at Pete and begun to say something—he'd gotten more cheerful as they got further from home—when his face went quiet.

"What's that?" he said, pointing.

Damn good eyes, Girenas thought, unslinging his binoculars from the stub branch where the case hung on. It was just townie myth that Indians had better vision; they did tend to notice more of what they saw than a townie, but then, living in town you had to pull in your senses or go nuts.

"Damn," he said softly. Everyone was up now, looking along with him. "Well, I guess we know where those bodies were coming from."

The last two weeks, they'd seen five—hard to be absolutely sure, since the parts were so scattered. In the binoculars he saw the end of a chase that had probably started a good long time ago. A group of women and children, thirty or so, broke out of a line of trees and ran upward into the grass. Behind them were men, ten or so if you counted teenagers. They wore leggings and tunics; he could see quill decorations, and bones and feathers woven into long braids. They carried spears, or darts set into atlatls, and they walked backward in a wide arc between their women and children and whatever was pursuing them.

Then a dart arced out toward them, and faint and far came a yelping like wolves. The men who boiled out of the riverside thickets in pursuit were thirty or more, all in their prime. Their naked torsos were painted with bars and circles of yellow and red, their hair drawn up in topknots through hide rings, their faces covered with more slashes of color.

The Islanders looked at each other. "We'd better decide pretty quick," Girenas said.

"Hell, doesn't look like a fair fight," Eddie said.

Well, I know what Eddie's thinking. He wants to get laid and none of the girls will oblige right now, and he figures some of those tribeswomen will be grateful. Plus he likes to fight.

Morris hesitated. "We don't know the rights or wrongs of it," he said.

Henry doesn't like to make a decision without thinking it over for a week. And he's no coward, but he hates to kill—more than the rest of us, that is.

"I know the wrongs of doing what they did to that kid we found," Sue said. "He couldn't have been more than eight or nine, and he probably lived for days after they left him like that."

Good point, Sue, Pete Girenas thought and nodded. "If it happens, it happens," he said. "If it happens where I can do something about it, it's my business. I say we go run those guys off. Any objections?"

Dekkomosu shrugged. "Shouldn't be too hard," he said.

"Mount up, then."

Their riding horses were well enough trained to come to the call by now. Girenas paused long enough to tie his hair back and pull on buckskin trousers, as well as snatch up his rifle, powder horn, and a bandolier.

"Jaditwara, you look after the camp," he said, and then vaulted into the saddle. "The rest of you, spread out and look lively."

The five of them went down the slope at a canter; he noticed out of the corner of his eye that Morris had snatched up bow and quiver instead of his rifle. *God damn,* he thought. Granted, Morris was actually pretty good with the thing, but it still wasn't a Westley-Richards. *No time for arguments now.*

The deadly game below had come near to its end; the hunters stalked through the high grass in bands, the better to swarm over a single enemy. The screaming alerted the Nantucketers to one such; two of the painted men with topknots were holding down a third of the braids-and-feathers people, sawing at bits of him with flint knives.

"Dekkomosu," Girenas said. "You and me."

The two victors heard that and the thud of hooves; they wheeled around. One snatched for the stone-headed hatchet in his belt and nearly had it out before the bullet punched into his chest. He went back on his heels and fell beside his victim, their blood mingling on the thick sod. The other turned and ran; Dekkomosu thumped heels against his horse, riding close before he dropped reins on its neck, sighted carefully, and fired.

Crack. The tall grass swayed back and mercifully hid what fell to the ground.

"Let's go!" Girenas heeled his mount; the Islanders galloped upslope, where the last few of the braids and-feathers men had been desperately fighting off their attackers.

Everyone froze at the crack of the rifles, and faces went slack with fear at the sight of creatures like giant deer, with humans growing out of their backs. Girenas pushed his horse forward, separating the combatants, then wheeled to face the topknot-and-paint men. They gave back before the line of five horses, snarling. One suddenly pointed and spoke in some fast-rising, slow-falling language while the two Islanders loaded and primed and pulled back the hammers of their rifles.

"Think he figured out we're not part of the horses," Girenas said. He raised his rifle and squeezed his knees. His well-trained horse froze. "Now, if I crease his topknot, that'll scare 'em. And if I blow his brains out, that'll scare 'em too."

Before he could squeeze the trigger, Henry Morris stood in the stirrups, drew his horn-hocked bow to the ear and shot. The arrow landed at the talkative warrior's feet, with a *shunk* sound as it buried half its length in the soft prairie soil.

Another frozen silence; Girenas chanced a look over his shoulder, and saw the five remaining men and boys staring at him, or just panting and letting sweat and the blood of their wounds run down their bodies.

He turned back; the talkative one had pulled the arrow out of the ground, tested the steel head on his thumb. He spoke again. An arrow was a lot more like an atlatl dart than a bullet was. *Goddammit, Henry, that was a* bad *idea.*

"They're going to rush us," Girenas said flatly, aloud.

The talkative warrior turned half away, as if to give the expedition's leader the lie, then whirled. The hatchet left his hand, whirred through the air, struck Morris's horse on the nose. The beast whinnied in shrill pain, put its head down, and bucked. The tall redhead went flying with a startled yell, and the topknot men attacked.

"Goddammit, Henry!" Girenas shouted. It seemed an appropriate war cry for this particular fight.

He shot, and the warrior folded around his gut with an *oooofff*! Girenas ignored him, since he wouldn't be getting up again. Another one was running forward to spear Morris on the ground, and there was no time to reload. Pete's horse bounded forward—it was half quarter horse and had great acceleration—and he threw himself out of the saddle, landing between the spearman's shoulder blades. The impact knocked the breath out of both of them, but the Islander was expecting it. He came up first, slammed the edge of his hand into the back of the Indian's neck, grabbed chin and hair and twisted hard. There was a green-stick *crack,* and the man went limp.

Girenas rose, whipped out his bowie, and looked around. The fight was over; the topknot warriors were running—the twenty or so left alive—with the three mounted Islanders after them. Puffs of smoke rose from their rifles, and now and then a man would go down. Girenas nodded, his breathing slowing, the diamond focus of combat opening out. They couldn't afford to have the topknot people dogging their tracks in blood-feud mode. Good hunters could outrun horses, over days or weeks.

He sheathed the knife, found his rifle and loaded, and whistled up his horse, all the time looking at the braids-and-feathers warriors. There were five left on their feet: two men in their prime, an older one with a wrinkled face and white threads in his black hair—call him forty or so—and a teenager. The women and children were still up on the rise, but beginning to talk. The men laid down their weapons and held up their hands toward the Islander; Girenas nodded, made as many as he could remember of the peace gestures—quite different— of the tribes they'd met, and moved to his injured comrade.

Morris was semiconscious, stirring and moaning a little. Girenas knelt by his side and opened one eye, then the other. *Mild concussion,* he thought. The leg wasn't ripped or bleeding, but Morris stirred and screamed as the ranger's strong hands manipulated it. *Oh, great, our doctor's injured.*

Awareness returned to the green eyes. "You with us, Henry?" Girenas asked.

"S-s-sure. Ah, Christ."

"That arrow was a bad idea, Henry."

"Yeah . . . Jesus, my leg!"

"Broken."

The older man slowly, cautiously felt it himself. "I'll say," he said. "Two places. Should heal if it's splinted. Look, Pete, I'm sorry; I screwed up. You've got a better sense of these things than I do. Won't happen again."

"Okay, man, no problem," Girenas said, his anger guttering away. "What about the leg?"

"It'll heal." Morris hesitated. "I'm afraid it's going to take a while, multiple fracture like this."

"How long?"

"Ah . . . two months. Possibly three. Of course, I *could* die," he went on, avoiding Girenas's eyes.

The ranger came to his feet, snorting disgust. The others rode back,

Sue quiet, Dekkomosu impassive, Eddie Vergeraxsson whooping and waving a couple of bloody scalps.

Girenas winced. Not many Indians in this era took scalps, but the Sun People tribes *did*. The locals were looking impressed and horrified, in various degrees.

"How's Henry?" Sue Chau asked anxiously. "I'll go rig a travois so we can get him back to the camp and the aid kit . . . but how *is* he?"

Girenas sighed. The travois ride would hurt like hell, which was just what Henry deserved.

"How is he?" he asked, looking around. True, it was a pretty spot. "Let's put it this way. We've found the place we're going to winter, I think."

CHAPTER EIGHTEEN

May, Year 9 A.E.
(April, Year 10 A.E.)

"Mmmmmm, 'dapa . . . Oh, *God* . . ."

Swindapa laughed softly in the darkness; the breath fluttered cool against the damp skin of Alston's neck. They wound arms and legs around each other; Marian sighed again with contentment at the closeness, the sheer satisfaction of touching and being touched. She tasted the sweat on Swindapa's neck and shoulder, nuzzling, hands stroking.

"Why couldn't we have the lamp on?" the Fiernan chuckled in her ear. "I like watching your face."

"Put it down to inhibitions," Marian laughed softly. Silhouettes showed through backlit canvas. "Bad enough you're going to yell later."

Growing up in a Fiernan greathouse, with scores of a single intermarried cousinage living from conception through birth to death under one big circular roof, did not breed an American sense of privacy. Swindapa had some inhibitions of her own, but none of them applied to making love.

Nice to have some time to relax, Marian thought, running her fingers down the other's spine. *Ship about ready to launch.* No sign of the Tartessians for weeks, so they'd cleared out. And right now, the camp was good and quiet; their daughters soundly asleep next door, tomorrow the day of rest—make-and-mend, no reason not to sleep in, so—

"Commodore!"

Swindapa groaned, gripped her tighter, and mouthed "Go away" silently. Alston rolled her eyes and carefully kept resentment out of her voice. *Uneasy lies the head that bears final responsibility, for everyone feels entitled to interrupt you*, she thought.

She went on aloud: "Yes?"

"Commodore, it's the local." The voice was Lieutenant Jenkins; he was OOD for this watch. "The one with the sore ankle? He's *real* up-set, trying to tell us something. I thought you'd want to know."

"It's two o'clock in the goddam morning," Marian whispered under her breath. In a normal tone: "Thank you, Lieutenant. That was entirely correct. I'll be right there."

They rose, splashed water on themselves from the basin on the table—cabin furniture hadn't been reshipped yet—toweled down, and dressed. The air was cooler on her face after the close, musky heat of the tent and their bed. She took a deep breath and pushed her mind to alertness. The moon was down and it was dark except for a heavy frosting of tropical stars overhead and a few watch fires along the edge of the camp.

And we just dismounted the cannon to reship them, she suddenly remembered. They were on the *Chamberlain*'s gun deck; they'd been lucky with the tidal scour in the outer passage, and it was deep enough to take the ship fully laden. But from the ship, they wouldn't bear on the shore, and they couldn't leave until the stores were all aboard. *Uh-oh.*

Jenkins was waiting patiently; his arm was still in a cast and sling, but he was walking well again, well enough to stand watch. X'tung*'a* the hunter was behind him, with a shaken-looking sailor behind *him,* rifle slung over her shoulder and cutlass at waist.

"Ma'am . . . he was just *there,* all of a sudden, right beside me on the parapet!"

"At ease, sailor. That's their specialty." And they could track a ghost over naked rock; she'd learned that hunting with them these past brace of weeks.

X'tung*'a* made an impatient gesture at the conversation in a language he didn't understand, then composed himself with an effort, squinting as Swindapa came out of the tent with a lantern. The pool of yellow light grew as she turned the screw that raised the wick; for a moment he forgot everything with the mercurial swiftness Alston had noticed among his folk, smiling with a child's delight at the wonder. Then he shook his head again and signed to her.

Alston crouched as he did, the posture for serious conversation among his people. X'tung*'a* pointed southward, then walked two fingers over his palm. He reached out and touched the pistol at the commodore's belt and made a scowling face.

"Ba'ad!" he said. "Many-many."

The walking gesture again, and then he pointed to a particular bright star. When he was sure she'd fastened on the right one his pointing finger traced an arc down to the horizon.

"Uh-oh," Marian said aloud. *If that means what I think it means . . .*

She mimed the walking movement, then traced the star down to the horizon and pointed around her. X'tung'a nodded vehemently, then made scowling grimaces and drew the Nantucketer bowie knife at his waist to make a cutting gesture next to his own throat.

"Tartessians," Marian said.

X'tung'a nodded again; he couldn't pronounce the word in any fashion an English-speaking ear found meaningful, but he did recognize it.

"Kawaka," Swindapa said softly behind her. "Shit," in Fiernan—not normally an oath in that language. She'd picked the usage up from speaking English so long.

"Goddam right there, 'dapa," Marian muttered. *This part's going to be tricky.* She pointed southward.

"Ba'ad many how many?" she asked, and opened and closed her fingers repeatedly.

X'tung'a shrugged and stood, pointing all around to the camp, then opening and closing his fingers in imitation of her gesture. *About as many as you, maybe more,* she translated mentally.

The problem was that the San just didn't count the way twentieth-century Westerners did, or the way Fiernans did, either. X'tung'a could probably describe every antelope in a herd of dozens after a single glance, but as far as she could tell, the concept of a number as an arbitrary symbol applicable to anything—a hundred men, or zebras, or trees—was utterly foreign to him. Each object in the universe was unique.

Marian Alston sighed and rose, smiling and gesturing thanks. "All right," she said. "As near as I can tell, we've got a serious problem. A group of Tartessians—almost certainly the ones we saw—is headed this way and they'll be here at dawn or a little before. X'tung'a thinks there are at least as many of them as there are of us. It's suspiciously well timed; they're arriving just the day before we planned to launch the ship—the cannon are mostly down on the beach."

Jenkins swore. "How'd they know that?" he said. "To get that close—"

"With a good telescope, they wouldn't have to get *that* close. There's high ground all around here." She held up a hand for silence, lost in thought.

Then she smiled. Swindapa sighed at the carnivore expression; she was a fighter herself at need, but she kept the Fiernan distaste for it. X'tung'a grinned back. His people didn't practice war, but they were no strangers to feud and vendetta, and the Tartessians had managed to pile up what she thought was a formidable store of bad karma in their visits to the region. The Bad Ones were about to get a nasty surprise.

"We can stand them off easily enough, now that we're warned," Jenkins said.

Swindapa shook her head. "No, Lieutenant. I don't think that's what the commodore has in mind."

"No, indeed," Marian chuckled. "And have them hanging about, sniping at the camp, harassing us while we relaunch the *Chamberlain*?" *Sniping at a camp with my daughters in it*, she added to herself.

Orders began to form in her mind. The hardest part would be getting across to X'tung'*a* exactly what was required.

"Lieutenant Commander, Lieutenant Jenkins, I want the camp turned out, but *quietly*. No lights, no alarms. Then—"

"Mnbununtu! How much further?"

The man the Tartessian captain called Mnbununtu winced in his mind at the hail, although his face might have been cut from scarred obsidian.

There were two reasons for his discomfort. The first was an old, niggling one—Mnbununtu wasn't his name. In the language spoken six thousand miles to the northwest, that word just meant "man" or "person." It was the word he'd used when the strangers landed on the beach where he'd been hunting and made an interrogative noise while pointing at his chest. Of course he'd said he was "a man." How could he have known they were human beings too? He'd thought they were *teloshokunne*, ghost-spirits; the tribe name "Tartessian" *sounded* like that. The word had stuck, though.

The second reason was an instinctive anger at the noise his companions were making. *Blind, log-footed buffalo,* he thought. Then: *No. That is an insult to all buffalo.*

Tanchewa—the name meant "leopard" in his tribe's language—turned and trotted back down the trail. The Tartessians had mostly been farmers or fishermen before they became sailors, and they were lost and frightened in this alien wilderness; many of them flinched at his swift, noiseless passage. He considered himself a peaceable man, on the whole, but he'd demonstrated more than once to the Tartessian crewmen that he wasn't to be trifled with. That memory remained.

Alantethol was in the middle of the sweating huddle of sailors. Not from fear—Tanchewa would never have followed him, no matter what the gifts, if he was a coward. It was the best position from which to command if something went wrong. Plans usually did, in his experience.

"Quiet, Captain," Tanchewa said flatly. He obeyed willingly on the ship, where Alantethol was the skilled one. The woods were a different matter. "We are close. But I am not easy in my liver."

"Why? The wild men?"

"The *mnbui*?" he said. The little brown hunters here were not exactly like the pygmies who dwelt near his village far to the northwest, but he thought of them as essentially similar. After all, they did not grow yams or keep goats, and those were the marks of civilization.

"Yes, them."

Tanchewa shrugged. "Perhaps. They are good trackers and hide well. But it is . . ." He stopped. Tartessian wasn't a good language to describe what he felt. ". . . something that makes my liver curl. We should go quietly, and swiftly, to fall on the strangers. Let me scout ahead first."

"Go, then. The Jester hold his hand from you, and the Lady of Tartessos protect."

Word passed down the line of sailors from the *Stormwind* and the *Sun Dancer*. They sank gratefully to their haunches, silent under the ferocious gaze of the quartermasters and steersmen, but taking pulls at their water bottles and scratching at itches. Tanchewa trotted back down the trail to the south, landing softly on the balls of his feet as he moved. As he put the head of the column behind him he slowed, drifting into the side of the trail that offered most shelter. The long killing spear was ready in his right hand, the small rhino-hide shield held in his left. Over his shoulder was his war bow, the same one he used to hunt elephant, and a dozen arrows the length of his leg.

Alone in the woods, he could feel the irritation and jangling of the crowd dropping away. These were not his woods; the woods of home were denser, hotter, with larger trees and many great rivers rich in hippo and crocodile, but he was still Tanchewa the Leopard, greatest hunter of all the People. He felt the night wind and took a deep breath of its scents, strong and rank with growing things and their decay. Sounds flowed past his ears; he did not consciously attempt to listen, instead sensing the *patterns* in the small tickings and rustlings, the squalls and creaks. In a little clearing he moved through the tall grass in a slow crouch, bent nearly double. You couldn't see detail at night, not even if you were Tanchewa, but always the *patterns* showed if they were disturbed.

He stopped, his eyes flaring wide. Then he turned and ran back northward with all his speed, hurdling obstacles with a long, raking stride, careless of noise. His lungs filled and he shouted, a long, high, carrying yell.

The Tartessians leaped to their feet. The weird yell coming from the south seemed to mean something to them; Marian Alston could hear officers calling orders. *Maybe it's Tarzan,* she thought. *Sounds like him.* She bared her teeth in harsh amusement at the thought; just the sort of thing the damned interfering bare-assed *bukra* of Burroughs's imagination would do.

"Now!" she shouted.

The mortar team dropped their round into the stubby barrel of the weapon. *Shoonk,* and a blade of fire speared man-high into the night.

Alston came up on one knee and raked back the hammers of her pistol with the pink-palmed heel of her hand.

Whonk. The star shell arced up through the leaves and burst. The bright acintic light froze the Tartessians in place for a crucial instant, startled into immobility, blinded by the light they hadn't been expecting. *Her* crews had been warned beforehand to look away.

Ninety Westley-Richards rifles volleyed at the enemy. Alston trained her weapon and fired, letting the weight bring the heavy pistol back into line before she used the second barrel. The Islanders were spread out along the trail behind fallen logs and folds in the hilly ground, twenty to sixty yards back. X'tung'*a* had picked the ground, and he seemed to know it the way she did her own quarterdeck.

BAAAAMMMM.

A dozen or so of the Tartessians were down, some screaming and writhing. Not bad, she thought with the part of her mind that was cold, detached analysis. Rifles weren't Guard crewfolk's primary tool, and it was dark. The enemy were leveling their muskets and firing back. They probably couldn't see a thing to shoot at, but there were a lot of them. Muzzle flashes winked at her like malignant red fireflies, and something went *crack* past her head, an ugly flat sound. Bullet-clipped leaves and twigs fell on her, and her mouth was a little dry. It always was, times like these.

Most of that was the knowledge that Swindapa was within arm's length and very definitely in harm's way. Campaigning with your lover had a nerve-racking quality all its own . . .

Ain't no friends like the friends you make in combat. Her father's voice, remembered from the porch on a spring day when she was barely up to his navel. *Hell, the* bukra *in my platoon, we was tighter 'n brothers, even them 'Bammy rednecks went around in white sheets back to home. Gooks didn't pay no never mind if you was white, black, or green.*

The Islanders were replying, a steady crackle of independent fire, and the mortar team switched to explosive rounds and began walking them down the trail. Beside her Swindapa leveled her rifle over a log and squeezed carefully, then reloaded without having to look down and watch her hands work. A Tartessian officer doubled over and fell limp in the midst of waving his men on. They were doing the best thing you could in an ambush—attack.

Or most were. A few turned and shoved their way into the brush on the other side of the track. Alston snarled to herself. Just about now . . .

Whudump! A crashing blast and stab of red fire like a sword blade into the dark, rank belly of the jungle. A Claymore was a very simple weapon, really; just a curved iron plate with the concave side facing the enemy, a layer of explosive, and a layer of lead shot inside a thin tin cover. Friction primers weren't as lasting or reliable, but they'd usually work when somebody's leg hit the trip wire—

More screams. Another *schoonk . . . whonk!* as the mortar team fired more star shell. The Tartessians came on recklessly, many of them throwing aside their guns and drawing cold steel, or carrying the guns by the barrels to use as clubs.

Whudump! Whudump! Whudump!

Alston's snarl grew wider as the flashes strobed, and the burnt-sulfur stink drifted through the hot night. There were Claymores between *this* position and the trail, too. The Tartessians froze again as men fell or stumbled back screaming and bleeding; they went to earth and began firing back. Loading a musket like theirs while lying down could be done, but you had to be a contortionist, and it was *slow*. Only a few of them had breechloaders.

"Ready!" Marian called through the shadow-lit night. "Take it slowly and do it right. Now!"

Beside her, Swindapa laid down her rifle and pulled an iron egg out of a pouch on her harness. A metal ring protruded from the top; she hooked her right index finger through it, twisted sharply and pulled. In the darkness Marian could hear the *scritch* as the friction primer ignited, the hissing of the fuse. Then the Fiernan rose and threw it with a snapping twist of arm and torso.

I hate those things, Marian thought. Most of Ron Leaton's weapons were unavoidably less advanced than their equivalents up in the twentieth. The grenades were unavoidably less reliable; they *scared* her.

More were arching out from the Islander ambush; they began exploding *crackcrackcrackcrack*, quick red sparks among the huddled Tartessians.

And there was a whistling *shunk* from behind her. Swindapa's drop back to cover behind the huge rotting fallen log started as gracefully as all her motions. It turned into a tumble and a cry of startled pain. A long black arrow was through the fleshy part of her thigh; she stared at it for an instant, wide-eyed.

From behind us. Marian knew, suddenly and crystal-certain. *Someone knows where our leadership is and they're trying to take it out.*

Her body was reacting without any need for her mind's prompting; she grabbed Swindapa under the arms and rolled over the log with her, ignoring the small shriek as the rough movement twisted at the shaft through the Fiernan's leg. Another arrow went *vhwwweept* through the space she'd occupied a second earlier, close enough to make a shallow cut across one shoulder blade before she was belly-down to the earth.

"'s not bad," Swindapa said through clenched teeth. "Not bleeding much. I can't use the leg."

Thunk. Another arrow, this one driven through the top curve of the log. A scream from nearby, as someone took a shaft in the back.

"One man behind us!" Marian called. "Torwnello, Reuters, Johnson, Aynaraxsson, about-face!"

"Torwnello's down, ma'am!" a voice called. "We're watching!"

More grenades were arching out behind her. She could ignore that for the moment, though; the Tartessians weren't going anywhere, and the bullets they were putting out were essentially a random factor. Let whoever it was come to her. Whoever it was was *good.*

Tanchewa threw down his bow. His eyes speared the gloom— *there.* The two women were on the other side of the log and had enough sense to lie tight along it. If he could kill the dark-skinned woman chief, the others might well flee, or at least be thrown into enough disorder that his comrades could escape. He took his shield by the central handgrip and charged, moving like his totem beast, feet landing light and sure among the vines and brush and fallen trees. Rifles barked at him, tongues of fire, and something scored along his ribs like a hot knife. That made him miss one stride, until the extent of the pain told him it was only a flesh wound—time enough to tend it later, if he lived.

Noise and motion in the fire-lit darkness; screams, the shit stink of death, the iron-copper-salt of blood, the rotten-egg smell of gunpowder. Chaos. Marian Alston let it flow through her as she reached over her shoulder and drew the *katana.* Distraction was a state of mind; if you weren't distracted, you would always see what was necessary and never be surprised. A rushing black shadow coming toward her. Smooth, very quiet, very fast—but not hurrying in the least, at full speed through brush, in near-total darkness.

She came to her feet with a long silibant hiss of exhaled breath, and the sword flowed upward to *jodan no kame,* high and very slightly to the right, hilt level with her eyes. Neither anger nor fear, beyond intention and desire. A knee relaxed and she swayed out of the line of the thrust. The sword floated down, diagonal cut, elbows coming in, wrists locking, gut muscles tensed and throat open for the *kia* as the long curved blade blurred. A sliver of silver as starlight caught the layer-forged steel.

"Dissaaaa!"

A jarring shock, flowing through her and gone, as the man's buckler shed the steel. He was pivoting, whirling, striking again in the same motion, one move flowing into another, shield, spearhead, the butt of the shaft. She parried again, blade down, right hand with the heel of the palm braced against the pommel. *Scrinnngg* as the tough wood slid along her sword. She felt the essence of the man she was fighting in that instant, the long-limbed quickness, the deadly balance.

Teki ni naru, Musashi had called it: to become the enemy.

They were moving together in a dance, the sword an extension of her back and shoulders, feet at right angles, weight centered over her *chi.* She let the rhythm of the combat form in her mind, a *gestalt* that made their interaction a single construct . . .

Now.

Alston sensed the rhythm of the attack and *knew* where the spearhead would come. *Bang* of steel on wood, and they were past each other. The sword flicking, reversing, stabbing—an *iado* move, to strike behind without turning. Soft, somehow thick sensation as the slanted-chisel point met skin. Sword looping up into the ready position as she turned, cut coming down with the stamping fall of her left foot.

"Dissaaaa!"

Crouched in the follow-through, blade out and level with the ground, she came back to herself. Seconds only had passed; Swindapa was lowering her pistol, the firefight was dying—

"We surrender!" someone shouted from the Tartessian position. "Please!"

Marian Alston looked down at the broken body of the tribesman, suddenly conscious of an enormous sadness. The face was contorted, the light painting it ghastly red as blood flowed from his mouth, but the features were still kin to hers—the features of the Dahomey, the Mandinka, the Yoruba, of tribes yet unborn in the tides of time. Of an ancestor, perhaps.

Strong, long-fingered hands clawed into the forest duff as the man tried to form words. A language she did not know, and they were gurgled through blood. Heels drummed for an instant, and he died in the usual human squalor.

Alston turned and shouted toward the Tartessians: "Throw down your weapons! Come forward with your hands up!"

Swindapa echoed it in their own language. When they obeyed, Marian shouted in her turn, for a corpsman. The medic came at a run, kneeling by the Fiernan and taking out his kit.

Swindapa winced and raised herself on her elbows. "Fast . . . he was so *fast,* I couldn't fire."

Alston knelt for a second to close the staring eyes. "Very fast," she said, with a wry quirk of her full lips. "But that's a race we all lose, in the end."

"You make the bluff," Alantethol said, despite the rough hemp of the noose about his neck and the hangman's knot under his ear. "Your law forbids you to torture prisoners of war. I will tell nothing you."

The eighty surviving Tartessians—less the wounded too injured to stand—stood sullen under the Islander guns in the waist of the ship. Alantethol and his officers stood on chairs, under the gaff of the *Chamberlain*'s mizzenmast. The lines from the nooses ran up over that, through beckets, and down to be secured to stanchions and belaying pins along the port rail. The ship rocked slightly at her moorings, and Alston could see eyes widening and tongues moistening lips as the men shifted to keep themselves balanced. That wasn't easy, with their hands tied behind their backs.

Marian Alston smiled—at least that was technically the name for her expression. Swindapa sat in a folding chair behind her, one leg thickly bandaged. The corpsman said it would heal within a month or two, with no loss of function. Two of the Islander crew were dead, and three more unlikely to live. That the Tartessians had suffered more altered Alston's determination not at all.

"You're right," she said, looking up at the sweat-slick face of the Tartessian captain, catching a whiff of the rankness of it mixed with the olive-oil-and-garlic odor of his body.

He was in fear of his life, but the aquiline features were set, the little gold-bound chinbeard jutting with the determination that firmed his mouth.

Alston set her hands on her hips and went on: "The thing is, Tartessos and the Republic are at peace. We have a treaty. You broke it, of your own will. So you're not prisoners. You're pirates. And we don't torture pirates, either. We hang them. 'dapa, repeat that in Tartessian, would you?"

The Fiernan sighed and did; her tone was regretful, but no less determined than her partner's.

Alantethol lifted his chin toward the east, where the first hint of dawn was paling the stars, lips moving in a silent prayer.

Alston went on: "On the other hand, if any of you were to tell me what arrangements you had with your ships, signals, and so forth, I'd pardon them . . . and give them sanctuary in Nantucket and a thousand dollars in gold. Oh, and I'd spare the others, too; I have the authority to do that. So, who'll save his life, and his friends, and be a rich man?"

Alantethol's mouth worked again; she stepped aside smartly to avoid the gobbet of spit. It arched past her to land on the scrubbed boards with a tiny *splat*. Considering what the human body did when it was strangled, the deck might well be a lot messier before long.

The translation took a few moments; Tartessian was a less compact and economical language than English. *Choppier than Fiernan, too,* she thought absently, eyes on the faces of the men standing with the nooses around their necks.

Brave man, she thought, looking at their commander. *Sadistic bastard*—the San had made clear how the Tartessians had abused their hospitality, and needlessly, too, when you considered their eagerness to please a guest—*but a* brave *sadistic bastard.* She wasn't all that impressed; physical courage was not a rare commodity, particularly not here in the Bronze Age, and particularly not among those picked for a voyage of exploration by as good a judge of character as Isketerol of Tartessos.

On the other hand, human beings were variable. Brave one day and timid the next; or a lion in the face of storm or battle but unable to contemplate the slow, choking death that awaited them. Some of the other Tartessian officers tried to spit at her as well as she walked down the line; some were standing with their eyes closed. One, younger than the rest, was silently weeping.

And one had a spreading stain on his tunic below the crotch. She caught the sharp ammonia stink of urine as she walked over and put one boot on the stool he was standing on.

"You first," she said, rocking it slightly. Her Tartessian was good enough for that. "Good-bye, pirate."

The man's lips opened just as the third leg of the stool came off the deck. He began screaming words through thick sobs; several of the others were shouting as well—curses and threats, she thought, directed at the man who'd talked.

"Marian!" Swindapa said quickly. "Two red rockets at dawn— they'll be standing off the coast. That's the signal for them to come in, that we've been captured."

And raped and murdered, most of us, Marian thought, her face a basalt mask as she let the leg of the stool thump back to the deck.

"Get them down," she said to the waiting master-at-arms. "Below, in irons—except for that one."

Alantethol seemed as much startled as furious as he was bundled past her. Alston sighed as she felt the tension ease out of her neck.

"Why is it," she said softly, "that cruel bastards like that think they have a monopoly on ruthlessness?"

"I don't know," Swindapa said. "I don't like to kill, myself. There are many things that I don't like but that are necessary anyway. Moon Woman orders the stars so." After a moment: "How many would you have hung?"

"All of them," Marian said, her voice as flat as her eyes. "And then started on the crew."

"Who's Mr. Me-Heap-Big-Chief-Gottum-Chicken-On-My-Hat?" Alice asked. "Honestly, the people you bring home to dinner sometimes, Will."

William Walker hid his smile. The northern chieftain *did* look a little absurd, in his high, conical helmet with a wood-and-boiled-leather raven on it; the way the wings flapped when he moved didn't help, either.

Hong came stepping daintily down the middle of the brick pathway; the horses in the stalls on either side raised their heads and snorted a little, as if they could smell the blood and madness in her eyes. Her riding crop tapped against her high, glossy boots and kidskin jodhpurs as she looked the visiting barbarian up and down.

"Hello, big fellah," she said in English. "If I pull on those long droopy mustaches, will the wings flap?"

Tautorun was a son of the high chief of a considerable confederation of proto-demi-God-knew-what in the Danube valley, in what would have become Hungary in the original history. They reminded Walker of his first followers, among the Iraiina of Alba. The language was similar too, sort of like the difference between Spanish and Portuguese up in the twentieth. Most people from Russia to Alba spoke similar dialects in this period, from what he'd been able to gather.

"This is High Chief Tautorun son of Arimanu, lord among the Ringapi," Walker said slowly in Iraiina, trying to make the sounds more like his guest's language—dropping initial *h* before *e* was one, he'd noticed. "Lord Tautorun, my wife the wisewoman Alice Hong."

Tautorun bowed, smiling and exchanging a few words with Alice before she sauntered off. If he thought her appearance strange—and he'd certainly never seen an Oriental woman before, much less one in pants—he gave no sign of it. No sign of being afraid of her reputation, either. They switched back to Achaean after that, which the visitor spoke quite fluently, albeit with a strong accent.

Smoother than the Iraiina ever were, Walker thought.

Rather *advanced* barbarians, in fact; they made his former father-in-law Daurthunnicar's bunch in the White Isle look like hillbillies from the deep hollows. Tautorun didn't wear a leather kilt, but instead trousers of well-woven cloth in a check pattern; his coat was wolf-skin, but beautifully tanned and sewn, as were his bull-hide shoes. The long leaf-shaped bronze sword at his side was as good as anything Agamemnon's smiths had turned out, the sheath tooled leather with chased-gold bands, and his jewelry was splendid in a lavish sort of way, arm-rings like coiled snakes and a necklace of gold, amber, and carnelian.

The visiting chief ran a thoughtful hand over his chin; the Ringapi even shaved there, although they were fond of long, sweeping mustaches. Tautorun's hung halfway to his collar, tawny like the hair that spilled out from under his ceremonial helmet. It was a considerably closer shave than he'd had before he was introduced to steel razors and lathering soap, of course, about which he'd been wildly enthusiastic—those and a number of other things.

As far as Walker could tell, the Ringapi were interested in more than trade—sniffing for opportunities, and feeling him out for an alliance. There had been naked greed in the barbarian's gray eyes for most of his tour through Mycenae and Walkeropolis, too.

Not least about the horses. "By the Lady Eponha," he said, viewing Walker's quarter horse stallion Bastard over the bar rails of the box. "I don't know why you've been buying horses from us, if you have many like *him*."

Bastard was getting a little long in the tooth, now—fifteen or so, and Walker had retired him from anything but stud duties years before. He was still a fine figure of a horse, though, a fast, sleek giant by the standards of 1242 B.C., and with luck he'd be siring colts for another decade.

I'm getting fond of horses again, he thought, taking a deep breath of the smells of a well-kept stable. *It's a lot more fun with some slaves to shovel the shit, of course.* And maybe the local attitudes were rubbing off on him. Certainly his kids old enough to walk were all horse-mad.

"We *don't* have all that many more like him," Walker went on aloud. "Several hundred three-quarter, half, and quarter breeds from him, though. I could give you one of his sons, for your return."

"That is a chief's gift indeed!" Tautorun said, hiding his eagerness as best he could. "I shall tell all at home of the riches and generosity of the Achaean lands."

Walker nodded. *And I'm smelling horseshit from more than the stalls, dude,* he thought.

Tautorun's people had always traded a little with Mycenae, through a long chain of middlemen; Walker had set up a base at the mouth of the Danube to speed things up, although that still meant paying protection money to the Trojans on the way. The new flood of trade had brought more information as well, both ways. The Ringapi lived on the Middle Danube, their lords charioteers dwelling in fortress-towns and taking tribute from scores of villages. They themselves were horse breeders and herdsmen as much as farmers, their trade stretching from the Adriatic to the Baltic along the ancient amber routes; they had more-tenuous contacts further still, east and west among distant kin from the English Channel to Central Asia.

They were also warriors, who kept an ever-more-greedy eye on the wealth of the Aegean countries, and they were being pressed by their neighbors—the tribes were on the move across much of Europe, to a rumble of chariot wheels and crackle of torched hill forts. According to the references he had (and thank *God* he'd managed to get a copy of the *Oxford Illustrated Prehistory of Europe* among the *Yare*'s cargo, when he hijacked her) a big *volkerwanderung* was due in another couple of generations. A bit like the fall of Rome with Attila the Theodoric and their horsey-set biker gangs of Vandals and Goths and Huns and whatnot.

Kingdoms would fall and cities burn all across these seas and far into Anatolia and the Canaanite country; from hints in the books and what he'd learned of the Ringapi and their neighbors, Walker suspected that that horde of Bronze Age Vikings that Ramses III fought would include a lot of Central and North Europeans as well as Achaeans, Sardinians, and odds-and-sods from everywhere. There was no reason why not; you could walk from Denmark to Greece in a month or two. An army or migrating horde could do it between spring and winter, provided they could threaten or muscle their way through and didn't mind leaving famine desert in their wake.

Or all that *would* have happened, without him. He certainly didn't intend to have barbarian hordes wandering around territory he planned to conquer himself and pass on to his heirs.

But on the other hand, they *could* be useful. Walker sat on a bench that looked out over an exercise yard where handlers were leading two- and three-year-olds around, and Tautorun sat beside him. It was a little chill and damp, but the horses in the building gave warmth, and southern Greece never got really cold by his standards, or by those of the man beside him. A slave came up with wine in gold-rimmed glass goblets, and the northerner drank deep—they were wildly enthusiastic about wine too, an expensive luxury up in the woods. Walker sipped and schooled his face to charm.

"I'm glad you've enjoyed my hospitality," he said mildly. "Keep the glassware, by the way; no, I insist . . . I hope you *do* tell of Mycenae's wealth and generosity when you return."

"To make trade grow faster?" Tautorun said shrewdly.

A little way from them, a brace of his retainers squatted on their hams, leaning their arms on their grounded spears. A squad of Walker's Royal Guards stood at parade rest near them, in their gray uniforms and armor, with their new breechloaders slung at their shoulders—Cuddy finally had acceptable copies of the Nantucketer Westley-Richards coming out of the workshops in some numbers.

"Trade, yes," Walker said. "We can use more horses."

Best not to go into too much detail about what they were using them for—mostly to pull reaping machines, although artillery teams were also a major user. Agamemnon's nobles, whose ancestors had been northern horse-barbarians, hadn't been happy about it, either. All that breed felt that putting horses to farming work was some sort of obscure social demotion for themselves, too.

Walker went on: "And we need metals, tin particularly. Raw wool, too, and hides, more than we can raise ourselves. If we can pacify the river route well, possibly other goods."

"And we your tools and weapons of *steel*," Tautorun said. "Wine and oil, this fire-wine, glass, fine cloth . . . there is no end to what we need."

No end to what you'd like to paddle your paws in, you mean, Walker thought and winced mentally at the thought of these goons rampaging through what he'd built up. They might be sophisticated barbarians, but they still had all that breed's love of destruction for its own wild sake, and they would smash even more through sheer ignorance.

"Well, we always need more slaves as well," Walker said. "You tell me you're often at war with your enemies—we'll buy all you can catch."

"That would be easier if we had better weapons."

Oh, wouldn't it just, Walker thought. They'd do anything to get their hands on guns. *Though . . . hmmm . . .*

"Of course. Yet we could scarcely hand over the secrets of our power, unless . . ."

He let his voice trail off.

"Unless—" Tautorun said eagerly, his voice a little slurred and his expression less guarded. It was amazing what spiking the wine with a little brandy did to those not used to it.

"We might be able to use fighting men soon," he said. "We've always hired mercenaries, but we need more. Possibly . . . possibly we could use *allies* as well. In the lands to the east of here."

The Ringapi chieftain's eyes grew bright with interest. "Ah, Hattiland," he breathed.

If there's a folk-migration building up, I might as well put it to use. Let 'em smash things up in the right places, keep the opposition distracted, and soak up bullets. We can always kill them all later. Maybe even civilize them, if they're good little doobies and useful to the Walkerian Dynasty.

The talk went on for some hours, until a chill nightfall. Tautorun took off the raven-crested helmet that marked him as a feeder of the Crow Goddess—She whom the Iraiina called the Blood Hag of Battles—and ran a hand through his barley-colored mane.

"Strong talk," he said. "Some would say wild—but this is a time of wolf and raven, of ax and spear, when new things walk the earth. Perhaps it's the time of the great War of the Gods that the songs foretell! I'll bear a word from you to the other chiefs of the Rangapi, and maybe a word from them to you in turn."

"And then men might go from here to there—skilled men," Walker said. "Men and goods, and oaths between us and the Ringapi lords."

"Yes, yes . . ."

"We'll talk further of this tomorrow," Walker replied. "Now let's feast."

He nodded; across the fencing of the paddock rose terraced gardens, and above those the white marble and bright windows of Walker's palace. Tautorun's eyes rested on it with a mix of envy, awe, and greed. He nodded.

"You set a noble table, too," he said, grinning. "My hand on it."

They stood and grasped wrists, squeezing a little; they were both strong men. "You've guested with me; perhaps we'll fight together someday," Walker said.

"That would be a fight to feed Her ravens and make the long speared Sun Lord smile," Tautorun said, shaking his right hand a little. He hesitated slightly. "That must have been a fight to remember too, the one that took your eye."

Walker's smile turned chill. "It was," he said. "I lost the battle, but got something better than one victory."

"It must have been a mighty booty, that you think it was fair exchange for such a wound."

Walker nodded. "I don't miss the eye. You see, I sacrificed it for wisdom."

Tautorun took a step back and shuddered slightly in his wolfskin jacket.

"Wave and smile, you son of a bitch, or I'll spit you here and now."

Marian Alston smiled, a somewhat grim expression, as she heard the bosun's mate hissing to the Tartessian standing by the rail and saw the light jab of the bowie knife resting over the prisoner's kidney. A thick scattering of the enemy prisoners stood there at the bulwark, and the officer who'd agreed to fink on his compatriots was standing on the rail with a hand on the ratlines. More Islanders were mixed in with them, in the clothes of the Tartessians, who sat in their loincloths under guard on the shore. They'd run the Tartessian flag up to the top too.

There was a slight hint of rose-pink over the jungled hills to the east and a layer of mist lying in the blue-green valleys. Already the air was warming, and sweat ran down her flanks under the uniform. Alston stood on the third rung of the rope ladder that lay along the starboard, landward side of the *Chamberlain*. That put her above the level of the deck and gave her a good view of the Tartessian vessels standing in through the narrow channel into Port Luthuli's roadstead.

Nice-looking ships, she thought for a moment. She could see how the hull form was derived from the *Yare,* the Nova Scotia–built topsail schooner that Isketerol and Walker had stolen. *'bout a five-to-one hull ratio,* she decided. Long and low and black with pitch, the sharp-prowed hulls were throwing a chuckle of bow wave under the dying breeze. Fast ships, then, although they were doing no more than three knots in these sheltered waters. The masts were tall and raked well back; two on the schooner coming in first, the *Sun Dancer,* three on the *Stormwind* following—that was about half the size of the *Chamberlain,* and brig-rigged, square sails on the fore and main, fore and aft on the mizzen.

Wish I was as certain as Heather and Lucy are that this is going to work, she thought wryly. The girls had given them a rousing send-off, although they'd been shocked underneath at Swindapa's wound. The Fiernan sat by the wheel on the quarterdeck, a kerchief hiding her bright hair and a cheese of gun wads supporting the injured leg. Alston felt naked, going into a fight without her partner by her side. It had been long years, since that first time down in the Olmec country.

The hyacinth eyes met hers, warm and fond. Alston nodded, and returned all her attention to the oncoming . . .

Targets, she told herself. *Think of them as targets and nothing else.* No boarding netting rigged, and their decks were crowded with men. *Maybe Isketerol had them sniffing around Australia,* she thought. *He knows about the gold there from the books Walker took.* That would explain stuffing men in that way.

The enemy ships were gliding closer. On each stern was a small platform with a statue on it, a grotesque juju with three legs, six arms, and a single staring eye—Arucuttag of the Sea, Lord of Waves, Master of the Storm, to whom the captains gave gold and man's-blood.

Closer, closer. How close before they could see through the fiction? And even when the schooner was well within range, the brig would be further out—it was the harder target. *Plus, I want to capture the ships, if I can.* For one thing, they and the prisoners would be valuable counters in whatever diplomatic game the Republic ended up playing with Tartessos. And God alone knew how she'd get the men back without another couple of hulls. It was tempting just to maroon them here, but that was either a sentence of slow death or a trip back home if other Tartessian ships called, both unacceptable.

Swindapa looked over at her, a question on her face. Alston shook her head, waiting. She raised her binoculars and focused on the man by the schooner's wheel, standing with his hands on his belt and a saffron-dyed cloak fluttering in the wind.

He had a spyglass; Isketerol's artisans were beginning to turn them out. She ignored the eerie conviction that he was looking at *her* and waited yet again, until she saw him lower the glass and open his mouth to speak. It might be some harmless order, but . . . and the distance was about right.

"Now!" she shouted.

Deck crew snatched up a line and heaved. It ran to a spring on the anchor cable, and the long hull of the clipper-frigate pivoted smoothly under that leverage, presenting her full broadside to the Tartessian ships.

A rumbling thunder as the bosun's pipe relayed the order and the waiting crews heaved on the gun tackle. She couldn't see the port side, but she knew exactly what the Tartessians were seeing, and it justified the gaping horror on their faces. The frigate's main battery was running out, the portlids swinging up to reveal the black maws of the eight-inch Dahlgrens. On deck, crewfolk were shoving and hustling the prisoners down the hatchways with savage enthusiasm. And—

BOOOOOOMMMMMMM—

One long, rolling crash as the gun captains jerked their lanyards and the twelve heavy cannon fired within a second of each other, at point-blank range.

"All yours, 'dapa!" Marian shouted and dropped down the rope ladder with reckless speed.

"Stretch out!" the middie shouted at the tiller of the longboat she landed in, her voice crackling with stress.

They heaved at their oars with panting, grunting effort that made the slender boats sweep forward, despite the weight of the Guard sailors who packed them to the gunwales, armed and cheering.

Four boats were pulling for the *Stormwind,* two for the smaller schooner. That looked to be out of action; she could see blood running in thin streaks through the ship's scuppers. *Christ, and I thought that was a figure of speech.*

Stormwind had taken bad hits too. Alston was relying on speed and surprise and the stunning effect of those first broadsides to keep them away from their cannon. The next thirty seconds would tell if it was enough.

"Thus, thus!" Alston shouted. Suddenly it was *there,* looming huge from the low-riding longboat. *"Up and at them!"*

"UP AND AT 'EM!" roared the laden boats.

A Tartessian cannon *did* fire, but too late—the ball went overhead, close enough for her to feel the ugly wind and know that fifteen seconds earlier it might have decapitated her as cleanly as a guillotine. Then they were up against the forepeak of the *Stormwind,* wood

grinding on wood. Marian leaped up and swarmed up one of the ropes
with a shout of "Follow me!"

Her head came level with the rail, to see a Tartessian bleeding from
half a dozen superficial wounds rushing at her with a boarding pike.
She drew her pistol one-handed, raked the hammers back against her
thigh and fired. The long steel head of the pike scored across her side
like a line of cold fire.

A flip put the barrels of the pistol in her hand. She smashed it into the
man's face, and his nose went flat in a spurt of blood. He roared and
reeled backward. That let her get her legs down on the *Stormwind*'s
deck and take a full-armed swing. Bone crumpled; she threw the pistol
in the next Tartessian's face and swept out her *katana*. That draw
turned into a cut, diagonally down from the left with her foot stamping
forward. The ugly jar of steel in meat and bone hit her wrists, and she
ripped the blade through its arc with a whipping twist of arms, shoulders, gut.

"Dissaaa!"

Something slapped her head around, stinging pain; the sensory data
were distant, nothing to pay attention to unless it crippled her—she
felt calm and utterly alive at the same time, information pouring in
through ears and eyes and skin and out in the movements of her sword
and orders. For a moment the two forces were locked together, blows
given and received chest to chest. Her *katana* jammed in bone, and
someone kicked her feet out from underneath her while it was stuck,
by accident or design.

Training saved her, making muscle go limp as she fell to the blood-
slick boards. She drew the shorter *wazikashi* and her tanto-knife, but
there was no way to parry the clubbed musket that a short, thick,
heavy-bodied Tartessian sailor was raising to beat out her brains.
Then the Tartessian screamed and fell back, his face half sliced off
by a boarding ax in the hands of a Chamberlain. The crewman was a
Sun People tribesman, and the battle madness of his folk was on him,
eyes showing white all around the iris, moving with a lethal, inhuman
fury . . .

Alston flipped herself back to her feet. "You!" she shouted, grabbing the bosun. The fighting had surged past her a little. "Get that!"

She pointed to a small stubby carronade standing to port of the
enemy ship's wheel, a flintlock piece with the hammer cocked—
ready, but the enemy had been surprised before they could use it. The
bosun nodded, understanding her gesture if not her voice in the overwhelming noise. He and she and half a dozen others grabbed the little
cannon and ran it forward.

"Way, there!" they called.

The Guard fighters parted, and there was a single moment to see the appalled faces of the Tartessians before she jerked the lanyard. It leaped backward, right up the quarterdeck and through the stern rail, but it had done its work . . . and it was loaded with grape.

The enemy gave way, turning and running down into the waist of the ship. Marian paused an instant to recover her sword, aware in some distant corner of her mind that the sensation of her feet sliding greasily in a pool of blood and body fluids would come back to her later. And the stink, the stink . . .

The Marines among the boarders fell out, reloaded their rifles, and volley-fired from fo'c'sle and quarterdeck, effective beyond their numbers in their crisp discipline and the ordered glitter of their bayonets. A Tartessian threw down his cutlass and fell to his knees, holding out his hand for quarter. There was an instant's wavering, and then the enemy's morale broke like a glass jar dropped on a granite paving stone.

"Cease fire!" Marian called as the rest of the enemy joined the first. "Belay fighting, there—cease fire!"

She stood, suddenly conscious of pain and of blood pouring in a wet sheet down her neck and her side. Her fingers went to one ear as a Tartessian in an officer's gaudy tunic came and knelt, offering his sword. She took it, wincing at the same time.

Well, there goes the earlobe, she thought, as the boarders began cheering, loud even after the memory of combat. One ran cat-nimble up the *Stormwind*'s rigging, slashed the crowned mountain of Tartessos down from the mast and ran up the Stars and Stripes.

The cheering spread across the water, and the Republic's flag was flying from *Sun Dancer* too. Alston felt her knees begin to buckle and clamped her fingers on the wound despite a sensation like a red-glowing steel spike thrust through the side of her head. Head wounds always made you bleed like a pig for some reason; the one in her side was deeper but not leaking as badly.

If this keeps up, eventually I'm going to be held together entirely by scar tissue, she thought, then called aloud:

"Ensign! Get the first aid going for the wounded and signal for the medics. Bosun, I want these prisoners disarmed and under hatches. You, there—"

Despite fatigue, despite the grief of losses and the pain of wounds, she felt a surge of sheer joyous relief. They were going home.

Home. Most beautiful word in the language.

CHAPTER NINETEEN

(February, Year 10 A.E.)
March, Year 10 A.E.

Thump.
William Walker jackknifed backward as the padded foot slammed into his leather-armored midriff. *Go-with,* he thought, and threw himself backward into a tumbling roll that brought him upright again in time to block a follow-up spinning back-kick. Ohotolarix closed in, moving lightly on the straw mats of the practice arena, grinning through the bars of his boiled-leather helmet, gloved hands up.

A roar went up from seats around the practice circle where the audience—officers and senior noncoms of his Royal Guard—cheered and yelled, shouting advice and comments. The Iraiina was a big man by the standards of this era, eight years younger than his overlord and a natural athlete. He bored in with a flurry of punches, back-fist strikes, then a sweeping takedown with his shin.

Walker grinned himself as he leaped over it, nearly chest-high, and his own foot lashed out—the showy jumping side-kick, rarely practical. Walker spun, then hooked a foot in under the short ribs. They went into a grapple, falling and rolling, hands finding and breaking leverage-holds. At last Walker caught his guard-captain in a scissors lock and mimed slamming the heel of his palm into his face, the killing blow up under the nose. He rose and offered the Iraiina a hand, pulling him up.

"You've gotten pretty good at the Sword Hand," he said.

"Indeed, lord," his Guard commander replied. He pulled off his helmet, shaking his thatch of sun-faded tow.

"It seemed like magic to me, that first time I saw it—you remember, I'd just lost a wrestling match to Hlokorax Winnahtaur's son? For that girl, what was her name . . . and you took him on and beat him in twenty seconds. *And* gave the girl back to me, and Hlokorax's knife. It was then I knew you were the *wehaxpothis* I must follow."

Walker laughed and nodded, slapping the other man on the back. He *did* remember that, quite vividly; it had been on the *Eagle*'s first visit to Alba, before he knew the language, but he'd still sensed something significant about the happening.

That's when I stopped daydreaming and began planning, he thought. The moment when the Event became really *real* to him. *That moment when Ohotolarix knelt and put his hands between mine.*

The two combatants walked out of the practice circle and headed down the corridor to the officers' bathhouse. It was as well equipped as the palace, if slightly less sumptuous, tile and brass rather than marble and gold.

Work 'em hard in the field, treat 'em like fighting cocks the rest of the time, Walker thought. That was the formula.

He made sure a lot of the officers were men who owed everything to him, too; younger sons of Achaean nobles without prospects, a lot of them, and promotions from the ranks—luckily, service in a king's guard was high-status work here. Some Albans he'd brought with him as well, and a few r. re who'd come along in the intervening years, ones who couldn't stomach the peace the Islanders had imposed in Alba. The odd foreign mercenary too; he made a mental note to check if there were any Ringapi in the ranks.

Slave girls took their sweat-sodden clothing, lathered them up, and turned on the hot water. After they scrubbed and soaked in the tub, they lay on massage tables while the attendants pummeled and thumped as they sipped fruit juice. It was hot and steamy here, the scent of steam and clean stone broken by the sharp medicinal odor of the massage oil.

Ohotolarix laughed. "I've even gotten used to being washed by women," he said.

Walked nodded; the Iraiina were a pretty prudish bunch, in some respects. After a silence broken only by the slap of the girls' hands on hard, taut muscle, he spoke: "Have you ever regretted following me here?"

The Iraiian shrugged, muscle rippling in his thick shoulders. To his way of thinking, that hadn't been a choice. He had put his hands between Walker's, and an honorable warrior followed his chief wherever he led, even into the Cold Lands beyond the grave.

By now he was used to the conditional-hypothetical way of thinking, though.

"Not often, lord. I confess, sometimes the summers here are too hot, and the people always too sly and tricksy, and they use too much garlic, and sometimes I long to see beech trees and snow and heather again, and smell a north wind whistling off the fens. But back in the northlands I'd never have been more than a *wirtowonax*"—an ordinary freeman of the tribe. "Here I'm great chief held in high honor, many men know my name, bards sing my deeds, and I have women and land, cattle and horses and gold of my own, with the best of lords to follow. And strong sons to sacrifice at my grave; four, not counting by-blows, and all of them alive!"

"Thanks to Hong," Walker noted.

How many kids myself? he thought. *Twelve that I've acknowledged. And Iphigenia is preggers, as Alice puts it.* Most of the Achaeans assumed that child would be his heir, but in fact he intended to pick whoever turned out best. *A good way to keep the kids very, very attentive and eager to please the old man, too.*

Ohotolarix made a slight grimace at Hong's name; he didn't like the Lady of Pain.

Well, thought Walker tolerantly, *not many people do like Alice, except the ones she's brainwashed.* Her Little Shop of Experimental Horrors out in the country had produced some strange results. *I do like her, but then, not many are as broadminded as I am.*

"What did you think of the Ringapi?" he said.

"Much like my folk, lord—richer, though. They'll fight well, in the old fashion. Their horses were good, of their kind, and they knew how to handle a chariot."

"I agree." He was silent for a while. "I'm thinking of sending a mission to their country, to establish a stronghold. I might want you to command that."

"Lord!" Ohotolarix was alarmed. "I'd miss the fighting!"

Walker shook his head. "No, just fight in a different area. And I need a man I can trust absolutely there."

That mollified the Iraiina; he thought the Achaeans were treacherous faithless dogs to a man, and by his standards he was right. "What's their land like?" he said.

"Great plains of grass, surrounded by mountains with thick forest. Timber and mines in the mountains, with the towns and villages on the flats, and great rivers running through it. Marshes with reeds and a lot of game, wildfowl, boar, aurochs. Colder winters than here, too cold for olives, but vines will grow there."

"It sounds a goodly land, lord." A laugh. "Why didn't we go there?"

"I considered it," Walker said. "But there are so many advantages to being by the sea." A pause. "Disadvantages too, of course."

The Iraiina's brows knotted; he wasn't a stupid man by any means, and he'd learned a good deal since his days as a simple warrior-herdsman.

"You don't think we'll have the victory in this war, lord?"

"I think we will have the victory, but I'm not *certain.* The Ringapi could be useful either way."

They talked until the next few contestants came into the baths—one was carried through limp, off to the medic—and the conversation became more general. There were a few halfhearted attempts to pump him for the inside skinny on the coming war, but he frowned those into silence—the need-to-know principle was something he worked hard at getting into their heads.

He did hint at promotions, which was true enough; he used the guard as a training ground for his officer cadre. When the men adjourned to their mess for a little further partying, Walker headed instead for the stables. He caroused with the guard officers fairly often; they were a pretty good set of guys, the hero worship didn't hurt and there was no loss of face—in this country even gods were supposed to come down and kick up their heels now and then. But today he felt thoughtful.

It was a bright winter's afternoon outside, just brisk enough to make him glad of the cloak as he walked across the parade ground and through the sere gardens at the base of the hill that held his palace. A hound waiting for him at the door sprang up and gamboled about as he came out, jumping up and licking at his hands until he cuffed it affectionately aside.

"Down, Rover, goddammit! Is there anything *I* miss about the twentieth?" he mused aloud—in English, which made it private. "Let's see—movies, deep-dish pizza, good barbecue sauce, air conditioning, CDs . . . and that's about it. Don't think you'd have liked it there, Rover. Down! Good dog!"

Thank God for Ohotolarix, who's a good dog too, he thought. The lunatic warrior code of his folk was deep in the Iraiina's bones; Walker understood the motivations thoroughly, without sharing them in the least. So long as Walker fulfilled the obligations of a chief, the Iraiina would be loyal unto death. It was good to have a few completely honest men around.

Particularly if you're . . . flexible and realistic yourself, Walker thought with a chuckle, swinging his arms. *Important to remember that people are different; you can't always judge other people's motivations by your own.*

He felt loose and relaxed, alert and strong all at once from the hard exercise and the hot water and massage.

On impulse he walked through to the stable complex. He kept some dried apricots on him and now fed them to a few of his favorite mounts. They came eagerly at the sound of his step, snorting, ears cocked forward.

I understand your *motivations, too,* he thought. Horses and dogs were more honest than human beings; they didn't *pretend* to love you because you fed them, they actually *did*.

Rover had been sniffing around; now he raised his head, cocked his own hairy ears, whined, and then growled slightly. Walker heard the noise a little later, and then a stablehand was backing into the hallway. Althea came after him, in riding clothes, slashing at him with her riding crop; at nine she was only a couple of inches shorter than the slave, showing promise of her father's height. The stable worker backed up, babbling excuses and sheltering his face with crossed arms that showed bleeding welts from the steel-cored leather; he knew better than to try and touch the girl, of course.

"Hey, what's up?" Walker said.

Quite a temper on that chick, he thought, looking at his daughter objectively. *In a couple of years, she's going to be quite a sight, too.* Long buttercup-colored hair fell down her back, shining from careful attention; her face was oval and regular, the eyes large and cornflower blue.

"This . . . this . . . this *fool* had Stamper taken over to the farriers to be shod today!" Althea said. "I wanted to ride him, and now I can't!"

The slave was from some tribe in the northern mountains and had most of his face covered with woad-blue tattoos; it didn't hide the depth of his fear as he turned and threw himself at Walker's feet.

"Lord, it wasn't my fault! Nobody said he'd be needed today, I swear by Rheasos the Rider!"

"Get out," Walker said, nudging him with a toe.

When the man had scurried away, he reached out and gripped his daughter by the back of the neck in an iron grip that brought a squeak of surprise. Then he effortlessly plucked the quirt out of her grasp and gave her three strokes with it, across the seat of her tight riding pants, hard enough to make her jump.

"Quiet!" he said, when she squalled.

"Yes, Father," she said, stepping back and rubbing her backside reflexively. Her blue eyes narrowed; not a hint of tears, he saw with approval. "Why did you do that?"

"Because you lost your temper," Walker said.

"Father! He's just a *slave.*"

"Oh, it's not the slave," Walker said. "Plenty more where he came from. *You're* the one who screwed up. What do I say about anger?"

"Oh." She frowned in thought. "I see, Father. Yes, that it's a good servant but a poor master."

"Right on, infant. You can't master anything unless you master yourself. If you ate sweets whenever you felt like it and didn't bother to exercise, who would you be?"

She giggled. "A big fat ugly sausage—Minister Selznick."

"And if you started hitting and killing every time you felt angry?"

"I'd be Auntie Hong!"

Walker shouted laughter, and the girl grinned. "That's funny but not true, Althea. Your Aunt Hong is . . . ah, sort of strange."

"Dad," Althea said, dropping into English for a moment, "she's a *sicko*."

"Well, yes, actually . . . who did you get that word from?"

"Bill—Mr. Cuddy."

"Ah, yes . . . and don't try to distract me, young lady. If you didn't control your anger, you'd be no better than all these wog lordlets. Think about it for a moment. It's good to have people *fear* you, but they shouldn't be afraid you'll start whipping them the moment some little thing goes wrong, or killing them for telling you something you don't want to hear. If you do, they'll lie to you—more than they would otherwise—and always tell you what they think you *do* want to hear. That's like being fucking *blind*, girl. And they may fear your temper, but they'll lack respect for *you*."

He bent over and caught her eye, his voice going cold. "And you will never, *never* do anything that might make people lose respect for us. Understand?"

She flushed and looked down at her booted toes. "Okay, Dad," she said in a small voice.

"Okay, then. Now go get yourself another horse."

Walker ruffled the dog's ears as his daughter trotted away. "Good kid," he said, sighing with contentment.

"Well, that's that," Marian Alston said. She looked down at the paper and the totals of her prize money and Swindapa's, neatly summed up and deposited to their account at the Pacific Bank. "It seems a little excessive."

Jared Cofflin quirked the corner of his mouth. "So were the cargoes on those boats you captured excessive. The government's share is enough to pay the repairs on the *Chamberlain* and a good chunk of the expedition's costs as well. And where they found the gold dust and nuggets God alone knows."

"She isn't talking, but I suspect Australia, then back via the Sunda Strait," Marian said. "And they were ships, not boats. Well, a schooner and a brig, if you want to get technical."

"Now you're sounding like Leaton," Cofflin said.

"No," Swindapa said, looking up from her seat by the fire across the room. "Not quite like Ronald."

Her goddaughter Marian Cofflin and Heather and Lucy were curled up on the settee with her, and the rest of the Cofflins' children sat on the rug at her feet as she read from a big leather-bound book. The rain had canceled the high school football game they'd originally planned to attend today. She marked her place with her thumb and went on:

"Marian just sounds like she loves ships. Leaton sounds like he wants to—" She visibly remembered Eagle People taboos about what could be said in front of children—"become very *intimate* with the machinery he loves."

Martha chuckled from the other side of the dining-room table, and there was a chorus of giggles from the children.

"It looks like we'll be getting that place in the country, sugar," Marian said. Martha raised a brow and the commodore went on: "We were talking it over—retirement place, and 'dapa would like to raise horses. Somewhere with a pier for a boat."

"We're going to have *ponies*!" Heather said; Lucy nodded vigorously, and the Cofflins' children looked at them with envy.

"That sounds nice. The question right now, though, is are we at war with Tartessos?" Martha said.

"I don't think so," Cofflin said. "I had Ian on the radio this morning, and he doesn't think so either, and neither does Christa Beale, and she's holding the fort as far as the Tartessos desk is concerned. Their assessment is that Isketerol wants to stay neutral for now and will claim—what did Ian say—plausible deniability and pay us a whonking great fine to get the men and ships back. Ayup, no war."

"Not *yet*," Alston said grimly. "It's coming, though. So I'd advise you to keep the ships, at least—we have to give the crews back, of course, but I think Isketerol can afford losing silver more than he can two good hulls."

"You think so?" Cofflin said. "Hmmm. You know, I'm not altogether sure that just having an alliance with Walker will push Isketerol into fighting us."

"It wouldn't, but there's more than that. Walker is pushing Isketerol, but it's a direction he wants to be pushed. Without us, Tartessos would be one of the two great powers—and the only one with access to the world ocean. With us, they're frustrated everywhere they turn, *and* we're helping the Albans catch up quickly. Walker will give him all the help he can; he's probably realized what we're doing in Babylonia by now."

Cofflin scowled. "I don't like fighting two wars at once."

"I don't like fighting any at all, but I also don't think we're going to have any choice," Alston said, sipping at her lukewarm cocoa. The late-autumn rain was beating outside the windows of the Chief's House, cold and on the verge of being slush.

Good old Gray Lady of the Northern Sea, Alston thought. *Living up to her Yankee ways.* She loved her adopted home, but there was no denying that the climate was lousy six to eight months a year. *Eight months of winter, four months of bad skiing.*

"We'll have to consider what we're going to do to convince Isketerol of the error of his ways," Cofflin said.

Off on the other side of the big room Swindapa's voice rose and fell musically: *"It was seven o'clock of a very warm evening in the Seeconee hills when Father Wolf woke up from his day's rest, scratched himself, yawned, and spread out his paws one after the other to get rid of the sleepy feeling in their tips. Mother Wolf lay with her big gray nose dropped across four tumbling, squealing cubs—like you little ones—and the moon shone into the mouth of the cave where they all lived."*

The children yipped and growled, pretending to be wolf cubs, and then settled down for the rest of the story. Jared looked at his watch.

"Speaking of Ron, we ought to duck over to Seahaven; he wants to show us some of his newest toys," the Chief said. "Swindapa? Martha?"

Swindapa shook her head. "I'm not back on duty until tomorrow, Doc Coleman says," she said, looking up and holding her place with a finger while the children tugged at her. "I want to find out what happens in this story too."

"And I'm going to go over these tax proposals for the Warrant," Martha said. "See you two at dinner."

"See you then," Alston replied, "and next Friday it's our turn to have y'all over."

They took their sou'westers and slickers from pegs in the front hall and ducked out into the steady drizzle. The streets were fairly busy; Nantucket was a working town now and didn't let a little water slow things down on a weekday afternoon. A hauler went by as they turned onto Center Street, and a string of horse-drawn wagons passed in the opposite direction. Cofflin nodded at them.

"New business," he said. "Taking down spare houses, then shipping 'em out to Long Island or Providence Base and putting 'em back up."

"Sensible," Marian said.

Nantucket's year-round population had increased, over ten thousand now, but there were still empty houses, and everything had to be built from scratch in the outports, as they were coming to be called.

They turned onto Main and waved to Joseph Starbuck, who was going into the Pacific Bank at the head of the street. Cofflin shook his head as they eeled through the dense crowds amid an odor of damp wool and fish from carts delivering to the eateries.

"Every time I see that place, I remember my first speech, up on the bank steps," he said. "The night of the Event, when we had all those lights in the sky and everyone was panicking. I might have myself, if I hadn't had to calm *them* down. And then the stars came back, and I thought everything was all right . . . until I noticed where the moon was."

"Same with me," Alston said. "It was the stars did it."

They turned right at Candle Street where it led into Washington, running southeast parallel to the line of the harbor and back from the new dredged channels and solid-fill piers. A leafless forest of mast and spar and an occasional smokestack showed over the tops of the buildings to their left; pre-Event boutiques converted to sail-lofts and chandlers' shops and warehouses, with a crowd dressed mostly in seagoing oilskins, with sweaters and rough pants and seaboots below that. They stopped for a moment while a dozen people manhandled a huge sausage of canvas onto a cart, and listened to a quartermaster dickering over the price of twenty-five barrels of salt beef.

"Salt whale, more like." the quartermaster said, her face going red. "Sell it to the fucking Marines, Andy! Four-fifty is piracy, nothing but. Three seventy-five a cask, and I want a written warranty."

"Three seventy-five? The *staves* are worth more than that. Have a heart, McAndrews, have I ever stiffed you before? Look, let's—"

Cofflin grinned as they walked on. "You know, that's something I don't regret," he said. "That we're making our own history again, instead of living off selling the image of it. The way this town was put under glass for the tourists always sort of got me, before."

"Not anymore," Alston said. "Smelling's believing."

The Chief gave a small snort. It *was* a little thick down here, especially since the rendery and tanneries had been moved out to this part of town. Fish, the collecting tanks for the offal—useful for fertilizer—and half a dozen crafts added to the aroma.

The buildings on their right were mostly post-Event, factories and workships in big timber-built shingled boxes, many with tall brick smokestacks, their plumes of woodsmoke adding a thick tang to the air. They passed signs: WASHINGTON MILLS SAILCLOTH AND CORDAGE and ZERO MAIN SEWING MACHINES; that one had a cart at the loading bay, with crates of its treadle-powered wonders being moved onto it—they were turning into a major export. Through the open bay doors they caught a glimpse of belts and shafting and whirring, clattering lathes and drill presses.

EAGLE EYE KNITTING, DON'S MARINE STEAM ENGINES AND GEARING, smiths and carpenters and plumbers and more; merchants' offices, SUN ISLAND SHIPPING, CHAPMAN AND CHARNES, TELENATRO AND FELDMAN . . . then the turnoff to the new shipyards on their left. That was where the *Chamberlain* was under repair in the spanking-new dry dock, and a second being was constructed.

Cofflin's face reflected a sober satisfaction at what his people had accomplished; this was prosperity, as the Year 9 defined it. Hard, demanding work, although God knew any sort of in-town labor was safer and softer than the fisheries. It all put food on the table and clothes on the back. Plus paying to keep civilization alive—schools and police and national defense . . .

"I'm worried about having Ian out so far," he said. "Missed him more than I anticipated; the man's right smart."

Alston nodded. "But he's doing a fine job where he is," she said. "I couldn't have negotiated that treaty with Babylon, and from the reports"—she'd spent several days reading the backlog as soon as the *Chamberlain* limped into Nantucket Harbor with her prizes at her heels—"he's building something solid there."

A spell of thoughtful silence, and then Cofflin spoke: "What are our chances, if it does come to an all-out fight?"

"Pretty good, but they'd be better in a few years," Marian said. "Walker and Isketerol both have less technological depth than we do, but they've got more breadth—much bigger populations to draw on, which compensates for the lower productivity. We're starting to pull ahead, though, and soon we'll have stuff that will take them a lot longer to match. Speaking of which, here we are—the magician's lair."

Cofflin snorted. "Let's see what rabbit Ron's pulled out of the hat for us this time."

Seahaven Engineering had started out its post-Event career in a big boat shed down by the end of Washington Street, near the shipyard. Much of the production had moved to a big new plant out by the Bessemer casting plant, but there was still a ceaseless bustle here. It smelled of hot metal, and whale-oil lubricant, and a little of the tingle of ozone from electric welders powered by the wind generators around town.

Jared Cofflin and Marian Alston created a bit of a stir when they walked in together and hung their dripping oilskins on pegs over a trough. A clerk showed them through the long showroom where Islanders and foreign merchants placed orders; through the great, hot, echoing brightness of the main machine shop, lit by sputtering, popping arc lamps high above.

The clerk opened a door, letting the noise of the shop floor into the wooden cubicle where Leaton had his office, and yelled their names over it. Cofflin hid a smile; he'd always liked Ron's management style, too.

The office was as cluttered as ever but bigger—an extension had been added for more bookshelf space, a draftsman's table with the rarity of an electric light. On a desk stood an even greater one—a working computer, under special license from the Town. It would be generations, if ever, before the Islanders could replace any of its components beyond the casing and the on-off switch, but Seahaven had need of it now.

The head of the firm was using the mouse to rotate a wire-drawing outline of some machine part; he clicked on Save and turned, sprang up from the littered table and advanced with outstretched hand.

"Jared, Marian!" he said eagerly. "Good to see you!"

"From the smile, I gather it must work, Ron," Jared replied as he shook his hand; then his own lips quirked. Leaton's enthusiasm was as infectious as a puppy's.

"Yes, indeed!" Leaton said. "We've got it in Bay Number Two. It was the ammunition problem that was toughest, but we're setting up a production-scale plant out of town by Casting Number One—closer to the powder mill, anyway."

Cofflin nodded while Leaton rummaged in a drawer; gunpowder manufacture was one thing they'd zoned right out in the countryside by Gibbs Pond from the beginning, and convenience be damned. The thought of a couple of tons of the stuff going off around here . . .

"Here it is," the machinist-turned-industrialist said, handing over a brass cartridge.

Jared Cofflin took it and turned it over in his hands. "Still .40?"

"Mmmm-hmmm. No reason to change it, and that way we don't have to do up new jigs and bits for the rifling benches and boring machines. Priorities, again . . . we're still short of tool steel, the high-carbon cutters work, but they wear out so damn fast. Okay, sorry. I'll stop complaining. The bullet's virtually the same as the Westley-Richards model too—a little more antimony and tin for hardening."

"What's this?" Cofflin said, flicking his thumbnail against the rim. Between it and the body of the shell was a thin rounded section.

"Miniature brass tube—we fabricate the base separately and then join it to the shell body with this. Makes it a hell of a lot easier to—well, not to get technical . . ."

Cofflin and Alston looked at each other and shared a dry chuckle. Leaton grinned and patted the air with his hands, acknowledging the hit. He was notorious all over the Republic for his readiness to shove technical detail into the ear of anyone who'd listen.

"All right, not to get *too* technical, it makes it a hell of a lot easier to fabricate. Here." He pulled a black cylinder out of the drawer. "Told you about this, didn't I, Marian?"

"Mmmm-hmmm." She turned it over in her fingers, a black tube with a thin hole down the center. "Compressed gunpowder," she said to Jared.

"What's the point?" Jared asked. "I'd think that would make it harder to fill the shell, since it's bottlenecked."

"It's the shape," Marian explained. "Ordinary black powder blows up as the grains burn from the outside in. This burns from the inside out, faster and faster 'till it's all gone."

Leaton nodded enthusiastically. "Nineteen hundred feet per second, as opposed to fourteen hundred for the old Westley-Richards," he said. "By the way, I'm working on a Gatling gun using the same cartridge—very promising."

"Nice work, Ron," Cofflin said.

"Stole the idea for the compressed powder: Lee-Metford, 1888. Metford rifling, too."

"You did the research."

They followed the engineer out into the shop, and then into one of the long timber bays. A stocky woman in a leather apron studded with pockets and loops for tools looked up and smiled greeting to Leaton, nodded to the Chief and Alston.

"Got 'em right here," she said, handing a rifle to Cofflin and another to the commodore. "First batch—all the collywobbles out, as far as we can tell."

"Interesting," Cofflin said, turning the weapon over in his hands. Most of it looked l..e the Westley-Richards, but instead of a side-mounted hammer there was a small rounded lever protruding from a curved slot on the right. Flush with the upper side of the weapon was a rectangular steel block that had a milled groove in the top and pivoted in a steel box set into the wood of the stock.

"Single-shot?" he said. Leaton nodded. "Why not a magazine gun?"

Marian replied for him. "KISS principle," she said. *Keep It Simple, Stupid;* the Republic had learned that early on. "This has got . . . how many?"

"Twelve moving parts," Leaton said. "See the screw at the back?"

"Ayup," Cofflin said.

"Undo that, and then you can strip it down for cleaning and repair by hand, like this"—he demonstrated—"no tools required. A blacksmith who's a good hand with a metal file could repair any of the parts, or duplicate them at need."

The engineer snapped the weapon back together again. "Here's how it works. You push down on the grooved block like this for the first round."

Cofflin obeyed; there was a soft, yielding resistance and a slight *click.* The block pivoted down from a pin at the rear, and now it made a ramp that led straight into the chamber.

"Slide a round into the breech." Cofflin pushed it down with his thumb. "Now put your right hand on the stock and pull the little lever back and down. That's half-cock—the weapon's on safety now. Pull it back all the way, and when you hear the next click it's ready to fire."

Cofflin took the rifle over to the waist-high bench that separated the workroom from the firing range. It was about a hundred yards long, with thick timber to either side and a wall of sandbags at the end to hold the man-shaped target. Nantucket's Chief put the weapon to his shoulder, giving a grunt of satisfaction at the smooth, well-balanced feel. Squeeze the trigger gently . . .

It broke clean, with a crisp action. *Crack,* and the butt kicked his shoulder; he lowered it again.

"How do I get the spent shell out and reload?" he asked.

Leaton chuckled like a child with a Christmas surprise to bestow. "Just pull the trigger all the way back so it hits that little trip-release stud behind it," he said.

Cofflin did, and started slightly as the breechblock snapped down and the spent cartridge was ejected to the rear and slightly to the right; he blinked as it went *ping* on the asphalt floor and rolled away. The technician scooped it up and dropped it into one of the capacious pockets that studded her leather apron, where it jingled with a good many others.

"Two springs, inside, I guess?" he said. "Well, that'll make it easier to use."

Marian slung a bandolier over her shoulder. "Easier and faster," she said, buckling back the cover flap. Brass cartridges showed in neat rows, nestling in their canvas loops. "Watch."

She brought the rifle to her shoulder and fired. *Crack,* and a puff of off-white smoke was added to the one he'd made. *Ting,* and the breech went down and the shell ejected.

Faster, all right, he noted. The old rifles went *bang* . . . beat . . . beat . . . beat . . . beat . . . *bang* when you were firing as fast as you could. This was more like *bang* . . . beat . . . beat . . . *bang.*

She repeated the process once more in slow motion. "See, there are only four movements to reload—take your hand off the stock, reach down for a cartridge, thumb it home, then thumb back the cocking lever and aim. That's about the same as for a bolt-action rifle."

Cofflin whistled, working his jaw to help his abused ears. "Fast is right," he said. "Four, mebbe five seconds between rounds?"

"Twelve aimed rounds a minute," Leaton agreed proudly, rubbing his hands together. "With a little practice. That's twice what the Westley-Richards can do, and this one's got more range and accuracy, as well."

"And it's waterproof, unlike the flintlocks, the rifle and the ammunition both," Alston said. "Virtually soldier-proof, too. Simple, rugged, easy to use and maintain. Until we can go to smokeless powder and a semi-auto, this is our best bet, I think."

"Ron," Cofflin said sincerely, "you've done it again. Congratulations!"

"Ah . . ." Leaton shuffled his feet. "Actually, it's the fruit of a weird taste in reading matter. It's German, originally—Bavarian, from the 1860s, I just modified the design a bit here and there. Guy named

Werder from Munich developed it, one of those all-round Victorian inventors and machinists. Obscure, but probably the best single-shot rifle ever made."

"Okay, tell me the bad news—production?"

Leaton grinned. "This time, the bad news is good, Chief. We can turn out two hundred a week, and the ammunition will be ample."

A thought struck Cofflin. "Wait a minute," he said, looking down at the rifle in his hands. *I certainly want our boys and girls to have the best, but . . .*

"Couldn't Walker duplicate this? He's copying our Westley-Richards now."

Marian nodded with a shark's amusement, and Leaton guffawed. "We hope he tries, Chief," the engineer said. "Yeah, he *could* duplicate the *rifle* without much of a problem."

The commodore took up the explanation. "But getting reliable drawn-brass cartridges and primers, *that* won't be nearly so easy. God damned difficult, as a matter of fact."

Leaton made a gesture. "He'll be able to do it, eventually," he said. "Bill Cuddy's a first-rate machinist, whatever else is wrong with him, and from the reports you've been sending me they've got a fair little machine-tool business going there. Still behind ours because they started out without our power sources or stock of materials, but growing fast. So, yes, he could duplicate the Werder and *eventually* the ammo if he gets a copy to reverse-engineer. Of course, Walker hasn't got our scale and most of his workers are rote-trained, not allrounders. Bottom line, it'll waste his resources for a good year, maybe three, if he tries to switch over—cutting into his Westley-Richards production pretty bad, we think."

"And if I know Walker," Marian Alston said with satisfaction in her tone, "he won't be able to resist trying to match anything we do, if it's remotely possible. An ego as big as the Montana skies."

The three Islanders shared a long, wolfish chuckle. Leaton turned to a cabinet, opened it, and handed Alston a revolver and belt. "This is by way of a belated coming-home present," he said. "Modeled on the Colt Python, but in 10 mm—.40. Black-powder, of course, but you'll find it an improvement over the double-barreled flintlocks, I think."

"Why, thank you, Ron," Marian said, giving the weapon a quick check. "Now, we have to talk priorities."

"Ayup," Cofflin said. "You want the expeditionary force to get first crack?"

Alston surprised him by shaking her head. "Not until they can make their own ammunition. I'm not going to put a thousand of my people seven thousand miles of irregular sailing-ship passage away from their sole and only ammunition supply. That's a point-failure source."

"Couple of months minimum for that," Leaton said. "The people you sent can handle the equipment, but some of it's fairly complex. Take a while to run up another set."

"Right," Alston said. "First we'll re-equip the Ready Force"—the Islander citizens doing their initial training—"the first-line militia battalions, and the ships'-company Marines. We can ship the surplus Westley-Richards to Kar-Duniash to equip local forces, and the Marines there can hand over theirs too when we get them Werders."

"Mmmm, sounds sensible," Cofflin said. He usually left specialists to handle their own areas of expertise—that was half the secret of doing the Chief's job right, remembering not to joggle elbows. The other half was picking the right experts to begin with, of course.

CHAPTER TWENTY

February–March, Year 10 A.E.
(April, Year 10 A.E.)

Ur Base's main communications room held several shortwave sets. They were talking in the clear; one of the few things they definitely *did* know was that Walker's radio had stayed behind in Alba when he left. He might be able to intercept a spark-gap Morse signal, but nobody in Mycenaean Greece was going to duplicate a voice set.

Colonel Hollard sat in the woven-reed chair and put the headset on, adjusting the mike.

"Ur Base," the radio technician said. "This is Ur Base. Come in, Dur-Kurigalzu. Come in, please."

"This is Councilor Arnstein's office in Dur-Kurigalzu. Receiving you loud and clear. Over."

"Roger that, Dur-Kurigalzu. I'm handing over to the colonel."

"Hello, Ian. What's up?"

"Hi, Ken. I'm calling about your lost princess; thought I'd check up on her. And there's some other news. How's she doing?"

"Not badly," Colonel Hollard said. "We gave her a guesthouse and hired those two Assyrian girls to do the cooking and suchlike. She's studying English, but pretty quiet otherwise. Not surprising, considering the trauma she went through. The kid's got guts."

"What about brains? Doreen thought she was very bright."

"Very is the word. Lot of culture shock, of course, but she's adaptable as well."

"Hmmmm."

"Sir?"

"Why so formal, Ken?"

"Well, I was wondering what you have in mind for her," Kenneth Hollard said. "We've gotten about all the intelligence data we can, and she's got no real place here. I was thinking about sponsoring her back on-Island—sending her to stay at my brother's place, maybe."

Arnstein chuckled. "Yes, she's a likable sort too, in that I-am-a-princess way, isn't she? No, I don't think we'll take her off the board just yet, Colonel. Doreen and I have been talking it over, and there must be *some* sort of use we can make of the last of the Mitannian royal line."

"Sir . . ." Hollard fought down annoyance; Arnstein was just doing his job. "Sir, she's already gone through a lot."

"I'm aware of that, Ken," Arnstein soothed. "And believe me, we're not going to do anything against her interests. But *we're* here for the interests of the Republic, not as a find-a-place-for-strays agency."

"Yessir. I'm going to be dropping in on her in a minute, anyway, as a matter of fact."

"Good," Arnstein said. "It would be best if she has positive feelings toward the Republic."

"I don't think she thinks in those categories, sir," Hollard said. "It's *giri*, here; personal obligations."

"Hmmmmm, you have a point. Mitanni was more of a feudal state than most of these ancient Oriental despotisms, as far as we can tell—which isn't very far. Damn, but I wish I had more staff qualified to do research in the archives here!"

"Sir, learning that script is a nightmare."

"You're telling me," Arnstein said. "How are the scribes coming?"

"Quite well."

"Good. I'll hire a couple and set them going on transliterations," he said. Akkadian could be written quite well in the Roman alphabet. "Good long-term project, anyway. I doubt cuneiform will be used for more than another century or so, and then anything that hasn't been written down in the new medium will be lost."

Hollard's brows went up. "You really think so?"

"Oh, yes. Not a certainty, of course, but highly probable, once paper and printing catch on—you can't print cuneiform, not really. You know, one reason I regret not being immortal is that I won't find out what's going to *happen* here."

"Councilor, I'd settle for knowing what's happening in Greece."

"That I can help you with."

Hollard leaned forward eagerly. "What?"

"We've finally gotten some informants into coastal Anatolia—your lost princess did help us there, the names of some merchants who trade through Hangilibat, and for a wonder they're alive. The latest intelligence is that this Hittite chief who's rebelled against King Tudhaliya—the one Raupasha told us about—has gone to Millawanda to confer with a 'chief of the Ahhiyawa.' "

Hollard made an interrogative noise, and Arnstein sighed. "Millawanda . . . Miletus. Port on the Aegean. Ahhiyawa . . . Achaea. Greece."

"Uh-oh."

"Uh-oh, is right. That damned war with Assyria took too long for comfort; the passes over the Taurus into Anatolia will be closed soon. We've got to get in contact with Hattusas, and then we've got to hit the enemy next spring."

"Yes, sir!"

"Which brings us back to Princess Raupasha . . ."

Colonel Kenneth Hollard was still mulling over the conversation when he walked into his quarters and heard a whine. He looked down. The wicker basket was overset and the hound puppy nowhere in sight. Until he looked in his footlocker, slightly open.

"Hell," he said, looking down. "Oh, well, I didn't like that belt anyway, or those slippers. Come here, you damned set of teeth and paws."

He clamped the puppy firmly in his arms, avoiding most of the attempts to lick his face, and took it back to the office. The beast was from the royal hunting pack's kennels; nobles here kept hunting animals, despite the general Babylonian dislike of dogs.

Of course, the king isn't a Babylonian, strictly speaking, he thought.

The royal family and a lot of the nobility here were Kassites who'd come down from the mountains during the breakup of Hammurabi's empire centuries before and seized power. They'd been pretty well assimilated by now, but they kept up some contact with the old homeland; Prince Kashtiliash had been fostered there for a couple of years, for instance.

"C'mon, pooch," he muttered to it, and the puppy went into wiggling ecstasy at the attention. "Got a nice girl I'd like to set you up with."

"That makes no sense!" Raupasha daughter of Shuttarna said.

The physician's apprentice Azzu-ena sighed. "I agree," she said, tapping the paper on the table between them. "But it is the way the Nantukhtar language is."

Raupasha looked down. She'd learned the *alphabet* quickly; it was childishly simple compared to the Akkadian cuneiform. The language it was designed to write was another matter. Azzu-ena knew more of it than she; of course, she was a learned woman, and *old*—perhaps even thirty. It was good to have her come and help with the studies; it made the house less of a silent prison. And it gave her someone to complain to when the irritation grew too much to bear.

"But the form of the words is exactly the same!" the Mitannian girl said. "*House dog* and *dog house*. Shouldn't it be *dog's house*, with that possessive ending?"

Azzu-ena frowned herself, scratching her big hooked nose. "You would think so . . . but in the English, most of the time, it is the *order* of the words that determines their meaning, not the declension and inflection as it is in Akkadian. Is it so in Hurrian?"

"Yes, and any other language I've ever heard of," Raupasha said. She sighed, and her lips firmed with determination. "I *will* learn this tongue! Quickly!"

"Why are you in such a hurry?" Azzu-ena asked. "I have been, because the knowledge I seek is in this tongue. Why do *you* drive yourself so?"

"Because . . ." Raupasha hesitated. *But there is no reason she should not know.* And it was good to have someone to talk to. "Because I must understand them, too. I would not always be their client and pensioner, well though they have treated me."

The maid padded in with a tray of the small round sweet cakes and a pot of cocoa. *Cookies,* she reminded herself. Or *biscuits.* Cocoa had a flavor like nothing on earth, soft and rich and dark and sweet all at once; she found herself craving it often and restrained herself sternly. She was not going to disgrace her blood before these strangers.

"And to have someone to talk to," she went on aloud. "You are not here at Ur Base all of the time, and the house slaves are so stupid!"

"Not stupid—they're peasants and far from home and ignorant," Azzu-ena corrected her, a smile taking any sting out of her words. "And please! Do not call them slaves. They are *employees* who receive a wage. The Eagle People hate the very word 'slave'; they are strange in that manner."

"They are strange in all manners," Raupasha said, pouring a little date syrup into the cups of cocoa and stirring them with a whisk. "So many weird taboos and laws of ritual purity—the way all excrement must be carried away out of sight, for instance, and all rubbish buried or burned, and even laborers made to *wash* every day as if for a ritual in a House of Exclusion."

"They have reason for that; they think that filth causes disease, and they may well be right. Likewise their hatred of insects."

"Oh!" Raupasha said. "Still, they are very strange indeed. I asked Lord Kenn'et the other day what his rank was in Nan-tuck-et, and he said he was a *citizen*. What means this word?"

"I am not sure," Azzu-ena said thoughtfully. "I *think* it means something like an *awelum*, a free man of a city."

"But he said something about the *citizens* choosing the king," Raupasha said. "Surely that means high nobles, generals, ministers, chief priests?"

"I haven't asked much of how they are governed," Azzu-ena said.

"Though of course you would, coming of a high family." She looked around. "And so they treat you, I see."

Raupasha nodded. The house here in the Nantukhtar base was smaller than her foster father's manor, but more comfortable than anything she had ever known. There were no frescoes on the walls, but there were framed pictures unbelievably lifelike, and windows of glass clear as solid air. Those were open now, and slatted screens of woven reed let in air without the glare of the afternoon sun. The tile floors were covered in fine rugs, for the Nantukhtar put them on the floor, rather than hanging them on the walls—an extravagance that gave her a guilty pleasure every time her toes worked into them. The furniture was beautifully made, much of it Babylonian—and that of the finest. And there was a kitchen and a *bitrimki*, a bathhouse, as fine as those of a king's palace in a great city like Nineveh or Dur-Kurigalzu.

"That is partly the lord Arnstein and his lady," Raupasha said shrewdly. "They think I may be of some use to them . . . I do not know what. If my family were still rulers, they might seek to make an advantageous marriage-alliance through me, but I have neither gold nor power to bring. Isn't it so odd that Lord Arnstein's wife is also his right-hand man . . . ah, you know what I mean!"

"Yes." A smile, turning the homely face of the female physician almost comely for an instant. "That is a strange custom to which I have no objection at all. Nor do you object that you are treated as suits your birth, rather than your wealth!"

Raupasha nodded. "But part of it is Lord Kenn'et, I think. He is an odd man—a great warrior, a slaughterer of Assyrians, yet his heart is moved to compassion, as if I were his kin." She scowled slightly. "As if I were a small child of his own kin, sometimes."

"That is the way of the Eagle People," Azzu-ena replied. "It is . . . contradictory. Their weapons slay like the hand of the plague-gods, and then they bind up the wounds of those they threw down." She paused and smiled slyly. "I have seen Lord Kenn'et only a few times. As you say, a great warrior . . . a man of great beauty, too. Tall as a palm tree and ruddy, strong and sturdy."

"Yes." Raupasha flushed, then coughed. "There is a thing I would ask you, Lady Azzu-ena."

"Ask." The Babylonian's face changed from happy gossiper to the impersonal attentiveness of a professional.

"I am troubled by my dreams. You are a person of learning, and I thought perhaps . . ."

"I am sorry, I am a physician, not a *baru*-diviner," Azzu-ena said sympathetically. "I can recommend a good one."

"No . . . it is not that my dreams are an omen, I think. It is only . . . I awaken, and before I am fully awake I see again the faces of my foster father and foster mother. They are smiling, and I am a child again and happy, but then . . . they change. I do not know why they should trouble me; their blood is avenged! Yet sometimes I fear to sleep because of it."

"That *is* perhaps an omen, or a fate laid on you . . ."

A knock came at the door. The maid went to it and then opened it quickly, falling to her knees.

"Don't *do* that," Colonel Kenneth Hollard snapped. The maid bounced up again, flustered. "Hello, Princess. Ms. Azzu-ena. May I come in?"

"My house is yours," Raupasha said. *If it is mine, really,* she thought.

Hollard was carrying a dog in his arms; a puppy, rather, flop-eared and spotted. Azzu-ena looked at it and raised her brows.

"Lord Kenn'et," she said. "I thought your people had a horror of touching dogs, even more than ours."

"Only unclean dogs," he said.

"Unclean?" she asked, baffled.

"Dogs that are left to run around towns and villages, untended and eating filth."

"Oh. You mean that dogs such as nobles keep for hunting, or shepherds, are *not* unclean."

"Ah . . . approximately, yes." He turned to the Mitannian girl, smiling. "I think you told me that dogs are not a pollution to your folk, either?"

"No," Raupasha said, shaking her head and stifling a giggle. The puppy was making a determined effort to lick the Nantukhtar commander's face, and then chewing at the leather strap across his chest that supported his belt and sword. *He is so grave and dignified, and it is worrying him like a piece of rawhide,* she thought.

"We honor them," she went on solemnly aloud, "For we say that they neither break faith nor lie. My foster father kept a kennel of hunting hounds, and we had mastiffs to protect the sheep."

"Well, this one's from King Shuriash's kennels," he said. "I thought you might like to have it."

Raupasha nodded and reached out eagerly. The puppy came to her with the indiscriminate love of its kind, and she *did* giggle when it licked her chin.

"I shall call him Sabala," Raupasha said. At his look, "It means 'Spotted One,' " she said, and looked a little baffled when he laughed.

She put the wiggling bundle of young dog down, pushing it away gently with a foot when it tried to chew on her ankle. It chewed the table leg for a while instead and then collapsed into sleep with its head on her foot.

Azzu-ena rose. "I must go," she said. "The time of my studies at the house of healing is come." She looked at her wrist, which bore one of the tiny timekeepers; Raupasha shook off a certain unease at seeing time divided so . . . relentlessly.

"Will you stay, Lord Kenn'et, and drink the cocoa with me?" Raupasha said, and then caught herself. *Do not be forward.* Her foster parents had warned her that the outer world was not so relaxed as their own manor.

The Nantukhtar hesitated. "For a short while," he said, looking at the mass of papers on the table. "I brought you a book."

"Ah . . . thank you, but I do not read your language well enough yet," Raupasha said with a sigh.

"This is something our *printing shop* made up for locals . . . for the people of the land," he said.

I do not think local *means exactly that,* Raupasha thought with a little resentment. *I think it means "backward," as one might speak of a hill tribe or the Aramaeans,*

She took the book eagerly anyway. The first page held a wonder that made her gasp, a drawing of a donkey so lifelike that she had to laugh—it was planting its feet and braying, pulling back against the hands that hauled on its bridle.

" *'A' is for* Ass," she read—there was an explanation in Akkadian in the upper right corner. A frown. "I thought that meant . . ." She tapped her rump.

"Ah . . . well, the word has two meanings—soldier's talk is sometimes a little . . . uncouth," Lord Kenn'et said. "I hope you like the book."

"Oh, yes! Only . . ."

"Only?"

"Well, I have been reading much. In my home, I had work—seeing to the spinners and weavers, and sometimes we would hunt gazelle. I hope you don't think that was unseemly; my foster father sometimes treated me like the son my father hoped to have."

Hollard laughed, and she blushed, remembering their customs. *Of course he doesn't think it's unseemly!* Raupasha scolded herself.

"Well, perhaps you could get out more here," he said.

"Is it allowed?" she said, her eyes drifting to the door. A warrior armed with a thunder-thrower . . . a *rifle* . . . was stationed there.

"Well, of course!" Hollard shook his head. "Yes, you can travel around. The guard's for your protection." He paused, knitting his brows in thought.

What a strange man, Raupasha thought. *He speaks to me as if I were his favorite sister, or sometimes as if I was a man.* It was strange, yes, but not unpleasing, most of the time. Sometimes it felt . . . insulting.

"How's this?" he said. "Would you like to learn to ride horses, as we do?"

"Oh, *yes!*"

"God damn it!" Walker shouted. "God damn it to fucking *hell,* I wanted them both alive!"

The officers were uneasy; they always were when their lord spoke in his birth-tongue. Most of them—the Achaeans among them, anyway—tried to forget that he had not been born among them. English was the tongue of sorcery, too.

The horses stamped and curvetted. blowing; they weren't tired by the gallop, only excited by the run and the belling of the hounds. The dogs milled about, uncertain, looking at the bloodied body on the ground and the man who stood at bay beyond it, his back to the crag. This pack was not used to hunting men.

Walker swung out of the saddle. The mountain soil crunched beneath his boots, and he was acutely conscious of the nervousness of the men confronting Agamemnon. The king's face was nearly purple; he'd run far and fast for a man his age and weight, after the chariot crashed. It was a warm late-spring day, but they were high enough now that it was a little cooler; Walker felt the mountain wind cuffing at his sweat-damp hair. Somewhere not too far away a goat bell tinkled.

The high king of Mycenae had turned at bay against a vertical rise of rock that broke out of the steep slope. To either side it gave to almost-vertical cliffs where a few straggly pines found root. He straightened as his breath came back to him, tears running down his cheeks into his white-shot gray beard.

"My son," he whispered, looking at the body before him. A sword lay not far from the dead man's hand; his face was young, beard a mere black down on his cheeks. "My son."

"I wanted that one alive!" Walker snarled to the guardsmen, and they paled.

"Lord, he attacked us," one of them said.

"Shut *up*. He was a stripling, and I *needed* him."

Damn. I could have married him off to one of my daughters, and that would have been perfect. I wish Odikweos hadn't been here and come along. The Ithakan was pale and silent in the rear ranks, a cluster of his own men around him.

"Lord King," Walker said, forcing unction into his voice. "It's a great pity your son was killed by accident—doubtless the gods required the sacrifice."

Agamemnon squared his shoulders, and suddenly he was no longer a fat old man weeping before a triumphant enemy. "Better he should die in battle than live as your slave, outlander."

"My father-in-law is distraught in his grief," Walker said loudly. *My father-in-law was making a break for it to raise a revolt against his lawagetas*, he thought, but the dynastic reminder would make the Achaeans happier.

He saw a few nods at that; Walker's infant son by Iphigenia would have as good a claim to the throne as anyone, now. He went on:

"Or he would not speak so of the father of his grandson. Come, my lord—we must return to Mycenae and arrange the funeral games."

"The gods' curse is upon the land," Agamemnon said hoarsely. "That I listened to you and brought evil witchcraft within the kingdom."

"Lord King—"

The older man ignored him. He reached up and touched his forehead, where a graze was bleeding. "This is the blood that is shed for the land," he said, holding the hand out for all to see. "The blood of Zeus the Father, the blood of Poseidaion, the blood of the kings. The gods know the value of the given sacrifice."

Walker knew suddenly what the older man intended. "Grab him! Now!"

A half-dozen men lunged forward, Ohotolarix first among them. Agamemnon took two steps to his right, spreading his arms to the sun.

"*It is accomplished!*" he shouted and leaped.

"God damn it to *hell!*" William Walker raved as the body struck, then bounced limp further down. *Got to make the best of it*, he told himself, taking control by sheer force of will. He walked three steps forward and turned, hand on sword hilt, eyes raking the score or so of men who stood before him.

"Now I come into my own," he said. "Who stands against me, dies." Everyone's eyes flicked to the body of Agamemnon, lying caught on the bushes a hundred feet down, and his heir, broken on the stone.

"Who is with me? Who? *Who?*"

A dynastic coup was nothing very new in Mycenae, and most of these men owed everything to him. One stepped forward, blade aloft: "Hail Walker, King of Men!"

The crowd took it up: "*Hail! Hail! Hail!*"

"Wonderful," King Shuriash said sincerely.

He beamed at the canal. It was a major one, or had been before it started to silt irrevocably, making its name of Libil-Higalla—"May It Bring Abundance"—a bitter jest.

In a few more years the banks would enclose only a stretch of shallow reed-grown water, and then the dry walls would join the hundreds of others that ran in futility across the flat plain of the Land. The villages on its banks were dying too. When a canal reached this state, there was no option but to abandon it and dig another. The fields would go back to desert—or, without a fresh washing and plowing every year, salt up, which was worse—and there would be hunger for the peasants until they were safely relocated. Hunger for them, lost rents for their landlords, lost revenue and strength for the king. And losing a canal was a bad omen.

Now two . . . *"machines," that was the word* . . . were chewing their way down the canal. On each barge was one of the Nantukhtar *steam engines,* with its tall iron stack puffing smoke, its mysterious wheels and belts driving an endless chain of saw-edged buckets. They splashed down into the water and gouged into the soft silt below, came up running with dark-brown mud, clanked and rattled back to dump their loads onto an endless belt that threw it to the side—left for the first dredge, right for the second. Waiting crews of peasants shoveled the rich muck into baskets and oxcarts, to spread on their fields before the fall sowing.

If a king's dignity had not forbidden it, Shuriash would have shouted his glee aloud and clapped hands. As it was, he grinned broadly and looked over at the Nantukhtar emissaries.

"You were right," he said to Councilor Arnstein. "With machines like this, I have no need to confiscate estates in Assyria, beyond what falls to me as king there."

With machines like this, he could reclaim land by the thousands of *iku*—tens of thousands, hundreds even. He was almost dizzy at the thought; his own engineers were dusting off tablets with plans stretching back centuries, even for the great Tigris-Euphrates canal that king after king had rejected as far too expensive.

Land was a king's strength, not only for what it yielded him in rents but as wealth to hand out to favored supporters and servants. Sometimes you almost wished for revolt, so that the estates of traitors could be escheated to the king. Reclaiming land was best of all; it could be granted without harm to any vested interest—that always produced anger—and by turning wilderness to productive fields the king showed that the great gods of the land favored his reign.

The royal party and its allies drew off into the shade of a grove—a grove that would live, now—and servants spread the meal. The king was merry today, and his attendants with him. From the Nantukhtar party came a new food; the *Nantukhtar paspasu,* the fowl of the Island country—*chicken,* in their tongue. *I must secure some for the royal gardens.* He could give out the live eggs to men he wished to favor, to enrich their estates.

The king washed the food down with cool wine and wiped his mouth on a cloth, belching his contentment.

"Come," he said to his son. "Walk with me."

They walked together under the rustling leaves of the date palms. The guardsmen hung back, close enough to dash forward if anything should happen, but too far to hear a low-voiced conversation.

"It is a good thing, my father," Kashtiliash said, nodding to the puffing, clanking dredge in the distance. "And the price is reasonable."

"A tenth of the harvest of the fields watered for ten years? That is not reasonable, that is a token," Shuriash said genially. "The Nantukhtar will seek their advantage from this elsewhere. Mainly, they will call in the debt when it comes time to fight in the Hittite country, next spring after the harvest. Although first we must settle the matter of Hangilibat."

"That is no more than they asked." The king nodded, and his son went on, "And this winter we will train the first five hundred men with *rifles*."

"Yes," Shuriash said, nodding judiciously. "So far the Nantukhtar have fulfilled all their promises." He cocked an eye at his heir. "That does not mean that our interest and theirs will *always* run like a well-matched chariot team." A jerk of his chin toward the canal. "Wonderful, but we cannot make its like; and if we come to depend on the makers, if we cannot so much as water our fields without their machines, we *need* them."

Kashtiliash nodded unwillingly. "We cannot make its like, *yet*," he said.

"A point, and a sharp one," Shuriash said. "Fear not, my son; I will not tear you from the arms of your warrior maid in anger at the Nantukhtar."

He bellowed laughter at the prince's stumble and flush. "Are you so besotted?" he asked. "Did you think I would not know? The eyes and ears of the king miss nothing, my son. Especially where the heir of the House of Succession is concerned."

"We . . . we did not want to set tongues wagging."

The king laughed again, a bantering note in it, but also a male companionship. "Except each other's, no? I'll not ask you if the rumors are true."

"She is . . ." Kashtiliash flushed still more darkly. "I thank you, Father."

"Indeed . . . as a second of third wife, she would be a good choice, to bind the alliance. And the sister of a man of high rank . . . Even if she's not a virgin; well, customs differ, and I suppose you could keep her in line, eh? And she looks able to bear strong sons."

Kashtiliash looked as if he had been chewing a bitter quince. "Father and lord, I do not think it would be that simple. Best think of other matters."

"Such as the rumblings among the priesthoods, eh?" Shuriash

shrugged. "I am pleased that you are not so preoccupied with writing poems and eating lettuce"—he laughed again; old tales said that strengthened a man's member—"that you haven't noticed they call me blasphemer, and the Nantukhtar they call wizards who summon demons."

"Are you concerned?"

"Not greatly. We have made alliance with the Nantukhtar, and the great gods of the land have smiled on us—have we not humbled Asshur, do the Elamites not tremble in fear, offering tribute and their king's daughter for my bed? What none of the kings my fathers could do, I have done, with the help of our allies. And there has been neither famine nor plague to mark the gods' anger. So long as it is so, we need not fear the temples. They are jealous because they no longer hold the only wisdom in the realm."

He clapped a hand on the shoulder of his tall son. "And you learn what the Nantukhtar have to teach, and mix it with our own wisdom," he said. "I am greatly pleased with your campaign in the north, my son. Soon it will be time for me to take the hand of Marduk at the New Year festival once more. Let the colleges of the temples concern themselves with that, and leave public matters to the king."

"I *knew* those would be worthwhile," Ian Arnstein said, tossing aside a well-gnawed drumstick. "Mmmm. Damned sight better than Colonel Sanders ever made."

Kathryn Hollard looked out at the dredgers. "They're a modification of the type Leaton designed for harbor work back in Nantucket Town," she said. "Kash was all over 'em while we were setting up—I think he really *understood* the principle."

Ian nodded. There were things that a very intelligent local could pick up on; steam engines, for instance, or even the internal combustion type. It was other things, like disease theory or anything involving electricity, that pushed their this-is-magic buttons.

"You know," Kathryn went on, "Kash really *is* smart. I'm pretty surprised the Assyrians beat him, in the first history."

Ian leaned back on a cushion, feeling benevolently full. "I'm not," he said. "What would you say is his strong point?"

"He's mentally flexible," Kathryn said immediately. "Good at grasping new concepts. Positively enthusiastic about them, in fact."

Ian nodded. "But this isn't an environment where that's much of an advantage, before we came," he pointed out gently. "In fact, it might be a *disadvantage*. In a really stable society like this, conservatism often works very well. All the best ways to use the things that they have have already been tried."

Colonel Hollard paused with a glass of pomegranate juice halfway to his lips. "You know, that's actually . . . rather brilliant, Councilor," he said slowly.

Doreen hit him with a pillow. "Don't inflate the Arnstein skull more than necessary, would you? It is a good point though. I've notice they're generally better at recording and systematizing than at innovation."

Kathryn tapped a thoughtful thumb on her chin. "Applies to military matters too, I suppose," she said. "The last big innovation here was when Raupasha's ancestors invented the war chariot, and that was, when . . . a thousand years ago?"

Arnstein nodded. "More or less. Not many big changes, and they have generations, centuries, to adapt to each one."

The two Hollards looked out at the dredge. "And now we're dumping the whole three millennia of changes on their heads all at once," Kenneth said. "Poor bastards."

"Anyone want the rest of these dried figs?" Doreen said. "No? You're right, Ken. The thing is, it's not even like the last couple of centuries in our history, the eighteenth and nineteenth and twentieth."

"Well, faster," Kathryn said.

"No, not just that. The locals are getting them without the long lead-in that Western civilization had; everything from the Greeks and then Christianity and Aquinian philosophy on through the Renaissance."

Kathryn narrowed her eyes in puzzlement. "What's religion got to do with it?"

Young, and a pragmatist, and a specialist, too, Ian Arnstein thought. He went on, "Quite a lot, actually. Judaism and its Christian heresy were important in implanting the idea that the universe was an orderly place, obedient to a single omnipresent, omnipotent system of laws with no exceptions—it leached the sacred out of the world, putting all the supernatural in one remote place. Call it preparation for the scientific worldview."

Doreen nodded and began repacking the picnic hamper, ignoring the scandalized looks of the royal servants. Their eyes grew even wider as the others pitched in to help.

"That's going to be more explosive here than just learning techniques, in the long run," she said. "I've been talking with their scholars a lot, and with some of them it's like watching a lightbulb go on inside when you give 'em the define-your-terms and why-does-that-follow routines."

Ian Arnstein looked over at the dredgers as they chewed their way through the soil of Kar-Duniash. *Symbolic,* he thought. *Undermining foundations is turning out to be our stock-in-trade.*

* * *

"I don't understand, man," the blacksmith said.

His shop was cluttered with work, mostly the finer ornamental type of wrought iron in various stages of completion. Walker lounged back against the doorpost; it was *hot* in there, with two big hearths and three smaller ones. All of them were glowing with coke fires, made from Istrian coal.

Work's kept him in good shape, though, Walker thought. Especially for a man in his fifties, now. His son was a nine-year-old miniature of his father, without the little granny glasses; he'd been proudly pounding on a miniature anvil until the king and his guardsmen arrived.

"I'm retiring you, John," Walker said patiently. He smiled like a wolf at the spurt of fear in the blacksmith's sad russet-colored eyes. *Well, he's learned his lesson.*

"No, no, nothing nasty," Walker laughed. "I'm just letting you retire. You've taught my people everything you know, and I don't trust you enough to put you in an executive job. So you're history here."

"You're letting us *go,* man?" the Californian said incredulously.

"Not back to Nantucket, of course. You know too much. Otherwise, yes, anywhere in the kingdom—provided you let me know. Hell, I'll throw in a land grant up in the hills if you want; you always were into that organic gardening horseshit, weren't you? And a pension."

Martins put the hammer down on his twister anvil and drank a dipperful of water from a bucket. "Yeah. Well, thanks, man. I'd like to get out of town, yeah. It ain't the best place in the world to bring up kids."

"Afraid they'll get contaminated, eh?" Walker laughed. He pushed himself upright. "If you get tired of rusticating, you can move back here. I'll even reserve a place in the guard regiment for your little Sam here, if he wants it."

Martins's face tightened in mulish stubbornness. Walker was still laughing as he walked out to the waiting carriage. John-taunting was an old sport. Not his favorite, but he'd miss it, in a way.

"Lord," Ohotolarix said in the bright sun outside. "A runner from the palace. Gla has fallen."

"Good news!" Walker said. That was the last rebel stronghold in Boetia, up by Lake Copais. "That leaves Thessaly, and once we've shown them the error of their ways, we're recovered from my late lamented father-in-law's flying leap."

Ohotolarix shuddered slightly. Walker could see his thoughts: *The sacrifice of a chief is powerful magic.* Too many others had thought so too, and it had set his plans back a year or more. Still, he wasn't in *that* much of a hurry.

He climbed into the open-sided carriage and signaled the driver. Iron-shod hooves clattered on the stone pavement, and the vehicle pulled away, with six mounted guards on either side. Walker linked his hands behind his head, blinking up into the cloud-speckled sky, humming.

"Oh, Jesus!" Kenneth Hollard said, feeling an almost irresistible impulse to cover his eyes and scream.

Raupasha was riding a horse around the exercise circle of Ur Base; she looked up and waved at him, smiling brightly. He had expected to see her in the saddle, since he'd given orders that she be allowed to train in riding. He hadn't expected to see her taking her retrained chariot pony over the obstacle course. She was laughing as she cantered, collecting the horse with rein and knees. It leaped, and she shifted her weight easily as it came down, leaning back slightly to steady it.

Oh, thank you, Jesus, Hollard thought, breathing again, as visions of falls and broken necks fled. At least she hadn't tried it with her reins knotted and arms crossed, the way officers and scouts had to.

"Lord Kenn'et!" she said, guiding her mount over to the adobe wall that surrounded the practice yard.

A grinning noncom took her bridle. "Not bad, Princess," he said.

The troops were making something of a mascot of her—the news of who'd killed the king of Assyria had spread quickly, and the story of her rescue was suitably romantic. *Her looks don't hurt either,* he thought. She was wearing Marine khakis, her long black hair was tied back in a ponytail, and her cheeks were flushed with fresh air and exercise.

"How is the princess doing?" he asked the Marine instructor.

"Not bad, sir. Good sense of balance, and she knew horses already."

Raupasha nodded as she swung down from the saddle. "Horses . . ." A pause while she searched for English words. "Horses part of . . . family."

Her accent was thick, but he was impressed with the progress she'd made in languages, too. Sabala was twining around her ankles, looking up with *notice-me-please* body language and wiggling even harder when she reached down to pat him. In the Akkadian they shared she went on:

"We had a few old chariot ponies on the estate—as old as me, or almost; the Assyrians didn't want any of the old *mariannu* families to have teams. Sometimes we'd hitch them up and I'd drive, with my foster father teaching me." A smile. "While I was in the chariot, I was a Great King like Tushratta, in the days when Egypt itself feared Mitanni."

A cloud passed over her face for a moment, the gray eyes darkening. "My foster father was a good man; perhaps he indulged me too much—treating me like the son his lord had wished and hoped for." Then she smiled again. "It is good to see you again, Lord Kenn'et. The gods send you good fortune."

"And you, Princess. They *have* sent us good fortune, as a matter of fact. Our . . ." *I don't think "commodore" has a precise equivalent,* he thought. "Our war commander has arrived safely back in Nantucket."

She put a hand on his sleeve. "That is good to hear, Lord Kenn'et. We have never met, but I owe this Marian-Alston also a great debt; and your . . . *Chief*"—she used the English term—"Jared-Cofflin also."

And you can pronounce their names better than mine, Hollard noted absently; nobody in this area could handle the *th* at the end of "Kenneth."

They turned and walked back from the stable complex along one wall of the base toward the central square and the command buildings. Ur Base was less crowded now, with most of the troops up north and most of the basic construction finished. However, there were still plenty of locals around, hired to work or sent to learn, and the streets were thick with wagons and carts. The guards at the entrance to the praetorium brought their rifles up to present arms as he passed, and he returned their salutes.

"Shall we play the chess again, Lord Kenn'et?" Raupasha asked gently.

Quick at picking up moods, this girl, Hollard thought. The went to his office and set out the board; there were plenty of board games here, but no others quite like this one.

"You are troubled," she said after a while.

He started out of his concentration and looked at the board. *I win in five moves,* he thought. He was a fair-to-middling player; the Arnsteins beat him like a drum, but he'd improved a good deal since he started playing with them. Raupasha had natural talent; she thought ahead and didn't have trouble holding different alternatives in her head.

"Yes," he said.

"Why are you troubled, Lord Kenn'et?" she said.

"I'm a little . . . uneasy," he said. "I promised you protection—"

"And you have given it," she said.

Hollard sighed. "Well, they're talking about asking you to do something for us," he said. "I'm not sure how compatible it is with what I promised you."

"You are a man of honor," she said firmly. "What is it that they— the lord Arnstein and his lady?—plan?"

"They want to put you on the throne of Mitanni," he said bluntly after a long pause. There was no way to sugarcoat it.

The olive face went pale, and her hands gripped the table until moons of white and pink showed in her nails. Her voice was calm when she went on: "Tell me more, Lord Kenn'et."

"You'd be a tributary of Babylon." That meant more or less a client state, in local terms.

She nodded. "I understand, Lord Kenn'et. King Shuriash must see to his own land's welfare. He could not afford to see Mitanni rise as it once was, or we too would be a threat."

She looked down at the table. "I am not . . . not sure if such a thing can be. We do not—did not—shut women of rank away like animals, as the Assyrians do. Yet we have no tradition of ruling queens. Do you Eagle People?"

"We don't have kings," he said.

She nodded; he'd explained how the Republic worked, although she'd found it stranger than atoms or germs. He continued: "But we don't bar any post to a woman. The question is, though, how *your* people would regard it. The whole object of this—from our point of view—is to find some way of bringing peace to the river district. The Arnsteins think that your people, the Hurrians there, would accept anyone connected with your old royal house, because they hated the Assyrians so."

Raupasha leaned her chin on a palm, her feathery-black brows coming together in a frown of thought. "That may be so. But the walls of the kingdom"—he puzzled at that and then realized she meant something like "structure of the state"—"were beaten into dust. Rebuilding them would be a long work."

"We'd help," Hollard said. "What we need most right away is an end to internal fighting and help with our war on Walker."

Abruptly Raupasha smiled, then laughed. It was an infectious urchin grin. "Right now, Lord Kenn'et, my sovereign majesty is such that I can't even stop Sabala from piddling on your floor."

"Goddam!" Hollard said. He was laughing himself as he picked the puppy up and headed for the door.

The third man staggered off with a small shriek; he'd have been screaming louder if he'd had the breath for it. His two predecessors were lying on the ground, one vomiting weakly, the other spluttering and beginning to regain consciousness as one of his friends flipped water in his face from a canteen.

The gathered Babylonians she was supposed to train in modern infantry tactics were watching her with round eyes; not many had seen one of the Eagle People before at close range. She'd offered a thousand pieces of silver and a chariot to anyone who could pin her shoulders to the ground. Experience had shown it was best to get the bull-baboon macho nonsense out of the way right off.

And none of them have seen the Empty Hand in action before, Kathryn Hollard thought grimly, wiping the blood off her skinned knuckles. *I am getting so tired of having to beat truths into these brainless dickheads before they'll* listen *to me.*

There were about a hundred of them, and they were supposed to function as cadre for the First Kar-Duniash Infantry. They were dressed in a local version of Islander uniform, pants and shirt and jacket, although the color was earth-brown rather than khaki proper. All of them were young and fit, which was helpful, and all of "good family," which was something of a drawback.

We should have started with peasants; at least they're used to doing what they're told, she thought.

"That should settle the question of whether it hurts your honor to serve under a woman," she said dryly. "Any more volunteers?"

A vigorous shaking of heads. "Now your prince will address you."

Kashtiliash's chariot drew up; he was in the same uniform, with a few additional touches—gold scales on the shoulders, for instance. Their eyes met for an instant, and one of the Kassite's eyelids drooped in a suspicion of a wink as he inclined his head toward the injured men.

Well, he *knows what I'm thinking.* Kathryn fought down her grin. *I think I'm falling in love. Christ, I'm an idiot. And I don't give a damn.*

"Men of Kar-Duniash," he said. "You have been chosen to be first to receive the fire-weapons of our allies. This is a great honor to you and your kindred." The young men perked up at that. Honor meant fame, not to mention estates and gifts. "In your hands will be the fire-weapons that swept the hosts of Asshur aside like sheep and ground the walls of their cities into dust."

A cheer broke out, and Kashtiliash raised a hand. "Cheer not! Here you will work, under the orders of the great warrior Kat'ryn-Hollard, who fought with me against the Assyrians and cut down assassins as they strove to end my life. He who does not obey, does not toil, on him will the wrath of the king descend. Hear and obey!"

The recruits went on their bellies, and Kashtiliash continued in the same vein for a while. She grimaced slightly; it would take something like this to get the scions of the kingdom's noble families doing what they were told, but generations of Yankees rose up in her blood at the sight.

"On your feet!" she commanded, when the prince's chariot was dust down the path toward the walls of Ur Base.

"Now we start the training," she began.

A voice from the ranks interrupted her. "When do we get the weapons of fire?"

"You. Step forward." A young man did, an eager grin on his face. "The weapons are called *rifles*," Hollard said.

"When do we receive the *rifles*?" he asked.

"First lesson. Sergeant Kinney!"

The noncom trotted forward, a large sack of wet sand in her hands.

"Front and center . . . what's your name?"

"Addad-Dan, O Commander."

"The first lesson, Dan, is that you *speak when you're spoken to!*"

The boy flinched. Sergeant Kinney walked behind him, opened the pack laced to his webbing harness, and dropped the sack inside. Addad-Dan staggered and grunted as the weight slammed onto his shoulders and gut.

"Twenty-five circuits of the parade ground!" Kathryn barked. "At the *run*, recruit! See to it, Sergeant."

"Ma'am, yes ma'am!"

Kinney was grinning, and she had a rifle sling with a loop wound around her right hand. "All right, hero, let's go for a stroll." *Whack* of the flat leather across the legs. "Move it!"

Kathryn Hollard set her hands on her hips and looked out over the shocked faces. "Here, there is no rank," she said. "None of you has *earned* any rank. Here, you are not the sons of great men; here, all you maggots are equally worthless! Your highest hope is to become a soldier—then, maybe, you may think of becoming officers. There are three things a soldier must do: he must obey, he must value his mission before his comrades, and he must value his comrades before himself.

"There are three skills a soldier must command: he must be able to march, to shoot, and to dig. We'll start with marching." She pointed off across the fields to a low ruin mound, a shapeless hill of weathered mudbrick where a settlement had once been. It was just visible on the edge of sight.

"You see that? We're all going there. Form up!"

She sighed at the shambling chaos that resulted. *This is going to take a lot of work.*

She suspected that her brother-commander had given her this assignment as something between a joke and a punishment; if she liked the locals, she was going to get a bellyful of them.

Well, at least I'll get to see Kash fairly often. Stick that in your pipe and smoke it, Colonel Brother Godalmighty Kenneth Hollard.

"Beautiful work," Kenneth Hollard said.

He swung the Werder to his shoulder and sighted. A squeeze of the trigger and . . . *crack*. There was a slight *tink* sound as the spent shell hit the packed clay behind him. The target at the other end of the range flipped backward, then up with a white board pointer showing where his round had hit—a couple of inches left of the center of mass, or what would be the center of mass if that was a man and not a human-shaped cutout.

Hollard felt a slight glow of pride; that would have put a man out of the fight for good and all, and at six hundred yards, too.

"Let me try, Lord Kenn'et! Let me try!"

"Ah . . . well, no reason why not, Princess," Hollard said. He ran her through the firing drill, which was simple enough.

They really did come up with something that's simpler *to use than the previous model*, he thought. From his reading of military history, that was a small miracle in itself. Of course, with Commodore Alston in charge . . .

Raupasha brought the weapon up to her shoulder eagerly, but she took the time to aim, and squeezed carefully. She was wearing Marine khakis without insignia and a floppy-brimmed campaign hat with the right side pinned up; wisps of fine black hair had escaped from the thong that held her long mane in a ponytail. Hollard smiled at that, and at her frown of total concentration.

Crack.

The target flicked up; the bullet had gone squarely through the head. *Hmmm. Not bad at all, at three hundred yards.*

"No, no, no!" he said aloud. "*Don't* show off. Through the center of the body, always. Heads are too easy to miss."

She gave him an urchin grin. The noncom who brought her more ammunition was grinning too.

Hollard sighed and turned to the Guard commander who'd brought in the cargo and reinforcements; Victor Ortiz had the shield and four gold stripes on his cuffs and epaulettes that meant captain's rank in the Guard, equivalent to Hollard's Marine colonelcy. They moved a few paces away. The firing range was too far from the riverside wall of Ur Base to see the masts of the three-ship flotilla, but he knew the crews and the base's laborers were hard at work. Another battalion of Marine infantry, heavy weapons to match . . . and a lot of long flat crates with Werder rifles in their coats of grease for his command, surplus Westley-Richards from the Republic's militia for their allies. More crates as well, Werder ammunition, and machinery for the ammunition shop.

"Praise the Town Meeting, from whom all blessings flow," Hollard said, his voice a mock-pious drone for a second.

"Praise the Chief and the commodore, who kicketh the Meeting's lazy butt and getteth them to move," Ortiz said, and raised his brows in a question.

"Yes, Ms. Raupasha does speak some English now," Hollard replied.

"I see . . . I've been briefed, of course."

"Good. That was a fast passage you made."

Ortiz preened a little, which was pardonable. "Sixty-three days, two of those stranded on the goddam mudbanks in this miserable river. We did over four hundred miles a day three days in a row, down in the forties, running our easting down."

"What news from home?"

"Not much. The fall harvest was good; the Girenas expedition is still alive, wonder of wonders. King Isketerol made a fulsome apology and paid a heavy fine to get his people back after that incident in South Africa—less thirty who applied for asylum, and got it—but he was a lot less happy when we kept the ships. That's it so far, but God knows how long it will last. Oh, and on a personal note, I'm the father of twin boys."

"Congratulations!" Kenneth Hollard said, pumping his hand. There was a trace of wistfulness in his voice; he'd been thinking that it might be nice to have a family of his own. *Not until this war is settled, I guess,* he thought. "How long *do* you think it will last?"

"God alone knows, *amigo.* Until that *hijo* Isketerol thinks he has a chance of jumping us—I'm anxious to get my ships loaded and back home, I can tell you."

"Me too," Hollard said, looking through the letters Ortiz had hand-delivered—some for security's sake, and two fat ones from his brother.

He looked forward to reading those. It was . . . *tranquil, that's the word* . . . listening to him tell of the goings-on around the farm. Not that farm life was any bed of roses; he'd helped out on his brother's grant often enough to know that. His mind's eye saw him, writing in the big log kitchen with a cup of sassafras tea by his elbow, snow falling outside the window, Tanaswada nursing the baby . . . and homesickness stabbed him with a moment's bitter pain.

"Well, I don't envy you sailing back into winter," Hollard said. He walked a few steps back toward Raupasha. "Princess! If you're going to shoot that many rounds, wear the earplugs."

She pouted, then obeyed. "Sergeant, see that the weapon is returned to stores when the princess is finished with it." To Ortiz: "We've actually got the locals producing a halfway decent beer. Care for a glass, Victor?"

"Lead on!"

"Wait a minute!" Raupasha called.

The Islander officers turned back. "Watch," she said.

Raupasha had a round of rifle ammunition pushed through the buttonhole of the left breast pocket of her khaki jacket. She fired, then slipped the bullet out of the hole and into the breech of her Werder in a single quick grab and push.

"That . . . how do you say . . . slices up? The loading time."

"That's *cuts down*," Hollard said.

"*Cuts down*, okay." She dropped back into Akkadian. "Wouldn't that be useful?"

"Mmmmm—sort of risky, leaving a bullet through a buttonhole like that."

"No, no," she said impatiently, giving him an exasperated look. "If you put a . . . a *row* of, not holes, but—what are these things in the bandolier called, that hold the bullets?"

"Loops," Hollard said automatically. Then his eyes went wide. "Loops—a strip of leather, say."

"Yes! Like this." The girl's finger traced a line from near her left shoulder nearly to her breastbone.

"Well, I'll be damned," Hollard said slowly. "Yes, say six—that would speed loading up considerably . . . no trouble to have the strip attached to the troops' jackets . . ."

Ortiz made an interrogative sound, having no Akkadian. Hollard explained, and the Guard officer's eyebrows went up in turn.

"You know, Ken, that's actually a pretty damn good idea," he said. "Smart girl."

They looked up at the Mitannian, who was cleaning the rifle under the noncom's direction with an air of total concentration spoiled by an occasional glance up under her brows.

"Ms. Raupasha," Ortiz said, bowing. "Would you care to join us in that beer?"

CHAPTER TWENTY-ONE

May, Year 10 A.E.

Bab-ilim; Gate of the Gods; Babylon the Great. Kathryn Hollard still felt a prickle of awe as she rode toward the northern gate. Turning in the saddle, she called out: "All right, let's show them what real soldiers look like!"

After four months, the Babylonians that she and the training cadre had been working with could march, at least. Rifles over their shoulders, arms swinging, booted feet striking the earth of the roadway in unison, the six hundred troops marched like a single organism toward the Ishtar Gate. A banner went at their head; blazoned with the gold sun disk of Shamash and the spade of Marduk. Outriders traveled before them, crying for the crowds to make way—and enforcing the order with their whips when necessary, through the horde pouring into the city for the springtime New Year festival.

The city she approached was not yet the Babylon of the Bible, the city rebuilt by Nebuchadrezzar and the site of the captivity of the Jews, that would not be—would not have been—for another six centuries. The current Babylon was mostly the city of Hammurabi the Lawgiver, sacked by the Hittites and refurbished by King Shuriash's ancestors. The Kassite kings dwelt more in their citadel of Dur-Kurigalzu a little to the west, but Babylon remained the greatest of their cities and the symbol of holiness and kingship in the land.

On this March morning it was warm but not hot, and for once the countryside of the Land between the Rivers looked halfway appealing with its leafy orchards and green-gold barley. Her command had been on a route march and field exercise for the last week; her body itched with dried salt and crusted alkaline dust.

Now and then she saw figures standing on the flat, flower-planted roofs of a nobleman's mansion looking toward the road and the novel sight of the First Infantry. Travelers crowded to the side of the road to let them pass, staring and gawking, and peasants stopped their work to look. Children ran alongside shouting. Kathryn smiled at them, and now and then threw a few copper pennies when the press grew too great. Even if they'd never heard of coined money, metal was valuable here—her action generally resulted in a squirming heap of naked youngsters, yelling and grabbing for the coins at the bottom of the pile.

A mile out from the real defenses of Bab-ilim was the wall that enclosed the suburbs proper. It was impressive enough, twenty feet high, studded with towers twice that. Within were clustered gardens, groves, here and there the colorful, blocky form of a temple, once an enormous walled enclosure around the Akitu shrine, where much of the New Year ceremony would take place. What she principally noticed were the trades considered too noisome to allow in the city proper: huge tanneries, rows of dye-vats, and the city's execution ground. It was small compensation that the roadway turned from packed clay to a broad avenue of baked brick.

And there was the growing stink of the city itself, probably the greatest in the world in this age, two hundred thousand souls or more—and all their livestock.

I'll get used to the stench again, Kathryn told herself. Of course, in a way that made it *worse.* And it was so *big.* Yes, any of the mainland cities she'd visited up in the twentieth dwarfed it, but those were fading memories. This was here, now, *real.* The continual clamor of wheels, feet, hooves, voices, was like a vibration in her flesh.

Then the city itself appeared, raised above the floodplain over centuries by the decay and rebuilding of the mud-brick buildings of which it was made—the living city raised on the bones of its ancestors, since time out of mind. The city wall proper rose like a mountain range that ran from right to left beyond sight, baked-brick ramparts sixty feet high and thirty feet thick and studded with towers every hundred yards or so. Another wall of equal proportions stood thirty feet within, and the gap between them was filled to the very top with pounded rubble and then paved with a roadway broad enough for three chariots to pass abreast. A moat drawn from the Euphrates ran at the foot of those man-made cliffs, a hundred feet across and twenty deep, the water green and foul.

Kathryn Hollard gave a silent whistle at the sight, impressed despite herself. *Oh, we could knock it down,* she thought. Given enough shells and enough time, of course. Trying to take or hold the city beyond. . .

The road itself rose on an embankment toward the city; crenellated fortress walls rose to flank it on either side, until they were marching through an artificial canyon. Great winged man-headed bulls marched in high relief along those walls, twice her height and made of molded brick, their bodies painted red, wings blue, stern hook-nosed faces with blue-black beards and golden crowns.

A lot like Kash's father, she thought, suppressing a grin. She shivered slightly and gripped the horse more tightly with her knees. *God, I miss Kash.*

The gate itself was a massive fortress with the road running over the moat on piers and then through it; a hundred-foot tower of reddish brick at each of the four corners, with an arched passageway sixty feet high between, sky-blue rosettes in molded brick covered by polished sheet copper, flanked by bronze lions twelve feet tall. The gate doors were made of huge cedar trunks thicker than her body and taller than a four-story house, brought from Lebanon in centuries past with incredible labor and trouble. They were sheathed in bronze, and the bronze was worked in low relief with gods, demons, dragonlike creatures, heroes slaying lions.

The Marine officer looked up. There in the dim heights of the gate tunnel were bronze grilles, and she could hear the crackling of flames. If anyone smashed those gates and tried to rush through this enormous tunnellike passageway they'd get a very warm welcome—boiling oil, boiling water, red-hot sand.

Royal guardsmen in crested helmets and bronze scale armor or Nantucket-made chain mail stood to either side—mostly with their backs to her, holding back the crowd with their round shields and spear held horizontally like a fence with living posts. Three more sets of gates divided the passageway before the travelers came out blinking into the brightness beyond.

More guards cleared a way through the street, named Aibur-Shabu, No Enemy Shall Pass, the broad processional street that ran north and south parallel to the Euphrates.

The crowds behind the leveled spears gaped and shouted and pointed, or rested with aloof patience and pretended detachment; she saw a noble standing in his chariot while his leather-clad driver wrestled the team into obedience; a priest robed and spangled with silver astrological symbols waited with folded hands, surrounded by his acolytes; a scribe pridefully held his jointed, wax-covered boards and stylus; what was probably an expensive courtesan glittering with jewels lolled voluptuously in her slave-borne litter, robes filmy and colorful, eyes painted into huge dark circles, peering with interest over an ostrich-plume fan.

One thing I regret, Kathryn thought, as she saluted the guardsmen's bowing captain, *is that I can't go incognito here.* It would be interesting to see the city when everyone wasn't gaping at *her*. Not possible—her height and features would mark her out. *Pity.*

The iron horseshoes of her mount rang on stone, hard white limestone thirty feet wide, flanked by ten-foot strips of red breccia veined with white on either side—unimaginable extravagance in this stone-less land. More soldiers were holding a passageway open through a tall gate in the wall, with inset brick pillars candy-cane-striped in red and blue. That was the entrance to the North Palace, where the Islanders would be quartered and the First Kar-Duniash would have their barracks.

"By the right . . . right *wheel*," Sergeant Kinney shouted behind her.

The battalion turned like a snake, men on the inside of the turn checking their pace and those on the outside striding longer with the smoothness of endless practice. They passed through another fortress gate and into the outer courtyard of the House That Was the Marvel of Mankind, the Center of the Land, the Shining Residence —in other words, the palace of King Shagarakti-Shuriash. There were times when Akkadian grandiloquence got on her nerves.

But you're thinking of living here permanently, she reminded herself. *And it does have its points.*

This was the outermost of five successive courtyards, paved with the same white limestone as the processional way and surrounded by three-story buildings on all sides.

"Halt!" Five hundred boots crashed down.

"By the right . . . right . . . *face!*"

Another crash, and she rode her horse out in front of the assembled ranks, reining in and turning to face them.

"Present . . . *arms!*"

The rifles came down off the shoulders with a slap and rattle of hands on wood and iron. Kathryn returned the salute crisply; they'd worked hard and earned it.

"Order . . . *arms!*"

Steel-shod butt plates rang on the stone paving. Her horse pawed the paving as well, curious at the unfamiliar surface. Kathryn controlled it with knees and her left hand on the reins, her right resting on her hip.

"Stand easy!" A rustle of relaxation. "Soldiers of the First Kar-Duniash, you've made a good beginning," she said, pitching her voice to carry. "You've also worked very hard. Dismiss to quarters!"

They gave a brief cheer and the formation dissolved as men slung their weapons, turned, chattered, hailed friends. Sergeant Kinney came up and took the bridle of her horse.

"I'll settle them in and see to the baggage train, ma'am," she said. "Good to have a rest."

"God's truth. I've got to go check in with the king."

She and her officers, including the provisional promotions from among the locals. She swung down, looking around as they fell in behind her and an usher led them on. Molded-brick shapes covered the walls up to the second story, all painted in yellow, white, red, and blue; after the predominant dun-mud-brick color of the land, it was a pleasant change. Above and on either side of the gates that linked the courtyards were huge terra-cotta faces, leering or smiling—protective spirits to frighten away demons.

A crowd of people were about, courtiers and smooth-cheeked eunuchs, soldiers swinging by with a clank and clatter, messengers, servants, scribes with their wax-covered boards and palm-size damp clay tablets for taking notes, officials, a flutter of girls from the king's harem—they weren't shut in there, although they were supervised fairly closely. All of them drew aside and murmured; she caught curiosity, awe, fear, the odd flat hostile glare.

The last gateway was flanked by granite lions tearing at recumbent enemies. On their backs were artificial palm trees of bronze and gold. Tall carved doors opened into the main throne room, a huge vaulted chamber fifty yards by fifteen. Here the bright light was muted to a glow through the high clerestory windows. Beams stabbed down through a mist of incense, a strong hieratic smell. The walls were hung with softly vivid tapestry rugs of kings past at war or sacrifice or the hunt, interspersed with heroes battling monsters, protective genies, flowered mountains.

Guardsmen stood at a parade rest copied from the Islanders, making a laneway down the center of the hall. The heads of their spears were steel now, reflecting more brightly than bronze would have; when sunlight caught one of the motionless blades it seemed to blaze with light. So too did the figure of the king on his throne, inlaid with lapis and gold; his crown was gold as well, shaped like a city wall. Kathryn's party came to a halt; the Babylonian officers prostrated themselves, the Nantucketers clicked heels, saluted, and bowed their heads slightly—citizens of the Republic groveled before no man.

Shuriash smiled. "Greetings, my valiant ones, and officers of my allies," he said. He looked at Kathryn. "My son, the prince of the House of Succession, declares that you have done well; that my soldiers learn the art of the fire-weapons."

"Oh King, your men have labored long and hard and have learned very well," she said. *True enough.* Not up to Corps standards by a long shot, but they'd started from a lower base.

"Know that you have the favor of the king," Shuriash said, beaming.

He signaled, and an official glided forward to put a chain around her neck. It was fairly heavy, solid-gold links and a beautifully worked pectoral in the shape of the Bull of Marduk, with eyes of lapis lazuli and chinbeard of onyx.

"My thanks to the king," Kathryn said, flushing in embarrassment.

"Many of your countrymen are here for the celebration of the New

Year festival," Shuriash said. "You will feast with the King's Majesty; may the celebrations make your heart glad. Now you have traveled far and will wish to refresh yourselves."

The Babylonians went on their bellies again, and the Nantucketers bowed and walked backward until it was possible to turn without lèse-majesté.

"Christ, I could use a bath," Kathryn muttered.

And Kash would be here. Tied up in ceremonial to the armpits, but they *had* to find some time.

"Trachoma," Justin Clemens said, holding back the child's eyelids. "See, the redness and swelling, and it looks like grains of sand are stuck in the soft tissue?"

"I am familiar with this disease," Azzu-ena said, nodding. "Very common—usually the clear part of the eye is distorted and opaque, at the end, bringing blindness with no cure. Is it *contagious*?"

She repeated the whole phrase in English, for the sake of practice. The sounds were hard for someone brought up to the Semitic gutturals of Akkadian, but she was slowly overcoming it.

"Very," Clemens said. "Spread by touching, by contact with cloth that has touched the eyes, and by flies. A disease of crowding and not enough washing."

The Babylonian's mouth quirked. "Like most?"

"Like most," Clemens said. It had become a bit of a running joke between them.

He was handling this clinic in an out-of-the-way chamber of the palace; an autoclave and water purifier were running in the next room, and an outer chamber was crowded with those waiting. He wrinkled his nose a bit at the rank smell of old sweat soaked into wool. No way around it, they hadn't invented soap here, and the palace bathing facilities were luxuries for the elite; so were enough clothes to change and do laundry frequently. And what water these people could get would be dangerous anyway.

The patients were mostly palace laborers and their families; he reserved this day for them. *And let the nobles fume and wait,* he thought. Looking after the locals wasn't his responsibility, but it bred goodwill . . . and the demand was overwhelming.

Some of the people waiting were from out of the city, kinfolk of the palace workers; that wasn't supposed to happen, but he wasn't going to turn them away, particularly the children. *I feel like someone trying to sweep back the ocean with a broom,* he thought helplessly, then forced himself to optimism. *Azzu-ena is learning—Christ, is she learning! And she isn't the only one.*

The Babylonian was taking notes, too, preparing a handbook in her native tongue—diagnosis and treatment of the most common ills, especially the ones that could be handled with local resources.

"What treatment?" she said.

"Well, penicillin, if we had enough," he said, which they didn't. "Antiseptic drops are the alternative."

He told the mother, and she gripped the boy child's head and tilted it back despite his squalls. *Damn, have to get deloused* again *after this,* Clemens thought, looking at the tousled black hair.

"Do you see what I do?" he asked the woman. She was thin, dark, looked about fifty and was probably in her third decade, with a weaver's calloused hands.

"Yes, great one."

He ran the dipper into the bottle, sealing the top with his index finger. Both were plain clay; if you handed out glass ones the recipients would sell them—food came first, and glass was an expensive rarity here. The solution inside was their all-purpose disinfectant, and it stung. The toddler wailed and struggled, but his mother gave him a tremulous smile. *Good teeth, at least,* Clemens thought abstractedly. Most people here did have them, at least until middle age; no sugars in the diet.

"Three times each day," Clemens said. "If you do this faithfully, it will be cured. Bring the child back to me when the medicine is gone. Do you understand?"

"Yes, holy one," the woman said, and suddenly she gripped his hand and kissed it; her own eyes filled and tears ran down her cheeks. "Thank you for saving my son's sight, holy one! He is our last child left alive, now he may live and father children of his own! Thank you—I have little, but what I have is yours."

"Go, go," Clemens said roughly, embarrassed. He went over to the table he'd set up and scrubbed his hands again. *I'm going to wear my skin off in this filthy country,* he thought.

"Lord," the palace usher said, looking about him with contempt. "You will miss the ceremony!"

"Just one more," he said. "Then we'll clean up and go."

It was another child, although barely so by local standards, a girl of twelve or thirteen. To Island-raised eyes she would have passed for nine—barefoot, dressed in a ragged gray shift with a shawl over her braids.

"What is the child's illness?" he asked the mother. Another skinny underfed weaver.

"A demon of fever, holy one," the woman said, bringing her shawl up under her chin in modesty; an upper-class woman might have covered her mouth as well. "For a night and a day now. She cannot eat the good bread."

Fever. Well, that was the all-purpose term here. He wiped down a thermometer and stuck it in the girl's mouth.

"Don't bite; just hold that under your ton—"

A desperate grab saved the instrument, and he looked into the hazed, defiant black eyes. Her mother raised a hand, but stopped at a gesture.

"Here is a date stuffed with pistachios," Clemens said. That was a treat rare enough to tempt someone with no appetite. "If you hold this thing in your mouth as I say, you may have it."

The girl considered, then nodded.

"Give me the date," she said.

"Here. But don't eat it yet."

This time the thermometer stayed in. Clemens got out his stethoscope and the blood-pressure apparatus and began his examination, throwing comments over his shoulder to Azzu-ena as she handed him the equipment he required.

Hmmm. A hundred and one degrees—no wonder she's cranky and off her feed, he thought. *Let's see . . .* There were so many diseases here, and many of them were just that—diseases, with no names in the books he'd studied.

Azzu-ena was craning over his shoulder. "That looks like a rash," she said. "Reddish patch."

"Mmmm-hmmmm." He pulled up the girl's shift; she pulled it down again and slapped his hand. Clemens sighed. "I am a physician. Eat your date."

More of the red patches, with little flecks of dried blood, as from a fleabite . . .

Clemens felt the color leave his face; for a moment the room swam, and he made a choked noise. Azzu-enu stepped forward, alarmed.

"No!" he said, his voice crisp. "Get back—don't touch me, don't touch her. Get into the other room." She hesitated, looking at him with astonishment. *"Go!"* She fled.

"You," he said to the usher. "Fetch soldiers. Have this part of the palace sealed—completely sealed, no one to enter or leave. Go, do it, then come back here." The usher drew himself up, tapping his staff.

Clemens caught his eye and spoke, his words slow and cold. "I am the one who saved the king's favorite. If you do not obey me in every particular, man of Kar-Duniash, the king will have you impaled. Do you understand me? For I speak the truth and I do not lie."

The usher's olive face went pasty; he backed away, bowing, hand before his mouth in the gesture of submission.

"What is it?" Azzu-ena called sharply through the door of the room that held the autoclave.

"Possibly the end of the world," Clemens said, his mind racing.

The dirigible's at Ur Base, he thought. *They can get here by tomorrow morning. All right, that's five hundred doses. Maybe, oh, God, maybe—*

He turned to the woman, kept his voice gentle as he looked into the enormous dark pools of fear that were her eyes. "Who is your man?" he said quietly. "How many other children do you have, and where do they dwell?"

"Ahhhh," Kathryn Hollard said, sinking into the tub until only her nose was above water, scratching vigorously at her scalp and the short-cropped sandy hair, reveling in the animal comfort.

Her quarters in the section of the palace turned over to the Americans weren't large, but they did run to the Babylonian equivalent of a bathroom; a big ceramic tub, with a drainpipe and a brazier in a corner to heat water. Sin-ina-mati had managed to wangle an appointment as her batman and had the whole thing ready for her, for which she was profoundly grateful. It was amazing how you could soak up dirt and dust and sand, and even if you kept your scalp stubbled and shaved everything else, the war against lice and fleas was never completely won. Still, she moved the gently exploring hand aside.

"Not now, Mattie," she said. "Not in the mood."

Sin-ina-mati pouted slightly and then grinned and tossed her the sponge.

"Ah, the handsome Prince Kashtiliash fills your thoughts," she said. "And you wish he would fill your—*ai!*"

Laughing, Kathryn held up her hand, ready to scoop more of the water at her. "Common knowledge now, is it?" she said, as Sin-ina-mati pretended to cower, laughing herself. "Hell, you can still scrub my back, Mattie."

"Not very common, but there's little secret here in the palace," the Babylonian woman said, bringing up a stool and sitting on it to use the sponge. "And I hear everything there is to hear."

"Happy to be back?" Kathryn said, taking the sponge before slipping down to soak again. She dropped back into English for an instant: *"Christ on a crutch, this country is parasite heaven."*

"I am happy to be back as a free woman, with silver of my own," Sin-ina-mati said. Serious for a moment: "I have paid my family's debts, and soon they will buy back their land that now they rent. Several families have asked me to tutor their children in the Nantukhtar letters, with generous fees. Thank you."

Kathryn nodded, slightly embarrassed. That was how the girl had ended up as a palace slave in the first place. Her peasant family had sold her off as the only alternative to starving for the whole bunch, from grandmother to nursing infants. That could happen here, if you were up against it, borrowed against the next harvest, and got seriously unlucky.

The gratitude made her uneasy, though. Sin-ina-mati's new status wasn't *her* doing; it was the Republic's policy. On the other hand, she'd learned firsthand that Babylonians didn't think that way. Everything was personal obligation or enmity to them, not personified abstractions like nations or governments. And she *had* gotten her a better job than carrying bedpans.

On still another hand, I'm also grateful that Mattie didn't get too . . . attached. She sighed. *It's certainly fun, once you get over the oh-ick-yuk-that's-strange bit, but now that I've tried it I can definitely say that it isn't* It, *for me. Beats the hell out of solitary vice, but no capital P Passion.*

It was always valuable to make a discovery about yourself, but this one was a pity, in a way. There would have been some advantages if it *had* been It, if she wanted to be career military, and so far she hadn't found anything that better suited her talents. *Although I like building things, too.*

She wiped soapy water out of her eyes and groped for her watch on the wicker table beside the bath. "Oh, hell," she said. "Got to get going—there's that thing over at the temple. Hand me that towel, would you?"

The occasion was full-dress. Luckily that wasn't very fancy for the Island military. The polished calf-boots, tailored khaki pants and jacket, scarf, and beret with the Republic's eagle-and-shield badge all looked fairly sharp without being too elaborate or labor-intensive. She buffed the badge until the gold of the arrows and olive wreath shone against the silver eagle, adjusted it, took a quick look in the mirror and buckled on her Sam Browne.

Coming up in the world, she thought, snapping out the cylinder of the new Python revolver that had come in with the Werders. *And not only better equipment.* A smile moved her lips as she flicked a fingernail at the silver lieutenant colonel's oak leaves on the collar of her uniform jacket.

"What is this?" Azzu-ena asked steadily. He could see the fear in her eyes, though; it was but a reflection of his own.

"Life," Justin Clemens said.

He swabbed the skin of her shoulder with alcohol, wiped it dry with the gauze, roughened it with the instrument and applied the vaccine, then taped another piece of gauze across it. When it was done he slumped in relief. The luckless laborers who'd been trapped in the waiting room were next, all six of them.

"Why have you isolated the mother along with the child?" Azzu-ena asked as he stood in thought.

"Because she's almost certainly infected by now—prolonged body contact," he said.

"What is the treatment for this disease?"

"There is no treatment."

"Not even the . . . penicillin?"

"That's useless against this. The vaccine prevents infection, but once the disease is established . . . among people like yours, who've never been exposed, as many as nine in every ten may die."

According to his medical history texts, Mexico had gone from twenty million people to one and a half million within a couple of generations after Cortez's men had arrived, bringing smallpox along with them. After what he'd seen on the post-Event mainland with influenza, mumps, and chicken pox, he believed every word of it. "Virgin field epidemic" had gone from a historical curiosity to a recipe for naked horror.

The woman's eyes went wide; these cities might not have known smallpox before, but they did have epidemics to give a basis for imagination.

"Is there nothing that can be done?"

"I don't have much of the vaccine, and I can't make any more here, and you don't—" *How do I explain about cowpox?* Which Babylonian cows did not have; he'd checked when he first arrived. *No time.* "I don't have the things I'd need. Nantucket is two months' sailing from here, and they could only send me a few thousand doses."

"You know this disease well?"

"From books. We wiped it out in our own land by vaccination."

"Nine in ten! Gods of plague have mercy!" She suddenly looked down at her arm. "This preserves, you say?"

"Yes, unless you're already infected, and I very much doubt it."

"Then why me?" Her gaze sharpened on him. "Will you not wish to preserve the king and his household?"

"I suppose we'll have to," he said wearily. "Since we can't preserve everybody. But I'll be *damned* if it's all going to go out for political reasons."

Suddenly she smiled and rested a hand on his shoulder for a moment. "You are a great healer," she said. "You will find something you can do."

He nodded wearily. "Apart from praying that we can isolate all the cases in time, there's only one thing I can do. It's far better than nothing, but I don't think it's going to go over very well."

* * *

"Lady Kat'ryn-Hollard," Kashtiliash said. "You have been promoted—finding favor with you own ruler, as well as ours! That is very well."

Kathryn felt herself flushing. He'd learned Islander military insignia, and he noticed. *For a big bad Bronze Age type, Kash is a sweetie,* she thought.

They turned casually down a side corridor, out onto a section of flat roof that turned into a balcony. From there they could see night descending on Babylon, a huge serried darkness against the horizon. The stars were still bright above; she knew that the streets down there—except for a very few broad, straight ones such as the Processional Way—would be canyons of blackness where nobody ventured without a light.

Kashtiliash was looking up at the stars. "I am thinking," he said after a moment, "of what you told me, of your island's voyage through the tide of years to this time, and how the very stars were different." He shook his head. "Yet always I had thought of my life as the *now,* from which all the future flowed. It makes the liver curl, to think of it instead as dry tablets tumbled in a ruin mound, a . . . fable."

She moved closer, and they laid arms around waist and shoulder; she was only an inch or so shorter than he, towering by this age's standards.

"We have a saying on Nantucket," she said. *"Don't think about the Event too much; it's bad enough without insanity stirred in."*

"Yet in the House of Succession I read the tablets of the ancients, the Sumerians . . . and they also saw stars different from these we see. It is curious, to think of the depths of time—curious and dizzying."

Kathryn nodded. *Not just a handsome face,* she thought, acutely conscious of the scent of him, a strong masculine musk.

"And I was thinking of you, my Kat'ryn-Hollard, and whether you have laid a witch's spell on me." He laughed softly. "You are nothing of what we think a woman should be, yet you are ever in my thoughts. My father thinks you the diversion of an hour; I dread his wrath if I tell him differently, yet I must—I have no choice."

"And everyone of *my* people thinks you're a disaster for me," she replied. They turned to each other and suddenly they were kissing hungrily.

"I strive to stay away, and I cannot stay away," he groaned after a long moment.

"What, all the women of your harem cannot console you?" she said.

"No more than the little servant maid can you," he said and laughed at the slight jerk of surprise. "Do you think I would not seek to know everything about you, Kat'ryn-Hollard?"

"No," she said—she'd rummaged shamelessly through the Arnsteins' files on *him*, certainly.

They kissed again, and he chuckled into her ear. "And I was raised
in a harem, Kat'ryn—a hundred women to one man may flatter the
vanity of a king and uphold his reputation, but . . ."

There was a long silence. "This is dangerous," she said, holding
back for a second and looking into his eyes.

"I know," Kashtiliash said, nodding. "I could not be elsewhere.
Could you?"

She felt her throat tighten as she shook her head. The room they entered was probably a clerk's in the daylight hours; there were baskets
of clay tablets and waxed boards, and a table.

Her whole body tightened; her skin felt as if it were a size too small
and was being pricked all over with miniature pins. When his hands
closed on her shoulders and slid down to cup her breasts, there was a
jolt beneath her diaphragm, almost like a blow, and she sagged
strengthless against the table.

"There is no time," he groaned.

"Then we'll make time," she said, her voice low and throaty.

Boring isn't the word *for it,* Kenneth Hollard thought.

The Islander officers were just behind the Arnsteins; they were behind a rank of King Shuriash's relatives; behind Hollard and the others were dignitaries, officials, priests, and God-knew-what. In the
great courtyard of E-sag-ila, the Temple that Raises Its Head, the
Palace of Heaven and Earth, the Seat of Kingship. It was impressive,
in its way, although not as much as the ziggurat that raised its head
across the street to the north—E-temen-an-ki, the Temple Foundation
of Heaven and Earth, soaring in seven steps three hundred and twenty
feet into the darkening evening sky. A great staircase ascended the
southern side, and from there ramps spiraled around each square step,
up to the blue-enameled shrine at the top. There, he'd heard, was a table of gold and a large bed . . . and a woman known as the Bride of
Marduk.

He glanced ahead. King Shagarakti-Shuriash would play the part
of Marduk later in the festivities, enacting the Sacred Marriage that
brought fertility to the land. *Lucky bastard,* he thought—it had been a
long time. . .

Right now the king was pacing forward, looking like an image himself in crown and robes, the mace of sovereignty in his hands. He was
reciting a hymn to Marduk, seemingly a verse for every step across
the huge stone-paved courtyard toward the temple gates.

Like parts of the king's palace, the Temple of Marduk had artificial
palm trees before the towering sixty-foot gates. Unlike the ones in the

palace, these were of solid silver and leafed with gold. The cedarwood of the gates was covered in silver as well, and the walls themselves were colored brick and bone-white gypsum. Within, the *sheshgallu,* the high priest, would have risen before dawn to cleanse himself with Tigris water and then spent all day before the image of the god, reciting from the *Enuma Elish,* the epic depicted on the gates.

Out here, the acres of courtyard were crowded with an orderly throng. Great banks of *kalu*—ritual singers—broke into choral song every time the king's recitation stopped, amid the tinkle and rattle of cistrum and cimbalomlike instruments. Incense smoked into the sky from censers of golden fretwork swung by the priests.

It was all stately beyond words; the problem was that with chants, songs, ritual gestures, it was going to take the rest of the afternoon to reach the temple, at which point the ceremony would actually begin. The dignitaries honored with an invitation had to go at the same pace. Colonel Hollard glanced aside at the crowd filling the open spaces of the courtyard and shivered slightly. Their faces were rapt, open, an abandonment of self beyond anything he could imagine.

Eventually they crossed the temenos, the sacred enclosure. The gates swung wide, and Kenneth Hollard missed his stride. *Jesus!*

Most of these Babylonian buildings were dim-lit inside; it made the bigger ones impressive, in a mysterious, smoky way. Esagila wasn't. The inside of the great hall *glowed,* light caught and reflected back and forth by the gold leaf that covered walls and the giant beams of the ceiling, sparkling from emerald and nacre and lapis. Hollard blinked, stunned for an instant. Then they were through the hall and into the sanctum itself, only the king and his most trusted guests there as witnesses. Hollard's eyes went up and up, past the man-high golden footstool, past the colossal foot and robe, to the golden, bearded face of the god that seemed to hover beneath the lofty roof, full-lipped and beak-nosed, the embodiment of power, telling all beholders to make peace with their mortality.

He shook himself mentally. *Come off it, that's just a statue.* Just a goddam big solid-gold statue. *No wonder the locals find it impressive, though.*

King Shuriash halted before the image of the god, one hand before his face and the other raised. The elderly *sheshgallu* came forward in his archaic wrap and relieved him of the symbols of his sovereignty—the tall crown of gold and jewels, the mace, the circle, all placed on a smaller chair before Marduk's. Then the high priest took him by the ear and made as if to force him to his knees. As a man rather than a king, Shuriash prostrated himself before Marduk and then rose only to his knees to proclaim:

> *I did not sin,*
> *O Lord of the countries.*
> *I did not destroy Babylon;*
> *I did not command its overthrow.*
> *The temple Esagila,*
> *I did not forsake its rites.*
> *I did not rain blows upon the weak,*
> *I did not humiliate the lowly.*
> *I was vigilant for the kingdom.*

Hollard found himself nodding. Shuriash actually meant it; for a monarch of the ancient Orient, he really was a pretty good sort. The priest slapped him sharply on both cheeks as the rite required, until tears came to his eyes; the king went on his belly once more, and then was lifted up, the high priest intoning:

> *Have no fear.*
> *The God Bel-Marduk will listen to your prayer*
> *He will magnify your lordship*
> *He will exalt your kingship*
> *The God Bel-Marduk will bless you forever;*
> *He will destroy your adversary;*
> *He will fell your enemy.*

One by one, the symbols he had laid down were returned to Shuriash. The chorus of singing priests burst out again, and within the confines of the temple their song was a wave of pure sound.

Hollard glanced aside at Raupasha, watching the intent sparkle of her dark-gray eyes. She was wearing what Doreen had dreamed up as the new Mitannian national costume, an open jacket of crimson silk embroidered with dragons in gold thread over a long, simple gown of indigo blue set with bullion medallions along the hem.

Looks damn fine, he thought. *She's filled out a little with proper food and exercise. Down boy!*

Then her eyes went wide, and her hand darted inside the jacket. Time seemed to slow as the slim hand came out with the bulk of a brand-new .40 Python in it, pointing ahead . . . toward King Shuriash. Toward his undefended back, bare to the allies he trusted.

Jesus, she's gone nuts! he thought. His hand lifted—and halted.

Instead, he pivoted himself, his own right hand clawing at the holster on his waist. The shot was not far from his ear, deafeningly loud. There were screams, cries of anger and rage; Shuriash was pivoting, features slack with amazement as he saw the priest leaping toward him with upraised knife. Raupasha's shot clipped a fingernail's width

of skin from the man's nose. The priest's face was twisted in an ec-
stacy of hatred, amok with fanaticism. The wound snapped his head
around for an instant, and slowed his rush.

"Die, blasphemer!" he screamed.

Prince Kashtiliash's actions had the smooth economy of an expert.
His sword slashed out and up, through the assassin's wrist. The priest
did shriek then, although Kenneth couldn't tell if it was with pain or
frustration. The sound cut off . . . literally, as the prince's second
stroke chopped halfway through his neck.

Then the two Hollards, the prince, and some of the nobles were
crowding around Shuriash, weapons poised and eyes glaring, putting
their bodies between him and any further danger, while priests and
onlookers scattered in terror. Hollard noticed that one of the few exceptions was Ian Arnstein, who'd seized his wife in a crouching hug
that put *his* body between her and danger. Time froze, for long in-
stants. The priest-assassin gave a final bubbling rattle, kicked heels,
voided, then died. His blood flowed out impossibly red in the light of
the shrine, creeping around the feet of those surrounding the king.

"Let me by," Shuriash snapped.

Reluctantly, his protectors spread apart, moving outward to make
their circle wider. Shuriash looked down at the priest.

"My thanks," he said to Kashtiliash, and nudged the body. "But it
would have been good to ask this one questions—hard questions, in a
hard way."

He caught Raupasha's eye and inclined his head. "My lady of Mitanni, I seem to owe you a life. I shall not forget."

Then he looked around. "Where is the *sheshgallu* of Marduk?"

The chief priest came forward, looking shrunken and old in his gorgeous robe and ziggurat hat. "My lord king, may you live forever—"

"If I do, it will be no thanks to your incompetence!" Shuriash
snapped.

"O Ensi of Marduk, there are so many priests in Babylon for the
akitu. . ."

Shuriash nodded. "That is true. You, you—" he pointed to guardsmen. "Take the corpse of this dead dog and put it where it may be
examined later. You, go speak to the people in the temenos; tell them
that the king has been spared by the grace of Marduk and the other
great gods assembled here in Babylon. Now, *sheshgallu*, it is time for
me to take the hand of the great god my lord, Bel-Marduk."

The high priest gaped at him. "You . . . you wish to go on with the
ceremony, King of the Four Quarters?"

Shuriash snorted. "Of course! If there was any aim to this plot besides killing me, it was to interrupt the *akitu*, that doubt might be

thrown on my right to rule as vice-regent of the great Bel-Marduk. This shall not be! The ceremony shall continue!"

There was a slight commotion at the doorway; it was a breach of decorum for anyone to enter the feasting-hall after the monarch. King Shuriash turned, his shaggy brows rising when Justin Clemens pushed past the guards. He smiled, though, despite the breach of protocol. The guards had known he would; the man who had saved the king's darling would not be denied audience even if his reasons were frivolous. Not for the first few times, at least.

Nobody thought his reasons were, once they saw his face. He came up to the table at the king's side and bowed.

"O King," he said. "I have grave news." He glanced around. "For your ears, and your heir's, and these officers of my people."

Shuriash looked at him keenly for a moment, then nodded. "Leave us," he said. There were murmurs from some of the ministers and generals. "Leave us, I said!" When the audience chamber was empty save for himself and his son and the Islander commanders, he went on: "I have given offense to powerful men. There had better be a good reason for this."

"O King, there is. There is *mutanu* in your city."

Shuriash's tanned skin went gray; so did his son's. *Mutanu* translated literally as "certain death." A better rendering into English would have been "plague."

"Are you sure?" the king said, grasping at a small image of Shamash that hung at his belt, a rare gesture for him.

"I am sure. It is. . ." He paused, groping for a word. "I do not know if you have a word for this *mutanu*. It starts with fever and a reddish rash, and then red sores erupt upon the body. If the victims live, they may be scarred. We call it *smallpox*."

Shuriash shook his head. "No, I do not know of this *mutanu*." His gaze sharpened. "You do? Have you brought this thing to the land of Kar-Duniash?"

Clemens licked his lips. *God, I wish I was sure,* he thought. "I do not think so," he said. "We have not suffered from this disease for a very long time. We have a means of making a person safe from it."

"Ah," Shuriash said. "That is well; that is very well."

Clemens shook his head. "Lord King, we have such a means at home in Nantucket, not here. Not our best means." In English, to the appalled faces of Kenneth Hollard and the other Islanders: "We've got enough vaccine on hand to immunize a couple of hundred people, no more."

"Is there another way, then?" Shuriash asked.

"Yes." Clemens hesitated, and the Babylonian made an imperious gesture. The doctor licked his lips again, tasting the salt of fear.

"Lord King, we can protect you and your family by the best method, for we have some of that medicine."

He winced internally. Still, there was no choice—they *couldn't* vaccinate the population at large, and if they were going to pick a few hundred, then it would have to be—coldly—based on who was most essential to the Republic's purposes.

"And my people?" Shuriash asked quietly.

"There is another way. It, too, protects against the disease, but . . . there are drawbacks."

Colonel Hollard snorted. "Spit it out, Lieutenant," he said.

"Lord King, the other method involves—" *How the hell do I say "attenuated virus" in Akkadian, goddammit?* He took another breath and began again. "It involves giving the healthy a weak form of the disease. In most cases, they recover with little harm and are henceforth immune."

Kashtiliash leaned forward, his brown eyes narrowed. "Most? That is a word as slippery as a fish dipped in sesame oil," he said.

Clemens nodded. "Of every fifty so treated, one will develop the strong form of the disease. Of those, one in two will die."

Shuriash seemed to swell where he sat. "You would kill"—he paused to calculate; Babylonian arithmetic used an eight-base system—"one in every hundred of my people?"

"King, if we do not, at least two in every *ten* will die! And that is . . . to rely on the favor of the gods." It wasn't easy to say "probability" in Akkadian either. "If this is truly the first time that this *mutanu* has visited your lands, then as many as *nine* in ten or more may die. And I think it is the first time; your *asu* Azzu-ena knows nothing of it, and her knowledge of your healing arts is very complete."

"Oh, *shit*," Hollard said, into the echoing silence that followed Clemens' words. "Why didn't I stay on Nantucket, where they don't *have* emergencies?"

CHAPTER TWENTY-TWO

May, Year 10 A.E.

"Dull duty," Guard Recruit Mandy Kayle said

"Sky Father give me 'dull' anytime," Petty Officer Samuel Taunarsson said. "I mean, God the Father and His Son," he continued, crossing himself. "And His Mother. Whether or not She is Moon Woman, too," he added for safety'n sake.

Above them the fabric of the balloon creaked in the predawn chill. She could see a few intact aircraft—they'd probably never fly again—pegged down under shelters at the little airport, and the big blimp-construction shed—empty right now. Despite that addition there was a forlorn air to Nantucket Airport, boarded windows and bindweed slithering out over the runways . . . as if the Event had left it stranded in its own little bubble of time. Kayle shivered slightly at the thought; she'd been nine years old the night of the Event, but she was *never* going to forget it. The world before, yes—there were times when she wasn't sure if her memories were real or dreams.

"Pressure?" Taunarsson said.

"Full, Petty Officer," Kayle said. The two-hundred-foot-long balloon was tugging at its moorings, rocking a little in a fresh westerly breeze. "At present weight, neutral buoyancy at five hundred feet."

"Drop stationary ballast," he said, and went to one side of the gondola. Kayle went to the other, her hand on the slipknot of a burlap sack of sand.

"One!"

Two fifty-pound bags hit the asphalt in unison with dull thuds.

"Two! Three!"

Ropes creaked sharply. The noncom nodded and stepped up to the head of the open oval gondola, picking up the handset. "This is *Eagle's Eye*. Communications check."

Evidently that went smoothly too, since he clicked the knob to a different channel and spoke again: "Ready, aye, ready."

From the gray-shot darkness over the side came the rare brilliance of an electric light; nobody was going to use an open flame near this much hydrogen.

"Paying up!" came the voice of the line team.

"Stand by to let go fore and aft!" Taunarsson called.

"Ready!"

"On the mark . . . *loose!*"

There was a bobbling heave, a sharp *tung* sound, and a steady *Clinkaclinkaclinka* as the mechanism let the cable run in a smooth, controlled surge. The Coast Guard fixed observation balloon *Eagle's Eye* rose and turned its nose into the wind as the fins caught the breeze. Kayle yawned and settled back on the bench by her duty station, keeping an eye on the pressure and altitude gauges.

Boring, she thought.

In the Year 2 the Kayles had taken up a sixty-four-acre Town grant farm out Milestone Road, about halfway to Sconset, a little south of Gibbs Pond. Sixty-four acres and forty crossbred Alban-Jersey dairy cattle, all of 'em needing to be milked twice a day, rain or shine, winter or summer.

Mandy Kayle was just old enough to remember times when the school year ended with a *vacation*. Even though her younger siblings, two blood and two adopted, got old enough to help, she'd been glad to shake the dust of the farm off her feet on her eighteenth birthday.

Shake the dust? Scrape the shit off my feet! Hell, this certainly beats working for a living. She'd probably get shipboard duty in six months or so. Maybe make petty officer and get into one of the middie slots, a commission in a couple of years. Standing on her own quarterdeck some day . . .

Or I could put in for flight training. Scuttlebutt had it that more ultralights were being sent far foreign, with the expeditionary force and possibly with ships for scouting.

She stood up to put on her sealskin jacket as they hit a thousand feet—it got brisk up here—and clipped on her safety line before Taunarsson could get on her case about it. He had a serious hair up the ass about regs; but then, he'd sailed with *Commodore Alston,* the lucky bastard.

"Vent water ballast, establish neutral buoyancy at five thousand feet," he said.

"Aye, aye," she replied.

That control was a wheel at the end of a pole in the middle of the gondola. She gave it three quick turns, then waited while the rumbling hiss started below and the *Eagle's Eye* surged upward again, her eye fixed on the altimeter and the converted fuel gauge that showed the level of ballast.

"Forty-five hundred feet," she said as her ears popped again.

"Ballast valve off."

"Ballast valve off, aye."

Silence fell, broken only by the clean, cold whistle of the wind around the balloon. The cable stretched away in a diminishing curve below them to the toy-small recovery gear, and Nantucket Island spread out, gradually rising from shadow to light as the sun heaved itself above the eastern horizon. The island was a lopsided triangle, gray-green set in blue and edged with white surf. She could see other land—Martha's Vineyard to the northwest, the mainland to the north—but her homeland was laid out below her like a map.

"Let's get to work," Taunarsson said. "You've got first watch."

"Aye, aye, Mr. Taunarsson," she said.

There was a thermos of hot cocoa in a box bolted to the side of the gondola that also held their boxed lunches; she poured for both of them, automatically adjusting for the continuous dip and sway of the tethered balloon. She'd been miserably sick the first couple of times, and she still remembered the petty officer's cheerful command—*Overside, and show the civvies what you think of 'em, Recruit.*

Then she broke out her binoculars, resting her elbows on the chest-high rail, careful to check that the strap was hitched around her neck and through the brass loop at the rear of her leather jacket before she took them anywhere near the edge of the little craft. What the lieutenant—hell, what the commodore—would say if she lost the irreplaceable pre-Event instrument just didn't bear thinking about.

Green-blue water shading out into dark blue, edged with whitecaps, stretching out all around to the edge of the world—back to greenish again over the sandbanks that dotted Nantucket Sound like silent hands waiting to grab ships' keels. The low shorelines of Cape Cod and Martha's Vineyard easily in view from here—there were threads of smoke coming up from both, probably from charcoal kilns and turpentine works, and a bigger one from the glassworks at Hyannis Base. What she and Taunarsson were *supposed* to look for were ships, and whales spouting, and schools of fish—so the Guard could pass the information on to whalers and fishers and tug captains—or people in trouble. Those were the things the Guard was for, along with exploring and fighting.

The scan was automatic by now. She could ignore the wind that brought red to her cheeks and ears, the almost inaudible murmur of the petty officer reading to himself as he went over a textbook—studying for a move up, of course. Mandy had a copy of that navigation manual herself. She could read it without moving her lips, but then, she hadn't learned to read as an adult—and in a second language at that.

Clouds in the north, she thought. Might be weather building up there. *Bit of a haze to the east.*

Out there the ocean stretched to Alba, to the Summer Isle, to the weird places along the Baltic that the *Douglass* had found—she saw herself standing in the prow of a whaleboat as it grounded on a sandy shore edged with pine; she saw painted men leaning on their spears, holding up strings of amber, drums beating in the dark forests . . .

Odd. There were *sails* out there; she could swear it. She flipped through the arrivals and departures checklist. Two brigs and a clipper were due in from far foreign this week, from the penal settlement on Inagua, Trinidad, and the Pacific, respectively. *Hell, there are* already *more than three there. Damn that haze.* And ships bearing up from the Caribbean usually ran in west of Madaket and picked up a tug there.

"Oh, shit," she whispered a second later.

"I'd forgotten how much I hated those things," Marian mumbled, then forced herself to full alertness and reached over Swindapa's sleepy murmur of protest to pick up the telephone. Her partner clung to her like a warm, drowsy octopus, sighing and stretching as Marian's hand fumbled in the dark through the clutter on the side table.

Matches, handkerchief, water glass, Greatest Chinese Invention of All time, right, there it is, telephone, she thought, yawning.

"Alston heah," she said. It had to be fairly important to use the still-limited telephone service. *"What?"*

Swindapa sat up in midstretch, eyes sharp and alert.

"Yes, of course notify the Chief, Sandy," Marian snapped. "At once. And sound the General Alarm and Turn Out. Yes, I'm authorizing it, goddamnit. Get to it!"

"What's happening?" Swindapa said steadily as they rolled out of bed and began to dress.

"Great minds think alike," Marian said, looking out the window.

The spring dawn was just breaking in the east, gilding the white pillars of the Two Greeks across Main Street from Guard House.

"It looks like King Isketerol decided not to wait for us to hit him first."

"It's *hanging in the air,*" Shaudriskol of Tartessos said, looking up at the tiny dot lazing in the morning sky. Light flashed off something beneath it, metal or glass.

"We knew they could do that," his uncle Zeurkenol said quietly. The kingdom had hot-air balloons as well, this last year. "Keep it down, don't startle the men. When we've taken the island, we too will command the skies."

It was a clear, fresh morning, and the whole fleet was cutting across the wind—pointing up from the southeast. The lookouts had cried out that the Jester had relented and Arucuttag of the Sea had brought them to landfall some time ago; small fires in metal bowls burned thank-offerings before the little model shrines on every quarterdeck. Even now, when Tartessian ships had spanned the oceans of Earth, it still felt a little unnatural to see nothing but sea for weeks.

He raised the far-seeing glasses to his eye, examined the coast, then looked down at the map carefully secured to a board, holding aside the oiled leather that protected it when it was not in use. The spy had stolen them a fine map indeed; *The Complete Map of Nantucket,* by something that the Eagle People called a *Chamber of Commerce*—like most men of rank, Zeurkenol had learned a smattering of En-gil-ish along with the new script.

His skin prickled a little at the sight of the low, sandy shore ahead; it was like sailing to the Otherworld—Nantucket, the home of everything mysterious, magical, eldritch . . .

"And the richest prize in all the world," he murmured.

"With the fate of the kingdom riding on our shoulders," his nephew added proudly.

"Don't flatter yourself, son of my brother," Zeurkenol said dryly. "Did you notice which regiments the king sent?"

"Wiseant, Boar, Wolf, Otter, and Bear," his nephew-aide said automatically. "They're . . . oh."

A substantial proportion of the new *standing army*—he used the Eng-il-its word when he thought, there being no close Tartessian equivalent; the closest you could come was *household guards*. First-rate troops armed with the new breechloaders, and with many other cunning new weapons. But all recruited from the new subject peoples in the lands south of the Pillars, tribal mercenaries from the mountains of the Riff. Fierce fighters and loyal to their salt, but there would be no politically destabilizing grief in the capital if they were lost.

"But the officers are of the best families in the City!"

"Yes," Zeurkenol said. "Not many unmarried men among them, either."

His nephew was young, no more than eighteen winters, but no fool. His eyes widened. All of them with hostages within the city walls. None of the New Men among them, either, none of the king's strongest supporters.

"You don't mean . . . the king *wants* us to fail? To die here?"

"Oh, no, never think it. The king strikes boldly here, and if we conquer, our rewards will be great . . . back in Tartessos, under his eye."

Isketerol was no fool, either, nor did he love blood for its own sake. There was not much to say against how the king *used* his new power, except that he *had* it.

I would be easier in my mind if I were sure his son would use it likewise, the nobleman thought.

The king in Tartessos might as well be a living god now, like Pharaoh. That was well for the city when the king was a very able man, although even the ablest made mistakes. The *next* king, though . . .

He pushed the thought out of his mind. There was a war to fight, and if he won it Tartessos would bestride the world.

"A general message," he said. It would be a repetition, but all the better for that—the troops were good fighting men but inclined to be a bit wild. "To all warriors ashore. Remember that the king has commanded that all nonfighters or those who surrender be treated well, as his subjects. There is to be no burning, no plunder, no forcing of women—any man found breaking these orders will be castrated and burned alive before the altar of Arucuttag!"

So the king had said, and like most of his orders there was wisdom in it. The loot of Nantucket would be beyond the dreams of avarice, even a king's dreams, but the skills and knowledge it held were a treasure far greater. Best to destroy as little as possible in taking them.

There was a crowd around the table in the map room; that was in the Middle Brick, the nearly identical building just south of Guard House. Marian looked down at the big relief map again, as more counters went into the clump hovering off the eastern end of the island. A cup of coffee was thrust into her hand, and she sipped automatically.

"How could they get this close undetected?" someone complained.

The Republic's military commander looked up, and the councilor flinched. "Because it's a very big ocean and we have only about forty deep-ocean ships and they're all over the world," she said. "And because the Meeting rejected my request that we keep a standing air patrol."

Fuel was scarce and hideously expensive, granted—so were spare parts. *But not as expensive as a surprise attack.*

"We don't have time for bickering," Jared Cofflin said.

Marian nodded. *Though from now on maybe we'll get less whining about how militia drill is a waste of time,* she thought coldly.

"From the reports, they may have something on the order of five or six thousand men," she said. "I'm ordering aircraft up, but I don't expect to find another fleet. At a guess, they slipped the ships out a few at a time to avoid attention from our people in Tartessos, and then picked up the troops in Morocco. What would have become Morocco; it was barbarian country in this milieu, and the Tartessians had overrun it. "Then they cut along the northern edge of the Trades, sacrificing speed for secrecy. Bold."

Swindapa came in; Marian returned her salute. "Commodore, the militia's assembling—we caught most people before they'd left for work."

Marian nodded; she could hear the noise in the streets, voices, wheels, hooves, teenagers on bicycles shouting *Turn out! Turn out!* as they pedalled. The Church bells had stopped their rythmic pulsing call some time ago. By law all adult citizens and resident aliens were in the militia, with arms and equipment kept ready at hand in their homes; and they'd just had a monthly muster-and-drill day last week.

"First Battalion is about ready to move out," Swindapa went on. "Less than an hour." Marian nodded with chill satisfaction; that was good time.

"What do we do?" Cofflin asked. "Meet them on the beach?"

Marian shook her head. "Not enough time," she said. "And they'll have the cover of their ship's guns on the landing zone. We can't get enough troops or cannon there in time, and they're going to out-number us badly as it is."

There were about twelve thousand people on the Island these days, but a large proportion of those were children or old people. They would all do what they could, from oldsters manning the aid stations and minding infants to Junior Militia carrying messages by bicycle. But of actual troops, the Island had barely three thousand.

"We have to keep Fort Brandt manned," she said, tapping the map.

That was the fortress on the site of the old Coast Guard station, near the lighthouse and the mouth of the harbor. Ron Leaton's best rifled cannon were there; nobody was going to take a ship in past *those,* and it was safe against any ground assault as well. That meant nobody was going to sail into the harbor and assault the docks; the noncombatants would gather there.

"That's a hundred and fifty people down," she said. "We have to crew the warships in harbor and get them to sea for our counter-attack." Three frigates, the new steam ram *Farragut,* and some smaller craft. "Say two thousand troops available all up to meet their landing force, and they'll be ashore before we're completely mobilized . . . how's the evacuation going?"

"Everyone's out of Sconset and halfway back to town," Jared said. "I checked myself. We used the mothballed school buses, most of them worked. The farmers and such are all coming in too; say another two hours for the last ones." A wintry smile. "Had some complaints 'bout leaving livestock and such. Dealt with it."

That was a massive relief; she needed the roads clear, and herds of cows and sheep blocking movement would be a nightmare.

"Captain Trudeau? The *Farragut*?"

The slender young man gulped air. "Ma'am, we're still fitting out. The guns aren't on board, we haven't shipped the masts . . ."

Alston's eyes speared him. "Your engines are installed?" A nod. "You have the protective plating for the paddle wheels in place?" Another. "Then my single question is, Captain Trudeau, *can you make steam*?"

He straightened. "Yes, ma'am."

"Good. Then go do it. Fast." He went out at a brisk walk.

Okay. We have three of the frigates, the Farragut, *and a bunch of smaller stuff. First we have to get them fully committed onshore.* Packed with soldiers, even the Tartessian transports would be dangerous.

Get them to empty those ships; then we hit 'em from the sea.

"Thank God for the *Eagle's Eye* and good weather," she said. Her finger traced a line out from Nantucket Town, heading east along Milestone Road. "Out here south of Gibbs Pond, where there's room for the Cherokee Brigade to make themselves useful. We'll stop them there."

"Ma'am!"

She looked up; the communications tech was scribbling. "It's the *Eagle's Eye*. Large numbers of small boats landing, and several Tartessian ships have beached themselves and are disembarking troops over the side . . . troops and artillery, ma'am."

The room drew a long breath with her. "All right, people, let's do it," she said. "Sandy, you've got the deck here."

"There go the air corps," Mandy Kayle said.

She'd watched the pilots arrive, by steam-hauler and bicycle, horse carriage and a single unprecedented school bus. Now the ultralights were lifting off in waves from the runways, ten and then ten more and then four. *Only two down for repairs,* she thought. *Good maintenance.*

The little plywood teardrops on their tricycle carriages hopped into the air almost immediately; they needed only thirty feet or so of rolling room even with their load of rockets and bombs. The motorized hang gliders circled like birds in a flock, building altitude until she could see the eagle wings painted onto the fabric of the arrowhead wings, the beaks and claws on the fuselages. One buzzed close enough that she could see a gloved hand come up to give her a thumbs-up signal, and then the little craft banked away and joined its comrades as they plodded at forty miles an hour toward the eastern end of the Island.

"Luck go with them," Taunarsson said. "Grant them victory!"

"Yeah," Mandy Kayle said.

Because if they aren't lucky, we're going to be needing luck our-

selves pretty damn soon. Her family's land was right in the path of the invasion.

"All right," Marian Alston said, looking down from the steps of the Pacific Bank.

It was the traditional—post-Event traditional, at least—place for public speaking in Nantucket. From here she could see the bulk of the Ready Force and the First Battalion, Republic of Nantucket Militia—eight hundred of them, all standing by their bicycles. Many of the faces turned up toward hers were still pale with shock . . . *but they're ready.* Rifles slung over their backs, extra ammunition and basic supplies on the carrying racks over the rear wheels, and heavy weapons on two-person tricycles.

She felt a moment's somber pride; building up the reserve force had been her work as much as anyone's.

"We're in a hurry, so I'll keep it simple," she said. "We're fighting for our homes, our families, our lives, and our freedom—In the most literal sense of the word." A low murmuring *onarl* ran through them, and she held up a hand. "Remember your training! We're going to win this as an organized force, not a mob. Trading your life one-for-one with a Tartessian is a bad bargain for the Republic. Listen to your officers and do your best; we all will, and that's how we'll come through this."

A short, barking cheer, and the long column began to move out, mounting up and pedaling up Main Street. They'd turn left on Orange and then out to Milestone Road; that ran all the way to Sconset. She turned to their commander, a Marine regular usually in the training cadre out at Fort Grant. He was a middle-aged man, from North Carolina originally, a sergeant in the corps before the Event, short and barrel-chested, with skin the color of old oiled teak. His vehicle would be one of the hoarded motor scooters, to give him mobility enough to oversee the operation.

"Major McClintock, push straight up Milestone and then fix them in place," she said, her finger tracing the folded map in his hand. "The rest of the militia will mass here and then move out in support." That would be the second through fourth classes, older and less fit. "You've got air reconnaissance and they don't, but they're going to outnumber you badly."

Unfortunately, Nantucket got wider as you went east; it was shaped like a lopsided triangle pointing westward . . . which was undoubtedly why the Tartessians had landed there. It gave them the maximum possible freedom of maneuver.

"They may try to flank you either north"—through the former moorland around Gibbs Pond, containing the vital powder mill—"or south, toward the airport. If you have to choose, hold on the north; it's hillier and easier to defend, but we need to keep them away from the *Eagle Eye*'s anchor rope if at all possible. Any questions?"

"No, ma'am," he said stolidly. A smile and a salute. "See you later."

"Take care."

The man hopped onto his scooter and his staff onto theirs; the *put-put-put* of their motors echoed as they sped away. The sun shone cruelly bright, scudding formations of white cloud from north to south above them. Alston looked up.

Rain, she thought. Flintlocks wouldn't shoot if they were wet, and the new weapons the Islanders were using would. *Please, God, send me some rain.*

A growl of engines came from lower down on Main Street, as the Cherokee Brigade approached; she smelled the not-unpleasant scent of burned alcohol, and crossed mental fingers.

All these cars have to do is work today, she thought. *And tomorrow if we're unlucky.*

Not all of them were Jeep Cherokees, in fact, although most were—that had been the most popular pre-Event model. All *had* been modified, usually with sheet-metal armor besides weapons. Swindapa's blond head showed beside the Gatling mounted on one. She saluted smartly, and Alston returned the gesture, silently thanking a God she didn't believe in that they were together. *And that Heather and Lucy are out with the other kids at Fort Brandt.*

She walked down the steps, checked to see that the strap on her Python revolver was secure, and swung herself down into the body of the car. The front held the driver and radio operator; she handed the second headset up to Alston, who settled it on beneath her helmet. Which reminded her . . .

"Helmet, 'dapa." Then into the microphone: "Alston to Rapezewicz."

"Loud and clear, Commodore."

"Status report, Sandy."

"Tartessians are still disembarking, but they've moved a holding force up to the top of the bluffs overlooking the beach."

Alston nodded. That was exactly as she expected, and—she looked at her watch—far too early for any Islander forces of note to have arrived there.

"Trudeau reports that he's jury-rigging some valving and warming his boilers; he'll be ready for sea in not less than two hours forty-five minutes. All the other ships will be by that time, too."

"Good." Alston nodded grimly to herself. About the best you could expect, from a cold start.

"*Eagle's Eye* has the First Battalion under observation; they're making good time. McClintock reports no contact as yet. And the air corps are beginning their attack run on the enemy ships."

Alston drew a deep breath. "All right, Sandy, keep me informed. Driver, move out!"

Private (First Battalion, Republic of Nantucket Militia Reserve) Garrett Hopkins chopped frantically at the oats and the sandy dirt beneath them with his entrenching tool. To either side of him the rest of his section were doing likewise, and dirt flew into the air as if a pack of giant gophers had moved onto this farm. He felt himself sweating, but it wasn't the exertion. He worked harder than this every day, on a loading team at the Bessemer works.

It was the knowledge that pretty soon people would be coming up through the fields ahead, trying to *kill* him. Kill *him*. This morning's toast and ham and eggs and porridge lay like a lump in his stomach, belching back up in gusts of gas, eaten in another world.

Trying to kill us all, or make us slaves, he thought, baring his teeth. His elder brother was a seaman, and he'd told the family about what he'd seen far foreign, in Tartessos and elsewhere. How the locals treated people there.

Enemy ahead of me, family behind me, the young man thought; his parents, his younger sisters, his brother's kids.

The oats were spring-planted and had a sweetish scent as his spade cut them, turning them to green mush on the steel; it was stronger than his own rank fear-sweat. The soil beneath was dark for four inches, then lighter sand. He jumped in when he couldn't reach down far enough, turning awkwardly as he dug beneath his feet; he stopped when the hole was chest-deep and tossed the spade up onto the piled earth in front of him. The blade and his hands packed it down; he checked as he'd been taught, making sure that he could see clearly in all directions but had room to duck down as well.

A glance over his shoulder—a board fence, then downslope their bicycles, and the road far behind and to the right, with a strip of scrub and trees along it. Ahead was the rest of this field of oats. More fences eastward toward the enemy, but he could see over them, and it struck him how pretty this part of the Island looked. The steel plant where he worked was useful, good honest work, but nobody could call it good-looking.

The sergeant—foreman at the Bessemer works—and a corporal went by, dropping board cartons of fifty rounds by each rifle pit. As he stopped by Hopkins's, he left a canvas bandolier of grenades as well, the new kind with spoon-and-ring detonators. Hopkins felt an instant's gratitude; the older type with friction primers gave him the willies.

"Make it count, Garry," the sergeant said, with a taut smile; his face was sweat-beaded too. "We need your right arm when baseball season starts again."

"Best outfielder on Seahaven Engineering's team," he agreed.

A voice came from the next hole. "A hero in your own mind. With a bat you couldn't hit your own feet."

He looked over and grinned at Evelyn Grant. *Never noticed she has a cute smile before,* he thought. *After this is over, have to do something about it.* That moment seemed infinitely far away and suddenly more desirable than anything in the world.

Longing turned to rage as he saw something tiny moving at the edge of sight, over toward Sconset. Black ant-figures in a strung-out line, trampling the barley planted there, then more distinct. Enemy. On *his* ground, *his* land.

A voice behind shouted: "Lieutenant says open fire at seven hundred yards—sixth fence out! Sixth fence—count it!"

He did, and checked the range estimate himself. Checked that his Werder rifle was loaded, checked that there were two grenades firmly planted in the sand near his right hand, checked that the six rounds in the strip of loops sewn to the left breast of his khaki tunic were in place, checked that the cover of the bandolier at his right hip was buckled back to show the staggered rows of shells. Then he noticed how dry his mouth was and took a sip from his canteen.

Thousand yards, he thought, when he put it down. They were only a thousand yards away, and he could see the flapping of a banner in their midst. The enemy were advancing in two lines twenty yards apart, with a spacing of twelve feet or so between each man. Not too different from the formation he'd been taught.

His head whipped around at the *crack* of a shot off to his right, and he heard someone reaming someone out for firing too soon. *Now they'll know we're here,* he thought.

The Tartessians checked a second at the sound, then a trumpet sounded, two rising and three falling notes. They came on at a trot now, and the spring sunlight blinked on their fixed bayonets. His mouth was dry again, and there was a tremor in his hands. He took a deep breath and forced it out, another, and felt a little better.

But I really *have to piss,* he thought. Suddenly it rammed home that not only were those men going to kill him if they could . . . *but I have to kill them to stop them. I* have *to.*

To quiet the thought he brought the rifle to his shoulder and checked again, this time that the sights were set at seven hundred yards. They weren't; the little arrow at the side had *200* under the pointer, the lowest setting—point-blank range. He shifted his thumb to it and clicked it up to *700.*

The sergeant came by again, stooping as he ran this time. "Check your sights, check your sights," he said. His Fiernan accent was thicker. "And for Moon Woman's loving sake, don't forget to adjust them as they get closer. Doesn't do any good to shoot unless you *hit*."

"Hope they don't *get* any closer," Hopkins muttered.

His tongue felt thick and dry despite the water he'd drunk, as he brought the rifle to his shoulder, leaning forward against the cool, damp surface of the firing pit. It soaked through the khaki jacket in spots—hung up fresh-smelling and spotless after his mother took it down to Squeaky Steam Cleaning when he came back from Drill Weekend last month.

Mom will be with her unit, he thought—she was in the last-ditch outfit, the over-fifties. *Jesus. I really hope she doesn't have to do this.*

The bright morning narrowed down to the little notch at the top of the rear sight, and the pip of the foresight through that. He could see the fence, gray weathered oak planks nailed to square posts. He'd earned a little extra money one summer over on Long Island, putting up fences like that. That had been the summer he'd lost his cherry with a Fiernan girl working on that farm, in a pile of clover that smelled like honey, like her.

A man was climbing over the fence; awkwardly, holding his rifle out in one hand for balance. Hopkins adjusted his rifle's aim automatically, and noticed things—the green tunic and bare hairy legs and strap sandals, dark bearded face with a round iron helmet, a heavy pack.

"*Fire!*"

His finger squeezed, as if the word had pulled a wire in his brain that ran down his arm to his hand. The Werder kicked against his shoulder and a puff of smoke rose from the muzzle, wafting away to the right as the wind caught it. *Bambambambambambam* as the rest of his platoon fired as well, and the hot shell ejected and bounced off his cheek, burning a little.

The slight pain jarred him out of the daze of seeing the foreigner pitch backward and lie still, one leg caught in the middle plank of the fence, tunic falling up to show a soiled loincloth.

Hopkins swallowed something that tasted like his breakfast ten days dead and reached down to reload. The voice in his head sounded like the Marine regular who'd taught him during his basic camp—harshly accented, with the staccato choppiness of someone born speaking one of the Sun People dialects, bored, slightly contemptuous.

Aim at his belt buckle and a little down, that's best for a chest shot. Don't get fancy. You usually won't be able to tell if you hit him. Shoot, reload, look for another target, shoot. Don't think, you Island-born think way too fucking much. Thinking rots your guts. Just shoot.

He shot, reloaded, shot. The Tartessians were much closer now, coming forward at a slow run. Another pitched forward just as Hopkins was about to fire at him. *Jesus.* Limp, gone, dead, thud facedown and lie there. Hopkins swallowed, tracked the man next to him, fired.

Crack. Ping. Reload, and the chamber was hot enough to scorch his thumb a little when he pushed the round home. The first line of Tartessians went to one knee, thumbing back the hammers of their rifles— just like the Westley-Richards he'd trained on first before they got the new Werders. Which meant—

"Christ!" He dropped the rifle onto the pile of dirt he'd been leaning against and ducked.

The volley, and ugly flat whizzing *craaak* sounds above him— whipcrack sounds, meant for *him.* Screams from nearby, louder screams than he could believe possible, someone he knew. The Tartessian war shouts were much closer; he forced his body to stand again, snatched up the rifle. The ones who'd fired were reloading, and the second rank of the Tartessian formation had run through them, sprinting forward. He could see a thick scatter behind them, all the way to the fifth fence—dozens, maybe hundreds, lying in the oats, sprawled still or thrashing or crawling back toward where they'd come from.

"You fuckers can all go back where you came from!" he shouted, firing again. The numbness that had gripped him since he shot the man climbing the fence was gone, replaced by a wild anger.

The man he fired at dropped his rifle, staggered, and stumbled away. The others around him threw themselves to the ground and a ripple of fire ran down their suddenly hidden ranks, only puffs of smoke showing where they were. Hopkins suddenly looked at the sights; they were readjusted to "400," and he couldn't remember doing it. Then he fired again, as the line that had fired first finished reloading and charged through their prone comrades. More fell, and the rest went to ground in their turn and opened up. This time the men behind them crawled forward; that would have given them better protection if the ground hadn't sloped gently upward, putting the Islanders above them.

Hopkins aimed at a trail of oats that was moving the wrong way, fired, fired again. *They're getting too close—*

Then a Tartessian rose and dashed—backward this time, away from the continuous crackle of rifle fire; he threw away his own weapon to run faster, and made perhaps ten yards before something slapped him between the shoulder blades like the hand of an angry invisible giant. He fell, lay still. More Tartessians ran; others crawled backward. Then there were shouts among them, and whole groups got up and ran back, while others covered their retreat as best they could, the same leapfrog drill they'd used in the attack, only reversed.

"They're running!" Hopkins whispered, as the last of them dashed past the torn-down fence where their attack had started and "Cease fire!" ran down the Islander firing line.

Then he stood, cheering, shaking the rifle over his head as the same savage howl went up from all his comrades.

"Silence in the ranks!" someone called, and he coughed and reached for his canteen. It was nearly empty, and he made himself take a small swallow. A corporal he recognized—she worked in the compressor-engine shed—came by.

"Where's Sergeant Folendaro?" he asked.

"Dead," she said and jerked a thumb.

Hopkins looked to the rear. There was a row of bodies there, with their khaki groundsheets spread over them; the lieutenant was standing nearby, looking at a map and talking to someone. He swallowed again.

"Anyway, Lieutenant says to check your bandoliers and sing out if you're short. Blocks down to cool. Gimme your canteen."

"Where's the latrine?" he asked, handing it over. She laughed.

"You're the fifth person's asked me that. No time. Piss in your hole if you have to."

She walked on. Hopkins found that he *did* have to; at least the sandy soil absorbed the stream quickly. He checked his bandolier as well after he'd buttoned his fly, and found to his astonishment that there were only forty rounds left.

I fired sixty rounds? he thought, incredulous. *No wonder the chamber's hot.*

He pressed the block down until it clicked into the open loading position and set the rifle on the mound of dirt in front of him; that way air could flow down the barrel and carry off some of the heat. Then he drew his bayonet and slid it under the rawhide bindings of the ammunition box that Folendaro—*he's dead, Jesus*—had dropped off earlier. Two swift jerks and it slit open; he pulled off the lid and began transferring the brass shells to the loops in his bandolier.

"Thank God for Ron Leaton," he called over to Evelyn Grant, who was doing the same.

"Yeah, that would have been a lot harder with the old Westley-R," she said, her voice hoarse. "I think we could have done it, but they'd have gotten closer and I didn't like the look of those bayonets, no sir."

"Say, Evelyn . . ."

"Yeah?"

"You want to catch dinner at the Brotherhood on Friday, then do the concert?"

She looked up at him, a cartridge poised between thumb and finger of her right hand.

"Jesus, Garry, you're asking me for a date *now*?"

"You know a better time? Hell, we could be *dead*."

"Yeah . . . okay, provided we're alive on Friday and they don't cancel the concert," she said, shaking her head. "I wonder what's going on everywhere else."

"We sure kicked their butts here," he said.

That's one way to put it. He could hear some of the enemy wounded calling out and could see a lot more bodies—he carefully didn't look too closely at the ones nearest, about a hundred yards out.

Further eastward was confused movement, and there were columns of smoke over toward Sconset. Something was coming down Milestone Road from that direction too.

"Uh-oh,'" he said.

"I know what 'uh-oh' means," Evelyn said, and ducked back into her foxhole, hunkering down.

The corporal came along the line, hurrying, dropping off canteens. "Lieutenant says watch out," she said unnecessarily.

"Uh-oh" means we're in the shit again, Hopkins thought. He loaded his rifle and thumbed back the cocking lever.

Click . . . click.

"Jesus, I'm starting to hate that sound," he muttered.

"Man-birds!"

Zeurkenol looked up sharply. Tiny shapes were rising into the air off to the southwest—right where the map said the *air-port* would be.

"Sound the alarm!" he said.

It snarled among the confusion of ships packed near the beach, and among the warcraft anchored further out. Zeurkenol looked up at the tops of his own ship; men there were unlimbering an antiair rifle, the same as the Westley-Richards but twice the size and mounted on a ring that ran around the mast. More of them would be on shore, and crewmen were scurrying for their personal weapons. There was nothing he could do but wait.

On shore the first of the antiair rifles spoke, from the low ridge above the beach. The engineers had built a roadway of planks to the Eagle People's asphalt road, and soldiers were marching up it. A dozen ships were beached, and twice as many more were swinging loads overside to rafts and boats, or pushing horses over the side—a few of the gods-abandoned beasts started swimming out to sea, but most of them had enough wit to follow the boats shoreward.

"Message to General Naudrikol," he said. "Remind him that we must secure the airport."

The signaler began to clack, turning its mirrored surface to flash the orders ashore. The dots grew closer, until they were giant painted birds, eyes and beaks fierce. The hunting hawks of the gods, of the Eagle . . .

Men do this, he told himself. *Not gods, but men like us. We too will ride the wind, when we have won the secrets they strive to keep for themselves.*

One was coming toward him on the flagship. It swooped downward, out over the crested blue water at scarcely more than bulwark height. The antiair rifles in the tops were barking at it, as rapid as a rifle with four hands to help load. Ordinary rifles began to crackle along the rail as well, and it was closer, closer, only a few hundred yards . . .

Raaaaawisshshhh!

Rockets fired from the stumpy second wings on either side of the bullet-shaped body; two, four, spraying forward in paths of red fire and gray smoke. The crews shouted with fear and anger—many of the mercenaries had laid under Tartessian rocket barrages when their homelands were overrun.

At least they won't simply choke with fear, Zeurkenol thought.

And then—marvelous, his heart sang!—the attacking aircraft nosed over and hit the water, became sinking debris. A savage cheer went up from the crew, in the instant before the rockets arrived.

One of the rockets twisted away, struck the water and burst in a club shape of spray. Another corkscrewed through the air, running through the rigging of the flagship, but by a whim of the Jester not striking anything. Two hit the ship, up near the bows, in a blast of fire and lethal splinters. There was a crash, and Zeurkenol heard the high screaming of wounded men as he picked himself up and looked about.

The flagship's skipper was an able man. Well drilled, the crew responded to the fire with water and sand. As he watched, smoke billowed up, and then steam.

He genuflected toward the idol of Arucuttag of the Sea that stood by the compass binnacle; the damage-control teams had caught the fires before they spread to sails and rigging, which would have been certain death for the ship. Then he called out. praise to them; they cheered him back.

A quick glance around showed yet more of the craft of the sky attacking his fleet; the air was full of smoke from the counterfire, loud with the crackle of guns, screams, and explosions. One went down burning as he watched, ignited by its own rockets; he sent up a silent promise of a sacrifice to Arucuttag. Another jerked and wobbled in the air; he was close enough to see the man steering it start and slump. By some freak of chance—he felt like beating Arucuttag's edolion with a stick, or cursing the Jester (neither advisable)—it flew straight on, rising slightly, until it crashed right into the rigging of a ship and exploded in a globe of flame.

Lady, spare us! That was the *Thunder Walker,* the main ammunition ship for the fleet!

Zeurkenol dove for the deck.

"Alston heah," she said, noting with a corner of her mind that the Gullah accent was creeping back. "We're at Quidnet."

The Cherokee Battalion drew up on the beach. *All twelve jeeps, not counting this command car,* Alston thought. About a platoon's worth of people in the crews. *Pretentious damned name.*

Everything was silence here, save for the ticking of engines; waves crashed gray-blue on the beach, gulls flew, curlews piped. *This would have been illegal before the Event, driving on the beach.* Southward from here was Sconset, where the invaders laired now. At this distance all she could see was smoke, and all she could hear was the distant *pop-pop* of firearms.

"Roger that, Commodore. Major McClintock reports he's pinned the main enemy advance along Milestone Road east of Gibbs, but they're feeling for his flanks—so far he's managed to block them, with *Eagle Eye*'s help. Enemy numbers are well over four thousand and they're putting more men into the fight, plus he reports mortars and light field artillery. He's going to try an attack now. Oh, and he says we need more Gatling guns."

Alston nodded. "Roger. Tell him I'm going to try and ease some of the pressure on him, and I'll tell Mr. Leaton about the Gatlings tomorrow." She looked up; the clouds were thickening. *Please. It rains here half the time anyway, why not today?* "What about the *Farragut*?"

"On schedule so far, Commodore. The other ships will be ready to sail as per."

"Keep it coming, Sandy. Over."

"Over, and good luck, Commodore."

Swindapa was chanting softly as she stood at the grips of the Gatling; there was a curious serenity to her face, a calm that helped Marian control the griping feeling in her stomach.

"Let's go."

With the tide going out, the sand was mostly hard-packed, good enough going for four-wheel-drive vehicles, even with the extra weight. Alston let the commander of the Cherokees take the lead in the first gun-car; he was a tall, lanky ex-ranger of some sort from Oklahoma, who actually *was* part Cherokee and had been over on the mainland for most of the time since the Event. He whooped and waved a hat with a feather stuck in the band as he passed, showing his teeth in what her daddy would have called a shit-eating grin.

"Watch it, cowboy," she muttered, as her driver fell in behind him; there were six other gun-jeeps behind *her*, and the others pulling the heavy mortars behind them in turn.

Swindapa's eyes stayed on the bluff to their right; much of it was covered with scrub, or twisted little Japanese pine stunted by the eternal winds and salt spray. Wisps of her hair escaped the braid and helmet lining, flaring bright when the sun broke through the cloud.

Alston watched her map and the odometer.

All right, we've got Sesachacha Pond to our right, now if we can just get close enough before they notice us—

"There!" Swindapa shouted.

She twisted the Gatling to the right, squeezing the trigger. The little electric engine whined, and smoke and flame spurted as Swindapa walked the burst toward what she had seen.

The fire was only a second too late. A line of fire lanced out from the brush fifty yards away, ending on the side of Captain Sander's jeep. A hollow *boom* followed, and the vehicle blew up in a spectacular globe of fire. The driver of Alston's car shouted and wrenched the wheel. Alston threw up an arm to shield her face; heat slammed across her like a soft, heavy club, and then they were through. The wheels on the right side thumped down on the wet sand, and more sand rooster-tailed forward as the driver slammed on the brakes.

Braaaappp. Braaaaaaap. More black-powder smoke, and a shining stream of .40 cartridge cases fountained across her. The other gun-jeeps had opened up as well, muzzle flashes like red knives through the smoke. Alston saw a man jump upright and run, a stream of bullets licking at his heels. He was wearing a pack-frame on his back, loaded with bullet-shaped rockets that had multiple fins at their rear; when the bullets hit him they exploded in a red flash that left a shallow crater in the sand where he had stood.

Another man came up to his knees, a green-bronze cylinder with flared ends over his shoulder. He pointed it at Alston's gun-jeep; he was only fifteen yards away, close enough for her to see his snarl of concentration. A man behind him flicked an alcohol-wick lighter, touched it to the dangling fuse of a rocket in the tube.

A bazooka, Alston thought, feeling her mouth start to drop open. *I'm about to be killed by a God-damned sheet-bronze bazooka.*

The *braaaaappp,* and a burst walked its way up the sand and into his torso. The tube kicked upward as he convulsed; it fired, and the backwash turned the loader into a shrieking torch that dashed seaward and collapsed in the waves. The rocket soared upward in a long arc and crashed into the water twenty yards offshore.

Riflemen were firing at her. After the rocket launchers, they didn't seem particularly dangerous—an illusion, but a comforting one. The gun-jeeps raked the inland slope with bursts, shredding the low scrub until the fire stopped, and then some, but no more of the Tartessians appeared.

"Forward," Alston said. Then she switched frequencies. "Major McClintock, come in. Commodore Alston here."

The headphones clicked. "McClintock here, over."

"Major, the enemy have some form of portable rocket launcher. We just ran into an ambush party using them."

"So did we, ma'am, just now," McClintock said grimly. "They're pushing us hard, Commodore."

"I'm moving forward to take some of the pressure off, Major," she said. Something cold struck the back of her hand—a raindrop. Her smile was equally cold. "And I think the Gray Lady is giving us some help at last."

"Fall back!"
Crack.
Garrett Hopkins ignored the rifle butt striking his bruised shoulder. The Tartessians were close now.

"And they're not stopping for shit," he said aloud. His voice sounded a little tinny and faint in his ears after the battering they'd taken.

The enemy went to ground again; the one-time field of oats was all trampled now, sodden to the point of being muck with the blood that had poured out on it. He'd never realized how *much* blood a human body had in it before.

"Fall back!"
This time the words penetrated the fog of methodical purpose that filled Hopkins's brain. He loaded once more and looked around. Off to his right Evelyn fired a last shot, reloaded, braced her shoulders against the rear of her foxhole, and began walking her feet up the side in front of her so that she could wiggle out on her back and then roll over to crawl until the ridge slope protected her.

Now that's smart, Hopkins thought. *You don't have to wave your ass in the air crawling out that way.* He began to do likewise but then heard a distant *shooonk* sound, repeated over and over again.

"Oh, sweet *Jesus*," he whimpered and collapsed into the hole, hands holding his helmet down. He'd learned what *that* meant today.

The first mortar shell landed ten yards away. Someone screamed on a single high note for a few seconds, then stopped as if the sound had been cut off by a knife. He heard the whistle of the next coming, coming right for his foxhole.

"Oh, shi—"

Blackness.

When he awoke, the pain was there, strong but somehow distant. He blinked for a moment before he realized that it was rain that was striking his face and that he was lying half out of the collapsed fox-hole, his legs buried to the knee. A few seconds later he realized that what was soaking him below the waist was blood—his own.

I'm dying, he thought, looking down at what was left of himself. Somewhere he knew he should be screaming, or fainting, but at that instant it just seemed another fact. *It's raining. I'm dying.* He knew, in the same abstracted way, that he was very lucky that the shock had hit him this way, and that it wasn't likely to last.

There was a noise to his right. He rolled his head; that took considerable effort, but he was curious.

Three Tartessians—one had a bandage around his head—were pulling Evelyn Grant out of her foxhole. She was alive, but her face was bloodied and her eyes were wandering with concussion from the near miss. One of the mercenaries raised his head and looked around, then said something in a fast-sounding language.

If Hopkins had been able to understand that remote ancestor of the Berber tongue, he would have heard the mercenary say, "No officers here—the Tartessian swine is dead."

The enemy soldiers pulled curved knives out of their belts and began cutting off the Islander's clothes. *I should do something,* Hopkins thought, and moved a hand around. His rifle was gone.

Of course, he thought. *They overran our position. They took the rifles.* Evelyn had waked up enough to struggle a little, and a Tartessian hit her on the side of the head. Then two of them grabbed her legs and pulled them back until her knees were nearly by her shoulders. The other laughed, kneeling and lifting the hem of his tunic.

"Ah," Hopkins muttered. "Got this."

The grenade seemed very heavy, and getting the pin out was difficult. He couldn't throw it.

He *could* let it roll out of his hand, onto the canvas bandolier of grenades the sergeant had given him this morning. There were still six of them left . . .

Blackness.

Alston leveled her binoculars, scanning the Tartessian position and then out to sea. *Eight warships,* she decided; visibility had closed in a little, gray sky over gray ocean. One was out of commission, masts down and firefighters abandoning the ship as she watched. The rest were keeping station, wearing into the strengthening north wind; they'd have to drop anchor or move off, if it got any stronger. There were twenty-five or so transports, some beached. The rest *were* anchored, and making heavy weather of it as the wind picked up.

Ashore . . . hundreds of men, on the beach or moving inland; some tents set up, probably headquarters, stores, and hospital, and a couple of temporary plank roads laid over the sand and up into Sconset itself, with traffic heavy. An artillery park, swarming with effort now, trying to bring some of the guns there to bear on her.

"Here," she said, and the gun-jeeps ahead of her fanned out, jouncing up the low slope to her right until a line of them commanded the ground between the ocean and Sesachacha Pond with interlocking fields of fire. Behind them the mortar haulers and unmodified models pulling tire-wheeled carts full of ammunition halted as well.

Their commander—commander of this whole force now that Sanders was toast—trotted up to the side of Alston's vehicle. Marian offered him a hand, and Captain Stavrand climbed up to stand beside her—a pale young man with large post-Event glasses in wire frames secured by a strap behind his close-cropped white-blond head.

"What a target, ma'am!" he said.

"Well, that's why we're here," Alston said with cold satisfaction. "Your heavy mortars outrange anything they've got on shore, and the Gatlings should be able to keep their infantry off. They can't beat up northward in this wind, so you're safe from their warships; and unless they can walk on water, they can't get over Sesachacha Pond. If they try to embark men in launches and row up to flank you . . . well, the mortars will work in that direction too."

"We can handle it from here, ma'am," he said confidently.

Alston might have smiled at the unspoken subtext: *So will you go away and let me do my job?* Under other circumstances, of course. Right now she simply nodded and looked over the Tartessian ships once more.

"Nothing heavier than five, six hundred tons," she murmured. "Heavy crews, though. Say a hundred, hundred and fifteen guns on seven keels, and some of the transports, add in another twenty . . . fairly light guns, but. . . . Whatever that god-awful explosion out on the water was, it didn't sink too many of them."

Alston cased the binoculars and looked behind her. The thick tubes of the six-inch mortars were going up on their support bipods; the loaders were setting up on the beds of the towing vehicles. That would put them high enough to drop the sixty-pound finned bombs down the waiting muzzles.

"With your permission?"

Marina nodded, and Stavrand vaulted over the side of her gun-jeep, back toward his weapons. The motion would have looked more impressive if his *katana* hadn't caught on the armored coaming, nearly tripping him.

"I hope the Tartessians give up now,"' Swindapa said thoughtfully. Her eyes had narrowed, watching the buzzing confusion of the enemy base area shake itself out; several hundred men were forming lines and trotting toward them.

"It's going to be very . . . *a'HiguinaYA'nazka* if they try to come at us here."

Marian recognized the term; it was untranslatable, meaning something between "repugnant" and "perverted." That was true enough; the only way the Tartessians could storm the gun-jeeps was head-on into automatic weapons fire.

"They probably will try," she said clinically. "They're remarkably stubborn. They're also trying to kill Heather and Lucy."

Swindapa nodded. "That's true," she said, and slapped the Gatling as if to say, *I'm here, aren't I?* "It's still *a'HiguinaYA'nazka.*"

"You're right," Alston said, and keyed the headset

"Rapczewicz here," Sandy's voice said. "*Farragut* and the rest of the flotilla nearly ready, Commodore."

Meaning, are you going to get your black ass back where it belongs, or am I going to have to handle it for you? Marian thought, her mouth turning up at one corner.

"I've gotten a good firsthand on the enemy fleet," Alston said, in half-apology. "What word from McClintock?"

"The enemy are pressing him very hard, but they're not getting through . . . yet," Rapczewicz said.

"Good." *Very* good. "I'm—"

BUDUMPFFFF.

The first of the heavy mortars behind her fired, a slap of pressure and hot air at her neck. The shell arched into the sky and moaned away, a falling note, then exploded a mile and three-quarters southward, not far from a stack of boxes under a tarpaulin. Black smoke gouted into the sky.

"Fire for effect!" Stavrand shouted.

"Let's go," Alston said to her driver. She felt a chill satisfaction as the sand erupted among the enemy. From here they could pound the enemy beachhead into ruin, and there was no way they could strike back. "Back to town."

Isketerol underestimated us, she thought.

He'd seen Nantucket, but only in the immediate aftermath of the Event, when they were still reeling. Since then the Republic had had a decade to find its feet and find out what it could do. Probably Walker could have told his Iberian friend better, but Walker had his own reasons to encourage the enmity.

The gun-jeep swayed as the driver backed, turned, and accelerated smoothly down the beach, taking the firmest sand, just up from the waterline. The rhythmic hammer of the big mortars slapped at her back again, and over that the raw sound of the Gatlings, as if a big sail were ripping under the stress of wind. Only this sound did not stop. . . .

The *Farragut* looked unfinished. "Hell, she *is* unfinished," Marian Alston said softly to herself.

Nevertheless, the war-steamer moved. Her hull form was similar to Marian's own *Chamberlain*'s, long and slender although not quite so large. The snaky low-lying menace of her was emphasized by the lack of masts; she would have three eventually, but those rested in the shipyard still. A tall black stack fumed from just forward of where the mainmast would stand, sending scuts of woodsmoke backward to her stern, the harsh smell thick in the air on *Chamberlain*'s deck.

The main difference was one hard to see from here: the *Farragut*'s bows didn't have the elegant clipper rake of the *Chamberlain*'s. Instead they were a single scimitar curve from waterline to forepeak, and low domed swellings showed where the heads of massive bolts held steel plates to beams.

More black-painted steel showed forward of the paddle wheels, sheltering them from fire when the ram was attacking a target. The wheels churned water into white foam that frothed out the rear of the boxes, as she towed the *Chamberlain*. Other steamers likewise towed the Republic's war fleet out past Brandt Point and through the breakwaters. The north wind would otherwise have pinned them in harbor, perhaps for weeks.

Compromise, Alston thought. It would be a long time before the Republic could build real oceangoing steamers and the worldwide infrastructure to sustain them. Two, perhaps three generations. In her official capacity she regretted that. Personally, she loved the tall white-winged ships she'd built and was glad that there would be another great age of sail.

Today there could be nothing but a bleak practicality. The weather suited her mood, a steady wet rain cutting visibility and blowing chill into her face. The crowd on the battlements of Fort Brandt were anonymous in rain slickers, but she waved anyway at their cheers. It was due them, and Heather and Lucy would be there to see their mothers off.

The sea was rougher as they passed beyond the breakwaters; the ocean between Nantucket and the mainland was shallow, which made for a harder chop in this sort of wind.

"Good," she said, cocking an eye at the sky and estimating with the speed of a lifetime at sea. "I'd say it won't come on to a blow for a while—not today, maybe tomorrow."

Lieutenant Jenkins shook his head. "Wouldn't a storm be a help, ma'am?" he asked. "Those ships the Tartessians have beached would be pounded to pieces, and the rest would have to slip their cables and run."

It was part of her duty to see that junior officers learned. Jenkins was a fine sailor, but not quite enough of a fighter yet.

"True enough, Lieutenant," she said. "But we're not beating off a pirate raid. This is war. I don't want to drive the Tartessian fleet away, I want to *crush* them, to wipe this force off the gameboard and then concentrate on doing the same in their home waters."

"Yes, ma'am," he said, nodding thoughtfully.

The ship had an odd, choppy roll under tow and pitched even more as *Farragut* turned east of north, to round Great Point and move south. She licked salt spindrift off her lips and thought: *Everything's ready.* Full crews—enough to fight both sides on the *Chamberlain*, the *Lincoln*, and the *Sheridan*, plus the smaller ships and schooners. Most of them knew what to do, as well.

"Message to the flotilla," she said, looking out over a sea of gray-blue, infinitely dappled with the rain. "The Republic expects every citizen to do his or her duty. Cast off, make sail, and take stations."

"Cast off!" Jenkins echoed her call through his speaking-trumpet. "Sail stations, sail stations, on the fore, on the main, all hands to stations! Lay aloft and loose all sail!"

Hands took up the lines on deck, and crewfolk swarmed aloft on the wet, swaying ratlines. A sudden thought struck her; when she'd been skipper of the *Eagle,* before the Event, she'd have been gut-anxious right now, afraid that someone would *slip.* The thought brought a slight smile. *How times change when the time changes.*

"Let fall!"

She looked up, squinting against the rain. The yards were studded with figures in yellow oilskins, putting the sails in gear. That had to be done in perfect synchronization with a following wind like this; otherwise the sail could hang up on an unloosed gasket, half on and half off, possibly ripping. Flax canvas just wasn't as strong as Dacron, no two ways about it. There was a thump above as the sails were pushed forward to hang below the yards.

"Gear manned and ready!" came the call from the decks.

"Sheet home the lower topsail! Belay!"

Order and response across the swimming deck, with the wind blowing streamers of water off the waves and over the rail behind her. Jenkins looked at the wind, and to the starboard at the ships nearer the distant white line of breakers on the beaches.

"Haul around on the weather tack and lee sheet! Tend the lee tack and weather sheet!"

She nodded approval as sail blossomed from the bottoms of the masts toward the tops. The *Chamberlain* heeled sharply to starboard as the wind took her, and her motion became a purposeful swoop diagonally across the waves marching out of the north.

"On deck, there!" The commodore looked up sharply at the lookout's hail. "Enemy in sight off the starboard bow—many sail!"

"I'm taking a look," she said. "Lieutenant Commander Swindapa has the deck."

"Ms. Swindapa has the deck, aye!"

She took the stairs to the main deck in three bounds, then jumped to the rail and grasped the wet, tarred rope of the ratlines in her hands. A quick swarming climb, and she was past the tops, up to the swaying junction of mast and topsail yard. There she braced herself and took out her binoculars one-handed, ignoring the long swoop . . . swoop motion of the mast as it traced a great oval in the sky, putting her over rushing gray water more often than the narrow deck.

The Tartessians. And they were making sail too, putting distance between themselves and the beach. Even with the rain there were fires there; she could see mortar shells bursting amid the wreckage of the beachhead, and further north the bright stab of Gatling fire through the gloom. She cased the binoculars and leaned out, gripped a backstay and braced her feet against the ribbed surface of the line to control her descent, then slid down to the quarterdeck in a long gliding flight.

She landed and caught Swindapa's quirked eyebrow. *All right, so I enjoy being able to do that,* Alston thought.

"Lieutenant Commander, message to the fleet. Enemy bearing"—she gave the direction and number. "All ships will follow flagship's lead en echelon; I intend to force a general engagement." Which she could, with the weather gauge and the *Farragut*.

Alston stepped over to the wheels and gave the course as Swindapa ducked into the radio shack. The four crewfolk heaved at the double wheels, and the *Chamberlain* lay further over, shipping foam on her starboard rail. Down below, the gun crews would be hanging on in the swaying dark, lit only by the dim glow of the battle lanterns, waiting.

Not long now, she thought, as the enemy's sails loomed higher and Nantucket sank astern. *Not long at all.*

The *Chamberlain* was leading the flotilla, heading south and east to put herself between the wind and the Tartessians and trap them against a lee shore. The enemy weren't cooperating, of course, cutting at right angles across the wind and nearly due east. That put the two fleets on an intersecting course, like the two sides of a triangle about to come to a point. As always at sea, after the long waiting the closing came with a sudden rush.

"Signal to the *Farragut*," she said. "Signal is *You may proceed.*"

The steamer turned out of line, giving a long, melancholy scream from its whistle that cut through the creak and thrum of a sailing ship under way. Its axe-bow butted a huge spray into the air, steel gray and ice white.

It's fairly rough, she thought. *Their gun decks are closer to the surface than the ones in these frigates. That will give them problems.*

The ram drew away with shocking speed, lunging across the waves. It had picked the fourth in line of the Tartessian vessels, to cut that one and the ships behind off from the foremost division. Alston watched the gunports on the port side of the Tartessian vessel fly open and the muzzles run out. Almost immediately the deep booming of cannon fire cut through the hiss of the rain.

"Too soon," she said. "They should have waited another minute."

Flying iron threw gouts of spray into the air a hundred yards in front of the *Farragut;* few of the balls skipped along the surface in today's weather. Thunder rumbled across the waves as well, like a huge series of doors thudding shut. *Ten guns,* she thought. *Twelve-pounders.* She and Swindapa and Jenkins were all looking at their watches. One minute ten seconds later the first cannon of the second broadside fired, and the rest within fifteen seconds more. *Not bad. Not as good as ours, though.* If you limited "ours" to the Guard frigates and schooners; God alone knew about the dozen civilian Reserve rag-tag-and-bobtail following behind.

Black smoke was pouring up from the *Farragut*'s stack. Once more broadside landed; then the paddle wheels thrashed into reverse, just before the steel-plated bow struck. It hit at a slight angle to the perpendicular, with the momentum of two six-hundred-ton bulks moving together at a combined speed of nearly thirty miles an hour.

The Tartessian ship shivered and pitched, stopping as if it had hit a reef. The foremast whipped forward and then snapped. Sails and mast fell down across the bows of the ship, and the rest of her rigging quivered and shook. And all that was nothing beside the brief glimpse of the damage to her hull as the *Farragut* reversed. Ribs had been smashed and the oak stringers stripped off the side of the ship in a swath fifteen feet long. The Tartessian war craft rolled back to port as the ram released her, and the sea poured in at once. The remaining two masts developed a list, and the open gunports were pointing down toward the sea.

The *Farragut* backed off. The next in line of the Tartessian fleet had yawed, turning further from the wind to bring her guns to bear.

They lashed the steamship and the water around it, but that necessarily presented her flank to the ram. With a dolorous whistle of steam, the *Farragut* began to pick up speed.

Alston turned her attention back to the four ships ahead. The *Chamberlain* was closing in on the first, no more than fifteen hundred yards now, less every second.

"Jenkins," she said, "we'll range up and give the leader a couple of broadsides at . . . mmmm, nine hundred yards." Fairly long range for the Tartessians.

"Then we'll touch up, cut across his stern, rake him—and give the ship following our starboard a broadside at the same time—range alongside, hit him another time or two, and board. Lieutenant Commander, convey my intentions to the rest of the flotilla. Marine sharpshooters to the fighting tops, action stations all."

The drum began to beat, a long, hoarse, rolling call. There was little to do, though, except for the Marines to scramble up the ratlines and take their places in the triangular platforms from which they would rake the enemy deck. Below, all was in readiness as it had been since they'd left port, decks clear, fearnought screens rigged and damped, corpsmen standing by for the casualties. The two Gatling guns clamped to the rails swung, loaders ready with more cylindrical drums of ammunition, gunners' hands on the cranks.

The enemy ship—*probably the flagship*—grew closer. It was a three-masted bark-rigged vessel; she counted twelve gunports and lighter weapons on deck. The same number of muzzles as her vessel, but surely a lighter weight of metal. The decks were black with men, though, and the rigging thick with them too—heavy crew.

Closer. Closer. Below: *"Out tampions! Run out your guns!"*

Drumming thunder below, squeal of carriages, and to her right the black port lids flipping up to show thick muzzles.

"Ready . . ."

"Fire as you bear!"

The two ships were running parallel, just under a thousand yards apart, their sails braced hard to starboard and the wind on their port. *BOOOOMMMMM,* a roaring world of sound as the twelve heavy cannon spoke as one, the *Chamberlain* heeling under their thrust, long blades of flame and clouds of smoke. Jenkins cast a quick look and then turned his eyes back to sail and helm; Alston noticed and felt a quick stab of approval.

"Thus, thus," he said to the helmsmen. "Don't close her—Zenarusson, keep your eye on your work! Thus!"

Her own attention was focused on the results. One ball raised a geyser of foam in the enemy's wake. The others all struck, solid smashing impacts on deck or hull. Then the Tartessian's cannon ran out, each muzzle seeming to point straight at her. She forced herself to objective appraisal; eighteen-pounders, probably.

BADUMMPF.

One gunport wasn't firing, the cannon dismounted, perhaps. The others snarled flame and disappeared backward, recoil hurling the great weights of metal back against the lines and tackle. Three paces in front of her, an iron cannonball cut a seaman in half, blood and matter spraying out in all directions. Alston wiped sticky wetness from her face, knowing that she'd feel it again, in her sleep. Her mind was a calculating machine right now. Two solid hits, from the thumping beneath her feet; a couple of misses, from the splashes in between.

Wounded crewfolk being hurried down the companionways, headed for the surgeon's station. A rattle of lines and blocks on the splinter nets overhead, cut by the passing shot. Bosun and petty officers and riggers swarming upward, knotting and splicing; no major sails down or uncontrollable, a quick flurry of hauling on deck to correct the yawing produced by a severed buntline.

As the guns spoke again, individually this time, the crews completed their leaping dance of reloading and ran them out again. A glance at her watch; ninety seconds, very fast. A slow crackle of rifle fire came from the tops above, snipers with scope-sighted weapons trying their luck. A staysail went flying loose, flapping and entangling. The Tartessian's head started to turn away from the wind, then came back.

Thumped them hard, Alston thought, as the enemy's guns answered. This time there was a screaming from the gun deck, dying away quickly. An eighteen-pounder ball clipped the mainmast, gouging a bite out of the white pine as neatly as a giant's teeth.

Again and again. Her eyes combed the Tartessian vessel, looking for hints . . .

"Brennan," she said to a middie. "To the gun captains; we're going to rake her."

A quick glance backward: the *Lincoln* was lying in the *Chamberlain*'s wake, trading broadsides with the next Tartessian in line. Back at her own opponent: outer and flying jibs down and a thin stream of blood flowing out of her scuppers.

"And the one behind her; we'll fire both broadsides. Then port guns reload with canister; we'll range in, sweep her decks, then board. Boarders and starbolins ready."

The youngster sprang off. She turned to Jenkins. "Now, Mr. Jenkins, if you please."

"Thus, thus!" he said. And "Haul all port, handsomely port!"

The bosun's calls and pipes repeated the call across the deck. The *Chamberlain* spun on her heel, taking the wind on her port quarter now, running before it to cut the Tartessian's wake. She held her breath . . .

"Yes!"

The enemy were too badly damaged to react quickly. The Islander frigate closed the distance with a lunging swiftness, throwing rooster-tails of salt water from her sharp bows. An almighty roar from astern distracted her for an instant; her head whipped around. Fire and a black swelling rising, bits and pieces of timber and probably of people . . . one of the Tartessian ships had blown up.

Back to her own work. Another grumble-rumble, as the portside guns ran out as well.

"Fire as you bear!"

Thudding reports ran back along both sides of the ship from the bows, smoke overwhelming sight for an instant, then blowing on in a mass ahead southward. The *Chamberlain*'s broadside had swept down the Tartessian's gun deck unopposed for a hundred and twenty feet. Even from here she could hear the screaming and could well imagine what damage had been done in those crowded quarters.

"Ready about!" she called.

"Ready . . . come about!" Jenkin's voice replied.

The wheels spun, and the deck teams heaved again at their lines. The *Chamberlain* turned, running east once more. Alston's legs moved automatically to meet the changing slope of the deck, going from horizontal to starboard-down. Close enough to the enemy to toss a ship's biscuit onto their bloody decks—still crowded with men, fighting forward toward the rails, a few even swinging grapnels. Now the Gatling teams spun the clamp-wheels that held their weapons to the starboard rail, lifted the heavy weapons free and rushed them across the deck, set up in a dance of trained hands, and opened fire in a stream that cut men down and sliced lines like a giant's sickle. The port guns ran out again, fired a point-blank wave of grapeshot, crews cheering.

"Boarders!" Alston roared through the smoke. "Boarders!"

The sides of the ships slammed together; grapnels flew, and crew-folk ran out along the spars to lash them together. Armed Guard crew were spilling out of the gun deck, and a column of Marines with their bayonets glittering.

"Boarders away!" Alston shouted. *"Follow me!"* Then she was on the rail, leaping, the slamming punch of impact through her boot soles as she came down on the lower deck of the Tartessian. A shambles, running with blood, dead and wounded everywhere, but more live ones coming at her. Another thud beside her—Swindapa, stumbling slightly on the slippery planks and going down to one knee. A Tartessian sailor lunged at her with a boarding pike, its long steel head a cold glitter in the rain.

Alston pulled the .40 Python from her right hip and shot him in the face at three pace's distance; he fell backward with a round red hole in the bridge of his nose, the back blown out of his skull. One man down, two, another, a miss, and the weapon clicked empty. She threw it into the face of the next and her hands went over her left shoulder and swept out her *katana*, cutting down with the same motion. Ruin flopped at her feet.

Swindapa had done likewise, lunging with a shriek. More Chamberlains were all around her, a tangled, tumbling melee for an instant, and then the enemy were down. She walked over to the shattered wheel, cut the line that held the Tartessian colors, and a crewman ran the Stars and Stripes up to the mizzen. A Tartessian lying with one hand pressed over a seeping redness on his stomach was holding out his sword to her in the other.

"Sur-r-ender," he gasped. "Not kill . . . any more . . . my people . . ."

Alston nodded; their eyes met, and for a moment she felt a kindred grief touch hers.

"Surrender!" she called, and the wounded man added his croak, calling loud enough to bring a grimace of pain.

Fighting died down and ceased. Middies and petty officers got the enemy rounded up and below, sent parties to secure the magazine. Alston looked westward, to where the sun was inclining behind the gray scudding wrack of cloud. The next Tartessian ship had struck as well, the flag of the Republic fluttering from the maintop and the *Lincoln* fast alongside. The one behind was rolling mastless as the *Sheridan* fired another broadside into her at point-blank range.

She took a deep breath. "Let's go finish this mess up," she said.

"In the name of the Council and People of the Republic of Nantucket, this Town Meeting will now come to order."

Jared Cofflin cleared his throat. Ian and Doreen had talked him into that one, then laughed every time they heard it. So had Martha, and so had Marian. *Swindapa and I were the only ones left out of the joke.* Eventually they'd looked it up. *Senatus Populusquae Roma—SPQR,* the letters on the standards of the Roman Republic, "the Senate and the People of Rome." *Very funny.*

The new Town Meeting hall was a lot bigger than the high school auditorium where they'd met for the first few years after the Event. It needed to be. Besides the increase in the population, attendance was way up. The issues decided here were a lot more important these days.

The new hall was out Madaket Road, west of town, not far from the old animal hospital, which given the occasionally zoo-like features of a Meeting, wasn't entirely out of place. It was a huge, timber-framed, barnlike structure, oak and white pine on a poured-slab foundation;

the interior was unadorned save for the lovely curly maple of the bleacher-type seating that surrounded the semicircular stage on three sides.

Behind the speaker's podium were more benches, where councilors and their staffs sat; behind them, covering the wall and as large as a medium-sized topsail, was Old Glory. Martha was sitting beside him on the foremost bench, and Marian Alston on the other, stiffly, with her billed cap on her knees.

Sotto voce she muttered, "We could have had another frigate for the price of this place."

He nodded, more an acknowledgment of what she'd said than agreement. They'd needed a new place for the Town Meeting, too.

Especially today. There were going on three thousand crowded in here, jammed onto benches that normally seated around two-thirds that, and sitting in the aisles as well. The rustle and murmur filled the shadows under the great beams of the roof, and there was a faint tang of animal rage in their scent.

Prelate Gomez walked to the podium and said a brief prayer. That got them quiet, and he went on, "Now we will have a minute of silence for those who fell defending their homes, families, and children."

Silence absolute and complete, except for a quickly hushed baby or two. Ninety-seven people had died during the long day of invasion, heavy losses for a community their size. That over a thousand Tartessians and their mercenaries had also died was very little consolation.

"O Lord God, let Thy wisdom descend on this gathering today, as Your Holy Spirit descended upon the apostles. Let us deliberate with that wisdom, and with humility and lovingkindness; banish fear and hatred from our hearts, that we may seek only what is best and pleasing in Thy sight. In the name of the Father, and the Son, and the Holy Spirit, Amen."

Amen, Cofflin thought, as the same murmur ran through the citizens packed on the benches. *But I'd bet we're going to have a fair bit of hate and fear here today.*

He gave the stout little Portuguese American cleric a nod as they passed. Even if he hadn't liked the man, he'd have made an effort to be polite. In theory the constitution mandated a strict separation of church and state. In practice, with about nine-tenths of the believers in a single denomination, its head necessarily had substantial influence. Believers in God, that was, and not counting followers of Moon Woman and Diawas Pithair.

"Citizens of the Republic," he began. "The first item on the Warrant is a declaration of war against the Kingdoms of Tartessos and Mycenae and any allies they may have. Is the wish of the Sovereign

People that a state of war exist between those two kingdoms and the Republic of Nantucket?"

The answer was a storming wall of sound that made him wish he could flatten his ears like a horse, or at least take a step backward. He let it run its course, waiting until it was dying of its own accord before raising a hand.

"Passed by acclamation," he said.

And that'll make a number of things simpler, he thought. The constitution also gave the chief executive officer a good deal more authority in wartime; he could mobilize the militia, for instance; commandeer ships and other property for another.

"Next item: disposition of the enemy prisoners of war."

A low savage growl went through the Meeting. Cofflin stepped aside for a moment and made a gesture with his hand. Marian Alston walked up to the podium. There was a cheer for her, and Cofflin reflected again how lucky the Republic was that Alston had not an iota of political ambition. Now she stared balefully at the crowd until the noise died.

"All those enemy personnel guilty of violations of the laws of war have been punished," she said flatly. "All remaining prisoners of war will be treated according to the laws of war or I will resign my commission."

That stopped the mutters of "Hang 'em all!" dead in their tracks; Cofflin grinned behind the bony Yankee dolor of his usual expression. Marian went on:

"And morality aside, mistreating prisoners is very stupid. It discourages people from surrendering. Now. We came through this as well as we did because we took precautions."

There was an uneasy shifting on the benches; Cofflin knew that was memories of how he and Marian and the others had had to beg and plead and wheedle to get the necessary money and supplies voted.

"Those precautions were adequate—but only just adequate. If it hadn't rained"—Cofflin nodded; flintlocks didn't like rain—"it might have taken several days and substantially higher casualties to mop up the enemy forces. Now we're in a war, and it's a big, serious war, and I can tell you that half measures are a *really* bad idea. I suggest that we all reflect on that."

The murmur that went through the crowd was slow and thoughtful, and Marian nodded—much better pleased with that, he guessed, than with the earlier cheers. Cofflin went back to the podium.

"Most of the prisoners aren't really Tartessians," he said. "They're from tribes the Tartessians have conquered. They're also trained fighting men, and fairly well equipped. Our military doesn't want them but they'd be very useful to our allies in the Middle East, and most of them seem to be ready to volunteer."

As Marian said, they were mercenaries—and the Republic's gold was as good as Isketerol's.

"The rest will be sent to a prisoner-of-war camp on Long Island, where they can grow their own food and meditate on their sins. Except for some who've requested political asylum in the Republic; the councilor for foreign affairs"—by radio—"strongly recommends that it be granted. Any objections?"

The meeting churned on. Cofflin sighed to himself; he might have far greater powers to act alone during wartime, but he still wanted to have a solid vote behind him. The Town Meeting system could drive him nuts at times, but when the Sovereign People finally made up their minds, nearly everyone got behind what had to be done.

He needed that, because there were going to be some very unpleasant necessities in the next few years. It was time to deal with Walker, before he dealt with them.

"I keep my promises, Sam," William Walker said.

The black ex-cadet nodded, blinking in the bright sun that reflected off the nearby ocean. On the docks of Neayoruk, two tall men stood face-to-face; McAndrews about the same height as the Montanan, with the same broad-shouldered, slim-hipped build, perhaps a little more heavily muscled. By now he wore *katana* and pistol as naturally as any; he'd been one of Walker's troubleshooters for years, commanding troops and helping out Cuddy and others on the organizational side.

And he doesn't approve of me at all, Walker thought. He never had, and leaving behind that girl of his in Alba, in the middle of a probably fatal childbirth, had cemented it.

Walker indicated the ship tied up to the stone pier. It was the type he'd started building in his second year in Greece, a copy of a *gullet,* two-masted, about a hundred and fifty tons burden, with a smooth oval outline and curved-cheek bows. The design was eighteenth-nineteenth-century Levantine, and they were handy little ships. This one carried eight guns and was loaded with weapons, powder, tools, books—none of them the very best Mycenae had to offer (the rifles were all muzzle-loaders, for instance) but a priceless load nevertheless.

The Egyptian in a linen robe standing nearby certainly thought so; he was nearly jiggling from foot to foot in his eagerness to be off, like a kid waiting for the washroom.

"Tell Pharaoh that Mycenae is anxious for alliance," Walker said, dropping back into Achaean . . . which, unlike English, the Egyptian envoy *did* speak.

McAndrews nodded again. Walker hid a grin. Meeting actual ancient Egyptians had been a shock for poor McAndrews. As anyone not besotted with radical Afrocentric horseshit would have known, they looked very much like Egyptians in the twentieth, except a little paler on average because three thousand years of Nubian and Sudanese genes hadn't arrived yet via the slave trade south down the Nile from above Aswan. Meri-Sekhmet, the emissary of Ramses II, was a sort of light toast color, with straight features and brown eyes. His body slave, on the other hand, was unambiguously *black*, which had been another shock to McAndrews.

I think he figures, now, that he can pass the technology on to the Egyptians and then through them to the Nubians. Good luck, you dumb bastard.

McAndrews shook hands, a bit reluctantly, then walked up the gangplank to oversee the crew, which included a number of specialists Walker had let him recruit—again, not the best but passable.

Meri-Sekhmet bowed and exchanged the usual endless pleasantries in atrocious Achaean Greek before he followed. The gangplank swung back and the ropes cast off; the twenty slaves in the tug grunted as they bent to their oars, sweat glistening on their naked, whip-scarred backs. Walker watched in silence as they towed the ship out beyond the stone breakwaters, out into the endless blue of the Laconian Gulf.

Helmut Mittler spoke, his voice still bearing the rough vowels of a North German. "I still say we should have liquidated him, sir."

Walker shook his head. "Remember Machiavelli."

"Sir?"

"Or Frederick the Great, for Christ's sake," Walker said, a little impatient. *Typical Kraut,* he thought. *All "how" and no "why." No wonder they got beat twice running.*

"Ah." Mittler's face cleared. "A prince should only break his word when it's greatly to his advantage—and to do that, he must haff a reputation for great probity."

"Exactly," Walker laughed. "McAndrews will tell Pharaoh that I'm a bastard, but an *honest* bastard, which will come in useful someday. So will Egypt, I think . . . if the damned Nantucketers succeed in linking up with the Hittites. And if the Egyptians are modernized enough to be a significant factor . . ."

"But not enough to be a threat," Mittler said, obviously running over the limitations of the cargo that McAndrews carried.

"Exactly," Walker chuckled.

CHAPTER TWENTY-THREE

May–August, Year 10 A.E.
(May, Year 10 A.E.)

Swindapa smiled as she stepped ashore at Pentagon Base, with the spring wind whipping her hair about her ears. She bent, touching her fingertips to the dust of the White Isle, then to lips, heart, and groin in the gesture of reverence.

It isn't home, not anymore, she thought. Home was the red-brick house on Main, the sea, her daughters, and Marian. Tears prickled behind her eyelids, unshed, and she smiled with a sad joy. *But it is the birthplace of my spirit. Though I may never return here whole-hearted, yet I cannot ever altogether leave either.*

In the history that bore Marian she had died a captive of the Iraiina, and her folk had gone down into a starless dark, overrun by the Sun People and remade in their image.

We saved them from that. O Moon Woman, great is Your kindness to us. Smile on Your children; send us a fortunate star to guide our feet. There was confidence behind the prayer; hadn't Moon Woman twisted time itself to give the dwellers-on-Earth a chance to make a better path?

"When do we get to see Grandma again, Mom?" Heather whispered up to her.

Swindapa stroked her head. "In a day or two, my child," she replied in Fiernan. Her daughters spoke it well; how not, when she'd sung to them in their cradles? "She's at the Great Wisdom, or coming to meet us."

There was the ritual of disembarking to go through, salutes, greetings. She looked curiously about her at the base; it had been nearly two years since she'd seen it, and it had grown like a lusty infant, seeming to change every time she turned around. The five-sided, earth-and-timber fort from when this was the Islander base for the war against Walker and the Sun People was still there, cannon snouting out from its ramparts. Two flags flew there, the Stars and Stripes and the crescent Moon on green that the Earth Folk had chosen.

Sprawling around it was the town that had grown up under its walls. Some called it Westhaven, some Bristol for the name of the place in the other future the Eagle People had come from.

It roared and bustled around them, full of excitement over the Islander fleet that had sailed in out of the dawn. The town had swallowed up the little Earth Folk hamlet that had stood here, but Pelanatorn son of Kaddapal stood there to greet them, grayer but still hale and looking stout and prosperous. His sister Endewarten spoke for Moon Woman here now, since their mother, Kaddapal, had taken the swan's road beyond the Moon—died, as the short-spoken English tongue put it. Four or five thousand others dwelt here now; mostly her birth-people, but perhaps one in four were Islanders, and there were hundreds of others from anywhere on this side of the water within reach of Islander ships.

The air smelled of their doings, of woodsmoke and coal smoke, of fresh-cut timber and brick-kilns and mortar, of hot iron and brass; it was filled with the clamor of hooves and hammers, the whirring of machines, the *chuff . . . chuff . . .* of steam.

They walked up toward the fortress in company with Commander Hendriksson, the base commandant; the town itself was under Nantucket law, mainly because Earth Folk custom had no way to deal with such a huddling of people without lineage ties. Lucy and Heather dropped back to walk with the commandant's children, their initial shyness dissolving in chatter. A policeman watched them go by; another thing the Earth Folk had not had before, or need for it.

But nobody need carry a spear when they drive their cattle to water, either, Swindapa thought. Aloud, she said: "Many more buildings."

"Mmmm-hmmm," the black woman replied, brought out of her thoughts. "All sorts, too."

The streets were mostly paved with brick, and over them traffic brawled and bustled. More manufactures had opened on the outskirts, where roads gnawed into field and forest, and the docks were thronged with ships. Swindapa smiled to see that some of them were captained as well as crewed by her folk. Those who studied the Stars made good navigators.

Many of the shops—carpenters, smiths, wainwrights, saddlers— had signs out advertising for apprentices, who would also be mostly Earth Folk. So were the workers in the new industries, the healer-helpers studying in the new hospital, and many of the students in the Islander school.

We learn, she thought. A haildom of Moon Woman stood near a Christian church. *And the Eagle People learn from us, as well. What comes of it will have the bone and blood of both of us in it.*

She smiled more broadly yet to see a charioteer chieftain of the Sun

People drive by, gawking in awe. He carried a steel sword at his waist, and his horses were shod in the same iron that rimmed the wheels of his war-car. But a Spear Chosen of the Fiernan Bohulugi rode past him on horseback, feet in the stirrups, a musket at his saddlebow, ignoring him with lordly contempt. The charioteer flushed, but the peace of the Alliance held his hand.

"I'd really better go on to the Great Wisdom first," she said to Marian. "The Grandmothers will be more ready to listen to you after I've listened to them. I'll take the children on, and they can visit with Mother and their cousins."

A smile replied, the same rare beautiful thing that had captured her heart.

"I'll miss you, sugar. A few days, then."

The road up from Pentagon Base was less of a rutted track now. *More of a rutted road,* Swindapa thought, as a warm spring shower cleared and she pulled off her oilskins and tossed them across the saddlebow, then looked around with delight on the mellow evening that brought them up onto the downland country, her oldest home.

Wind chased cloud-shadow over the great open roll of the countryside, fluttering the grasses and the leaves of the beech trees in patches of forest on hilltops. It was intensely green and fresh, and even when the scents—cut grass, horse, damp earth—were the same as in Nantucket, they were different in a subtle way her nose knew even if she had no word for it. Here and there she saw a barrow-grave of the ancients rising as an island of green turf, perhaps speckled with the gray-brown or white of sheep. The whitewashed wattle-and-daub walls of the round houses, great or small, were marked with intricate patterns of soot, ochre and saffron that told stories her eyes could read. Clumps of greenweed starred the pasture with yellow gold, and there were crimson tormentil, betony, hawkbit, the blue of clustered bellflowers; butterflies exploded upward at the clop of horses' hooves, meadow browns, marbled whites.

Every now and then she reached out to touch the shoulder or arm of her mother; strange to have her riding a horse, wonderful that it was beside her. And the horse itself had come west-over-sea from what the Sun People called Jutland, brought by Fiernan traders now that the beasts had so many more uses than war.

"Are you still happy, child of my womb?" Dhinwarn said.

"Oh, very," Swindapa replied. "Into what star-path-through-shadow (life, living) isn't rough-going-storm-cold (weeping-laughing) woven? Mostly, very happy."

It was good to speak Fiernan again. Enough to begin thinking in it, even if that meant groping for a word now and then when she used an Islander concept.

Her mother grinned at her. "Even without—" she made a gesture with one finger.

Swindapa chuckled, held up her hand in the same gesture, added the other fingers together, and moved the hand rhythmically.

"Without nothing, and it's never tired at that!" she added, and they shared a bawdy laugh.

Marian would be so *embarrassed,* she thought, smiling fondly.

"I see you are happy; Moon Woman has set stars at your birth that called you to a strange way, but not a bad one," Dhinwarn said. She shook her head. "It's strange and frightening, this *love-between-only-two people* the Eagle People have. Yet not a starless thing or a turned-back path."

"No, wonderful and terrifying," Swindapa agreed. It had scared her at first, that her whole life should be so wrapped up in only one other. "There's nothing so warm; it's like being *inside* the fire, without being burned."

Heather and Lucy raced by on their ponies, waving and shouting to their mother; an uncle pursued them, swearing and laughing at the same time.

"Those two are fine girls," Dhinwarn said. "You should bring them here more often."

"As often as the stars set a path for it," Swindapa said.

She looked around at the countryside. Not everything was as she remembered, even from her last visit. There were new crops amid the familiar wheat and barley and scrubby grass of fallow fields. Machines were at work, cultivators and disc-plows pulled by oxen—or sometimes by shaggy ponies that had once drawn only chariots. The whir of a hay-mower's cutting bar made a new thing in the long quiet of the White Isle.

More stock, she thought. *More fodder to overwinter it. New byres and sheepfolds, too. Bigger beasts, some of them.* Something teased at her eye, until she realized it; she'd seen scarcely a single woman spinning a distaff as she walked or sat. *Thread comes from the machines now.*

Some of the small square fields had been thrown together for the convenience of the animal-drawn reapers the Eagle People had brought, too, changing the very look of the land. If you looked closely, there were other changes; iron tools in the hands of the cultivators, more and more colorful clothes and cobbled shoes on the dwellers, brick-walled wells, the little outhouses that the Islander medical missionaries had advised and the Grandmothers agreed to make part of the purity rituals, here and there a chimney, or a wagon with a load of small cast-iron stoves, or a wind pump.

"More changes than you would think, and more every year—like a rock rolling downhill," Dhinwarn told her, sensing her thought. "Some are discontented, thinking they break old harmonies. Others say no, best of all so many more of our children live and grow healthy."

Her smile grew slightly savage. "And because we listened first, we grow faster than the Sun People in all ways, wealth and knowledge and numbers. Many of them come west now—not to raid, but asking for work or learning."

Swindapa nodded. "We had to become other than we were, or cease to be at all," she agreed.

They spoke more, but her voice was choked off when the Great Wisdom itself rose above the horizon on the east, looming over the bare pasture as it had been made to do so many centuries before. She had seen the pictures on Nantucket, of the great stones shattered and abandoned, their true purpose lost. There were times when that image seemed to overwhelm her memories, but here the Wisdom stood whole and complete, the great triathlons and the bluestone semicircle . . .

She began to sing under her breath, the Naming Chant that called each stone by its title, and listed the Star-Moon-Sun conjunctions that could be sighted from it—not only the great ones, the Midwinter Moon that chased the flighty Sun back to Its work of warming the Earth dwellers, but the small friendly stars that governed the hearth or the best time to take a rabbit skin.

Marian never could sink her mind into this, she thought. *Odd, for she knows the Eagle People's counting so well. Perhaps it's that she can't see that a word can be a number too.*

Beside her Heather and Lucy grew quiet until she finished, their lips silently following along on some of the simpler bits. When she was done and waved them ahead they clapped heels to the ponies and rode off to the north, toward the Kurlelo greathouse, shouting greetings to cousins they hadn't seen for a quarter of their short lives. Swindapa stood in the stirrups and shaded her eyes with a hand.

The huge round, half-timbered shape of the greathouse, with its conical roof of thatched wheat-straw, looked subtly different. A metal tube at the apex . . .

"You put in a copper smoke-hood!" she said, delighted.

Her mother nodded and took off her conical straw hat. "It's much easier on the eyes now," she said. "*And* warmer in winter. Better for the girls doing the Chants, too." She smiled. "We've so much more time for that! More time for songs and stories, for making bright-please-eye-warm-heart-joy-in-hands things."

Swindapa's smile died as she remembered that this was not only a visit. It was a meeting, and the news was of war. The Grandmothers didn't decide such matters; that wasn't their business, save where the Sacred Truce was concerned. But those who *did* decide such matters would listen carefully to their opinions.

"Uhatsna InHfija, Inyeta, abal'na," the elder of the Grand mothers in the circle began, as the last of those who felt they should be here drifted into the smaller round hut and ranged themselves about its hearth. Her owl-headed staff nodded in her hand.

There were a score and one in all, a lucky number, although nobody had arranged it thus. Swindapa breathed in the scent of woodsmoke and thatch and cloth and sweat . . . yet even this wasn't as it always had been. The smells included soap, the bitter scent of hops, and one of those sitting around the whitewashed wall was wearing glasses.

"A good star shine on this meeting. Moon Woman gather it to her breast. We're here to talk, let's talk," the Eldest said.

She picked up the sticks in her hands, tapping lightly along their colored, notched lengths. Each notch and inset in the yard-long wands marked some happening, or feeling, or shade of meaning. They squatted on their hams around the fire, shadows flickering on their faces— wrinkled crone, stout matron whose drooping breasts were proud sign of the children she had borne, Swindapa the youngest of them but the one whose path had wandered beyond Time along the Moon-trail. Others, star-students, Rememberers, Seekers.

The Grandmothers of the Great Wisdom.

The Eldest spoke, with her voice and with the flashing sticks: "Would that the Eldest-Before was with us, who first greeted the Eagle People, was here."

She saw so far, so much. I'm lost without her.

Another set of sticks took up the tapping rhythm. "You sat by her feet a long time. We'll listen to you; there are many here, we'll find out what Moon Woman wants. Everybody rides the Swan sometime."

Love, trust.

Greatly daring, Swindapa took up her rods. She'd made them herself, on the voyage over. They looked different; more angular, in parts, with strange colors. That showed her spirit . . .

"I've seen the changes here. Most of them are happy."

Doubt, uncertainty, a tremulous joy, children laughing, cattle lowing, peace.

More tick-tapping, weaving in and out. An older woman spoke: "Happy for now. In the many-cycles to come, who knows."

Doubt, nagging worry—concern.

The eldest: "Eldest-Before saw only a darkness without stars before the feet of the Earth Folk, before the Eagle People came from out of time."

Relief, joy, an aching not noticed until it went away.

Another: "We thought we'd have peace, but now the Eagle People are talking of a war, far away, with people who never harmed us. Is that the path Moon Woman's stars reflect, now?"

Distaste, wariness, doubt, doubt.

"Moon Woman shines in all the lands—who aren't Her children? The Eagle People came from very far to help us, shouldn't we do the same for others?"

Resolution, resignation.

"Earth Folk have never carried spears so far. Bad enough to fight for our own hearths."

Blood, mothers burying children, burning, grief, wrongness.

Swindapa took up the exchange. Her people were great rememberers. So:

"Once the Earth Folk lived from the Hot Lands to Fog-and-Ice place. We didn't carry spears beyond our own neighborhoods, but the *dyaus arsi,* the Sun People, they carried them everywhere. One fight, another, everyone hoped each would be the last. And when the Eagle People came, we'd gone back so far our heels were wet in the ocean at our backs. Not everything is good, just because we always did it."

Resolution, fierceness, sadness.

Another voice: "There's too much of the *dyaus arsi* in the Eagle People, for my taste. They are a restless breed; even in their Wisdom Working they cut everything up, then stick the bits together to suit them. Bossy, rude, turn-up-the-nose-we-know-best. I don't like this Father-Son-Spirit teaching they bring, either."

Irritation, disquiet, longing for peace, for the endless turning-in-harmony-growing.

Swindapa: "Yes, they descend from the Sun People, but with some of us in them, too. And an acorn doesn't look much like an oak; you can't eat an apple until it's ripe."

Patience, waiting-becoming, patience.

Another: "There's more than one road to the same place. Call an apple an ash, it's still an apple—the Father-Son-Spirit-Mother doesn't teach as Diawas Pithair did. If the Eagle People are greedy and fierce, they don't take it out and stroke it the way the charioteers do."

Wonder, acceptance.

Dhinwarn: "They gave my daughter back to me, when she was taken from the Shining World. They beat back the Burning Snake for her, that had eaten all her dreams."

Love, warmth, hearthache-assuaged, joy.

The words went back and forth, until the words faded out of it and there was a tapping chorus of agreement, woven in and among the humming song. After a while they began to sway, and then they rose, dancing in a spiral. The spiral wove out of the hut, and an owl hooted and flew above them as they swayed and hummed toward the Great Wisdom.

"This is more Ian and Doreen's kind of work than ours," Swindapa said, drawing her horse a little aside.

Marian cocked an eye at her and chuckled. "First you grumble about how we're always fighting," she said. "Now we're playing at diplomats, and you complain about *that.*"

Swindapa smiled herself, then sighed and shrugged. "I don't like going among the Sun People much," she said.

Marian nodded sympathy. "Don't let them make you *il'lunHE peko'uHOtna*, then," she said.

That meant something like *gloomy;* or perhaps *dark-spirited* or *Moon-deprived.* Even after these years, she still found the Earth Folk language a tangle; she suspected that you had to grow up speaking it to truly understand it well. Still more the dialect of Swindapa's home, where they piled pun upon allusion upon myth in a riot of metaphors.

"You're right, my *Bin'HOtse-khwon,*" Swindapa said. "But I miss the children."

"So do I, sugar, but they're happy enough at your mother's place for a while."

The Islander party drew rein at the edge of the woodland trail, looking downward. The sun of the summer evening cast long shadows across them, and over the landscape that stretched away to the marshes by the Thames—the Ahwun'rax, the Great Chief River. In one course of the tides of time, this was the border of southern Buckinghamshire, not far from Windsor. Here it was the tribal lands of the Thaurinii folk, the *teuatha* of the Bull.

The stockaded *ruathaurikaz* of their chieftains stood atop a low chalk cliff above the river. Faint and far, a horn droned. Below, at the foot of the heights, lay that which made this clan more important than most. The river split around a long oval-shaped island; from the south bank a bridge of great timbers reached to the isle, and another from there to the north shore. Boats lay at anchor downstream of them; even from here Marian could see that some of them were quite large, one a modern design, probably out of Portsmouth Base or Westhaven.

Around the fortlet lay open pastureland where shaggy little cattle and horses and goatlike sheep grazed. Fields were smaller than the grazing, wheat and barley just beginning to show golden among the green; hawthorn hedges marked them out, or hurdles of woven willow withes. Farmsteads lay strewn about, dwellings topped with gray thatch cut from river reeds. Men at work in the fields, women hoeing in gardens, all stopped and pointed and stared, the racket of their voices fainter than the buzzing of insects. Not far away a girl in a long dress and shawl squeaked as she heard the thud of hooves and rattle of metal. She almost dropped the wicker basket of wild strawberries in her hands, then took to her heels, yelling.

Apart from that there was no sign of alarm, no signal fires or glints from a gathering of spearheads; instead the folk gathered to stare and point, some crying greetings. The peace of the Alliance lay on the land of the Thaurinii, with not so much as a cattle raid to break it. There had always been more trade here than in most steadings; the boats marked it, and the sign of many wagons on the roadway.

Dust smoked white under hooves and wheels as they rode down the gentle slope. The sun was hot for Alba, and sweat prickled her body under the wool and linen of her uniform. Behind her the Marine guard drew into a neat double rank of riders, with the Stars and Stripes of the Republic at their head. Behind them were the two-wheeled baggage carts and the attendants that Sun People respectability required.

The horn dunted again from the chieftain's steading, and the narrow gate swung open. No chariot came out of it; the reports were accurate, then—this particular tribal hegemon was progressive, as such things went in the Year 9. Instead of the traditional war-cart, he and his rode horseback, with saddles and stirrups made to Nantucketer models. They did carry weapons, but that was to show respect to warrior guests, swords slapping at sides in chased bronze scabbards or the more common axes across saddlebows, painted shields across their backs.

Likewise their finery, bright cloaks and tunics in gaudy patterns, kilts pyrographed in elaborate designs—or, for some, Islander trousers. The leader wore a tall bronze helmet with great ox horns mounted on it, the totem of his tribe. Beside him was a younger man whose helm was mounted with a metal raven, its wings flapping as his horse cantered; that was bravado, a declaration that he claimed the favor of the Crow Goddess, the Blood Hag of Battles. Behind the chieftain and his retainers walked trumpeters blowing on long, upright horns. Their bellowing echoed back from trees and river and palisade and a storm of wildfowl took wing from the water.

Marian flung up her hand. The trumpeter behind her blew his bugle, and the little column came to a halt. A wind from the river flapped out the red-white-and-blue silk of Old Glory, and the gilt eagle above it seemed to flap its wings as well.

"I am Commodore Marian Alston-Kurlelo," she said in the local tongue. "Daughter of Martin, War Chief of the Eagle People."

That harsh machine-gun-rapid speech came easily enough to her now; the complex inflections and declensions were simple, compared to her partner's language.

"We come in peace," she went on, "to speak for the Republic to the chieftains of Sky Father's children." They'd undoubtedly heard of the mission and its message by now, but the forms had to be observed.

The older man nodded. He was tall for this era, an inch or two more than Marian. His brown beard was in twin braids and his hair in a ponytail down his back, the traditional Sun People styles. The face was handsome in a battered way; in his mid-thirties, early middle age by contemporary standards. The little finger of his left hand was missing, and his tanned skin was seamed with thin white scars; all in all he looked tough enough to chew logs, but the green-hazel eyes were friendly enough. Unlike those of some of his followers . . .

"I am Winnuthrax Hotorar's son," he replied. "Rahax of the Thaurinii folk. Be you guests and peace-holy beneath my roof and among my people. May the long-speared Sky Father hear me, and the Horned Man, and the Lady of the Horses. May your crops stand thick and your herds bear fruitfully; may your wi—" He coughed, paused, and ammended the traditional "May your wives bear many sons." "May your household prosper."

"Long life and fruitful fields, weather-luck and victory-luck and undying fame be yours, Winnuthrax son of Hotorar," Marian said ceremoniously. "May many descendants make sacrifice at your grave in times to come. May the God of my people guard you and all yours."

Winnuthrax smiled, nodded, and dismounted. "Your God is a powerful God," he said, as Marian joined him. A youth came up with a platter of bread and salt, and a cup of mead. "As we learned on the Downs."

"You were there?" she said, sprinkling the bread and taking a bite. The two leaders pricked their thumbs and squeezed a drop of blood into the mead, then shared the cup.

"Indeed, I led my tribe's war band to the battle on the Downs, following the wizard," he said casually. "Likely I'd have laid my bones there if I hadn't taken an arrow through my shoulder. Your Eagle People healers found me after our host fled, and it healed clean. Otherwise you'd be dealing with my son here. Eh, Heponlos?"

The young man with the raven-decked helmet nodded. When he removed the helm, she saw he was short-haired and that his beard was cropped close to his jaw—Eagle People styles.

"So I know your God is strong to give victory," Winnuthrax said. He inclined his head politely to Swindapa. "And so is Moon Woman, of course, lady. . . . Some of my people here have taken the water-blessing of your Eagle People skylord, He of the Cross, and the crops haven't suffered, so the land-spirits don't mind. I'd make Him sacrifice too, but His priests and priestesses say He won't have those who don't forsake others."

Marian nodded and walked by the Thaurinii chieftain's side as they led their horses up the slope to the stockade. She wasn't surprised at the chief's lack of resentment; the Sun People tribes didn't feel any lasting grudge at being beaten in a straight-up battle, and the Americans hadn't ravaged their homes or harmed their families—quite the contrary—they'd prevented reprisals by the Fiernan Bohulugi, who *did* carry grudges. There were plenty of the easterners who resented the Alliance, but it was for other things.

"You've prospered, chieftain," Marian observed as they walked.

The broad shoulders shrugged. "We've always been traders here as well as fighters—there's blood of Moon Woman's people in us, for all that we're Sky Father's children now. More trade of late, yes; and some of our young men have taken work on your ships, or in your war bands. The gold they win buys us new things, and those who return bring new knowledge and seemly ways."

His son tossed off a creditable salute and smiled when Marian returned it in reflex.

"Hard Corps, fuckin' A," he said in English that was heavily accented, but fluent. "Corporal Heponlos Winnuthraxsson, Marine rifleman aboard *Frederick Douglass* on the Baltic expedition, ma'am."

"Thank you, but we've sworn an oath to the Eagle People God to lie with none but each other," Marian said politely.

"As you wish, of course," Winnuthrax said, raising his mead-horn. He looked a little relieved; the obligations of Thaurinii hospitality hadn't been designed with this sort of cross-cultural contact in mind. The servant girl he'd summoned looked relieved as well . . . or possibly that was a look of disappointed curiosity rather than anxious relief.

"*I think it's 'disappointed curiosity' this time,*" Swindapa whispered in her ear, grinning.

Marian snorted. "You're much prettier," she murmured back. "And you don't have nearly as many fleas."

Something like this happened every time they guested overnight at a Sun People chieftain's steading, but her partner still found it endlessly entertaining. Then again, the Fiernan language didn't even have a *word* for monogamy; it was something Swindapa did out of love, because her partner cared about it. Marian looked at the servant girl's neck; no scars, although she'd probably been wearing a collar until a few years ago. The prohibition on slavery in the Alliance treaty hadn't been as hard to enforce as she'd once feared, but she suspected from the reports and her own observations that the abolition was often more a matter of form than fact, particularly in the backwoods.

Oh, well, Rome wasn't built in a day. Not everyone who worked in the Republic or served in its ships and regiments stayed on; plenty went back home, like her host's son. That brought its own problems, but it carried the seeds of progress.

The hall of the Thaurinii chiefs reminded her strongly of the others they'd guested in over the past month, a sameness that underlay differences of detail. The walls were wickerwork thickly daubed with clay, between a framework of inward-sloping timbers that turned into the crutch-rafters that carried the thatch of the roof. The chief's seat was in the middle of the southern wall, a tall chair of oak and beech, its rear pillars carved in the shape of the Twin Horsemen, their most notable feature their erect luck-bringing philli. A second chair was for the most honored guests; everyone else sat on stools, or on benches, or the floor, with sheepskins and blankets beneath them if they were lucky.

She noticed one difference there; the floor was mortared flagstones, rather than dirt covered by reeds. There were still fire pits down the center of the floor, but there was also an iron heating stove with a sheet-iron chimney, both probably turned out here in Alba at Islander-owned plants. The feast had been mostly traditional—roast pork, mutton, beef, and horsemeat with bread—but there had been potatoes and chicken as well.

The Thaurinii differed from the more easterly tribes in some other respects too; the women of the chief's family had eaten with them, although they were withdrawing to the other end of the hall now that the serious drinking was supposed to begin. Probably residual Fiernan influence. She and Swindapa were being treated essentially as warrior-class men, of course, but she was used to that. Irritating, but not unbearably so.

Progress, she thought. *Longest journey, single step, and all that.*

Leaping shadows from the fire pits gleamed on the gold or copper that rimmed whole-cowhorn cups, on bright cloth and gold torques around hairy necks, on the weapons and shields hung on the walls between bright crude woolen hangings—she hid a smile at the printed Islander dish towels that held pride of place. Sun People art was often quite good of its kind, but when they fell for Nantucketer stuff they tended to nose-dive into the worst kitsch available. The air smelled of woodsmoke, cooking, a little of sweat and damp dog, but not very unclean—there had been a bathhouse here before the Event, although Winnuthrax had improved it with soap and a real tub since.

They're really not such bad sorts, Alston told herself. *Of course, they're warlike and macho to the point of insanity, and cruel as cats to anyone who isn't a blood relative or an oath-sworn ally, and they'd a thousand times rather steal something than make it themselves, but they have their points.* They were brave, and many of them were even honest . . .

Winnuthrax leaned over to refill her horn. Marian sighed; headache tomorrow, but at least they weren't breaking out distilled liquor— when that met a tradition of heroic imbibing, the results could be gruesome.

"So, this is the same war as the one in the distant hot lands, closing in on the wizard Hwalker's lands? Some of my folk enlisted with your Marine war band for that—two young men outlawed for kine-reaving outside the bans, Delauntarax's daughter who ran away—but she was, ah, strange—and half a dozen who were just restless or poor or all together. The Cross-God priest at Seven Streams mission brings their letters to us sometimes and reads them. Much good fighting there, gold, good feasting, strange foreign lands to see. If I were younger, I'd be tempted myself."

"I *am* younger, and I *am* tempted," his son Heponlos said.

"No, and again, no," his father said, exasperated. "You are my heir."

"You could pick one of my uncle's sons and ask the Folk to hail him."

"No!"

Winnuthrax sighed, and then shrugged. "Well, you can see there's no shortage of young men anxious to blood their spears."

Marian nodded. "Yes, this is the same war—but a different part of it. Isketerol of Tarktessos is an ally of Walker's, and he attacked us this spring. We slaughtered them then, and now we take the fight to their homeland. We don't require your aid under the Alliance, but we ask it as oath-friends."

"Hmmm." Winnuthrax rubbed at his beard and then cracked something between thumb and forefinger. "Well . . . yes, that's what I've heard."

A feral light gleamed in his son's eyes. "Tartessos swims in gold, they say; wine and silver and oil and cloth, many fine things."

Marian felt Swindapa's faint snort beside her. *Yes, I know,* she thought. *They* are *a bunch of bandits. But for now, they're* our *bunch of bandits.*

"It'll be a serious war," she said.

"But you'll be supplying weapons?"

She nodded, a trifle reluctant. The charioteer tribes would do anything to get their hands on firearms; the Republic kept modern ones— as "modern" was defined in the Year 9, meaning breechloaders—out of their hands as far as possible.

"Hmmm. Well, I'll speak to the folk, talk to the heads of household, and hear their word," Winnuthrax said.

He was a long way from an autocrat; war-leader, yes, but there was an element of anarchic democracy to these tribes, at least as far as free adult males were concerned.

"Let it never be bandied about that the Thaurinii don't stand by their oaths and their friends, and you've dealt well with us, that's beyond dispute." He sighed again. "And enough of business—tomorrow, I can show you some boar worth the trouble of carrying a spear!"

This time it was Marian who sighed. Swindapa had taken the Spear Mark as a teenager, uncommon but not rare for a Fiernan girl; she actually *liked* hunting big dangerous pigs with a spear. Marian Alston liked hunting, but sensibly, with a gun. Still, you had to keep face. Sun people hospitality was like that; sacrifice, chanting and blood and fire, to put the guest in right with the tribal gods; sonorous ancestral epic; gluttonous feasting, drinking, boasting . . .

All very Homeric, but a month is about all I can take, she thought. Nearly over, thank God, and then she could get back to the sort of rational preparation she felt comfortable with.

"No, boss, I *can't* do that," Bill Cuddy said. "Not a straight copy."

He was sweating, a little. Usually Walker was sensible enough, but his temper was more uncertain than usual after the reverses in the East. It was times like these you remembered that he only had to shout, and the guards would come in and kill you—or even worse, hand you over to Hong.

There are times I really wish I hadn't listened to Will, Cuddy thought, forcing himself to meet the cold green eyes and shrug. *Yeah, I've got a mansion and a harem and I'm richer than god, and the work's interesting, but sometimes . . .*

The windows of the private audience room were open; outside, the blue-and-white-checked-marble veranda had an almost luminous glow under the afternoon sun, and the trails of hot-pink bougainvillea that fountained down the sides of man-high vases were an explosion of color. The warm herbal scents of a Greek summer drifted in, and the sound of cicadas, almost as loud as the city-clamor of Walkeropolis beyond. A servant entered and removed the remains of a pizza—Walker had eaten at his desk today, things were moving fast—and another knelt and arranged a tray of hot herbal tea, cold fruit juice, watered wine, and munchies. Bill Cuddy didn't feel at all like eating, even those little pickled tuna things on crackers with capers, which he was usually pretty fond of.

Walker indicated the rifle that lay on his desk, acquired at enormous expense via the Tartessian intelligence service in Nantucket.

"That doesn't look too complicated."

"No, boss, it ain't. It's a fucking masterpiece of simplicity; Martins could make one of these by hand, filing it—parts wouldn't be interchangeable, but it'd work. So, yeah, I can make the rifle, no sweat. It'll cut into our Westley-Richards output, total production'll go down for six months, maybe a year—but not all that bad. Besides the loading mechanism and ammo, it's pretty much the same gun—bit better ballistic performance, is all."

"You're telling me you can, and then you can't?" Suddenly Walker smiled, an open, friendly grin, and thumped his forehead with the heel of his hand. "Oh, wait a minute—it's the ammo, right?"

He spun a brass cartridge on the table next to the rifle; the polished metal caught the sun that came through the French doors and spilled flickering shadows across furniture inlaid in ivory, silver, and lapis lazuli.

"Yeah, boss. Look, I could turn out small quantities, yessir. Machining rounds from solid bar stock, maybe—but that'll eat materials, and Christ, it'll tie up an entire lathe all day to turn out a couple of hundred! The drawing and annealing plant to turn out *millions* of those fuckers—no way. Not in less than three, four years—and to do that, I'd have to pull all my best people off other stuff, *and* off teaching. I mean, Jesus fucking Christ, boss, I just don't have the range of machine tools that Leaton does, or electric power sources or—and he doesn't have to teach all his trainees to goddam *read* first!"

"Okay," Walker said grudgingly. "God *damn.* This is going to hurt morale—the men aren't used to the other side having more firepower." A wry smile. "And I'm used to having you pull miracles out of your hat."

The smile didn't reach all the way to the eyes; Cuddy felt himself beginning to sweat again. "Well, yeah, we can't do *that* ammo yet, but I've had an idea."

"Oh?" Cool interest this time, complete focus.

"Yeah. Actually I was busting my ass trying to figure out how we were going to do what Leaton did, and it occurred to me—why not do an end run instead? So I looked up some stuff I remembered from that book you've got, the one by the dude called Myatt, some Limey Major or something . . ."

"The *Illustrated History of Nineteenth-Century Firearms*?" Walker said, nodding unsurprised. They'd already gotten a *lot* of use out of that one.

"Yup. So I thought, they must have had a lot of problems with drawn-brass stuff to begin with, maybe they had something else? Something that didn't work quite as smooth but that still did the job?"

Walker nodded again; that was also something they had a lot of experience with.

"So here it is."

He reached down into the leather briefcase at his side and handed over a round of ammunition. Walker took it and turned it over in his hands. It was made a little like a shotgun shell, built up of iron and brass and cardboard.

"The thing like the iron top hat, that's the base," Cuddy said. "Primer we can do—I've been dicking around with mercury fulminate for nine years now; you should crucify me if I hadn't made *some* progress. Percussion cap in the base, then you *wrap* a strip of thin brass around that, and then that holds the cardboard tube with the bullet and powder."

The lynx eyes speared him. "Tell me the disadvantages."

"It's not as strong as the regular type. Not completely waterproof, either. And the brass, when the chamber's *real* hot, it may glue itself to the walls and jam, or tear apart when the extractor hits. But it'll *work*, boss. I can duplicate this rifle, all it needs changed is the shape of the chamber, and I can turn out this ammo in quantity—simple stamping and rolling, and then handwork assembly-line style."

"Cuddy, you're a fucking genius!" Walker leaned back in his swivel chair, a dreamy smile on his face. "You say it would have screwed us if I'd ordered you to go ahead on duplicating the ammo?"

"Up the *ass,* boss, totally. Not just losing production, but it would have dicked up our expansion program by tying up my people."

A harsh chuckle from his overlord. "One gets you ten, that's *exactly* what they planned!" His hand struck the desktop with a gunshot crack. "That bitch Alston thinks she has me typed—and she's smart, I *nearly* did that."

Cuddy swallowed and looked away. Alston was the only thing that could make Walker's eyes look, for a moment, entirely too much like Alice Hong's for comfort.

Walker went on, "What about the Gatlings?"

Cuddy shook his head again. "No way, bossman. The ammo isn't strong enough to be hopper- or clip-fed." His grin went wider. "But."

"But?"

"But the same book had an idea the Frogs used, back around Gatling's time. You take a whole bundle of rifle barrels, say seventy-five of them, and clamp them together. You load them with plates in a frame—the plates hold the ammo. Load a plate in, wham, hit the trigger, take the plate out, put in another one." He held up a hand. "Yeah, heavier and slower than a Gatling, but it'll work."

"Cuddy, you are my *main man*! Get right onto both of them. Top priority."

Cuddy rose, nodding; he paused to greet Helmuth Mittler on the way out. He and the head of Section One weren't all that close—the ex-Stasi agent reminded him too much of cops who'd busted him in the past, those pale eyes with the I've-got-the-goods-on-you look. Still, the former East German did good work . . . and it was just as well to keep on the good side of him, he was important at court too.

Maybe I'm not sorry I listened to Will after all, Cuddy thought. His bodyguard fell in around him as he walked down the corridor. *Tonight I'll celebrate. Susie. Yeah, Susie.*

Susie—her own name was unpronounceable—was the most enthusiastic girl he'd picked up here; like a demented anaconda in bed and she worshiped him like a god.

Of course, I did win her off Hong, he thought. *Probably quite a contrast.*

It was all a matter of contrasts. He'd felt hard-done by, that first six months after the Event; now things were fine. Susie felt her life had taken a turn for the better when he won her from Hong . . . all a matter of contrasts, and of being adaptable.

"Guys, this is crazy," Peter Girenas said.

The tall redheaded man shrugged, smiling. "Pete, crossing North America in the Year 8—9, now—that's crazy. Staying where we like it, that's sensible."

The bluff where the Islanders and their newfound friends had wintered looked better now that spring had melted the last of the snow and green grass covered the mud in fresh growth. The row of log cabins had their doors and windows open to air; they'd been crowded but not impossibly so. Now most of the Cloud Shadow People were back in hide tents; there were plenty of hides, with more pinned to the logs to dry.

Henry Morris was still limping, very slightly; he probably would for the rest of his life. His wife, Raven Feather, stood beside him, smiling, with their baby in her arms. Henry was dressed for the hunt in leggings and long leather shirt; so were the two young men beside him, but they carried bows, rather than atlatls and darts. Bows they'd made themselves, under Morris's skilled direction.

"Dekkomosu. . . ." Giernas began.

The Lekkansu—*former Lekkansu, now a Cloud Shadow warrior,* Girenas thought—smiled and shook his head.

"My heart's full of love for you, brother," he said softly. "But not for your people. I'll stay here, where I don't have to meet them soon. And where I can help these people who've taken me in."

"Look, Henry, it's okay now . . . but what if you decide you've made a mistake? What if you get sick?"

"If I get sick, I'll heal or I'll die," Morris said. "And if I decide I'm making a mistake, well, I'm closer to the Island than you are, aren't I?"

"Okay, okay," Girenas said. "So, that's fair; we leave you your share of the gear and all the mares in foal, and one of the stallions. Good enough?"

"Good enough," Morris said. He advanced and shook Girenas's hand, embraced Sue Chau, thumped Eddie Vergeraxsson on the shoulder.

Girenas swung into the saddle. Their six packhorses and remounts were ready. So was Eddie, of course, and Sue. Beside her Spring Indigo rode, their child across the saddlebow in a carrying cradle he'd made overwinter himself. Girenas turned his horse's head to the west. Ahead the spring prairie waved in a rippling immensity of green, starred with flowers, loud with birdsong.

"Let's get going," he said to his party. "Long way to California. Hell—" he turned in the saddle and looked back at Morris. "You'll never find out what happens!"

Morris waved, laughing. "I'll know what happens here," he called. "And that's as much as any man can know!"

CHAPTER TWENTY-FOUR

May–August, Year 10 A.E.

"He should have called off the ceremony," Clemens said desperately.

"He could not," Azzu-ena said. "A king who does not celebrate the New Year is no king, or so the people think."

He turned away from the beds. There were twenty in this room, but only ten were occupied—the only patients he was absolutely sure were going to recover. There were over a hundred in the wards now, and the guardsmen were bringing in dozens more every day. Twenty *deaths* a day, that he was sure of—he was also sure that more victims were being hidden by their relatives.

He bent over one and drained a pustule into the little ceramic dish. Then he scrubbed down, shed gown and mask, and moved into another chamber, where a long line of palace servitors and royal guardsmen waited. A couple of Kathryn Hollard's New Troops were there too, to keep order and make sure nobody bolted.

"Bare your arms," he said to those waiting, ignoring the fear and the hopeless resignation.

God damn this inoculation, he thought as the first of them shuffled forward. Apart from the small percentage who would develop the full-blown disease, everyone he inoculated would be contagious for at least a week, which meant they had to be kept in strict isolation. Which meant they'd be useless until then, and he needed immune people for a hundred different tasks.

"At least the king agreed to detain all the people from other cities," Azzu-ena pointed out, taking up a roughening scraper and small scalpel beside him. "And make them take the inoculation before they are allowed to depart."

"That's something," he said grudgingly.

Unless some of them are asymptomatic carriers, he thought. *Christ, have mercy.*

The line shuffled forward, and Justin Clemens forced himself to remember that he was saving ninety-nine lives for each human being he killed.

"Release!" the ground-crew officer barked.

The hundred and fifty of the New Troops detailed to the landing crew let go of the ropes, and the *Emancipator* bounded up from the temenos of the great temple—the only open space in Babylon big enough to moor it. The crowd gathered to watch was small, for fear and illness kept most away. The dirigible rose, a cloud of dust whipping across the stone pavement; Kenneth Hollard threw up a hand and squinted to save his eyes. It circled as it fought for altitude, and artificial raindrops fell as some hand released ballast. Then it was up and rising, its silvery-gray hull catching the light and making the red Guard slash stand out even more vividly.

He turned away, shaking his head. "Must be really heavily laden," he said. "Vicki Cofflin told me she hates to valve ballast like that."

"Well, they've got a long way to go—it's nearly six hundred miles to Hattusas," his sister said in turn.

Kashtiliash shook his head. "And all that distance in an afternoon and a night," he said softly. "Great gods, to command such power!" He moved a hand through the air. "Strange, for air to carry such weight."

They watched for a few minutes, until the *Emancipator* had dwindled to a dot in the northwestern sky.

"What's the news on the smallpox?" Hollard asked.

"Not good," Kat said grimly, and the prince nodded. "Clemens says the isolation policy isn't working, or it's just slowing the spread from prairie-fire to forest-fire speed."

"The only good thing is that we have no news of outbreaks elsewhere, which there would be if the *contagion*"—Kashtiliash used the English term—"had escaped from the city. Nobody is allowed out of the city without fourteen days in the *quarantine camps*."

"At which people are not happy," Kat added.

Kashtiliash nodded. "Plague is a sign of the anger of the gods," he said, rubbing a hand over the back of his head. "I *think* that I understand what your *asu* says of the small animals that cause disease. I have seen them through the *microscope* with my own eyes—and I trust you Nantuktar.

"That is, my thoughts believe. My liver trembles and yearns to appease the gods. I fear that there are only a handful who are convinced even in their thoughts. More who fear your magic worse than the plague, or are loyal to the throne despite their terror. But the priesthoods, many of them—"

Kashtiliash looked up and frowned, then continued in a different tone. "What is this?"

The crowd hadn't dispersed. Instead they were gathering into clumps, staring and muttering. The prince turned to command an aide and waited impatiently while the man trotted away; he kept a hand clenched on the hilt of his sword, the other resting on the butt of the revolver that he'd been presented as part of the New Year ceremonies.

"Lord Prince," the aide said, panting—moving fast in bronze scale armor was never easy, and the day was growing warm—"there is unrest."

"What sort?"

"Lord Prince, there are agitators amongst the crowd—priests of Nergal and Enna. They claim that the sickness is brought by our brave allies"—his sidelong glance wasn't as friendly as his words—"and spread by their magical ships of the air."

"Disperse them," the prince commanded tersely. "Arrest any man who speaks so. Spread the command. Go!"

The aide went; a minute later the guardsmen spread out and advanced with leveled spears, shafts reversed to show the small bronze knobs on the butt ends. Their officer shouted the royal command to disperse. Normally that would have been enough—more than enough. This time it wasn't. The crowd eddied and milled, and then things began flying through the air—lumps of donkey dung first, then bricks. A soldier wobbled out of line, dropping spear and shield and clapping his hands to his face, blood leaking out between his fingers.

The others were cursing and shouting, plying the spearshafts with a will. More bricks flew, and a few of the crowd tried to wrestle the weapons away from the troopers. Another command from their officers, and the six-foot shafts flipped around, showing sharp bronze or Island steel. Still the crowd did not disperse—not until another order rapped out and the guardsmen advanced shield to shield, their points jabbing in earnest this time. Bodies lay on the pavement after they passed, and the townspeople turned and ran.

The Hollards and the prince looked at each other, and at the rioters lying still or moaning and curling around their wounds.

"Oh, *shit*," Kenneth Hollard said and pulled the hand-held radio from his webbing. Outside the wall of the great open yard, a growing clamor came from the streets.

"Ian. Wake up."

Ian Arnstein did, blinking gummy eyes and swinging his feet down from the bunk. The sleeping arrangements of the dirigible were pullman style, bunks that were strapped up against the ceiling when not in use.

Right now they were in use, and only the night watch was awake. The interior of the *Emancipator*'s big gondola was quiet under the drone of the engines—they were running on four, to save fuel. Soft light blinked from the instruments forward and from bulbs overhead. For a moment he simply stared at them, his mind whirling back through the years to days when electric bulbs were a commonplace, not a wonder. Then he rubbed his face and yawned. Doreen was sleep-rumpled too, but on her it looked fairly good.

Chill air seeped through the permeable sides of the craft. He shivered a little, pulled a blanket around his shoulders, and accepted the cup of hot cocoa that his wife put in his hand.

"What's going on?" he asked.

"Ken's on the radio from Babylon," she said. "It doesn't look good."

"Oh, Lord," he muttered. "I'm coming, I'm coming."

He pulled on his clothing—wool pants and sheepskin jacket and cap—then made his way up the central corridor. Outside, the moon was shining on the peaks of the Anti-Taurus range, north of what would have been the Turkish border in the twentieth century. He stopped for a moment to look and shiver. The *Emancipator* was rising only gradually, threading her way between the mountains rather than soaring over them, and they were close enough to look *big*. Snow glistened salt-white on the higher peaks, and he could see a long streamer of it blowing off one only a few thousand yards to his left. Below that were dense forests, deep black-on-black in the moonlight.

Brrrr, he thought—it was spring, but nobody had told that high mountain country below. *I'll be glad when we get into the plateau.* He went on to the forward control area of the gondola. The same view was spread out on three sides there, but it looked less intimidating with the ordered activity of the flight crew. Vicki Cofflin and her second-in-command were bent over the navigation table.

"Where are we?" he asked.

"Hi, Councilor," she said. "Right here—north of what would be Diyarbakir, heading northwest toward Hattusas. On course. Should get there about an hour before dawn, another three hours or so."

"Okay, then," Ian said, feeling the last tendrils of sleep leaving him. "Let me at the radio and we'll find out what's gone wrong now."

He sat in the chair next to the communications officer and accepted the headset from her. "Arnstein here," he said, conscious of a very slight grumpiness in his tone.

"Colonel Hollard here," came the voice in his earphones. "I'm afraid we have a . . . bit of a situation."

"What do you mean?" Arnstein snapped. It wasn't like Ken to be slow coming to the point.

"We've got a full-blown revolt here in Babylon."

Damn. He wasn't altogether surprised, though. These people didn't believe in accidents. If something went wrong, it was gods or demons responsible, offended by some lapse of piety or let in by the breaking of a taboo.

"That isn't the worst of it, of course," Hollard went on.

"What *could* be worse than—wait a minute, do I want you to tell me?"

"No, but I'm afraid you need to hear it."

Ironic, Kathryn Hollard thought. This was the rooftop-cum-balcony where she and Kash had met the week before. Now it was their command post.

From here she could see the flame-shot darkness of Babylon the Great. This northern district by the river and the Ishtar Gate wasn't too bad; the Royal Guard had it under firm control, and the Marine battalions were marching in down the Processional Way, along with the rest of her New Troops. Elsewhere fires were burning; she could see one three-story building about a quarter of a mile away clearly, backlit by flames. Flames shot out of the slit windows, and then the flat roof collapsed, the heavy adobe tumbling down on anyone still left within. Faint in the distance came the surf-roar of the crowds, screams, the clash of metal . . . and now and then the faint popping crackle of firearms.

The smell of it came too, carried on the cool night wind, the rank scent of things not meant to burn. Fire was a terror in these densely packed cities without running water. Let it get out of hand, and a firestorm could consume everything within the walls.

King Shuriash lay on a bed in one corner, his breath slow and heaving. Justin Clemens rose and tucked away his stethoscope. Priests and *ashipu* came closer to the bedside, their chants a soft, wailing falsetto under the distant mutter of conflict.

"Definitely a stroke," he said as he came over to the high commanders. "And a bad one. I've made him as comfortable as I can, but there's nothing I can do. It would be a mercy if he didn't regain consciousness; there's extensive brain damage, I suspect."

Prince Kashtiliash's face was like one of the carvings of protective genii outside the palace as he went to bend over his father, but there was gentleness in the touch of his hand on the grizzled black hair.

"The king is fallen," he said grimly to the generals and courtiers gathered around him when he returned. "I rule in his place, until he awakens—and if he does not, I am the king. Does any doubt it?"

A few glanced at each other, but nobody spoke. Instead, one by one, they went to their knees and then to their bellies; there was a rustle of stiff embroidered fabric, clinking from the officers in their scale corselets. One by one they muttered, "*La sanan, sa mahira la isu!* The king who has no rival!"

When they rose, he nodded and went on, "We must put down this rebellion, and we must do it swiftly."

"Indeed, O Prince." That was Kidin-Ninurta, his diplomat face carefully blank. "Cannot our friends, our new allies, assist in this?"

Kenneth Hollard nodded. "We will give what aid our ally requests."

"I will request as little as I may," Kashtiliash said. Kathryn caught the slight relaxation from several of the nobles and military men. "I would not have it said that my reign rests on foreign blades, no matter how close and friendly the alliance. Yet to bring troops into this city is to risk their lives from the disease."

Servants came in carrying a large table, a map unrolled upon it. Kashtiliash grunted as he recognized the view, drawn from above the city.

A general stepped forward. "The west bank is mostly quiet. The main trouble is in the older parts of the city—here, here, here. Around the temples of Enna and Nergal particularly." He hesitated.

"Speak. I do not blame the bearer for the news," Kashtiliash said.

"Lord Prince, we have found many bodies dead of the new plague as we push forward in those areas. The men . . . they are brave men, Lord Prince, in the face of spear and sword."

"But they fear the plague demons—as would any men with sense."

He walked to the edge of the rooftop and rested his hands on the balcony. "Cordon off those areas," he said. "Barricade the streets; tear down buildings where necessary, to create gaps." There were substantial areas of Babylon where you could go from roof to roof almost as easily as walking at ground level.

"Use the troops who have been through the *inoculation*. Let no one into these areas. Women, children, and men surrendering may come out—provided they submit to the *inoculation* themselves. Send them then to the *quarantine camps*. Shout these terms over the barricades."

He used a good many English terms in those sentences, but they were ones most people in the palace had picked up perforce over the last week.

"And there shall be no more foolishness in the rest of the city. All the troops shall be *inoculated*, one company at a time. While they wait, the others shall cordon off the city *so*"—his finger slashed across the map, dividing the mass of Babylon into segments.

"We shall take one area at a time, and in that area the soldiers shall go from house to house. Any sick shall be sent at once to the *hospital*. All others shall be *inoculated* . . . that word is too cumbersome. We shall call it the 'scratch of safeguard.' Yes. All shall receive the scratch of safety and be isolated after. So the Throne commands!"

"We obey," the nobles and high priests of the temples not in rebellion murmured. *"La sanan, sa mahira la isu!"*

Kenneth Hollard drew himself to attention and snapped a salute. Kathryn did likewise, and from Kashtiliash's nod, from something about his eyes, she thought he sensed the difference in the gesture.

"Lord Prince," the elder Hollard said. "The troops you have to cordon off the rebel areas are very few and will remain so until more are inoculated . . . have received the scratch of safeguarding."

Kashtiliash nodded. "That, my ally, is where you and your men—your troops—shall assist." He paused. "And if you would, your boats of steam could also be of help. We will need the blackwater, a great deal of it."

Colonel Hollard inclined his head. "Of course, Lord Prince . . . but why?"

Kasthiliash turned to Lieutenant Clemens. "You say that the bodies of the dead are dangerous?"

"Very, Lord Prince."

"Then we will need the blackwater oil for funeral pyres. A great many."

Ian Arnstein whistled as the Marine commander finished. "Well, you're right, I did need to hear that," he said.

"Your orders, sir?" Hollard said.

"Orders?"

"Do you want the *Emancipator* to turn back? Our base here is in . . . well, considerable danger."

"Do you need the airship to control Babylon?"

"Ah . . . no, sir. Bombing from the air is sort of a blunt instrument for crowd control."

"Then we'll continue to Hattusas."

"Sir . . . the plan was to have a secure base in Babylonia and overland supply lines. As it is, I have to divert virtually all our forces to helping Prince Kashtiliash reestablish order here."

"Colonel Hollard, Walker isn't going to wait, so we'll just have to do the best we can with what we have. I'll lay the groundwork with the Hittites, and you work on getting things back on track down there."

A pause. "Yes, sir, Councilor."

Arnstein nodded, then cleared his throat as he remembered that the other man couldn't see him. "Looks like Prince Kashtiliash is taking charge decisively."

"Damn right, Councilor. I knew he was capable, but this is the first time we've seen him out of his father's shadow . . . and to tell you the truth, he's starting to look better as a possible brother-in-law."

"God forfend, Ken. The Meeting's sort of sensitive about citizens of the Republic as monarchs abroad, you know."

"I do know, oh, yes, indeed. I'd better let you get some sleep, then. I've got a busy night ahead of me."

"Take care; I can't spare you."

"That's mutual, Councilor. Good night to you and Doreen, then."

Arnstein clicked off and removed the headset, yawning again. "Not really much point in going back to sleep," he said. His mouth quirked as he looked at his wife. "Sorry, darling. Looks like I've gotten us out onto the end of a long limb, here."

"Do you think Ken was serious about the prince and his sister?"

"I have a horrible suspicion he was. After all, Kashtiliash is going to be *king,* now."

"Great King, King of Sumer and Akkad, King of the Four Corners of the World, King Who Does As He Damned Well Pleases."

"Unless he PO's so many important people that they kill him," Ian agreed. "But he's already *getting* the rebellion, and we're helping him put it down. So he's going to be in a very strong position indeed."

"Gevalt."

"Truer words were never spoken," Ian said. "Okay, we might as well go over this speech in Hittite. Thank God they've got a lot of Akkadian-speaking scribes up there!"

"Strange to see him so helpless," Kashtiliash murmured, so softly that only the woman by his side could hear him. "He always seemed a tower, or a mountain himself, eternal and strong—a wall of safety for me."

Kathryn nodded. "Perhaps you should stay here," she said. "You could be close by if he awakens and still direct the operations— messengers will find you more easily than if you're moving about."

"No, Kat'ryn, I must show myself to the troops. They are shaken— the arrows of the plague gods frighten them as the chariots and spear-men of Assyria did not."

"You're concerned with their loyalty?" she said, alarmed.

"Not the troops who fought under me in the north, no," he said, shaking his head. "The city militia, yes; and if this trouble lasts, per-haps some nobles and their followers. I am guarding my younger half brothers most carefully, lest one be spirited away to use as a rallying point for rebels. But the men I lead to Asshur's walls are with me; and they will stand by you Nantukhtar too—they remember how many of their lives you saved, with your guns and with your *asu* Clemens' arts. It is their fear I must put down, not rebellion."

She nodded reluctantly. "And I'll have to lead the first Kar-Duniash," she said. "They're not trained for street fighting and they're not used to operating as a unit, yet . . ." She hesitated. "It doesn't hurt you with your men, that you and I are . . . together?"

He grinned wider. "No, never. They say that Kashtiliash is the very Bull of Marduk; not only does he slay the lioness of the marshes with his spear of bronze, he brings the lioness who came from the sea to his bed with the spear of his manhood!"

Kathryn snorted. *That* is *the way the sexist bastards would look at it,* she thought.

"Let's get to work, then," she said briskly.

"Yes," he said. His voice turned gentle for a moment. "Good-bye, Father."

"They come!" the royal officer said, clutching at his upper arm where an arrow had gone through just below the short sleeve of his scale-mail shirt. "We could not hold them—too many. People of the city and temple guardsmen."

Even in the dark Hollard could see that there were fewer than the hundred-odd followers that the Babylonian should have had. Some were limping, some bleeding, and a number had their arms over the shoulders of comrades who bore their weight. Their wheezing breath was loud in the shuttered quiet of the street, but he could hear the snarling brabble of voices not far off and the thudding sound of feet.

"Fall in behind us, then," he said. "Our healers will see to your wounded. Hold yourself ready if I have need of you."

The Babylonian nodded, panting still, and staggered off for the rear.

This was one of the wider streets in this section of town—all of twenty feet across, with two- and three-story adobe buildings rearing up on either side. It stank, like a black open-topped sewer. There was no light but the crescent moon; he could hear a Fiernan-born Marine muttering an invocation.

"O'Rourke!" he said.

"Sir?" the company commander said.

"Take parties"—he tapped the first two fingers of each hand to either side—"evacuate those buildings, then blow them. Put the charges on interior walls so they'll fall in."

O'Rourke looked up thoughtfully. "I think I should put some snipers on the roofs further back as well, Colonel, sir," he said. "If I was a hell-born rioter with sedition and mischief on my mind, I'd have people on these roofs on either side when I tried to storm a barricade, so I would."

"Do it."

O'Rourke nodded, snapping off a salute and grinning whitely in the shadows, then walked off shouting orders. Marines raced back to the supply wagon and came out of it carrying small, heavy barrels, with lengths of fuse cord over their shoulders. More hammered in the doors, and the householders poured into the street, cursing or crying or clutching children and some snatched-up treasured possession. Hollard winced slightly—these people were about to lose everything they owned—but needs must when the devil drove, as the commodore said.

O'Rourke came dashing out, laughing again. There was a multiple massive BUDUMPF from both sides of the street, and the buildings collapsed inward with a long rumble that shook the ground.

"Put up those snipers . . . wait." Hollard stopped, thought, looking over the gap the explosions had created. Too far to throw, but . . . "We've got some of the new rifle grenades, don't we?"

"That we do," O'Rourke said and grinned wider. "Splendid thought, Colonel, sir. Two squads?"

"Do it. Let's get moving here! Lieutenant Mleckzo, get us some light."

And I hope to God the other company commanders are doing the right thing.

He looked over his position. The infantry were deployed in front of him, shoulder to shoulder across the roadway in three rows. They were buckling back the flaps of their bandoliers, some licking a thumb and wetting the foresights of their rifles. Others under Mleckzo's direction were hammering the handles of torches—bundles of oil-soaked reeds wrapped around sticks—into walls and setting them alight. A ruddy glow spread over the roadway, catching on the cold glitter of fixed bayonets and the yellow brass of cartridges.

"Colonel, sir, aren't we supposed to get a Gatling?" O'Rourke said, coming up beside him and dusting off his tunic.

"Yes, we were," Hollard said.

"Good," O'Rourke said. "The more one-sided, the better."

"I'm not looking forward to firing on these people," Hollard said softly; there were things you didn't say in front of the troops. "We're supposed to be here to help them, as well as the Republic."

O'Rourke looked at him with surprise in his eyes. "Well, we *are* helping them, sir," he said, his voice equally low. "We finished off the Assyrians for them, we're doing our best to stop this epidemic, and the fools would be fighting us."

"They're scared, Paddy," Hollard said. "Scared people don't think very straight. Now the smallpox has hit them, and some of the priests told them we were to blame. Why shouldn't they believe it? They've seen us fly and throw thunderbolts, why shouldn't they believe we can cause a pestilence?"

O'Rourke put a hand on his shoulder. "Sir . . . Ken . . . if you're going to be in this line of work, it's best not to think about some things too much. We can handle it here."

"Thanks, but if I can order it, I can watch it," Hollard said quietly. "Carry on."

Hooves rattled behind them. Hollard turned quickly, but it was the Gatling coming up, with an outrider in front of it. He let out a sigh of relief; it was extremely unlikely that any mob could storm this position, but the Gatling made it a lot less likely still.

The six-barreled weapon was mounted behind a sheet-steel shield, drawn by a two-horse team, with another drawing an ammunition limber behind it. Each team was guided by a Marine riding the left horse, and the mounted crews trotted behind. He recognized Sergeant Smith, transferred from mortars to the newly arrived weapons, and she grinned at him as she swung down from the saddle and saluted.

"Sorry we're late, sir," she said. "Had a little brush with some rioters who got through."

"Very well," he said. "Get set up—we left a gap in the middle of the line for you."

"Sir, yessir."

The noncom barked orders of her own, and the crews unhitched the teams, then ran the weapon forward, hands pushing on the wheels.

"Feed me!" Smith snapped, when the iron-and-brass machine was level with the front line of prone infantry. She sat on the little bike-saddle mounted on the trail and traversed the weapon experimentally.

The crew lifted one of the drum-shaped magazines and fitted it into the loading slot on top of the Gatling's breech. Smith swung the crank at the side back a half turn and then forward; there was a clunk-*clank!* sound, and the barrels turned two spaces.

"Ready, sir!"

Hollard nodded. The mob sound was much closer now; they'd stopped when they heard the blasting charges bring down the houses, but they were coming on again. *Run away, you idiots!* he pleaded within himself. Then his eyes panned across a slight figure helping run the limber forward. Oddly, there were no markings on the plain uniform, and the Marine was wearing a hat rather than a helmet. And . . . was that a *dog* with her?

"Can't be!" he muttered and stepped closer. "Jesus Christ—Raupasha! What the *hell* are you doing here?"

She looked up at him, pushing up the brim of the campaign hat.

"I am starting payment on a debt, Lord Kenn'et," she said, meeting his eyes without wavering. "And you cannot send me back to the palace, because that would be more dangerous than staying here!"

Hollard opened his mouth. A voice rang out: "Heads up! Here they come!"

"Did you have to bring the *dog*?" he heard himself say, and a part of him marveled at the banal absurdity.

Raupasha smiled. "I had to. He kept barking; someone would have heard."

"Well, stay out of the bloody way, then," Hollard snarled, turning back to his work, surprised at the furious heat of his own anger.

Figures were moving down the road, shadows in the darkness. He raised his eyes and brought up his binoculars. *Ayup.* Figures flitting from rooftop to rooftop as well; it was as if there were two sets of streets, one on the ground and one at roof level.

I wonder how they control burglary here, he thought, and went on in a calm, carrying voice:

"Second and Third Platoons will fire and reload. Volley fire on the word of command only. Sergeant Smith, you will fire three three-second bursts at the command for volley fire. Understood?"

"Sir, yessir!"

A knot gripped the pit of his stomach as he saw the crowd milling, thickening as more and more pushed up, the sound of their voices growing. He could hear men shouting, probably haranguing the others and whipping them up to attack.

"Christ, I hate this," he muttered, then laughed harshly. O'Rourke made an interrogative sound, and Hollard went on, "I was just thinking how much I hate shooting people who can't shoot back—but when we finally get at Walker, I'm going to hate it even more, because his goons *will* be able to shoot back."

A long, baying snarl, and the mob was running at him, filling the street. There was a slight quiver along the line of bayonets ahead of him—picking targets. O'Rourke looked at him, and Hollard nodded.

The company commander filled his lungs. *"Fire!"*

BAAAMMM!

The rifles fired a lacing of red needles into the gloom. *Run away,* Hollard pled silently. *Please, run away. Don't make us do this.*

The Gatling opened up, the operator turning the crank three times; *braaaaaaapppp,* like a giant tearing canvas between his hands, and a stream of brass cartridges poured out of the bottom of the weapon. *Braaaaaaapppp. Braaaaaaapppp.*

Jesus, I'm glad it's dark.

Then there was a long *whhhtt* from one of the buildings ahead, and an arrow went by him, more sensed than seen in the flickering light of the torches. A Marine stumbled back from the firing line, fumbling at the shaft stuck in his hip, moaning. More arrows flitted past, a few hitting the timber of door frames and quivering like angry bees.

"Corpsman! Corpsman!"

Stretcher bearers trotted forward. As they did, the squads stationed on the rooftops opened up. A distinctive muffled *badaff* marked the rifle grenades, and then vicious red cracking sounds as they burst on the rooftops. Something caught fire from one, and then muzzle flashes stabbed out at the figures outlined against the flames, slow, deliberate, aimed fire.

Not all of them were dead; something arched down from a rooftop, trailing red sparks, and burst in a puddle of flames on the roadway. The fire was slow and red-sullen, not the quick rush of kerosene—sesame oil. It still burned, and a Marine's uniform started to burn, until comrades rolled him and beat out the flames. Another call for corpsmen went up, and Kenneth Hollard ground his teeth in rage.

"Smith! Rake that side of the street!" Hollard snapped. "O'Rourke, keep an eye on the mob."

The crowd had stopped as the torrent of lead plowed into it; scores were down, dead or screaming or moaning and twitching. The rest wavered and eddied. The Gatling crew ran their weapon back out of the infantry formation and wheeled it around to the left, the noncom in charge spinning the elevation wheel. Then the harsh tearing sound of the machine gun began again, long bursts this time as she worked the crank. The stream of bullets worked down the length of the rooftops on that side of the street, tearing through the soft adobe bricks and sending spatters of it back down into the roadway. More than a few bodies followed, tumbling down to thump into the packed clay.

And at last they *were* running, back the way they had come—except for the piled dead and wounded.

"Captain O'Rourke, we'll move forward now," he said. "Let's get them pinned back in the quarantine area."

Where they'll all die unless they come out and accept inoculation, he thought, then pushed the knowledge away.

"I think we should have parties moving forward on the roofs to either side, sir," O'Rourke said.

"See to it, Paddy. Have a couple of working parties bring out some ladders, too."

Babylonians kept those for accessing their roofs, taking them down at night when they weren't sleeping on their roofs to escape the heat.

"Yes, sir. Good idea."

The Marines moved forward in a line of bayonets, the Gatling crew dragging the bodies aside so their weapon could pass.

Hollard picked his way through the bodies. *I should get some of Kash's people here to pick up the wounded rioters. . . . How long to*

*get the situation here under control? Couple of weeks, if Kashtiliash
does the right things. Then—*

A rifle fired not ten feet behind him. He spun, to see a Babylonian
falling back onto the pile of dead where he'd lain concealed. Two
more were up and charging, bronze knives in their hands, faces contorted and screaming. And they were *close*. Hollard clawed at his
holster, the Python coming free with glacial slowness. An attacker's
head exploded, close enough to spatter across his arm and torso. He
shot the third at point-blank range, the muzzle blast of three quick
shots burning the wool of the man's tunic, his body jerking under the
impacts.

Raupasha was standing, lowering the Werder from her shoulder.
Even in the darkness, he could see the smoke rising from the muzzle.
Her dog crouched at her feet, growling.

"Ah . . . it seems you've paid off your debt, Princess," he said
slowly, waving away the concerned faces that turned toward him.

"No," Raupasha said, her face pale and eyes wide. "I've just
begun."

"Well, now that we're here, we have a slight problem—how do we
keep the locals from spearing us or running away before we can talk?"
Doreen Arnstein said. "Sort of hard to get them into the Anti-Walker
League if they stick sharp pointies into us first."

The Anatolian plateau lay two thousand feet below them, dawn's
long shadows stretching across it, stretches of green cropland and dun
pasture amid a rocky, rolling landscape with high forested mountains
to the north. It was bleak enough, but less so than the arid barrens Ian
remembered from visits to Turkey in the twentieth; the raw bones of
the earth less exposed by millennia of plows and axes and hungry
goats.

Ian shrugged against his heavy sheepskin jacket. "I'm thinking,
I'm thinking," he said.

The city of Hattusas, capital of the Hittite Empire, lay below. It was
smaller than Babylon—he estimated its total area at around four hundred acres—and it lacked the gargantuan ziggurats that marked the
cities of the Land Between the Rivers. Yet it had a brooding majesty
of its own, surrounded by cyclopean walls of huge irregular blocks in
the shape of a rough figure eight. On a rocky height at the eastern edge
of the city was a great complex of palaces, some with ornamental gardens on the flat roofs and trees planted about them. Elsewhere were
twisted streets of buildings; castlelike fortresses and temples, scores
of them. The smoke of sacrifice rose up from them, and crowds were
packed densely into the sacred precincts.

He suspected that they were packed everywhere in the city that had any associations of sacredness, with the *Emancipator* cruising overhead. They'd opened some of the slanting windows, and he could hear the turmoil as well as see it. The gates were open, and people on foot were streaming out of the city, followed by laden wagons and preceded by a few chariots whose owners lashed their teams to reckless speed.

"We don't have time to be subtle," he said. "What we've got to do is put a messenger in, someone they'll listen to, and then open negotiations."

Everyone on board turned to look at the Babylonian emissary, Ibi-Addad, who turned gray and began to raise protesting hands.

There was panic in the streets of Hattusas. Tudhaliyas, Great King of Hatti, Living Sun, stood on the battlements of his palace and listened to the screams and cries below. Sweat ran down his own long, swarthy face, running into his trimmed beard.

There was reason enough for fear; years of evil news, as if the gods had deserted the land of Hatti. Three years ago he'd suffered his great defeat at the hands of Tukulti-Ninurta of Assyria. Well before that, rumors of black sorcery and menace came from beyond the Western Ocean, among the Ahhiyawa. Then the rebellion of Kurunta, possibly in league with them; just a week before rumors had come of how an army sent to bring him to obedience had been annihilated by evil magic—and on its heels, news of a barbarian invasion in the northwest. But that was nothing beside this. The *thing* floated over the city of the king like some great fish of the air, needing not even wings to hold it up, though it was as long as a temple square—five hundred paces, at least. The rising sun shone on its gray covering, on the blood-red slash across it, on cryptic symbols that seemed to breath menace. A sound drifted down from it, a great buzzing as of a monstrous bee.

"It is coming this way, My Sun," one of the courtiers said. "Perhaps you should . . ."

"Flee in terror?" Tudhaliyas said ironically.

He was a man of middle years, dressed now in garb for hunting or war—knee-length tunic covered by a cloak thrown over one shoulder, tall pointed hat, curl-toed boots, wool leggings, with a sword at his belt and the mace of sovereignty in his hands. His hair was long and black, his square, hard face shaven close and much tanned and weathered.

"If this is evil spirits, then Teshub and the Sun Goddess Arinna and Hebat and the other gods and goddesses of the land will protect us," the king said.

"Unless our sin is too heavy, unless we have incurred pollution," someone whimpered.

"If our sin is heavy, if we have incurred pollution, then running will not help us," he said. "If this is a miracle of the gods, running may bring their anger. Stand fast!"

Most did, his guards among them, even when the *thing* came closer and closer still amid a great hissing and buzzing. His sweat turned cold as the monster shape cut off the sun, and his eyes blurred with fear. Then they sharpened. Were those the shapes of *men* behind windows like those of a house? He'd assumed that whatever it was, it was alive—did anything else besides living things move with intelligent direction, of its own accord?

Yes, he thought. *A ship, a cart, a chariot—all these move. But . . .*

A voice bellowed out, making him take a step backward.

"WE COME IN PEACE! HAVE NO FEAR! WE COME IN PEACE!"

"The gods have condemned us!" someone screamed, groveling and beating his head on the flagstones. The bronze-scale armor of the warriors rattled, eyes rolled, tongues moistened lips. Tudhallyas raised his voice in cold command.

"The gods do not speak our Nesite tongue with a Babylonian accent," the king said. "I am the One Sun, and I will answer."

He stepped forward, parting the ranks of his guards until he stood alone in an open stretch of rooftop; that would have been impossible, were they not so shaken. There he had to grab at his hat; a great wind was coming downward from the *thing,* as if a mighty storm blew. Closer, he could see that below the sleek gray shape was another, this shaped like a boat with windows cut into its hull . . . and it was made of wicker. That reassured him, despite the alienness of every detail.

He cupped his hands and shouted upward: "If you come in peace, from whom do you come?" He spoke Akkadian, which all educated men learned.

"WE SEND AN EMISSARY! GREET HIM IN PEACE, ACCORDING TO THE LAWS OF GODS AND MEN!"

Another door opened in the boatlike structure, this one in the bottom, and he could see the shapes of men there. Suddenly the *thing* snapped into perspective. A man came *out* of the hole, dangling in a canvas chair at the end of a rope; another rope uncoiled beneath it, striking the pavement near the king.

"PLEASE TAKE THE ROPE AND STEADY IT!"

The bellowing made it hard to distinguish voices, but if that was a man's voice, it was another man than the first. And it spoke Akkadian. He looked behind him and signaled two guardsmen forward. They laid down their spears and shields gingerly and came forward to take the rope. It was perfectly ordinary cord, thumb-thick, woven of fiber; perhaps that reassured them. They grasped it firmly and pulled in lengths hand over hand as the man in the canvas seat was lowered down.

Ah, thought Tudhaliyas dazedly. *That is to prevent him swaying back and forth like a plumb bob.*

The canvas seat came within a few feet of the rooftop, and Tudhaliyas saw a man like other men—he felt disconcerted and obscurely angry, a part of his fear flowing away. The man hopped out, and the two guardsmen released the rope with a yell as it burned through their fingers. Looking up, the king saw that the *thing* had bounced upward a little, bobbing in the air like a feather.

The man was of medium height, dressed in a ceremonial robe and hat of the type men wore in Kar-Duniash or Assyria. His accent was of Babylon, though, as he advanced two steps and went down in a smooth prostration.

"O King, My Sun, live forever!" he cried.

Tudhaliyas' eyebrows shot up of their own accord. That was the accent of the God-voice that had bellowed down over the city.

"Who *are* you?" he blurted. "You may rise," he added automatically.

"O Great King, your slave is Ibi-Addad, son of Lakti-Marduk, a servant of your brother Great King Kashtiliash of Kar-Duniash, King of Sumer and Akkad, King of the Universe, to whom there is no rival."

This is madness, thought Tudhaliyas. Nothing so . . . so *real* could have come out of that *thing*. And . . .

"King Kashtiliash?" he blurted. "What of his father, Shagarakti-Shuriash?"

"Alas, O King, the father of King Kashtiliash has been gathered to his fathers."

The sun fell across their faces. The *thing* was soaring upward once again, turning and droning away to the south. Tudhaliyas felt some self-possession return as it departed.

"You will explain this to me, servant of the king my brother," he said sharply.

Ibi-Addad sighed. "O King, may the gods make your days many, *that* is going to be a difficult task."

The cannon still reeked a little of sulfur and death. Kathryn Hollard stood by it with one hand on a barrel, the metal still warm from discharge, watching as the long line of captives shuffled out of the area beyond the barricade. She felt sandy-eyed and exhausted after the night's fighting, but still far too keyed up to think of food or sleep. Columns of smoke still rose, but they were under control now, and none were too near. The reek of burning lay across the city, mingling with the usual stench.

She did take a swig from her canteen and handed it to Prince . .

No, she thought. *He's the king now.*

. . . King Kashtiliash where he stood at her side. A few of his entourage were shocked at the informality; she could hear them gasp.

She would have laughed, if it hadn't been for the endless chain of civilians shuffling forward to surrender. Each one passed through a corridor of spearmen, stopping at the end to bare an arm for the inoculation—this station was manned by one of Clemens's retrained dancing girls—many moaning or sobbing as they did so, still convinced that it was a device of demons. Others came from the riot-torn districts on stretchers, the pox pustules clear on their faces.

Kathryn swallowed slightly; she'd gotten used to the butcher-shop horrors of the battlefield, somewhat, but this was something completely different.

Kashtiliash caught her look and walked a little aside, signaling her to follow with a slight movement of his head.

"You did very good work last night," he said. "If I had had to use only my own forces, many more would have died."

She shrugged, with a weary smile. "The First Kar-Duniash *is* your own, Lord King," she said.

"They are as you made them, and they did well," Kashtiliash said, sighing and rubbing his fingers across his brow. "Would that this had not been necessary."

"Amen," she said.

"It is strange," he said meditatively. "If I thought of it at all, before you—your people—came to the Land, I thought of Kar-Duniash as the center of the world."

"Everyone does that," Kathryn Hollard said.

Kashtiliash shook his head. "No, but we had reason. No realm we knew was more ancient than the land of Sumer and Akkad, or richer, or more learned, or more skilled in all the arts and knowledge. Oh, perhaps Egypt, yes . . . Mitanni was a thing of a day, the Hittites rude hillmen who learned from us, the Assyrians our onetime vassals. Of the world we knew, we were the center."

He sighed. "And now I must see us as you Nantukhtar see us—poor, ignorant, dirty, diseased. I have more of the English than you might think, and I have heard your brother and the *asu* Klemn's speak, and heard reports of what your soldiers and wisemen say. *Locals,* is that not the word? As we might term a hill-tribe, or a band of the truffle-eating Aramaeans."

"Lord Prince . . . Kash . . ."

"No, my Kat'ryn, I do not say *you* regard *me* so—although they say that Ishtar gives blindness along with love. But it is not only that you Nantukhtar think of us so, but that it *is* so, which karks me. I have listened; your physicians can cure so many illnesses that we suffer; in your land no man goes hungry, and even peasants live like nobles; you have arts that make ours look like some child's fumbling, when he pinches out a little clay ox from the dirt of the fields; and you command a power that can kick apart our proudest cities like a hut of reeds."

"Kash . . . we just have a longer history. If we see further, it's because we stand on the shoulders of giants—your peoples' not least among them."

The Babylonian was silent for a long moment, then he nodded. "I have thought this also; it keeps my heart from bitterness."

"And we grow and beget and suffer and die too," she said.

"That also." His hand clenched on the hilt of his sword. "I swear by my father, and by the gods of the land, that I will not leave my kingdom and people poor and ignorant and powerless, not while there is strength in my hands."

Kathryn Hollard felt a sudden cold chill. It was only a little way from that oath to resentful hatred for the Republic and all its works . . .

"I'll help," she heard herself say. "All that I can."

He smiled. "That is very good. And now that I am king . . . many things may be arranged more as we desire them."

CHAPTER TWENTY-FIVE

May–August, Year 10 A.E.

"Yes, sir. We're ready to move out from the bridgeheads on the upper Euphrates. Once Hangalibat is secured—it's still pretty chaotic up here, Chief—we can get in direct contact with the Hittites. From what Councilor Arnstein's saying, things are going pretty well there."

"There's nothing like having your back to the wall to make people reasonable, and they were pretty impressed with the *Emancipator*. Propaganda value alone is going to make that a cost-effective project. . . . now spit it out."

"Sir?"

"Whatever it is that you're reluctant to talk about, Colonel Hollard. Oh, by the way, for the duration of this war, you're a brigadier general."

Jared Cofflin lowered the microphone of the shortwave set. It was a pleasant late-spring day on Nantucket, not long before Daffodil Weekend. From the second-story radio room he could see some, nodding in yellow glory like a promise of peace.

But there is no peace, he thought to himself.

Martha looked up from her knitting. "I suspect it's about King Kashtiliash," she said.

"Ah . . ." Hollard's voice came through again. "It's King Kashtiliash, sir. He wants to marry my sis-, ah, Lieutenant Colonel Hollard."

Oh, Jared Cofflin thought. *Oh, shit.*

"There's no law against marrying noncitizens, dear," Martha pointed out. "In fact, it generally confers automatic resident alien status on the spouse—and there are hundreds of cases."

"Yes, but usually the spouse moves *here*. And Kashtiliash is a head of state."

"Swindapa is a . . . well, a Kurlelo Grandmother."

"That's different. And there's a law against citizens seizing power or aiding foreign governments."

"Yes, but Kathryn Hollard isn't proposing to do either. The legitimate government of an ally is proposing to *give* her a position, and she's not proposing to use it in a way contrary to the interests of the Republic."

"You caught that, Brigadier?"

"Yessir. All right, I've got the text of a goddam proposed marriage contract the two of them drew up. You want me to read it?"

"Go ahead," Cofflin said. After he'd listened, he whistled softly. "Well, I'm surprised he agreed to all that."

There was a slight smile in Kenneth Hollard's voice. "He's got it bad, sir. *And* it's mostly to his advantage, too—this bit about a Nantucket tutor for any kids they have, and sending them to the Island for schooling as well. That's not unusual here—fostering, that is."

"Marian," Cofflin said, "you've been listening?"

"Mmmm-hmmm," another voice said. "You getting this, Hollard?"

"Yes, ma'am. A bit scratchy but clear."

Swindapa's voice came in: "I think it's sweet."

Hollard chuckled. "Lieutenant Commander, I don't think *either* of the people concerned is what you could call 'sweet.' "

"Ian?" Cofflin said. "You're not saying anything?"

"I wasn't surprised, and the rest of you are just talking yourselves around to accepting it," Arnstein replied, infuriatingly reasonable. "Could we do that, and get on to things that still aren't settled? Tudhaliyas is dithering, and this barbarian invasion is looking more and more serious."

"And I'm just about ready to go," Marian Alston cut in. "If what I'm planning comes off, the equations in the Middle East all change, too."

Jared Cofflin sighed. *I wonder how people like Churchill and FDR kept all their balls in the air at the same time.*

"Alaksandrus of Wiulusiya is the key," Tudhaliyas said.

Ian Arnstein nodded, shivering slightly. His scholar's ear looked past the Anatolian pronunciations and supplied Hellenic alternatives—or Achaean, the archaic Mycenaean Greek he'd learned after the Event. *Alexandros of Wilios.* Later Greek would drop the '*w*' sound altogether; it would be Ilios—Troy, as it was also known. Inquiring, he'd learned that the kingdom in question was on the northwestern coast, just south of the Dardanelles. The people were closely related to the *Ahhiyawa;* and yes, that was a powerful kingdom west across the Aegean.

Doreen leaned over and whispered in his ear, "This is getting too creepy for words."

Ian nodded. So far the Hittites had been vastly impressed—except for King Tudhaliyas, who Ian thought wasn't impressed by much of anything. He'd supplied mooring for the *Emancipator,* comfortable quarters, lavish gifts . . . and an endless tale of woe. Tudhaliyas had brains and guts, but he was a complainer. In fact, it would be fair to say he whined.

Still, I get to see the capital of the Hittite kings, he thought. *The great stone walls, the pointed-arch gates with monoliths of frowning gods carved beside them . . . And then I get sucked into the Trojan War, or a reasonable facsimile thereof.*

"Alaksandrus is your vassal, isn't he?"

"He is supposed to be," the king nodded.

They were sitting in an audience room flooded with light; unlike Babylonian architecture, Hittite ran to big square external windows, although they didn't have window-glass, of course. Nor did they have chairs, except for royalty.

Why, O Lord, do so many countries back here have this ridiculous rule? They know how to make chairs, and chairs aren't particularly difficult to make, so why don't they? He was sitting on a stool, and his back wasn't enjoying it.

Otherwise it was quite pleasant, stuccoed inside and done in geometric designs in ocher and cinnabar, with carpets that looked astonishingly Turkish draped over built-in benches. Even more pleasant, nobody had made any objections to Doreen's being present. The king's wife was too. Zuduhepa was *Tawannannas,* a title in its own right; the next king's wife wouldn't inherit it until Zuduhepa died herself.

Arnstein unrolled his map. "Troy is here?"

After the exclamations and explanations, the royal couple nodded. "And that is where the . . . barbarians have invaded?"

"To the north of it, but they come closer every day. As I said, Alaksandrus is the problem. For years he has been scanting his tribute and sending excuses when I summon his men and chariots for war—perhaps that was why the Assyrians beat me, three years ago."

"O King," Doreen said, "you need not fear Asshur again. With my own eyes I saw their cities burn."

"Would that I had been there to see it!" Zuduhepa said, clenching a fist.

She was a slight woman about ten years younger than the king, with huge, dark eyes and a towering headdress on her abundant black hair; the rest of her was invisible under layers of embroidered gown. The hand that clenched on the table bore rings set with turquoise and unfaceted emeralds.

"Would that I could have seen Tukulti-Ninurta flayed, castrated, and impaled!" she went on. "Or brought bound before my lord, beaten with rods—"

The king cleared his throat. "We heard of his death and overthrow and questioned refugees, but the tales seemed . . . exaggerated."

He glanced out the window; the *Emancipator* had made more than one journey, ferrying personnel and supplies up from Babylon. It had also taken Tudhaliyas's own envoys south and back. He nodded.

Ian smiled, reading the Hittite monarch's thoughts: *Not only do I need these Nantukhtar to ward off the menace to the West, but if I do not learn some of their arts, Kashtiliash will overshadow me as an oak-tree does a radish.* Tudhaliyas had been dropping broad hints as to whether Jared-Cofflin had a marriagable daughter he would care to wed to his son, Arunuwandas.

It's nice to be loved, but just about as pleasant to be needed.

"And Alaksandrus's faithlessness hurts the realm," Tudhaliyas went on. "For the Wiulusiya are very skilled horse breeders and tamers."

Yes, Arnstein thought as he took a fig out of a bowl to hide his shiver. Homer had called them the "horse-taming Trojans."

The Tawannannas cut in: "Alaksandrus son of Pirusia is a hothead—no better than a pirate, carrying off plunder and women from foreign parts."

That fits the legends too, Ian thought. And three thousand years from now a younger Ian Arnstein would read Homer's immortal words, and now—

"Now the Man of Troy screams for help," the king said. "But the question is, Will he obey? Will he cooperate? Has he even now begun to put out feelers to the enemy, as I suspect? And as I *know* my traitor cousin Lord Kurunta of Tarhuntassa has done?"

Ian looked at the map again. Besides controlling the Bosporus, the Trojan kingdom also controlled a couple of the best land routes up onto the Anatolian plateau.

"That will be awkward," he said. "These barbarians who're invading—What are they like? Where do they come from?"

Tudhaliyas shrugged. "We're not sure. None of them speak any language that we can comprehend; none of the ones we've captured, at least."

He clapped hands, and one of the guards by the door ducked out. A few minutes later two more entered the room, pushing a prisoner before them. The man was tall, taller than either of the burly Hittite guards, and had his hands tied behind his back—his elbows, rather, which looked extremely uncomfortable. His chin had been shaved at some point and was now sprouting oak-brown stubble; his long hair and droopy mustaches were much the same color, and his eyes were dark blue. The remnants of his clothes were plaid, in garish colors. Trousers and shirt and jacket, Ian noted with interest. He also carried a powerful stench, but that was probably the result of imprisonment. A partially healed wound crusted one side of his head, and his eyes were a little bright with fever.

Another trooper lugged along a sampling of equipment. The Arnsteins' eyes narrowed. A broken-off spearhead, with a flame-shaped head and short socket; round-tipped bronze sword with flared-wing hilts cast on; a conical helmet with a model of a raven attached.

On a suspicion, Ian addressed him in the Iraiina language: "Who are you, warrior, and what is your clan and tribe?"

The man started violently and spoke in machine-gun-rapid language. Ian strained and could *almost* follow him; it was like the haunting pseudo-familiarity of Italian to someone who could speak Spanish.

"You know them?" Tudhaliyas said.

"Not them," Doreen answered. "Relatives of theirs, very far to the north and west . . . Ian, I'd say this guy was some sort of Central European, by his looks. Probably, and if he's typical."

Ian nodded thoughtfully, tugging at his beard. Physical appearance tended to follow the same geographical lines here as in the twentieth, roughly—but only roughly, of course.

"These also we took, but they don't seem to belong with the rest," Tudhaliyas said hopefully.

"I'll say they don't," Ian said thoughtfully, as a carpet was laid on the table and the plunder set forth.

Steel knife, he thought. A bowie, to be exact. Steel spearheads. And resting in the center, a double-barreled shotgun, flintlock variety. The prisoner stirred uneasily as Doreen took it up, then shouted and tried to dive for the floor when she pulled back the hammers, pointed it at him and pulled the trigger.

Click-*ting,* and a shower of sparks from the right-side pan; the flint was missing from the hammer on the left. The prisoner raised his head cautiously, opening his eyes.

"Well, that tells us something," Ian said as the man was led away again. *Namely, that this man has seen firearms in action but doesn't know enough to know that one wasn't loaded.*

Tudhaliyas and his queen had tensed as well. "No thunder," he said shakily.

"Well, there goes the gunpowder monopoly we thought we'd have, once," Doreen muttered in English, putting the weapon down. "Damn Walker, anyway."

"No, it needs . . . food," Ian said. They were speaking Akkadian, and Akkadian didn't have a word for gunpowder. Yet.

"Well, that settles it," he said to the Hittite monarchs. "Your barbarian invasion is definitely linked to Walker—Walkheear."

Tudhaliyas shuddered. "The Wolf Lord," he muttered. "We've heard a good deal of *him*. Not least from Ahhiyawa refugees, since he killed their king and took his throne. It's said he has a witch-queen who sacrifices men to a Dark Lady in abominable rites and from their blood brews—ah, that she practices magic."

Ian and Doreen exchanged a glance. She'd kicked him under the table more than once in their joint diplomatic career, and probably Zuduhepa had just given her husband the same service, reminding him that the newcomers probably practiced similar sorcery, only this looked to be on *their* side.

Ian cleared his throat. Hong *did* practice all manner of abominations when she got the chance, and from her file and her record in Alba, she probably did dress them up in cultic garb. Walker would cheerfully turn that to use, of course.

"Walker is a rebel against our rulers, just as Kurunta of Tarhuntassa is against you," he said.

"So here we have Lord Kurunta of Tarhuntassa in rebellion against the Great Throne, probably with the Wolf Lord's aid; and these barbarians invading us from the northwest, also with the Wolf Lord's aid," Tudhaliyas said. "And we have Wiulusiya, which may not be a loyal vassal . . . and Tarhuntassa will make it difficult to receive aid from your people in Babylon, since the best road—Carchemish—runs on the edge of his territory."

Ian sighed. It was becoming increasingly obvious what they'd have to do. *The Republic calls,* he thought, and surprised himself at how little irony there was in it. *I'm getting patriotic in my old age.*

"Well, always interesting to see a new town," Doreen said in English, reading his expression.

"No," Ian said. "I need someone here to coordinate . . . and besides, my dear, if things go wrong . . . well, it would be a hard day for David if we were *both* there, wouldn't it?"

Doreen scowled. "You fight dirty," she said.

"Of course," he replied. "I fight to *win*."

The Hittites were beginning to look uncomfortable with this consultation in a language they could not speak. "My Sun," Ian said to Tudhaliyas, "we have a means of . . . flying over . . . difficulties. And soon we should knit all the strands of our strength together, testing our opponents as we do."

"Sorry to interrupt your honeymoon, Sis," Brigadier Hollard said, reining in his camel in beside hers. He lifted his hat and wiped at the sweat on his face and neck with an already sodden bandanna.

Kathryn, Lady of the Land, Commander of Chariots, grinned back at him. "Wouldn't want to wear things out so soon," she said with a chuckle.

The Marine column was singing as they swung along the dusty dirt track:

Oh, we're marching on relief through Iraq's burning sands
A thousand fighting Islanders, the General, and the band;
Ho! Get away, you bullock-man, you've heard the bugle blowed!
The New Corps is a'comin', down the Hittite road!

"Burning sands is a bit much for Hangilibat," Kathryn said judiciously. "More like 'dry semi-arid.' "

Hollard looked around. *Fair enough,* he thought. Moderately rolling plains, cut by tributaries running down from the Anti-Taurus far to the north to feed the Khabur and then the Euphrates; that was why it was also called the Rivers. There was actual grass on the ground even here; sparse, clumpy, beginning to frizzle up toward summer, but grass nonetheless. Even a few fields plowed into it, and the odd low thicket of waxy-leaved scrub oak.

Or there *had* been fields plowed into it; a lot of the land was deserted, and they'd seen precious little livestock. Supply would be a real problem if the force got any bigger; they had two battalions of Nantucket Marines, six hundred of Babylon's New Troops, some specialists, a contingent of the Royal Guard—also retrained on Westley-Richards breechloaders—and . . .

"Lord Kenn'et!"

Raupasha's chariot drew up beside them; the girl leaned back, the reins in one expert hand, her grin brilliant through sweat-caked dust, the gray eyes shining. The horses snorted and shied a bit at the smell of camel, but a word and pressure on the reins controlled them. She was escorted by Marines, a section of mounted infantry with their rifles at their knees. They were mostly young too; half of them were grinning in sync with the girl's infectious enthusiasm.

She was wearing Marine khakis herself—rather incongruous with the golden fillet of royalty—a Python revolver at her belt and a Werder in a scabbard attached to the frame of the war-car, and he suspected that the gangling spotted hound standing with its forepaws on the front of the chariot and its ears flapping in the breeze was unorthodox too.

"Hello, Princess," he said. "What's new?"

"More men rally to us," she said with delight. "The Hurri-folk *do* accept me!" She flushed a little, and he squirmed at the look in her eyes. "I wasn't altogether sure they would, Lord Kenn'et, but you were right."

"How many does that make now?" he asked, then answered himself. "About three thousand." They came and went, but the total kept going up.

"These brought seven chariots," Raupasha said. "And a hundred footmen! You must meet their leaders when we camp tonight, Lord Kenn'et, and Lady Kat'ryn. When we reach Dur-Katlimmu, they will hear the word of the Great King concerning Mitanni, and I think they will hail it well. I go!"

She turned the chariot in a curve tight enough to bring one wheel off the ground and dashed back down the dusty column, her Marine escort swearing and thumping their heels against the ribs of their horses.

Kathryn leaned over and poked him in the ribs.

"Joan of Arc syndrome, ayup?"

"Well, she's living her daydreams," Hollard said. "What worries me is how we're going to feed all the let's-restore-the-good-old-days-of-Mitanni types she's gathering in. Even with those camel-drawn heavy wagons, we're getting a long way from where our steamboats can reach. But yeah, it'll be convenient; most of the non-Assyrian notables will be there and we can plug them into the new order. With luck we can install her at Dur-Katlimmu"—the largest approach to a city the area had, and the former seat of the Assyrian governor—"install a garrison, and then press on. We're getting real close to areas where this rebel against the Hittite king is operating, and he's in cahoots with Walker."

Kathryn nodded grimly. "Real work," she said. "Kash wishes he could be here, but he's got to consolidate back in Babylon. He said he's going to build a temple in thanks that we Nantukhtar aren't all like Walker."

"He should," her brother agreed.

A click and buzz came from the radio on the back of the tech riding next to him. He edged his camel closer, ignoring its complaints, and took the handset.

"Hollard here," he said. Kathryn watched his expression, and her own went blank.

"Great minds think alike," he said when he replaced the instrument. "Seems the Wolf Lord wants to steal a march on us. Those barbarian allies of his are moving on Troy."

"Troy VI, right enough," Ian muttered to himself.

"Councilor?" Vicki Cofflin asked.

The *Emancipator* was wallowing as she came in toward the city. A hundred or more hands were ready to take the released lines and guide the huge, light craft into the lee of the city's walls—the past three weeks had made them accustomed to it, even if they still tended to make warding signs and spit. He could see the harvesters at work among the fields, orchards and silvery green olive groves among them, and tracts of bright pasture where the city's famous horses were raised. Most of the villages and all the manors of the surrounding lords were empty, though, and a last trickle of refugees was making its way into the six great gates. The grain was coming in too, as fast as it could be cut. The courtyards of houses and the rooftops had been turned into threshing floors.

"Archaeological reference, Ms. Cofflin," Ian said. "Everyone wondered which layer of the site of Troy was *the* Troy, of the Trojan War."

"Yes, but we still aren't *sure* that there *would* have been a Trojan War if we hadn't showed up, are we, Councilor? Maybe it was all just a story, the first time 'round?"

He snorted, and looked down. *Yup.* The king was waiting for him, anxious as ever.

"Sorry, Lieutenant. Don't want to bore you with this sort of thing."

"Oh, hell, no, Councilor. It's a lot more interesting than, say, listening to LG's talk about President Clinton."

He gave her bland smile a look of suspicion—"LG" stood for "Lost Geezer," a not-very-complimentary term the younger generation used for elders who couldn't get over the Event—and then chuckled before he turned and walked back toward the exit ramp with what he hoped was appropriate dignity for meeting a king.

Alaksandrus of Troy had been a surprise. He was a long-nosed, sandy-blond man who reminded Ian of Max von Sydow, as far as looks went. The language he spoke was close enough to Mycenaean Greek that he could understand it without much difficulty; and he spoke the Achaean dialect as well.

What was really surprising about him was his eagerness to cooperate, once he'd gotten over the terror of the dirigible. He cut an imposing figure in his polished bronze breastplate, boar's-tusk helmet with a tall horsehair plume nodding behind, and a metal-reinforced kilt. A few brushes with the invading host from the north—the Ringapi, they called themselves—and their thunder-weapons had knocked most of the swagger out of him. There was something slightly touching about the eagerness with which he'd greeted a chance at salvation.

And something guilt-inducing, as well, Ian thought. *I hope I'm not giving him too many false hopes, just to get him to buy us time.* The way the ordinary people of the city cheered him through the streets was even harder to take. Refugees from the north had described all too vividly what happened in towns and farms the Ringapi took. Even more feared was Walker the Wolf Lord.

The airship's oak landing rails touched the ground, and the rear ramp went down. Ian walked down it, thankful that he didn't have to wear the elaborate caftan that an ambassador's dignity required in Babylonia. A force of Marines directed the unloading of the cargo, with a host of Trojans working like . . .

Don't say it, don't say it, save it for your next chat with Doreen! Ian told himself, bowing to the king.

"When will your troops arrive?" Alaksandrus asked.

Ian sighed internally, keeping a bland smile on his face. "As soon as possible," he said. "We've brought in a good many by air."

It was a sign of how worried Alaksandrus was that he no longer marveled at that but simply accepted it—and railed against its limitations.

"Each trip brings so few," he fretted. The horses of his chariot team seemed to catch the infection and stamped and tossed their heads against the expert touch of the young driver.

"It brings powerful weapons," Arnstein soothed. *And me, more often than I like, because we have to keep you sweet, you old lady in a brass breastplate,* he thought, and pointed.

A heavy seven-foot tube was being lowered onto a waiting timber cradle with oxcart wheels mounted at either end. The dirigible creaked and groaned as it was relieved of the weight, straining upward against the mooring ropes. The cradle groaned as well, and the twelve yoke of oxen bellowed as they were goaded into the traces. The six-inch mortar began to creak its way across the plain of Ilion and toward the South Gate with its great square bastion. The walls of Troy didn't enclose as much ground as Hattusas or Babylon, but they were impressive in their own right, stone-built and better than four stories high, with towers higher. Unlike most he'd seen, they sloped inward slightly.

Captain Chong trotted over, gave the king a bob of the head and Ian a salute. "That's the second battery complete, sir," he said in English. "If these trained pigs of locals don't bog it down, in an hour or so we'll have it mounted."

Ian nodded; he was no expert, but he'd been impressed by the speed and competence of the Marine effort.

"Tell your captain of warriors that my own are worried about the earth ramp," Alaksandrus said. He pointed toward Troy. "They feel it is a scaling ladder that we are building for an enemy."

All around the city, thousands were laboring to build an earth berm up against the stones; thousands more piled earth and rubble from demolished homes against the interior wall, as well.

Chong shrugged when Ian interpreted. "Sir, tell him that without backing and something to absorb the shot, that curtain-wall will get converted into rubble if anyone brings some guns within range of it." He smiled, a savage expression. "Of course, that'll put them within range of *my* guns. Mortars, anyway."

I do wish Alaksandrus would make up his mind what he's more worried about, Ian thought several hours later when he sat down with the shortwave set in his quarters. The Marine operator looked at him and handed over the earpieces and microphone.

"Hard day with the king, sir?"

"Is it that obvious?" he asked—rhetorically.

"Hatussas, Hatussas, come in," he said. "Hatussas—"

"Hatussas here," his wife replied. "Hi, Ian. How's His Gibbering Majesty? I was expecting the Basil Rathbone of the Bronze Age, from Tudhaliyas's description."

"It's not really funny, Doreen," Ian said. "I think he was at least a self-confident pirate until he led his troops to try and stop the Ringapi crossing into Anatolia. He still can't give me a coherent explanation of what happened, except that it involved a lot of explosions and then the Ringapi chariot corps hunting his like hounds after foxes." He paused. "What happens when they win isn't funny at all."

"Yeah," Doreen said quietly. "Anyway, the latest from Colonel—pardon me, Brigadier—Hollard is that—"

"Sir!" A Marine burst into the room. "Sir, the enemy's in sight."

"Oh, shit," Arnstein muttered.

The horde that poured down the flat coastal plain from the north toward Troy was enormous—more people than the whole Republic of Nantucket, the Island, and outports put together.

I've seen as many people at a football game in L.A., Ian tried to tell himself.

That memory paled to nothing before this vision of warriors in gaudy armor in chariots, warriors on foot in plain gray undyed wool with their spears over their shoulders and shields slung at their backs, dusty women trudging beside big ox-drawn carts with their babies on their backs, chieftains' women riding in carts with leather awnings, children running about shouting or crying, herds of cattle and herds of sheep and herds of horses . . . and prisoners trudging behind the wagons, yoked neck to neck with Y-shaped wooden poles.

The noise was like distant surf mixed with a grumble of thunder. The smell of the horde came before it, dust and manure and massed sweat, with somehow a scent of burning. The sound changed but didn't diminish as they settled in, ringing the small hilltop city with a wall of campsites and brush corrals.

"They can't stay," Alaksandrus said, standing beside Arnstein. "They *can't*. There's no food out there! We brought almost everything in and burned what we didn't."

Ian nodded. Troy stank of the beasts driven inside it, and of the peasants who camped in every open space, including on some of the roads.

"I'm sorry, Lord King," he said, "but there comes their supply line."

He pointed at the ships that were sailing in out of the west, their sails gilded by the setting sun.

"The Wolf Lord's ships," Alaksandrus said desolately. Ian brought up his binoculars and looked. They were medium-size sailing vessels, not enormously different from the ones Nantucket or Tartessos turned out; a little lower in the freeboard, perhaps, and he saw differences in the sails that he couldn't name. What all of them had in common was the wolfshead banner at their mastheads, red on black.

A curious change came over the Trojan king; he sighed, and a weight seemed to lift from his shoulders. "A man without hope is a man without fear," he said. "Let's see what his herald has to say."

"You think they'll send a herald?"

"It's usually done." A small quirk of the melancholy lips. "I always did. Surrender is cheaper, if you can get it."

"What are your intentions, Lord King?" Arnstein asked.

Alaksandrus's lips quirked again. "Fight," he said. "Your men may get here before we have to give up—the city's well provisioned, and one can always hope for plague in the besieger's camp."

Things moved with glacial slowness; every so often Ian would look up at the *Emancipator*. He could go . . .

The herald had brass lungs and spoke the Trojan dialect well; he was also dressed in a uniform of gray tunic and trousers, black boots and belt—definitely not one of the horde.

"My lord summons you to parlay," he said. "Outside the walls."

"Does your lord take me for a suckling babe?" Alaksandrus yelled back.

"Do you distrust his word of honor?"

A derisive laugh arose from those crowded near the square towers that marked the gate bastions. The herald nearly wheeled his borrowed Ringapi chariot about to leave, then visibly controlled himself.

"Each party may bring six men. The meeting shall be there—" he pointed to a small hillock in plain view. "Thus neither side may gain unfair advantage."

Alaksandrus nodded slow assent. Ian felt himself doing likewise. It was the old curse; he had to *know*.

The sun was almost to the western horizon, backlighting the masts of the ships anchored offshore with boats going to and fro to unload barrels and sacks. Ian noted other developments with interest; from this ground level position he could see that the prisoners of the horde, and many of its members, were digging a trench and earthwork all around the city.

It would make life much easier, he thought, *if villains were stupid poltroons. Unfortunately, Walker isn't. Mean as a snake, yes. Stupid, no, and nerve enough for three.*

The Trojan party walked forward; three of the guards were Marines with rifles. The group standing to meet them seemed to be mixed, barbarian Ringapi flamboyance and Walker's men in their grimly plain outfits in about equal numbers—and two extra figures whom he took for midgets and then realized with astonishment were children, tow-headed and about ten years old. It wasn't until he was within talking distance that the tall figure in the center threw back the hood of his cloak and Ian Arnstein saw again that boyish, square-jawed, hated face.

Not so boyish anymore, he thought savagely. The left eye was gone, courtesy of Marian's *katana,* and a V of scar ran up under the eye patch. Some lines there, too, and a weathered outdoors look. *Looks healthy, dammit.*

The woman beside him hadn't aged too much either, but the changes in her face—Ian shivered slightly. Objectively speaking, she was a petite, pretty, well-kept Oriental woman in her thirties. But somehow it was if the skull beneath the skin was far more visible now.

"Well, if it isn't the Professor!" Walker laughed delightedly.

Ian replied with a curt nod, making sure that the Python was there under his jacket. For a moment he considered pulling it out and using it—Walker's death was, he decided coldly, worth his own—but it would be foolish. William Walker was far more experienced and deadly at personal violence than Ian Arnstein was ever going to be.

Even the commodore had taken only his eye, the last time they were within arm's reach of each other.

Walker shrugged at his silent glare. "Okay," he said, then dropped into Achaean. A scholar's corner of Ian's mind noted that it was virtually devoid of accent now.

"Here are my terms," he said. "If the city surrenders and admits *my* troops, I'll keep the Ringapi out—they'll be content to move east, provided the city gives them half its gold and silver—and the lives, personal freedom, and remaining property of the inhabitants will be safe; they can have the status of freemen in the kingdom of Mycenae. If you resist, I'll turn my allies loose to sack it when I take it. And I will take it."

King Alaksandrus followed the man's words well enough, but

Ian could see that their lack of the formal phrasing annoyed him, even now.

"What of the king, and the nobles?" he said.

"Deportation to Sicily, or other places of my choice," Walker said. "I'll grant them fiefs equivalent to their lands here, which are forfeit to the crown; they can take a moderate amount of their personal property. And never, never return, under pain of death. The Royal Guard to be split up and enlisted in my regiments."

Ian nodded; that would disperse the Trojan notables, and in a generation or two they'd merge and vanish with the gentry wherever Walker settled them. Assuming that Walker intended to keep his word.

"And if you don't surrender, I won't have the king"—Walker's eye speared Alaksandrus, with a slight smile at the plain armor that was supposed to disguise him—"or his family and nobles killed. I'll turn them over to the Despotnia Algeos, and she won't have them killed either. Show them your masterpiece, Alice."

Alice Hong's smile wasn't a snarl. It was bright and cheery, and far, far worse for that. She pulled the concealing cloak and mask off the figure standing beside her. Ian Arnstein took one look, and knew that however long he lived he would wish he hadn't. He quickly turned his eyes above Hong's head, concentrating on not humiliating himself by vomiting or fainting.

They're trying to shake you, Arnstein. You will be calm. Or at least *look* calm, if that was the best he could do. Far and faint he heard a child's voice mutter in accented English, "Oh, *yuk-o*, Auntie Hong!" Somehow that made him feel even more furious, but it also made him more able to ignore Hong's cheerful explanations:

"—problem of preventing infection with the exposed bone here and here, but—"

"Take that . . . *thing* away," Alaksandrus said. He spat, and then spoke one word: "No."

"No?" Walker said. "Last chance. Or—" he indicated the vaguely humanoid figure that didn't move except to breathe, as if each breath were fresh torment.

"No. And the gods my ancestors will receive me if I fall; I will not be taken alive. Your threat is empty."

Walker shrugged and made a sign with his hand; Hong stooped and draped the cloak about the unmoving figure with an obscene tenderness.

"I'm just as glad," he said casually. "The troops need a little blooding." He looked at the city. "Somebody's been giving you advice, I see. But being able to take it doesn't help if you can't dish it out as well." He looked at Ian. "Special offer for you, Professor. I could use a man like you—and I know how to reward service, too. Who knows?

You might like working for me more than that old fossil Cofflin. We might turn out to be *simpatico,* you and I."

"Now you're getting *nasty,*" Ian said quietly. "I'll wait, thank you very much."

"For what, the Riders of Fucking Rohan to come galloping to the rescue with their horns blowing and slaughter us insensitive orcs?" he jeered and waved an arm in an expansive gesture. "Sorry, Professor, no TV cameras. This is Big-People Land—out here, things don't work that way."

Arnstein met his eyes. "Your father," he said flatly, "was a hampster. Your mother smelled of elderberries. Now go away, you silly Greek knigget, or I will taunt you once again."

Walker's face was equally cold for an instant. Then he smiled again. "Don't catapult any cows at us," he said. "You're probably going to need them all, if you're lucky."

CHAPTER TWENTY-SIX

August–September, Year 10 A.E.

"Command us, Lord Kenn'et!"

Hell, Kenneth Hollard thought, looking at the motley crowd assembled behind Raushapa's chariot. *And I thought the Babylonians were ragged.*

Many of the men gathered under the flag of Mitanni—suggested by the Arnsteins, and consisting of a white chariot wheel on a blue background, with crossed thunderbolts behind—were *literally* ragged; peasants in rags armed with anything at all, down to and including rocks snatched up a few minutes ago.

Some had better equipment, which looked as if it had spent the past twenty years or so buried under the stable floor or hidden in caves. Wheels on chariots were actually wobbling, the horses were mostly elderly crow bait, and the bronze helmets and armor were green with verdigris where recent polishing hadn't revealed dents, nicks, and ominous-looking holes. Their smell was formidable, too, although there he had to grant that everyone was getting a bit gamey, with water short and a lot of work in the hot sun.

There were better than three thousand men and nearly a hundred chariots all up, though, and from their roaring cheers when Raushapa harangued them in Hurrian they seemed enthusiastic enough.

"Translate for me," he said when she'd finished, stepping up into the chariot beside her. Sabala's leash was tied to the railing, and the hound barked hysterically until Raupasha called him sharply to heel.

"Men of Mitanni," he began. That brought another long cheer. "Men of Mitanni, your kingdom has been restored, now that Asshur is thrown down."

This time he was afraid the cheers would make somebody pop a blood vessel; a couple *had* fainted, although that might be the heat.

"We were traveling to Dur-Katlimmu to enthrone your queen." Impatient, he held up a hand. *They can certainly cheer; can they fight?* "Now a force of the Hittite rebel Kurunta of Tarhuntassa approaches, to deny you that."

This time the sound was a low growl. The Assyrians were hated bitterly, but the Hittites had left plenty of grudges as well.

"With him march men of the Wolf Lord of Ahhiyawa," he said, watching their unease. Rumors had penetrated this far, at least. "He has strong weapons and powerful magic, but so do your allies. Watch, and see."

A shiver of anticipation ran over them; they'd all heard what happened to the Assyrians. Hollard jumped down and walked over to the baggage train. The Islander section of it was mostly huge wagons pulled by twenty pair of camels; the beasts were groaning and complaining, as usual.

A squad of Marine technicians had stacked their rifles and were hard at work assembling the ultralight that had come in with the latest shipment from the Island. As he watched they gave a unified *hup-ho!* and heaved the arrowhead-shaped wing up on top of the three aluminum struts above the little teardrop-shaped fuselage. That creaked on its tricycle undercarriage and creaked again as they busied themselves with the bolts. The pilot was going over the engine that drove the prop behind her seat, but came to her feet as he drew near.

"Sir!"

"At ease, Kayle," he said. *God, she looks pathetically young.* "How does it look?"

"It's a nice simple little engine, sir," the Guard pilot said. "I double-checked the filters to make sure no sand had gotten into it. And, ah, sir . . ."

"Yes, Kayle?"

"Sir, we're not fitting the bomb racks?"

"Kayle, this is a scouting mission. I want information, *capiche*?"

"Sir, yessir."

Kayle pushed her goggles back up on her forehead, threw her scarf over her shoulder, and climbed into the tiny cockpit. She tested the controls—essentially a set of wires that warped the wing—and chopped her hand forward. The crew bent and pushed the wing onto a stretch of open ground with no large rocks and turned the nose of the ultralight into the wind. The engine coughed, sputtered, then began its insectile drone.

The crew kept hold of the wingtips until the pilot shouted to them to release, and the little aircraft bounced forward. Faster, with dirt and dust trailing back in a broad plume, and then on the fourth bounce it was airborne, banking up into the cloudless aching-blue sky.

A long soft sigh of wonder came from the Mitannians as the eagle-painted wings banked and headed northwest to where the camel scouts had brushed the enemy patrols. Raupasha sighed herself as she stood beside him.

"To fly like that!" she said. "The *Emancipator* is a wonder, but *that* would be like having the wings of your Eagle god, Lord Kenn'et."

"It is fun." He found himself grinning at the girl's eagerness, and then a thought struck him like ice water injected directly into the stomach.

"It will make me feel much safer, when I lead my people into the fight," she said sunnily.

Oh, shit.

Captain Chong smiled behind the slit of the sandbagged observation bunker, one of dozens built along Troy's wall. The rising sun was behind them, giving a good view of the shoreline a half mile away; the city would be only a jagged black outline against a ball of fire to observers there. The Ringapi camp sprawled between, its campfires hazing heaven with their smoke. He cranked the field telephone sharply and pressed the Send button.

"Up two," the Marine said. "Ranging round, fire!"

There was a *whump* from the Citadel, a long droning whistle, and then a slamming *crump* from the beach. Dirt and sand gouted skyward.

Ian Arnstein raised his glasses. The cannon were still being towed shoreward on rafts from the Achaean ships anchored offshore. *Not many black hulls pulled up on the beach,* he thought, watching the doll-tiny men straining at their oars. The ships Walker had built were too big to do that; many of them were three-masters. There were a few of the traditional long, low penteconters, and he saw one that looked like a late-medieval Venetian galley, huge oars pulled by four men each and a brace of big guns pointing forward. That chilled him a little; it was just like Walker to commission a vessel of the sort that had made galley slaves common. Before then rowers were almost always free men.

"The ships are just out of reach," Chong said. "Three rounds, for effect!" And then "Cease fire!" regretfully, as the boats towing the rafts turned around and began thrashing the water toward the ships they'd just disembarked from.

"Then they can't get their guns close to the walls?" Ian said hopefully.

"I didn't say that, sir," Chong said. "They just can't land them *here.* We're on the highest ground around, so we can hammer them as they come ashore. They'll have to take them out of range and then bring them within range of the walls by night one at a time. It'll cost them heavily, but I've got only four tubes and my ammunition is limited. Eventually they'll get the guns in protected positions close enough to hit us."

"What then?" Arnstein asked, licking dry lips.

The Chinese-born officer buckled his binocular case with a snap. "Then they pound us into dust," he said quietly.

Arnstein nodded. *But we're buying time,* he thought. It was a little comfort; not much, but a little. *Walker doesn't deal with frustration well. If we stand him off, he'll get mad and stay longer than he should. Probably he just showed up to get things started.*

The bulk of the renegade's troops were obviously elsewhere, judging by the numbers he could see. *Doing what?* he wondered—and then wished he hadn't.

You wanted adventure and travel, Mandy Kayle thought, licking lips dried by the airstream. *All right, Ms. Hotshot Pilot, you've got it. Endless deserts full of homicidal locals.*

The tawny landscape rolled away beneath her, with here and there a line of greener vegetation to mark a watercourse or arroyo. The wind blew past at forty-five miles an hour, barely a crawl up here at two thousand feet. She could see the dust plumes now.

"*Eagle Eye II* here," she said; it was a pilot's privilege to pick her own call sign. "*Eagle Eye II.* I have the enemy under observation."

"You're coming through loud and clear, Two."

"Enemy are three miles to your northwest, proceeding in two columns of unequal size. Estimate the larger column to consist of"—she juggled control stick and binoculars, tipping the *Eye* to the right to improve her view—"local troops, chariots one-fifty, repeat one-fifty, infantry three thousand, archers and spearmen, with oxcarts and pack donkeys to match. Over."

"Excellent work, *Eye.* Over."

Details sprang out at her: a charioteer's long black hair spilling from under his helmet, ax flashing as he gestured with it; the plodding pace of infantry, breathing their own dust; a ripple of light on spearheads through the dust. The other column . . .

"Proceeding to close on second column."

She pushed the stick forward and to the side, working the pedals with her feet. There was the familiar lovely swooping sensation, the rattle and hum of air through the rigging, the snap of her scarf behind her. More grit at this level, but she kept the goggles up for a better view.

"Second column is troops with firearms! Repeat, troops with firearms!"

Men marching in order, in a column of fours behind a standard-bearer; mounted officers in modern saddles. Big wagons pulled by horses as well. And . . . one, two . . . *six* cannon. Something else too, something she couldn't quite identify.

And they'd seen her, right enough, men pointing, their mouths moving silently through the lenses of her binoculars. Moving to order, their packs thrown down, blocks throwing up their rifles in unison. Muzzle flashes winked up at her . . .

Her mouth went drier, and she could feel her stomach trying to crawl up into her lungs for safety. There were an almighty *lot* of bullets coming her way; she sucked the stick back and reached up to push the throttles all the way to their not-very-powerful maximum.

"Sir, they've got breechloaders. Awful damned good ones, too."

She banked sharply, jinked, threw the responsive little craft around the sky. She was standing it nearly on edge when the enemy pulled a tarpaulin off a wagon bed and swung a thick-barreled *something* on a yoke mount that let them point it rapidly to any portion of the sky. As she hung at the top of the curve, she was miserably certain that it was pointing directly at the part of the sky she occupied right then and there. It fired; she was expecting some sort of shell, but instead there was a muzzle flash like a rifle's, only many times repeated, and a torrent of smoke, enough for a whole company volley.

"What *is* that—"

Her speculation was cut short by the arrival of the malignant lead bee swarm. Rounds went *ptunk!* through the taut fabric of *EEII*'s wings, and cracked into the plywood of the fuselage like nails driven by a mad carpenter. Her skin went cold for a second; any one of those could hit *her* and go through her the long way. Then her heart stuttered as a bullet *pinged* off metal; let one of them hit the wrong part of the engine, and she'd have no choice but a gliding landing—and saving the last bullet in the Python at her waist for herself.

"Automatic weapon. I say again, the enemy have—"

The dead tone in her earphones when she pressed the switch alerted her. She joggled the switch, and nothing happened but a faint frying sound. *Must have been hit.* There went another of their precious pre-Event radios; more important, she'd have to deliver the news herself. That provided a perfect and honorable excuse to stop flying this very unfriendly patch of sky.

The *EEII* was at extreme rifle range now; she turned the nose back to the southeast, aiming the point at the distant column of dust that meant home and the Republic's protecting arm.

Wizt-wizt-wizt-wizt . . .

This time she felt the little craft shudder as it was hit. The engine coughed and stuttered, and then took up its buzzing with a ragged edge, like her heartbeat. Something struck like fire and ice in her lower back, and her foot fell off the rudder bar. She reached behind her and felt a warm wetness.

And, she realized, sensation in her foot and toes as well. A wave of irrational thankfulness hit her. Not a spinal injury. *And a lot of good that does me if I bleed to death!*

Marines were running past outside the aid tent as Justin Clemens reached behind his back to tie on his surgical gown. He glanced up; the ultralight was returning . . . but wobbling in the air and trailing smoke.

"Business in the shop, people!" he said and felt hands touch his; Azzu-ena finishing the ties with neat bowknots.

He turned to do hers as well, his mask still down around his neck. Everything looked ready, the doctors and assistants were running in and scrubbing down, and the little kerosene burners under the autoclaves were hissing. *God damn this heat and all this grit,* he thought. *We'll need plenty of gauze coverings to keep it out of the working areas.*

"I should have stayed in Babylon," he grumbled.

"Why?" Azzu-ena said, checking instruments on a tray beside their table, her fingers flicking rapidly. "The epidemic is over, and you are a figure of fear. King Kashtiliash is building the water towers you requested, but you would do him no favor by staying there. Let memories cool."

Clemens nodded. The system would purify even Euphrates water, and it would run to public fountains. And the next shipment from Nantucket was supposed to include a complete vaccination-preparation setup for Ur Base. Then, by God, he would vaccinate the whole of Kar-Duniash, if he had to chase them down and do a flying tackle on each and every one.

The stretcher bearers came in, with the bloodied form of the pilot lying facedown. The back of her uniform tunic was sopping; Azzu-ena took a pair of scissors and cut it away as he leaned forward, pulling up his mask. His hands probed the area between pelvis and spine.

"Bullet, no exit wound, internal bleeding too, we'll have to open her up!" *And hope it didn't destroy her liver.* "Saline, ether, stat, get someone her type in here, let's get a move on here, people!" he snapped, then turned and saw Brigadier Hollard crouched by her head; she was still conscious, but her eyes were wandering.

"What the hell are you doing here!" Clemens roared. "You're not sterile, you're endangering the patient, get the hell out!"

"Shut up," Hollard hissed, his voice flat and deadly enough to stop even Justin Clemens in midphrase.

". . . *Auto, some sort of automatic, mounted on a wagon—*"

"I've got it, Kayle," Hollard said gently. "Rest now. They'll patch you up."

Then he was gone from the tent in four long strides.

"Remember Lord Kenn'et's words!" Raupasha shouted. "Against the Hittites, fight like lions—against the wizard's men, chariots are to flee and footmen to fall flat." There was an unhappy murmur, and she put metal into her voice. "There is no honor in putting yourself in the way of a *bullet*."

The emergency demonstration with a couple of sick donkeys had been impressive; she just hoped it hadn't killed the men's spirit.

"Follow me, men of Mitanni!" she said. "Once again you are called to war, you descendants of men who bestrode the universe. Teshub and Indara Thunderer are with us!"

She signaled to the driver and he pulled the heads of the horses around, clicking to them.

"Not too fast," she said, putting the thought of Sabala's pleading eyes out of her mind; strange that it should strike her now. "We have a better team and a better chariot; we are to lead, not lose them in our dust."

As she spoke she pulled the rifle from its scabbard that her friend Fusaro had made for her back at Ur Base. *Strange, to have a leatherworker as a friend, but that is the Eagle People way.* The weapon was balanced and deadly in her hands, and she'd always been a good shot—first with the bow and then with rifles. And with this rifle, all she needed was to be deft and have a keen eye, and to be as formidable as any. It was a heady feeling.

The coat of light chain mail Kenn'et had insisted on—*Mitara, Lord of Justice, preserve him!*—was only enough weight to anchor her securely; the chariot bounced far less than the ones she had grown up with, making more of a sway than a blow against her feet. She squinted under the brim of her helmet and saw the Hittite host approaching.

Rebel Hittite host, she reminded herself. Tudhaliyas was an ally of Nantucket, therefore of hers. Then: *I am afraid, but I can master it.* The conquering of fear was as heady as the *soama* of the ancient stories, the drink that made her ancestors as one with the gods.

Now they were close enough that she could see men through the dust and flash of movement. Three-man Hittite carts, driver and warrior and shield bearer, heavier than hers, horses' sides covered by leather blankets sewn with scales, the crews armored as well. All that weight might well slow them enough that her poor followers with their knackers-yard horses wouldn't be at too much of a disadvantage. The footmen would be; those following the rebel lord's chariots were fully equipped, nearly every man with helmet and good shield, long spear, sword, leather tunic boiled in vinegar or wax. When the infantry met, it would go hard for her folk. That grieved her, but the battle was to be won; so her foster father had taught her, and the Eagle People. She knew the price of defeat too well.

She brought her rifle up, looked back at the wedge of chariots that followed her. Some were out of the fight already, tumbled with wheels off or axles broken. Most followed, and she waved them to her right. They swung after her, and she brought the weapon up and aimed, knees flexing.

Crack. A miss, and an arrow went *whirrrt* through the chariot; they were within a hundred yards. But Hittites weren't archers of note, they preferred the javelin and thrusting spear. She pulled a bullet from the bandolier looped around her body and thumbed it home.

Crack. A man flung up his arms and fell backward out of his chariot, tumbling as the speed of the galloping horses threw his body against the ground. That would have broken bones even if his wound was slight.

Raupasha daughter of Shuttarna shouted in exultation.

"They're behind the locals, all right, behind and to the right," O'Rourke said. "We stung 'em."

"What arms?" Kenneth Hollard asked, handing up his canteen. The camel-mounted commander of the Scout company leaned down and took it, drinking with appreciation. The day was growing hotter as the sun rose toward noon.

"Breechloaders for certain. Most of them Westley-Richards like we were using last year," he said. "But they've got something very nasty as well, not a Gatling but something of the sort. Several of them. Cost us."

He inclined his head. Wounded Marines were being lifted off camels and onto stretchers; some were being laid out with blankets over their faces.

"And a battery of fieldpieces—twelve-pounder Napoleons would be my guess—and something else, further back, that they didn't use."

"Numbers?"

"Around a thousand, I'd say—not counting teamsters and such. They moved from column into line very fast indeed, Brigadier, sir. Fire and movement, extended order."

"Thanks, Paddy. Pull your people out, get them something to eat"—he'd had the field kitchens set up along with the hospital; you needed both—"and then dig in, and we'll see what happens. With luck, they think this force is simply locals, an ultralight, and you."

"With luck indeed."

Hollard looked along the line where his Marines were digging in, and the man-tall hillocks over to his left where the New Troops of Babylon waited. *One good thing is that soil doesn't show up very well here,* he thought. *Another is that khaki blends in very well indeed.*

He walked forward to the spot where part of the heavy-weapons company was setting up. He'd pushed the Gatlings well forward, giving them interlocking fields of fire along his front and open ones to the flanks. The sergeant in charge paused with a rock the size of a loaf of bread in her hands.

"Bit different from Babylon, nae, sir?"

He nodded, and she hesitated. "Sir, ask you a favor? Sir, it's a letter. In case Skyfather calls me."

He took it: *Delauntarax of the Thaurinii, in Alba* was written in a shaky hand. Vague, but the Postal Service was used to that; things got through eventually.

"Keep masked until the word comes down, and it'll be the other side who go to feast in the sky," he said, tucking it into a pocket.

She nodded. The crew threw a khaki-colored groundsheet over the Gatling on its two-wheel mount and scattered handfuls of dirt over that. Having dug their own holes, the infantry were doing likewise.

Hollard walked out in front of his own line and examined it carefully. The *maskirovka* was good—a useful Russian word much emphasized in the tactical manual put together by a committee of retired types with several centuries of combat experience between them. It was another advantage the Islanders had. He'd met plenty of Bronze Age hunters who were *extremely* good at hiding out, but few of the warrior types thought that way. Most of them had styles that deliberately drew the enemy's attention, and by their codes trying to hide was shameful.

Inconspicuous, he thought, looking at his own position. *Looks exactly like about one company, hastily dug in.*

Besides the *maskirovka,* they'd used the irregularities of the ground well; the supplies and hospital tent were out of sight altogether, behind swellings that turned them into dead ground.

He looked back and forth. Troops dug in, reserves at hand, weapons placed by the book . . . now all he could do was pray.

"They come," Raupasha said, jumping down from her chariot before the hillock that held the expeditionary force's command personnel. That wasn't much: Kenneth Hollard, his six-person staff, and a clump of communications technicians and runners.

The horses were flaring their nostrils to draw breath, foam splattered their necks and shoulders, and several arrows stood in the frame of the vehicle. Kenneth Hollard saw with a sudden stab of alarm that she was holding one hand to her side, with blood on her fingers.

"You're hit?" he said.

"It is nothing, Kenn'et," she said. "A graze. One of the Hittite charioteers had a gun—the type with two barrels, that shoots many bullets . . ."

"Shotgun," he said automatically.

"A shotgun. But he aimed badly, and I did not." She pointed behind her. "They come."

He nodded. The Hittites were whooping forward about half a mile away, and the Mitannians retreating fast and to the right. Thank God they'd kept enough wits to remember what he'd said; he didn't want friendly forces masking his fire when the fecal matter hit the air-circulating device. And from the dust—bless the dust here, you couldn't move troops without raising it, and it was a boon to the man standing still—Walker's men were coming in on *their* right a mile further back, ready to support their local allies.

"You should get back to the hospital tent and have that seen to," Hollard said sternly, then smiled. "I don't want it festering."

"No, it would spoil the coronation if I smelled like a corpse three days dead," Raupasha laughed. "Teshub and Indara be with you, Kenn'et, and hold their hand over you."

"Amen," Hollard muttered.

She saluted and gave him an urchin grin as he returned the gesture—she had earned it, today and in Babylon. Then she walked away; the driver handed off his team and went after her, carrying the scabbarded Werder and the ammunition, and following the princess with an expression about as doglike as Sabala's.

Have to find her a husband, I suppose, Hollard thought. Though . . . most of the local aristocrats and princelings wouldn't be very happy with a woman who had been contaminated with Islander ideas of independence. *Not necessarily or all the time,* he thought. *Look at my new brother-in-law. So we should be able to dig someone up for her.* The thought was obscurely irritating, and he pushed it aside. Business to attend to.

Now to see if his plan worked. Usually they didn't, in combat. The exceptions were where you'd completely suckered the other side, a successful ambush or flank attack. That was when you won big.

The Hittites were coming full-tilt for his position. He leveled his binoculars; chariots in front at the trot, footmen running behind—standard formation, for the Near East in the thirteenth century B.C. The Hittites would be more prone to try and ram right in than most, using the chariot for shock. He caught one man with a sun disk on the top of his conical helmet, shouting orders and waving a sword; not

Kurunta of Tarhuntassa himself, but probably a relative—the Hittite Empire was a family business, cemented by a stream of daughters from Hattusas sent out to marry vassal kings, and vice versa. The snipers had been briefed to look for that insignia.

Closer, closer. Hollard's lips skinned back as he scanned to his left. Walker's men were coming on briskly, advancing in company columns at the double, with their rifles across their chests. Trotting along were what looked like fieldpieces, six-horse teams, and light gleaming off iron and brass.

They're using the Hittites to unmask and develop our position, he thought, plus using them to simply soak up bullets. Reasonably well-trained men and a commander with some grasp of tactics, then. Possibly one of Walker's Islander renegades. He hoped so; it would be a positive pleasure to string one of *them* up. They'd all been sentenced to death for treason in absentia years ago, too.

Hollard judged distances; you went by which features of a man's body you could see easily, when legs became separate from the generalized antlike blob, when you could see arms swing or a face. The Hittites were closing rapidly, but the Walkerites were hanging back— over two thousand yards, extreme rifle range but well within that of heavy-weapons fire.

He reached for the radio at his belt and clicked. "Captain O'Rourke."

"Here, sir."

"Let them have it, Paddy."

"With a will, Brigadier, sir, with a will."

BAAAAMMM!

A hundred rifles volleyed from the Scouts' deliberately badly camouflaged rifle pits. *Maskirovka* was more than just hiding; it was *deception*, disinformation. It wasn't what you didn't know that killed you, it was what you thought you knew that wasn't so. A dozen Hittite chariots went down; a few of them flipped completely over, pitching forward and squashing the screaming crews like bugs beneath a frying pan.

Schooonk . . . whonk!

The Scouts' mortar opened up as well. A shell landed in the middle of the dense-packed Hittite infantry, and men fell, opening out in a circle around the explosion like an evil flower with a crimson blossom. The riflemen were firing independent-rapid as well and at less than four hundred yards mostly hitting. Men and chariots were going down all across the Hittite front; he saw arrows fly out, few covering even half the distance, and there were puffs of smoke from some of the chariots—smoothbores firing shot, even more futile than the bows. The charge wavered, which was exactly the wrong thing to do, like most half measures. They should either run as fast as they could, take cover, or keep charging. A running man could cover four hundred yards in a disconcertingly short time, if you were on the receiving end.

Horns and trumpets sounded. Hollard brought up his binoculars; the man with the sun disk on his helmet had survived and was going into a frenzy of signaling. In between he fired shotguns, handing them off to a loader as he did so—a new use for the three-man Hittite chariot crew, and quite ingenious. The chariots reversed themselves and galloped away, and the infantry flattened themselves to the ground.

Schooonk . . . whonk! More mortar shells falling among the prostrate men. He sympathized, in a way; that was the most unpleasant part, having to wait helplessly and hope you were lucky. Mostly he felt detached. Down underneath he could feel fear, not so much fear of death as of certain mutilating wounds, and more fear for the lives that depended on his decisions.

"Here they come," he said aloud, and his staff nodded soberly.

The Walkerites were deploying, going from column into a two-line formation, well spread out, swinging in to envelop the little Islander position.

"Right, about six hundred up, say three hundred in reserve," he said.

Through the binoculars he could see men manhandling weapons forward. They were on field-gun carriages with shields, like the Islander Gatlings but not quite the same. Fairly light, or they couldn't be brought forward that fast—keeping up well with the infantry. A battery of six real field guns galloped forward and then deployed, the teams turning and then being unhitched and led to the rear, crews leaping down and running the ammunition limbers forward, ready to form a chain to hand rounds up to the loading teams.

Budumm. A sound like a heavy door closing and a long puff of smoke from one of the enemy cannon; it ran back under the recoil. No surprise; the Republic couldn't make a mobile gun with a recoil-absorbing carriage yet either. Then a savage snapping *crack* of red fire in the air not far behind Paddy's position, and a wide oval of dust as the casing fragments and lead balls hit the ground.

Muzzle-loaders, twelve-pounder smoothbores, he thought, watching the swab-ram-fire loading drill. *Firing shrapnel, time-fused shells.* They were getting off more then two rounds a minute. Good practice.

Somewhere his soul winced; he'd put Paddy's unit out there as bait, and they were going to pay again, the way they had this morning. The rifle fire dropped off as the Scouts hugged the bottoms of their holes; the area around their position was turning into a haze of dust an smoke as the enemy fell into a regular rhythm of load-run-up-swab-ram-fire, rounds coming forward from the limbers like a bucket chain at a blaze.

Price of doing business, he told himself, as the cry of "corpsman!" went up and the stretcher teams went forward. He'd authorized enlisting local volunteers to carry wounded, to free his own troops for the fighting, and they were going in as bravely as men could be asked to do.

"Captain Lautens," he said into the radio. He wished Chong were here—he knew the man's work—but Lautens hadn't screwed up so far. The artillery commander's voice replied crisply:

"When you unmask, go for those whatever-they-ares brought forward with the infantry; they're your first priority."

"Sir, yessir. We're ready."

"Good man."

Closer, closer . . . One of the mystery weapons stopped, turned. The shield hid whatever it was the crew did at the breech, but he could see rifle rounds sparking off it in snapping white flicks of light, leaving lead smears across the metal. *Has to be steel for that,* he thought; a wrought-iron shield would be too soft. Then the muzzle flashes, and a distant *braaaaapp* of sound. The bullets struck sparks all around the Scout company's mortar position, off rocks and the barrel of the weapon. The crew had gone to earth in their slit trench, as he'd ordered in advance—they were there to lure the enemy, not hurt him.

"Take a note of that shield," he said to the lieutenant who was in charge of Intel. "Multiple barrels, I'd say." Hadn't there been some French weapon? "Rate of fire's not as high as a Gatling, but it's definitely useful."

Fairly close now, the long line of men jogging forward, their artillery firing over their heads. Those heads went up, an apprehensive movement—valuable clue to the reliability of their fuses. Now they went down on one knee, bringing their rifles to their shoulders . . .

"Paddy, your people are out of it—have them cease fire and take cover. All company commanders," he said into the radio. *"Now!"*

Canvas covers flew off, and the whole of the Islander position erupted in smoke and red strobing flashes. The Marine riflemen were firing at maximum speed, mad-minute snatch-and-shoot; the Gatling gunners turning the cranks and grinding out a storm of lead like water from a high-pressure hose. An endless string of firecrackers might have sounded something like that, if they'd been thrown by the hundreds. The steady, heavy thuds of the artillery came through it, and he saw one of the enemy rapid-fire weapons disintegrate, wheel and barrel and shield flying in separate directions . . . probably with pieces of the crew mixed in.

* * *

"Clamp! Clamp and tie off."

Clemens hated spouting wounds. Azzu-ena's hand came down into the cavity with the long scissorslike instrument; the blunt tips found the vein and pinched it closed. An assistant slid her fingers in with the loop of catgut ready. They stayed out of his way with practiced skill.

"Number four!" he called, and someone put it into his hand. It was a small silvered mirror on the end of a thin curved handle. He slid it in carefully . . .

"Got it! Extractor."

The number four went into his left hand, and he used the tiny smeared picture to guide the needle-nosed instrument in his right. Ease it closed, and the feel of metal under the heads. Jiggle. *Yes!* A surge of triumph as he eased it out, brought the bent, distorted lump of metal up before his eyes. *Good. Didn't break up.* He examined the track of the wound again, checking for bits of cloth and killed tissue that would rot if left in.

"Irrigate and swab," he said when he was sure. "Close him up."

The final running stitch, the assistants painting with disinfectant and bandaging. He checked the blood pressure; no real need for a transfusion, although he'd have ordered one back on the Island, just in case. Here there were too many who *really* needed it, and no refrigerated whole blood on hand—you had to do it live.

"Next!"

"That's it, Doctor," the orderly said.

Clemens staggered slightly, like a man who'd run down stairs in the dark and expected a few more at the bottom than there were. He looked around; four of the other surgeons were busy, but no fresh cases were coming in—nothing but routine bandaging, at least.

"Take a break," he said, then walked out of the tent and into an area shaded by an awning, scrubbed and dried off, and collapsed onto a bench and pulled down his mask. Azzu-ena sat beside him and handed him an enameled mug of water. He took it, relishing the slightly chlorine-tasting lukewarmness of it.

"You're getting good," he said.

She blushed slightly and rubbed at her big hooked nose. "I've had a good teacher."

He hesitated and opened his mouth to speak. Instead he froze, looking up. There was a screaming in the air, and an arching trail of smoke from the north, where the burble of small-arms fire continued. The screaming grew louder, and he found himself acting without making a decision at all, sweeping the Babylonian into his arms and diving for the ground, his body covering hers.

* * *

"Damn," Kenneth Hollard said mildly. "Moral courage."

"Sir?" one of the staff officers said. She had a slight Fiernan accent, so he amplifed.

"The enemy commander has moral courage. He's not afraid to admit he got suckered and cut his losses and retreat."

The smoke obscured his view, but through the gaps the wind made he could see the enemy infantry pulling back—one line lying prone and firing, the other turning and dashing to the rear for fifty yards, then falling to the earth and giving covering fire while their comrades did the same, or dragged back the not-too-badly wounded. The rapid-fire weapons did the same, the three that were left; the field guns were still firing, the crews snatching up the trails as they recoiled and running them back with the momentum, stopping and firing again, repeating the process. *And* the enemy commander had uncommitted reserves.

"Order our people forward, sir?" the staffer asked. Hollard shook his head again.

"We'd take a heavy butcher's bill doing that," he said. "And they can move backward just as fast as we can move forward." He looked up; it was well past noon. "They'd break contact in the dark; we don't have the numbers to overrun them."

He looked over to his left, to the range of rocky hills. A little further away than he'd like, but ground was ground—you couldn't rearrange it to suit. He might not have the numbers required to simply overwhelm the enemy, but he *did* have a card up his sleeve.

That was your one really bad mistake, he thought at the enemy commander. *Too eager.* Too convinced that he had to move forward with maximum speed to snap up the tempting target of an isolated Nantucketer force. *You should have scouted the whole area thoroughly— used your Hittites for it.*

Kenneth Hollard reached for the radio; the Babylonian New Troops had only one, their commander's. Just then a moaning whistle brought his head up sharply. A trail of fire and smoke rose up from the rear of the enemy position. It moaned across the sky; he turned to watch it overshoot his command post, heading for the rear area.

I'm not the only one who had a surprise up his sleeve, he knew with angry self-reproach.

"All units, go to ground and take cover," he barked into the handset. "Rocket bombardment incoming!"

The staff and runners jumped for the slit trenches. Hollard vaulted into one too, but braced himself forward on one knee to observe. The rocket launchers had looked like wagons with their canvas covers on. Those were back, the boxy frames that held the six tubes elevated by a crank. As he watched, a man snapped a lighter under a dangling fuse and then turned and ran, diving to the ground a hundred feet away. The rockets lit with a dragon's hiss, firing one by one in no particular order as the combined fuse split into individual ones and reached the powder but *fast*.

He dropped into the bottom of the narrow trench and brought knees to chin, letting his flared helmet cover as much of him as possible. Now it was simply luck. The sky overhead shrieked as if in torment, and then the multiple *CrackCrackCrackCrack* and surf-roar of impact began.

"First Kar-Duniash!" he shouted into the receiver.

"Here." Kathryn Hollard's voice, calm but with an underlying tension.

"Go for it, Sis. Those things can reload fast—he can punish us and pull out behind it."

"Will do."

The doctor and the *asu* came to their feet, brushing themselves off. Justin Clemens looked around; there was a crater in the empty land two hundred yards away, but nobody seemed to be hurt. Not here; up north the sky was woven with a web of smoke trails and a continuous rippling roar of explosions.

They would be very busy soon. Justin Clemens felt his hands begin to tremble and his breath grow short. *Elevated blood pressure and stress*, he told himself, which helped very little.

"Ms. Azzu-ena," he croaked.

She looked at him, dark eyes alert; she knew that meant formality, in English.

"Wwww . . . Would you please marry me?"

Her eyes flared wide; whatever she'd been expecting, it wasn't *that*. Then they filled with tears, and she opened her mouth to reply.

"Here they come!"

The cry brought their heads up. Horse-drawn ambulances were jouncing down the rough ground from the north, toward the laagered wagons and the tents. They turned and dashed back into the operating theater, heading for the vats of disinfectant.

"I have no dowry!" she hissed, as they ran their arms under the stream.

"I wouldn't say that," he said. "I wouldn't say that at all."

We're nearly behind them, Kathryn Hollard thought.

The enemy advance had swept past the hiding place of her force. But they had three-quarters of a mile to cover before they reached the position where rocket launchers were vomiting fire back at the Islanders. One had blown up in a spectacular globe of red-gold flame as it was being reloaded, but that left five. The wind swept smoke toward them, smelling of burnt sulfur and death.

"Men of the First Kar-Duniash!" she said, looking down the line.

Eight hundred of them, crouching with their bearded faces turned first toward the sounds of battle and then toward her. *God knows, there are times when I wanted you all dropped into hell and the door locked and the key in Dr. Hong's pocket,* she thought. She *had* hung four in Babylon for rape and looting during the street fighting, and then she'd had to pistol the brother of one of the convicted when he tried to murder her.

"For your king and your salt and given oaths," she said. "The battle cry is *Kashtiliash*! Now follow me!"

She scrambled forward, and there was a multiple clatter and scrape of hobnails on rock; they were following. Kathryn felt her breath release; after Babylon she'd been fairly sure—but there they were under the eye of their prince. On either side the line shook itself out, two-deep and spread out—nothing fancy, but it wound over the irregularities of the ground like a living serpent tipped with a glittering line of steel points. The months in the desert hadn't been wasted, then.

They were down onto the flat, and all she could see was the smoke and distant figures, all she could hear was the crackle of rifles, the thudding bark of artillery, the hiss of the rockets like an angry cat larger than worlds.

"Trumpeter, sound *Double time*," she said. The notes rang out, brassy and sweet in the hot, dry air. *We're coming, big brother.*

A gun suddenly swiveled around and turned toward her; despite the distance, the muzzle looked big enough to swallow her head. A flash of flame-shot smoke, the rising whistle sound, and it burst over the ranks to her left. Men tumbled and fell, still or writhing like broken-backed lizards in a cat's jaws.

"Trumpeter, sound *Fire and advance*."

The first rank went to one knee, and their rifles came up. A staccato ripple of fire and smoke ran down the line as four hundred rifles fired, and then their wielders were going through their loading drill. She trotted through the rotten-egg-smelling fogbank of their discharge and saw the second rank dash through the first and run ten yards ahead, going to one knee in their turn. Men were turning their way in the enemy ahead, pulling back like a door swinging. The enemy commander was refusing his flank, turning his formation into an L as he pulled back, with the short end facing her. Facing her, the men in it prone and shooting back.

A weapon like a fat cannon pointed at the First Kar-Duniash and a whole file of men went down, bullets slapping into flesh, sparking and ra!sing puffs of dust around their feet, going *tinnnnk* into helmets like a smith's punch.

"Trumpeter, sound *Charge*! Kashtiliash! Kashtiliash!"

"KASHTILIASH!"

She swept out her Python pistol and cocked it with her thumb.

"Charge! Charge!"

Kenneth Hollard looked down as the stretcher was carried up the rear ramp of the *Emancipator*. He recognized Sergeant Smith, despite the mass of bandages that covered her torso, and bent over her. Her eyes were wandering with morphine, but they recognized him . . . or at least focused on his face.

"Good work," he said, and then switched to the Sun People tongue of Alba. "You fought well, warrior."

"Pithair," she murmured, smiling faintly. That meant "father," and he didn't think she was invoking her god. He was certain when she went on, *"Is it well, at last, Father?"*

"Dahig'tair," he began. *Guess she's seeing someone else,* he thought, laying a hand on the clammy coldness of her forehead. "Daughter, it is very well."

She sighed and closed her eyes, and the bearers carried her up the ramp and into the long gondola, fitting her stretcher into the racks and transferring her IV to the holder. Lieutenant Vicki Cofflin came back from the control stations in the bow, turning sideways to pass a corpsman doing something to one of the wounded. A sharp smell drifted backward under the exhaust fumes of the idling engines; it was the odor of disinfectant, and somehow of pain.

God, I hate visiting the wounded. You had to, of course; men and women in pain needed to know that they were valued for what they'd done.

"We're ready to go, sir," the commander of the *Emancipator* said, saluting. "We'll have them in the hospital at Ur Base in a few hours, and then we'll be back with the loads you specified."

She nodded down and forward; water wagons were on either side of the gondola's underbelly, with hoses running from the dirigible's keel ballast tanks. "Thought we could spare the water, seeing as we're heavily laden and heading right back into home base," she said.

He returned the salute and shook her hand. "This thing is *damned* useful," he said. "I might want you to do some high-level reconnaissance when you get back. In the meantime, I need a temporary lift and the use of your radio—need to talk to your uncle."

The *Emancipator*'s powerful generator and altitude gave its shortwave set as much range as the one at Ur Base, or Republic House, Nantucket Airport, for that matter.

"Aye, aye, sir. Welcome aboard."

He climbed the ramp behind her, squeezed past the corpsmen, and held on to a stanchion as the mooring ropes were released. The *Emancipator* turned and circled upward swiftly, swaying a little, and he saw the huge orca-shaped shadow dwindle as the mooring crews went stumbling backward from the blizzard of dust and grit.

Hollard's ears popped; he looked northwest, straining his eyes for a sight of the retreating enemy. All he saw was smoke from the grass fires the battle had started. Vicki Cofflin broke his concentration.

"Sir."

He started a little.

"Sir, we're neutral at thirty-five hundred. That's as high as I'd care to go, with the wounded aboard."

Hollard nodded and turned back, sliding into the communications officer's chair and slipping the earphones onto his head. She was turning dials for him, and a crackle of static foretold success.

"That should do it, sir, if you want to try."

"Hollard here," he said. "Hollard here. Over."

"Republic Home here, receiving loud and clear. Just a moment, Brigadier Hollard . . ."

"Portsmouth Base here. Commodore Alston is monitoring this frequency . . . coming in loud and clear."

"This is the Chief." The familiar dry twang sounded in his ears. "Hear you had a bit of a dustup."

"Yes, sir," Hollard replied. "I'll be making a full report soonest. Bottom line, we ran into a force of Walker's Achaeans. We won, but we didn't break them, and they're better equipped than we anticipated. We suffered thirty-two fatals, our local irregulars about three times that, and the First Kar-Duniash about twice."

He looked off to the northwest, where the enemy force was withdrawing, like a wounded lion into a thicket, sullen and hurt but not seriously weakened.

"Preliminary prisoner interrogations indicate this was one regiment of a brigade that's been operating in support of Kurunta of Tarhuntassa, out of Miletus, for the past couple of months." He pulled a pad out of his thigh pocket. "Here are some specs on the equipment."

When he finished, Alston's soft Sea Island accent came on the circuit. "Damn," she said. "He found a way around the ammunition problem we thought he'd waste time on. We outsmaahted ourselves, yeah."

"Ayup," Jared Cofflin said. "Not the first time—we'll just try to make it the last. What's your appraisal, son?"

"Sir, we're in for a harder war than we thought. We're going to need more of everything, and we'll have to raise and equip more local troops. The First Kar-Duniash did very well . . . in fact, I think now that my sister's, ah, Lieutenant Colonel Hollard's—

"No need to get formal, son."

"—marriage was extremely fortunate. This was probably a probing attack to see if they could take over in Mitanni. But we need to link up with the Hittites, we need to raise the siege of Troy and get Councilor Arnstein out, and we need to field a substantial force here to counter the Achaeans."

"Marian?" Cofflin's steady voice asked.

"Essentially correct," she said. "Though I'd add that it's a very high priority to break the Tartessian blockade in the Straits of Gibraltar, so we can get some sea power out there, cut Walker off from Anatolia."

Hollard felt himself nodding. "That's God's truth, Chief."

Cofflin sighed. "If only we'd killed Walker . . ."

"We will," Alston said flatly. "In the meantime, Brigadier Hollard, I suggest that you proceed as you outlined. I'm preparing for the naval wing of our strategy, but that's going to take time, too. For one thing, if we *do* win in the Straits, we'll need basing facilities— Alba's too far away."

"Ma'am, yes ma'am."

"Consult with Councilor Arnstein and Ms. Arnstein on the political side," Cofflin said. "We have to keep those alliances as tight as we can and build all the influence we can."

"Roger on that, sir. I'll be getting the Mitannian situation organized over the next couple of weeks—it's crucial." He looked at his watch. "As a matter of fact, there's a meeting with Ms. Raushapa's supporters scheduled quite soon. I'll have a full report to you and the commodore when I get back to Ur Base next week."

"Good work, son, and Godspeed. Tell your people that from me and all of us, as well—our thoughts are with them, the whole Republic's are."

"Thank you, sir."

"You're doing reasonably well so far," the commodore added. "Just don't lose sight of the forest for the trees."

"Thank you, ma'am."

And don't screw up, he added to himself. *Right, let's get the little princess secure on her throne . . .*

"Thank you, Lieutenant," he said, relinquishing the comm seat to its usual owner. "Let's get me back on the ground."

"Yessir." In a commander's tone, smooth and firm for someone young: "Off superheat, valve the maneuvering cell."

A hissing in the background that he'd scarcely noticed went a and hot air ceased to flow into the big central cell in the airship's fuse-lage. The *Emancipator*'s circling began to take her downward, like running along a huge, smooth invisible ramp in the sky. The orderly layout of the expeditionary force camp below swelled.

"Engines negative ninety."

Crewfolk heaved at the wheels; the dirigible's motion changed as the engine pods swung to point their fans at the sky, and the descent accelerated as they pushed it downward.

"Maintain. Altitude nine hundred . . . seven hundred . . . throttles back half. All right, sir, time for you to drop out on us."

Hollard nodded and walked back to the center of the gondola. Two of the crew helped him into a harness much like a parachute's. An-other dropped a long coil of rope toward the ground; it seemed to shrink as it fell away, turning from wrist-thick hemp to a gossamer thread by the time it raised a puff of dust below, at the edge of the air-ship's shadow. Marines sprang to hold it.

"Rope through here, sir"—a *click* as the mechanism engaged—"and you squeeze this to slow down. Squeeze to slow, let go to go faster, sir."

"Thank you, sailor," he said, and stepped out over the hole. "Gung ho!"

A long, swooping fall, exhilarating and frightening at the same time, like rock climbing or rappeling on an obstacle course. He squeezed at the handgrip as the faces below him swelled, then hit the quick-release catch in the center of his chest as the earth hit his boots. The Marines holding the line let go with a rush, and the dirigi-ble climbed, turning for the southeast and accelerating as the engines pivoted down to the horizontal.

"Magnificent!"

Brigadier Kenneth Hollard turned and stepped into the chariot; Raupasha was driving herself now, and moving easily—it *had* been a graze, along her side.

"Magnificent," she said again. "I would love to do that myself someday, Kenn'et."

"That might be arranged," he said, laughing and ruffling Sabala's ears and then shoving the dog firmly away—the hound was a dedi-cated crotch-sniffer, like most of his breed. "Your people are going to hail you here, then?"

"Yes," she said, her mood turning serious. "Today we shed our blood together, as the true *mariannu* of old did; today we—and you— on a victory over an ancient enemy."

The Mitannians were gathered in the lee of a low, smooth hill; it some shade, now that the sun was inclining toward the west. They lit campfires, a surprisingly orderly array, and they rose with a crashing cheer as the chariot swept up the hill. His brow raised when some of them brandished flintlock shotguns as well as spears and looted Hittite weapons. *Well,* he thought, *we were going to try and talk Kashtiliash into authorizing some Mitannian New Troops as well. Probably it could be done . . .*

Raupasha drew rein with a flourish and raised her free hand to silence the roaring waves of sound. She waited until the quiet was tense with expectation and then broke into impassioned speech. In Hurrian, of course, of which complex agglutinative language he spoke perhaps three phrases, including "princess," "please," and "thank you."

Spears thrust up into the growing dark as men leaped and danced with joy; another paroxysm of sound struck when she grabbed Hollard's wrist and raised it high, then wrapped his hand around hers. The contact was very pleasant, and he beat down a touch of guilt as she let go again, giving his palm a squeeze.

Then the heads of the war bands began to come forward, to kneel before Raupasha and place their hands between hers; he was a little uneasy as they took his right hand and pressed it to their foreheads afterward. That took most of an hour, and Raupasha spoke again, raising his hand with hers once more.

"They seem really pleased," he said to her. She nodded, raising shining eyes to his. "What was that last part about?"

"They were more than pleased, Lord Kenn'et," she said solemnly, "when they heard that you would be my consort, to father a new line of kings for Mitanni, sons who would make us glorious as of old."

For a moment the world seemed to stop. Hollard closed his eyes. *Oh, sweet Jesus, and in public, how'm I going to get out of this, Kashtiliash will go ballistic, Kathryn will cut my testicles off, and Councilor Arnstein will flay me, and what the Chief and the commodore will say—*

There were no adequate words. But he had to try.

"Oh, *shit!*"

EPILOGUE

August, Year 10 A.E.

"Ma'am, she sails like a cast-iron pig," Captain Trudeau said. "The *Farragut*'s my ship, she's the most formidable thing on the World Ocean and I love her dearly, but she's crank, she's wet, she's not fit to be let out on the Atlantic on a dark night."

Commodore Alston clasped her hands behind her back and rose slightly on her toes; she'd always done that when she needed to think. Right now the bright surface of the Southhampton Water was full of ships; her own *Chamberlain*, all six of the Republic's frigates, and brigs, schooners, things less nameable, score upon score of them, with swarms of small craft crisscrossing the waters between the anchored ships and the docks. All the naval power of the Republic and its Alliance gathered to make an end to the Tartessian pest, with thousands of warriors ashore ready to embark on the troop ships along with the First Nantucket Militia and the Second Marines.

Not far away, the *Eagle* lay at a single anchor, waiting to unfurl her wings and take the string westward for home, with a light cargo and returning passengers; even when most of an expeditionary force was going one way, some duty or necessity always called in the other.

It was a bright August day, the sort that pre-Event travel posters of England always showed and nature rarely did, with a breeze out of the north that ruffled the intensely blue water into a rippled skin ridged with white, pitching the ships at their anchors and bringing a smell of salt, silt, and woodsmoke from the great volunteer camp around Portsmouth Base. Southbound wings made the sky overhead clamorous, almost enough to mask the noise of the encampment.

She narrowed her eyes against the brightness and considered the *Farragut*. With her masts shipped and without the protective plating she looked more normal; and still menacing, with the two four-inch rifled guns on fo'c'sle and quarterdeck on their track mountings and the canvas-shrouded Gatlings clamped to her rails, and the high bridge across her paddle boxes.

"That's even without the ram plating fitted?" she asked.

"That helps, but not all that much," Trudeau said, his eyes bright blue in a swarthy face. "Nothing short of ripping out her engines and completely rebuilding the bow *would* help, as far as her deep-water performance is concerned. She ships water over the bow like a submarine if there's any sort of sea, even under steam—God only knows what she'd do in a real blow."

"And She's not talking," Alston said. "Hmmm. Reserve buoyancy's low, too—hard to recover from being pooped."

Trudeau came to the defense of his ship. "Apart from shipping water over the bow, she's a honey with her paddles going. Very maneuverable."

Alston nodded. Unfortunately, that didn't solve their problem. Even burning coal, which could be gotten here in Alba, her engines were and would remain fuel hogs—reliable, and they gave her a good twelve knots, but useless for oceanic voyages. There was little point in having a steam ram-gunboat that arrived at the scene of action with her fuel bunkers dry, particularly when, for all her three masts and ship-rig, she wasn't too handy under sail.

"Well, I'm afraid you'll have to nurse her along," Alston said. *The design had to be a compromise; the characteristics of a ram and a blue-water sailor just aren't all that compatible.* "You got her head across the North Atlantic. I've every confidence you'll be able to get her down the Bay of Biscay and to Gibraltar with us, God, Moon Woman, and the weather willing."

The two American-born touched wood; Swindapa made the Fiernan triple-touch gesture of reverence.

"And the dockyard's ready to help with the installation of the bow plating, Captain Trudeau," Alston went on.

Trudeau saluted. "Yes, ma'am—although that makes her even worse."

Swindapa sighed as he departed, then said, "It's time, love."

They went below, through the twitter of pipes and the ritual calls of an officer leaving the ship, into the great stern cabin. Dhinwarn sat on the big bunk, her daughter's adopted children on either side, looking up as she told a story with an arm around either shoulder. They looked slightly incongruous in sailor suits next to her Fiernan string skirt, which was what they'd been wearing for the past couple of months, the Great Wisdom—or less. The girls bounced to their feet as their mothers came in.

"Mom . . ."

"Mom . . ."

Heather and Lucy looked at each other, and visibly decided it one more try.

"Do we *have* to go?"

"Yes, you do," Marian said, forcing a gentle smile. *Come on, woman, you're a commodore. You're not allowed to bawl. It'd scare the troops. It'll only be for a few months.*

"Come on, now, you don't want to miss the tide," she said.

"Yes we do! We want to go with you!"

"We could stay below if there's trouble!"

"We could carry powder up from the magazine!"

Swindapa crouched and hugged Heather as the child ran to her, stroking the red head and its braids. "We want you safe," she said.

Marian nodded, cupping a hand under Lucy's chin. "We're going into action," she said. "You wouldn't want us worrying about you, now, would you?"

"Can't we stay with Grandma, then?" Lucy said, her great brown eyes filling with tears. "We'd be closer to you."

Dhinwarn laughed. "That would be dancing-rightly with me," she said in Fiernan; she understood English a lot better than she spoke it.

"No, sweetlin', because you'll have to be at school again soon," Marian said. "You'll be staying with Uncle Jared and Aunt Martha until we get home. That won't be too long, surely; perhaps we can be back for Christmas."

"Promise?" Heather said.

Marian kissed her brow. "No, because I can't be sure. Now come on, honey, sugar. Make us proud."

They took the girls' hands; both bravely stifled tears as they led them back to the quarterdeck. Their sea chests were there—sources of immense pride, with their names neatly stenciled on the sides, Guard-fashion: HEATHER ALSTON-KURLELO and LUCY ALSTON-KURLELO, and GUARD HOUSE, NANTUCKET TOWN underneath. So was the other luggage, souvenirs, boxed presents from their Kurlelo relatives, their favorite stuffed animals.

Captain Nguyen of the *Eagle* was there as well, saluting and then repeating the gesture smartly down at the two nine-year-olds. "Ready to go aboard?" he said.

The Alston-Kurlelo daughters looked at each other and shed a little f their solemnness. *Uh-oh,* Marian thought. *It just occurred to them at they get a voyage without their mothers to squash the things they lly like to do as too dangerous—and they think they can pull their rmer act on Nguyen.*

ou might want to keep them in irons below until you make the t Point Light," she said. "They're as mischievous as apes, h of them, and what one doesn't think of to get into trouble r will."

!" A wail of indignation.

ng sailors hoisted the luggage and went over the side and

down the rope ladder to the *Eagle*'s captain's gig. After a final exchange of hugs and kisses, so did Heather and Lucy. Nguyen shook their mothers' hands after his salute.

"Don't worry, Commodore, Ms. Swindapa. I'll see them and *Eagle* both home safely."

"I'm sure you will, Mr. Nguyen," Alston said.

Swindapa nodded silently, a single tear track running down the honey-tan of her cheek. It took more than rings on the cuffs to convince a Fiernan that they shouldn't cry when they were sad. The bosun's pipe twittered Nguyen over the side, and Marian stood with a hand shading her eyes. She smiled crookedly as her daughters swarmed up the side—they *were* agile as apes, and a summer spent rambling the countryside with their Fiernan cousins hadn't hurt a bit —and stood by the rail, waving again and again.

Orders echoed over the water, crisp and precise:

"Up and down!"

"Avast heaving!"

"Anchor at short stay!" There was a clatter of steel on steel, and the capstan crew paused.

Then: "Break out the anchor!" and they heaved again, slowly at first, and then suddenly no longer straining against the flukes' hold on the bottom.

"Anchors aweigh!"

Sail broke out from the bottom of the masts toward the top, and the ebbing tide and freshening offshore breeze took *Eagle* and heeled her slightly, a wave appearing at her bow.

"Shift colors!" came faint but clear, and the jack and ensign came on smartly; then the steaming ensign broke out on the gaff.

"Mr. Jenkins," Marian said.

He saluted, smiling, and turned to bark orders. The bosun's pipe twittered, and a team bent to the quarterdeck carronade.

Boom!, softer and deeper than a long gun, and the puff of smoke blew away to the south and leeward. The two girls jumped up and down as the signal gun saluted their departure, waving both arms from *Eagle*'s fantail railing until all sight was lost.

"Fair voyaging," Swindapa said softly. "Always fair voyaging, and a fortunate star, and may partings never hurt them worse than this. And may they never have to sail to war."

"Amen," Marian Alston said, and settled her billed cap firmly on her head. She wished that with all her heart, but she suspected it wasn't very likely. "Final dining-in for the fleet captains tonight," she said.

Swindapa nodded. The Republic's fleet would sail to war as soon as the *Farragut*'s final killing tool was installed, and there was a moa pit-roasting ashore for the last gathering of the commanders.

"So much has happened here," she said, looking ashore to where she'd been roped from her collar to a stake, naked and filthy and shivering, when the *Eagle* first arrived in these waters.

"We'll be back," Marian said. "And we'll be home, and this will be memories, too."

"The war isn't over yet," Swindapa said. "So much at stake."

"But we haven't lost yet either," Alston smiled. "And we're not going to."

> For it is not the bright arrival planned
> But in the journeying along the way
> We find the Golden Road to Samarkand.

THE SUNRISE LANDS

by S.M. STIRLING

A generation has passed since The Change
that rendered technology inoperable around
the world, and western Oregon has finally
achieved a degree of peace. But a new
threat has risen in Paradise Valley, Wyoming.
A man known as The Prophet presides over
the Church Universal and Triumphant,
teaching his followers to continue God's
work by destroying the remnants of
technological civilization they encounter—
and those who dare use them.

**Available wherever books are sold or at
penguin.com**

S.M. Stirling

THE PROTECTOR'S WAR

Eight years after the Change, survivors have banded together in tribal communities, committed to rebuilding society. In Oregon's Willamette Valley, former pilot Michael Havel's Bearkillers are warriors of renown. Their closest ally, the mystical Clan Mackenzie, is led by Wiccan folksinger Juniper Mackenzie. Their leadership has saved countless lives.

But not every leader has altruistic aspirations. Norman Arminger, medieval scholar, rules the Protectorate. He has enslaved civilians, built an army, and spread his forces from Portland through most of western Washington State. Now he wants the Willamette Valley farmland, and he's willing to wage war to conquer it.

And unknown to both factions is the imminent arrival of a ship from Tasmania bearing British soldiers...

"[A] VIVID PORTRAIT OF A WORLD GONE INSANE."
—STATESMAN JOURNAL (SALEM, OR)

Available wherever books are sold or at
penguin.com